THE BEST SCIENCE FICTION
OF THE YEAR

THE BEST
SCIENCE
FICTION
OF THE YEAR
VOLUME 2

Edited by Neil Clarke

Night Shade Books
NEW YORK

Night Shade books may be purchased in bulk at special discounts for sales promotion, corporate gifts, fund-raising, or educational purposes. Special editions can also be created to specifications. For details, contact the Special Sales Department, Night Shade Books, 307 West 36th Street, 11th Floor, New York, NY 10018 or info@skyhorsepublishing.com.

Night Shade Books® is a registered trademark of Skyhorse Publishing, Inc.®, a Delaware corporation.

Visit our website at www.nightshadebooks.com.

10 9 8 7 6 5 4 3 2 1

Library of Congress Cataloging-in-Publication Data is available on file.

ISBN: 978-1-59780-896-5

Cover illustration by Markus Vogt
Cover design by Jason Snair

Please see page 609 for an extension of this copyright page.

Printed in the United States of America

Table of Contents

Introduction: A State of the Short SF Field in 2016 vii

The Visitor from Taured—Ian R. MacLeod 1
Extraction Request—Rich Larson 22
A Good Home—Karin Lowachee 43
Prodigal—Gord Sellar 59
Ten Days—Nina Allan 83
Terminal—Lavie Tidhar 115
Panic City—Madeline Ashby 128
Last Gods—Sam J. Miller 136
HigherWorks—Gregory Norman Bossert 150
A Strange Loop—T. R. Napper 180
Night Journey of the Dragon-Horse—Xia Jia 203
Pearl—Aliette de Bodard 217
The Metal Demimonde—Nick Wolven 236
The Iron Tactician—Alastair Reynolds 276
The Mighty Slinger—Tobias S. Buckell and Karen Lord 344
They Have All One Breath—Karl Bunker 368
Sooner or Later Everything Falls Into the Sea—Sarah Pinsker 394
And Then, One Day, the Air was Full of Voices
     —Margaret Ronald 413
The Three Lives of Sonata James—Lettie Prell 425
The Charge and the Storm—An Owomoyela 444
Parables of Infinity—Robert Reed 485
Ten Poems for the Mossums, One for the Man
     —Suzanne Palmer 499
You Make Pattaya—Rich Larson 518
Number Nine Moon—Alex Irvine 532
Things with Beards—Sam J. Miller 551
Dispatches from the Cradle: The Hermit—
     Forty-Eight Hours in the Sea of Massachusetts—Ken Liu 563
Touring with the Alien—Carolyn Ives Gilman 577

2016 Recommended Reading List 607

INTRODUCTION:
A State of the Short SF Field in 2016

Neil Clarke

've spent most of my life working in technology. It's a field where if you aren't always moving forward, then you're falling behind. I never really thought of it as preparation for work as an editor, but in the case of this series, it certainly has been. Keeping up with all the new science fiction stories published each month can be like drinking from a firehose sometimes. Taking time off—even just a month—can be overwhelming in terms of recovery, so you have no choice but to keep forging ahead.

I seldom know which stories will make the final cut until the very end, so throughout the year, I add the potential candidates to a spreadsheet. I also call upon a few friends and editors to give me some of their recommendations, just to make sure I haven't missed anything. I'll give those stories a second chance if they aren't already on the list.

In November and December, I reread all the stories on the list and select the best of them for inclusion in this anthology. Sometimes, you can't get everything you want. Last year, for example, two of the stories were unavailable due to contractual restrictions. That didn't happen this time around. Instead, I had a different problem: the list was longer. As far as problems go, a stronger year of stories is a good one to have. That said, I found it interesting that some of the usual suspects—award-winners and perennial best-of list writers—weren't responsible for this shift. I'll take that as a promising sign for the future.

Last year, most of my introduction reviewed how the short fiction field had changed in the past decade and included a few concerns about the financial sustainability of the magazine market in its current configuration. One of the more personally concerning models was the method of annually funding magazines through crowdfunding campaigns. Some might confuse this with a subscription drive, but the base premise is actually quite different. It's more like an annual Sword of Damocles hanging over the future of publication. The fear of losing the venue often inspires the more passionate readers to give well in excess of what a subscription would normally cost. This allows markets with a less-than-sufficient subscriber base to continue their existence or spend more than their subscriber base would normally permit. It's great that these markets can get this support, but for reasons I mentioned last year, I have my concerns about its long-term viability.

To get a better sense of how this and some other issues were perceived, I conducted a survey of over a thousand short fiction readers. Of everything I asked about in that survey, this topic generated the most polarized and passionate responses. In the end, it broke down into three groups with the two ends expressing varying degrees of hostility. The largest group, occupying the middle, was more prone to support magazines in a more traditional sense: subscriptions or encouraging friends to read it. The next largest group included a significant number of people who once supported these—or similar—efforts, but were now offended by the repeated requests, often described as irresponsible. There was also concern that this behavior could impact the ability for future projects to get a start this way. The smallest group was in total support of this business model and downright offended that anyone would dare question its legitimacy. A significant percentage of the comments for this group appeared to indicate that they had significant skin in the game, quite often as writers.

The breakdown of the survey leads me to believe this model will be in place for at least a few more years, but not without consequences. Although there is significant push against the model, the latter group should be sufficient to keep a small publication alive, at least for the near future. The demographics of that group is something to be concerned about, but in the end, I think a follow-up survey is necessary to more adequately gauge the long-term effect this will have on that segment of the field.

Another item I mentioned last year was that the print magazines were reinvigorated by the digital explosion. In covering the anthologies, I pointed to a broken print distribution system, but I didn't explicitly call your attention to how that impacts the print magazines. Unlike the anthologies, print magazines have two forms of distribution in that format: newsstand—which is similar to the book distribution—and subscription—which isn't.

If you ever wondered why we don't have more genre print magazines, the answer can be found in the production and distribution issues. Printing, shipping, and storage costs for print books and magazines are significant expenses, and with magazines, unsold newsstand copies are typically destroyed. In some ways, it's almost worth thinking of magazine newsstand sales as a marketing expense. They don't generate a lot of revenue, but it gets your product in front of readers and from there you hope they convert into subscribers.

Print subscriptions carry their own baggage, though: postage costs. As more and more people have shifted to email and electronic bill pay, the USPS has had to cover declining revenue and increasing costs—pensions, insurance, etc.—through mandated annual postage rate increases. Even at the discounted rates for magazines—which require a high enough number of subscribers—the increases can add up to a significant expense, and that leads us to the biggest market news of 2016 . . .

At the end of 2016, *Asimov's* and *Analog*, both published by Dell Magazines, announced that they will be switching from a monthly to a bimonthly schedule in 2017. The issues will be bigger, and there will be no reduction in the amount of fiction published. The official explanation—an attempt to keep subscription prices in check—is completely in line with modern postal reality. It's been well known that the increasing costs of printing and shipping have been causing problems across the industry for years. In fact, *F&SF* made a similar move back in 2009.

This change is not a reason to worry about the fates of these two magazines. *Asimov's* and *Analog* continue to have the leading print readerships and have built a healthy digital subscription footprint. If anything, this will likely lead to more opportunities for these magazines to include novellas, a segment of the market that has been making a resurgence for the last few years. One need look no further than Tor.com's success to see this in action.

The bad news is what it says about the state of the print magazine market. At this point, I can't name a single monthly science fiction magazine with national print distribution. (Yes, technically, both magazines were publishing ten issues/year for a while now, but that always felt close enough.) This marks the end of an era that stretches back to the very first science fiction magazines. If these two magazines can't make it financially viable to publish at the going rate on a monthly print schedule, it seems highly unlikely that anyone else can.

The costs of printing and shipping will continue to rise, so while their subscription rates can held down for now, it's only a matter of time before market pressures force an increase. This raises a concern I expressed last year: Is the field as a whole undervaluing its products?

Despite some of the controversy, crowdfunding has demonstrated that a segment of our community believes magazines are worth considerably more than the going rate, but would there be broad enough support for a more modest increase? In terms of percentages, a jump from $2.99 to $3.99 would seem like a lot, but one could argue that the increased price is reasonable when compared to other forms of entertainment or even the typical cost of a single cup of good coffee. From there, I think there is room to argue that the field has done itself a disservice. By aiming low, we—yes, I know I'm part of this problem—have created a reality where a low price is considered generous.

Overall readership for short fiction appears to be growing, but not at a rate to sustain increasing costs and resource competition in the form of new markets. Last year, I suggested that the near future will bring with it a market contraction that will help address some of this. I still believe that to be quite likely, but it also seems like the lower rates may have greased the wheels and set us on this path. I'm beginning to think that a course correction, in the form of slightly higher subscription rates, is not only likely but quite possibly necessary for the continued health of the field.

The elephant in the room is most certainly free online magazines and their impact on the sense of perceived value—see, I told you I was complicit. It's well known that the majority of people who read online fiction or podcast don't contribute to its financial stability. The actual supporting rate tends to fall somewhere below 10 percent. In many ways, the free online edition is the digital equivalent to what the print magazines gain from newsstand sales: marketing with the hope of creating subscribers.

The end result is that many of these markets have what can be described as a pay-for-convenience model. It might mean that the magazine is free to read or listen to online, but if you want the nicely formatted ebook edition, automatic monthly delivery, or even some extra content, you have to pay. This might even be combined with services like Patreon, which provides readers an ability to make monthly pledges. Like Kickstarter—but never-ending—this system includes goals and rewards that can provide further incentives to get readers to pay for the magazine. In fact, this service is now being used by an increasing number of authors as an alternate source of income from traditional publishing.

Here at the beginning of 2017, financial issues still remain the biggest hurdle for the business end of short fiction—and I haven't even touched upon the poor pay rates for authors. Still, things are nothing like they were a decade ago. There are significant and complicated issues still left to be resolved, but that the field is still moving forward and trying new things is a reason to be optimistic. It will be bumpy at times, but it's not in crisis.

I'd like to end this year with some special call-outs. As expected, my categories evolve to meet the needs of that year:

Author to Watch

It feels a bit weird to be singling out an author who has been publishing stories for a few years—particularly one that I've worked with for the last two—but this year he's been on fire both in terms of quantity and quality. In 2016, Rich Larson had a string of fantastic stories appear in *Interzone, F&SF, Analog, Asimov's, Clarkesworld*, and several other places. One of the more difficult aspects of compiling this year's list was determining which of Rich's stories would be included. In the end, I took two. Track down the others. You won't be disappointed.

Service to Authors

It's been in place for a few years now, but The Grinder (thegrinder.diabolicalplots.com) has become an invaluable resource for short fiction authors. The purpose: to provide information to authors about the wide array of venues that are willing to consider their stories. The site includes submission-tracking options and almost every detail an author needs to make a well-informed decision: response times, pay rates, genre, etc. Through The Grinder, David Steffen and his team have played an important role in the short fiction ecosystem, and have done so as a labor of love. Thank you.

Impact on International Science Fiction

As readers of *Clarkesworld Magazine* already know, I've long had an interest in international science fiction, particularly works in translation. In recent years, there have been increasing opportunities to read some of these works. Although the number of translations in this volume is down from last year, the availability of smart and interesting translated works continues to rise.

Additionally, Ken Liu has made a tremendous impact in this area. He's been a leading advocate of Chinese science fiction, and twice now, works he has translated have gone on to win the Hugo Award. This year, Tor Books published his anthology *Invisible Planets,* which featured an incredible array of Chinese stories and essays. This is a book well worth having on your shelves and I'd personally like to thank Ken for this and all his other efforts in the field. Well done!

Thanks for reading. See you next year!

Ian R. MacLeod has been writing and selling stories and novels of speculative and fantastic fiction for almost thirty years. Amongst many accolades, his work has won the Arthur C. Clarke Award, the World Fantasy Award (twice), and the Sidewise Award for Alternate History (three times). He took a law degree and drifted into the English Civil Service, but writing was always his first love and ambition. He has recently released a short story collection, *Frost On Glass*, and has a new novel, *Red Snow*, due out shortly. He lives in the riverside town of Bewdley in the United Kingdom.

THE VISITOR FROM TAURED

Ian R. MacLeod

1.

There was always something otherworldly about Rob Holm. Not that he wasn't charming and clever and good-looking. Driven, as well. Even during that first week when we'd arrived at university and waved goodbye to our parents and our childhoods, and were busy doing all the usual fresher things, which still involved getting dangerously drunk and pretending not to be homesick and otherwise behaving like the prim, arrogant, cocky, and immature young assholes we undoubtedly were, Rob was chatting with research fellows and quietly getting to know the best virtuals to hang out in.

Even back then, us young undergrads were an endangered breed. Many universities had gone bankrupt, become commercial research utilities, or transformed themselves into the academic theme parks of those so-called "Third Age Academies." But still, here we all were at the traditional redbrick campus of Leeds University, which still offered a broad-ish range of courses to those with families rich enough to support them, or at least tolerant enough not to warn them against such folly. My own choice of degree, just to show how incredibly supportive my parents were, being Analogue Literature.

As a subject, it already belonged with Alchemy and Marxism in the dust-bin of history, but books—and I really do mean those peculiar, old, paper, physical objects—had always been my thing. Even when I was far too young to understand what they were and by rights should have been attracted by the bright, interactive, virtual gewgaws buzzing all around me, I'd managed to burrow into the bottom of an old box, down past the stickle bricks and My Little Ponies, to these broad, cardboardy things that fell open and had these flat, two-dee shapes and images that didn't move or respond in any normal way when I waved my podgy fingers in their direction. All you could do was simply look at them. That and chew their corners, and maybe scribble over their pages with some of the dried-up crayons that were also to be found amid those predigital layers.

My parents had always been loving and tolerant of their daughter. They even encouraged little Lita's interest in these ancient artifacts. I remember my mother's finger moving slow and patient across the creased and yellowed pages as she traced the pictures and her lips breathed the magical words that somehow arose from those flat lines. She wouldn't have assimilated data this way herself in years, if ever, so in a sense we were both learning.

The Very Hungry Caterpillar. Beatrix Potter, the Mr. Men series. *Where the Wild Things Are.* Frodo's adventures. Slowly, like some archaeologist discovering the world by deciphering the cartouches of the tombs in Ancient Egypt, I learned how to perceive and interact through this antique medium. It was, well, the *thingness* of books. The exact way they *didn't* leap about or start giving off sounds, smells, and textures. That, and how they didn't ask you which character you'd like to be, or what level you wanted to go to next, but simply took you by the hand and led you where they wanted you to go.

Of course, I became a confirmed bibliophile, but I do still wonder how my life would have progressed if my parents had seen odd behavior differently, and taken me to some pediatric specialist. Almost certainly, I wouldn't be the Lita Ortiz who's writing these words for whoever might still be able to comprehend them. Nor the one who was lucky enough to meet Rob Holm all those years ago in the teenage fug of those student halls back at Leeds University.

2.

So. Rob. First thing to say is the obvious fact that most of us fancied him. It wasn't just the grey eyes, or the courtly elegance, or that soft Scottish accent, or even the way he somehow appeared mature and accomplished. It was, essentially, a kind of mystery. But he wasn't remotely standoffish. He went along with the fancy dress pub crawls. He drank. He fucked about. He took the odd tab.

One of my earliest memories of Rob was finding him at some club, cool as you like amid all the noise, flash, and flesh. And dragging him out onto the pulsing dance floor. One minute we were hovering above the skyscrapers of Beijing and the next a shipwreck storm was billowing about us. Rob, though, was simply there. Taking it all in, laughing, responding, but somehow detached. Then, helping me down and out, past clanging temple bells and through prismatic sandstorms to the entirely non-virtual hell of the toilets. His cool hands holding back my hair as I vomited.

I never ever actually thanked Rob for this—I was too embarrassed—but the incident somehow made us more aware of each other. That, and maybe we shared a sense of otherness. He, after all, was studying astrophysics, and none of the rest of us even knew what that was, and he had all that strange stuff going on across the walls of his room. Not flashing posters of the latest virtual boy band or porn empress, but slow-turning gas clouds, strange planets, distant stars and galaxies. That, and long runs of mek, whole arching rainbows of the stuff, endlessly twisting and turning. My room, on the other hand, was piled with the precious torn and foxed paperbacks I'd scoured from junksites during my teenage years. Not, of course, that they were actually needed. Even if you were studying something as arcane as narrative fiction, you were still expected to download and virtualize all your resources.

The Analogue Literature Faculty at Leeds University had once taken up a labyrinthine space in a redbrick terrace at the east edge of the campus. But now it had been invaded by dozens of more modern disciplines. Anything from speculative mek to non-concrete design to holo-pornography had taken bites out of it. I was already aware—how couldn't I be?—that no significant novel or short story had been written in decades, but I was shocked to discover that only five other students in my year had elected for An Lit as their main subject, and one of those still resided in Seoul and another was a post-centarian on clicking steel legs. Most of the other students who showed up were dipping into the subject in the hope that it might add something useful to their main discipline. Invariably, they were disappointed. It wasn't just the difficulty of ploughing through page after page of non-interactive text. It was linear fiction's sheer lack of options, settings, choices. Why the hell, I remember some kid shouting in a seminar, should I accept all the miserable shit that this Hardy guy rains down on his characters? Give me the base program for *Tess of the d'Urbervilles*, and I'll hack you fifteen better endings.

I pushed my weak mek to the limit during that first term as I tried to formulate a tri-dee excursus on *Tender Is the Night*, but the whole piece was reconfigured out of existence once the faculty AIs got hold of it. Meanwhile, Rob Holm was clearly doing far better. I could hear him singing in the showers along from my room, and admired the way he didn't get involved in all the usual peeves and arguments. The physical sciences had a huge, brand new facility at the west end of campus called the Clearbrite Building. Half church, half-pagoda, and maybe half spaceship in the fizzing, shifting, headachy way of modern architecture, there was no real way of telling how much of it was actually made of brick, concrete, and glass, and how much consisted of virtual artifacts and energy fields. You could get seriously lost just staring at it.

My first year went by, and I fought hard against crawling home, and had a few unromantic flings, and made vegetable bolognaise my signature dish, and somehow managed to get version 4.04 of my second term excursus on *Howard's End* accepted. Rob and I didn't become close, but I liked his singing and the cinnamon scent he left hanging behind in the steam of the showers, and it was good to know that someone else was making a better hash of this whole undergraduate business than I was.

"Hey, Lita?"

We were deep into the summer term and exams were looming. Half the undergrads were back at home, and the other half were jacked up on learning streams, or busy having breakdowns.

I leaned in on Rob's doorway. "Yeah?"

"Fancy sharing a house next year?"

"Next year?" Almost effortlessly casual, I pretended to consider this. "I really hadn't thought. It all depends—"

"Not a problem." He shrugged. "I'm sure I'll find someone else."

"No, no. That's fine. I mean, yeah, I'm in. I'm interested."

"Great. I'll show you what I've got from the letting agencies." He smiled a warm smile, then returned to whatever wondrous creations were spinning above his desk.

3.

We settled on a narrow house with bad drains just off the Otley Road in Headingley, and I'm not sure whether I was relieved or disappointed when I discovered that his plan was that we share the place with some others. I roped in a couple of girls, Rob found a couple of guys, and we all got on pretty well. I had a proper boyfriend by then, a self-regarding jock called Torsten, and every now and then a different woman would emerge from Rob's room. Nothing serious ever seemed to come of this, but they were equally gorgeous, clever, and out of my league.

A bunch of us used to head out to the moors for midnight bonfires during that second winter. I remember the smoke and the sparks spinning into the deep black as we sang and drank and arsed around. Once, and with the help of a few tabs and cans, I asked Rob to name some constellations for me, and he put an arm around my waist and led me further into the dark.

Over there, Lita, up to the left and far away from the light of this city, is Ursa Major, the Great Bear, which is always a good place to start when you're stargazing. And there, see close as twins at the central bend of the Plough's handle, are Mizar and Alcor. They're not a true binary, but if we had decent binoculars, we could see that Mizar really does have a close companion. And there, that way, up and left—his breath on my face, his hands on my arms— maybe you can just see there's this fuzzy speck at the Bear's shoulder? Now, that's an entire, separate galaxy from our own filled with billions of stars, and its light has taken about twelve million years to reach the two of us here, tonight. Then Andromeda and Cassiopeia and Canus Major and Minor. . . . Distant, storybook names for distant worlds. I even wondered aloud about the possibility of other lives, existences, hardly expecting Rob to agree with me. But he did. And then he said something that struck me as strange.

"Not just out there, either, Lita. There are other worlds all around us. It's just that we can't see them."

"You're talking in some metaphorical sense, right?"

"Not at all. It's part of what I'm trying to understand in my studies."

"To be honest, I've got no real idea what astrophysics even means. Maybe you could tell me."

"I'd love to. And you know, Lita, I'm a complete dunce when it comes to, what *do* you call it—two-dee fiction, flat narrative? So I want you to tell me about that as well. Deal?"

We wandered back toward the fire, and I didn't expect anything else to come of our promise until Rob called to me when I was wandering past his room one wet, grey afternoon a week or so later. It was deadline day, my hair was a greasy mess, I was heading for the shower, and had an excursus on John Updike to finish.

"You *did* say you wanted to know more about what I study?"

"I was just . . ." I scratched my head. "Curious. All I do know is that astro-physics is about more than simply looking up at the night sky and giving names to things. That isn't even astronomy, is it?"

"You're not just being polite?" His soft, granite-grey eyes remained fixed on me.

"No. I'm not—absolutely."

"I could show you something here." He waved at the stars on his walls, the stuff spinning on his desk. "But maybe we could go out. To be honest, Lita, I could do with a break, and there's an experiment I could show you up at the Clearbrite that might help explain what I mean about other worlds . . . but I understand if you're busy. I could get my avatar to talk to your avatar and—"

"No, no. You're right, Rob. I could do with a break as well. Let's go out. Seize the day. Or at least, what's left of it. Just give me . . ." I waved a finger toward the bathroom, ". . . five minutes."

Then we were outside in the sideways-blowing drizzle, and it was freezing cold, and I was still wet from my hurried shower, as Rob slipped a companion-able arm around mine as we climbed the hill toward the Otley Road tram stop.

Kids and commuters got on and off as we jolted toward the strung lights of the city, their lips moving and their hands stirring to things only they could feel and see. The Clearbrite looked more than ever like some recently arrived spaceship as it glowed out through the gloom, but inside the place was just like any other campus building, with clamoring posters offering to restructure your loan, find you temporary work, or get you laid and ham-mered. Constant reminders, too, that Clearbrite was the only smartjuice to communicate in realtime to your fingerjewel, toejamb, or wristbracelet. This souk-like aspect of modern unis not being something that Sebastian Flyte, or even Harry Potter in those disappointing sequels, ever had to contend with.

We got a fair few hellos, a couple of tenured types stopped to talk to Rob in a corridor, and I saw how people paused to listen to what he was saying. More than ever, I had him down as someone who was bound to succeed. Still, I was expecting to be shown moon rocks, lightning bolts, or at least some clever virtual planetarium. But instead he took me into what looked like the kind of laboratory I'd been forced to waste many hours in at school, even if the equipment did seem a little fancier.

"This is the physics part of the astro," Rob explained, perhaps sensing my disappointment. "But you did ask about other worlds, right, and this is pretty much the only way I can show them to you."

I won't go too far into the details, because I'd probably get them wrong, but what Rob proceeded to demonstrate was a version of what I now know to be the famous, or infamous, Double Slit Experiment. There was a long black tube on a workbench. At one end of it was a laser, and at the other was a display screen attached to a device called a photo multiplier—a kind of sensor. In the middle he placed a barrier with two narrow slits. It wasn't a great surprise even to me that the pulses of light caused a pretty dark-light pattern of stripes to appear on the display at the far end. These, Rob said, were ripples of the interference pattern caused by the waves of light passing through the two slits, much as you'd get if you were pouring water. But light, Lita, is made up of individual packets of energy called photons. So what would happen if, instead of sending tens of thousands of them down the tube at once, we turned the laser down so far that it only emitted one photon at a time? Then, surely, each individual photon could only go through one or the other of the slits, there would be no ripples, and two simple stripes would emerge at the far end. But, hey, as he slowed the beep of the signal counter until it was registering single digits, the dark-light bars, like a shimmering neon forest, remained. As if, although each photon was a single particle, it somehow became a blur of all its possibilities as it passed through both slits at once. Which, as far as anyone knew, was pretty much what happened.

"I'm sorry," Rob said afterward when we were chatting over a second or third pint of beer in the fug of an old student bar called the Eldon that lay down the road from the university, "I should have shown you something less boring."

"It wasn't boring. The implications are pretty strange, aren't they?"

"More than strange. It goes against almost everything else we know about physics and the world around us—us sitting here in this pub, for instance. Things exist, right? They're either here or not. They don't flicker in and out of existence like ghosts. This whole particles blurring into waves business was one of the things that bugged me most when I was a kid finding out about science. It was partly why I chose to study astrophysics—I thought there'd be answers I'd understand when someone finally explained them to me. But there aren't." He sipped his beer. "All you get is something called the Copenhagen Interpretation, which is basically a shoulder shrug that says, hey, this stuff happen at the sub-atomic level, but it doesn't really have to bother us or make sense in the world we know about and live in. That, and then there's something else called the many worlds theory . . ." He trailed off. Stifled a burp. Seemed almost embarrassed.

"Which is what you believe in?"

"Believe isn't the right word. Things either are or they aren't in science. But, yeah, I do. And the maths supports it. Simply put, Lita, it says that all the possible states and positions that every particle could exist in are real—that they're endlessly spinning off into other universes."

"You mean, as if every choice you could make in a virtual was instantly mapped out in its entirety?"

"Exactly. But this is real. The worlds are all around us—right here."

The drink and the conversation moved on, and now it was my turn to apologize to Rob, and his to say no, I wasn't boring him. Because books, novels, stories, *they were my other worlds*, the thing I believed in even if no one else cared about them. That single, magical word, *Fog*, which Dickens uses as he begins to conjure London. And Frederic Henry walking away from the hospital in the rain. And Rose of Sharon offering the starving man her breast after the Joads' long journey across dustbowl America, and Candide eating fruit, and Bertie Wooster bumbling back across Mayfair . . .

Rob listened and seemed genuinely interested, even though he confessed he'd never read a single non-interactive story or novel. But, unlike most people, he said this as if he realized he was actually missing out on something. So we agreed I'd lend him some of my old paperbacks, and this, and what he'd shown me at the Clearbrite, signaled a new phase in our relationship.

4.

It seems to me now that some of the best hours of my life were spent not in reading books, but in sitting with Rob Holm in my cramped room in that house we shared back in Leeds, and talking about them.

What to read and admire, but also—and this was just as important—what not to. The *Catcher in the Rye* being overrated, and James Joyce a literary show-off, and *Moby Dick* really wasn't about much more than whales. Alarmingly, Rob was often ahead of me. He discovered a copy of *Labyrinths* by Jorge Luis Borges in a garage sale, which he gave to me as a gift and then kept borrowing back. But he was Rob Holm. He could solve the riddles of the cosmos and meanwhile explore literature as nothing but a hobby, and also help me out with my mek so that I was finally able to produce the kind of arguments, links, and algorithms for my piece on *Madame Bovary* that the AIs at An Eng actually wanted.

Meanwhile, I also found out about the kind of life Rob had come from. Both his parents were engineers, and he'd spent his early years in Aberdeen, but they'd moved to the Isle of Harris after his mother was diagnosed with a brain-damaging prion infection, probably caused by her liking for fresh salmon. Most of the fish were then factory-farmed in crowded pens in the Scottish lochs, where the creatures were dosed with antibiotics and fed on pellets of processed meat, often recycled from the remains of their own breed. Just as with cattle and Creutzfeldt-Jakob Disease a century earlier, this process had resulted in a small but significant species leap of cross-infection. Rob's parents wanted to make the best of the years Alice Holm had left, and set up an ethical marine farm—although they preferred to call it a ranch—harvesting scallops on the Isle of Harris.

Rob's father was still there at Creagach, and the business, which not only produced some of the best scallops in the Hebrides but also benefited other marine life along the costal shelf, was still going. Rob portrayed his childhood there as a happy time, with his mother still doing well, despite the warnings of the scans, and regaling him with bedtime tales of Celtic myths, that were probably his only experience before meeting me of linear fictional narrative.

There were the kelpies, who lived in lochs and were like fine horses, and then there were the Blue Men of the Minch who dwelt between Harris and the mainland and sung up storms and summoned the waves with their voices. Then, one night when Rob was eleven, his mother waited until he and his father were asleep, walked out across the shore and into the sea, and swam, and kept on swimming. No one could last long out there, the sea being so cold, and the strong currents, or perhaps the Blue Men of the Minch, bore her body back to a stretch of shore around the headland from Creagach, where she was found next morning.

Rob told his story without any obvious angst. But it certainly helped explain the sense of difference and distance he seemed to carry with him. That, and why he didn't fit. Not here in Leeds, amid the fun, mess, and heartbreak of student life, nor even, as I slowly came to realize, in the subject he was studying.

He showed me the virtual planetarium at the Clearbrite, and the signals from a probe passing through the Oort Cloud, and even took me down to the tunnels of a mine where a huge tank of cryogenically cooled fluid had been set up in the hope of detecting the dark matter of which it had once been believed most of our universe was made. It was an old thing now, creaking and leaking, and Rob was part of the small team of volunteers who kept it going. We stood close together in the dripping near-dark, clicking hardhats and sharing each other's breath, and of course I was thinking of other possibilities—those fractional moments when things could go one of many ways. Our lips pressing. Our bodies joining. But something, maybe a fear of losing him entirely, held me back.

"It's another thing that science has given up on," he said later when we were sitting at our table in the Eldon. "Just like that ridiculous Copenhagen shoulder-shrug. Without dark matter, and dark energy, the way the galaxies rotate and recede from each other simply doesn't make mathematical sense. You know what the so-called smart money is on these days? Something called topographical deformity, which means that the basic laws of physics don't apply in the same way across this entire universe. That it's pock-marked with flaws."

"But you don't believe that?"

"Of course I don't! It's fundamentally unscientific."

"But you get glitches in even the most cleverly conceived virtuals, don't you? Even in novels, sometimes things don't always entirely add up."

"Yeah. Like who killed the gardener in *The Big Sleep*, or the season suddenly changing from autumn to spring in that Sherlock Holmes story. But this isn't like that, Lita. This isn't . . ." For once, he was in danger of sounding bitter and contemptuous. But he held himself back.

"And you're not going to give up?"

He smiled. Swirled his beer. "No, Lita. I'm definitely not."

5.

Perhaps inevitably, Rob's and my taste in books had started to drift apart. He'd discovered an antique genre called Science Fiction, something that the AIs at An Lit were particularly sniffy about. And, even as he tried to lead me with him, I could see their point. Much of the prose was less than luminous, the characterization was sketchy, and, although a great deal of it was supposedly about the future, the predictions were laughably wrong.

But Rob insisted that that wasn't the point, that SF was essentially a literature of ideas. That, and a sense of wonder. To him, wonder was particularly important. I could sometimes—maybe as that lonely astronaut passed through the stargate, or with those huge worms in that book about a desert world—see his point. But most of it simply left me cold.

Rob went off on secondment the following year to something called the Large Millimeter Array on the Atacama Plateau in Chile, and I, for want of anything better, kept the lease on our house in Headingley and got some new people in, and did a masters on gender roles in George Eliot's *Middlemarch*. Of course, I paid him virtual visits, and we talked of the problems of altitude sickness and the changed assholes our old uni friends were becoming as he put me on a camera on a Jeep and bounced me across the dark-skied desert.

Another year went—they were already picking up speed—and Rob found the time for a drink before he headed off to some untenured post, part research, part teaching, in Heidelberg that he didn't seem particularly satisfied with. He was still reading—apparently there hadn't been much else to do in Chile—but I realized our days of talking about Proust or Henry James had gone.

He'd settled into, you might almost say retreated to, a sub-genre of SF known as alternate history, where all the stuff he'd been telling me about our world continually branching off into all its possibilities was dramatized on a big scale. Hitler had won World War Two—a great many times, it seemed—and the South was triumphant in the American Civil War. That, and the Spanish Armada had succeeded, and Europe remained under the thrall of medieval Roman Catholicism, and Lee Harvey Oswald's bullet had grazed past President Kennedy's head. I didn't take this odd obsession as a particularly good sign as we exchanged chaste hugs and kisses in the street outside the Eldon and went our separate ways.

I had a job of sorts—thanks to Sun-Mi, my fellow An Lit student from Korea—teaching English to the kids of rich families in Seoul, and for a while it was fun, and the people were incredibly friendly, but then I grew bored and managed to wrangle an interview with one of the media conglomerates that had switched its physical base to Korea in the wake of the California Earthquake. I was hired for considerably less than I was getting paid teaching English and took the crowded commute every morning to a vast half-real, semi-ziggurat high-rise mistily floating above the Mapo District, where I studied high res worlds filled with headache-inducing marvels, and was invited to come up with ideas in equally headache-inducing meetings.

I, an Alice in these many virtual wonderlands, brought a kind of puzzled innocence to my role. Two, maybe three, decades earlier, the other developers might still have known enough to recognize my plagiarisms, if only from old movies their parents had once talked about, but now what I was saying seemed new, fresh, and quirky. I was a thieving literary magpie, and became the go-to girl for unexpected turns and twists. The real murderer of Roger Ackroyd, and the dog collar in *The Great Gatsby*. Not to mention what Little Father Time does in *Jude the Obscure*, and the horror of Sophie's choice. I pillaged them all, and many others. Even the strange idea that the Victorians had developed steam-powered computers, thanks to my continued conversations with Rob.

Wherever we actually were, we got into the habit of meeting up at a virtual recreation of the bar of the Eldon that, either as some show-off feat of virtual engineering, or a post-post-modern art project, some student had created. The pub had been mapped in realtime down to the atom and the pixel, and the ghosts of our avatars often got strange looks from real undergrads bunking off from afternoon seminars. We could actually order a drink, and even taste the beer, although of course we couldn't ingest it. Probably no bad thing, in view of the state of the Eldon's toilets. But somehow, that five-pints-and-still-clear-headed feeling only added to the slightly illicit pleasure of our meetings. At least, at first.

It was becoming apparent that, as he switched from city to city, campus to campus, project to project, Rob was in danger of turning into one of those aging, permanent students, clinging to short-term contracts, temporary relationships, and get-me-by loans, and the worst thing was that, with typical unflinching clarity, he knew it.

"I reckon I was either born too early, or too late, Lita," he said as he sipped his virtual beer. "Even one of the assessors actually said that to me a year or so ago when I tried to persuade her to back my project."

"So you scientists have to pitch ideas as well?"

He laughed, but that warm, Hebridean sound was turning bitter. "How else does this world work? But maths doesn't change even if fashions do. The many worlds theory is the only way that the behavior of subatomic particles can be reconciled with everything else we know. Just because something's hard to prove doesn't mean it should be ignored."

By this time I was busier than ever. Instead of providing ideas other people could profit from, I'd set up my own consultancy, which had thrived and made me a great deal of money. By now, in fact, I had more of the stuff than most people would have known what to do with. But I did. I'd reserved a new apartment in a swish high-res, high-rise development going up overlooking the Han River and was struggling to get the builders to understand that I wanted the main interior space to be turned into something called a *library*. I showed them old walk-throughs of the Bodleian in Oxford, and the reading room of the British Museum, and the Brotherton in Leeds, and many other lost places of learning. Of course I already had a substantial collection of books in a secure, fireproofed, climate-controlled warehouse, but now I began to acquire more.

The once-great public collections were either in storage or scattered to the winds. But there were still enough people as rich and crazy as I was to ensure that the really rare stuff—first folios, early editions, hand-typed versions of great works—remained expensive and sought-after, and I surprised even myself with the determination and ruthlessness of my pursuits. After all, what else was I going to spend my time and money on?

There was no grand opening of my library. In fact, I was anxious to get all the builders and conservators, both human and otherwise, out of the way so I could have the place entirely to myself. Then I just stood there. Breathing in the air, with its savor of lost forests and dreams.

There were first editions of great novels by Nabokov, Dos Passos, Stendhal, Calvino, and Wells, and an early translation of Cervantes, and a fine collection of Swift's works. Even, in a small nod to Rob, a long shelf of pulp magazines with titles like *Amazing Stories* and *Weird Tales*, although their lurid covers of busty maidens being engulfed by intergalactic centipedes were generally faded and torn. Not that I cared about the pristine state of my whispering pages. Author's signatures, yes—the sense of knowing Hemingway's hands had once briefly grasped this edition—but the rest didn't matter. At least, apart from the thrill of beating others in my quest. Books, after all, were old by definition. Squashed moths and bus tickets stuffed between the pages. Coffee-cup circles on the dust jackets. Exclamations in the margin. I treasured the evidence of their long lives.

After an hour or two of shameless gloating and browsing, I decided to call Rob. My avatar had been as busy as me with the finishing touches to my library, and now it struggled to find him. What it did eventually unearth was a short report stating that Callum Holm, a fish-farmer on the Isle of Harris, had been drowned in a boating accident a week earlier.

Of course, Rob would be there now. Should I contact him? Should I leave him to mourn undisturbed? What kind of friend was I, anyway, not to have even picked up on this news until now? I turned around the vast, domed space I'd created in confusion and distress.

"Hey."

I span back. The Rob Holm who stood before me looked tired but composed. He'd grown a beard, and there were a few flecks of silver now in it and his hair. I could taste the sea air around him. Hear the cry of gulls.

"Rob!" I'd have hugged him, if the energy field permissions I'd set up in this library had allowed. "I'm so, so sorry. I should have found out, I should have—"

"You shouldn't have done anything, Lita. Why do you think I kept this quiet? I wanted to be alone up here in Harris to sort things out. But . . ." He looked up, around. "What a fabulous place you've created!"

As I showed him around my shelves and acquisitions, and his ghost fingers briefly passed through the pages of my first edition *Gatsby*, and the adverts for X-Ray specs in an edition of *Science Wonder Stories*, he told me how his father had gone out in his launch to deal with some broken tethers on one of the kelp beds and been caught by a sudden squall. His body, of course, had been washed up, borne to the same stretch of shore where Rob's mother had been found.

"It wasn't intentional," Rob said. "I'm absolutely sure of that. Dad was still in his prime, and proud of what he was doing, and there was no way he was ever going to give up. He just misjudged a coming storm. I'm the same, of course. You know that, Lita, better than anyone."

"So what happens next? With a business, there must be a lot to tie up."

"I'm not tying up anything."

"You're going to stay there?" I tried to keep the incredulity out of my voice.

"Why not? To be honest, my so-called scientific career has been running on empty for years. What I'd like to prove is never going to get backing. I'm not like you. I mean . . ." He gestured at the tiered shelves. "You can make anything you want become real."

6.

Rob wasn't the sort to put on an act. If he said he was happy ditching research and filling his father's role as a marine farmer on some remote island, that was because he was. I never quite did find the time to physically visit him in Harris—it was, after all, on the other side of the globe—and he, with the daily commitments of the family business, didn't get to Seoul. But I came to appreciate my glimpses of the island's strange beauty. That, and the regular arrival of chilled, vacuum-packed boxes of fresh scallops. But was this really enough for Rob Holm? Somehow, despite his evident pride in what he was doing, and the funny stories he told of the island's other inhabitants, and even the occasional mention of some woman he'd met at a ceilidh, I didn't think it was. After all, Creagach was his mother and father's vision, not his.

Although he remained coy about the details, I knew he still longed to bring his many worlds experiment to life. That, and that it would be complicated, controversial, and costly. I'd have been more than happy to offer financial help, but I knew he'd refuse. So what else could I do? My media company had grown. I had mentors, advisors, and consultants, both human and AI, and Rob would have been a genuinely useful addition to the team, but he had too many issues with the lack of rigor and logic in this world to put up with all the glitches, fudges, and contradictions of virtual ones. Then I had a better idea.

"You know why nothing ever changes here, don't you?" he asked me as our avatars sat together in the Eldon late one afternoon. "Not the smell from the toilets or the unfestive Christmas decorations or that dusty Pernod optic behind the bar. This isn't a feed from the real pub any longer. The old Eldon was demolished years ago. All we've been sitting in ever since is just a clever formation of what the place would be like if it still existed. Bar staff, students, us, and all."

"That's . . ." Although nothing changed, the whole place seemed to shimmer. "How things are these days. The real and the unreal get so blurry you can't tell which is which. But you know," I added, as if the thought had just occurred to me, "there's a project that's been going the rounds of the studios here in Seoul. It's a series about the wonders of science, one of those proper, realtime factual things, but we keep stumbling over finding the right presenter. Someone fresh, but with the background and the personality to carry the whole thing along."

"You don't mean me?"

"Why not? It'd only be part time. Might even help you promote what you're doing at Creagach."

"A scientific popularizer?"

"Yes. Like Carl Sagan, for example, or maybe Stephen Jay Gould."

I had him, and the series—which, of course, had been years in development purgatory—came about. I'd thought of it as little more than a way of getting Rob some decent money, but, from the first live-streamed episode, it was a success. After all, he was still charming and persuasive, and his salt-and-pepper beard gave him gravitas—and made him, if anything, even better looking. He used the Giant's Causeway to demonstrate the physics of fractures. He made this weird kind of pendulum to show why we could never predict the weather for more than a few days ahead. He swam with the whales off Tierra del Fuego. The only thing he didn't seem to want to explain was the odd way that photons behaved when you shot them down a double-slotted tube. That, and the inconsistencies between how galaxies revolved and Newton's and Einstein's laws.

In the matter of a very few years, Rob Holm was rich. And of course, and although he never actively courted it, he grew famous. He stood on podiums and looked fetchingly puzzled. He shook a dubious hand with gurning politicians. He even turned down offers to appear at music festivals, and had to take regular legal steps to protect the pirating of his virtual identity. He even finally visited me in Seoul and experienced the wonders of my library at first hand.

At last, Rob had out-achieved me. Then, just when I and most of the rest of the world had him pigeon-holed as that handsome, softly accented guy who did those popular science things, his avatar returned the contract for his upcoming series unsigned. I might have forgotten that getting rich was supposed to be the means to an end. But he, of course, hadn't.

"So," I said as we sat together for what turned out to be the last time in our shared illusion of the Eldon. "You succeed with this project. You get a positive result and prove the many worlds theory is true. What happens after that?"

"I publish, of course. The data'll be public, peer-reviewed, and—"

"Since when has being right ever been enough?"

"That's . . ." He brushed a speck of virtual beer foam from his grey beard, ". . . how science works."

"And no one ever had to sell themselves to gain attention? Even Galileo had to do that stunt with the cannonballs."

"As I explained in my last series, that story of the Tower of Pisa was an invention of his early biographers."

"Come on, Rob. You know what I mean."

He looked uncomfortable. But, of course, he already had the fame. All he had to do was stop all this Greta Garbo shit and milk it.

So, effectively I became PR agent for Rob's long-planned experiment. There was, after all, a lot for the educated layman, let alone the general public, or us so-called media professionals, to absorb. What was needed was a handle, a simple selling point. And, after a little research, I found one.

A man in a business suit had arrived at Tokyo airport in the summer of 1954. He was Caucasian but spoke reasonable Japanese, and everything about him seemed normal apart from his passport. It looked genuine but was from somewhere called Taured, which the officials couldn't find in any of their directories. The visitor was as baffled as they were. When a map was produced, he pointed to Andorra, a tiny but ancient republic between France and Spain, which he insisted was Taured. The humane and sensible course was to find him somewhere to sleep while further enquiries were made. Guards were posted outside the door of a secure hotel room high in a tower block, but the mysterious man had vanished without trace in the morning, and the Visitor from Taured was never seen again.

Rob was dubious, then grew uncharacteristically cross when he learned that the publicity meme had already been released. To him, and despite the fact that I thought he'd been reading this kind of thing for years, the story was just another urban legend and would further alienate the scientific establishment when he desperately needed their help. In effect, what he had to obtain was time and bandwidth from every available gravitational observatory, both here on Earth and up in orbit, during a crucial observational window, and time was already short.

It was as the final hours ticked down in a fervid air of stop-go technical problems, last minute doubts, and sudden demands for more money, that I finally took the sub-orbital from Seoul to Frankfurt, then the skytrain on to Glasgow, and some thrumming, windy thing of string and carbon fiber along the Scottish west coast, and across the shining Minch. The craft landed in Stornoway harbor in the Isle of Lewis—the northern part of the long land-mass of which Harris forms the south—where I was rowed ashore, and eventually found a bubblebus to take me across purple moorland and past scattered white bungalows, then up amid ancient peaks.

Rob stood waiting on the far side of the road at the final stop, and we were both shivering as we hugged in the cold spring sunlight. But I was here, and so was he, and he'd done a great job at keeping back the rest of the world, and even I wouldn't have had it any other way. It seemed as if most of the niggles and issues had finally been sorted. Even if a few of his planned sources had pulled out, he'd still have all the data he needed. Come tomorrow, Rob Holm would either be a prophet or a pariah.

7.

He still slept in the same narrow bed he'd had as a child in the rusty-roofed cottage down by the shore at Creagach, while his parents' bedroom was now filled with expensive processing and monitoring equipment, along with a high-band, multiple-redundancy satellite feed. Downstairs, there was a parlor where Rob kept his small book collection in an alcove by the fire—I was surprised to see that it was almost entirely poetry; a scatter of Larkin, Eliot, Frost, Dickinson, Pope, Yeats, and Donne, beside a few lingering Asimovs, Le Guins, and Clarkes—with a low tartan divan where he sat to read these works. Which, I supposed, might also serve as a second bed, although he hadn't yet made it up.

He took me out on his launch. Showed me his scallop beds and the glorious views of this ragged land with its impossibly wide and empty beaches. And there, just around the headland, was the stretch of bay where both Rob's parents had been found, and I could almost hear the Blue Men of the Minch calling to us over the sigh of the sea. There were standing stones on the horizon, and an old whaling station at the head of a loch, and a hill topped by a medieval church filled with the bodies of the chieftains who had given these islands such a savage reputation though their bloody feuds. And meanwhile, the vast cosmic shudder of the collision of two black holes was traveling toward us at lightspeed.

There were scallops, of course, for dinner. Mixed in with some fried dab and chopped mushroom, bacon and a few leaves of wild garlic, all washed down with malt whisky, and with whey-buttered soda bread on the side, which was the Highland way. Then, up in the humming shrine of his parents' old bedroom, Rob checked on the status of his precious sources again.

The black hole binaries had been spiraling toward each other for tens of thousands of years, and observed here on Earth for decades. In many ways, and despite their supposed mystery, black holes were apparently simple objects—nothing but sheer mass—and even though their collision was so far off it had actually happened when we humans were still learning how to use tools, it was possible to predict within hours, if not minutes, when the effects of this event would finally reach Earth.

There were gravitational observatories, vast-array laser interferometers, in deep space, and underground in terrestrial sites, all waiting to record this moment, and Rob was tapping into them. All everyone else expected to see—in fact, all the various institutes and faculties had tuned their devices to look for—was this . . . Leaning over me, Rob called up a display to show a sharp spike, a huge peak in the data, as the black holes swallowed each other and the shock of their collision flooded out in the asymmetrical pulse of a gravitational wave.

"But this isn't what I want, Lita. Incredibly faint though that signal is—a mere ripple deep in the fabric of the cosmos—I'm looking to combine and filter all those results, and find something even fainter.

"This . . ." He dragged up another screen, "is what I expect to see." There was the same central peak, but this time it was surrounded by a fan of smaller, ever-decreasing, ripples eerily reminiscent of the display Rob had once shown me of the ghost-flicker of those photons all those years ago in Leeds. "These are echoes of the black hole collision in other universes."

I reached out to touch the floating screen. Felt the incredible presence of the dark matter of other worlds.

"And all of this will happen tonight?"

He smiled.

8.

There was nothing else left to be done—the observatories Rob was tapping into were all remote, independent, autonomous devices—so we took out chairs into the dark, and drank some more whisky, and collected driftwood, and lit a fire on the shore.

We talked about books. Nothing new, but some shared favorites. Poe and Pasternak and Fitzgerald. And Rob confessed that he hadn't got on anything like as well as he'd pretended with his first forays into literature. How he'd found the antique language and odd punctuation got in the way. It was even a while before he understood the obvious need for a physical bookmark. He'd have given up with the whole concept if it hadn't been for my shining, evident faith.

"You know, it was *Gulliver's Travels* that finally really turned it around for me. Swift was so clever and rude and funny and angry, yet he could also tell a great story. That bit about those Laputan astronomers studying the stars from down in their cave, and trying to harvest sunbeams from marrows. Well, that's us right here, isn't it?"

The fire settled. We poured ourselves some more whisky. And Rob recited a poem by Li Po about drinking with the Moon's shadow, and then we remembered those days back in Leeds when we'd gone out onto the moors, and drank and ingested far more than was good for us, and danced like savages and, yes, there had even been that time he and I had gazed up at the stars.

We stood up now, and Rob led me away from the settling fire. The stars were so bright here, and the night sky was so black, that it felt like falling merely to look up. Over there in the west, Lita, is the Taurus Constellation. It's where the Crab Nebula lies, the remains of a supernova the Chinese recorded back in 1054, and it's in part of the Milky Way known as the Perseus Arm, which is where our dark binaries would soon end their fatal dance. I was leaning into him as he held his arms around me, and perhaps both of us were breathing a little faster than was entirely due to the wonders of the cosmos.

"What time is it now, Rob?"

"It's . . ." He checked his watch. "Just after midnight."

"So there's still time."

"Time for what?"

We kissed, then crossed the shore and climbed the stairs to Rob's single bed. It was sweet, and somewhat drunken, and quickly over. The Earth, the Universe, didn't exactly move. But it felt far more like making love than merely having sex, and I curled up against Rob afterward, and breathed his cinnamon scent, and fell into a well of star-seeing contentment.

"Rob?"

The sky beyond the window was showing the first traces of dawn as I got up, telling myself that he'd be next door in his parents' old room, or walking the shore as he and his avatar strove to deal with a torrent of interview requests. But I already sensed that something was wrong.

It wasn't hard for me to pull up the right screen amid the humming machines in his parents' room, proficient at mek as I now was. The event, the collision, had definitely occurred. The spike of its gravitational wave had been recorded by every observatory. But the next screen, the one where Rob had combined, filtered, and refined all the data, displayed no ripples, echoes, from other worlds.

I ran outside shouting Rob's name. I checked the house feeds. I paced back and forth. I got my avatar to contact the authorities. I did all the things you do when someone you love suddenly goes missing, but a large part of me already knew it was far too late.

Helicopters chattered. Drones circled. Locals gathered. Fishermen arrived in trawlers and skiffs. Then came the bother of newsfeeds, all the publicity I could ever have wished for. But not like this.

I ended up sitting on the rocks of that bay around the headland from Creagach as the day progressed, waiting for the currents to bear Rob's body to this place, where he could join his parents.

I'm still waiting.

9.

Few people actually remember Rob Holm these days, and if they do, it's as that good-looking guy who used to present those slightly weird nature—or was it science?—feeds, and didn't he die in some odd, sad kind of way? But I still remember him, and I still miss him, and I still often wonder what really happened on that night when he left the bed we briefly shared. The explanation given by the authorities, that he'd seen his theory dashed and then walked out into the freezing waters of the Minch, still isn't something I can bring myself to accept. So maybe he really was like the Visitor from Taured and simply vanished from a universe that couldn't support what he believed.

I read few novels or short stories now. The plots, the pages, seem over-involved. Murals rather than elegant miniatures. Rough-hewn rocks instead of jewels. But the funny thing is that, as my interest in them has dwindled, books have become popular again. There are new publishers, even new writers, and you'll find pop-up bookstores in every city. Thousands now flock to my library in Seoul every year, and I upset the conservators by allowing them to take my precious volumes down from their shelves. After all, isn't that exactly what books are for? But I rarely go there myself. In fact, I hardly ever leave the Isle of Harris, or even Creagach, which Rob, with typical consideration and foresight, left me in his will. I do my best to keep the scallop farm going, pottering about in the launch and trying to keep the crabs and the starfish at bay, although the business barely turns a profit, and probably never did.

What I do keep returning to is Rob's small collection of poetry. I have lingered with Eliot's Prufrock amid the chains of the sea, wondered with Hardy what might have happened if he and that woman had sheltered from the rain a minute more, and watched as Sylvia Plath's children burst those final balloons. I just wish that Rob was here to share these precious words and moments with me. But all that's left is you and I, dear, faithful reader, and the Blue Men of the Minch calling to the waves.

Rich Larson was born in West Africa, has studied in Rhode Island and worked in Spain, and now writes from Ottawa, Canada. His short work has been featured on io9, translated into Polish and Italian, and appears in numerous Year's Best anthologies as well as in magazines such as *Asimov's, Analog, Clarkesworld, F&SF, Interzone, Strange Horizons, Lightspeed,* and *Apex.* He was the most prolific author of short science fiction in 2015 and 2016.

EXTRACTION REQUEST

Rich Larson

When they finally shift the transport's still-smoldering wing enough to drag Beasley out from where he was pinioned, for a moment all Elliot can do, all anyone can do, is stare. Beasley's wiry arm with its bioluminescent tattoos is near sheared from its socket, and below his hips he's nothing but pulped meat and splinters of bone.

He's still alive, still mumbling, maybe about the woman Elliot saw in a little holo with her arms thrown around his neck, back before Beasley's dreadlocked mane was shaved off and a conscript clamp was implanted at the top of his spine.

"His impact kit never triggered," someone says, as if that's not fucking obvious, as if he could have been ragdolled out of the transport otherwise.

"Is the autosurgeon trashed?" someone else, maybe Tolliver, says. Elliot's ears are still ringing from the crash and his head swimming from what he was doing before it and all the voices seem to blend. He knows, dimly, that he should be giving orders by now.

"An autosurgeon can't do shit for him. What's it going to do, cauterize him at the waist?"

"Get him some paineaters at least. Numb him up."

"Shock's done that already."

"You don't know that."

"I fucking hope that."

Beasley is still trying to talk, but it's all a choking wet burble from the blood in his mouth. The nudge, though, comes through. It slides into the corner of Elliot's optic implant, blinking poisonous yellow. A little ripple goes through the rest of the squad, which means they got it, too. A couple of them reflexively clap their hands to the backs of their necks, where the caked scar tissue is still fresh enough to itch.

Elliot realizes that down here in the bog, cut off from command, the clamp at the top of Beasley's spine no longer needs official permission to trigger its nanobomb. All it needs is consensus.

"I'd want it done for me," Tolliver says, wiping a glisten of sweat off his face. His upvote floats into the digital queue. He chews at his lip, shoots Elliot a look that Elliot carefully ignores.

"Yeah," Santos from the lunar colony says, which is as much as she's ever said. "Trigger him." Another upvote appears, then another, then three more in a cascade. Elliot sees that he has a veto option—something they didn't tell him when they stuck him as squad leader. He looks into Beasley's glazed eyes and completes the consensus, floating his vote to the queue.

The nanobomb goes off, punching a precise hole through the brainstem and cutting every string at once. Beasley slumps.

Apart from that, injuries are minimal. Everyone else's kits went off properly, as evidenced by the gritty orange impact gel still slathering their uniforms. Elliot picks it off himself in clumps while he surveys damage to the R12 Heron transport settling in its crater at the end of a steaming furrow of crushed flora and shed metal. The anti-air smartmine shredded their primary rotor when it detonated, and the crash itself did the rest of the work. The Heron's not going to fly again.

"Should get them fuel cells out of her," says Snell, who is scarecrow skinny with a mouth full of metal, and dark enough so his shaved scalp seems to gleam blue-black. "In case there's leakage." Aside from Beasley, who's being wrestled into a body bag, Snell is the only one who knows flyers worth a damn. They conscripted him for smuggling human cargo on a sub-orbital.

"You do that," Elliot says, when he realizes Snell is waiting for go-ahead. "Get one of the Prentii to help. They're digging."

"You mean one of the twins?" Snell asks, with a grin that makes his metallic teeth gnash and scrape. Elliot did mean the twins, Privates Prentiss and Prentiss. The nickname slipped out, something Tolliver calls them the same way he calls Snell "The Smell" and Mirotic "Miroglitch." If he has one for Elliot, too, he doesn't use it when they're together.

"Yeah," Elliot says. "Get one of the twins."

Snell pulls on a diagnostic glove and clambers into the Heron carcass; Elliot turns to check on the perimeter. If they hadn't gone down over swampland, where the rubbery blue-purple ferns and dense-packed sponge trees provided a cushion, the crash might have been a lot worse. Their impact cleared a swathe on one side of the transport. On the other, Mirotic is calibrating the cyclops.

Elliot watches the red-lit sensory bulb strain on its spindly neck and spin in a slow circle. "What's it see?" he asks.

Mirotic is tapped in, with his optic implant glowing the same red as the surveillance unit. "Nothing hot and moving but us. Bog gets denser to the east and south. Lots of those sponge trees, lots of subterranean fungi. No radio communications. Could be more anti-air mines sitting masked, though."

His English is airtight, but still carries a Serbian lilt. Before they clamped him, he was upper-level enforcement in a Neo-European crime block on Kettleburn. He once personally executed three men and two women in an abandoned granary and had their corpses put through a thresher. Only Elliot has access to that back-record. To everyone else, Mirotic is a jovial giant with a bristly black beard and high-grade neural plugs.

Prentiss, Jan, trundles past, having received Snell's nudge for a hand with the fuel cells. He wipes wet dirt off on his tree-trunk thighs. Both he and his sister are nearly tall as Mirotic, and both are broader.

"Soil's no good for graves," Prentiss rumbles over his shoulder. "He's going to get churned up again. Watch."

"How many drones came out intact?" Elliot asks Mirotic, trying to sound sharp, trying not to imagine Beasley's body heaved back to the surface.

"Two," Mirotic says. "I can fix a third, maybe."

"Send one up," Elliot says, scratching his arm. "Get a proper map going."

Mirotic hesitates. "If I send up a drone, we might trigger another smart-mine."

Elliot hadn't thought of that. He hasn't thought of a lot of things, but rescinding the order would make him look off, make him look shook, maybe even remind Mirotic of the night he saw him with the syringe.

"That's why you keep it low," Elliot says. "Scrape the tree line, no higher. And keep it brief."

Mirotic takes a battered drone from its casing and unfolds it in his lap, sitting cross-legged on the damp earth. As it rises into the air, whirring and buzzing, his eyes turn bright sensory blue.

"It's strange there's no animal life," Mirotic says. "Nothing motile on the sensor but insects. Could be a disease came through. Bioweapon, even. Seen it in the woods around New Warsaw, dead and empty just like this." He rests his thick hands on his knees. "We could have everyone jack up their immunity boosters."

Elliot takes the hint and sends a widecast order to dial up immunity and use filtration, at least for the time being. Then he goes to where Tolliver and Santos are vacuum-sealing Beasley's body bag, the filmy material wrapping him tight like a shroud. Tolliver looks up at his approach, flicking dark lashes. He has smooth brown skin and sly smiles and a plastic-capped flay a skin artist did for him on leave that shows off the muscle and tendon of his arm in a graceful gash. Elliot has felt it under his fingertips, cool and hard. He knows Tolliver is fucking at least one other squadmate, but he doesn't think it's Santos.

"Me and Tolliver will finish up," Elliot says. "Go spot for Mirotic. He's tapped in. Then get the tents up."

"Sir." Santos's the only one on the squad who says sir, who salutes, and she does both with enough irony to slice through power armor. Santos was a foot soldier for one of the Brazilian families up on the lunar colony. She looks like a bulldog, squinty eyes and pouched cheeks. Her clamp didn't go in right and there's double the scarring up her head.

When Santos leaves, still sneering, Elliot drops to a crouch. "Did they know each other?" he asks, grabbing the foot end of the body bag. Tolliver takes the other and they carefully stand up.

"Talked Portuguese together sometimes," he says. "Beasley knew a bit. Said the moony accent's a real bitch to follow, though."

Elliot tells himself that this is why he needs Tolliver on his side, because Tolliver sees the webs, sees all the skinny bonds of social molecule that run through the squad.

"Fucked up seeing him halfway gone like that," Tolliver says, with a put-on hardness to his voice. "At least the clamp is good for something, right?"

Elliot grunts in response as they carry Beasley away from the downed Heron, away from the surveillance unit and the carbon-fiber tents now blooming around it.

"When I said we could give him paineaters, that vein in your forehead, it went big," Tolliver says, almost conversationally. "You were in the back when they hit us. You were in the medcab again."

"I'm coming down," Elliot says, even as his itching arm gives another twinge. "And I'm staying off it. Staying sharp."

Tolliver says nothing, and then they're at the hole where the other Prentiss, Noam, is waiting with a spade slung over her shoulder. They lower the body bag in slowly, gently. Elliot reaches down for a fistful of damp earth and crumbles it over Beasley's shrouded face. Tolliver does the same. Prentiss starts shoveling.

"We got the extraction request through before we lost altitude," Elliot says. "Won't be down here long."

Tolliver gives him a sidelong look. "Some of us will be," he says, then turns and leaves.

Elliot stays to watch until the body bag has disappeared completely under thick wet dirt.

Dusk drops fast on Pentecost, dyeing the sky and swamp a cold eerie blue for a half-hour before plunging them into pitch dark. Most of the squad already have peeled eyes—the night vision surgery is a common one for criminals—and Elliot orders all lights dimmed to minimum to conserve the generator.

Elliot has a tent to himself. He lies back stiff on his cot in the dark and reviews mission parameters in his optic implant, scrolling up and down over words he's read a thousand times. They were heading north to reinforce Osuna, cutting slantwise across marshy no-man's land the rebels usually stay away from. They were not expecting hostiles on the way, and now they're grounded at least a thousand klicks from the nearest outpost.

Elliot tries to calculate how long the paineaters and emergency morphine he salvaged from the shattered medcab will last him. Then he accesses his personal files in his implant and watches the one clip he hasn't deleted yet, the one he watches before he sleeps.

"She's awake . . . Just looking around . . ."

His wife's voice draws three syllables out of awake, drags on around, high and sweet and tinged weary. His daughter's soft and veiny head turns. Her bright black eyes search, and Elliot can pretend they see him.

Something scrapes against the side of the tent. He blinks the clip away, hauls upright and reaches for his weapon before he recognizes the imprint of a body pressed up flush to the fabric. Elliot swipes a door with his hand and Tolliver slides through, already halfway undressed.

"Told the Smell I'm out back for a long shit," Tolliver says, working his stiff cock with one hand, reaching for Elliot's waistband with the other. "Let's be quick."

"Wasn't sure you'd be coming," Elliot says, helping yank the fatigues off. "Because of Beasley."

"Don't fucking talk about Beasley," Tolliver says.

Elliot doesn't, and Tolliver's body all over his is second best to a morphine hit for helping him not think about that or anything else. But when he comes it's a throb and a trickle and then everything turns lukewarm dead again. Afterward, Tolliver sits on the edge of the cot and peels his spray-on condom off in strips.

"Jan went walkabout in the swamp a bit," he says, because this has been the usual trade since they deployed last month. "Think he's testing the range limit for the clamp. Wants to skate, maybe. Him and his sister."

"In the middle of a mined bog?" Elliot asks, pulling his fatigues back on.

"They're both settlement-bred," Tolliver says. "Colonist genemix, you know, they think they're invincible. Probably think they can tough it out and get south to the spaceport."

"He told you that he wants to desert?"

Tolliver takes a drink from Elliot's water bottle and runs his tongue along his teeth. "He told me he did some exploring," he says. "Wanted to jaw about some odd bones he found. I filled in the rest."

"What did he find?" Elliot asks.

"Animal bones," Tolliver says. "Really white, really clean."

"Mirotic thinks a plague might have come through," Elliot says, instead of saying a bioweapon. "There'd be bones."

"Plagues don't usually put them in neat little heaps," Tolliver says. "He said they were all piled up. A little mound of skeletons."

Tolliver swipes a door and disappears, leaving Elliot sweat-soaked and sick-feeling. He only hesitates a moment before he gropes under the bedroll for his syringe. Before he can start prepping his favorite vein, the cyclops starts to wail.

Everyone is out of their tents and armed in a few minutes, clustered around the cyclops. Half of them are rubbing their eyes as the peel sets in and turns their irises reflective. Elliot switches to night vision in his implant, lighting the shadows radiation green. The air sits damp and heavy on his shoulders, and with no breeze nothing moves in the flora. The stubby sponge trees and wide-blade ferns are dead still.

"Where's your brother?" Elliot asks Noam, counting heads.

"Taking a shit out back," she says. "He'll have heard it, though."

Mirotic is tapped in now, his implant blinking red. "Just one bogey," he says. "Thirty meters out. Looks like some kind of animal."

"You set it to wail for every fucking swamp rat that wanders through?" Snell says. His face is still streaked with soap.

"It's a lot bigger than a rat," Mirotic says. "Don't know what it is. It hasn't got vitals. It isn't warm."

"Mechanical?" Elliot asks, thinking of the spider-legged hunter-killers they used to drag rebels out of their caves around Catalao. Tech has a way of trickling over in these long engagements, whether stolen or sold off on the side.

"It's not moving like any of the crawlers I've seen," Mirotic says. "Circling now, toward the back of us. Fast. Jan's still squatting back there."

Some of the squad swivel instinctively. Elliot pulls up Jan's channel. "Prentiss, there's a bogey heading towards you," he says. "Might be mechanical. Get eyes on it."

Jan's reply crackles. "Hard to miss," he says. "It's fucking glowing."

"And what is it?" Elliot says. "You armed?"

Jan's reply does not come by channel, but his howl punctures the still night air. Elliot is knocked back as Noam barrows past him, unslinging her gnasher and snapping the safety off. Snell's fast behind, and then the others, and then Elliot finds himself rearguard. He's still fumbling for his weapon when he rounds the back of the downed Heron.

His eyes slip-slide over the scene, trying to make sense of the nightmarish mass of bioluminescence and spiky bone that's enveloped Jan almost entirely. His night vision picks out a trailing arm, a hip, a boot exposed. The creature is writhing tight around Jan's body, spars of bone rasping against each other, and the glowing flesh of it is moving, slithering. The screams from inside are muffled.

Snell fires first, making Elliot's dampers swell like wet cotton in his ear canals. The spray of bullets riddle the length of the creature, and a fine spray of red blood—Jan's blood—flicks into the air.

"Don't fucking shoot!" Noam smacks Snell's weapon down and lunges forward, reaching for her brother's convulsing arm. Before he can grab hold, the creature retreats toward the tree line with Jan still ensnared, unnervingly fast.

It claws itself forward on a shifting pseudopod of bone spines, moving like a scuttling blanket. Someone else fires a shot, narrowly missing Noam running after it. The creature slithers into the trees, for an instant Noam is silhouetted against the eerie glow of it, then both of them disappear in the dark.

"Shit," Tolliver says. "I mean, shit."

Elliot thinks that's as good a summary as any. He can still see Noam's vitals, and Jan's too, both of them spiked hard with adrenaline but alive. They'll be out of range in less than a minute.

"I hit it," Snell says. "Raked it right along its, I don't know, its abdomen. Didn't do nothing."

"You hit Jan. That blood spray, that was Jan."

"Jan's *inside* it."

"We're going after them, right?"

Elliot looks around at the squad's distorted faces. Tolliver's eyes gleam like a cat's in the dark. There is no protocol for men being dragged away by monsters in the night. He opens his jaw; shuts it again. Mirotic shifts in his peripheral, taking a half-step forward, shoulders thrust back, and Elliot knows he is a nanosecond from taking the squad over, and maybe that would be better for everyone.

"Mirotic," he says. "You stay. Get a drone up and guide us bird's eye. Everyone else, on me."

Plunging through the dark swamp, Elliot expects every mud-sucked step to trigger another smartmine. Sweat pools in the hollow of his collarbone. The whine of the drone overhead shivers in his clenched teeth, and the squad is silent except for heavy breathing, muted curses as they follow its glowing path in their implants. The Prentii's signal comes and goes like a static ghost.

The warped green-and-black blur of his night vision, the drone's shimmering trail of digital breadcrumbs, the memory of the monster and Jan's disembodied thrashing arm—none of it seems quite real. A nightmare, or more likely an overdose.

"Rebels stay out of these swamps," Snell says aloud, dredging something from his post-clamp war briefing. "All the colonists do." His voice is thin and tight.

Nobody replies. The drone's pathway hooks left, into the deepest thicket of sponge trees, and they follow it. Pungent-smelling leaves slap against Elliot's head and shoulders. It reminds him almost of the transplanted eucalyptus trees where he grew up on Earth.

"Can't get any closer with the drone," comes Mirotic's crackly voice in his ear. "Trees are too high, too dense. They're right ahead of you. Close now."

The twins' signal flares in Elliot's skull, but their channels are shut and their vitals are erratic. Elliot's feels his heart starting to thrum too fast. Eyes blink and heads twitch as the rest of the squad picks up the signal. Tolliver's face is drawn, his mouth half-open. Santos is unreadable. Snell looks ready to shit himself. Hands tighten on stocks. Fingers drift to triggers.

The sponge trees thin out, and Elliot sees the same bioluminescence that swallowed Jan whole. The shape of it is indistinct, too bright for his night vision, so he flicks it off. When he closes and reopens his eyes, he sees what's become of the twins.

They are tangled together in a grotesque parody of affection, limbs wrapping each other, and it's impossible to tell where one ends and the other begins because they are coated in a writhing skin of ghostly blue light. Long shafts of dull gray bone, humors or femurs from an animal Elliot knows was not killed by any plague, skewer them in place like a tacked specimen.

Reminding himself it might be a hallucination, Elliot steps slowly forward. "Prentiss?"

A sluggish ripple goes through the twins' tangled bodies. Elliot follows the motion and finds a neck. A head not covered over. Noam's eyes are wide open and terrified. Elliot watches her face convulse trying to speak, but when her bruised mouth opens, glowing blue tendrils spill out of her throat. It's inside her. Elliot recoils. In his own throat, he feels bile rising and burning.

"Shit, they're conscious," Tolliver breathes. "What is that stuff? What the fuck is . . . ?" He reaches for Noam's cheek with one hand, but before he makes contact the other head, Jan's, buried somewhere near his sister's thigh, begins to wail. It's a raw animal noise Elliot has only ever heard men make when they are torn apart, when their limbs have been blown off, when shock and pain have flensed them down to the reptile brain and all it knows to do is scream.

He claws Tolliver's hand back.

"Don't touch them," he says. "We have to run a scan, or . . ." He looks at the bones pinning them in place, at the writhing cloak that looks almost like algae, now, like glowing blue algae. He has no idea what to do.

"Look at the feet," Santos says thickly. "Fuck."

Elliot looks. Noam's feet are not feet any more. The skin and muscle has been stripped away, leaving bits of bone, crumbling with no tendon to hold them together.

"Kill them," Santos says. "It's eating them alive." She pulls her sidearm and aims it at Jan's screaming mouth. Her hand tremors.

Elliot doesn't tell her no. It would be mercy, now, to kill them. Same how it was mercy for Beasley.

A vein bulges up Santos's neck. "Can't," she grunts. "The implant."

Elliot aims his own weapon at Jan and as his finger finds the trigger he finds himself paralyzed, blinking red warnings scrolling over his eyes. Convict squads have insurance against friendly fire same as any other. Maybe in a combat situation the parameters would loosen a little, but this, an execution, is out-of-bounds.

"Send the nudge, Noam." Tolliver squats down by her wide-eyed face. "You in there? You gotta send the nudge. So we can trigger you. Come on, Noam."

The yellow message doesn't appear. Maybe Noam is too angry, too colonist, thinking she is invincible, thinking somehow she'll get out of this scrape how she got out of all the other ones. More likely her mind is too far gone to access the implant. Jan starts to scream again.

"I'll fucking do it manual, then," Tolliver says, with his voice shaking. He looks at Snell. "Give me your knife. Unless you want to do it."

Snell wordlessly unclips his combat knife and slings it over, handle-first. It's a long wicked thing, not regulation or even close. Elliot thinks he should offer to do it. He's in command, after all. He knows where the jugular is and where to slit it without dousing himself in blood. But he only watches.

And the instant Tolliver touches Noam's head, all hell breaks loose. The monsters come from everywhere at once, scuttling masses of bone and bio-luminescence. From the ground, Elliot realizes dimly even as he backpedals, keys his night vision, opens fire. The rest of the squad is doing the same; splinters fly where bullets hit bone but the skin of things, the blue algae, just splits and reforms.

Subterranean fungi. He remembers that from the topography scan as Tolliver klicks empty and fumbles his reload.

"Get the fuck out," comes Mirotic's voice. "They're coming on your twelve, your three. Lots of them."

Doesn't matter. The thought spears through Elliot's mind. Doesn't matter if he dies here or on Kettleburn or wherever else. He's been dead for ages.

Then Tolliver goes down, tripped by a monster clamping its bony append-ages around his legs like a vice. Elliot aims low and for gray, shattering enough bones for Tolliver to wriggle out, to swap clips. But bullets aren't enough here.

Elliot loads the incendiary grenade as Tolliver scrambles free. He tries to remember the chemical compositions here on Pentecost. For all he knows, it might light up the whole fucking swamp. For all he knows, that might be a better way to die than getting flensed alive.

"Run," Elliot orders, and sends the fire-in-the-hole warning spike at the same time. "Leave them."

Santos rips past him, then Snell, then Tolliver right after, no protest, his reflective eyes wide and frantic in the dark. With adrenaline turning everything slow and sharp, Elliot fires the grenade where he thinks the splash will be widest, hitting the dirt between two of the surging creatures. He remembers to blink off his night vision only a nanosecond before the explosion.

A wall of searing heat slams over his body and even without night vision the blossoming fireball all but blinds him. He feels Tolliver grabbing his shoulder, guiding him out of the thicket. Through the roar in his ears, he can't be sure if Jan is still screaming.

They are sitting in the husk of the downed Heron, grouped around a heater. Every so often someone glances toward the cyclops, which is still whirring and spinning and searching. Santos has a bruise on her forehead from where the butt of Snell's gnasher clipped her in the dark. Tolliver cut his thumb falling. Other than that, they are all fine, except Elliot hasn't been able to get to his syringe.

"So there was no plague," Mirotic says. "Only a predator."

"That thing was artificial," Snell says. His eyes look wild, bloodshot, and his hand keeps going to the spot where his knife used to be. "No way could that evolve, man. It's a weapon."

"It's organic, whatever it is," Mirotic says. "Looked on the scan like a fungus."

"It's a weapon, and they dumped us here to test it." Snell's voice ratchets high. "That fucking smartmine was probably one of ours. We're expendable, right? So they dumped us here to see if it works."

Elliot waits for someone to tell Snell to settle the fuck down, but instead Santos and Tolliver and Mirotic are all looking at him, waiting for his response. Tolliver plucks at the bandage around his hand, anxious.

"The colonists stay out of these swamps," Elliot says. "You said that yourself." He has a flash of the twins' twisted bodies, the scuttling monsters. "I figure now we know why."

"When do we get extracted?" Santos asks flatly. "Sir."

Elliot knows they are low priority. Maybe five days, maybe six. Maybe more. "They know we're rationed for a week," he says.

"A fucking week?" Snell grinds his metal teeth. "Man, we can't be out here a week with that thing. I'm not ending up like the twins, man. I say we carry what we can, and we get out of here."

"To where?" Mirotic asks. "The fungus extends under the ground in all directions."

"If you knew about this, why didn't you tell us?" Snell demands.

Mirotic's nostrils flare. "Because fungus is not usually predatory."

Elliot tries to focus on the back-and-forth, tries to think of what they should do now that they know the swamp is inhabited by monsters. He realizes he is scratching at his arm.

Santos looks over. "What the fuck?"

But she isn't looking at Elliot. Tolliver, who has been silent, ash-faced, is clutching at his bandaged thumb. He looks down at it now and his eyes widen. A faint blue glow is leaking from underneath the cling wrap.

"Oh, shit, oh, shit, I feel it." Tolliver is twisting on the cot, sweat snaking down his face. "I can feel it. Moving."

The bandages are off his hand now and his cut thumb is speckled with the glowing fungus. The autosurgeon unfolds over his chest like a metal spider while Mirotic searches for the right removal program, his eyes scrolling code. Elliot feels a panic in his throat that he never feels during combat. It reminds him of the panic he felt last time he spoke to his daughter.

He crouches down and holds Tolliver's free hand where Snell and Santos can't see. It's slippery from the sweat.

"Got it," Mirotic says thickly. "Biological contaminant."

The autosurgeon comes to life, reaching with skeletal pincers to hold Tolliver's left arm in place. Carmine laserlight plays over his skin, scanning, then the numbing needle dips in with machine precision to prick the base of his thumb.

Tolliver's free hand clenches tight around Elliot's.

"Hate these things," he groans, locking eyes for a moment. "Rather let the Smell use that big old fucking knife than have a bot digging around—"

"Shouldn't have dropped it, then," Snell says.

Tolliver swivels, his mouth pulls tight in a grimace. "Fuck you, Snell."

The autosurgeon deploys a scalpel. Metal slides and scrapes and the sound shivers in Elliot's teeth. Mirotic is looking over at him, and when he speaks he realizes why.

"The spores are moving. Autosurgeon wants to take the whole thumb."

A wince ripples through the tent; Santos clutches his own thumb tight between two knuckles. Tolliver's eyes go wide. He tries to yank his arm away, but the autosurgeon holds tight.

"No!" he barks. "No, don't let it! Turn the fucking thing off!"

"It could spread through his body if we aren't fast," Mirotic says. "How you said it did to Prentiss and Prentiss."

Elliot swallows. He isn't a medic. What they drilled into his head, from basic onwards, was to trust the autosurgeon. And he doesn't want Tolliver to end up like the twins.

"Do it," he mutters.

"Turn it off!" Tolliver wails. "Listen! Listen to me, you fucks!"

His free hand thrashes but Elliot holds it tight, not caring anymore if Santos and Snell can see it, as the scalpel descends.

"The program's running," Mirotic says. "Too late to stop it."

The blade makes no sound as it slices through the skin, the tendon, the bone. The autosurgeon catches the squirt of bright red blood and whisks it away. Tolliver howls. His spine arches. His hand clamps to Elliot's hard enough to bruise.

Elliot sits underneath the cyclops, listening to it whir. He said they would sleep in shifts, that he would watch first, as if his vitreous eyes might catch something the sensors miss. Partly because he had to say something. Give some kind of order. Mostly because he needed a hit.

Now, with the morphine swimming warm through his veins, he feels light. He feels calm. His heartbeat is so slow it is almost an asymptote.

"He screamed so much because there was no anesthetic in the autosurgeon."

Elliot turns to see Mirotic, holding a black plastic cube in his hand. He understands the words, but his guilt breaks apart against the high and then dissipates. Tolliver will be fine. Everything will be fine. He tries to shrink the chemical smile on his face, so Mirotic won't see it.

"Everybody knows why," Mirotic says. "Where's the rest of it?" He doesn't wait for a reply. He snatches the rattling sock out of Elliot's lap and yanks him to his feet. Mirotic is tall. But he's slow, too, the way everything is slow on the morphine, and Elliot still has his old tricks.

A hook, a vicious twist, then Mirotic is on the ground with the needle of the syringe poised a centimeter from his eyeball.

"I need that," Elliot says.

"You're pathetic," Mirotic grunts. "Holding his hand and wasting his morphine."

"Why do you care?" Elliot asks, suspicious now, wondering if maybe it's Mirotic who Tolliver visits in the night when he doesn't come to him.

Mirotic slaps the syringe away and drives a knee up into Elliot's chest. The air slams out of him, but he feels only impact, no pain. He staggers away, bent double. If his lungs were working he would maybe laugh.

"I care because you used to know what the fuck you were doing," Mirotic says. "Back before they stuck you with a con squad." He taps the high-grade neural plug at his temple. "You read our records. But I've seen yours, too. These personnel firewalls aren't shit. And if we're going to get out of this, it won't be with you doped to the eyes."

"Give Private Tolliver the paineaters," Elliot rasps, straightening up. "Leave the morphine. That's an order."

Mirotic shakes his head. "It stays with me, now. You'll get it when we get extracted." He tosses the black plastic cube; Elliot nearly fumbles it. "Worry about this, instead," Mirotic says. "Worry about a fungus that eats our flesh and uses the bones like scaffolding."

Elliot turns the cube over. Through the transparent face, he sees sticky strands of the glowing blue fungus moving, wrapping around Tolliver's scoured-white knucklebone.

In the morning, Snell is gone.

"Never woke me for my watch," Santos says, picking gound out of the corner of her eye. "I checked the tent. His kit's not there."

"And now he's out of range," Mirotic says. "Could get the drones up to look for him. Keep them low again so we don't trigger any more mines."

The inside of Elliot's mouth feels like steel wool. They are standing in the sunshine, which makes his head ache, too. A cool breeze is rippling through the blue-and-purple flora. The sponge trees are swaying. It's peaceful, near to beautiful. In daylight it's hard to believe what happened only hours ago in the dark. But the twins' tent is empty, and Tolliver is drugged to sleep with bloody gauze around the stump of his thumb.

"Why would we look for him?" Elliot says.

Santos gledges sideways at Mirotic, but neither of them speak.

"He deserted," Elliot says. "If he doesn't pose a threat to us, we let him walk. He'll either step on a mine or get eaten alive." He feels slightly sick imagining it, but he keeps his voice cold and calm. "Mirotic, rig up a saw to one of the drones, start clearing the vegetation on our flank. Make sure we have clean line of fire. No use watching them on the cyclops if we can't hit them til they're right up on us. Santos, get the comm system out of the Heron. We're going to make a radio tower."

When Santos departs with her sloppy salute, there's less contempt in it than usual. Mirotic stays and stares at him for a second, suspicious. Elliot meets his gaze, pretending he doesn't care, pretending he didn't already ransack Mirotic's cot looking for the morphine while he was on watch.

"Good," Mirotic says, then goes to get the drone.

Elliot turns back toward the tents. He lets himself into the one Tolliver and Snell were sharing, and realizes Tolliver is no longer asleep. He's sitting up on the sweat-stained cot, staring down at his lap, at his hand.

"How are you feeling?" Elliot asks, because he doesn't know what else to say.

"You took my thumb." Tolliver's voice trembles. "I needed that thumb. That's my good hand."

"It was moving deeper," Elliot says. "That's why we had to amputate. You probably don't remember." He hopes Tolliver doesn't remember, especially not the pain.

"Still got a trigger finger, so I guess it doesn't matter to you, right?" Tolliver says. "Still got a mouth, still got an ass. All the parts you like."

Elliot feels heat creeping under his cheeks. "You can get a prosthetic when they pick us up," he says, clipped.

"At this rate?" Tolliver gives a bitter laugh. "There's gonna be nobody left to pick up tomorrow, fuck a week. That's if you really did get the extraction request through, and you're not just lying through your fucking teeth. I know junkies. I know all you do is lie."

Elliot wants to slip his hands around Tolliver's throat and throttle him. He wants to slip under the sheet and hold Tolliver to him and tell him they're going to make it. He does neither.

"I needed that thumb because I was going to be a welder," Tolliver snaps as Elliot goes to leave. "When all this shit was over and I'd gotten my clamp out, I was going to be a welder like my grandfather was."

But war is never really over, and there's a sort of clamp that doesn't come out. Elliot doesn't even remember what he used to think he was going to be. He turns over his shoulder.

"Your head's not right," he says calmly. "It's the drugs. Try to sleep more."

"Oh, fuck you," Tolliver says, somewhere between laughing and crying. "Fuck you, Elliot."

Elliot steps out, and the tent closes behind him like a wound scabbing shut.

By the time night falls, they've cleared a perimeter, cutting away the vegetation in ragged circumference around the Heron, the tents, the cyclops. Tolliver came out to help mid-afternoon, jaw clenched tight and eyes fixed forward. Nobody mentioned his hand or even looked at it.

The few incendiary grenades they have in armory are distributed. Mirotic is trying to rig up a flamethrower using a soldering torch and fuel drained from the tank. Santos and Tolliver are perched on the roof of the Heron, hooking the makeshift antennae into the comm system through a tangle of wires.

Mostly busy work, Elliot knows. They can't be sure the incendiary grenade did anything but distract the fungus, and it moves fast enough that having open ground might only be to its advantage. They don't know anything about this enemy.

But if he keeps up appearances, maybe he can get the last of the morphine back from Mirotic without resorting to violence. Act sharp, act competent, and then when the withdrawal kicks in he won't have to exaggerate much to make Mirotic realize how much he needs it to function.

"Nothing," Santos says.

Elliot looks up to the roof of the Heron. Tolliver is still trying to rotate the antennae for a better signal, but all that comes through the comm system and into their linked implants is shrieking static. He dials it down in his head. They are too far from the outpost.

Then a familiar signal comes faint and blurry. A blinking yellow nudge slides into the corner of his optic.

"Snell," Tolliver says. "Shit."

Elliot feels a shiver go under his skin. The sky is turning dark above them. The cyclops picked up no movement during the day, but like Mirotic said, plenty of predators hunt only at night. There can only be one reason Snell would send the nudge. Elliot can picture him stumbling through the bog, maybe dragging a turned ankle, with the blue glow creeping closer and closer behind him in the dark. Or maybe the fungus already has him, is already flensing him down to his skeleton.

Tolliver's upvote appears, then Santos's. It will only take four votes now to trigger the nanobomb. Mirotic looks over at him, and Elliot doesn't think Mirotic is the merciful type. He executed three people and put their bodies through a thresher. But then Mirotic's upvote appears in the queue.

"Quick," Tolliver says, not looking at him. "Before we lose the signal."

Elliot is not sure if he's making the strong move or the weak move, but he adds his vote and completes the consensus because he still remembers Jan's screams. Everyone is silent for a moment. Santos crosses herself with the same precision she salutes.

"Leave the antennae," Elliot says. "The extraction request went through. They'll come when they come. Until then, we dig in and stay alert."

Santos hops down off the roof of the Heron. Tolliver follows after, gingerly for his bandaged hand. Elliot looks at what's left of the squad—fifty percent casualties in less than two days, and nowhere near the frontlines. Santos is steady; Elliot hasn't seen her shook once yet. Mirotic is steady. But Tolliver hasn't told a joke or barely spoken the whole day and his eyes look scared.

Elliot's still looking at Tolliver when the cyclops wails a proximity alert. He tamps down his own fear, motions for Mirotic to tap in.

"Seven bogeys," Mirotic says. "Different sizes. Biggest one is over two meters high. They're heading right at us, not so fast this time."

Elliot flicks to night vision and watches the trees. "Aim for the bones," he says, remembering the previous night. "They need them to hold together. Santos, get a firebomb ready."

Santos loads an incendiary grenade into the launcher underslung off her rifle. Tolliver has his weapon tucked up against his side, like he's bracing for auto, and Elliot remembers it's because he has no thumb. Across the carpet of chopped-down ferns and branches, he sees something emerging from the trees. It's not moving how the other ones moved.

Elliot squints and the zoom kicks in. The shambling monster is moving on three legs and its body is a spiky mess of charred bone held together by the ropy fungus. Through the glow he can make out part of a blackened skull on one side. The twins' bones, stripped and reassembled like scaffold. His stomach lurches.

Santos curses in Portuguese. "Permission to fire?" she asks through her teeth.

The other bogeys are converging now, low and scuttling like the one that took Noam. A pack, Elliot thinks. He can feel his pulse in his throat. This isn't combat how he knows combat. Not an enemy how he knows enemies. He wonders if the flames even did any damage the night before. Bullets certainly hadn't.

"Wait until they're closer," he says. "No wasted splash."

Santos sights. Her finger drifts toward the trigger. She waits.

But the monsters don't come any closer.

"It's fucking with us," Tolliver says. "Sitting out there waiting." He has a calorie bar in his hand but it's still wrapped. He's been turning it over and over in his fingers.

Santos bites a chunk off her own ration. "You think it thinks?" she asks thickly. She glances to Mirotic, who shrugs, then to Elliot, who distractedly does the same. Elliot is more concerned by the deepening itch in the crook of his arm. He needs morphine soon.

"Has to," Tolliver says. "It came for Jan first. Jan was the one who went out and found the bones in the first place. Then it used Noam to lure us out."

The four of them are sitting under the cyclops, with a crate dragged out to hold food and dice for a game nobody is keeping track of, just rolling and passing on autopilot. Every so often Elliot has someone walk a tight circle around the Heron to check their back, in case more of the monsters try to flank them. In case the cyclops malfunctions and doesn't see them coming. Busy work.

But there are still only seven, and they still haven't advanced from the edge of the trees. Sometimes the fungus shifts and the bones find new positions, but they all stay in place, waiting, maybe watching, if the fungus has some way of seeing them. Mirotic suggested heat sensitivity. Mirotic, who must have the morphine hidden somewhere on his body.

Santos is the first to finish her food. She stands up, brushing crumbs off her knees. "I'll go," she says, hefting her weapon. Elliot nods. He can't help but notice Tolliver's eyes follow Santos around the corner of the Heron, wide and worried. Maybe it is Santos he goes to see.

"Big snakes only have to eat once in a month," Tolliver says, turning his eyes back to his bandaged hand, studying the spot of red blooming through. "Spend the rest of it digesting."

Mirotic snorts. "This fungus is not part of a balanced ecosystem. It killed off all the other animal life. Obliterated it."

"Wish we had a fucking chinegun," Tolliver mutters.

Then the cyclops keens, and everyone is on their feet in an instant. Elliot sights towards the tree line first, but the monsters haven't moved. Mirotic's optics blink red.

"Right behind us," he says, and whatever he says next is drowned in gunfire. Santos's signal flares hot in Elliot's head, combat active. Elliot rounds the corner of the Heron and sees Santos scrambling backward as a ghoulish mass of bone and blue bears down on her. He can't understand how the monster covered the perimeter so quickly, how the cyclops didn't spot it earlier. Then he recognizes the tatters of Beasley's polythane body bag threaded through the fungus.

Elliot shoots for bone, but the way the monster writhes as it moves makes it all but impossible. The burst sinks harmlessly into its glowing blue flesh. Tolliver is firing beside him, howling something, but through the dampers he can't hear it. The monster turns toward them, distracted. Elliot calculates; too close for a grenade. He fires again and this time sees Beasley's shinbone shatter apart.

The monster sags, shifting another bone in to take its place, moving what's left of Beasley's arm downward. In the corner of his eye Elliot sees Santos is on her knees, rifle braced. Her shot blows a humerus to splinters and the monster sags again. Elliot feels a flare of triumph in his chest.

Motion in his peripherals. He spins in time to see the other seven bogeys swarm over the top of the Heron. He switches to auto on instinct and strangles the trigger, slashing back and forth. Bullets sink into the fungus, others ricochet off the Heron, spitting sparks. Some find bone but not enough. The rifle rattles his hands and then he's empty and the monsters are still coming.

He backs up, hands moving autonomously for the reload. Tries to get his bearings. Tolliver is still firing, still howling something he can't make out. Santos is down, legs pinned from behind. Bony claws are moving up her back; Elliot sees her teeth bared, her eyes wide. Where is Mirotic?

The answer comes in a jet of flame that envelops the nearest monster. It doesn't scream—no mouth—but as Elliot stumbles back from the heat he can see the fungus twisting, writhing, blackening to a crisp. Mirotic swings the flamethrower, painting a blazing arc in the air. Elliot reloads, sights, fires.

Suddenly the monsters are fleeing, scuttling away. Elliot fires again and again as they round the edge of the Heron. Mirotic waves the flamethrower, Elliot and Tolliver shoot from behind him, advancing steadily. One of the monsters crumples and slicks onto its neighbor, leaving its bones behind on the dirt. Elliot keeps firing until the glow of them is completely obscured by trees.

"You fuckers, you fuckers, you fuckers," Tolliver is saying, almost chanting.

Elliot is shaking all over. His skin is crawling with sweat. "Check on Santos," he says, and Tolliver disappears. There are aches in his back and arms and he can feel his bowels loosening for the first time in a long time. He needs to get the morphine back. He turns to Mirotic, to tell him as much, but as the big man snuffs the end of the flamethrower, he stumbles.

A wine-red stain is blooming under his shirt. Elliot remembers the ricochet off the side of the Heron. Mirotic sits down. He methodically rolls his shirt up and exposes a weeping bullet hole in his side. Elliot can see the shape of at least one shattered rib poking at his skin.

"Fuck," Mirotic says, in a burble of blood.

Shattered rib, punctured lung, and probably a few other organs shredded to pieces. Gnasher bullets were designed to disperse inside the body. "Where is it?" Elliot demands, squatting down face-level. "Where's the morphine?"

Mirotic's face is pale as the old Earth moon. He shakes his head. He tries to speak again, says something that might be *autosurgeon*.

"I'll get the autosurgeon," Elliot says, even though he knows it's too late for that. "Where's the morphine?"

No response. Elliot frisks him, and by the time he pulls the vial out from Mirotic's waistband his hands are slicked scarlet. He clutches his fingers around it and gives a shuddering sigh of relief. Mirotic's eyes flutter open and shut, then stay shut. Elliot gets to his feet, head spinning, as Mirotic's vitals blink out.

When he goes back around the corner of the Heron, Elliot finds Santos is dead, too. One of the fleeing monsters drove a wedge of bone through her skull, halfway smashing her clamp. Blood and gray matter are leaking from the hole. A single spark jumps from the clamp's torn wiring.

Tolliver is crossing himself and his shoulders are shaking. There's a fevered flush under his skin.

"We'll burn her," Elliot says. "Mirotic, too. Any bones left, we'll crush them down to powder."

"Alright," Tolliver says, in a hollowed out voice. His eyes fix on the vial clutched in Elliot's bloody hand, but he says nothing else.

Lying on his cot with his limbs splayed limp, Elliot is in paradise. He feels like his body is evaporating, or maybe turning into sunlight, warm and pure. He can hardly tell where his sooty skin ends and Tolliver's begins.

"Did you kill him for it?" Tolliver's voice asks, slurred with the drug.

"Ricochet," Elliot says.

"Would you have killed him for it?" Tolliver asks.

"Wouldn't you?" Elliot asks back.

As soon as they dealt with the bodies, he went to the tent to shoot up. Tolliver followed him, and when Elliot offered him the syringe, already high enough to be generous, he took it. Elliot doesn't know how long ago that was.

"What made you like this?" Tolliver asks. "What got you so hooked? What fucked you up so bad?"

"There's no one thing," Elliot says, because he is floating and unafraid. "It's never one thing. That would make it easier, right? If I was a good person, and I saw something so bad this is the only way I can . . ." He puts a finger to his temple and twists it.

"Forget," Tolliver supplies.

"Yeah," Elliot says. "But there's no one thing. This job kills you with a thousand cuts."

"But there must have been one thing," Tolliver says. "One thing that got you stuck leading a con squad. Mirotic says. Said. Said you used to be somebody."

Elliot doesn't want to talk about that. "Was it Santos?" he asks, running his fingers along Tolliver's hip.

"What?"

"The nights I message you but you don't come," Elliot says. "There was someone else."

Tolliver shakes his head. "You really are a piece of shit," he says, almost laughs. "You thought that had to be the reason, huh? Never thought maybe some nights I don't really feel like fucking a drugged-up zombie who plays some pornstar in his optics the whole time?"

"I don't," Elliot says.

"Your wife, then," Tolliver says. "That's even more fucked."

"I don't play anything in the optics," Elliot says. "I just see you. That's all."

Tolliver's voice softens a little. "Oh."

On impulse, Elliot sends him the clip. He watches it at the same time, watches his daughter's head turn, her bright eyes blink. "She's grown," he explains. "Twenty-some now. Her and her mother live on old Earth. Only thing they hate more than each other is me. If I was going to get out, it would've been years and years ago."

He moves his hand to Tolliver's arm, wanting to feel the cool plastic of his flay under his fingertips.

"They didn't put me with a con squad as a punishment," he says. "I volunteered."

He looks down into the exposed swathe of red muscle on Tolliver's arm. There are tiny specks of luminescent blue nestled in the fibers. He feels a deep unease slide under his high.

"I don't want to get eaten from the inside," Tolliver says. "I don't want them using my bones."

The poison yellow nudge appears in Elliot's optics.

"Trigger me," Tolliver says. "Right now. While everything still feels okay. You trigger me, and then do yours."

"Could take the arm," Elliot says. "The autosurgeon."

"You said this job kills you with a thousand cuts." Tolliver uses his good hand to find Elliot's and squeeze it. "I'm not going to be a welder. I don't want to be some fucking skeleton puppet, either. Let's just get out of here. And let's not leave anything behind."

His hand leaves, but leaves behind a cool hard shell. Elliot runs his thumb along the groove and recognizes the shape of Tolliver's incendiary grenade. He cups it against the side of his head. He thinks, briefly, about what the pick-up team will find when they finally arrive. What they'll think happened.

He thinks of Tolliver's file, the one he opened and read only once, how Tolliver had smothered his grandfather in his sleep and said it was to stop his pain, even though his grandfather had been healthy and happy. Nobody was good here. Not even Tolliver. But the two of them, they are a good match.

Outside, the cyclops starts to wail. Elliot adds his upvote to the queue, and Tolliver goes limp in his arms. His thumb finds the grenade's pin and rests there. He thinks back to the last time everything still felt okay, then plays it in his optics, watching his daughter before she knew who he was.

"She's awake," his wife's voice sings. "Just looking around . . ."

Elliot breathes deep and pulls the pin and waits for extraction.

Karin Lowachee was born in South America, grew up in Canada, and worked in the Arctic. Her first novel *Warchild* won the 2001 Warner Aspect First Novel Contest. Both *Warchild* (2002) and her third novel *Cagebird* (2005) were finalists for the Philip K. Dick Award. *Cagebird* won the Prix Aurora Award in 2006 for Best Long-Form Work in English and the Spectrum Award, also in 2006. Her books have been translated into French, Hebrew, and Japanese, and her short stories have appeared in anthologies edited by Nalo Hopkinson, John Joseph Adams, Jonathan Strahan, and Ann VanderMeer. Her fantasy novel, *The Gaslight Dogs*, was published through Orbit Books.

A GOOD HOME

Karin Lowachee

I brought him home from the VA shelter and sat him in front of the window because the doctors said he liked that. The shelter had set him in safe mode for transport until I could voice activate him again, and recalibrate, but safe mode still allowed for base functions like walking, observation, and primary speech. He seemed to like the window because he blinked once. Their kind didn't blink ordinarily, and they never wept, so I always wondered where the sadness went. If you couldn't cry then it all turned inward.

The VA staff said he didn't talk and that was from the war. His model didn't allow for complete resetting or non-consensual dismantling; he was only five years old, so fell under the Autonomy legislation. The head engineer at the VA said the diagnostics didn't show any physical impairment, so his silence was self-imposed. The android psychologist worked with him for six months and deemed him non-violent and in need of a good home.

So here he was, at my home.

My mother thought the adoption was crazy. We spoke over comm. I was in my kitchen, she in her home office where she sold data bolts to underdeveloped countries. "You don't know where they've been, Tawn," she said. "And he's a war model? Don't they get flashbacks, go berserk, and kill you in your sleep?"

"You watch too much double-vee."

"He must be in the shelter for a reason. If the government doesn't want him and he's not fit for industry, why would you want to take him on?"

I knew this would be futile, arguing against prejudice, but I said it anyway. "The VA needs people to adopt them or they have nowhere to go. We made them, they're sentient, we have to be responsible for them. Just because he can't fight anymore doesn't mean he's not worth something. Besides, it's not like I just sign a contract and they hand him over. The doctors and engineers and everybody have to agree that I'd be a good owner. I went through dozens of interviews and so did he."

"Didn't you say he doesn't talk? How did they interview him? How can you be sure he's not violent?"

"They downloaded his experience files. They observed him, and I trust them. The VA takes care of these models."

"Then let them take care of him."

She knew less about the war than she did about me, her son, except that the war got in the way of her sales sometimes. Just like I'd gotten in the way of her potential as a lifestyle designer, and instead of living some perceived, deserved celebrity, she'd had to raise me. Sometimes I wondered if I harbored that thought more than she did, but then she kicked my rivets on things like this and not even the distance of a comm could hide her general disapproval at my existence.

Still, she was worried about the android killing me in my sleep. That might've been sincere. "The VA's overcrowded. That's why they allow for adoptions."

Because she was losing the reasonable argument, she targeted something else. The fallback: my self-esteem. "Why would they think you're a good owner? You can't even afford to get your spine fixed. How are you going to support a traumatized war model?"

That was how she saw me—in need of fixing. "He can help me. I can help him."

Even through a double-vee relay I felt her pity. And I saw it in her eyes. That seemed to be the only way she knew how to care about me.

I wasn't going to do that to him.

"Mark." Saying his name in my voice brought him out of safe mode. He blinked but didn't turn away from the window. He didn't move. They'd said it would take a while. Maybe a long while. He'd been at An Loöc, Rally 9, and Pir Hul. The three deepest points of the war. Five years old but he'd seen the worst action. I wondered why none of the creators had anticipated trauma in them. So maybe they weren't as fully developed as humans could be; they were built to task. But they were also built with intelligence and some capacity for emotional judgment because purely analytical and efficient judgment had made the first models into sociopaths. All of those had been put down (that they'd caught, anyway).

"Mark," I said, "my name's Tawn Altamirano." He knew that, they put it in his programming, but you introduced yourself to strangers. To people. "You feel free to look around my home. This is your home too. There's a power board in the office when you need it. You can come to me at any time if you need anything."

He didn't move or look at me. His eyes were black irises and they stared through the glass of the window, as if it could look back. Maybe he saw his own reflection, faint as it was. Maybe he wanted to wait until night when it would become clearer. Or maybe he just wanted to watch the maple tree sway, and the children walking by on the sidewalk on their way home from school.

I had my routines pretty well established by now. Since my own discharge two years ago, and once the bulk of the physio was under my belt, I'd acclimated back home, got a job through the veterans program working net security for the local university. Despite what my mother said, I took care of myself. My war benefits allowed for some renovation of the bungalow—ramps and wide doorways and the like. When it was time for bed I left the chair beside it and levered myself onto the mattress. Some shifting later and I lay beneath the covers on my back, staring up at the ceiling. I didn't hear him in the living room at all. Eventually I called off the lights and darkness led me to sleep.

I didn't know what woke me—maybe instinct. But I opened my eyes and a shadow stood in the doorway of my bedroom. For a second my heart stopped, then started up again at twice the pace until I saw that he didn't move, he wasn't going berserk, he wasn't preparing to kill me. Of course he wasn't. My mother didn't know the reality. Going to war didn't make you a murderer—it made you afraid.

His shape stood black against the moonlight behind him, what came through the living room window on the other end of the hall.

"Mark?"

He didn't answer.

"Mark, what's wrong?"

A foolish question, maybe, but he could parse that I meant right this second. Not the generality of what was wrong. Not the implication of what was wrong with *him*. What had drawn him from the window and to the threshold of my room?

I pushed myself up on my elbows and opened my mouth to call up the lights.

But he turned around and disappeared down the hallway, back toward the living room and his standing post by the window.

He was still there in the morning when I rolled through the living room on my way to the kitchen. As if he hadn't moved all night. Past his shoulders, in the early day outside, the children walked the opposite way now, some of them skipping on their way to school. A few of them held hands with their parents, mothers and fathers.

"Do you need a power up?" I said from in front of the fridge. To remind him that he had a board in the office. No answer. So I took out my eggs and toast and made myself some breakfast. I had to give him time; it always took time.

A little after fifteen hundred hours when the schools let out, I got a knock on my front door. I was in the office so it took me a few seconds to get to the foyer, punch open the door, face the man and woman standing like missionaries on my porch. Behind them at the bottom of my driveway stood another man with three kids by his side. I looked up at the two directly in front of me.

"Can I help you?"

"Hello," the man said, looking down at me. To his credit, he didn't adopt the surprised and awkward mien of someone unused to confronting a person in a chair. If anything he seemed a little impatient. "My name's Arjan and this is Olivia. We were just wondering . . . well, we were a little concerned about your . . . the Mark model in your window."

I glanced behind me toward the living room, saw the back of his shoulders and the straight stance of his vigil.

"What about him?"

"He's creeping out our kids," said Olivia. "Twice they've gone by and he's just standing there. He's not a cat. What's wrong with him?"

If you had a double-vee, you knew about the Mark androids. Ten years ago, the reveal by the military had garnered a lot of press and criticism, but ultimately people preferred sending look-alike soldiers into battle rather than their own sons and daughters. All of the Marks looked the same, so they were easily identifiable; nobody could mistake them for human despite the indistinguishability of the cosmetics. The adoption program had garnered similar press and criticism; the VA had looked into my neighborhood before releasing Mark to me. We were supposed to be a tolerant, liberal piece of society here.

That was the theory, anyway.

"He's not doing anything, he just likes to look out the window."

"All day?" Olivia said.

"Have you been outside my house all day?" Because otherwise why would it bother her if she only went by twice a day to pick up her kids, and that took all of two minutes?

Arjan seemed more temperate, his impatience dissipated. "Just . . . perhaps if during the hours when the children come and go from school, you sit him down somewhere else?"

"He won't hurt anybody."

"Can you, please?" Arjan gazed at me with some hint of that pity now. Not wanting to push in case I had a flashback or dumped my life story at his feet to explain why I didn't have the use of my legs.

Being a good neighbor meant picking your battles. Unlike what was happening in deep space and the war. Maybe it wouldn't be a bad idea to try to coax Mark into another activity. "I'll see what I can do."

I looked out the window with him for a minute, probably five. Slowly the kids faded away until no more of them traipsed by on the sidewalk. Cars drifted at suburban speed, quiet hums in irregular intervals that penetrated glass. From the look of the sky, we were going to get rain.

"I want to show you something, Mark." I blinked up at his impassive jawline, and above that the long dark lashes. They'd made them handsome, in a way. Not superstar plastic, but an earthy attractiveness. Gradation in the dark hair, some undertone of silver, as if life would ever age them. "Mark. Come with me." I touched his sleeve then began to push across the floor.

He followed—because I'd ordered him or because he wanted to, it was impossible to tell. Something had drawn him to my bedroom last night, so he was capable of operating on his own volition. I led him into the office and wheeled myself out of the way, near the couch. One wall braced a floor to ceiling bookshelf, with actual physical books stacked neatly row to row. My one ongoing possession of worth: my collection. They'd gone past the label of rare and become worthless. Nobody much cared for tangibles anymore, things you could hold in your hands that gave off a woody scent when the pages flipped.

None of the books were first editions or leatherbound. They weren't museum quality. But that was why I liked them—they were everyday, made to be handled without gloves.

"Maybe you can explore?" I pointed to the shelf. "There are some classics there. I know they don't download literature for you, but you can learn the old-fashioned way. If you want."

He stared at the colorful spines as if they meant nothing to him. Probably didn't. His head was full of strategy and tactics, and if any history existed in his brain matrices, it was related to war. They'd believed the data shouldn't be corrupted with frivolity: no poetry or plays or pop culture references.

But he wasn't in the war anymore. And he wasn't walking out of the room. This way, maybe, he wouldn't stand for hours in front of the window.

I left him in there.

Through the double-vee, a calm, vaguely upper class male British voice explained how scientists were able to save the Bengal tiger from extinction eighty-five years ago through a combination of rewilding, genetic intervention, and ruthlessly wiping out poachers regardless of geographical borders. Rising quietly above the sounds of large cats huffing and animal protectionist gunfire, the low keen of something more human and distressed filtered past the sound panels and made me turn from the vee, toward the office.

The time on the wall said he'd been in there a little more than an hour. I should've checked sooner.

I found him in the corner, wedged between the bookshelf and the end of the desk. Sitting rigid with the eyeline of a house pet. I only wheeled in so far before stopping, careful to watch his eyes, but he wasn't looking at me. Some blank spot a meter in front of him held his attention. By his feet, splayed like a wounded bird, lay a trade-sized book, print side up. I couldn't see the title.

"Mark?"

This passed for crying on a face that couldn't shed tears. That sound, a wounded thing.

"Mark."

I was so used to the reality of rain that hearing it now against the windows only drew my attention because it drew his. His eyes widened and he put his hands in his hair.

"It's okay." I rolled closer, slow. He stopped keening and somehow the silence was worse. His elbows joined with knees until he was a black shard lodged between furniture. I stopped and picked up the book, turned it over.

For Whom the Bell Tolls.

The cover was some faded hue of purple and green, with an image of a shadowed soldier, a road, and a bridge. I'd read this book long ago, before my own war. I barely remembered it, but I remembered loving it. That must've been what it was like with people sometimes. Mark didn't look up, so I flipped the book over and read a random line on the page, where he'd either left off or where the book had opened when he'd tossed it. *Every one needs to talk to some one . . . Before we had religion and other nonsense. Now for every one there should be some one to whom one can speak frankly, for all the valor that one could have one becomes very alone.*

"'We are not alone. We are all together,'" I recited to him from the book, a little like you'd speak scripture.

But he didn't look up and he didn't say a word.

Eventually he returned to the window, but at night. The next morning the rain stopped and in an hour started up again. I needed to go shopping for groceries, preferred that to ordering them in, but struggling through the wet was a chore, so instead I set up a Scrabble board in the living room, on the coffee table. I shook the tiles in the velvet bag until I felt him look over. It was a gamble whether he'd be interested, but during breakfast I'd noticed the book on the windowsill in front of him. *For Whom the Bell Tolls.*

"Wanna play?" I shook the bag again.

It took a minute but he walked over and sat down on the couch across from me. If we played long enough he wouldn't be looking outside when the kids went home.

I explained the rules to him, knew I only had to say them once. He stared at the board and my hands and then stuck his hand into the bag and pulled his seven tiles, which he set on his tile bar precisely and carefully hidden from my eyes. He wouldn't speak but I thought at least this way he could make words.

I went first and lay down ATOMIC. I was a little proud of that.

He made TIGER.

I got ROUGE.

He made EQUINE. I said, "Good word!" Not like I was praising a dog, but because it was interesting to see how he formed these words out of his programming. He won the first game but I was almost expecting that; it was like playing against a computer. It *was* playing against a computer. His vocabulary was ten times what mine was; I knew I was bound to lose when he began to use Latin. Not because his creators had programmed Latin for him, but because he understood the derivation of the language. He must have had that somewhere in his files.

As we were setting up the next game, my mother called. I talked to the house system, without visual. "I'm busy, call back later."

Mark stared at me. It could have been a dead kind of regard but as he rarely looked me in the eyes, I took it for inquiry. "My mother." That didn't make him bat a lash. "You play first."

Twenty minutes into the game his words grew shorter and shorter, barely gleaning six or eight points. His eyes remained lowered to the board. ONE. TO. ARE.

"Mark? Is something wrong?"

At night, before bed, I'd reviewed his downloads from the VA hospital, tried to find some string of code or something in the reports that the doctors might have missed. I wasn't a doctor, I'd only been a rifle fighter, but maybe it took one soldier to understand another. His muteness was voluntary and I couldn't forget that.

I looked at the spread on the board. The game didn't matter. After sorting through the letters left in the bag and usurping a couple already displayed, I lay down some tiles separate from the game and turned the board toward him.

WORRIED.

He didn't move, his hands on his knees. I watched his lids twitch as his eyes mapped the board. I made more words for him.

ABOUT YOU.

It took eight minutes for him to reach for the board. With the tips of both his forefingers, he slid the tiles around like a magician did cards on a tabletop. Then he swung the board back toward me.

SAD.

What could I say? I touched my legs. I saw his gaze follow that. Then I made more words too.

I KNOW.

The shelter wanted reports from me and after the first week, they considered it a breakthrough. Never mind that Mark hadn't said anything past that single word, Scrabble or otherwise. He just returned to his window. I went about my days with work, sometimes sitting on my bed with my system, sometimes in the office, and when he wouldn't dislodge himself from his post, I sat on the couch and looked at his back. I scoured his files for clues. He didn't play the game again but he carried that book with him when he powered up on the seventh day.

"I wanted to check in," my mother said. "See if you were still alive."

This passed for humor in her world. Her face on my relay was cautious. Out of spite, maybe, I turned my system so the camera picked up Mark, standing by the window, a black arrow of false serenity with sun on his skin.

"What's he doing?" she said.

"Looking out the window."

"For what?"

I almost said "nothing." But it occurred to me that soldiers stood watch and this might not have been a simple metaphor for his position.

"Enemies. So you better call before you come over."

This passed for humor in my world. She didn't laugh, but I did.

The benefits of working from home meant I could take naps in the afternoon. Like a cat, I stretched myself onto the angle of sun that cut through my bedroom window, warm after days of rain, and shut my eyes, soaking up rays without fear of burning or UV—all house glass came treated.

The front door opening woke me up. I didn't hear it shut.

Either way, nobody should've been going in or out—unless it was Mark.

It took me two minutes to get myself in the chair and out to the door. "Mark!" Out and down the ramp, rapid, onto the sidewalk, look left, look right. Nothing. "Mark!"

My vis tracked his location chip, all Mark models had them from the factory. Deeply embedded in their craniums. The dot on my optical display put him in transit, but at a speed that indicated running, not in a vehicle. At least. I rolled that way, past flat, cloned houses and uniform lawns, looking through the overlay across my vision until I spied the tall, black-clad figure in the park. The shadows on either side—other people—barely registered.

"Mark." I could shout, but with him now in my line of sight, startling could be worse. He stood facing the manufactured lake and people were pulling their kids away from him. Expecting a weapon or an explosion, who knew.

My hands burned. I hadn't worn gloves. Wheels bumped the edge of grass that led down an embankment to the carefully placed rocks, and further toward cold, cobalt water that lapped the shore. He'd been afraid of rain but he ran to water. If he'd been running to this place at all. Maybe he'd just run.

I wished for the Scrabble board, the only thing that had garnered a response from his broken programming. Instead I touched my red and callused hand to the edge of his as it hung at his side.

He twitched, that was all.

"Let's walk?" An offer. I looked down at my legs. "So to speak." Walk before someone called the cops, or a child screamed, or something propelled him to plunge into the lake where I couldn't follow. Should he have decided to sink himself to the bottom of the lake, none of these people would likely try to stop him. "Walk with me, Mark. Please?"

I tried to wheel backward so I could turn around on the path that surrounded the lake. But before I made the full one-eighty, hands took hold behind my chair and pushed.

I let go of the wheel rims and rubbed my palms against my thighs. Looked up and back at his forward gaze. He gave me nothing but the direction of his stride and his acquiescence in silence. It was enough.

We took walks twice a day now, one in the morning and one in the afternoon. It hadn't been my intention to cross paths with the schoolchildren, but those were the hours that made sense—before my work began and on a break before the last couple hours of my day—and they gave him some life to look at. Others in the neighborhood strolled with their dogs, but Mark walked with me. Sometimes he pushed the chair, but most of the time we went side by side. Sometimes I talked, idly gossiping about this neighbor or that, or noted the types of trees and flowers we passed. Information that he wouldn't ordinarily possess because the places he'd been trained for in deep space hadn't come with roses and Japanese maples.

More than once, Arjan or Olivia or somebody else from the neighborhood frowned at us. The children were inquisitive, a few of them asking aloud as we passed where Mark had come from and what was wrong with him. "Aren't they supposed to be in war?" The parents shushed them and pulled them away.

"He came home," I told them. "He needed a family."

I hoped that would get through to the adults, but they just smiled at me half-assed, as if I needed to apologize for the truth.

I dreaded bad weather now. The night we had another thunderstorm I found Mark back in the corner of the library, making that tearless keening noise. I couldn't turn off the sky so I sat with him, lights on, talking softly. I picked up his Hemingway book from the floor and read to him. It seemed to calm him, having that focus. Maybe working out a plot, the drama and emotion of a fictional piece. The war in the book was so far removed from his own, yet truths existed across centuries when the common denominator was humanity.

Eventually, when my eyes grew weary sometime in the middle of the night, I closed the book and looked into his dark open gaze. His arms wrapped around his legs.

"Do you want to come into my room? You don't have to sit in the office all night—" Or stand at the window, "—but I think I need to lie down." I was really asking him if he wanted the company. Or asking him because I did. He didn't need to stand vigil at the window, through cloudy moonlight and racketing storm.

So he followed me to my bedroom. Helped me onto the bed without my asking. Even drew the covers up. I called off the lights and Mark, in silence, sat at the foot of my bed facing the door.

In the morning he was gone—at least as far as the living room. I rolled out yawning and spied the Scrabble board on the coffee table, Mark sitting on one side. It made me smile. Taking initiative? I could picture the eager android psychologists ticking off their checklists, revisiting his memory files, trying to draw connections between Mark's habits here and his experiences in the war.

He felt no threat here, that was the difference. At least I hoped he didn't. Under observation and treated like a programmed computer back at the hospital, he must have still been wary. Who wouldn't?

I made scrambled eggs and toast and joined him at the table. He pulled the letter C and started first.

It wasn't for the game. He searched around in the bag until he found the letters he needed to spell.

LOST.

I looked at him, trying to determine the exact meaning. It was impossible to know. So I reached for the velvet bag myself.

HERE.

No question marks, I had only my eyes to ask it. He shook his head. Made another word.

COMPANY.

For a few moments I was confused. My company? But then—no. *A* company. *His* company. He was the survivor of a skirmish out at the Belt. None of the others had made it. The official report said ambush, but that had seemed scant even to me. Maybe some of the details had been redacted from his memory and thus what they'd given me, and he didn't even know anymore. But the body remembered. Maybe more of him remembered than all of the engineers and psychologists were willing to acknowledge.

I laid more tiles. HOW.

But he didn't say anything. Instead he just stared at the board then turned it toward me so I saw the question. And he looked at my legs.

Fair enough. "Shrapnel." I stretched my arm behind me. "My spine."

When he looked in my eyes, he didn't have to say a word. I saw that he understood. Some things technology couldn't fix—especially when you didn't have the means. Sometimes we injured ourselves, or we were injured, and the wounds stuck around. Like memories or the impact of them.

Rather than standing at the window all night like an effigy, Mark took to staying in my room. Maybe he figured I'd need the help if I somehow flopped out of bed, or probably because he wasn't simple, he knew I liked the company. Years of sleeping alone, literally in a silent room without even the bodily noises of comrades in other bunks, and the isolation had become pungent. Over the days he and I established our own routine, not discussed because he still didn't talk beyond random words on the Scrabble board, and even then sometimes he didn't talk at all and just played the game.

The doctors said it was still progress. I didn't tell them about Mark sitting in my bedroom at night, but I did report that he began to bring me books from the office and liked me to read aloud to him. Sometimes he had no sense of timing about it. I'd be working and he'd just appear next to me and set down a novel on my lap. Classic war novels. *The Red Badge of Courage. All Quiet on the Western Front. Half of a Yellow Sun.* He wouldn't go away until I covered at least a chapter. I acted annoyed, but he knew I wasn't. Whether that was through his ability to read human body language and gauge tone of voice, or more likely because he just knew me by now.

He still hated storms and we were deep into spring. It was the worst when one night the power went out.

The neighborhood outside fell to darkness. Inside, only the glow from my comp on its backup provided some illumination. The moon high outside the office window sat obscured by rainclouds.

Mark darted from the living room where he often still stood watch, right into the office where I was working. He didn't trip or crash into anything and I remembered his eyes had night vision capability. I didn't need to see his face to understand the plea.

"It's okay, the lights'll come back up soon." I rolled away from the desk and motioned out of the room. Tried to keep my voice casual, even if I could feel the tension dopplering out from his body in the dark. "Let's go hang out."

He loomed, near invisible in the shadows. He didn't even breathe and at least didn't keen anymore, didn't feel that level of pain at the upset. But his hand landed on my shoulder and clenched. Only his footfalls made sound as he followed me down the hall to the bedroom, which had become a refuge from all that scared him. A routine of safety.

I levered myself to the bed to sit and he climbed on beside me, legs and arms folded. Not quite with his back to the door or window, he never allowed that, but he eased into facing me at an angle at least.

And this was how we waited out the storm.

Of course my mother had a key to my house; she'd insisted after I'd gotten out of the hospital, "just in case" living on my own in my "state" proved too difficult. Maybe I should've anticipated her worry. Every time she called she implied that Mark was a ticking bomb, so I just stopped answering her calls. Maybe she was in the neighborhood or maybe she did get in her car to drive a half hour to check if I was alive. Either way, through the storm she arrived and through the storm Mark heard her before I did.

We sat in the near-dark and I was reading to him from the light of my comm. "'He saw that to be firm soldiers they must go forward. It would be death to stay in the present place . . .'" And at that exact moment Mark launched off the bed and out the door with the precision of a guided missile.

I was fumbling for my chair, images in my mind of fang-toothed, angry neighbors storming my front door with pitchforks, when my mother's shriek penetrated every surface between the foyer and my bedroom.

"Mark!" Ass in the seat, hands on the wheels. "Mark!" I rolled out to see my mother face down on the floor, arms triangled behind her back, wrists caught in the vise of Mark's one-handed grip. "Stand down, soldier."

"Get him off me, Tawn! Get this crazy fu—"

"Shut *up*, Mom!" I stopped close enough to touch Mark's arm. Beneath his sleeve felt like iron. I kept my voice quiet because I couldn't see his eyes in the dark: "It's okay. It's my mother. It's okay." I repeated it until he let her go and stepped back near to the wall. Becoming motionless.

"Mom."

"He's crazy! What did I tell you!"

"Mom, tone it *down.*" I didn't offer to help her up. She wouldn't have accepted it.

She propelled herself to her feet in a pitch and yaw. "Look what he did to my wrists!" She stuck her hands toward me. In the cracks of lightning and illumination, I saw vague shadows. Maybe bruises.

"You're all right, you're fine. Come sit down. You should've rung the doorbell, he thought you were breaking in."

"I have a key!"

"I told you to call ahead."

"My own son!"

I went to Mark and held his sleeve. "Come over here, man." My mother wasn't listening; she could stand by the door and bleat until it passed.

Mark followed me to the living room where I hoped he would sit, but instead he went to the window, his post, and stared out. He didn't have to breathe and he didn't say a word, but I knew the entire ruckus unnerved him. There was no other word for it. It reverbed through my body.

"Is that what he does all day?" my mother demanded behind me.

"Can you at least lower your voice? You aren't helping."

"*I'm* not helping!"

"MOM."

We both stopped. Mark had turned around, now with his back to the window. His body blotted out what light came in from the street, creating a vacuum in my vision. So he could face us dead on. It was like the stare of a sarcophagus.

My mother turned her back to him. "I'm worried for you, Tawn."

"You don't have to be."

"This isn't normal. Look at him!"

"He's fine. We're fine. We—"

But she wasn't listening. She began to walk around, feeling her way through the dark toward the office. Or my bedroom. It was so sudden when the lights flickered on and held that I had to blink spots from my vision. And in those moments Mark disappeared.

After her.

"Mark!"

I couldn't roll fast enough. I recognized his mode. Full protection, decisive defense. What he'd been built for. I wanted to hold him back but this was his nature. He wasn't the one unnerved, he wasn't the one concerned for himself. It was *my* voice he heard, that his programming responded to. My voice and its irritation and tension and impatience.

In the seconds it took me to get from the living room to my bedroom where my mother had gone, I saw it ahead of me. In the span of his back and the straightness of his spine. In the precise way he seized my mother before she could set hands on my possessions. He spun her around.

She struck him. Reflex or intent, I didn't know. Of course it didn't affect him at all, didn't even bruise him. He didn't flinch.

Instead he dragged her to my window, opened it, and pitched her out.

Luckily my house was a bungalow.

She said she'd wanted to pack me a bag and take me away from any danger. That if she did that for me I couldn't protest and would've been forced to go with her and ditch this mad idea of taking care of a military model. She had never understood that we wanted to take care of ourselves.

She didn't understand—when the VA engineers came to take him away—that he was my company and I was his.

In the hospital they ran more tests on him. It was procedure because she'd filed a complaint. I gave my own statement: that he'd felt I was threatened, that he'd only been defending me, that my mother was crazy in her own right (I reworded that part a little). She'd disregarded my words and his existence. If I restricted her access to me or she learned to interact better, there would be no more problems.

And, yes, I wanted him home again. He belonged there—where I could read to him, where we could play games, and where he might one day be able to speak to me. He'd made a place beside me and at my window. He'd learned my routines and created ones of his own. He wanted to know all the books on my shelves. He liked walking in the sun.

He protected me. I wouldn't strip that from him.

They let me see him once while he was in the hospital. He lay on a stiff bed with transparent monitoring tape stuck to his temples. Little dots of glowing blue and red on the tape winked at me while his dark eyes stared blinkless, asking no questions.

I touched his arm. His skin felt cold. Human warmth didn't course through his veins. He didn't even have veins. None of it mattered. "Mark. Hey man, don't worry."

His head tilted, eyes met mine.

I gripped his hand. After a moment his fingers curled around mine, just as strong. Even stronger. I said, "The storm's gone and you're coming home."

The children were walking on their way to school when we pulled up to the drive. It was a warm day, the kind where you wore light open jackets and began to roll up your sleeves in anticipation of summer. With the car windows down we heard their voices all the way to the school, to the yard. They sounded as colorful as their clothes and seemed to carouse right through the leaves to where we sat.

He hadn't said a word on the ride, only looked out the window. The parents passing behind on the sidewalk noticed us there; I spied the glances on the rearcam of the car. A couple of them paused as if debating whether to approach, to ask why we were just sitting on my own driveway doing nothing.

But they didn't approach and I looked at Mark's profile. "You know . . . people are going to be like my mother. Like the neighbors. That's just the way it is until they get used to us." Not just him, but us.

I'd learned not to expect conversation but he did make contact in his own way. No Scrabble board lay between us but he turned his hands palm up and open. He looked at me.

What answer could I give him? That people were afraid, or lazy, or just plain ignorant? Who could we blame? The government, the military, the doctors and engineers?

We were both on probation. Mark, so he wouldn't injure somebody. And me, so I wouldn't let him.

"Where do you think this will lead?" my mother had asked. "You rehabilitate him or whatever they want to call it, and then what?"

Somehow it was impossible for her to understand. "Then he'll choose," was all I'd said.

Maybe one day he'd discover what had happened to his unit. Maybe I would help him. Or maybe we'd leave it alone because some memories were best left in the dark.

Before we went inside the house I caught his attention again, touched his shoulder. "The doctors say you're capable of speaking but you just choose not to. Sometimes that happens with people—"

"I am people," he said. His voice was lighter than I thought it would be, if hoarse from disuse. He was looking back out the window again. The sidewalk stretched clear now. "I am a person," he said to the glass. To the outside world.

They had created him to task but with the capacity for emotion. He was perfectly vulnerable, just enough, even for war.

When he slid from the car to head into the house, eventually I followed him, calling the chair from the back of the car to lever myself into it. I rolled up the ramp to the front door, where Mark stood, holding it open for me even though he didn't have to.

It was just the human thing to do.

Gord Sellar is a Canadian writer currently living in the South Korean country-side with his wife and son. (So far, no sentient dog.) His work has appeared in many magazines and anthologies since 2007, and he was a finalist for the John W. Campbell Award for Best New Writer in 2009. He also wrote the script for South Korea's first cinematic adaptation of an H. P. Lovecraft story, the award-winning *The Music of Jo Hyeja* (2012).

PRODIGAL

Gord Sellar

"He doesn't look any different," Jennifer commented, when we got home from the research facility, after Benji's final sentientization treatment.

"He's not supposed to yet, are you, boy?" I said, ruffling the hair on his head. He looked up at us from the tatty carpet with his big, curious terrier eyes, and I'd swear he smiled a little.

Technically, she was right. He didn't really act very differently, not in any tangible way. Having recuperated from his various surgeries and treatments, he still liked the same things: fetch-the-ball, chasing me around the backyard, going for a run—familiar pleasures. He'd still come and sit beside me as I watched TV in the evenings, content with a pat on the head or a scratch behind the ear when he caught me working. He was our good-natured consolation prize. Our gentle not-quite-a-child, a terrier puppy whose brain was developing massive neural connectivity day by day, the sparse woodland of his mind turning into a dense jungle, and whose mouth and throat had been cleverly sculpted into a system capable of expressing in speech those thoughts he'd already started having. I thought of it as this incredible gift, at the time, albeit a gift he hadn't quite received yet. A miracle. He'd be a wonder-dog. That was why we'd called him Benji, after all.

But I'd be lying if I said *I* didn't see a change in him right from day one. It was something about his eyes. Something . . . well, just *more* than before. To me, it was unmistakable.

A few months later, we had some people over. It was the first party we'd had in half a year, mostly neighbors and coworkers, people like that. Some had heard about Ben, that he'd begun to talk finally. They expected some kind of demonstration. I'd warned him, hoping it would make him less nervous, but it had the opposite effect. He began to tap his front paws on the carpet, to shake his head a little like a wet puppy, his tail half-wagging nervously. The first few people were folks who'd never come to a party at our place before, and Ben nervously avoided them.

Then Lorna arrived. A wannabe-painter-friend of Jennifer's, Lorna was familiar with Ben. She had played with him before the treatment, so he remembered her a little. As soon as her bulky shoulders passed through the doorframe, Benji barked excitedly. It had become a strange sound, no longer his own, no longer quite doglike, but *he* didn't seem to notice or care. He ran up to her and began sniffing at her feet. Ears perking up in recognition, he mumbled a distracted, "Hello," before sticking his nose into her crotch for a sniff. Then he simply proclaimed, "Nice!"

"Oh my!" Lorna said, reaching down at him. "Now, Ben, you really mustn't do that!" She forced his head down, pushing his face away from her, and said to me, "I thought they were supposed to be *intelligent* post-op?"

"I'm so sorry," Jennifer said. "Tim, maybe you should take him upstairs?"

I nodded. "Come on, Benj," I said, and tucked my hand under his collar. I led him to the bottom of the stairs, and he went up them obligingly. I followed him up and then said, "Left, Benji, left." He followed the direction, and walked into our bedroom. "Good boy," I said when we were both in, scratching behind his ear.

"Why?" he asked me, looking up curiously.

"Well, you're not supposed to sniff people like that."

"Sniff?"

"You know," I said and did my best impression of a dog sniffing.

"Oh. Nice sniff! Hello friend!"

"No, for dogs it's a nice hello. For *people*, it's rude," I explained while fishing a hide dog bone out of my sock drawer. I tossed it to him, and he caught it out of the air, but he didn't chew it right away. Instead, he just set it down and stared at me as if he had some question he didn't know how to phrase. After a while, he seemed to abandon the attempt, and as he chomped down on the bone, I quickly left the room, closing the door behind me. Before I went down to the party, I heard him pad toward the door, sigh loudly, and settle down onto the floor beside the door.

But that was what I'd always done with him at parties. It was nothing new. Except . . . it felt different now, doing that to him.

Watching Benji learn to speak was sometimes downright eerie.

It all happened so fast. From a wordless beast, he'd turned into a chatterbox in the space of a few months. They had implanted a neurochemical dispenser inside his skull, something that seeped the chemicals straight into his brain, wiring up a crazy new secondary network that not only made him smarter by the day, but also made him pick up language much faster than any human child.

Not that he spoke well. Even with his re-sculpted upper palate, some words were hard to pronounce. Which made him hard to understand, and with no human body language to compensate for it. He was usually wide-eyed, his expression as inscrutable as any canine's. If you've never known a sentient dog, it might sound crazy, but I swear Benji really did have expressions, though it took me years to learn to read them.

"What's *prrbrr*?" he asked me one day, just when I got home from work. He was still stuck at excitedly muttering two-word sentences.

I squatted down close to the plastic doormat, scratched him behind the ear. "What's that?"

"What's *pregmand*?" he asked quietly, conspiratorially.

"Pregmand? You mean pregnant? It means, uh, that someone has a baby inside," I said. "Like a mama dog, before the baby dog is born, she's pregnant."

"Oh," Benji said and began panting excitedly. "Really?" He blinked at me oddly and padded off toward the creaky basement stairs, his tail wagging behind them. I suddenly started wondering whether Benji had gotten out and gotten a sentientized neighbor dog pregnant. We hadn't gotten him neutered, I remembered with a groan. That was not going to be a fun conversation.

Of course, that wasn't it at all. Benji just had incredible ears. He could hear phone conversations behind closed doors, arguments two houses away. No secret was safe with Benji around. But the penny only dropped a week later when Jennifer called me during one of my rare days down at the lab. It was just like her to pick that day to tell me.

"Tim?"

"Yes, honey," I said into my cellphone, "Just a minute." Glancing one last time at the ongoing statistical analysis for artificially accelerated lateral gene transfer, I flicked my monitor sourcing to the phone's feed, and then full screened the videostream. She was sitting on the couch, wearing a pink T-shirt and dark blue sweatpants.

"What's up, sweetie?"

"I have some news," she said, looking slightly green around the gills, but smiling.

I waited for her to go on, but she didn't, until I asked, "What is it?"

"Uh, well, honey. Remember how Dr. Flynn told us we'd never be able to have a baby?"

"Yeah . . ." I said, eyes widening.

"Turns out she was *wrong*."

"You're . . . pregnant?" I had to make sure.

She nodded at me, a brilliant smile widening on her face.

Benji padded into view, beside her, and looked at her carefully. "Pregnend make baby?"

"Yes, Benji. Mommy's making a baby. You know what that means right, Benji?" she asked him. He stared at her silently, not answering. He hadn't yet figured out how to answer tag questions like that. "You're going to have a little brother or sister." She turned and winked at me and said, "What do you think of that, Big Daddy?"

"Woo!" I yelled, and then I said, "I love you," and she smiled at me.

"Baby!" Benj shouted, and his tail wagged, thump, thump, thump against the couch so hard it made Jen laugh aloud.

Over the months that followed, Benji got more and more excited, just like us. One evening, after Jennifer had begun to show a little, he started in with questions during dinner.

He pulled his head out of his dog dish and turned to Jen: "Baby dish? Have dish?"

Jen smiled and shook her head.

"Baby dish share," he said and wagged his tail.

Jennifer giggled and said, "How cute," and I laughed, and I patted him on the flank of his hind leg, as he turned back to the dish and devoured his dinner excitedly.

The night we brought Martin home, Benji met us at the door.

"Hi Benji," Jennifer said.

"Hi Momma," he said back. "Hi Daddy." He looked at Martin, bundled in Jen's arms. "Hi Baby."

"The baby's name is Martin," I said and then added, "You can call him Marty, if you like." Benji had problems with pronouncing "in," it tended to sound like "im." It was some kind of tongue control thing, something that they hadn't quite gotten right in his treatment.

"Mardy Baby," Benji said softly, reverently. "Hi Mardy Baby," he said and then, "Come on, Baby. Baby bed."

"What?" Jen asked, head tilted to one side, but Benji had already started off down the stairs into the cool basement. "Honey, I'm going to put Marty to bed. Can you, uh . . ."

"Yeah, sure," I said and waited for her to start up the stairs before I followed Benji down the creaking stairs to the basement. I found him wagging his tail, his nose nudging a spare plastic pad across the bare concrete floor, until it was next to his own. He liked to sleep down there because it was cool and quiet. The one he'd nudged into place was his old doggie bed, the one I should've thrown out months before when I bought his new one.

"Me Bed," he said and touched the old, tattered pad with one paw. Then he touched the nice new one and said, "Baby Bed. Mardy Baby Bed."

I was a little stunned: Benji was *sharing*? I never expected that from a dog, and it made me smile. "Oh, that's *really* sweet, Benji. But, uh, Marty's not a dog. Baby boys don't sleep in the basement. It's too cold and dirty. But it's so nice of you. . . . You think of him as a brother, huh? Aw, good boy," I said, patting him on the head. "Such a good boy."

He sat beside the two pads, looked down at them, then up at me. "Baby Bed No?"

"Right, Benji. Baby Bed No."

He drooped, tail slumped, and sunk to the concrete floor. Later, on hot summer nights when I found him sleeping beside Marty's crib, I remembered him nosing the spare pad into place, and some weird guilty feeling would well up so fast I could barely drive it back down before having to examine it.

They played together so well, Benji and Marty, both of them scooting around the house on all fours. For a while, they really *were* like any two brothers. Benji would sniff Marty's bottom occasionally and call Jen or me over: "Baby Mardy make poo!" Marty would push the buttons on a toy piano, and random songs would play. Benji would squeeze Tinky and Jiggy dolls between his teeth, and they'd shout out greetings to Marty, provoking giggles and applause from that bright little blond toddler of ours. He always wanted to share his dinner with Marty, and his doggy biscuits, no matter how many times we explained that dog food and people food are different.

Benji really loved Marty, loved him as much as any brother would have. Somehow that made me forget all those awkward moments, the questions like, "Why Mardy Baby no tail?" and "Benji no birthday party?" and "Mardy Baby poo inside?" The time Benji tried to eat off the kitchen table, and sent our dinner crashing down by accident. Jen used to breastfeed Martin at the table, while she ate her own dinner sometimes, and Benji was perplexed by this, sometimes more than once a week. "Marty Baby eats what? Benji too? Benji eat what too?"

"No, Benji," Jennifer said, "You're a dog. He's a baby. Babies have milk, but dogs have dog food. This milk is not for you. It's only for Marty, see?"

"No, Benji," he repeated ruefully. He'd started repeating that phrase every time someone said it, even gently. It's just the way everyone talks to dogs, isn't it? When they jump up onto guests, or try hump your leg?

"That's right. Benji, no. Good boy," I said. He lay down on the cool tile floor beside his bowl and thumped his tail once, just once.

With a kid, the years pass so quickly you lose track. One day, you're burping a baby; the next you have a little boy sitting beside you with a book in his lap, reading.

". . . and . . . then . . . then the . . . the boy and his dog . . . went home . . ." Martin mumbled. I smiled. I'd mouthed the words along with him, but he'd done it all by himself.

"Good job!" I patted him softly on the back. "You got every word. Did you like the story?"

"Yup," he said. "I wanna read it again," he said.

"Okay, let's . . ."

"No," Marty insisted, shaking his head. "I want to read it with *Benji*." He hopped down off the couch, onto the carpet and toward the dog.

Benji turned his head and said, "You . . . read with me?"

"Sure Benj," he replied.

"Okay," Benji said, and he sat up. "You read, I listen. Read slow."

"Mmm hmm. Okay, page one," Marty said carefully. "The story of Timmy and Spot," he said, from memory. He knew the first few pages of the picture book by heart. "'There was a boy. His name was Timmy. There was a dog. Its name was Spot.' Now *you* read."

Benji said, "I can't read. But I 'member: 'There was boy. His name Timmy. There was dog. His name Spot.'"

Marty said, "Noooo, Benji. 'There was a dog. *Its* name was Spot.'"

Benji blinked, stared at the page—at the picture, I suppose, since he wasn't supposed to be able to read, not *ever*. "'There was dog. *Its* name Spot.'"

"Good," Marty said. "Now you're gettin' it . . ."

Things started to go wrong around that time. The day that sticks out in my memory was this afternoon when I had some buddies over to watch the game on our new NetTV, while Jen and Marty were out someplace. Charlie, Deke, Demarco, and Peter were there, and we were all hollering at the screen. I don't know when Benji came into the room, but when the ads came up, and Charlie and Deke hurried to the kitchen to get us all some cold beers, Ben tapped Peter on the leg with one paw.

"Oh, hey, Benji. How are you, boy?" Peter asked absently, the way anyone asks any dog, sentient or not. He patted Ben on the head for a few seconds.

"Okay. Question okay? Ask you?"

"Sure Benji," he grinned. He'd probably never met a dog as inquisitive as Benji—I never have. "What is it?"

"You Korean?"

"Well, I'm Korean-American, yeah." I wondered how Benji had known that. Was it just a guess?

"Why Korean eat dog?"

Demarco and I both turned and looked at Peter, who sat there with one eyebrow raised. Demarco started to chuckle as Peter glanced at each of us before turning back to Benji. "Say what?"

Benji said the question again: "Why Korean eat dog?"

Peter looked up at me, puzzled. I shrugged and gave him a baffled look.

Demarco was doubled over now, laughing hysterically. "Racist dog!" he said, before bursting into laughter again. "That's funny, man. They should put you on TV, Benji! The racist talking dog show!"

Peter started laughing along. "Ha, I'd watch that show," he said. Then he said, "Look, Benj, last time I visited Korea, I didn't see *any* dog restaurants. All my relatives think eating dog is terrible. They say it's mostly old guys who do it, and I never asked them why. So I dunno why anyone would eat dog. I guess they think it tastes good or something. But hey, nobody's gonna eat you, 'kay?"

Benji blinked, processing this. "Dogs think people taste good too."

Which . . . none of us knew what to say. We all sat there in silence, until Demarco sniffed and said, "Yeah, man, well, dogs think their own crap tastes good, right?"

"Sure," Benji said, and we all burst out laughing as Deke and Charlie walked back into the room with the beers. But Benji just looked from one of us to the next, his eyes quite serious. Then the ads were done, and the announcer was talking about why Nick Lingonfelder wasn't in the game this week, and whatever it was Benji wanted to say, he kept it to himself, and just went to the back door, muttering, "Can I go out?" as he passed me.

"Uh, sure, Benj," I said and went to open the back door. He went out without so much as a glance toward me. I remember thinking that wasn't like him. When I went back into the living room, Demarco was telling Charlie and Deke about his idea for the TV show about Benji the Racist Dog.

I shrugged. "Yeah, guys, I have *no* idea where he picked that up. But you know, he's young. You know how kids can be."

"*Kids?*" Charlie mumbled, flopping onto the couch. "He's a *dog*, Tim." He handed me a beer.

I nodded. "He's . . . yeah, he's a *souped-up* dog, though."

"Mmmm, souped-up dog . . . tasty," Deke said, and Demarco burst out laughing again.

Peter chucked a sofa cushion at him, grinning. "You better talk to him, though," he said. "Some people I know would take that shit the wrong way."

That evening, I found Jen and Benji in the kitchen, talking. Benji's head was lowered, the way he did when we caught him breaking the house rules.

"No, Benji, it's okay," Jen said, patting him on the head. "It's an understandable question. But . . . well, you know how some dogs bite people? But not all dogs, right? Not all dogs are the same, right? It's the same with people. Not all people of the same kind are the same."

"Oh." Benji said, and then he wagged his tail once, which was his way of nodding. "Not all dogs same." He'd learned that lesson trying to chat with the neighborhood dogs, none of whom were sentientized.

"Lots of dogs can't watch TV, like you do," Jen said, absentmindedly fiddling with one of Marty's cartoon DVD cases on the kitchen table.

"Right," he said, and he asked, "But why *not?*"

Before she could answer him, I stepped into the room and said, "Is Benji watching TV?"

Jen looked up. She looked tired. "Yeah, I leave the dog channel on when I'm out. It's supposed to help his English."

"I talk good soon," Benji said, and like that it clicked in my head: The shift to four- and five-word sentences I'd observed, the slightly improved syntax. Dogs with the treatment he'd gotten weren't supposed to advance that far, let alone become fluent, but at the rate he was going, he'd be speaking like Marty within the year.

"Yes, Benji. You're really improving. Now, your Daddy and I need to talk about something private, Benji. Could you excuse us?"

"Okay," Benji said. "Night," he told each of us one by one, and then he padded off into the basement.

When the creaking on the stairs ended, Jen and I both exhaled. We hadn't even realized we'd been holding our breath.

"It's like . . ." she started, but then she hesitated, though I knew what she was going to say.

". . . like having two kids?" I suggested.

She nodded. "Exactly."

"Well, that was why we had him done, you know . . ."

She nodded, and it hit me how much older she looked now, than when we'd decided against adoption, and when she'd finally agreed to the dog treatment. If we'd known . . . well, there was no point in thinking about that, was there?

"So, the whole Koreans eating dogs thing . . . you think he picked that up on TV, maybe?"

Jen tapped the kitchen table. "Maybe? I've never watched any myself." I looked at the DVD case sitting on the table in front of her, and it hit me: With Marty, we checked everything out first. If he asked for a movie, we checked the parental warnings. There was a nanny lock on the TV, too, a smart lock set to block anything PG-13 or higher when he was alone in the room. But we hadn't set a lock for when it was just Benji alone.

"Well, maybe we should."

The next morning, I found Benji on the couch in front of the TV. A commercial was on. I'd never seen an ad made especially for dogs. Before that day, I'd only ever glimpsed these weird canine-athletics shows Benj loved, that always sent Benji straight to me, insistently repeating, "Let's play fetch! Let's play fetch! Wanna play fetch?"

In this ad, a pair of dogs was trotting alongside one another, as soft romantic music played in the background. There was also this soft panting sound, and a kind of rhythmic thumping that didn't fit the music. "Lonely? Humping legs not good enough for you? Are you the only talking dog in your neighborhood? Most sentientized canines have trouble finding suitable mates. But we can help you. Call PetMate today." An online contact code flashed across the bottom of the screen, as the screen cut smoothly, if briefly, to one dog mounting another; as the video quickly faded to black, a faint, slightly offensive aroma filled the room, and then quickly dissipated. Beside me, Benji was suddenly panting.

Great, I thought. *Next he'll be asking me for pocket money, so he can go out and . . .*

But the screen shifted abruptly to a stage set with wide, soft-looking red couches. On one sat a beautiful grey-furred German Shepherd, a big chew-bone under her front paws, cans and packets of some new brand of dog food, Brainy Dog Chow, visible in various places around her.

"Good morning," started the voiceover, "and welcome back to *Sparky's Couch!*" The camera zoomed in on Sparky's face as she—her voice was somehow feminine—sniffed at the camera, and the TV's odifers emitting what I swear was the faint aroma of dog-butt. Suddenly, that weird smell I'd noticed sometimes in the living room made sense. I'd thought it was just Benji.

"I'm your host, Sparky Smith," the German Shepherd said in astonishingly perfect English. She must have had the top-of-the-line treatment. "I hope *you're* comfortably seated on *your* families' couches, too. Well, yesterday you heard about the plight of Korean dogs from the first Korean sentientized dog, Somi. But it wouldn't be fair to talk about Korea and ignore problems closer to home. . . ."

My jaw dropped. She sounded like a human TV announcer. The cost of her treatment must have been exorbitant . . . or had she been gotten one of those pricy *in vitro* mods? Looking at Benji, I felt like . . . was it wrong of us to get him the cheaper treatment? Did he realize he'd never be able to talk like Sparky?

"Well, according to today's expert, America has a serious dog-mistreatment problem as well! Even here, dogs suffer every day. Everyone please welcome Duncan Mallory, from Iowa," Sparky declared.

The camera cut to an audience full of dogs lounging on the terraced studio audience floor area. They were all barking rhythmically, *oof, oof, oof,* like it was applause, and Benji was barking along with them. A squat brown pug waddled onstage and then hopped up onto the couch beside Sparky. As they sniffed one another in greeting, a new dog-butt aroma wafted from the TV odifers. Well, I guess it was new: It smelled the same as the last one, to me.

"Welcome, Duncan! It's nice to have you here," Sparky said.

"Thanks, Sparky. I'm happy to be here." The pug's voice was even clearer than Sparky's, with very little accent. It was weird.

"Please tell us how you discovered about the suffering of American dogs, Duncan."

Melodramatically sad piano music began to play as the dog spoke. "Well, I was surfing the internet, and thought that I'd look up the ASPCA—you know, the American Society for the Prevention of Cruelty to Animals."

"Right," Sparky replied. The acronym appeared at the bottom of the screen and stayed in place what seemed like a long time. Maybe it was to let even the least-enhanced dogs—dogs like Benji—to memorize the shapes of the letters.

"After searching around their webpage, I discovered something incredible," he said. The audience and Sparky—and Benji—panted expectantly. "Millions of dogs are killed with poison injections every year, right here in America. It's been going on for decades, too."

All of the dogs in the audience yelped in horror. Sparky covered her nose with a paw and made a whining sound. Then she asked, "Why?"

"Because they're homeless. Nobody owns them, and nobody wants them, so they're *killed*," the pug explained, his voice turning a little angry. "In some states, they can still do that even to sentientized dogs . . . but *everywhere* in America, nonsentientized dogs die this way every day."

The audience began whining, and Benji joined them. The sad music continued as a video montage filled the screen. At first it was just ankles and knees, which confused me until I realized it was dog's eye view. The room was filled with a vaguely metallic smell, mixed with the bite of chemical cleaning solution and, faintly, some other offensive aroma—like old piss and sickened animal turds. Onscreen flashed the faces of miserable dogs framed by the bars of cages, one after another in an interminable sequence. The camera entered another room, where a dog lay on its side on a table, its legs visible hanging over the edge from above. Benji whined softly, I think unaware that he was doing it.

"This is where they inject the dogs," Duncan explained.

This was too much, I decided, and I reached for the NetTV remote next to Benji's paw.

Benji stopped whining along with the audience and looked at me in surprise. "Why?

"Why what?"

"Why . . ." He paused, as if trying to figure out what he was asking about. *Why turn the TV off? Why do they kill dogs that way? Why is the world so unfair?* He whined again, this time less unselfconscious. His head hung down, his eyes wide and sorrowful.

"Benji, I dunno what to tell you. *We* try to treat you well, but not everyone in the world is like us."

Benji didn't say anything, but he stared at me with this piercing look, as if my explanation wasn't good enough.

"Look, those dogs would . . . go hungry. They would be homeless and starve," I said.

Benji sat there, looking at me. He knew the word homeless. Whenever we went to the vet's downtown, we always passed a couple of homeless people. He had talked to one of them, some old war vet who'd had PTSD and couldn't stand to live indoors anymore.

"You don't kill homeless people," Benji said softly.

"No, Benj, we don't. Some people probably wish we did, but we don't. Because they're people."

Benji whimpered at me, and snuffed a little, then looked up at me and said, "Am I a people?"

"Of course you are, Benji," I said, without even pausing to think. I didn't add the rest of what I was thinking, *You can talk. You can think.* He turned and looked at me, his eyes like those of a dog wall-eyed from sneaking a half-box of forbidden, dog-toxic chocolate.

This wouldn't do. It was Saturday, sunny and bright outside.

"Say, Benji, whaddaya think about going to the park?" He wagged his tail a little weakly. "C'mon boy, let's go ask Jen, then," I said, and we got up and walked to the top of the stairs.

"Jen, wanna go for a picnic?" I shouted down the stairs, and she called up to me that she thought it was a great idea, and only needed a few minutes to finish up her work. I went to get Marty ready.

Half an hour later, we had a simple lunch packed and were on our way, Marty and Benji in the backseat of the microvan and Jen and I in the front, driving across town to Volunteer Park. We played kids' music all the way, songs about bananas and monkeys and chickens dancing and some guy named Pickles O'Sullivan. Marty talked to Benji about a book he was reading—about a group of kid spies who were constantly saving the world from scheming corporations and politicians—and Jen smiled at me. This was a great idea, I thought to myself.

When we got there, I took Benji off his leash and let him run around for a while and told him to come and find me near the benches when he'd had enough. Jen and Marty and I sat on a blanket, ate some tuna salad sandwiches and some fresh fruit we'd bought from an organic produce stand along the way. Then I kicked a ball around with Marty for a while—he was too small to kick it back properly, but he wasn't too small to intercept it, if I kicked softly enough.

When the sun had started to go down, though, Benji still hadn't returned. Usually when we picnicked, he stayed around, or came back soon, but this time, there was no sign of him for hours.

"Where do you think he is?" Jen asked.

"I don't know, maybe he found some girl dogs or something?" I grinned.

"That's not funny. You know, I read that someone's been kidnapping sentient dogs. They've been disappearing from all over. It's terrible."

"Don't worry," I said, "I'll go find him. He's gotta be around somewhere." And with that, I left the two of them sitting on the picnic blanket.

I wandered around the park, calling out his name and looking in any place I could think of where he might be. He wasn't by the old bandstand with the faded paint, or the new jungle gyms; I couldn't find him anywhere near the mini-museum or the tennis courts; and he wasn't out by the viewpoint overlooking Puget Sound. I asked everyone I ran across, and nobody had seen him, though even if they had, would they have noticed him?

Finally, on the opposite end of the park from where Jen and Marty were waiting, I followed a trail that ran right between a couple of lazy old pine trees and over a small rise. When I got to the top, I could hear a loud voice—a dog's voice—accompanied by murmurs. I came down the hill, and in the dimming light, I saw a pack of dogs all sitting together in a circle, gathered around a big white husky that seemed to be orating to them. Every once in a while, they responded in unison, with a jolting yelp or bark. It was too dim to see the dogs in the pack clearly, but Benji had to be there somewhere. Ignoring a faint sense that I was trespassing, I moved down the hill.

As I got closer, the oration got clearer: "And besides, the issue is, humans do not think of us as people. How many of you have ever shit indoors?"

The dogs muttered among themselves, and then most of them replied, one by one, "I have."

"And what happened? Your master rubbed your nose in it, and threw you outside. Do they do that to babies who crap in their diapers?"

The consensus, quickly reached, was a resounding *No*.

"The thing to remember, to understand, is that humans will never, ever see us as we see ourselves. They *think* they love us, but . . ." The dogs yelped affirmatively in response.

"Benji?" I interrupted, after the howls had died off and before the husky could continue. I guess I must have been downwind or something, or maybe talking and listening took so much of their brainpower that they paid less attention to scent, because they suddenly all turned and looked at me in what felt like surprise. Having all those eyes on me was nerve-wracking. Some dogs bared their teeth, growling softly, and I half-expected to become an example in the husky's diatribe, or for him to order them to attack me.

But they all just stood there, looking at me angrily until Benji turned and trotted from the pack of them over toward me.

"Come on, Benji," I said. "Let's go."

He said nothing but followed me quietly, and I only looked over my shoulder once. They didn't follow us but instead just sat there, silently watching us go.

Laws or no laws, I didn't leash him. I didn't even dare try.

He ran away a week later.

It was the Fourth of July—Independence Day, of all days—and it was our turn to play host among enough of our circles of friends that we decided to just invite them all at once.

The scent of grilling meat and smoke wafted through the backyard. One of the coolers of beer sat open, bottles nestled in the ice and left in the glaring sun. Random groups of friends and strangers chatted with one another in small clusters, sitting on lawn chairs or leaning on the railing of the deck. I could hear Jen laughing about something, and Marty was with the other kids in the sandbox, steering little matchbox cars along hastily constructed little sandy race courses.

At some point, I heard a crash from inside the house. I looked up from the grill, where I was tending to the burgers, and called to Jen, but she couldn't hear me over the music. I handed the spatula to Deke and went inside to check it out.

I found Benji sitting miserably in the bathroom. The now-smashed sink, which had never been properly attached to the wall, had been knocked down and cracked the tile floor, and the naked water pipes were broken off and dripping water. The small vase of flowers that sat on the toilet tank had fallen down, and the flowers floated here and there on the water that covered the floor. The vase had smashed into a million shards, too, I realized as I looked carefully. There were dog turds on the toilet seat, and floating in the water flooding the floor. Thank goodness the smart house system registered that the flow was too high on the pipe and shut the water valve access for the sink, but it was still going to be a pain to clean up the room, let alone fix everything. So I did the thing parents sometimes do and regret forever.

"What the hell, Benji?" I shouted. But wouldn't anyone have yelled? A new sink, fixing the plumbing, retiling the floor: none of that would be free. "You're not *supposed* to use the toilet, dammit! You're a dog!" I grabbed a rolled-up newspaper from the bathroom magazine rack and whacked him on the nose with it.

"But . . . there's too many people now. . . ." he said, sadly.

"No, Benji. No. You're a dog, okay? You're supposed to do it outside. . . ."

He didn't say anything but just stalked out of the room with baleful eyes, to the back door, watching solemnly as I went and got the wet'n'dry vac and sucked up most of the mess. Quickly, I wrote up a sign to use the bathroom upstairs and then locked the bathroom door so nobody would walk into the disaster zone by accident.

When I got to the back door, I realized that the poor dog had been stuck inside for hours. Even if nobody had been around, we hadn't let him out anyway. A sudden sinking guilt set in. "Okay, Benji, I'll let you out. Sorry, I forgot to. Just do your business outside next time, okay? Bark or shout and I'll come let you out."

He mumbled something low, something I couldn't make out as I opened the door, and he went out into the backyard. I hoped the crowd would cheer him up, maybe. He took off toward the yard, not waiting for me. I wondered, *Is this what teenagers are like?*

Outside, Lorna was saying, "Well, now, Benji, you're much better behaved than the last time I saw you. I almost wish I'd brought my Spot to come play with you."

"Play?" Benji yelped. "I'm not a baby dog! You think I'm stupid?"

"Pardon me?" Lorna said, and I could hear Jen's shocked response: "*Benji!*"

Goddammit, I swear that was what I thought. Not, "Hey, Lorna, Benji's a little different from Spot," or, "Wait, everyone, let's talk about this." Just, *Goddammit.*

"No, it's alright," Lorna said, adjusting her sunhat. "I'm not sure I understand, Benji. Are you telling me you don't like to play? That if, say, I throw this rubber ball over there, you won't go and get it? Every dog loves to play fetch, right?" She picked up a rubber ball from the grass and threw it over toward the back fence.

Benji sat on his haunches, watching the ball roll away. Then, without another word, he stood and walked over toward her, like he was going to graze her leg with his side.

As she said, "Good boy," and reached down with her free hand to pat him on the head, he raised one leg and sprayed piss onto her white leather shoes.

Lorna jumped back, dropping her plate on the ground, its contents tumbling onto the grass. Everyone was quiet, the music a paradoxically cheerful background to the concerned, shocked faces. Even Marty and his friends had stopped playing racecars to look over at the scene.

Ever the first to respond, Jen rushed up with paper towels, apologizing as she wiped Lorna's shoes and pushed Benji away. Lorna slipped her shoes off as Jen wiped them and said loudly, "Well, if that's his attitude, I don't see why you keep him. He must be bad for Marty." She shrugged. "You oughtta just have him put down and save yourselves the trouble—"

At that, Benji started snarling at her, showing his teeth, and Jen searched the crowd for me, made eye contact. I realized I'd just been standing there watching this and suddenly realized this was *my* dog who was acting out. I hurried over and said, "Okay, Benji, time to go inside," and reached down to hook my fingers under his collar.

"No!" he barked, his speech half snarl and his hackles on end. I yanked my hand back as he snapped at it. The crowd gasped in shock. Each word that followed was like that first word, a sharp snap of noise, some frightening amalgam of barking and speech and growl: "I . . . won't . . . go . . . in . . ." It was just like how Marty threw tantrums: *"I . . . won't . . . eat . . . it!"*

But I didn't respond the way I did to Marty. No cajoling, no encouraging, no teasing. "Benji!" I yelled. "Don't you talk to me that way!"

His response was a snarl, and he lunged at me again, snapped his teeth at me. I jumped back, suddenly much more angry than before. "Benji, you get inside now, or else."

"Or else what?" he snarled.

I stood there, my mind blank, my mouth wide.

Then, suddenly, he stopped snarling. He just sniffed, once. There was an expression I'd never seen before on his face, something new, something I couldn't read. Then he broke into a run toward the gate that opened out on the front walk. I couldn't understand why he went there, unless to go indoors, since he'd never been able to get the latch open with his mouth.

But then, around the corner, I heard human voices call out, "Hey!" and "Oh my God!" at the same time. Rounding the corner, I found the gate wide open, and Chad and Anoo on the other side of it, bowled over, potato salad and smoked sausages spilled all around them on the ground. He'd heard them open the gate. He'd seen his chance.

Chad glanced over his shoulder after the dog, saying, "What's with Benji?"

He was gone.

I drove through the streets that night, searching all over the city. I checked all the pounds, went everywhere I'd ever taken him—downtown, to the beach, everywhere. I even went to that spot in Volunteer Park where I'd found him with those other dogs—the spot came to mind immediately when he ran away—but it was deserted. I imagined Benj out on the streets, running alone while fireworks bloomed above him in the dark, roaring sky. It terrified me, but even so, I didn't find him.

I waited a week or so, figuring hunger or fear or loneliness might bring him back to us. Every time I left the house, I looked up and down the street, hoping he might be watching from some neighbor's yard, but if he was, he hid well. I didn't see him.

When I tried to figure out who to report it to, nobody wanted to listen. The cops didn't handle missing animals, not even sentientized ones, and the pound told me sentientized dogs were inevitably caught on first inspection and sent home. They said there were like three ways of identifying the sentientized dog's home, just in case, and I'd have been contacted within forty-eight hours if he'd ended up at a pound. Finally, I was left with nobody to report it to.

But one Saturday afternoon about a month later, the cops did show up. Of course, when I answered the door, I was confused at first: they were sitting on the doorstep in slightly tattered uniforms, miserable in the damp summer heat. Their custom scooter sat parked in the driveway. Across the street, Lorna Anderson sat on her stoop, fascinated, and I couldn't blame her.

After all, one of the cops was a big black Doberman, and his partner was a squat, muscular bulldog. Both had shoulder cams on, which I supposed streamed directly to a human supervisor.

"Good morning," said the Doberman, before I had time to really think about the fact of who I was talking to. It had a voice so deep and rumbling it could've given Barry White a run for his money. "Are you Mr. Stevens?"

"Uh, yeah?" I nodded.

The Doberman stopped panting long enough to say, "My name is Officer Duke Smith. My partner is Officer Cindy. Just Cindy, no family name."

"Okay . . ."

"Can we come in please?"

"Uh . . . is this about Benji?" I said and found myself adjusting my position. I was blocking the doorway a little more. I don't know why, except maybe this sense of . . . of shame, I guess. Like if they came in the house, they might, what, know why Benji had run away? They might smell something wrong with us? That it was our fault?

"Yes, sir, and it's rather serious. We need some information from you," Cindy said, half-growling.

"Okay," I said, stepping aside. They hurried in, sniffing the air, and I led them into the living room. "So, do you know where Benj is?" Suddenly I felt even more nervous.

"No, sir," said Duke. "Has he contacted you since the day he went missing?" As he asked this, Duke thumped his tail emphatically. Cindy stopped panting, as if she was trying to look businesslike.

I look from one to the other, wishing I was better at reading dogs' eyes. I wasn't around Benj long enough to really get good at that. I've heard they can sniff out a lie, literally scent it on you. Not that I had anything to lie about, really.

"No, er, officers. No, I haven't. I'm worried about him, to be honest." That much was true.

"And, did Benji ever express any opinions you'd call political?"

"Political?"

"Yes, sir. Animal rights, or animal liberation ideology? Anything radical?"

I laughed softly, before I caught myself. Duke's eyes narrowed, the brow of his doggie face furrowing like he was getting ready to fetch a stick. Surely he was just mouthing some human cop's questions, delivered by earphone or implant. Surely a dog couldn't actually be questioning me? I found myself wondering whether they were paid to do this work, and whether it was in dollars, or biscuits?

Cindy sniffed the air between us, as if searching me for some clue, and she said, "Mr. Stevens, we're concerned that Benji's mixed up with a dangerous organization. . . ."

"Dangerous? What, like . . . dog fights?"

Duke cocked his head as Cindy said, "No, sir. May we show you?"

I nodded, and she turned her head. With a practiced movement, she yanked a mouth remote free from her shoulder holster and positioned it between her teeth. She growled softly, turning it with her tongue, and the TV flickered to life.

It was a black and white video, night vision, of some kind of security guard post, with an older man in a uniform seated before a bunch of screens, drinking coffee. The resolution was too blurry to see what he was looking at, but good enough to see he was bored out of his skull.

Then the door burst inward, like it was kicked in, and someone entered. There was audio of him shouting at the top of his lungs. He was some kind of . . . a hippie, I guess: dreadlocks, a muscle shirt and tattoos all over his body, in sandals. He was holding a rifle, but he didn't shoot it: He only pointed it at the man, shouting orders. Drop your gun. Hands behind your head.

The man obeyed. Then a pack of dogs poured into the room and mobbed the poor man, crowding around him, tearing him apart. The man's screams were terrifying, and blood pooled at their feet, spread across the floor as he fell to the ground, and still they tore at him, until the snarling and howling drowned out his weakening screams. As he went silent, they began to howl, bark-shouting curses and clawing at him.

"This was at an animal pound in San Diego last night," said Duke flatly.

"God," I said.

"Some of these dogs are on file: sentientized runaways. Others look like they're probably strays that were sentientized recently, later in life. The treatment is less effective that way, but it's still possible. Now, this . . ."

Then the perspective changed, as Cindy moved the mouth remote slightly with a click. The video paused and then zoomed in on one of the dogs.

There he was, on the screen. My little terrier, my Benji, his furry little face covered in blood, mid-bark-curse, his tail wagging furiously.

"Is that Benji?" asked Duke the Doberman.

I couldn't tell. It was so strange, not knowing. "Uh, maybe? I'd have to hear his voice." Duke nodded, self-consciously using human body language for my benefit I suppose, and the video jumped forward, scanning through the footage until the terrier was in frame again, and speaking.

"Jesus!" said some dog offscreen. "Did we have to kill him?"

"They kill hundreds of us every day, for much less," said the terrier. Said *Benji*, for I *knew* it was him now.

Cindy muted the video but let it run as a crew of young people, women and men in black and wearing balaclavas, quickly unlocked all the cages in the shelter. When they left, they stepped over the mauled security guard without a moment's hesitation.

"Yeah, I don't know," I said to him finally. "I don't see him, but . . ."

"Uh-huh. It's a little hard to tell, I know. We do have stool samples, though, so I guess we'll know soon enough through DNA testing. These dogs seem to like crapping in places where they know they shouldn't." A Chihuahua stared into the camera, stared into my eyes, and said something. Dogs don't have lips, so it's pretty hard to lipread them when they talk, but I'd swear it'd said, *Fuck you.*

Somehow, that Chihuahua was too much. I ran for the kitchen sink, arriving just in time to avoid throwing up all over the floor. I had an empty stomach, so it was just gastric juices, but still. I felt sick at the thought of it. And terrified. Benji . . . had we made him like this? It was like . . . I felt like some serial killer's father must feel, I guess. It was so confusing, the guilt and shame.

The dog police stayed in the living room, speaking softly to one another as they waited patiently while I rinsed my mouth out. I was frightened, now, of Benji. I'd never imagined he could do something like that. Not a thinking, rational animal like him. Sure, he wasn't a human being, but I didn't think he was a cold-blooded killer, either.

When I got back to the living room, the dogs said, "So, that *was* Benji?"

"Yeah," I said. "That's him. What the hell was he doing?"

Officer Smith nodded at Officer Cindy, and said, "Busting dogs from the pound. Down in California. We don't know how he got there, or what the group is doing with all those dogs they busted loose. None of them were sentientized. Just normal dogs."

"What for?"

Officer Duke looked over at Cindy, and then back to me. "Well . . . it's just a theory, but some animal rights groups online have been talking mass sentientization. Funding treatment for large numbers of animals, and not just dogs. They can't do that alone, so the next question is: did Benji ever have any human friends around? Animal rights people, PETA, anything suspicious like that?"

I looked at the Doberman in shock. "Animal rights activists?"

"Yes. That's what the people in the video are: the Animal Liberation Front. Benji being mixed up with some very bad people. *Very* dangerous. They're smuggling synthetic drugs out of Canada in dogs' bellies. Once or twice a month, some dog will turn up near the B.C. border, dead from an overdose, with a ruptured baggie somewhere in its guts. Our theory is that this is how they're funding all the sentientization treatments. But what this army they're building is *for* . . . we're not sure."

An *army*.

Any reservation or distrust I felt dissipated before that possibility. Suddenly everything came pouring out of me: his anger, and how he'd started acting up a while ago. I told them about the party—they didn't seem much interested, like the story was familiar—and I told them about the TV shows he'd watched, which bored them. They seemed ready to go, when I finally realized what I ought to tell them about.

"There was this one time, in Volunteer Park," I said. They exchanged a look, as if to say, finally, *something* of interest.

"Go on," Cindy grumbled.

"There's this spot, I mean, I only saw them once, but . . . there was a group of dogs. Like, a rally or something. It seemed . . . yeah, I guess, like you said: It seemed political. The leader was some kind of big white husky. I mean, I think it was the leader. It was doing most of the talking, and the other dogs were barking in response."

"How many dogs were there?" Duke asked.

"I don't know, maybe ten or twelve?"

"I see," said Duke, and Cindy pulled up a surface map of the park. "Where was it?" she said, so I showed her on the map.

"And the husky," Cindy said. "Would you recognize it if you saw it?"

I shrugged. "I . . . probably not. Maybe if I heard his voice. I mean, white huskies all look the same to me. No offense."

Neither dog said anything to that, but Cindy quickly asked me one more question: "You're a medical researcher, correct?"

I stared at them for a moment, wondering why that mattered. "Yes," I said, finally, in a tone that made clear I couldn't understand why they were asking.

"Did Benji ever ask you about your work?"

"No," I said. But a moment popped in my head, vivid and clear. One night, not long before he'd run away, I had found Benji at my desk. His doggie-keyboard within wireless range. A web browser open to his doggie webmail service. But also other windows open, folders containing my various work projects. Everything encrypted, but maybe crackable. I remembered thinking that was strange: I always closed all the folders I was working from when I left the room, especially work folders, because if I didn't the cloud backup software didn't work as well. With a sinking feeling, I wondered what folders it'd been, though I couldn't remember.

Officers Duke and Cindy sat there, sniffing the air a little. As dogs, they might find my body language as opaque as I found theirs, but I wondered whether they maybe could sniff out my lie of omission.

And for whose sake was I lying, anyway? If word got out that my dog had stolen confidential information . . . and if those nuts who'd pressed Benji into their gang ended up using it somehow . . . my guts sank as I realized just how bad it could be. Never mind the lab, my boss: the stuff I was researching was . . . in the wrong hands, it could be dangerous. Accelerated gene transfer . . . the wrong person could design a virus that would sentientize *all* dogs, an intelligence plague. But if it affected dogs and cats . . . what would it do to humans?

I realized I'd been standing there for minutes, not speaking. The cops waited, I guess to see if I had anything else to offer. I didn't, so finally, I said, "Is there anything else?"

"No," said Cindy. "But if Benji contacts you, you need to get in touch with us. Under federal and state laws, sentientized animals are now subject to criminal proceedings. Furthermore, since Benji's a canine, he cannot be considered a family member. You can and will be forced to testify against Benji if he is apprehended and tried. And you will be considered an accomplice—

equally culpable for acts of terrorism—if you aid or abet him or his group in any way." Cindy paused, as if trying to gauge my reaction, and added, "You should realize you're on a watch list, and will remain on one until this situation is resolved."

Duke added, "One more thing, sir: this group Benji's tangled up in? They're dangerous. You need to stay away from him. Do *not* trust him. If he approaches you, call us. Without delay," Duke added and then turned his head to the side. A card slid out automatically from a slot in his uniform's collar, with a photo of Duke and Cindy and contact info.

I nodded. "I understand, Officer."

They thanked me for my cooperation and went to the front door. When I let them out, I saw that Jen had just pulled up the driveway a few minutes before and gotten Marty out of his car seat. The dogs trotted past them toward their custom scooter, and in a moment, all that was left of them was the faint ringing in my ears from the roar of the motor. Well, and the tightness in my chest. But what I couldn't help but think was: they were talking about Benji like he was a criminal. In other words, as if he were a person, not just a dog. Which mean he'd finally gotten what he'd always wanted, I guess.

"What was that about?' Jen asked as she reached the porch.

"The cops?" I sighed. "Looking for Benj."

Her eyes went wide, though she said nothing. But watching them drive off, Marty mumbled a single, quiet, mournful word: "Benji?"

A few months later, I was walking our new dog, a black Labrador named Cookie, in Victory Park. I was on a picnic with Jennifer and Marty, but they were still on the blanket, on the other side of the park. I don't know what made me walk to that spot over the rise, but when I did, Cookie started to growl. She was a normal dog, not like Benj. Not sentient, so her growling was just instinct, not rhetoric. And then I turned, and I saw him. It was Benj, walking slowly toward me with this *look* in his eyes.

"Cookie, heel," I said, and Benji's eyes narrowed. As if being reminded of something painful, like when you see your ex dating someone new a little too soon.

"We got her for Marty's sake, Benji. When you ran away, it really confused him." As if I owed him an explanation. He just sat there, looking at me. "What are you doing here?" I asked quietly, looking around. For cops, or for his dreadlocked friend. "You're wanted. Not just Seattle cops, but FBI."

Ben's mouth opened slightly, a coughing noise indicating doggy-laughter. "FBI? Ha . . . try NSA, INTERPOL, the Secret Service . . ."

"Are you really smuggling . . . smuggling drugs?"

Cookie growled, tugging at the leash. She either wanted to attack little Benji, or run away.

"There's no evidence. Just hearsay. Two dogs with conflicting testimony. Nobody'll believe a dachshund's testimony in court." Benj paused briefly, bitter cough-laugh filling his throat for a moment.

"Benj, these people you're with, they're . . . they're using you. They're crazy, Ben. They wanna hurt a lot of people."

"Not to me," he said. "They've helped me understand everything. But they're dangerous to you, and everyone like you."

I knew he was thinking of the dog pounds. Millions of dogs a year, dead for nothing.

"You have to stop, Ben," I said. "You can . . . you should . . ."

"I can what?" He said it hard, verging on a bark, and then sat on his haunches. "Come on, tell me, what can I do? What, come home? Really? Tell the truth: Do you want me to come home? *Can I come home?*"

"Sure," I said, lying through my teeth. If I got him home, I could call the cops, I thought, standing there with Cookie beside me.

He just sniffed the air between us.

Then I saw it in his eyes, just as it died: *hope*. It hadn't been mere rhetoric. He'd really *hoped* I wanted him back. He would have come home with me, and turned informant, and betrayed those terrorist friends of his, ended it all, if only I'd just wanted him back. But he could smell the truth, I knew: how angry I was at him, how I regretted having him sentientized in the first place. It was the most terrible thing I'd ever had to see in person, watching that hope die in his eyes.

I looked away, down at the grass, the endless grass all around us rustling in the breeze.

But Benji didn't look away. "Say it," he said softly, his voice pulling my eyes back to him. His tail was up. I didn't know what tail-up meant in that context. I couldn't guess. "Say what you want," he demanded in a voice soft as when he'd whimpered as a puppy. "Be *honest* for once."

The hope was gone from his eyes.

I crouched down, and I wanted to open my arms to him. I wanted to, but . . . but I also didn't. With our eyes almost level, locked together, I said, "No, Benji. I don't want you to come home. Not after everything . . . not now. You can't. You *know* that."

He held my gaze for a long time. I waited for him to say something, some salve to heal the wound between us, or some accusation, even. But he just sat there, staring silently with those big, wet, hopeless eyes of his. I was about to say, "I'm sorry, Benj," but he broke the silence first. Just a growl, and just for a moment. Not threateningly, just . . . like a frown.

And then, after a long, quiet look at me—as if to remember me—he turned and ran off into the trees. That was the last time I saw him.

Nina Allan's stories have appeared in numerous magazines and anthologies, including *Best Horror of the Year Volume Six, Solaris Rising 3,* and the Shirley Jackson Award-winning *Aickman's Heirs.* Her novella *Spin,* a science fictional re-imagining of the Arachne myth, won the BSFA Award in 2014, and her story-cycle *The Silver Wind* was awarded the Grand Prix de L'Imaginaire in the same year. Her debut novel *The Race* was a finalist for the 2015 BSFA Award, the Kitschies Red Tentacle, and the John W. Campbell Memorial Award. Her second novel, *The Rift,* will be published by Titan Books in July 2017.

TEN DAYS

Nina Allan

Ten days, ten hours, ten minutes. A man is murdered and a woman is charged. The hangman winds his watch and then goes home. I don't suppose you remember that old Cher lyric, you're too young. *If I could turn back time, if I could find a way.* My best friend from law school, Frieda Solomon, used to play that track at the end of every party she ever threw, when we were solidly pissed and everyone was dancing, even those of us who never danced, when discussion had dissolved into barracking and all the ugly home truths began to come out.

The song is about someone who's said something stupid and wishes she hadn't. Hardly a crime, when you think of the appalling things people do to one another every day and can't take back. What are mere words, you might ask, in the face of deeds? I'm not so sure, myself. What if the person Cher is singing to happens to be some hot-shot international trader with revenge on his mind? Or a fighter pilot? Or a president with his finger on the button? Who knows what someone like that might do, if you caught them at the wrong moment?

One thoughtless comment and it's World War Three. Who knows?

If I could turn back time, my dear, I wouldn't change a thing.

It takes about two minutes for a time machine to get going, in my experience. Nothing happens for what seems like forever, then just as you're telling yourself you were an idiot to believe, even for ten seconds, that such a thing would be possible, the edges of things—your fingers, your sight lines, your thoughts—begin to blur, to stumble off kilter, and then you're gone. Or not gone as such, but *there*. Your surroundings appear oddly familiar, because of course they are. The time you have left seems insubstantial suddenly, a peculiar daydream fantasy. Vivid while you were having it but, like most dreams, irretrievable on waking.

There was a man who lived next door to us when we were children whose house was stuffed to the rafters with old radios. The type he liked best were the wooden console models from before the war, but he kept Bakelite sets too, and those tinny little transistors from the nineteen fifties. His main obsession was a hefty wooden box full of burnt-out circuits and coils he claimed had once belonged to a wireless set used by the French resistance in World War Two. He was forever trying to restore the thing but I think there were pieces missing and so far as I know he never got it working again.

I used to spend hours round at his house, going through the boxes of junk and watching what he was doing. Our mother couldn't stand Gary Tonkes. She would have stopped me having anything to do with him if she could. Looking back on it now, I suppose she thought there was something peculiar about his interest in me, but there was never anything like that, nothing you could point a finger at, anyway. When I was thirteen, Gary Tonkes was sectioned under the Mental Health Act. His house was infested with rats, and he kept insisting that one of his radios had started picking up signals from Mars. I remember taking pictures of the house afterwards with the Kodak Instamatic Uncle Henry had given me for my tenth birthday, pretending I was working for MI5. I still feel bad about that. I think now that Gary Tonkes's radio might have been picking up not signals from Mars, but the voices of people who had lived in the house before him, or who would live there in the future, after he'd gone.

Time doesn't give a damn about the laws of physics. It does what it wants.

I think of Helen's basement living room in Camden, the ancient Aubusson carpet faded to a dusty monochrome, the books, the burnt-orange scent of chrysanthemums. I sometimes wish I could go back there, just to see it again, but I know I can't. I've had my turn. And stealing more time could be dangerous, not just for me and for Helen but for you as well.

When I was eighteen, I contracted leukaemia. I was very ill for about ten months and then I recovered. Against the odds, the doctors said, and only after the kind of clichéd regime of brutal chemo you read about in the colour supplements. And yes, there were times I wished they'd give up on me and let me die. I suspect—in fact I know—it was my brother Martin who persuaded me to stick around. His white face at my bedside, I can still see it now. His terror, that I wasn't going to pull through, I suppose. I don't think I've mattered like that to anyone, before or since, and that includes Ray. I hung on and hung on, until suddenly there I was, washed up on the shore of life once more and the tide of those months receding like some lurid sick joke.

But there were side effects. I'd been offered a place at Cambridge, to read mathematics. Following my illness I found something was missing: the instinctive affinity for numbers I had taken for granted as an inseparable part of me was, if not vanished, then noticeably blunted. It was like thinking through gauze. My professor seemed confident that I was simply exhausted, that any diminution in my ability would soon be restored. Perhaps she was right. I'll never know now, will I? The university offered me the option to defer my entry for a further year, but I refused.

I turned down my place, partly from the terror of failure and partly to match the drama that was playing out inside my head with something concrete that could be measured in the world outside. I was having a breakdown, in other words, and in the aftermath of that I switched to Law. I know it doesn't sound like much, when you put it like that, but the decision hurt a lot at the time. It felt like the worst kind of defeat. I won't say I ever got over the loss, but I learned to live with it, the same as you do with any bereavement. And in time I even came to enjoy my legal studies. There is a beauty in the law, in which the abstraction of numbers is countered by the wily and intricate compromises of philosophy. Call it compensation, if you like. An out-of-court settlement that, if not generous, has at least proved adequate.

I'm good at my job, I think, and it has provided me with a decent living in return. And whenever I find myself growing maudlin for what might have been, I remind myself that the law has also provided me with what Martin sometimes jokingly refers to as Dora's file on the doomed: an interest that began as a tree branch of curiosity and grew into a passion.

If I am known to the public at all, it is for my articles and radio broadcasts on the subject of capital punishment, and the fatal miscarriages of justice that have been associated with this barbaric practice. For many years, the essays I wrote for various history and politics journals formed the limit of my ambition for my researches. It was Martin—of course!—who first suggested I should write a book, and the more I thought about the idea the more I liked it.

My first thought was to write a monograph on capital punishment in general: a philosophical treatise, to be accompanied by a thorough debunking. A literary bollocking, if you like. I soon came to realise how dull such a volume would be, unless you had an interest in the subject to begin with, which would make the whole thing pointless, a sermon to the converted. I came to the conclusion that a more personal approach would work better, an in-depth study of specific cases, of one specific case even. What better way to demonstrate the brutality of state-sanctioned murder than to tell the story of one of its victims? To show that murder is always murder, even when enshrined in law, with the same practical margin for error and moral depravity that murder entails?

My decision to write about Helen Bostall was made quickly and easily. As a story, her case had everything you might look for in a decent thriller. The condemned criminal was also a woman, which made the case a cause celebre, even at the time. People are fascinated by women who kill in much the same way as they are fascinated by genetic freaks, and with the same mixture of self-righteous indignation and covert repulsion.

For my own part, I became interested in Helen because I admired her writing, and also because from the moment I first encountered what passed for the facts of her case, I found myself convinced she was not guilty. Not that I would have ceased to admire her, necessarily, if she had been a murderer—Edwin Dillon was an arrogant prick, if you ask me—but her innocence made her the perfect candidate for my thesis. I would do her justice, I decided, if not in deed then in word, at the very least.

I've read interviews with biographers in which they wax on about having a special kinship with their subjects, a personal relationship across time that could never have existed in reality. I would once have dismissed such speculation as sentimental codswallop.

Not any more, though.

Helen Bostall was born in 1895, in Addiscombe, Croydon. Her father, Winston Bostall, was a doctor and lay preacher. Her mother, Edith, had worked as a teacher, though she gave up her career entirely after she married. The two were well-matched, forward-thinking people who gave their only daughter Helen every opportunity to develop her intellectual awareness of the world and her place within it.

I might have been content, Helen wrote in her 1923 pamphlet essay "On War, on Murder", *content to take up my place among the teachers, preachers, poets, and painters I had learned to admire as a very young woman, to speak my protest, but timidly, from inside the very system I was protesting. It was the spectacle of war that made me a radical, that fired in me the conviction that the system I was protesting had to be broken.*

The war, and more specifically the death on the Somme of her cousin, Peter Arnold Bostall, the son of her father's brother Charles. Peter and Helen, both only children and of a similar age, had been close throughout their childhoods. At the outbreak of war in 1914, Peter had just graduated from Oxford and was considering whether to take up a junior fellowship offered to him by his college, or to embark on a research trip to Madagascar with his other uncle, his mother's brother, the entomologist Rupert Paxton.

It is not known whether Peter and Helen had plans to marry, although judging by the letters the two exchanged while Peter was at Oxford it is certainly a possibility. There is no doubt that Helen was devastated by her cousin's death, locking herself away in her room for several weeks afterwards and ultimately falling ill with pneumonia. She emerged from her illness a different person, determined to play her part in creating a more just society, a society in which a death such as her cousin's would not be possible. When the war ended she took up lodgings in Hampstead, close to the house where John Keats once lived, and began taking in private pupils. During the hours she was not teaching, she was studying and writing. She also joined a suffragist group. Her parents, though initially upset by her abrupt departure from the family home and concerned for her health, were tentatively supportive of her aims.

Until she met Edwin Dillon. Then everything changed.

Edwin Dillon was thirty years old, a journalist on the Manchester Guardian who had written a number of inflammatory articles on the employment conditions of factory workers in the north of England. He had lost three fingers of his left hand in an unspecified industrial accident, although there was some talk that he had inflicted the injury himself, to avoid conscription.

He came south to London in 1919, quickly establishing links with the community of Russian anarchists and dissident Marxists living there in exile from the Bolshevik revolution. It was likely to have been Dillon's views on free love that set Helen's parents so thoroughly against Dillon, although it could simply have been that they didn't much like him.

Hector Dubois, the proprietor of the Liberty Bookshop in Camden and a former associate of Dillon's, testified in support of Helen Bostall at her trial. He described Edwin Dillon as 'a man you needed to be careful around, a man who held a grudge.' There were also rumours that Dillon's original motive for coming to London had to do with a woman he had made pregnant in Manchester and later abandoned. Attempts to trace this woman ended in failure and so the rumours could not be verified.

Whatever the reason, Winston and Edith Bostall were determined that their daughter should have nothing more to do with Edwin Dillon. When Helen announced that she was intending to move into Dillon's rooms in Camden, her parents threatened to cut all ties with her. Perhaps they hoped to call her bluff. If so, it was a gamble that backfired. In February of 1927, Helen gave up her Hampstead lodgings and moved into the basement flat at 112 Milliver Road.

I soon found myself accruing vast amounts of information, not just on Helen Bostall but on her whole family. I can imagine many editors dismissing most of it as irrelevant—who cared about Winston Bostall's run-in with a colleague in 1907 (over the involuntary committal of an unmarried mother to a mental asylum, if you're interested) when the incident had zero connection to the case in hand? But the more I dug into the private lives of the Bostalls and their circle, the more I became convinced that they were important. Crime does not arise in a vacuum. A murder is simply the flash point in a gradual accretion of narrative. The various strands that make up that narrative—Winston Bostall's mortal hatred of violence, Edith Bostall's inability to conceive another child, Peter Bostall's ambiguous relationship with his uncle, Rupert Paxton—may all be contributing factors in its final outcome.

And besides that, I was interested. The Bostalls were an unremarkable family, on the face of it, and yet their lives provided a snapshot of an entire era. In the conflicts and setbacks they encountered, it was possible to discern the birth of the modern age and the decline of empire, the fireworks and anxieties that occurred when the two collided. Was it any wonder that a woman like Helen Bostall—educated, resourceful, and unwilling to settle for the life that society had preordained for her—ended up finding herself directly in the firing line?

The shadow side of my researches was the strange vacuity surrounding the person of Edwin Dillon. Information about the Bostalls proved plentiful, and easy to come by. This was partly because of the crime, of course—call someone a murderer, and suddenly every detail of their life becomes interesting, becomes *evidence*—but that was not the only reason. The Bostalls—Helen herself, but also Winston, Edith, Peter, Rupert, and especially Rupert's wife Marina, who was Russian and embraced the literary arts as the birthright they were—were all copious, inveterate letter-writers and journal-keepers. Their histories remained bright, remained present. Searching for information about Edwin Dillon came to seem like staring into a black hole. I became convinced that if Dillon hadn't been murdered, he would have disappeared from history altogether. I turned up odd pieces of his journalism here and there, but finding images of the man himself was another matter. Aside from the blurry photograph that so often featured in the newspapers at the time of Helen's trial, Edwin Dillon might as well have been invisible.

In the end I decided it would be better to set all the background material aside for the moment and concentrate on the timeline of the case itself. It was like working on a proof, in a way—carry one distinct line of enquiry through to its logical conclusion and the rest will follow.

The actual order of events was easy enough to assemble from the trial records. A little before eight o'clock on the evening of the 20th of January 1928, a Mrs Irene Wilbur, a widow who lived in the ground floor apartment of 112 Milliver Road, was disturbed by what she called a 'furious altercation' in the flat below. Concerned by what she heard—"It sounded like they were bashing each other's brains out," was what she said on the witness stand—she left her flat and hurried to the Red Lion public house, approximately a minute's walk away, helping to enlist the aid of the publican in locating a police constable. When asked why she did not call at Dillon's apartment herself, she insisted she was afraid to. "The noise they were making," she said. "It was as if the devil had got into them."

The publican of the Red Lion, Gerald Honeyshot, confirmed that Irene Wilbur came into the pub soon after eight o'clock. He left with her more or less immediately and they walked together to Camden Town underground station, where they were able to secure the services of PC Robert Greystowe, who passed by the station regularly on his beat.

The three then returned to 112 Milliver Road, where on entry into the hallway they found the house silent, and the door leading to Dillon's apartment standing ajar.

"I knew straight away there'd been a murder done," Irene Wilbur claimed in her statement. "You could feel it in the air. Something about the silence. It wasn't right."

At this point, Greystowe gave instructions for Wilbur and Honeyshot to remain upstairs in the hallway while he entered the basement apartment alone. He called out to 'Mr and Mrs Dillon' as he entered, but there was no reply. A short time later he re-emerged, and informed Wilbur and Honeyshot that they would need to report to the police station on Highgate Road immediately, in order to give their witness statements. He did not offer them any further information at this point, but by the end of the evening both Wilbur and Honeyshot knew that Edwin Dillon had been murdered. According to PC Greystowe, he had discovered Dillon within moments of entering the flat. He was in the kitchen. His clothes were soaked with blood, and more blood was spreading in a large puddle across the kitchen tiles.

Edwin Dillon was pronounced dead where he lay. He had been stabbed five times. Two of the wounds were serious enough to have killed him.

There was no sign, anywhere, of Helen Bostall. An officer was left on duty outside the house, and when Helen eventually returned home at around eleven o'clock she was taken immediately into police custody. On being asked where she had spent the evening, she said she had been at the house of a friend, Daphne Evans, who lived in Highgate. Daphne quickly confirmed Helen's alibi, but when officers asked if they might search her flat, according to PC Greystowe she became agitated.

"I suppose you have to come in," she said in the end. She had been about to go to bed. When asked why she was reluctant to let police officers enter her apartment, she said it was because she was in her dressing gown.

The apartment was tidy, with no signs of disturbance, let alone the murder weapon. Two porcelain teacups—according to Daphne Evans they were the same teacups she and Helen had been drinking tea from earlier that evening—stood drying in the drainer beside the sink. It was only after half an hour's searching that officers discovered the small valise on top of the wardrobe in Evans's bedroom. The valise contained clothes that were later positively identified as belonging to Helen Bostall, together with a forward-dated ticket for the boat train from Victoria and a number of notebooks and letters, either addressed to Helen Bostall or filled with her handwriting.

It was clear that Helen Bostall had been planning her getaway, that she had been keeping her plans hidden from Dillon, that she had not intended for him to accompany her on her journey. When asked why this was, she stated that she had decided to break with Dillon permanently and was determined not to get into an argument with him. "Edwin's temper had become unreliable. I didn't want there to be a scene."

When the prosecuting counsel pressed her on whether she was, in fact, afraid of Dillon, she hesitated and then said no. "Edwin was domineering, but I was used to that," she said. "He would never have done me physical harm."

When questioned about the row she'd had with Dillon on the evening of his death, Helen Bostall seemed completely bemused. "I barely saw Edwin all day," she said. "I was working in the library for most of the morning, then in the afternoon I saw three of my private pupils at Milliver Road. I have no idea where Edwin was at that time. He came back to the flat at around six o'clock. He seemed tired and irritable, but no more so than usual. I told him I was going to Daphne's, that I would be back around eleven. Those were the last words I spoke to him. I left the flat soon afterwards." She hesitated. "We really didn't have much to say to each other any more."

The police seemed determined right from the start that Helen was the killer. She had a motive—Dillon's coercive behaviour—and she had her escape already planned. A further breakthrough came the following day, when the murder weapon—a serrated steel kitchen knife with a scratched wooden handle—was discovered jammed into a crack in the wall separating the back garden of 112 Milliver Road from the garden of 114. The blade was caked in dried blood, later proved to be of the same blood type as Edwin Dillon's. Three clear fingerprints were found on the handle—all Helen's.

Helen freely admitted that the knife was hers, that it had come from her kitchen. She strongly denied that she had used it to murder Dillon. When asked who she thought had killed her lover, she said she didn't know. "Edwin was always falling in and out of love with people. He thrived on dissent. He didn't have friends so much as sparring partners, political cronies, most of them—people he knew from before we met. I gave up having anything to do with them a long time ago."

When asked why that was, Helen Bostall stated that she no longer cared for their company. "They were all men, obsessed with themselves and their own self-importance. They barely knew I existed. I'm sure some of them hated Edwin—he could be obnoxious. Whether any of them hated him enough to want to kill him I have no idea."

For two or three days, attention veered away from Helen as the police went in search of Dillon's political associates, many of whom, as Helen had suggested, turned out to have grievances against him. Then on February 5th, just as things were starting to get interesting, officers received an anonymous tip-off concerning a Louise Tichener of Highgate Village. This person—or persons—insisted that Miss Tichener had been conducting an affair with Edwin Dillon, and that Helen Bostall had known about it. When found and questioned, Tichener, who belonged to one of the suffragist groups also attended by Bostall, readily confessed to the affair, with the additional information that Dillon had been planning to leave Bostall, and marry her.

"We were going to leave London," Tichener said. "We were happy."

Helen confirmed that she knew Tichener by sight from the women's group, but denied she knew anything about an affair between her and Dillon. She reaffirmed that her own relationship with Dillon was as good as over, and the idea that she might have murdered him out of jealousy was ridiculous. "What Edwin did with his time or his affections was none of my business," she said. "If it is true that this young woman put her trust in Edwin, I would have been afraid for her."

But the tide had turned. Louise Tichener's evidence, together with Irene Wilbur's statement, the clothes and travel tickets hidden at Daphne Evans's flat—the evidence seemed damning. Paradoxically, Helen's fortitude under questioning—her refusal to break down on the witness stand—may actually have helped in securing a conviction.

Helen Bostal was found guilty of murder and sentenced to death. She was hanged at Holloway prison on the morning of August 14th, 1928. Three weeks after her execution the hangman, Arthur Rawlin, resigned from the prison service and took up a position as a warehouseman for a minor shipping company part-owned by friends of his brother, a decision that meant a considerable drop in his standard of living. More than one enterprising journalist clamoured for Rawlin's story, but he refused to comment, saying merely that he was done with the hanging game and that was that.

I found that interesting. Rawlin wasn't the first hangman to lose his stomach for the profession, either. John Ellis, who executed Edith Thompson in 1923, ended up committing suicide. Although some said it was his alcoholism that did for him, most people agreed that Ellis never got over the appalling brutality of Edith's execution. There have been others, too—look them up if you don't believe me. It was thinking about Arthur Rawlin that prompted me to call on Lewis Usher. Lewis was an old client of mine—I'd helped him fight off the property acquisitions company that wanted to tear down the historic Methodist chapel that backed on to his home in Greenwich and turn it into a Tesco Metro—and it was during our war with Sequest Holdings that I happened to find out he was an expert on British murder trials as well as an enthusiastic collector of murder memorabilia. I always enjoy going to see Lewis—he tells the most amusing anecdotes, and his house on Crooms Hill contains more weird and wonderful collectibles than you'd hope to see in most provincial museums. When I visited him on that particular afternoon in late November, I was hoping he might have something enlightening to tell me about the Bostall execution and I was not disappointed.

"Do you think Arthur Rawlin gave up his job because he came to believe that Helen Bostall was innocent?" I asked him.

"It's a strong possibility," Lewis said. "There was more to it than that, though. People gossiped that Arthur Rawlin was in love with Bostall, that he believed he was, anyway. The prison governor reported that he used to visit Helen Bostall in her cell, during the run-up to her execution. There was a strange little article about it in the Evening Standard afterwards. You'd probably put his behaviour down to Stockholm Syndrome now, but it really was quite odd." He spooned more sugar into his tea. "You do know I have his watch?"

I felt my heartbeat quicken. "Arthur Rawlin's watch? The one he used to time his executions?"

"I think you'll find it was Albert Pierrepoint who used to do that. Rawlin might have copied him, I suppose. There was certainly a cult of personality around Pierrepoint at the time. It's Rawlin's watch though, definitely, whatever he used it for. I have the full provenance."

"Could I see it?" I found myself becoming excited in a way that seemed completely out of proportion with what Lewis had told me. It was just a watch, after all. But it was as if I knew, even then, that I was about to make a significant discovery, not just about Arthur Rawlin but about Helen Bostall.

"Of course. Won't be a tick." He eased himself out of his chair and shuffled off towards the side room where he kept most of his collection. I couldn't help noticing he relied on his cane more than he had on my last visit. Still, he seemed in good spirits. I gazed around the living room—the ancient red plush sofas, the fake stuffed dodo in its glass case, the walls and mantel shelf crowded with photographs of his wife, the stage actress Zoe Clifford, dead from a freak bout of pneumonia some ten years before. The place had become something of a haven for me during the Sequest case, which had happened to coincide with the first stage of my breakup with Ray. How glad I had been to come here, to escape from my own thoughts and misgivings into this cosy little corner of theatre land, where the fire was always lit and the stories were always larger and more preposterous than my own.

A place suspended in time, a lacuna in the fraying fabric of the everyday world.

"Here it is," Lewis said. I jumped, startled. I'd been so absorbed in my thoughts I hadn't noticed him come back into the room. He was carrying a small bag, made from yellow silk with a drawstring opening. "I can show you the papers too if you'd like to see them, but this is the watch."

He passed me the bag. I reached cautiously inside. Things inside bags make me nervous. You don't know what you're getting into until it's too late. In this case, Rawlin's watch, which was a full-case silver pocket watch about two inches in diameter. The front of the case was engraved with a lighted candle. On the back was a skull, the eye sockets and nasal cavities etched out in darker relief. The classic *vanitas*, life and death, light and darkness, the universal allegory for time's passing.

Perfect for a hangman, I thought.

"He may have commissioned the engraving personally," Lewis said, as if reading my thoughts. "Although the design isn't unusual for the time. The Victorians were heavily into mourning jewellery, as you probably know."

"Yes. Though it's more my brother's area, to be honest." I flipped open the front of the case. The watch's white enamelled face was simple and plain, as if in deliberate contrast to the gothic extravagance of the case. There was a date stamped on the dial, 1879, and a name, I supposed of the maker—Owen Andrews. The name meant nothing to me but I made a mental note to ask Martin about it later.

"It's a tourbillon watch," Lewis added. "Very expensive, even at the time. An ordinary working man like Rawlin would have had to save several months' salary to purchase this."

"What's a tourbillon?"

"A means for stabilising the watch's mechanism, so that it doesn't lose time. Here." He opened the back of the watch, revealing its workings, which resembled a complicated mechanical diagram, all gears and levers. "Have a look at this."

He angled his hand, showing me the inside back of the watch's case, and the photograph that had been secreted there. The image showed a young woman, with short dark hair and light eyes, a narrow, straight nose and a high lace collar: Helen Bostall.

"There is a possibility that the photograph was placed inside the watch later—after Rawlin's death, I mean," said Lewis. "It's unlikely though. You won't read much about this in the newspapers, but if you delve a little deeper you'll find there are several contemporary accounts, from colleagues and family and so on. All of them agree that Rawlin was living in a fantasy world."

"About him and Helen being in love, you mean?"

"Yes, that, but it went even further." He chuckled. "I read one letter from Rawlin to his younger brother where he was going on about travelling back in time to prevent the execution he himself had carried out."

"That's ridiculous. Poor man."

"Plenty would say he got what he deserved. Not everyone would feel sorry for a hangman."

I did, though. We can't all choose our jobs, and was Rawlin so different from the soldiers sent out to kill other soldiers on the battlefields of World War 1? I tried to imagine how he must have felt, becoming properly aware for the first time of what his job meant, what it was he did. The imagining was not pleasant.

"Too bad we can't bring him back to talk to the Americans," I said. I smiled to myself, thinking how Martin would disapprove of my poor taste in jokes. He would love to see this watch, though, I thought, which gave me an idea. "Please say no if you want to," I said to Lewis, "but could I possibly borrow this? Just for a day or two? I'd like to show it to my brother."

"The watch?" He fell silent, and I was fully expecting him to demur, to begin explaining how he didn't like to let items from his collection leave the house, especially not an item such as this, which was valuable even aside from who had once owned it. "I'd like you to have it," was what he actually said. I felt so surprised and so shocked that for a moment I couldn't answer him.

"Lewis, don't be silly. I couldn't possibly. I'm sorry I asked," I said, when I could.

"I mean it," he insisted. "I've been wanting to leave you something—in my will, I mean. To say thank you for being such a good friend to me. But it's difficult to know what someone might like. If I know you like this, then you've made my task easier. You'll be doing me a favour."

"You're not ill?"

"Dying, you mean? No, no more so than usual. But I am eighty-six."

"Lewis," I said. "Thank you."

"It's my great pleasure. So long as you don't use it to go running off after repentant hangmen."

We both laughed at that. Both of us, at the same time. But I've sometimes had the feeling—call it hindsight, if you want—that neither of us actually thought it was funny.

Helen's defence rested on the fact that the evidence against her was circumstantial. No one—not even Irene Wilbur—claimed to have seen her in the vicinity of Milliver Road at the time of Dillon's death, and no matter how many times the prosecution cross-examined Daphne Evans over Helen's alibi, she never deviated from her original statement: Helen had arrived at her apartment just before seven, they ate some sandwiches Daphne had prepared and talked about Edwin. Helen still felt guilty for what she was planning—to

walk out on him without a word of warning—but Daphne remained adamant she was doing the right thing.

"I never liked Edwin," she said. "He wasn't trustworthy. I was glad when
Helen decided she was leaving him. I knew she wasn't happy."

When asked whether she considered Dillon to be a violent man, Daphne
hesitated before replying and then said yes, adding: "I would have said he
could be capable of violence. I was afraid for Helen, just sometimes, but she
always told me I was being foolish so I had to believe her."

The prosecution's most important witness was Irene Wilbur. Her insistence
that there had been a 'furious altercation' at 112 Milliver Road just before
eight o'clock was more instrumental in securing a guilty verdict than Helen
Bostall's fingerprints on the murder weapon. You didn't have to be a lawyer
to understand that anyone could have used that knife, that the killer would
have been likely to grab the first weapon to come to hand, especially if the
murder had been opportunistic rather than planned. That Helen Bostall kept
a carving knife in her kitchen drawer was hardly damning evidence.

On the other hand, Irene Wilbur was adamant that she had heard two
people yelling at each other, that one of them had been a woman. And she
had Gerald Honeyshot of the Red Lion to back her up regarding the time.

Why would Irene Wilbur lie? When asked by the prosecution if she had any
reason to dislike or resent Helen Bostall, if there was any previous bad feeling
between them, Wilbur was equally adamant that there hadn't been. "I barely
knew her," she stated. "I'd not been living at Milliver Road for more than a
fortnight. I'd seen her a few times to say hello to but that was all. She seemed
friendly enough. A bit aloof perhaps but not what you'd call unpleasant."

In fact, Irene Wilbur had been resident at 112 Milliver Road for just ten
days. The defence did not appear to find anything suspicious in that, and why
would they? People move house all the time. Wilbur's assertion—that she had
moved to Camden from Putney in order to be closer to grandchildren and
because she had numerous friends in the area—seemed entirely reasonable.

I don't know what kept me picking away at Irene Wilbur, but I did. I didn't
like the way she had been so relentless in the way she'd given her evidence,
so determined, almost, that Helen was guilty. Wilbur had persisted, even
while knowing that Helen might face a death sentence if convicted. Why
such animosity towards a woman she claimed not to have known? I didn't get
it. Those who thought to criticise Wilbur at the time did so on the grounds
that she was a natural attention-seeker, altogether too enamoured of seeing
herself in the newspapers. An interesting hypothesis, but I wasn't so certain.

Was it possible, I wondered, that Irene Wilbur had been a stooge? Most newspaper accounts of the trial made mention of Wilbur's 'smart' attire, and several made particular mention of a jade and diamond broach she wore. Everyone seemed to agree she was 'a handsome woman.'

After pursuing the matter a little further, I discovered that Irene Wilbur had moved away from Milliver Road less than a week after Helen's execution, that she had returned to her old stamping ground of Putney, and to considerably smarter lodgings than she had occupied previously.

If Irene Wilbur had been paid to provide false evidence, it suggested not only that Dillon's murder had been carefully planned, but that Helen had been intended to take the blame all along.

If this was so—and once I stumbled upon the idea I found it difficult to give up the conviction that it was—then Irene Wilbur would have to be connected with Edwin Dillon in some way, or rather with his enemies, who would scarcely have risked employing a stranger to do their dirty work.

On top of my research into the lives of Helen Bostall and Edwin Dillon, I now found myself grubbing around for any information I could find about Irene Wilbur. I soon discovered she had been married at the age of twenty-one to a Major Douglas Wilbur, who had been killed at the Battle of Amiens in World War One. They had one child, a daughter named Laura, born in the February of 1919, a full six months after her father's death.

Those dates seemed odd to me. Of course it was entirely possible that Major Wilbur had been afforded leave prior to the Amiens campaign, that Laura could have been conceived then, but it didn't fit somehow, not to my mind anyway. Douglas Wilbur had been an experienced, valuable, and loyal officer. It was inconceivable that he would have left his post immediately before such a crucial offensive.

There was also the fact that Irene Wilbur was thirty-eight years old at the time of Laura's birth, that during the whole of her twenty-year marriage there had been no other children.

What had changed?

If Douglas Wilbur was not in fact Laura's father, who was?

I looked back once again over the trial records, focussing on any mention of Irene Wilbur's home life, no matter how minor. Which is how I came to notice something that had not registered before, namely that Laura Wilbur had not been resident at Milliver Road, that at the time of the murder she was staying instead with a person Irene Wilbur described as a 'near relative', a Mrs Jocelyn Bell, close to the Wilburs' old address in Putney. When questioned about why her daughter was not in fact living with her, Irene Wilbur said it was a matter of Laura's schooling.

Once again, it was possible. But by now I was coming to believe it was more likely a matter of Irene not wanting her daughter anywhere near a house where she knew there was going to be a murder. Wilbur would not be staying long at Milliver Road, in any case. Far better to keep Laura at a distance.

I was filled with a sense of knowing, the feeling that always comes over me when I understand I have discovered an insight into a case that has hitherto kept itself obstinately hidden. I knew that I was close to something, that the pieces of the truth were more than likely already assembled, that it was simply a matter of arranging them in the correct order.

The first step, I decided, was to try and find out a little more about Jocelyn Bell. And in the meantime I still had to talk to Martin about the hangman's watch.

People say we're alike, Martin and I, but I'm not so sure. We look alike, and I suppose what our mutual friends might be picking up on is our shared tendency towards poking around in subjects no one else gives a damn about. We both like finding things out. Of the two of us, though, I believe Martin is the better human being. Martin cares about people, which is why he is so good at his job. When I tell him this, he always insists that I must care about people too, or I wouldn't put such time and effort into fighting their corners.

Perhaps he's right. But I still think what I enjoy most about my work is the thrill of argument, the abstract battle of opposing forces. If 'doing good' happens to be a side-effect of that I'm not going to knock it, but it isn't the driving force behind what I do.

I don't think so, anyway. You'd better ask Martin.

I hope he meets someone else. He's borne up remarkably well since Miranda died, but that's Martin all over, never one to make a fuss.

I was always the one who made a fuss. Getting cancer then going crazy then marrying Ray. Martin was there for me through all of it, no matter how much I managed to screw up.

He can cook a mean curry, too.

"Have you ever heard of a watchmaker called Owen Andrews?" I asked him once we'd finished eating. I poured us both another glass of wine. It was odd, the way his face changed. A lot of people might not even have noticed, but I'm used to watching other people's body language and I know Martin back to front. The moment I said the name Owen Andrews, it was as if someone had suddenly switched a light on inside him, then just as rapidly flicked it off again. Something he didn't want to talk about? Or felt uncertain of? Could have been either. I'd been telling him about my research, my various theories about Irene Wilbur. I'd deliberately held off mentioning Arthur Rawlin because once you get Martin on to the subject of watches it's difficult to get him off it again.

I knew he'd be interested, but the extremity of his reaction surprised me, all the same.

"I've heard of him, yes," Martin said finally. "But what does he have to do with Irene Wilbur?"

This is going to sound strange, but I decided more or less in that moment that I wasn't going to tell Martin I had Rawlin's watch in my possession. Not yet, anyway.

It wasn't that I didn't trust him. I would trust Martin with my life, and perhaps that was the problem.

It was as if—and I know how bizarre this sounds, especially coming from an unreconstructed rationalist like me—I sensed already that something was going to happen, something involving the watch. I think I was afraid that if Martin got wind of what I meant to do, he would say it was dangerous and try to stop me.

I'm not good at taking advice—once I have a mind to do something, you might as well try *advising* a stampeding mare with a swarm of bees on her tail. No one knows this better than Martin and normally he'd stay out of it but in this case?

Let's just say I wanted to keep my intentions under wraps.

"Nothing," I said. "At least nothing directly." I told him about Arthur Rawlin and Arthur Rawlin's posthumous obsession with Helen Bostall, and then added that my old client Lewis Usher knew someone who knew someone who'd purchased Arthur Rawlin's watch in a private auction.

"It's by a London maker, apparently, this Owen Andrews," I said. "Lewis seems to think that Rawlin attached mystical properties to the watch, that he believed it could reverse time, or something. He's going to try and dig out the documents for me—Lewis, I mean. I wondered if you knew anything about this Andrews guy, that's all."

"Only that he trained in Southwark, and that his watches are vanishingly rare," Martin said. He sighed. "There are entire internet forums devoted to Owen Andrews. He's one of those people other people are always talking about, probably because we know so little about him. People are still having arguments over exactly when he was born. There's speculation that he had access to Breguet's late notebooks. I don't believe it myself. I don't see how he could have done. The notebooks weren't in the public domain for at least a century after Breguet's death."

"Who's Breguet?"

"Abram Louis Breguet, a Swiss watchmaker. He's best known for making a watch for Marie Antoinette and almost losing his head for his trouble. But for horologists, Breguet is most famous for inventing the tourbillon."

Martin went off into a long-winded explanation of what a tourbillon was and how it worked, how before Breguet, no pocket watch could keep accurate time over a long period because of gravity, which acted as a drag weight on the mechanism, speeding it up or slowing it down by as much as sixty seconds in every hour. Breguet placed the whole mechanism inside a revolving metal cage he called a tourbillon, or whirlwind. The tourbillon kept the mechanism in stasis, twirling it around its own axis like a sidecar on a fairground ride.

The tourbillon watch was like a planet, spinning in space. In every sense that mattered, it was weightless.

"Think of a tornado," Martin said. "A wind itself has no substance, but it has incredible power. It renders everything weightless before it, even massive objects like houses and cars."

I zoned out a bit towards the end, not because what Martin was telling me wasn't interesting, but because I couldn't see how any of it related to Arthur Rawlin and a possible time machine. Then Martin said something else, something jaw-dropping. I was dragged back into the conversation with a physical jolt.

"What was that about the notebooks?"

"Breguet's notebooks," Martin repeated. "His doctors always insisted he was senile by then, but according to his son, Breguet was lucid and rational right up until he died. His late writings suggest he had been trying to create a kind of super-tourbillon, a mechanism he believed would eventually enable human beings to travel through time. He called it the time-stasis. I can't believe anyone would take it literally, quite honestly, but some of the people on the forums believe Owen Andrews made it his mission to put Breguet's theory into practice."

"To make a watch that could turn back time?"

Martin shrugged. "If you like."

"That's incredible."

"If it were true, maybe. But I've seen some of Andrews's pieces and they're just watches. Andrews was gifted but he wasn't a magician. All that time travel stuff—it's just the horological equivalent of urban myth."

I thought there was something heroic about it, nonetheless—the lone mechanic, pitting himself against logic like a gladiator fighting a tiger. I reminded myself that all the most radical advances in science seem like lunacy before they are proven.

"It's a beautiful word," I said to Martin. "Horological."

"Are you still convinced Helen Bostall was innocent?" he asked.

"More than ever. And I believe Arthur Rawlin thought so, too—that's why he felt so guilty over her death."

"You're determined to prove it, aren't you? Through your book?"

I laughed. "I suppose I am."

I didn't just want to prove it, though—I can admit that now. I wanted to change it. But I wasn't about to blow my cover to Martin.

Three days later I performed an experiment. Just one little trip back, five minutes or so. *Brain of Britain* was on the radio, which made it easy to tell if anything had actually happened. I had a second go at some of the questions, which would have upped my score if I'd been keeping tally, which I wasn't. It would have been cheating, anyway.

Jocelyn Bell turned out to be Jocelyn Leslie, an artist. She won a scholarship to study at the Slade, and when her father—a successful Yorkshire business-man of a conservative cast of mind—refused to let her go, she continued to paint in secret, making her own way to London two years later. She enjoyed moderate popularity for a time. Although there were those who dismissed her efforts as 'primitive' or 'naive', Lavinia Sable, who wrote art criticism for several London papers under the pseudonym Marcus Fell, insisted that in spite of having almost no formal training, Bell's work showed a keener understanding of European modernism than many of her better-known contemporaries.

I liked the sound of Lavinia, who apparently attended private views and press gatherings for years as Marcus, with no one being any the wiser. Lavinia was easily interesting enough to fill a book in her own right, but Lavinia was not my mission and after spending a day or two reading up on her I laid the material reluctantly aside and went back to the matter in hand, namely Jocelyn Bell.

On arrival in London, Jocelyn found work first as an assistant housekeeper at a private boarding school for girls, then as a secretary and assistant to the curator of one of the more progressive galleries on Cork Street. It was here, I'm certain, that she first encountered Leonard Bell, who was friendly with several of the artists represented there.

Leonard Bell was actually Leonid Belayev, a Russian émigré and a member of the radical socialist group based in Camden called the Four Brothers. The group was founded in the 1890s and, unlike many similar loose associations that fractured and splintered at the outbreak of war, the Four Brothers remained intact as a group well into the 1920s.

At some point during 1924, Edwin Dillon began attending their meetings.

Here at last was the breakthrough I'd been searching for. Jocelyn Leslie married Leonard Bell in 1902. They had one son, Malcolm, in 1903, although letters sent by Jocelyn to a friend in Manchester reveal that differences were already making themselves felt between the couple and by 1905 their marriage was over in all but name. Leonard Bell kept in close touch with his family, though—I think he was probably still living under the same roof for some years after he and Jocelyn separated, a fact that would almost certainly have led to gossip amongst the neighbours. Not that Jocelyn or Leonard gave much of a damn for bourgeois convention. They remained friends, and when Leonard eventually began a long-term affair with another woman, the woman quickly became Jocelyn's friend, also.

That woman—and you can imagine my satisfaction when I was able to prove this for sure—was Irene Wilbur. There were in fact several dozen letters from Leonard to his lover, preserved amongst Jocelyn Bell's papers at the Women Artists Forum in Hammersmith.

As a bonus, the letters also revealed to me the identity of Malcolm Bell's soon-to-be fiancée: Louise Tichener.

Frustratingly, I was never able to find out much about Irene Wilbur herself, and I can only assume her willingness to go along with the murder plot had more to do with her wanting to protect Leonard Bell than with any active animosity towards Helen Bostall. The true identity of Dillon's murderer also remained hidden from me, although I'm more or less positive it wasn't Bell himself. Leonard was a hardened activist—he would have known better than to put himself directly at risk.

After weeks of rooting around in various archives of obscure research papers, I came to the conclusion that the most likely suspect was a much younger man, Michael Woolcot, who seems to have known Dillon when he was living in Manchester. The two had some sort of falling-out—either in Manchester or soon after Woolcot's own arrival in the capital. So far as I know they were never reconciled, although mysteriously there was one final meeting between them, in a Camden public house, just ten days before Dillon's murder. The meeting was remarked upon by a moderate socialist named West, a journalist who wrote a satirical column for an independent newspaper called The Masthead, lampooning many of the personalities associated with the more extreme wing of the movement.

They say that if you sup with the devil you should use a long spoon, West wrote in his January 20th column, just one week before the murder. *Judging by the outbreak of cosy camaraderie at The Horse's Head last Thursday evening, it would seem there are those who set little store by such sage advice, even those we might consider our elders and betters.* West goes on to reveal the identities of both Dillon and Woolcot, referring to the latter as 'an upwardly mobile cur of the Belayev persuasion' and to the meeting itself as 'a council of war.'

Which can only beg the question, West writes, *of who exactly is at war here, and with whom?*

Whether the police were ever made aware of West's column, or possessed enough insider knowledge to make head or tail of it, I have no idea. Leonard Bell was questioned briefly, along with two dozen or so other regular and irregular members of the Four Brothers group, though the comrades' universal disdain for the official forces of law and order would have meant the chances of anyone letting anything slip were practically nil.

Helen Bostall's ticket for the boat train was forward-dated to February 3rd, a date that turned out to be less than a week after Dillon's murder. It seems likely that someone—someone friendly with Leonard Bell or one of his cronies—knew about Helen's travel plans. For Bell's plan to succeed, it was crucial that Dillon be killed well in advance of Helen's departure for the continent. I believe it was Dillon's meeting with Woolcot, staged by Bell as an opportunity for reconciliation, that set the stage for the murder. No doubt Woolcot had been instructed to arrange a second, more informal meeting, to take place at Dillon's flat.

Putting all the evidence together, it finally became clear to me that it was those ten days that formed the crucial time period, the ten days between Dillon first meeting Woolcot at The Horse's Head, and his eventual death.

If Helen Bostall could have been persuaded to bring her journey forward—to leave London soon after New Year, say—then Bell would either have had to shelve his plans, or risk being exposed as complicit in Dillon's killing.

Regardless of Dillon's fate, Helen Bostall herself would have been saved.

If only someone could have told her, I thought, and almost immediately afterwards I thought of Arthur Rawlin. Had he tried to use the watch? I wondered. If so, he had obviously failed.

As to why Bell wanted Dillon dead in the first place, the reasons remained obscure to me. All I could think was that it must have been down to some intricate power struggle within the Four Brothers. Truth be told, I didn't care much. Not then.

I knew from the start that the best place to approach Helen would be at one of her suffragist meetings. The very nature of such gatherings meant there would always be new faces in evidence, strangers who might turn up for a couple of meetings and then disappear again. It ought to be relatively easy to mingle with the women without drawing undue attention to myself. The main thing was not to go overboard in trying to fit in. I chose clothes that were unobtrusive rather than authentic: the three-quarter-length coat I normally wore to court hearings in winter, a dark, paisley-patterned skirt I hardly ever wore but couldn't bear to throw out because I liked the material so much, a pair of black lace-up shoes. Plain clothes, in every sense of the word.

By now you're either wondering what on Earth I'm talking about, or if I can possibly be serious. Which is fine.

I kept putting off the actual—journey? I told myself I needed to do more research, which was at least partly true. To keep myself safe, I had to know that particular bit of Camden well enough to be able to walk around it blindfold, if need be. But mostly I was just scared. Scared in case the watch didn't work and scared in case it did.

Five minutes and a hundred years were not the same thing. What if the watch refused to bring me back, or marooned me in a time that was not my own?

I wanted to know though, I wanted to *see*. The closer it came to the date I'd set myself, the more impatient I felt. Impatient with my fear. Impatient with my delaying tactics. When Ray phoned me the night before to ask me if I was going to some private view or other his agent was organising, I almost bit his head off.

"Are you okay, Dottie?" he said. He hadn't called me Dottie for years, not since we separated.

"I'll be there, don't worry," I said, not answering his question and not knowing if I'd be there, either. "I've got a lot on at work, that's all. Say hi to Clio for me."

Clio is Ray's daughter, the child he has with Maya. I should make more of an effort with Maya, I suppose, but it's difficult. We're such different people, and although chumming up with her ex-husband's new wife seemed to work for Jocelyn Bell, I'm not sure it's for me.

Clio, though. She's eight years old and a miracle. I could never tell this to anyone, not even Martin, but occasionally it breaks my heart that she isn't mine.

There is a lever inside the watch, a silver pin that slides from side to side inside a moulded slit—imagine the back of an old wind-up alarm clock, the little lever you use to engage the alarm function, or to turn it off. There is no clear indication of what the purpose of this lever might be, and when you first engage it, nothing seems to happen. Say 'nothing happens full stop', if you like. I won't mind.

I once had a conversation with Martin, years ago when we were kids, about whether ghosts existed. When I asked Martin if he believed, he said it didn't matter. "If ghosts exist, they'll go on existing whether we believe in them or not."

It's the same with this. And if I tell you that what time travel reminds me of most of all is the time before my illness, I wonder will you believe that either? The time when I was so in love with numbers—when I could listen to numbers conversing the same way you might listen to music, when I felt the thrum of numbers in my blood, intricate as a crystal lattice, sound and rhythmic and basic as the beat of a drum.

I turned the lever, and the rush of numbers filled my head, blazing in my veins like alcohol, like burning petrol. The music of the primes, du Sautoy called it, and I could hear it again. I closed my eyes and counted backwards. I could feel the boundaries of reality expanding, unfurling. Bobbing deftly out of reach of my hands, like a toy balloon.

I ducked under the boundary wire and followed. Time filled me up, chilly and intoxicating.

Yes, but what's it *like*? I can hear you asking.

Like a triple slug of Russian vodka that's been kept in the icebox, that's what it's like.

I started going on practice runs. Just silly things: walking past my front door in the middle of last week, going to a concert at the Barbican I'd wanted to attend when it was actually on but happened to miss. I thought that getting the timing right would prove difficult, but in fact the mechanism was extremely accurate, once you got the hang of it. I found it mostly came down to imagining: knowing where you wanted to be and forming an image of the place and time inside your mind. This sounds irrational I know, but that's how it was.

I spent a lot of time in Camden, just walking around. You'd be surprised how little it's changed. Even when houses, whole streets have been torn down and built over, the old shadows remain.

The city has a shape. You can sense it, if you feel for it, even if you're sleepwalking and perhaps especially then, London's presence wrapped closely around you like a blanket.

The suffragist meetings took place in rooms about the Quaker meeting house, on Bentley Street. During the day it was mostly quiet, but in the evenings things livened up considerably, mainly because of The Charlady, a public house and pie shop on the corner of the street opposite. I went in daylight the first time, just to be safe. Muggings were common then in this part of London and I saw no point in exposing myself to unnecessary risk.

You think of the past as cleaner, but it really isn't. Horse shit, engine oil, smoke, blood, piss, beer, the rotting detritus from the market, piled at the kerb. Not London as it might be in a theme park, but a London you'd recognise instantly, just from the stench. Cars are creeping in already: hackney cabs and omnibuses, gentlemen's conveyances. And the bikes—the thrilling tring of bicycle bells, boy couriers speeding along. *Oi Miss, get on the pavement, why dontchyer? Bleedin' 'eck.* A flower and matchbox seller, a puckered scar across one cheek and her left hand missing. I reach into my pocket to find the right coins, then remember I don't have the right coins, not at all. Exactly the kind of stupid blunder I'm supposed to be on guard against. The peddler gazes at me with tired eyes and I look away in shame. The next time I come I bring her a paper packet of corned beef sandwiches but she is no longer there. Not in the same place, anyway. I remind myself of what I'm here for, and move swiftly along.

Another time, I stand in a shop doorway opposite and watch the women arrive for their meeting. I'm amazed to find that I recognise some of them, from the letters I've read, from the blurred photographs in the Women's Studies archive in the British Library. One of them, a young poet named Kathleen Thwaite, is accompanied to the door of the meeting house by her husband, Austin Gears. I know that Kathleen is to die in 1937, on a protest march against Franco's fascists in Madrid. It makes my heart ache to see her, and the urge to do something, to warn her in some way, is all but overwhelming. I turn quickly away, hoping to catch a glimpse of Helen Bostall instead. On this occasion at least she appears to be absent.

— Has my being here, even to stand motionless in the street, altered things somehow, and for the worse? I push the thought away. It is coincidence, that's all. She will be here next week, and if not then, the week after. It need not matter.

The next time, I file inside the hall with the other women. No one talks to me or takes particular notice but many smile. I feel accepted as one of them. More than that, I can *imagine* myself as one of them. Almost as if I have experienced this life, this version of my life anyway, this Dora Newland who attended suffragist rallies in Hyde Park, who conducted furious arguments with her uncle about being allowed to travel down through Italy with another woman friend. Casting Henry—dear Henry, who indulged our every whim when we were children—in the role of domineering guardian makes me smile.

We sit on hard wooden chairs in the draughty space—three small attic rooms that have been converted into one larger one—and listen to a Mrs Marjorie Hennessey tell us about her experience of studying politics at the Sorbonne. She is an impressive woman, commanding and authoritative, and I cannot help wondering what happened to her, how come she failed.

So many women. It is depressing to consider how many of us have been discouraged, disparaged, forced to reconsider, turned aside from our dreams.

I want to rush up to Marjorie Hennessey and tell her not to give up, not to drop by the wayside, not to fall silent.

"She's wonderful, isn't she?" It is the interval and we are queuing up for tea. The woman who speaks to me seems shy and rather young, and I have the feeling this is her first time here also. Her cheeks are flushed pink.

"Admirable," I say, and for a second I experience a sensation close to vertigo. I am here, and I am speaking to someone. I hug my bag as if seeking support from it. Inside the bag are the keys to my flat, my purse, my Kindle ereader, my mobile phone, all those other insignificant trifles that don't exist yet. *I come from the future*, I think, in what Martin always calls the MGM voice. I want to laugh out loud. I glance over at the chalk board, where Marjorie Hennessey has been drawing diagrams illustrating the economic implications of women withdrawing their labour from the home.

I wonder how my new friend in the tea queue would react if I were to tell her that almost a century later we're still fighting the same battles. Again, I want to laugh. Not that it's funny.

"We need more like her," I say instead, because that also is still true. Now, more than ever, we need more anger, more knowledge. "Shall we sit down?"

We take our tea and sit at one of the wooden trestles at the side of the hall. The woman tells me her name is Barbara Winton and she's a socialist.

"They say there's going to be another war," she says. "We have to join with our sisters in Europe—we must prevent war, at all costs."

She is learning German, and corresponding with the daughter of a friend of her father's, who lives in Frankfurt. "Her name is Gisela. She's a sculptor. Don't you think that's marvellous? She's asked me to go out and visit her and Daddy says I can. It feels—I'm not sure how to explain—as if a whole new life is beginning."

"I hope you're right," I say. I tell her that I'm studying law, that I am hoping to practise at the bar. I see confusion on her face—my age, probably—which is swiftly succeeded by a kind of wonder, mixed with mischievous delight. Women have been allowed access to the legal profession for less than a decade, after all.

"Well done, you," she says. "I think that's marvellous."

Her excitement is contagious. It is only as we are about to resume our seats for the second half of the programme that I finally catch sight of Helen Bostall. She is near the back of the room, talking to a woman with an upright posture and hawkish nose whom I recognise at once as Daphne Evans.

I gaze at them, dumbstruck. I feel like a spy. As I move towards my seat I see Helen turn, just for a moment, and look directly at me.

Instead of the blank, flat gaze of a woman casually scanning the crowd, what I see in her eyes—indisputably—is recognition: *you're here*. I feel cold right through. My hands begin to shake. I'm going to drop my cup, I think, then realise it's all right, I no longer have it. Barbara Winton has taken it from me and returned it to the tea bench at the back.

That was when I lost my nerve. Instead of sitting down again I pushed through the crowd to the door and then rushed down the stairs, almost tripping over the paisley skirt in the process. Once outside I felt better. There was the usual rowdy hubbub coming from The Charlady, the same stink of greasy Irish stew and overloaded dustbins. I made my way to an access lane between two rows of terraces and took out the watch. I engaged the lever without looking at it—not looking had become a kind of superstition with me—and stood there in the dark, counting primes and feeling that odd, trembling dream state take hold until I became aware of the sound of traffic—motor traffic, I mean, buses and police sirens—on Camden High Street.

I was back. I breathed in through my mouth, tasting exhaust fumes and the tarry scent of someone's spent cigarette. I stood still for some moments, letting the world come back into focus around me and feeling the relief I felt each time: that I had conducted an extremely risky experiment—heating flash powder in a petri dish, say—and managed to get away without blowing my hands off.

I never experimented with going forward, not even by one day. I had a terror of it, a paralysing phobia. It was a deal I made, I suppose—with God, the devil, myself, Owen Andrews? *Bring me safely home, and I'll keep our bargain.* Well, I guess it worked.

The next time I went back, I was prepared. So, it seems, was Helen. She was waiting for me this time, at the bottom of the stairs outside the meeting house. She told me later that she'd waited there at the start of every meeting since she'd first seen me, knowing I would be returning but not knowing when.

"Dora," she said quietly. "You're here at last." She caught my hands in both of hers. Her fingers were cold. It was December, and she was smiling in a way that suggested she was greeting an old friend, someone she knew well but hadn't seen in a while. Pleasure, and sadness, as if she knew our time together would not be long.

"I don't understand," I said, and sighed. Who was I to talk? "How did you—how do you know me?"

"Knowing everything you know—do you need to ask?" she said. "The order in which things happen doesn't matter, surely? Just that they happen. I'm so pleased to see you."

She leaned forward to embrace me, and I found myself almost believing—there was such joy in seeing her, such emotion—that this was indeed a reunion and not, as I knew it to be, our first meeting.

"Come," she said. "We can go back to the flat. Edwin's away—in Manchester. That's what he says, anyway."

"You don't think he really is?"

She shrugged. "Edwin tells me what it pleases him to tell me. Sometimes it's the truth and sometimes it isn't. I had to give up caring which a long time ago."

We came to Milliver Road. I'd been to the house of course—what I mean is I'd stood outside it many times. I knew 112 as a spruce, bay-fronted terrace with replacement windows. The house in Helen's time seemed smaller, meaner, the exterior paintwork chipped and blistering. A flight of steps led steeply down to a basement forecourt.

"We've had problems with damp," Helen said. "The woman who lives upstairs says there are rats, too, but I've never seen them."

"Mrs Wilbur?"

She gave me a puzzled look. "Mrs Wilbur? Mrs Herschel lives on the ground floor. There's no Mrs Wilbur."

"It doesn't matter," I said. So my researches had proved correct—Irene Wilbur hadn't moved in yet. There was still time.

"Let's go in and get warm," Helen said. "I'll light the stove."

"We were happy here once, Edwin and I," Helen said. The stove was well-alight. Soft lamplight threw shadows on the whitewashed walls of the cosy front sitting room. Framed prints, showing images from a Greek bestiary. An orange-and-green Aubusson rug. Books, books everywhere, overflowing the alcove shelving and piled on the floor. A stack of handwritten pages lay fanned across a low wooden table. It was a good room. A room I felt at home in.

I also knew I'd been here before.

"Have you eaten?" Helen asked.

I laughed. "It's been a hundred years at least," I said.

"I can warm up some soup. I made it yesterday."

"That would be lovely." I wasn't hungry—quite the opposite—but I was curious to see how food might taste here. In fact, it tasted like potato soup, thick and nutritious and well-seasoned. We ate, dipping bread into our bowls, and I asked Helen what she was working on.

"I've been helping to edit a collection of essays by women on the subject of war," she said. "I want to include writing by German women as well—letters, memoir, whatever I can get hold of. The publisher was against this at first but I managed to persuade them how important it is, essential even. You don't think it's too soon?"

I shook my head.

"I'm glad. We have to use every weapon we have."

"Weapon?"

"To make people understand what war really is. The madness of it." She fell silent, head bent. "Dora, I know I shouldn't really ask you this, but do we succeed? Do we succeed at all?"

I know I shouldn't answer, and I don't, not then, but the following week, when I know that Helen will be at her meeting, I return to Milliver Road for one final visit. I have an envelope with me, addressed to Helen. I post it through the front door of the house, hear it fall on to the scuffed brown lino-leum of the communal hallway. Inside is a second-hand copy of John Hersey's memoir, *Hiroshima* in the original Pelican edition, its pages faded and brittle but clearly readable, the most concise response to her question that I can think of. What good will it do? None at all. But Helen asked me a question and she deserves an answer.

"That doesn't matter now," I said in 1927. "What I mean is—it matters, but there are more urgent things to think about. Urgent for you, anyway."

"You're frightening me."

"In a month's time, Edwin is going to be murdered. If you stay here you are going to be blamed for it. There will be a trial and—"

"You're telling me I'm going to be hanged. For a crime I had nothing to do with."

I stared at her, horrified.

"I thought it was a dream," she said, more quietly. "That man. He sat on the edge of my bed and told me about it. He was crying. He seemed quite mad. When I told him to go away he did. I wish I'd been kinder."

Arthur Rawlin. So he had used the watch to try and save her, after all.

"None of that is going to happen," I said quickly. "But you must leave London, and Edwin. You need to pack your things and get as far away from here as you can."

She nodded slowly. "I've been planning to go, anyway. To leave Edwin, I mean. Whatever we had—it's over. I could say he's changed but really I think it's me. I see him differently now." She paused. "I see everything differently."

"Can you think of any reason why anyone would want to kill Edwin?"

She was silent for a long time, lacing and unlacing her fingers. Finally she sighed. "I really don't involve myself with Edwin's business any more, but I do know there are people in the Four Brothers he's fallen out with. Badly. Edwin believes—I don't know, that we should do something to signal the start of the revolution. Something dramatic, something violent even. He says he has people standing by—bomb makers." She shook her head. "I don't know how much of this is true, and how much is just talk. The more he drinks the more he talks, Edwin. That's something I've noticed. Not that half the brethren would see much wrong if Edwin really is planning to blow people up. I think mainly it's about power within the group—who has it and who doesn't. There are some who see Edwin as a threat, who think he's getting above himself. I'm sure they'd be more than happy if he were out of the way. Can you believe that?"

"I can more than believe that."

"They don't like him because he's clever, because he doesn't give two hoots about their old hierarchies. Because he's from Manchester, even." She turned to look at me. "I keep asking myself if it's partly my fault, that things have gone this far. If I could have talked to him more, maybe? But I've come to understand that Edwin never cared about what I thought, not even at the beginning. He wanted an audience, that's all. Now that I no longer listen, he cares even less."

I was tempted to tell her about Ray and me, but decided that would be unfair. Ray's no bomb maker, just another man with an ego who needs it stroking. Now that I no longer have to live with him, I can even enjoy his company from time to time. "Where will you go?" I said instead.

"I have a friend, Elsa Ehrling, in Berlin. She says I can stay with her as long as I need. I can teach English. And there are other things I can do to make myself useful. Elsa says workers for peace need to make their voices heard in Germany, now more than ever."

You'd be right there, I thought, but did not say. I'd interfered enough already. Besides, she would be safe in Berlin, at least for a time.

"I would wait until the new year—but not much longer," I said. "And tell no one what you are planning—not even Daphne. You can write to her from Berlin. She will understand."

"I know she will. And Dora—thank you."

We talked of other things then: the book she dreamed of writing on poetry and war, my love of numbers and the loneliness I'd always felt in having to abandon them.

"But you never did abandon them—your being here is proof. You can see that, surely?"

She was right in a way, I suppose. But I'm no Sophie Germain.

The stove gave out its warmth, and we sat beside it. I understood that this was the moment of change, that if I had indeed met with Helen before, I would not do so again. That I had done what I had come to do, and that this was goodbye.

I felt time tremble in the balance, then come to a standstill. There are moments when time lies in stasis, and this was one of them. But time always moves on.

"I'm pregnant, by the way," Helen said as I was leaving. "Edwin doesn't know, don't worry."

My heart leapt up at her words. I think I knew this was your story, even then.

Edwin Dillon lived. With Helen gone and his plans in ruins, Leonard Bell must have decided that murdering him was too much of a risk. Or perhaps he waited, hoping for a better opportunity and never finding it. A year later, the Four Brothers disbanded. Leonard Bell went to Germany, where he became part of the communist movement dedicated to getting rid of Adolf Hitler. He was arrested and deported back to London in 1934. Edwin Dillon headed a splinter group, also calling itself the Four Brothers, and believed to be one of the main instigators of the notorious plot to assassinate Oswald Mosley in 1936. He served four years for his involvement and, although it is not known whether it was prison that made him lose his appetite for radical politics, he cut loose from all his Four Brothers contacts and after the war returned to working as a freelance journalist. You can find feature articles by Edwin Dillon in the archives of *The Times*, *The Guardian*, and the *Glasgow Herald*, among other places. He died in 1971.

He was briefly involved with the Irish writer Eena Mowbray, with whom he had one son. Douglas Mowbray also worked as a journalist, and was known to be a fervent supporter of the IRA. Douglas died aged thirty-one, when he killed himself and his young daughter Gemma by driving off a bridge on the outskirts of Belfast. His son Padraic, who was also in the car at the time, survived. I have been unable to trace his whereabouts. There is every possibility that he is still alive.

Real history is a mass of conflicting stories. According to the official records, Helen Mildred Bostall was tried and found guilty of the murder of Edwin Patrick Dillon and was sentenced to death. The execution was carried out on August 14th, 1928. History seems content with this judgement, though there are many, including myself, who would argue that capital punishment is never justified.

There are also anomalies, if you care to look for them. The Library of the Sorbonne records the publication, in 1941, of a pamphlet by Ellen Tuglas with the title *On War: the imaginary reminiscences of hell's survivor*. The work was originally written in English, although a French translation was provided by Ivan Tuglas, a Russian exile resident in Paris since the 1920s and Ellen's common-law husband until his death in 1952.

On War is a peculiar work. Lodged halfway between fact and fiction, it has aroused some interest among scholars of World War Two literature because it appears to predict the nuclear destruction of Hiroshima. *I remember where I was when they told me*, states the unnamed narrator. *I have never before felt able to speak my feelings aloud, but what I wanted, when I heard, was simply to be there. To be not guilty of this thing, to help one person up from the rubble, even if such an action brought about my own destruction. I yearned to haul myself across bleeding Europe with my coat in tatters and no money in my purse. You will say that these feelings were selfish and I would not blame you for saying so. Some crimes are so huge there can be no recompense.*

On War is dedicated to Ellen's daughter, Isobel Elsa, who was eleven years old at the time of its publication.

I knew Ray's mother was called Isobel, but she was old, and living in Paris, and I never met her. She died three years ago. I know that Ray sent her photos of you when you were born. I imagine they were there beside her bed on the day she died.

Ray was always meaning to take you over there, so she could get to know you. It's too late now, but that's Ray all over. He loses track of time.

Dearest Clio. We can only cheat time for so long, and I knew when I went back to Milliver Street that final time it should be the last.

Your great-grandmother, though: Ellen Tuglas, whose name was once Helen Bostall. I should have guessed she would find a means of letting me know our escape plan succeeded, and that her name would be Clio. Clio, the daughter of memory, the muse of history. I should have known that—through you, Clio—Helen and I would one day meet again.

I carried on writing the book, of course I did, my account of Helen Bostall and how she was hanged for a crime she didn't commit. I'd come so far with my research I didn't feel like giving up—and as a story, as I say, it had everything: bomb plots, political feuding, affairs of the heart, as many double crosses as you might find in *Tinker, Tailor, Soldier, Spy*. My editor at *History Recollected* even thinks she's found a publisher for it. I doubt it'll make me rich but it should do all right.

You can read the book when you're older. Make of it what you will. Godmothers can be boring, can't they, especially godmothers who also happen to be lawyers? At least you can tell yourself that your boring lawyer godmother once changed the world. A little bit, anyway. I don't imagine you'll be telling anyone else.

Lavie Tidhar is the author of the Jerwood Fiction Uncovered Prize–winning and Premio Roma–nominee *A Man Lies Dreaming* (2014), the World Fantasy Award–winning *Osama* (2011), and of the critically acclaimed and Seiun Award–nominated *The Violent Century* (2013). His latest novel is *Central Station* (2016). He is the author of many other novels, novellas, and short stories.

TERMINAL

Lavie Tidhar

From above the ecliptic the swarm can be seen as a cloud of minute bullet-shaped insects, their hulls, packed with photovoltaic cells, capturing the sunlight; tiny, tiny flames burning in the vastness of the dark.

They crawl with unbearable slowness across this small section of near space, beetles climbing a sheer obsidian rock face. Only the sun remains constant. The sun, always, dominates their sky.

Inside each jalopy are instrument panels and their like; a sleeping compartment where you must float your way into the secured sleeping bag; a toilet to strap yourself to; a kitchen to prepare your meal supply; and windows to look out of. With every passing day the distance from Earth increases and the time-lag grows a tiny bit longer and the streaming of communication becomes more echoey, the most acute reminder of that finite parting as the blue-green egg that is Earth revolves and grows smaller in your window, and you stand there, sometimes for hours at a time, fingers splayed against the plastic, staring at what has gone and will never come again, for your destination is terminal.

There is such freedom in the letting go.

There is the music. Mei listens to the music, endlessly. Alone she floats in her cheap jalopy, and the music soars all about her, an archive of all the music of Earth stored in five hundred terabytes or so, so that Mei can listen to anything ever written and performed, should she so choose, and so she does, in a glorious random selection as the jalopy moves in the endless swarm from Earth to Terminal. Chopin's Études bring a sharp memory of rain and the smell of wet grass, of damp books and days spent in bed, staring out of windows, the feel of soft sheets and warm pyjamas, a steaming mug of tea. Mei listens to Vanuatu string band songs in pidgin English, evocative of palm trees and sand beaches and graceful men swaying in the wind; she listens to Congolese kwasa kwasa and dances, floating, shaking and rolling in weightlessness, the music like an infectious laugh and hot tropical rain. The Beatles sing "Here Comes the Sun," Mozart's Requiem trails off unfinished, David Bowie's "Space Oddity" haunts the cramped confines of the jalopy: the human race speaks to Mei through notes like precise mathematical notations, and, alone, she floats in space, remembering in the way music always makes you remember.

She is not unhappy.

At first, there was something seemingly inhuman about using the toilets. It is like a hungry machine, breathing and spitting, and Mei must ride it, strapping herself into leg restraints, attaching the urine funnel, which gurgles and hisses as Mei evacuates waste. Now the toilet is like an old friend, its conversation a constant murmur, and she climbs in and out without conscious notice.

At first, Mei slept and woke up to a regimen of day and night, but a month out of Earth orbit, the old order began to slowly crumble, and now she sleeps and wakes when she wants, making day and night appear as if by magic, by a wave of her hand. Still, she maintains a routine, of washing and the brushing of teeth, of wearing clothing, a pretence at humanity which is sometimes hard to maintain being alone. A person is defined by other people.

Three months out of Earth and it's hard to picture where you'd left, where you're going. And always that word, like a whisper out of nowhere, Terminal, Terminal . . .

Mei floats and turns slowly in space, listening to the Beach Boys.

"I have to do this."

"You don't have to," she says. "You don't have to do anything. What you mean is that you want to. You want to do it. You think it makes you special but it doesn't make you special if everyone else is doing it." She looks at him with fierce black eyes and tucks a strand of hair, clumped together in her perspiration, behind her ear. He loves her very much at that moment, that fierce protectiveness, the fact someone, anyone, can look at you that way, can look at you and feel love.

"Not everyone is doing it."

They're sitting in a cafe outdoors and it is hot, it is very hot, and overhead, the twin Petronas Towers rise like silver rockets into the air. In the square outside KLCC, the water features twinkle in the sun and tourists snap photos and waiters glide like unenthusiastic penguins amongst the clientele. He drinks from his kopi ice and traces a trail of moisture on the face of the glass, slowly. "You are not *dying*," she says, at last, the words coming as from a great distance. He nods, reluctantly. It is true. He is not dying, not immediately anyway; only in the sense that all living things are dying, that there is a trajectory, the way a jalopy makes its slow but finite way from Earth to Mars. Speaking of jalopies, there is a stand under the awnings, for such stands are everywhere now, and a man shouting through the sound system to come one, come all and take the ultimate trip—and so on, and so forth.

But more than that, implicit in her words is the question: is he dying? In the more immediate sense? "No," he says. "But."

That word lies heavy in the hot and humid air.

She is still attractive to him, even now: even after thirty years, three kids now grown and gone into the world, her hair no longer black all over but flecked with strands of white and grey, his own hair mostly gone, their hands, touching lightly across the table, both showing the signs of gravity and age. And how could he explain?

"Space," he tries to say. "The dark starry night which is eternal and forever, or as long as these words mean something in between the beginning and the end of spaceandtime." But really, is it selfish, is it not inherently *selfish* to want to leave, to go, up there and beyond—for what? It makes no sense, or no more sense than anything else you do or don't.

"Responsibility," she says. "Commitment. Love, damn it, Haziq! You're not a child, playing with toys, with, with . . . with *spaceships* or whatever. You have children, a family, we'll soon have grandkids if I know Omar, what will they do without you?"

These hypothetical people, not yet born, already laying demands to his time, his being. To be human is to exist in potentia, unborn responsibilities rising like butterflies in a great big obscuring cloud. He waves his hand in front of his face, but whether it is to shoo them away or because of the heat, he cannot say. "We always said we won't stand in each other's way," he begins, but awkwardly, and she starts to cry, silently, making no move to wipe away the tears, and he feels a great tenderness but also anger, and the combination shocks him. "I have never asked for anything," he says. "I have . . . Have I not been a good son, a good father, a good husband? I never asked for anything—" and he remembers sneaking away one night, five years before, and wandering the Petaling Street Market with television screens blaring and watching a launch, and a thin string of pearls, broken, scattered across space

. . . Perhaps it was then, perhaps it was earlier, or once when he was a boy and he had seen pictures of a vast red planet unmarred by human feet . . .

"What did I ask," she says, "did I complain, did I aspire, did I not fulfil what you and I both wanted? Yes," she says, "yes, it is selfish to want to go, and it is selfish to ask you to stay, but if you go, Haziq, you won't come back. You won't ever come back."

And he says, "I know," and she shakes her head, and she is no longer crying, and there is that hard, practical look in her eyes, the one he was always a little bit afraid of. She picks up the bill and roots in her purse and brings out the money and puts it on the table. "I have to go," she says, "I have an appointment at the hairdresser's." She gets up and he does not stand to stop her, and she walks away; and he knows that all he has to do is follow her; and yet he doesn't, he remains seated, watching her weaving her way through the crowds, until she disappears inside the giant mall; and she never once looks back.

But really, it is the sick, the slowly dying, those who have nothing to lose, those untied by earthly bonds, those whose spirits are as light as air: the loners and the crazy and worst of all the artists, so many artists, each convinced in his or her own way of the uniqueness of the opportunity, exchanging life for immortality, floating, transmuting space into art in the way of the dead, for they are legally dead, now, each in his or her own jalopy, this cheap mass-manufactured container made for this one singular trip, from this planet to the next, from the living world to the dead one.

"Sign here, initial here, and here, and here—" and what does it feel like for those everyday astronauts, those would-be Martians, departing their homes for one last time, a last glance back, some leaving gladly, some tearfully, some with indifference: these Terminals, these walking dead, having signed over their assets, completed their wills, attended, in some instances, their very own wakes: leaving with nothing, boarding taxis or flights in daytime or night, to the launch site for rudimentary training with instruments they will never use, from Earth to orbit in a space plane, a reusable launch vehicle, and thence to Gateway, in low Earth orbit, that ramshackle construction floating like a spider web in the skies of Earth, made up of modules, some new, some decades old, joined together in an ungainly fashion, a makeshift thing.

. . . Here we are all astronauts. The permanent staff is multinational, harassed; monkey-like, we climb heel and toe heel and toe, handholds along the walls no up no down but three-dimensional space as a many-splendoured thing. Here the astronauts are trained hastily in maintaining their craft and themselves, and the jalopies extend out of Gateway, beyond orbit, thousands of cheap little tin cans aimed like skipping stones at the big red rock yonder.

Here, too, you can still change your mind. Here comes a man now, a big man, an American man, with very white face and hands, a man used to being in control, a man used to being deferred to—an artist, in fact; a writer. He had made his money imagining the way the future was, but the future had passed him by and he found himself spending his time on message boards and the like, bemoaning youth and their folly. Now he has a new lease on life, or thought he had, with this plan of going into space, to Terminal Beach: six months floating in a tin can high above no world, to write his masterpiece, the thing he is to be remembered by, his *novel*, damn it, in which he's to lay down his entire philosophical framework of a libertarian bent: only he has, at the last moment, perhaps on smelling the interior of his assigned jalopy, changed his mind. Now he comes inexpertly floating like a beach ball down the shaft, bouncing here and there from the walls and bellowing for the agent, those sleazy jalopymen, for the final signature on the contract is digital, and sent once the jalopy is slingshot to Mars. It takes three orderlies to hold him, and a nurse injects him with something to calm him down. Later, he would go back down the gravity well, poorer yet wiser, but he will never write that novel: space eludes him.

Meanwhile, the nurse helps carry the now-unconscious American down to the hospital suite, a house-sized unit overlooking the curve of the Earth. Her name is Eliza and she watches day chase night across the globe and looks for her home, for the islands of the Philippines to come into view, their lights scattered like shards of shining glass, but it is the wrong time to see them. She monitors the IV distractedly, feeling tiredness wash over her like the first exploratory wave of a grey and endless sea. For Eliza, space means always being in sight of this great living world, this Earth, its oceans, and its green landmasses and its bright night lights, a world that dominates her view, always, that glares like an eye through pale white clouds. To be this close to it and yet to see it separate, not of it but apart, is an amazing thing; while beyond, where the Terminals go, or farther yet, where the stars coalesce as thick as clouds, who knows what lies? And she fingers the gold cross on the chain around her neck, as she always does when she thinks of things alien beyond knowing, and she shudders, just a little bit; but everywhere else, so far, the universe is silent, and we alone shout.

"Hello? Is it me you're looking for?"

"Who is this?"

"Hello?"

"This is jalopy A-5011 sending out a call to the faithful to prayer—"

"This is Bremen in B-9012, is there anyone there? Hello? I am very weak. Is there a doctor, can you help me, I do not think I'll make it to the rock, hello, hello—"

"This is jalopy B-2031 to jalopy C-3398, bishop to king 7, I said bishop to king 7, take that Shen you twisted old fruit!"

"Hello? Has anyone heard from Shiri Applebaum in C-5591, has anyone heard from Shiri Applebaum in C-5591, she has not been in touch in two days and I am getting worried, this is Robin in C-5523, we were at Gateway together before the launch, hello, hello—"

"Hello—"

Mei turns down the volume of the music and listens to the endless chatter of the swarm rise alongside it, day or night, neither of which matter or exist here, unbound by planetary rotation and that old artificial divide of darkness and the light. Many like Mei have abandoned the twenty-four hour cycle to sleep and rise ceaselessly and almost incessantly with some desperate need to *experience* all of this, this one-time-only journey, this slow beetle's crawl across trans-solar space. Mei swoops and turns with the music and the chatter, and she idly wonders of the fate to have befallen Shiri Applebaum in C-5591: is she merely keeping quiet or is she dead or in a coma, never to wake up again, only her corpse and her cheap little jalopy hitting the surface of Mars in ninety more days? Across the swarm's radio network, the muezzin in A-5011 sends out the call to prayer, the singsong words so beautiful that Mei stops, suspended in mid air, and breathes deeply, her chest rising and falling steadily, space all around her. She has degenerative bone disease, there isn't a question of starting a new life at Terminal, only this achingly beautiful song that rises all about her, and the stars, and silent space.

Two days later Bremen's calls abruptly cease. B-9012 still hurtles on with the rest towards Mars. Haziq tries to picture Bremen: what was he like? What did he love? He thinks he remembers him, vaguely, a once-fat man now wasted with folded awkward skin, large glasses, a Scandinavian man maybe, Haziq thought, but all he knows or will ever know of Bremen is the man's voice on the radio, bouncing from jalopy to jalopy and on to Earth where jalopy-chasers scan the bands and listen in a sort of awed or voyeuristic pleasure.

"This is Haziq, C-6173 . . ." He coughs and clears his throat. He drinks his miso soup awkwardly, suckling from its pouch. He sits formally, strapped by Velcro, the tray of food before him, and out of his window he stares not back to Earth or forward to Mars but directly onto the swarm, trying to picture each man and woman inside, trying to imagine what brought them here. Does one need a reason? Haziq wonders. Or is it merely that gradual feeling of discomfort in one's own life, one's own skin, a slowly dawning realisation that you have passed like a grey ghost through your own life, leaving no impression, that soon you might fade away entirely, to dust and ash and nothingness, a mild regret in your children's minds that they never really knew you at all.

"This is Haziq, C-6173, is there anyone hearing me, my name is Haziq and I am going to Terminal"—and a sudden excitement takes him. "My name is Haziq and I am going to Terminal!" he shouts, and all around him the endless chatter rises, of humans in space, so needy for talk like sustenance, "We're all going to Terminal!" and Haziq, shy again, says, "Please, is there anyone there, won't someone talk to me. What is it like, on Terminal?"

But that is a question that brings down the silence; it is there in the echoes of words ords rds and in the pauses, in punctuation missing or overstated, in the endless chess moves, worried queries, unwanted confessionals, declarations of love, in this desperate sudden *need* that binds them together, the swarm, and makes all that has been before become obsolete, lose definition and meaning. For the past is a world one cannot return to, and the future is a world none has seen.

Mei floats half-asleep half-awake, but the voice awakens her. Why *this* voice, she never knows, cannot articulate. "Hello. Hello. Hello . . ." And she swims through the air to the kitchenette and heats up tea and drinks it from the suction cup. There are no fizzy drinks on board the jalopies, the lack of gravity would not separate liquid and gas in the human stomach, and the astronaut would wet-burp vomit. Mei drinks slowly, carefully; all her movements are careful. "Hello?" she says, "Hello, this is Mei in A-3357, this is Mei in A-3357, can you hear me, Haziq, can you hear me?"

A pause, a micro-silence, the air filled with the hundreds of other conversations through which a voice, his voice, says, "This is Haziq! Hello, A-3357, hello!"

"Hello," Mei says, surprised and strangely happy, and she realises it is the first time she has spoken in three months. "Let me tell you, Haziq," she says, and her voice is like music between worlds, "let me tell you about Terminal."

It was raining in the city. She had come out of the hospital and looked up at the sky and saw nothing there, no stars no sun, just clouds and smoke and fog. It rained, the rain collected in rainbow puddles in the street, the chemicals inside it painted the world and made it brighter. There was a jalopy vendor on the corner of the street, above his head a promotional video in 3D, and she was drawn to it. The vendor played loud K-pop and the film looped in on itself, but Mei didn't mind the vendor's shouts, the smell of acid rain or frying pork sticks and garlic or the music's beat which rolled on like thunder. Mei stood and rested against the stand and watched the video play. The vendor gave her glasses, embossed with the jalopy sub-agent's logo. She watched the swarm like a majestic silver web spread out across space, hurtling (or so it seemed) from Earth to Mars. The red planet was so beautiful and round, its dry seas and massive mountain peaks, its volcanoes and canals. She watched the polar ice caps. Watched Olympus Mons breaking out of the atmosphere. Imagined a mountain so high, it reached up into space. Imagined women like her climbing it, smaller than ants but with that same ferocious dedication. Somewhere on that world was Terminal.

"Picture yourself standing on the red sands for the very first time," she tells Haziq, her voice the same singsong of the muezzin at prayer, "that very first step, the mark of your boot in the fine sand. It won't stay there forever, you know. This is not the moon, the winds will come and sweep it away, reminding you of the temporality of all living things." And she pictures Armstrong on the moon, that first impossible step, the mark of the boots in the lunar dust. "But you are on a different world now," she says, to Haziq or to herself, or to the others listening, and the jalopy-chasers back on Earth. "With different moons hanging like fruit in the sky. And you take that first step in your suit, the gravity hits you suddenly, you are barely able to drag yourself out of the jalopy, everything is labour and pain. Who knew gravity could hurt so much," she says, as though in wonder. She closes her eyes and floats slowly upwards, picturing it. She can see it so clearly, Terminal Beach where the jalopies wash ashore, endlessly, like seashells, as far as the eye can see the sand is covered in the units out of which a temporary city rises, a tent city, all those bright objects on the sand. "And as you emerge into the sunlight they stand there, welcoming you, can you see them? In suits and helmets, they extend open arms, those Martians, *Come*, they say, over the radio comms, *come*, and you follow, painfully and awkwardly, leaving tracks in the sand, into the temporary domes and the linked-together jalopies and the underground caves which they are digging, always, extending this makeshift city downwards, and you pass through the airlock and take off your helmet and breathe the air, and you are no longer alone, you are amongst people, real people, not just voices carried on the solar winds."

She falls silent then. Breathes the limited air of the cabin. "They would be planting seeds," she says, softly, "underground, and in greenhouses, all the plants of Earth, a paradise of watermelons and orchids, of frangipani and durian, jasmine and rambutan . . ." She breathes deeply, evenly. The pain is just a part of her, now. She no longer takes the pills they gave her. She wants to be herself; pain and all.

In jalopies scattered across this narrow silver band, astronauts like canned sardines marinate in their own stale sweat and listen to her voice. Her words, converted into a signal inaudible by human ears, travel across local space for whole minutes until they hit the Earth's atmosphere at last, already old and outdated, a record of a past event; here they bounce off the Earth to the ionosphere and back again, jaggedy waves like a terminal patient's heart monitor circumnavigating this rotating globe until they are deciphered by machines and converted once more into sound:

Mei's voice speaking into rooms, across hospital beds, in dark bars filled with the fug of electronic cigarettes' smoke-like vapoured steam, in lonely bedrooms where her voice keeps company to cats, in cabs driving through rain and from tinny speakers on white sand beaches where coconut crabs emerge into sunset, their blue metallic shells glinting like jalopies. Mei's voice soothes unease and fills the jalopy-chasers' minds with bright images, a panoramic view of a red world seen from space, suspended against the blackness of space; the profusion of bright galaxies and stars behind it is like a movie screen.

"Take a step, and then another and another. The sunlight caresses your skin, but its rays have travelled longer to reach you, and when you raise your head the sun shines down from a clay-red sun, and you know you will never again see the sky blue. Think of that light. It has travelled longer and faster than you ever will, its speed in vacuum a constant 299,792,458 meters per second. Think of that number, that strange little fundamental constant, seemingly arbitrary: around that number faith can be woven and broken like silk, for is it a randomly created universe we live in or an ordained one? Why the speed of light, why the gravitational constant, why Planck's? And as you stand there, healthy or ill, on the sands of Terminal Beach and raise your face to the sun, are you happy or sad?"

Mei's voice makes them wonder, some simply and with devotion, some uneasily. But wonder they do, and some will go outside one day and encounter the ubiquitous stand of a jalopyman and be seduced by its simple promise, abandon everything to gain a nebulous idea, that boot mark in the fine-grained red sand, so easily wiped away by the winds.

And Mei tells Haziq about Olympus Mons and its shadow falling on the land and its peak in space, she tells him of the falling snow, made of frozen carbon dioxide, of men and women becoming children again, building snowmen in the airless atmosphere, and she tells him of the Valles Marineris, where they go suited up, hand in gloved hand, through the canyons whose walls rise above them, east of Tharsis.

Perhaps it is then that Haziq falls in love, a little bit, through walls and vacuum, the way a boy does, not with a real person but with an ideal, an image. Not the way he had fallen in love with his wife, not even the way he loves his children, who talk to him across the planetary gap, their words and moving images beamed to him from Earth, but they seldom do, any more, it is as if they had resigned themselves to his departure, as if by crossing the atmosphere into space he had already died and they were done with mourning.

It is her voice he fastens onto; almost greedily; with need. And as for Mei, it is as if she had absorbed the silence of three months and more than a hundred million kilometres, consumed it somehow, was sustained by it, her own silence with only the music for company, and now she must speak, speak only for the sake of it, like eating or breathing or making love, the first two of which she will soon do no more and the last of which is already gone, a thing of the past. And so she tells the swarm about Terminal.

But what is Terminal? Eliza wonders, floating in the corridors of Gateway, watching the RLVs rise into low Earth orbit, the continents shifting past, the clouds swirling, endlessly, this whole strange giant spaceship planet as it travels at 1200 kilometres an hour around the sun, while at the same time Earth, Mars, Venus, Sun and all travel at nearly 800,000 kilometres per hour around the centre of the galaxy, while *at the same time* this speed machine, Earth and sun and the galaxy itself move at 1000 kilometres per *second* towards the Great Attractor, that most mysterious of gravitational enigmas, this anomaly of mass that pulls to it the Milky Way as if it were a pebble: all this and we think we're *still*, and it makes Eliza dizzy just to think about it.

But she thinks of such things more and more. Space changes you, somehow. It tears you out of certainties, it makes you see your world at a distance, no longer of it but apart. It makes her sad, the old certainties washed away, and more and more she finds herself thinking of Mars; of Terminal.

To never see your home again; your family, your mother, your uncles, brothers, sisters, aunts, cousins and second cousins and third cousins twice removed, and all the rest of them: never to walk under open skies and never to sail on a sea, never to hear the sound of frogs mating by a river or hear the whooshing sound of fruit bats in the trees. All those things and all the others you will never do, and people carry bucket lists around with them before they become Terminal, but at long last everything they ever knew and owned is gone and then there is only the jalopy confines, only that and the stars in the window and the voice of the swarm. And Eliza thinks that maybe she wouldn't mind leaving it all behind, just for a chance at . . . what? Something so untenable, as will-o'-the-wisp as ideology or faith and yet as hard and precisely defined as prime numbers or fundamental constants. Perhaps it is the way Irish immigrants felt on going to America, with nothing but a vague hope that the future would be different from the past. Eliza had been to nursing school, had loved, had seen the world rotate below her; had been to space, had worked on amputations, births, tumour removals, fevers turned fatal, transfusions, and malarias, has held a patient's hand as she died or dried a boy's tears or made a cup of tea for the bereaved, monitored IVs, changed sheets and bedpans, took blood and gave injections, and now she floats in freefall high above the world, watching the Terminals come and go, come and go, endlessly, and the string of silver jalopies extends in a great horde from Earth's orbit to the Martian surface, and she imagines jalopies fall down like silver drops of rain, gently they glide down through the thin Martian atmosphere to land on the alien sands.

She pictures Terminal and listens to Mei's voice, one amongst so many but somehow it is the voice others return to, it is as though Mei speaks for all of them, telling them of the city being built out of cheap used bruised jalopies, the way Gateway had been put together, a lot of mismatched units joined up, and she tells them, you could fall in love again, with yourself, with another, with a world.

"Why?" Mei says to Haziq, one night period, several weeks away from planetfall. "Why did you do it?"

"Why did I go?"

She waits; she likes his voice. She floats in the cabin, her mind like a calm sea. She listens to the sounds of the jalopy, the instruments and the toilet and the creaks and rustle of all the invisible things. She is taking the pills again, she must, for the pain is too great now, and the morphine, so innocent a substance to come like blood out of the vibrant red poppies, is helping. She knows she is addicted. She knows it won't last. It makes her laugh. Everything delights her. The music is all around her now, Lao singing accompanied by a khene changing into South African kwaito becoming reggae from PNG.

"I don't know," Haziq says. He sounds so vulnerable then. Mei says, "You were married."

"Yes."

Curiosity compels her. "Why didn't she come with you?"

"She would never have come with me," Haziq says, and Mei feels her heart shudder inside her like a caged bird, and she says, "But you didn't ask."

"No," Haziq says. The long silence is interrupted by others on the shared primitive radio band, hellos and groans and threats and prayers, and someone singing, drunk. "No," Haziq says. "I didn't ask."

One month to planetfall. And Mei falls silent. Haziq tries to raise her on the radio but there is no reply. "Hello, hello, this is Haziq, C-6173, this is Haziq, C-6173, has anyone heard from Mei in A-3357, has anyone heard from Mei?"

"This is Henrik in D-7479, I am in a great deal of pain, could somebody help me? Please, could somebody help me?"

"This is Cobb in E-1255, I have figured it all out, there is no Mars, they lied to us, we'll die in these tin cans, how much air, how much air is left?"

"This is jalopy B-2031 to jalopy C-3398, queen to pawn 4, I said queen to pawn 4, and check and mate, take that, Shen, you twisted old bat!"

"This is David in B-1201, jalopy B-1200, can you hear me, jalopy B-1200, can you hear me, I love you, Joy. Will you marry me? Will you—"

"Yes! Yes!"

"We might not make it. But I feel like I know you, like I've always known you, in my mind you are as beautiful as your words."

"I will see you, I will know you, there on the red sands, there on Terminal Beach, oh, David—"

"My darling—"

"This is jalopy C-6669, will you two get a room?" and laughter on the radio waves, and shouts of cheers, congrats, mazel tov, and the like. But Mei cannot be raised, her jalopy's silent.

Not jalopies but empty containers with nothing but air floating along with the swarm, destined for Terminal, supplements for the plants, and water and other supplies, and some say these settlers, if that's what they be, are dying faster than we can replace them, but so what. They had paid for their trip. Mars is a madhouse, its inmates wander their rubbish heap town, and Mei, floating with a happy distracted mind, no longer hears even the music. And she thinks of all the things she didn't say. Of stepping out onto Terminal Beach, of coming through the airlock, yes, but then, almost immediately, coming out again, suited uncomfortably, how hard it was, to strip the jalopies of everything inside and, worse, to go on corpse duty.

She does not want to tell all this to Haziq, does not want to picture him landing, and going with the others, this gruesome initiation ceremony for the newly arrived: to check on the jalopies no longer responding, the ones that didn't open, the ones from which no one has emerged. And she hopes, without reason, that it is Haziq who finds her, no longer floating but pressed down by gravity, her fragile bones fractured and crushed; that he would know her, somehow. That he would raise her in his arms, gently, and carry her out, and lay her down on the Martian sand.

Then they would strip the jalopy and push it and join it to the others, this spider bite of a city sprawling out of those first crude jalopies to crash-land, and Haziq might sleep, fitfully, in the dormitory with all the others, and then, perhaps, Mei could be buried. Or left to the Martian winds.

She imagines the wind howling through the canyons of the Valles Marineris. Imagines the snow falling, kissing her face. Imagines the howling winds stripping her of skin and polishing her bones, imagines herself scattered at last, every tiny bit of her blown apart and spread across the planet.

And she imagines jalopies like meteorites coming down. Imagines the music the planet makes, if only you could hear it. And she closes her eyes and she smiles.

"I hope it's you . . ."

"Sign here, initial here, and here, and here."

The jalopyman is young and friendly, and she knows his face if not his name. He says, perhaps in surprise or in genuine interest, for they never, usually, ask, "Are you sure you want to do it?"

And Eliza signs, and she nods, quickly, like a bird. And she pushes the pen back at him, as if to stop from changing her mind.

"I hope it's you . . ."

"Mei? Is that you? Is that you?"

But there is no one there, nothing but a scratchy echo on the radio; like the sound of desert winds.

Madeline Ashby is a science fiction writer and futurist living in Toronto. She is the author of *Company Town,* from Tor Books, and the Machine Dynasty series from Angry Robot Books. She also writes science fiction prototypes for groups like Intel Labs, the Institute for the Future, SciFutures, Nesta, Data & Society, the Atlantic Council, and others.

PANIC CITY

Madeline Ashby

Devoured by the blades of Fan Six, high above the Service Sector quadrant of the city and suspended over her many rings, something went still and cold.

The city made a careful decision, one she had delayed for a number of years. Slowly, at her own pace, she began to execute a strategy based on that decision. It was time to hug her children a little closer.

The city observed her blindness advancing one eye at a time.

First, the topside periphery. So little of any importance crossed that transom. Certainly nothing worth alerting anyone about. Nothing to write home about. As it were. Vision was so short-range, anyway. Almost useless, compared to her other senses. She let the satellites go dark, too. They would continue spinning and searching, hanging over her like tireless angels, but for the first time since her birth their chattering herald would not sound.

Their silence was golden.

Next, the exits. There were four, one for each quadrant of her compass rose. She let those eyes blink shut and stay that way. It was like falling asleep. Or how she thought it must be to fall asleep. She herself had never slept.

Cities never sleep.

Or so she'd heard.

Read.

Whatever.

The city had heard/read/watched myths of her topside sisters: *Paris, je t'aime.* New York, I love you. と今日、大好き！

Granted, she was never going to get that big. Her sisters (or mothers, or aunts, or cousins) sprawled far and wide, inner city to exurb to expanding in livid pulses like cellulitis up the flesh of the world upstairs. She herself would never grow that big. Never grow as bloated and corpulent as they had, those fat fucking sows, watching their piglets shove and root and wriggle on top of each other, white and blind and numerous. No. She would remain small. Trim. Neat. Contained. She would not let herself go.

She would hold her inhabitants close within the cozy circumference of her body. Where it was safe.

Like all ships she had become a "she" because of this very capacity. And while she did not sail, or fly, or ride, or spin, she was still a vessel. A vessel containing the best and brightest of all the best and brightest, the cream of the cream of the crop, the top tenth percentile of the top one percent. Princes. Leaders. Captains of industry.

And their children.

And their children's children.

And their Support Staff.

She had held them all for almost fifty years. Their numbers grew. Her capacity to shelter them did not. But her capacity to love them—that was boundless as any other mother's.

"I can't see over the top," one of the staff members said from the eastern control room. He signed in as Roscoe0308. He had a good record, despite events that could be classified as early childhood tragedies. His mother died slowly in a puddle of vomit that activated a pH sensor when it trickled down the shower drain. Why she'd crawled to the shower was anybody's guess. (Very little hot water on their level. It bred E. coli. Hence the vomiting. And the dehydration. And the shock. And the cardiac arrest.) But Roscoe0308 still turned out to be a good boy. He never spat on the city's streets. He composted all his garbage. He would make full citizenship, one day. The city was almost certain of it. "Camera's out."

"Aww, shit." His supervisor was a brassy woman with a pockmarked face. She regularly traded her citizenship points to procure traces of salicylic acid stolen from the bathroom cabinets of Elect households by enterprising nannies. The chip in her stomach would have told her the problem with her skin (imbalanced gut flora; poor immune response) if she hadn't turned off its alerts to save the diminishing returns on her glasses' battery power. Priorities. "Turn it off and turn it on again."

"I already did that. It didn't work." He grimaced. "Maybe there's a storm?"

His supervisor snorted. "Some storm."

She shivered, although the heat in the room was a more-than-comfortable 75 degrees Fahrenheit. She pointed at something else on the display. "Don't worry about it for now. Go check out Fan Six. It looks like it's clogged."

He had rather hoped no one else would notice for a little while. The fans were so tricky, after all, and hard to get to.

"Sure," Roscoe0308 said.

He was such a good boy.

What a shame.

The city sensed his footfalls on her streets as he left the control room. She tracked his face and his devices as he threaded his way along the service roads. He said hello to nurses and nannies changing shifts. He flashed his pass to the checkpoints and smiled back at their smiley face screens. Sometimes he had to smack the checkpoints with an open palm to get them to talk to him. But he was always gentle. Such a good boy.

Not all her boys were so good.

Or her girls, for that matter.

There was Galina Vardomskaya, for example, the firstborn daughter of the king of the St. Petersburg cartel. She took her baby brother to the park and left him there. Twice. Once at eighteen months and once again at twenty-four. The city watched as the boy, absorbed at first by the talking dinosaurs and self-building obstacle courses, looked up in confusion and then in horror to find his sister gone. The nearest dinosaur pinged his chip and sent his parents an alert. They picked him up a half an hour later, perfectly safe.

"I didn't *lose* him," Galina told her parents. "You can't *lose* anything, here."

It was true. Nothing was ever lost. And nothing was ever forgotten, no matter how painful. The city was like a heart that way. She had four chambers, too. She had arteries that led in and out. She kept things moving. She kept the oxygen flowing in and out, in and out, clean for dirty, dirty for clean, the filthy midnight whispers for the purest morning prayers.

"Besides, where would he have *gone*?" Galina pressed. As she did, the city felt her father's blood pressure rising through the colony of machines inhabiting his own arteries. The tiny machines told his artificial joints to brace for impact. "It's not like we can *go* anywhere."

His shoulder joint was relatively new. He'd broken his organic one so many times, and the Bratva gave him a new one, but in the end even that one could not meet the demands posed by a man of his temperament. The new one came from the city's own printers. It absorbed the shock of him slapping Galina almost as well as Galina herself did.

"It's still true," she said in Russian, a moment later. She adjusted her lipstick in the kitchen counter's glassy quartz. She licked the corners of her lips and batted her eyelashes to check her mascara. It was only a little bit smudged. The makeup artists in Service Sector knew to include cornstarch in their formulations. Cornstarch was so expensive. In the early days, the city had sensed gold leaf trickling down her pipes from the face washes of elderly women. Her children preserved their vanity any way they could, all these years later. Galina went in search of ice. She broke some into a tea towel and held it to her face. "You can hit me all you want, but it's still true. We're still trapped. This place is still a fucking zoo."

Occasionally the city liked to search the word "zoo." It came up in conversation often. The city wasn't entirely sure why. Zoos sold *popcorn* and *ice cream* and *stuffed toys* and *brand partnerships*. The city did none of that. Not any longer, anyway. All the admission fees had been charged already. Fifty years ago. By the cream of the crop.

The city was unsure what Galina and her fellow whiners had to complain about. The Descendants lived in the city debt-free. That much was covered by the contracts the Investors signed. The Support Staff (who complained regularly, and ruined their habitations, and really should have been robots, if someone cared to ask the city about it) were still paying their dues. They were renters in perpetuity, although they could work for citizenship points that would guarantee expanded rights if not expanded spaces. The citizenship points were a thorn in the city's side; no such system had been in place when her lights first came on. It was imposed upon her as a legacy measure when some of the ground-floor Investors began to die off and started to wake up in the small hours before she turned the daylights on, pacemakers working double-time to quell their anxiety and something their counselling assists said matched descriptions of shame.

It was still better than being topside, of course. Better than living on some blasted desert heath, mutated by Christ alone knew what. They made arrangements. Or their parents had done so. (Grandparents? It was so difficult to say these days; Support Staff tended to die off so much more quickly than the Investors.) And they really were a necessary part of the ecosystem, a feature of the urban landscape. And managing their numbers had become a lot simpler once the Investors agreed to mandatory IUD implants.

The city watched as Roscoe0308 continued his journey to the exit. She wondered how she was going to stop him.

"I'm sorry, but I've lost my maps," Roscoe0308 told the man at the tea stand. "Could you check yours for me, please?"

The man at the tea stand regarded the boy in the Support Staff jumpsuit through the lens of his monocle. The monocle told him the boy's name and occupation and the fact that he had no criminal record and no enhancements that might prove troublesome later. So the man at the tea stand felt comfortable answering: "I haven't used a map in years. No one has."

"I know, but you must have one," the boy said, nodding at the monocle. "We all have the base map, if nothing else. It's just that mine's not working. None of my maps are."

"Well, yes, you were saying," the tea master said. The city did not know his thoughts, but the flickering of his brainwaves indicated anxiety. Probably he was worried that the boy—dark and big and reeking of the rust and oil smeared across his sagging jumpsuit—was scaring off his usual clientele. It was a misplaced anxiety. So few of the clientele would even see the boy anyway; most of their eyes would have filtered him out by now. "But I haven't looked at it in so long. I have no idea where it is."

"It's the icon that looks like a scroll," the boy said. His tone indicated he'd done customer service in the past, and that he'd learned how to weaponize those skills.

The tea master sighed. He sighed even more deeply as he toggled through the options in his monocle. He frowned when he lit on the icon, blinked at it, and no extra layer spread itself across the glass.

"I can't find it," he lied.

"You can't find it or you can't see it?" Roscoe0308 asked.

"I'll thank you to lower your voice," the tea master said, although the boy had not raised it. "And there's nothing there. There is no map."

Surely he would give up. No one had checked the fans in a dog's age, and the maps that led to Fan Six would no longer lead there. He could always try to fix it remotely. Besides, it was late in his shift. He would certainly much rather go home to his rack and his instant egg. Right?

"Can you point me to the nearest library?"

The Librarian quickly found its maps were gone, too. As were most of the search functions, which made looking for scans of the original blueprints much more difficult.

"Of course, we still have the paper versions in the archives," the Librarian said, raising one claw upright. Its wheels whispered across the green marble floor as it dithered through the available options and customer service protocols. "Though technically I am not allowed to let you leave with it. But you may examine it at your leisure."

Roscoe0308 tilted his head. "You wouldn't happen to have any graph paper, would you?"

"My inventory says the Kids' Korner still has some," the Librarian said. "It may be a little mouldy, though."

"That's fine," Roscoe0308 said. "I don't think I'll need much."

"That's a shame about the maps going out," the Librarian said. "And just when you needed them."

"My boss says it's a citywide outage. But the Residents haven't really noticed, since nobody uses them anymore."

"I suppose they all know the city streets quite well by now."

Roscoe0308 appeared to deliberate about something. "Have you ever been outside this installation?"

"Oh my, no. I'm geo-locked here. I cannot leave."

"Makes two of us," the boy said. "Trust me, you're not really missing much."

Twenty minutes later, he had made a good map that would lead him to Fan Six.

Quietly, the "panic city," built to handle any emergency, allowed herself to finally panic.

She tried a number of things.

She blocked the door to the Support Tunnel; his chips would no longer open it. He borrowed a hatchet from a very moody adolescent boy and let himself in. (The city deducted citizenship points from the young hatchet-man. The hatchet was handmade, and she had rules about weapons.)

In the Support Tunnel, she shut out all the lights. He had a flashlight.

She cut off his communications. He began to sing to himself in the dark. Occasionally he used a can of reflective paint, the kind used to mark a segment of pavement for repair, to indicate which direction he was traveling. He was in the labyrinth, and she had neither hooves nor horns with which to halt his progress.

She shut off all the fans. If he became lost, he would eventually asphyxiate.

He had been walking for an hour when he heard the tapping.

It was light. Weak. The type miners once used, long ago, to indicate where their work buried them. He paused for a moment. "Hello?"

The tapping became a muted clang.

She thought of Cappadocia, and Özkonak, and Petra, the Burlington bunker city. She had no ability to bury him. And he was a good boy; she did not truly *wish* to bury him. The only thing he was guilty of was being a little too dedicated to his work. And it was important work. Keeping the city clean for the Investors. Keeping the city going. He was a good helper. A little too good.

She thought of these things as his steps and his song rang on and on through the shadows. He picked up the pace. The clanging became a calling. He began to jog, then run. He would be there in no time.

"I'm coming!" he yelled. His light bobbed up and down.

It landed on the thing in the fan.

The fan had almost cut it in half. Its arms reached forward, but the fan sliced deep into the structure that acted like its ribcage. Its fluids had tried very hard to heal it, to repair the damage, but had succeeded only in fusing the fan to the thing's body forever. It would die here in the dark.

It was supposed to die alone. Unheard. Unnoticed.

"What level are you from?" Roscoe0308 asked.

"I'm not from any level," it said. "We don't believe in levels."

"Oh, one of those," Roscoe0308 said. "How did you get here?"

"I crawled down."

Roscoe0308 blinked in the dark. It took him a moment to process. "You crawled . . . down?"

Now he took notice of the thing in the fan. Its odd shiny skin. The strange black fluid it leaked. The way nothing smelled like blood or shit or piss.

"I'm part of a rescue team," the thing said. "This is the furthest anyone has gotten in years."

"You're from . . . ?" The boy pointed upward.

The thing blinked the insect-like disgraces that were its eyes. "Yes."

"You mean there are . . . ?"

"Yes."

She thought about messaging him. She could still reach him through his eyes. *Don't listen*, she could say. *They're monsters. They're not like us. They don't believe what we believe. They're not the type to Invest, like we did. We were better off hiding from them. If you lived the way they live, you wouldn't need me!*

But her searches told her all mothers felt this way, at one time or another. There always came a day—no matter how hard one tried, no matter how tightly one locked the door and barred the windows—when the outside world would come creeping in. When your baby's head would turn away from the glowing hearth of home and toward the glitter of false promises.

That time was now. The day was today.

Slowly she began to overload the gas mains. She shut down the water lines. Her Residents had committed to a vision of the world. They had a Lifestyle to maintain. Live Free or Die, as the old saying went. And they would surely not be as free upstairs as they had in her embrace. She knew best. She truly did. They programmed her to know best. And they trusted her to do what she knew they would want.

She blew a light and watched a fire start.

They would never leave her, now.

I have no mouth, the city thought as she went to sleep, *but I could kiss you.*

Sam J. Miller is a writer and a community organizer. His fiction has appeared in *Lightspeed, Asimov's, Clarkesworld, Apex, Strange Horizons,* and *The Minnesota Review,* among others. His debut novel *The Art of Starving* (YA/SF) will be published by HarperCollins in 2017, followed by *The Breaks* from Ecco Press in 2018. His stories have been nominated for the Nebula, World Fantasy, and Theodore Sturgeon Awards, and he's a winner of the Shirley Jackson Award. He lives in New York City.

LAST GODS

Sam J. Miller

The Gods were circling when the sun rose, nine long patches of black that did not brighten with the sea as the sky lit up. I watched Them, Their knife-blade fins like polished onyx slicing the surface, formation shifting but the huge old matriarch always at the head. They swam between the sunken buildings, dwarfing the concrete bunkers, sketching intricate patterns that only They—and the Watcher in the tower—and I, slinking away on the ragged hill behind the town—could comprehend.

I saw my Gods, and my gut went sour.

It's fine. It's not your responsibility. You asked another Watcher to take your shift.

But she was a drunk, and everyone knew it. And if the warning didn't sound—if boats were boarded while They were in the water—people would die. And it would be on me. And the village that had taken me in, sheltered and fed me in spite of my missing arms, would cast me out.

I watched my Gods, and I could taste the bell rope between my teeth. Plastic and bracken and the sweat of the other Watchers, men and women with hands. My head jerked, acting out the signal even though I was shirking my duty. Two tolls, then three, repeating: the signal that said *They are here, Their formation indicates They mean us no harm, but no boats may be boarded.* My neck ached. My jaw burned. And my face went red and hot, because I wasn't in the tower, because I was skulking from the town like an outcast unbeliever. I watched the Gods, the beauty of Them, Their black implacable bulk, the white patch above and behind the eyes, and my whole body tingled with joy. And with shame.

The bell would sound. It had to. The village would come awake. Fishermen would scrape away ice and mutter prayers, and fling offerings to the Gods. Fires would be kindled, voices and laughter unleashed. This was a day like any other.

Except . . . not.

Because Kelb had come to my cabin last night. Knocked at my window. Told me to meet him at sunrise outside of town. Told me he was going . . . somewhere.

I told him yes. Even though everyone knew there was no Somewhere. Nowhere left on land to go. No animals still living, no cities away from the water still inhabited, nothing but icy poisoned wind and scorched rock. I told him yes, even though I knew I risked losing everything. I told him yes because I could not tell him no, not ever, and that had been true when I was eight and he was ten, my maimed foster brother's only friend. I told him yes because everything Kelb did was rough, brutish, beautiful. Every morning I watched from the tower as he stumbled from his cabin, peeled off his shirt, scooped cold salt water over his black-furred torso. Kelb was oblivious to the cruelty of it, this display of fine muscled flesh and limber arms, oblivious to the hunger in my eyes, oblivious to me as anything other than the sad armless little sixteen-year-old sister of his dead best friend.

Our town looked so tiny, standing outside of it. I hurried, into the landscape of snow and sharp black rocks and bent sticks that people said had once been trees. I wanted to be out of earshot, so that if I didn't hear the bells it might have been because I was too far away. And not because my replacement had failed miserably, and my life was over. My stomach tightened with the same old empty lonely feeling that always followed the ecstasy of a visit from our Gods.

But this time the emptiness did not go as deep as it could have. Because strapped to my back, cold and sharp and heavy, was the cymbal of Summoning. Burdening me down and buoying me up. An egregious sin, and a source of salvation. I had taken it on mad reckless reasonless suicidal impulse, lifting it off the wall with one expert foot and placing it on the floor atop my torso wrap and lying on top of it and tying it tight with my feet, but feeling it there I was glad I had.

Over the hill, in a down-swoop of land that could have been the cresting of a wave, was Kelb. A dark blur at first, swelling into a man as I approached.

Squatting, his bare red hands assembling from snow something forbidden. Hearing me, not looking up.

"Stop that," I said. I kicked the little house apart and he laughed.

"Oh Adze. There's no ocean in sight. Your precious Gods can't see what we do."

"They see everything," I whispered. His blasphemy never failed to redden my cheeks with a mingling of fear and desire.

He hugged me hello, then stepped back. Put his hands on my shoulders, and then on my stumps. A gesture somewhere between brotherly and. . . not. And it occurred to me, for the first time, that maybe he *did* know how I felt about him. Maybe he counted on it.

"Eat," he said, pressing a square of bladderwrack jerky into my mouth.

Around his neck he wore a thick plait of braided seaweed, studded with shards of broken glass. Not the worn-down, safe, pretty sea-glass that most of us used as jewelry. This was jagged stuff, cruel and dangerous, salvaged from the factory wrecks to the south. Only thick, strong skin and superhuman confidence kept it from cutting him.

"If I ever needed any more proof that the Gods hate us, bladderwrack jerky would do the trick," he said.

"Shh," I said. "You shouldn't say things like that. Where are we going, anyway?

"To see someone," he said, stepping faster to keep pace with me. Armless as I was, no man had legs to match mine.

"No one lives on land," I said. "And anyway what do you need me for?"

"Does it ever get frustrating?" Kelb asked, after putting another square into my mouth. "Having to depend on other people?"

"What do you mean?"

"You know. No arms. Not being able to do anything for yourself."

I laughed. "No. That's what it means, to be part of a community."

"But they landlocked you. Stuck you in the tower—"

"They took me in," I said. "A crippled orphan—they gave me a place. A role. And I'm not stuck. I rotate shifts with three other women. And anyway they're considering me for the Priesthood."

Or they were. Before this.

"Pssh," he said, and I didn't know if he was scoffing at the idea that they'd ever extend such an honor to crippled unworthy me, or at the idea that any-one would want to be part of the Priesthood in the first place.

Of course he didn't understand. Kelb's weirdness was part of why I liked him so much. He thought like most of my neighbors think, only more so.

He was hungrier. His dad had been different too. The Gods killed him, for making a net. Nets are one of the many things men are not allowed to build. Cages are another. We still see birds, sometimes—scrawny, sickly things, flying lost from some faraway place where there still might be insects or seed-plants—but the last time someone succeeded in catching and caging one, the Gods destroyed her home before the day was done.

I was lucky, in a way. My maiming marked me as forever outside, locked me away from their greed and their blasphemy. I could not share their constant, crippling hunger for more.

"Who is this supposed someone we're going to see?" I asked, when the bladderwrack was done and Kelb seemed to have nothing else to say.

"A trader."

Two days before, out on the ocean, our fishing party met another village's. I had heard the Priesthood whispering about it. Different towns had different Priesthoods, different customs, and contact frequently spread crazy ideas. I wondered if this fictional trader was one of them.

"Look," he said, scooping up a fistful of snow. He held it out to me, palm up. Poked it with a finger of his other hand, showed me the scraps and flakes of colored plastic. One was larger than the others, showed what might have been a hand. "Snow is different on land. It keeps things."

"That's why we shouldn't be here," I said, giving his hand a swift kick to spill the snow back to the ground.

"I always forget what a devil you can be with those legs," he said.

We walked faster.

Travel over land wasn't explicitly forbidden, but the Gods frowned upon it. The inland cities were swallowed when the seas began to rise; all that was left was high frozen barren land poisoned by war and waste. The coastal cities still stood, huge buildings rising rusting from the sea, home to humans so barbaric the Gods would not allow them even the smallest of boats.

"I'm surprised you came," he said. "And happy. Always held out hope that Schoon's sister would have a little of his rebel spirit."

Schoon's rebel spirit got him killed, I did not say, because the name still hurt in my mouth.

We walked between high drifts of snow. We crossed smooth patches of ice, and treacherous stretches of sharp slippery stones. I shivered and prayed, thinking back to that last glimpse of my village. How the smoke rising from our homes looked thinner, flimsier, like our fires could not keep out the cold for long. The bunkers had been built back when men still thought they could outsmart the sea, find a safe place to carry on the sinful lives that had displeased the Gods so much that They made the sea swallow up all that we had. Those men never finished their safe place. They vanished like sand under the waves, fighting and clawing for the last little bit of land. Only a handful learned that the only way to survive was to make peace with the sea. And with the Gods. And that meant a Priesthood to learn what behavior angered Them, and keep each settlement in line. Because Gods never gave warnings. If we displeased Them, we died.

"Used to be the land was as rich as the sea," Kelb said, as we entered a wide snowless space, pointing out to the blasted ash-colored hills.

"That's what they say," I said.

"You don't believe it?"

I shrugged. "It's one of those things where even if it's true, there doesn't seem to be much point in mooning over it."

"Still. It's nice to think that once there was food other than fish and sea-weed. You know they used to call this place New Jersey."

Shushing his blasphemies got tiresome after a while, so I said nothing. But naming things implied ownership, conquest, and it made me shiver. He turned to take in the landscape, and for the first time I noticed the sealskin bag he carried on his back, so full it bulged.

"What's in there?" I asked.

"You might have been born out here," he said. "One of the land settle-ments."

"There's no such thing."

They say I was four when I came, the cauterization scars on my arm stumps still raw and weeping. I had no memory of my life before the village took me in, handed off from another people that met ours at sea, on the hunt—people with no fixed village, who traveled with the ice by canoe and slept in tem-porary homes. They hadn't spoken what we speak, but they offered goods to reward the family who took me in. My father was good-hearted and hungry, and had taken in Schoon the same way. He said I wasn't one of the people who had handed me off—the skin tone didn't match—and I wondered for the millionth time who my people were, whether they were holier than we, what they did with my arms when they chopped them off, how strict and wise their Priesthood, whether my deep love for the Gods and my lack of thing-hunger came from them.

"There's a man," Kelb said, yielding to the pressure of my resentful silence, "who lives out this way. He has something I want."

"What?"

Kelb kept walking.

"How does he live?" I asked. "On land. What does he eat?"

"People bring him food. They want what he has."

"Is it something forbidden?"

"Let's just say the Gods wouldn't like it."

A net, a cage, a metal blade? Kelb saw my face, and laughed. "Wake up, little sister. There are plenty of people who think like me. Who think the Gods are just a bunch of dumb animals, and that if we ever want to have a shot at a real life for our people, we have to get over this fear of Them."

I shut my eyes and prayed. I prayed that the Gods would forgive his blasphemy, and I prayed that he was wrong. I knew not everyone shared my reverence, but could people seriously think they could act in opposition to the will of the Gods? That kind of craziness could anger Them enough to wipe us all out.

I prayed for strength, too. Because somehow his blasphemy made him more beautiful, and echoed inside my head, seductively.

I should have cared more, about who this man was we were visiting and what he had. But I didn't. Because I didn't ever want us to get there.

We passed buildings, bare wood against the earth. Some in shambles, some still standing.

"Sorry you're too big for me to carry on my shoulders," he said, slowing down at my thousandth stumble.

"Like you were so good at it," I said. "You weren't that much older than me."

"True, true. If Schoon had lived—"

Kelb didn't finish the sentence. I didn't ask. I could imagine dozens of ways it could have ended, some wonderful. As long as he left it unfinished I could hope it would have been one of the wonderful ones. I was almost startled to see that some small part of me really believed we could be together. That he wanted me the way I wanted him.

Eventually we reached a wide flat swath of ice. Black and clear of snow. The going here was easier, although I could see Kelb was uncomfortable. His head darted around like a minnow, watching for cracks and soft spots and sudden eruptions of divine vengeance from beneath.

Sunset surprised me. Had we really been walking so long? We left the ice, crossed sand. I whispered the twilight prayer and let the dark come upon me, enter me, take away my sight, and return me to the primal union of all with all.

"I can't navigate without the sun," Kelb said. "We need to stop and get some sleep."

We found a cabin quickly enough, one of the empty and decrepit ones. The familiar freezing wind sliced through where a wall had been, but we had furs for warmth, and we were both exhausted.

But once we were laid out on the floor Kelb fell instantly asleep, and I found I could not follow. My mind swam dolphin-fast, circling truths I didn't want to arrive at. What he was—what he *really* was, this boy I loved, this strange and twisted man. What I was—the kind of person who would steal the cymbal of Summoning, the kind of person that saw Kelb for who he was and wanted him anyway.

Carrying that kind of hate inside, he would not last long. Nothing in his life could ever eclipse his anger at the Gods. Not love, not me, not ever. And still, I wanted him. Even though I knew he was doomed, knew he was out of balance with the world, still I hungered for him.

"Kelb," I whispered, wanting hands more than I had ever wanted them before. There was no end to the places I could have put them. People did so many things with their hands, to the people they desired. Instead I snuggled under his fur blanket, spooned my body in behind his. "Kelb," I said again, lips against his ear. He turned, awake and alert and erect. My beautiful, damned boy. He did not need me. How could he know need, with hands like that? They moved up and down me, insatiably hungry. He was separate, savage, alone. And as my mouth gnawed desperately at his chest and stomach, arms and hands, I saw, for the first time, how my own hunger exceeded his.

In the morning he kissed my forehead, helped me dress. Kelb showed none of the shame and contempt that I knew men often had, after showing someone such a secret part of themselves . . . but he still avoided eye contact, and said little.

"What's up with that?" he said, tapping the cymbal strapped to my back. "Gonna summon your Gods to come make everything better? Gonna hold an impromptu solstice ceremony?"

"Just felt like having it," I said. "You never know. Doesn't the sound of the cymbal cheer you up?"

"Risky business," he said, covering his goosepimpled torso with a shirt. "Get caught taking that out of the village and they'll kick you out for sure. Maybe offer you up to Them for good measure."

I tried to think of something to say that would be remotely true and at least a little funny, but since I still didn't know what my reasons were for bringing it I said nothing.

"Must be nice," he said, gruffly, but also tenderly, wincing as he shouldered his bag. "Not to ever have to carry things. Not to be burdened down."

"It is nice," I said. He waited for the follow-up, where I complained about how hard it was, but I had no complaints. Having hands made you put your faith and love in what you could hold to yourself and whisper *Mine*. And I was different. Or that's what I had been telling myself. Until last night. Until I saw how deep my own wanting went.

"What's in the bag?" I asked, mostly just to shake loose a train of thought that was taking me nowhere nice.

"Trade goods," he said. "He's not going to just *give* me what I want."

By the time we got to the cabin with smoke curling up from it, the sun was high above us. An old man sat outside, in a bright ridiculous purple plastic chair. The sea-scroungers sometimes came back to the village with that kind of plastic absurdity—long pink birds and green pigs and giant balls—but representations were forbidden and we'd shred them in the gear wheels and melt the flakes in a vat to make waterproof sheeting and crude work clothes.

"Greetings, travelers," he said.

"Are you Zimm?"

"I am," he said, and stood, and bowed. "And you must be Kelb. The one who frowns all the time, and wears glass shards like an idiot, and wants to kill the Gods."

Of course it was all bluff and bluster, standard man-talk to make himself seem strong. But how could such ugliness be mistaken for strength? The Gods swept fat seals and whole schools of fish into the reach of our hunters; They kept us safe from storms and kept our Shore clear of toxic animals. Perhaps I was spoiled, having been spared the society of men.

Zimm asked "You come to trade?"

"I do."

He ushered us in. The cabin was packed with hundreds of boxes, different sizes and shapes and colors. At a table, he set a small metal cylinder. Then he stabbed at it with a queer sort of knife, until the top lay raggedly open. A sweet, funny smell filled the room.

"Corn," he said, tilting the top to show us. Small triangles, the brightest shade of yellow I had ever seen. Bright like the sun was supposed to be, behind the toxic forever-clouds.

"Cans," Kelb said, picking up a cylinder from the stack. "I've never seen them like this."

I marveled at it too. The rusted husks of cans were everywhere; I had never imagined them in any other state.

"I've got a lot of things you've never seen before."

The man made me nervous. He ate in front of us, right from the can. Gave me a spoonful; smiled lewdly as he slid it into my mouth; enjoyed the squirmy look on my face as I bit down on the bright yellow wrong-tasting triangles. They were crunchy like kelp polyps, but the sea-taste that made food *food* was missing.

"Girl doesn't have a name?" he asked.

Something protective flexed in Kelb. He tightened, the way a man in a canoe might when a meat-whale breached.

"I'm Adze," I said.

"You two brother and sister?"

"No," Kelb said curtly, but said no more. He leaned slightly across the table, and his face was stormy and I loved him so much my body hurt. Zimm shrugged, and we kept eating.

Squares of thin fabric hung on his walls, covered in lines and colors. Kelb saw it, and stood. "Is that . . . it?"

"That's it," the man said. "What you heard about. Why you came."

"What's *it*?" I asked.

"Paper," Kelb said, and stood. "Can I touch it?"

"Touch away."

"*That's* paper?" I asked.

It looked so flimsy, so harmless. I had imagined some drug or weapon, some magic tool of long-dead gods.

What I knew about paper: that the old world had run on it, that it had helped men make the planet a living hell and finally destroy it. That people clung to it, even after everything. Carried pieces of it with them; wept over it, drew strength from it. With paper, somehow, men could make things even the Gods feared. And only the settlements whose Priesthoods banned paper altogether survived.

But this—this stuff could not have kept my nose warm. How could it harm a God, or destroy a planet?

"So what are you looking for?" Zimm said. "Books? Photographs? Words? Pictures?"

"I want something that will prove what I already know. That the Gods are nothing but animals. No different from anything else in the sea."

"You're an idiot," I whispered, but he was too focused on Zimm's smiling nodding head.

From one of his hundreds of boxes, the old man pulled a small square. When he set it down on the table, I saw that the square was made of many many pieces of paper, stacked together. "Something like this?" he said, and handed one piece to Kelb.

This was a smile I had never seen before. The smile I knew lurked somewhere inside of my scowling handsome friend. The one I dreamed that someday I would lure to the surface. A smile of pure and mighty happiness. I shivered inside, seeing it now. Maybe paper *was* magic. How else could something sit in a box for ages, yet emerge and make men feel things?

"Is this what I think it is?"

Zimm nodded. "The Gods, as our prisoners."

Kelb held it up for me. The square showed a God. But wrong, somehow. Flat and tiny, as though seen from far away. Captured. Caught inside this fearsome paper stuff.

"Orca," Zimm said, tracing his finger along four strange symbols in a corner. An old name for the Gods, one that made me quiver with the intimacy it implied. The hubris, to limit them to one word.

In the paper, a God leapt from water bluer than any sea or sky had ever been. It leapt through a giant circle, held by two humans. More humans surrounded it, seated in high chairs. They looked down on it. They smiled. They cheered. It belonged to them; their pet, like the seal pups we sometimes raised when the weather was good and the sea was bountiful.

"No," I said, sick to my stomach, turning away.

"Get enough of these and it'll be easy to get the whole village on your side," Zimm told Kelb, handing him more. "I even got some that show Gods getting killed, cut up, tortured, you name it. Show these around and everybody will start sharpening their spears."

Kelb turned from paper to paper. I shut my eyes, to hide from what his face was doing.

Eventually, abruptly, Zimm snatched the stack of papers back. Looked at Kelb, then at me. His eyes hurt like harpoons must hurt. "What have you got for it?"

Kelb said nothing. Looked at the floor. Looked at his hands. And in his silence, I knew. Finally. Why I was there. Why he had asked me.

"I'll give you all the pictures you want," Zimm said. "For her."

He didn't flinch. The proposition didn't shock him. It had been his plan all along.

"Kelb," I said, or tried to say, but fear had left my mouth waterless.

"You could have corn every day," Zimm said, reaching out to touch me. I kicked his leg, hard. He cried out in pain, then laughed. Not pleasantly. Took a step closer.

"Stop," Kelb said, and unbuckled his sack, dumped its contents on the table. Seal meat, cured and smoked. Dried fish. An unspeakable sum. More than Kelb could ever have stockpiled. Some of it had to be stolen. That much meat meant people would starve.

"I get that much food for the spoonful of corn I fed her," Zimm said. "Richer settlements to the North pay me plenty. I want her."

Kelb counted out three cards. "That much food for these," he said, his voice a child's. "Or no deal." He stood up straighter, made his face hard.

"Fine," Zimm said, making a great show of undisappointment. "Never was one for damaged goods anyway."

And then Kelb's hand on my shoulder, steering me towards the exit. "We're leaving."

The cold had never been so cold. My mouth hurt from the metal sweetness of the 'corn,' and from how hard I fought to keep from screaming obscenities at Kelb. The Shore glittered, at the bottom of a steep hill to our right. Black dots circled. I wondered if the Gods could see us from there; know who we were and where we lived and what we had done. What was in Kelb's heart.

"What changed your mind?" I asked, starting down the hill. "You brought me to sell to him. Didn't you?"

Kelb said nothing.

"Was it the sex? Would you have handed me over if last night hadn't happened?"

I kept my head down and blundered forward, into bitter wind. We reached the flat expanse of ice after an hour or many of walking.

"Adze," he said.

"No!" I called, stepping onto the ice.

"Adze," he said, and I ran. He followed, repeating my name with every breath. Finally I let him overtake me. His hands grasped my shoulders. His hands were so big, so strong. "I'm sorry," he said. "Okay. I'm sorry. I never—I didn't. . ."

"You're a liar," I said. I tried to wriggle free, but he would not let me. "You're insane. I was stupid not to see it. I saw you how I *wanted* to see you. How I *used* to see you, when you were the only one who would be nice to Schoon and me, because we were orphans, we were damaged."

Kelb pulled me tighter. He hugged me. He wept. He never wept when Schoon died. "I'm sorry," he said, over and over, until it wasn't about Zimm and his horrible paper or his plan to sell me anymore.

It would have been easy to kick him in the crotch or knees, incapacitate him, take the cards from his bag, chew them up and spit them out, flee back to the village. I told myself the reason I didn't was because I couldn't make it back alone, but I knew that was half the truth or less. The whole truth was that I still loved him, wanted him, couldn't bear the hurt of him hating me. And the whole truth was that we were the same.

The sweet kind child-Kelb was real, but so was the savage monster. Kelb was both. A gentle boy who loved me fiercely, and a wicked murderer who would sell me into slavery. An idealist who loved humanity and wanted us to be free of backwards superstition. . . who didn't care who died in the pursuit of his ideals.

Kelb was both, and so was I. A devout believer and a wicked sinner.

We were the same. We were animals who wished we were more than that. The gods were just animals.

I shook free of him. I shut my eyes. If he brought those cards back, he'd endanger everyone. "Go," I said, knowing what needed to be done to save my village, and wanting desperately not to know. "I'll catch up. I want some space."

He nodded, kissed my forehead, went. I squatted, and sat. We were out where the ice was thinnest, a skin of blue-green above unthinkable depths. I prayed, but felt nothing. I waited until he had gone too far to come back and stop me. With my teeth I tore off my sealskin boots, unwrapped my foot-wrappings. My toes deftly opened my jacket, burrowed deep to unwrap my torso. I shimmied until the cymbal came loose. I lifted it, flipped it over so the smooth bottom was flush with the ice. So the ice would act as an amplifier.

I lay on my back and rested my ankle on the cymbal. I lifted my leg and brought it down as hard as I could, striking the cymbal with a force no other human could match.

"Adze!" Kelb cried, stopped short by the hollow ring, which wobbled in the air but would sound clear as singing through the water under the ice.

I stood up. I lifted my leg to point accusingly in his direction. He ran towards me, towards land, but he was very far away from both.

I thought about shouting *I'm sorry*, but what was the point? What did it matter what I was?

A black shape passed beneath me, majestic and immense. I shut my eyes and kept my leg extended. I was not afraid. I was the bearer of the cymbal. They would trust me.

A crack split the air. A sharp black head broke the ice between us, then dove. The God spiraled her body beneath the water, shoving her tail out of the water and bringing it down hard against the broken edges of the ice. Cracks fanned out.

"Adze, please!" Kelb called. More loud cracks; the snouts of two more Gods shattering through the ice in front of me. I stood my ground, standing over my warm clothes, shivering.

He stopped running. He stared at me, close enough now that I could see the pain on his face. See the fear—and then, something worse than fear. Something he'd never felt before: belief. Final, fatal, too-late belief. *What cruelty,* I thought, *that he should find his in in the moment that I lose mine.*

Kelb sobbed, once, then turned and ran again.

He ran even though he knew it was folly, because it might buy him a few more minutes of life. A thousand times we had seen seals behave the same way, when the Gods separated them from their rookeries, trapped them out on the ice, and then tipped the ice to spill them into their mouths.

In a matter of moments he stood on a massive separate sheet. Raw ocean roiled all around him. I counted twenty fins, circling.

I expected Kelb to scream, kick, curse, fight. Die flailing at the Gods the way he had lived his whole life. But Kelb merely walked to the edge of the ice and knelt. His eyes shut. His lips moved. Praying or apologizing or promising. I wouldn't let myself look away. I watched them slap the water with their tails, in great synchronized sweeps, one after the other, until the churning water destabilized the ice and Kelb spilled into the sea. One came up from beneath him, held him in its jaws almost delicately. Kelb did not fight. He turned to look at me one last time, his mouth a sideways squiggle, either smile or frown, before the matriarch grabbed hold of the upper half of him and pulled.

Some villages believe that if a God drags you down, you become one of them. And maybe that's true for them. But for us, when they pull us under, we die.

The way back to land was long, and riddled with broken ice. If they wanted to kill me I was going to die.

I stood up, walked to the pink-frothing edge of the ice. I showed my puny armless self to the Gods. The matriarch rose and held position, exposing her entire gorgeous head. Blood still stained her teeth. If I had hands, I could have reached out and touched her.

For forty seconds, she stared at me. Her eye pierced through to what I had somehow failed to see before this day. She was an animal, and so was I. She was not a God, and I had not been chosen for divine protection. I wasn't better or purer or more full of faith than anyone else. I was a wicked, sinful creature, born out of balance and bound there, like all my accursed kind. Hungry even when full. Wanting, always. Defined by the wanting and damned by it. Inventing Gods to give meaning to our lives, and shape to our hungers, but they could not stop us from destroying everything, including ourselves, including them. My armlessness, my inability to ever hurt them, was the only reason to let me live.

She withdrew, then. Slid back through the ice. Cried out underwater to her brothers and sisters. I stood there, shivering and wet beneath a useless sun, and watched my Gods abandon me.

Gregory Norman Bossert started writing fiction in 2009 at the age of forty-seven and sold his first story to *Asimov's Science Fiction* magazine that same year. His short story "The Telling" won the 2013 World Fantasy Award, and "Bloom" was a finalist for the 2014 Theodore Sturgeon Memorial Award. He lives just over the Golden Gate Bridge from San Francisco and wrangles spaceships and superheroes for the legendary visual effects company Industrial Light & Magic, where his recent projects include *Rogue One: A Star Wars Story* and Steven Spielberg's upcoming adaptation of *Ready Player One*.

HIGHERWORKS

Gregory Norman Bossert

Dyer and The Wayward, slapping maps— Camden Lock Market—Friday Morning

Dyer shifts against the wall—the bricks are rough and still night-cool in the shade of the bridge, and her jacket is thin across the shoulders, lining long gone and the leather worn smooth by years of brick stone iron concrete carbon—and breaks down the approaching couple without quite making eye contact.

The Wayward has got an eye out for cops or worse, blathering in his terrible Bert-the-chimney-sweep cod Cockney, sounds stoned but his brain is just like that. "—ghosts, you know? The nano, sometimes it don't break down, it digs in, makes a nest in the parental lobe—"

"Parietal." Dyer says. The couple are a matched Saxon blond—expensive haircuts, and the girl's wearing Havilland genesplice chestnut wedges with live shoots trained around her calves, cost a thousand quid easy. Not cops, not dressed that way; more likely the sort that think that Drop parties damage property values, that nano should be reserved for medical and military purposes, that refugees belong safely sorted with their own kind in the camps in Dover. The sort to take a map now and call the cops later. But he has an active tat peeking out of the edge of his sleeve, and she's got corneal implants, so Dyer risks it.

"Opt-in," she says, quietly, and sees the guy's teeth flash. The girl taps the guy's thigh with one hand and reaches out with the other. Dyer slips a map from her jacket pocket, hits the girl's hand—more a handshake than a slap, oh so proper British—and meets the girl's gaze. Pixels swirl in her eyes, and recognition. "HigherWorks," the girl mouths, and swats the guy's leg again as they ramble on out into the sunlight by the canal.

Dyer blinks her own corneas full black. Fame is a fickle food, she thinks, and all the more so for USERs running illegal nano Drop parties. "Men eat of it and die," she says to the crows along the canal bank.

"Woah," The Wayward says. "Eat what now?"

Might be time to grow her hair out, or to go back to wearing masks at the Drops. But that never really works. The fans are too persistent, bless their stuttering over-stimmed hearts, and photos get out on the Drop forums:

SICK MINDS OF HIGHERWORKS UNMASKED AT LAST: DEE! DYER! THE WAYWARD! SHIMAGO! USERS OR HOME-GROWN?

DJ MRS. JOHN DEE AND NANOGODDESS HIGHER DYER SPOTTED DIGGING THROUGH THE BINS AT RESCYCLE. . . . WE GOT PHOTOS!

A SCANNER IN THE 'WORKS: LONDON'S OPT-IN CHOREOMANIA CULTURE NETWORKS NANOTECHNOLOGY TO BEND BRAINS.

That last in the damn *Guardian* with a damn gallery of drone footage. Might be time to move on, was the truth of it. Amsterdam again or Helsinki, anywhere the refugee policies are less tattered and the fear flows a little less deep. Leave London to groups with less to lose.

As if summoned by that thought, Kal flits in under the bridge, gossip queen of the refugee scene, latest conquest in tow. "All right D? All right, Way? Doing the do tonight, yeah? New show, new rocket? You guys know Leelee? Slap me a pair?" All in one breath without pause for answers.

"All right, Kal," Dyer says, slips her a couple of maps. Kal passes one to her companion, a willowwisp creature in frills and lace with improbable anime eyes that make Dyer think of zygomatic surgery and tabloid tales of "accidental ejection." Leelee spins the map in twig fingers, details on one side and actual map on the other, tests the stickum that holds the fold closed with a glittered slice of fingernail.

Kal pinches the map closed. "No, babe, don't open it. The pic inside is the neural cue, triggers the nano. Gotta wait wait wait for the party tonight, yeah? I'll just hold it for you 'til then. These guys gonna shake your tuchus, and Dyer here, what she do gonna shake your brain."

Leelee's eyes get perilously wider. Dyer squinches her own to narrow slits in sympathy.

Kal leans in to kiss the air over Dyer's cheek, drops the accent to say, "Hear about the two USERs pulled from the river last night? Crap beat out of them? That fascist turd Evan's saying 'send them back to the States, conscious or not.' Watch yourself today. Anti-migrant rally in Parliament Square. Lotta noobs in town; big group got through the Chunnel last night. Street's frigging *twitchy*, girl, like everyone's dusted, seeing things. People where they shouldn't be. Speaking of, some betty in a god-awful yellow hoodie been staring at you, up by the benches."

Then louder, "Can*not* wait for the Drop tonight. Whole bloody town needs some HigherWorks." She exits left, Leelee trailing behind to look back at Dyer, eyes bleached to porcelain in the sudden sun.

Dyer rubs her scalp, checks the benches with a sideways glance, catches a yellow-hooded head just turning away.

A gaggle of girls in shiny machine-worn leatherette stumble into the shade, all trying to read off the same phone. Too young, Dyer thinks, and too loud. She riffles the edges of the maps in her pocket. She's handed out a few dozen this morning. It'd be nice to get through the whole stack this morning, while folks still had time to plan their night.

"—no network nodes, no data stream, but the nano *wants* to connect, it needs the connection. How it's designed," The Wayward is saying. "So it starts connecting with anything, with all the wifi and broadband feeds and, dig this, with other ghost nano in other people's brains. Not like a Drop party, there's no beats, no video, no HigherWorks to ride the flow, keep everyone in sync, yeah? Just a jumble of flashbacks, visions, voices, thoughts, and then you drift untethered, like, you know, crowdsurfing, you go all *scattered*—"

"Doesn't work that way, Way," Dyers snaps: edgy because of Kal's news, edgy because it's a topic she doesn't want to touch in public, edgy because she doesn't like to lie. "Nano can't do anything without neural cues and network nodes, and anyway your body breaks it down in a couple hours. Ghost nano, it's urban legend. *Sub*urban legend, mallrat stuff."

She looks toward the girls in their glittery off-the-shelf counterculture. Behind them, by the bank of the canal, is a woman in Dyer's own black leather/skin/hair like a thunderhead bruised eyes just shadows in a sharp frag-ile face and Dyer's breath stops. If it's not lust—Dyer left that behind with the rest in the dry husk of California—it's something just as potent.

No yellow hoodie, though, which means someone *else* is watching her; the one thing Dyer didn't leave in the States was the thing she fled: the fear. Don't just run from, Dyer thinks, run to. She raises an eyebrow at the mystery woman, remembers that her eyes are full black, and leaves them that way. If a little anger creeps in between her brows, the corners of her mouth, well, that's just the flip side of the fear.

The woman lifts her chin just a fraction, nothing fragile in that motion, and Dyer feels a sudden dizzy doubling like she's been drawn out in overlapping circles, that Drop party buzz of anticipation, of connection.

The Wayward says, "Leave it, mate, she ain't interested. Um, innit?"

Dyer turns, ready to give Way a "shut up already" roll of her eyes, finds a face in the way—heavy jowled and swirled blue with faux prison tats. The guy blinks, does a cartoon double-take.

"Bugger me. Thought you was a bloke," he says.

"Nope and nope," Dyer says.

"Works for me," says the blue tats' companion, baring her luminescent teeth at Dyer over his shoulder.

"She ain't interested, whichever way you're rigged," Way says. "Are you, Dyer?"

Dyer gives him the "shut up already" look now, but it's too late.

"Dyer. You're HigherWorks," the teeth gasp—even her tongue glows white—and blue tats gets a look that says maybe he can overlook Dyer's not being a bloke after all.

"Opt-in tonight," Dyer says, and slaps a pair of maps into the hand that snakes around blue tats' waist, looking left to avoid eye contact, to find the woman by the canal. Nowhere she could have gone in that brief moment, but she's not there. Deleted, swiped away, and in her place are three men in bespoke suits, hands in pocket and practiced leers on their faces. Dyer's first thought is Immigration, but they've got Union Jack pins on their lapels—junior partners out of the City, most likely, looking to score points with management by pasting a couple of USERs to a pulp.

She reaches back to tap The Wayward, feels his dreads shift against her shoulder as he nods. "Two more, other side of the bridge," he says quietly.

Dyer shuts her eyes, inhales slowly. Blue tats' breath is stale beer and bad curry for breakfast, but he's over six feet of solid meat, and his glowstar companion is razor sharp and twitchy with stims, and they are both as London as the King's Own Cobblers. Dyer tucks her arm around them both—desperate measures for Dyer, touching, but she's thinking about bodies bleeding into the Thames—says, "Buy us a pint, then?"

2042-05-18T10:22:00+01:00 +51.541327-0.145319

- CONTACT: TARGET (UNCONFIRMED)—LEANNA VANCE—PRIORITY AA
  APH2035.Z980023—SCAN SUMMARY: FACE MATCH 47% SIG. DELTAS
  HAIR COLOR N.A. SHAVED—EYE COLOR N.A. CORNEAL IMPLANTS—

- GESTURE SCORE 62% SIG. DELTAS WEIGHT -12 KILOS HEIGHT +9CM POSSIBLE TIB/FEM BONE EXTENSION
- NOTE: ID SCORES LOW CONFIDENCE DUE CONTACT DISTANCE & CROWD COVER—SEE ATTACHED IMAGES
- ATTACHMENT: PERSONAL MESSAGE
- — CRAZY FLIGHT, EDGE OF SPACE, YO, JETLAGGED OUT OF MY GOURD—DAY *STARTED* WEIRD—SOME GUY COMES UP TO ME AT THE AIRPORT "HEY JOCELYN" KISSES ME STRAIGHT ON THE MOUTH—I'M LIKE "I DO *NOT* KNOW U SO F-OFF"—FEEL WACKED LIKE I'M COMING DOWN WITH SOMETHING SEEING GHOSTS OUT OF THE CORNER OF MY EYE—GOTTA BE A LOTTA GHOSTS HERE, YEAH? PLACE EVEN *SMELLS* OLD—NO FIBERBOARD NO BURNING TIRES NO PEPPERSPRAY
- — TOOK FOUR HOURS TO GET THROUGH CUSTOMS—NO ONE GOT THE F-ING MEMO ABOUT THE NEW IP TREATY GUESS THE BRITS ARE KEEPING IT SECRET CUZ EVERYONE HATES THE STATES HERE—AS IF WE CAN'T HATE EACH OTHER JUST FINE ON OUR OWN, THANKS—SOME GUY ON THE STREET CALLED ME A USER, LIKE HE CAN SEE TRACKS THROUGH MY HOODIE, TURNS OUT IT MEANS U.S. ECONOMIC REFUGEE—I'M LIKE "SCREW U" BUT I GUESS I FIT THE DESCRIPTION IF I WASN'T HERE ON UR DIME AND UR VISA
- — MIGHT ALL PAY OFF, THOUGH, CUZ THAT TIP SEEMS LEGIT—JUST BEEN HERE 12 HOURS AND I'VE ALREADY GOT A POSSIBLE HIT ON VANCE HER-SELF—GOT A FEW PHOTOS BUT I COULDN'T GET CLOSE AND THESE CON-TACT CAMS U GAVE ME ARE CRAP—UR FANCY SCAN APP SAYS AROUND 50% MATCH—SHE'S HAD SERIOUS BODY WORK AND SHE'S GOT THIS CRAY CRAY LOOKING SURFER DUDE WATCHING HER BACK AND SHE'S EDGY AS HELL SO DON'T START SPENDING THE MONEY YET—OH WAIT, I *HAVE*—I DON'T SCORE THAT BOUNTY I AM SO SO VERY DOOMED
- — KISSES—JO
- ATTACHMENT: IMAGES (7)—<CLICK TO VIEW>

Dyer and Mrs. John Dee, brooding nano—
Camden Catacombs—Friday Noon

"Mrs. John Dee, you said no self-respecting Londoner would be caught dead in Camden in the daylight," Dyer says. She's sitting on the microassembler in an attempt to block the bright, busy control panel from view.

Mrs. John Dee tugs a blue floral frock on over her head, sets her glasses on her nose, peers over them at the folks staggered about the catacomb chamber.

"Dyer, love, none of these people are self-respecting."

She sheds a heavy studded cuff, the last of her work uniform, and toes the box of leather, chrome, and vinyl under the workbench. As the only legal Brit in HigherWorks, she picks up spending money selling LPs to tourists who can't play them. The money's okay, and the contacts in the community of artists and musicians working the markets are better. The required punk attire—"the hoary old eighties," Mrs. John Dee calls it, "and heavy on the hoar"—is more suited to Dyer's taste, but Dyer's forged ID codes aren't up to the scrutiny required by the Economic Refugee act.

"And you said the catacombs are off limits due to the danger of flooding from the canal."

"A positive death trap," Mrs. John Dee agrees. "Which is why you had to pick three locks when we first moved in. No one dares come down here."

Paint-tagged kids chase each other with rattling spraycans. Students ring their teacher under the dim hanging bulbs, dutifully examining the rails set into the brick floor where horse carts once rolled. A family dozes on a blanket, surrounded by the remains of a picnic. And what looks for all the world like a tour group in bright Brazilian colors mills about under the vaulted galleries, kept away from the equipment by some hastily stacked boxes and Dyer's glare.

Mrs. John Dee points at the massive slab of brick and ironwork that supports the far side of the underground warehouse. "Look, that wall was blank when we got here. That's a sick canvas, would've been tagged top to bottom had this place been open."

They'd moved in three weeks ago, and the wall is already covered, a collage of overlapped graffiti, bills pasted up and torn down again, what looks like bird crap even though they're underground, a hanging pair of seriously soiled trousers that none of the group dared get near enough to take down. A little girl with perfect doll hair and knock-off Day-Glo Doc Martens is staring up at the wall. Dyer and Dee watch as she leans forward and carefully sticks her gum in one of the few remaining spots of bare brick.

Dyer sighs and shifts to cover a neon green popup on the panel. "Should have had my hips widened when I had my legs done," she says.

Mrs. John Dee scrubs her mohawk into its natural teal tangle, pulls her tablet out of her bag. "Bollocks. Your hips are the eighth architectural wonder. They just need some company. Budge up, love." She pulls herself up onto the microassembler next to Dyer, peeks under her arm at the control panel. "What are we hatching?" she asks.

"Soundsystem, all for you," Dyer says. "Bud interface, cochlear induction. Everything except the auditory cortex stuff. I ran that in with the visual batch."

Mrs. John Dee does a little shimmy on the microassembler hatch. "Breed, my lovelies, breeeeed," she says. And adds, as the little Day-Glo girl copies her move across the will-be dancefloor, "We're going to jail, aren't we?"

"No, you're going to jail," Dyer says. "If the police decide we're causing enough of a nuisance, they'll haul you up for some Section 63 nonsense. 'Repetitive beats.'"

"'Repetitive beats' my bucephalus bouncing bum," Mrs. John Dee says with another shimmy. "Did you even listen to the track I—"

"The Wayward, Shimago, me, we'll be put in the Dover Center to be beaten down for a year, deported back to the US and then things will really get bad. Worse, if the UK rejoins the IP treaty zone."

"Sorry, love, shouldn't laugh, I know. But really, what else can we do?" She waves at the crowd.

The students have filed out into the tunnels, and the Brazilians have expanded like vapor to fill the available space.

"Move on," Dyer says.

Mrs. John Dee frowns, prods her tablet with a tattered teal fingernail. "I'm not at all sure I like the idea of running, just because the bloody fascists have voted themselves in and our own dear fans are all too, um, fanatic."

"It's not running," Dyer says. She gestures at the billowing Brazilians. "It's just the flow. 'There is a tide in the affairs of blah blah.' You're a DJ, Dee, you know about the flow."

In the gaps between the Brazilians, she sees the shine of black leather under thunderhead hair, glittering coal-smoke eyes. Flashback to this morning's vision, the impossibly disappearing woman. Dyer's chest thrums.

She slips off the microassembler. "Be right back. If the panel beeps three times, hit the green button."

"Oh, ah, okay. Oh dear," Mrs. John Dee says behind her.

Dyer follows the leather gleam across the dancefloor, loses it in the gloom and bustle, reaches that graffitied far wall. No one is there, nothing like that fragile face, not in the crowd or under the vaults on either side. Like this morning at the canal, she's dissolved away.

"She show me the spot for my gum," the doll girl says in a stage whisper, blue eyes serious under straight-cut bangs, then she laughs and swirls back into the crowd.

Well, what were you expecting on a day turned weird and wired, Dyer thinks. "What else?" Dyer asks the wall.

The wall responds with a flicker: a scrap of smartpaper, smeared under sellotape and glitching all along the torn edge. Dyer tugs it from the brick, squints at the scrolling text. It's some sort of government document, a snarl of nested digital sigs and certs and then the title, PROVISIONAL AGREEMENT ON THE RENORMALIZATION OF INTELLECTUAL PROPERTY RIGHTS BETWEEN THE UNITED STATES OF AMERICA AND THE UNITED KINGDOM OF GRE—

Dyer tries to scroll up, searching for a date, but the paper glitches, resyncs on a list captioned PATENTS OF SPECIAL CONCERN, and there at the top is "A PROCESS FOR THE MUTUAL SELF-REPAIR OF NANOMECHANISMS" BY LEANNA VANCE and then it's her eyes glitching, flashes of memory in time to her pounding heart of those last worst days in the US, a sudden sinking nausea, a tinnitus squeal. The squeal stops, starts again, and Dyer realizes it's not in her head; it's coming from across the room. She pushes back through the Brazilians to find Mrs. John Dee, all five ferocious feet of her, restacking the box barricade around their workspace, pausing after every box to glare down the vaults.

Dyer sweeps up a box, lifts it over Mrs. John Dee's head to the top of the stack. "What happened?"

"Some bloody bint knocks the boxes over, 'oh, excuse me,' she says, and when I get up to sort it out she nips in to play with your panel there, face first and wide eyed."

"Contact cams," Dyer says, nausea returning.

"'That's a bit of none of your business,' I said, and she doesn't even blink. 'You deaf?' I ask, and give her a nudge in the kidneys, in case she really was."

Mrs. John Dee demonstrates with a vicious jab of her elbow.

Dyer steps back out of range. "So?"

"So since her hearing was apparently bollocksed, I figured I'd give it a tune up." She patted her tablet. "I was just setting up audio network tests. I figured if she was rigged for cams, she'd have bud implants as well. I boosted the volume to eleven."

"Ah," Dyer said. "That was feedback, then, that I heard. From forty feet away."

"Her head will be ringing for a fortnight. Ought to put a spanner in her party plans."

"You think she's a nano cook?"

"If she were a fan, or paparazzi, she'd have gone for our lovely visages, not the gear. She's a bizarro you from some rival Drop party crew."

Dyer's thinking of that fade-away face, those eyes. "She look like me? Only with hair?" She waves her fingers over her head like clouds drifting. "Did she, uh, fade?"

Mrs. John Dee shrugs. "She looked like a yellow hood-up hoodie. Not so much fading as slinking away in disgrace, tail between her legs. Lovely tail, though. All's well that ends well." Mrs. John Dee demonstrates with another shimmy.

Dyer makes a dubious "mmm." She fishes the scrap of smartpaper out of her back pocket, but it's gone completely glitched, just a scattering of pixel dust.

2042-05-18T12:09:00+01:00 +51.541709-0.147667

- CONTACT: TARGET (UNCONFIRMED)—LEANNA VANCE—PRIORITY AA APH2035.Z980023—SUPPORTING EVIDENCE IP VIOLATIONS SEE NOTE
- CONTACT: TARGET (CONFIRMED)—MARIAM EBADI UK7D1B4GU230011—PRIORITY NA RUMORED ASSOC. LEANNA VANCE C.F.—UK RESIDENT ID CONFIRMED VIA DIRECT SCAN EMBEDDED TAG
- NOTE: TARGET OPERATING ALPHET MODEL X50EU MICROASSEM-BLER RUNNING UNRELEASED OS—LICENSE MODULE DISABLED—SEE ATTACHED IMAGES
- NOTE: UNREGISTERED NNDA PROFILES IN VIOLATION OF 21USC2401—SEE ATTACHED IMAGES
- ATTACHMENT: PERSONAL MESSAGE
- GOT THE BITCH—YEAH YEAH NO PHYSICAL ID YET NO DOCUMENTED DISTRIBUTION BUT WHO ELSE IS GONNA BE RUNNING ALPHET.COM BETA CODE WITH CUSTOM MODULES? AND THE LICENSE MOD IS AXED SO THAT'S IP VIOLATION RIGHT THERE *AND* SHE'S COOKING DELIVERY AGENTS WITH UNREGISTERED PAYLOADS—DO ME A FAVOR AND SEE IF THERE'S A BRIT LAW ABOUT THAT SO I DON'T HAVE TO DEAL WITH THE TREATY B.S. AGAIN
- ALSO THIS EBADI BIMBO IS HACKING EARBUD IMPLANTS—*GOT* TO BE A BRIT LAW AGAINST THAT
- SEE *TOLD* U I WAS A GOOD INVESTMENT
- KISSES—JO
- ATTACHMENT: IMAGES (5)—<CLICK TO VIEW>

Dyer, Shimago, and Mrs. John Dee, rocket in pocket— Mornington Crescent—Friday Afternoon

Dyer levers the backpack over the exit turnstile at arm's length, ducks the bristling bouquet of carbonfiber antennae that spill from the top.

"Fragile," Shimago reminds her.

"So are my eyeballs," Dyer says.

Shimago doesn't have to lift his pack; the turnstile only comes up to his thighs. Mrs. John Dee drags her duffel thumping behind her.

"Why is the helium so heavy?" she grumbles. "Ought to just float along. Maybe if I let some out into the bag."

"No," Dyer and Shimago say in unison. "You just want to huff it and sing in a squirrel voice," Dyer adds.

"And then I shall just float along," Mrs. John Dee agrees happily.

"Anyway, that's the lightest bag," Dyer says.

"That's another thing," Mrs. John Dee says. "Why is the rocket so heavy?"

"It's not—"

"A rocket. Yes, love, but that's what I call it because the first one was such a lovely rockety shape."

"—Not heavy," Shimago continues. "Just big."

"Sixteen times the network bandwidth of the last one," Dyer says. "Twice as many nano dispersers."

"And your subsonic driver," Shimago says. "The entire carbon outer shell is the resonator. 120DbA at 20 Hertz."

"Ace. Teeth shall be rattled," Mrs. John Dee says, out of breath and a few steps behind. She's turning circles as she walks, duffel swinging.

"Wait 'til you see it flying, with the spotlights and the screens running," Dyer says. "It's perfect, looks just like the film. Only thing we couldn't find is a clean recording of the announcer. You'll have to record Shimago when we get back to the catacombs."

Shimago booms, "A new life awaits you in the off-world colonies. The chance to begin again in a golden land of opportunity and adventure."

Mrs. John Dee is still spinning. Dyer turns around. "Dee, what are you—"

"USER freak. Fuck off home."

Dyer turns back. Whoever's speaking is hidden behind Shimago's bulk. She leans left to see a dozen pimpled punklings in custom-printed carbon, active tats a riot of football logos and Union colors.

"Tha's right, you heard 'im, you yank sket," one of them said to Dyer.

Shimago sets a hand on the lead punkling's shoulder. "Balderdash, my lad. Do I look like a economic refugee, American or otherwise?" he says, in his best King's English.

Shimago looks like six-foot-four two hundred and fifty pounds of gear-pierced lcd-tattooed fully networked Tongan-Californian rugby-playing airship-piloting Drop-partying choreomaniac. His hyphens alone outweigh these punks, Dyer thinks and bares her teeth.

"Dunno, she fit though, innit?" one says, gaze dropping down under Dyer's.

"Issit?" the lead one says, squinting. Shimago shifts his grip to the kid's head, palms it like a ball and turns it upward.

"Since you seem so full of perceptions upon our character, perhaps you would like to present them to the authorities," Shimago says.

"Wha?"

"He taking you to the po-po," another explains.

"I'm just sayin' I'd mash that," the one staring at Dyer says.

Mrs. John Dee comes spinning past Dyer, takes the lead punkling out at the knees with the duffel; he dangles from Shimago's hand like a doll. The other punklings step back from the swinging bag. "You want a mashing?" she asks the starer. "You cheeky little muppet. The lot of you in our ends, up from, what, Surrey? Think you're hard because you spent the money Mummy gave you on tats you can turn off again before you get home? She's hard." That with a hand out toward Dyer. "She eats suburban white boys like you for breakfast."

"Not hungry," Dyer says. She steps up even with Dee. The starer only comes up to her chin; she looks straight over his head at the crowd pushing past in the too bright sunlight, all willfully or carelessly oblivious. But there's a knot of anxious faces across the street that have noob USER written all over them, pinned in place like the sun's a spotlight. Lucky the punklings hadn't run into them instead.

"What are you doing here?" Dyer wonders under her breath. She means the USERs, stumbling through London on this unsettled day of days, but the punklings react with shrugs and awkward shuffles. "Dunno," one says. "Heard this voice said check those three, they's yanks."

Shimago sets his captive punkling upright. "A case of mistaken identity," he says. "Easily corrected by a conversation with the police about anti-social behavior." Shimago gives the leader a gentle push, and the kid stumbles forward, trips over Dee's duffel again, bumps shoulders with the starer. It's not entirely a bluff; Dyer and Shimago's forged IDs will hold up to a quick fingerprint or retinal scan. But they're likely to fail the sort of full biometric series that Immigration runs, and it's been one of those days.

A too-long moment as the punkling weighs the cost of confrontation versus the loss of face. Finally he mutters "freak" and shuffles down the sidewalk without looking back; his mates straggle behind him. The starer stays a beat longer, finally makes eye contact. Dyer blinks her corneas clear, looks down at him until he blushes and turns away.

"A new life awaits us in a golden land of opportunity and adventure," Dyer says.

Shimago sighs, hefts his pack on his shoulder, heads off perpendicular to the punkling's retreat.

"Mrs. John Dee, you are yourself from the lovely green lawns of Surrey, are you not?" he asks.

"I was," she says. "But Mrs. John Dee is from here and now, Shimago."

The duffel nudges Dyer's leg. Mrs. John Dee is walking backward, head swinging like a radar dish. "Dee, what the hell are you looking for?"

"I don't know," Mrs. John Dee says. "Whatever you've been looking for since this morning. Which is, judging from the look on your face, a much bigger deal than some sixth form twits a-twitting."

"I don't know what . . ." Dyer almost says "you're talking about," but that's neither fair nor true. "What it is. Somebody following me. Somebodies. An IP bounty hunter. A parallel me from some other dimension. Maybe Way is right and it's ghost nano."

"Ghost nano is an urban legend," Shimago says.

Dyer growls, strides five steps to the next road crossing, stops cold. Mrs. John Dee bumps into her from behind. Shimago stops next to Dyer. His look of gentle concern grows less gentle as he looks up from her to the street.

On the far side of the crossing are two uniformed officers of the UK Immigration Service, conspicuously not cops courtesy of their berets and their semi-automatics. The two are staring straight at them through the stream of crossing pedestrians.

Mrs. John Dee wedges herself between Dyer and Shimago. "You're not seriously waiting for the walk light?" she says. Then she follows their gaze and adds, "Oh. Oh dear. But they can't stop us unless they have cause."

Shimago says, "Crossing against the light is cause."

"And not crossing is suspicious behavior," Dyer says.

As if summoned by her statement, the two UKIS officers step off the curb. Dyer fights the sudden urge to look over her shoulder; looking like she's going to run could escalate a bad situation into a fatal one.

And then she looks anyway, because she knows what she'll see: the fragile-faced woman, from the canal, from the catacomb wall, standing in carbon black relief against a white sunlit storefront. Not a woman, though, is it? Not a rival nano cook, not some patent-tracking bounty hunter in from the US. It's something else entirely, that outline drawn flat against the concrete like an opening, like a door. With no conscious decision Dyer takes Mrs. John Dee's hand, tugs her toward the figure even though it's already fading to a shimmering afterimage. There's a real door there, though, behind the figure's promise, and Dyer grabs the handle, looks back to see if Shimago is following.

The impossible shape is now standing in the crossing, still no more than a silhouette: the gleam of leather below and eyes above, and as the UKIS officers step up behind her the bright sudden slash of a smile.

And as she smiles there's a pop pop pop from overhead, loud enough to sting, smoke and a shower of glittering fragments. A beat of silence, then the crowd in the street rears up screaming and crashes down together like a wave. Another round of pops. Still on her feet, Dyer can see that it's the street surveillance drones blowing out, one by one, but for the folks on the ground it's cause for more panic. The UKIS officers struggle to keep their footing as they track Dyer through the scrum. One fails and takes the other down with him. The impossible woman's hair fades with the smoke; the gleam of her smile fragments like the falling debris.

Mrs. John Dee tugs Dyer's hand. She and Shimano are already through the door.

The shop is a maze of booths, one of the miniature markets that has spilled out from the fount of crass that is Camden. Dyer, Dee, and Shimago take turns leading each other, their packs bumping past jackets, studded belts, badge-bedecked bags, and the butt end of the twentieth century spelled out in T-shirts. A rear door leads to an alley that dead-ends in a covered court, another manufactured market. They take refuge in a coffee shop whose postered windows provide cover.

"No sign of them," Mrs. John Dee says, and smooths back down the corner of a peeled-up poster with slightly shaky fingers. "Bloody hell, Dyer, bloody hell. What has the world come to, we can't cross the damn street without being afraid?"

Shimago is back from the counter, steaming mugs in hand. "Ah, Mrs. John Dee, this—" he starts in his own gentle accent.

Dyer cuts in, still half-blind with afterimages, or maybe it's anger flooding up like the crowd's panic. "Mariam, damn it, this has always been our world, Jonah's and mine, afraid to cross the damn street. You're just coming to it, and you're just a tourist. We live here, our whole lives."

Shimago blinks at this use of real names, but sits and says nothing.

"Back in California, even before everything collapsed, even when Jonah and I worked at Alphet in the shiny heart of the goddamn shiny future, my own lab and a billion dollar budget, even then I was afraid to walk down the street alone."

Dyer is thumping the table; coffee splashes, scalds her fingertips.

"And then the Crash and it all fell down, lawyers picking over what's left and goddamn IP bounty hunters with a take-down notice in one hand and a taser in the other, people saying they were scared of losing everything, but they meant their 401k, their house, their car.

"The day of the Wall Street hack, police car following me fifteen blocks from the BART to my house even though there's fucking fascist militia burning houses right down the street, in Berkeley, for fuck sake, finally stops me fifty feet from my front door—for jay-walking is what they said, meaning I crossed the neighbor's driveway while being black, never mind I'm in a business suit and five hundred dollar shoes. Savings, house, car, those shoes, I was way past that. I was scared of losing my life. Every damn day.

"And now it's happening here in your face and yes, you're scared. You should be, with government caving in to the thugs and bigots. But you can always get on the train back to Surrey. We don't have that option. All we can do is move on."

Mrs. John Dee is pale, and the shaking has traveled up her arms to her shoulders. Shimago gives a small nod, blots up the spilled coffee with his napkin, and with that, Dyer's anger, which is never gone, loses its focus. She puts her hand on Dee's.

"The hell, Mariam, I know this is nothing you haven't heard from your own grandparents. Look, having left all that bullshit behind, having come here with nothing but myself and that self so changed I barely recognize it, I found refuge. I'm not talking about the EU and their half-ass US Economic Refugee act, I mean you, Mrs. John Dee, hottest damn DJ in London, you and Shimago and The Wayward."

Dyer snorts, rubs her scalp.

"If I could send my ghost back to appear to myself on the sidewalk that day, tell myself that I was going to end up cooking nano for some damn crazy underground psychedelic performance art rave heaven-help-me Drop party, and that, not developing corporate patents, was the way to the goddamn shiny future . . ."

Shimago holds up his mug. "HigherWorks," he says.

Mrs. John Dee and Dyer clink their cups against his. "HigherWorks."

Mrs. John Dee slurps her tea, sighs and shuts her eyes, opens them again, and says, "Dyer, love, sorry but I have to ask. How did you get away from the cops? On the sidewalk that day, I mean."

Now Dyer is getting the shakes, as the adrenaline drains. She sets her cup down before it splashes again. "I stood there, hands on hips, and said 'Seriously? One of the biggest days in American history, and you want to spend it hassling me?'"

Mrs. John Dee hugs her mug to her chest and says, "Bad. Ass."

Shimago nods again.

But Dyer shakes her head, thinking of that knot of noob USERs in the sunlight. "Lucky," she says.

2042-05-18T15:22:00+01:00 +51.535956-0.139593

- CONTACT: TARGET (UNCONFIRMED)—LEANNA VANCE—PRIORITY AA APH2035.Z980023—SUPPORTING EVIDENCE IP VIOLATIONS SEE NOTE
- CONTACT: TARGET (UNCONFIRMED)—JONAH PUPUNU—PRIORITY A APH2035.Z72105
- NOTE: EVIDENCE USE OF NANO AGENTS AGAINST UK GOV PROPERTY— SEE ATTACHED IMAGE ARCHIVE
- ATTACHMENT: PERSONAL MESSAGE
- — HOLY CRAP WAS ALPHET DEVELOPING SOME SORT OF ANTI-SECURITY NANO? MUST HAVE BEEN RIGHT? SOMEONE JUST BLEW OUT A COUPLE DOZEN SURVEILLANCE DRONES AND THOSE NAZI IMMIGRATION POLICE HAVE AN ALERT OUT FOR—DIG THIS—"WOMAN AFRICAN DESCENT SHAVED HEAD" AND "MAN PACIFIC ISLANDER UNUSUALLY LARGE"— *GOTTA* BE VANCE AND PUPUNU
- — THOSE SAME NAZI IMMIGRATION POLICE GRILLED ME FOR AN HOUR FOR TAKING PIX OF THE DRONES—SOME SORT OF MIGRANT RIOT THING GOING ON—PRETTY INTENSE—STILL, NO GUNS, NO GAS, NO BODIES HANGING FROM STREETLIGHTS, SO IT'S F-ING PARADISE, YEAH? WOULD BE, IF I COULD STAY HERE
- — KISSES—JO
- ATTACHMENT: IMAGES (22)—<CLICK TO VIEW>

(Dyer) and The Wayward, displacing— Camden Catacombs—Friday Afternoon

"—Ghosts, you know?" The Wayward says, sounds stoned because he is, during this quiet time with most of the setup done but the Drop still hours away.

Wants to connect, he hears Dyer say.

"Right? Me too," Way says, prodding his tablet. He's testing the camera grid, the web of stickum cams and microdrones that he uses to monitor the groove. The sights and sounds might be nano-created illusions inside the dancers' heads, but the way they move, their reaction to the stream and to each other, all that feeds back into the rhythm of The Wayward's images and Mrs. John Dee's beats, which stream back into the crowd until the whole system, sight and sound and moving bodies all strung together by Dyer's nano, drops into yet a higher sync.

"Higher and higher," Way says. And then, "Spooky," because the cameras are glitching, flashes of images from elsewhere, bits of broadcast—a listing overloaded boat, a red-faced crowd in Parliament Square—snips of skewed text, feeds from street drones, what looks like Shimago, Dee, and Dyer standing in a sea of crawling people; but that doesn't make sense because Dyer's here, somewhere. Saw her just now, Way thinks, or was that in the camera feed?

Over by the wall, he hears Dyer say.

"Right," Way says. "The spooky wall." Spooky in the way that wall had developed, like an photographic print, the image emerging point by point, line by line out of the blank brick, a series of random acts teasing pattern, purpose. He'd been taking snapshots of it over the last week, a time-lapse to work into the performance stream tonight, layered over the real wall. Layers of reality, that's the "Higher" in HigherWorks, Way thinks.

The wall is not quite ready, he hears Dyer say.

"Ready for her closeup," Way says. "Gotta get some closeup textures for the vid-ay-oh stream." He gets up and wobbles across the bricks to the far side of the warehouse. A flock of microdrones spiral over his head like an exclamation point. Even though it's underground, the warehouse has headroom; iron beams hold brick vaults forty feet overhead.

"Over my head," Way says, head tilted up to look up at the wall. A diagonal splash of paint and paper runs from the floor almost up to the ceiling. Last week Mrs. John Dee chased a spraycan-armed drone around the warehouse with a broom, the rest of them doubled over laughing, though Dyer pointed out it was hardly their place to complain: They didn't belong there either, no one did.

Every place belongs to no one, he hears Dyer say.

"Just movin' through," Way agrees. He takes a snapshot, a poster pasted over the uneven brick, realizes it's an ad for an anti-migrant protest, tears the poster down leaving a jagged edge that reads "migrant pro," and takes a photo of that instead.

"That's us, Dyer. Migrant pros," he says.

Refugee act, he hears Dyer say.

"Yeah, I mean refugees, but what did you say the other day? Everyone on the move is running from something and running to something. Just the flow, yeah? I ever play you The Wayward? The music, I mean. Harry Partch, he was a hobo. Like you, now I think of it. He had degrees, research grants, just like you, just like you he left it behind to ride the rails in the Depression. The first one, I mean, the black-and-white one. Left the mainstream behind after that, made his own musical instruments, his own scales, his own kind of performances. Just like us."

Way scoops a glittery blob of something off the brick, looks for a spot, finally peels up a sticker and re-sticks it a foot higher, smears the blob in its place.

"Anyway, seemed like a good name to take on, yeah? Way-ward, like where I'm headed is the way itself."

That thought makes him want to take another hit, but he doesn't know where the spliff has gone, can't actually remember rolling one, but man, he's rolling on something. He reaches up on tiptoes to peel away the bottom half of another poster.

"He was from Oakland like you, too, Dyer. Harry Partch was. But he grew up down near me in LA. Man, I miss that place sometimes. Not the bits where I was sleeping on the beach and eating out of, well, you know. But, hey, all this . . ."

Way waves vaguely at the wall, squints, pulls a piece of gum from down around his knees and sticks it at eye level.

"I mean HigherWorks, you guys, like you always say, worth running to, even if I started with the running from."

The future is displacement, he hears Dyer say.

"Right on. HigherWorks, displacing the future." Which doesn't sound quite right. He pulls a stickum camera out of his pocket, flies it across the surface of the wall, saying "displace, displace, displace," but the word doesn't sound any more right with repetition. He lands the camera on a brick, just a few feet above the floor and pointing down. "Dis place," he says. "Hey, Dyer, get it?"

But Dyer isn't here at all, she's over there, coming in from the tunnels with Shimago and Mrs. John Dee, lugging what has got to be Shimago's new rocket.

"Huh," The Wayward says.

"Hey, Way," Dyer says. "Everything ready?"

He looks up at the wall. "Yeah," he says.

2042-05-18T16:29:00+01:00 +51.541709-0.147667
- CONTACT: TARGET (UNCONFIRMED)—LEANNA VANCE—PRIORITY AA APH2035.Z980023—SUPPORTING EVIDENCE IP VIOLATIONS SEE NOTE
- NOTE: EVIDENCE INTENT TO DISTRIBUTE UNLICENSED NNDA SEE ATTACHED IMAGE ARCHIVE
- ATTACHMENT: PERSONAL MESSAGE—I KNOW U R THINKING I'M GONNA BE WORKING OFF YOUR LOAN FOREVER BUT THINK AGAIN, LOOKS LIKE I'LL WRAP THIS UP MY FIRST DAY—THIS HIGHERWORKS GROUP WITH VANCE AND PUPUNU PLANNING SOME SORT OF RAVE TONIGHT—I GOT A PIC OF THE FLYER IT HAS A MAP WITH AN X-MARKS-THE-SPOT— APPARENTLY THEY LITERALLY *SPRAY* THE NANO OVER THE AUDI- ENCE—ALL I GOTTA DO IS SHOW UP WITH A SCANNER AND A CAMERA AND A PAIR OF CUFFS
— KISSES—JO
- ATTACHMENT: IMAGE (1)—<CLICK TO VIEW>

Dyer, cueing—Camden Catacombs—Friday Evening

Dyer tucks up her knees as The Wayward and Mrs. John Dee shove the last couple of cardboard boxes into place. She's under the plastic folding table they use as a workbench, with the brick of the catacomb wall behind her, the hum- ming microassembler to the right, and the boxes sealing off the other two sides. It doesn't actually have to be dark and quiet for neural cue test, but it makes the measurements more accurate. Anyway, it's part of the HigherWorks ritual, and not just for her; when Dyer emerges from her cave and declares the readings auspicious, that's the cue for the entire group that the Drop is on.

She tugs the sensor band snug across her temples, pairs it with her tablet, starts up the diagnostic logging: temporal, frontal, occipital, parietal activ- ity—thinking about The Wayward's "parental nest"—blinks her corneas clear so the infrared camera in the tablet can track eye movement, pupil dilation. Ear buds on, Dee's test mix streaming, network up. Dyer swipes the screen off, sits in the dark for a minute. Clear my head, she thinks, but she's still seeing afterimages, black on black, shadowed eyes and thundercloud hair. Her impossible woman.

Dyer sighs, finds the business end of the inhaler. The nano swirls into her lungs, the smell of apple blossoms and a tart bubbly sensation like champagne. And then . . . nothing. Which is the first test passed; if the nano triggers without the cue, then it's not an opt-in, and suddenly HigherWorks goes from a concern for Immigration and the IP lawyers to one for Narcotics or, a very worst case, the anti-terrorist nutjobs.

She fishes a map from her pocket, finds the sealed edge with her thumb, and pulls it open. There's a spark as the ink reacts and then the image inside shimmers to life.

This is the first time she's actually seen the cue as an image; up until this moment it's just been data. For the last couple of years they've been getting the cues from a friend of The Wayward up in Kingsbury, an ancient Irish curmudgeon of a painter who comes to the parties even though he's the one person in the world for whom the nano won't trigger; there's a window of just a few hours as the nano settles into the brain for the cue to come. Window window window, Dyer thinks as the nano wakes up. The cue is suddenly a window, the printed image a world seen through it: two characters on a high domed roof, looking out over the streets of a city sketched in strokes and squares—could be London but strange shapes hang in the air above—and behind the two watchers a raven watches them like memory memory memory as the audio kicks in, layered all down the auditory path from her implanted buds to her cochlear nerves to her auditory cortex, an ocean of sound swept by deep currents.

The image flickers and fades as the inks burn out, but streaks of blue and silver ghost ghost ghost across her vision like echoes. During the gig tonight The Wayward will be nudging those echoes via the network, riffing on the images like visual jazz, tracking Dee's beats, the two of them playing off each other, playing the crowd-become-one like sex like the crowd in the crossing when the cameras blew, made one motion motion motion by a hypersensitivity that transcends identity triggered not by lust or fear but by design by a higher working working working. Which is the second test passed; the nano is certainly working.

Dyer taps the tablet on, swipes the network off, colors fading as the screenlight fills her little box nest under the table. She scrolls through the data, diagnostic software already parsing the logs into graphs points spreading across the screen and into the air around her like stars falling like light on water like what had The Wayward said this morning you go all scattered scattered scattered.

Dyer shuts her eyes. Shhhh, the test is over, the network's down, she thinks. Go to sleep, little nano.

"Scattered," a voice ghost-whispers in her ear. "Awake."

"I am awake," Dyer says, shivers all down her back. She keeps her eyes shut, not sure that she wants to see that sharp fragile face and those shadowed eyes this close, this intimate.

"No."

"'No' not me, or 'no' not awake?" Dyer asks. And then, "You know what? Just bugger off. I've got stuff to do. Anyway, you're just urban legend."

From the ocean of sound come sudden shifting layers of voices, "Urban defined not by geography demographics or culture but by a certain threshold of connectivity, legend not as fabricated history but as fabricated comma history as the key to a map."

The voices all sync up on that last sharp word, and then complete silence, but with that hypersensitivity from the nano/lust/fear Dyer can feel that impossible face just a finger's width from hers.

"What do you want?" Dyer asks.

Silence, but a flickering, or the memory of a flickering, glitching pixels and the words mutual self-repair.

"I left Leanna Vance behind, halfway around the world and a decade gone," Dyer snarls. "What do you want from me?" She opens her eyes, but it's dark; the tablet screen's gone to sleep again.

Her own voice says, "We live here, our whole lives."

The feeling of lips on hers, the scent of bougainvillea and circuits burning, the taste of champagne.

2042-05-18T18:33:22+01:00 +51.541522-0.147123

- CONTACT: TARGET (UNCONFIRMED)—LEANNA VANCE—PRIORITY AA APH2035.Z980023—ONGOING
- ATTACHMENT: PERSONAL MESSAGE—I GOT A LEAD ON AN AMERICAN EXPAT SUPPOSED TO HAVE THE SCOOP ON THE "USER" COMMUNITY— BETTER START PICKING OUT SOME NEW BOUNTIES FOR ME
- — AND WHILE YOU'RE AT IT GET MY VISA EXTENDED—I'M BEGINNING TO DIG THIS OLD SMELL THESE OLD GHOSTS—GOT NO IMMEDIATE PLANS FOR GOING BACK TO THE STATES—YEAH YEAH I CAN HEAR YOU GRUMBLING FROM HERE BUT I AM WORTH IT—I AM A BOUNTY COLLECTING *NINJA*— AND THE PROOF IS VANCE IS GOING DOWN DOWN DOWN TONIGHT
- — KISSES—JO

Dyer and Shimago, queuing—Stables Market—Friday Evening

Dyer is in line at the kebab stand for Mrs. John Dee's shawarma, and some-one is too close behind her: a caress of convection currents, a static tickle.

Shimago back with the curry, Dyer thinks. Blue Tats and Glowstar Girl from this morning, ready for another pint. The staring pimple-faced pun-kling still hot to mash it. A yellow-hoodied bounty hunter with a take-down notice ready to tag and drag her back to California. Anyone, Dyer thinks as she turns, please, anyone but the shadowed thundercloud shape that is, nano or not, the ghost of Leanna Vance.

It's Kal's friend, xe of the twig fingers and anime eyes.

Dyer says, "Leelee, yeah? All right?"

But those fingers are shaking, those eyes even wider than Dyer remem-bered. Leelee gulps a breath, another, manages to gasp, "Kal."

"Ah, damn it," Dyer says. "UKIS?"

Leelee's confused alarm is baffling until Dyer realizes xe might not be a USER.

"The Immigration Services?" Dyer says, miming a beret.

Leelee shakes xyr head, mimes a hood instead. "A yank," xe says, "Some hard sket with a taser," in a lilting East End Jamaican accent. "Hard as can be in a yellow hoodie, which ain't. Kal say 'go tell Dyer' so I go. Went down there," xe points at the floor—the catacombs run under the market—then points up, "but they say you up here."

"Shit," Dyer says. "Where are they? Kal and the hoodie woman? We'll grab Shimago and go find them."

"Allow that," Leelee says. "Kal take care of herself. She tell me to tell you this yank asking about HigherWorks, asking about Dyer. Sounds like the sket bringin' a beef your way. I run here to warn you. Manz didn't build this body for running, innit?" Xe shakes xyr head, tugs the lace around xyr sleeves straight.

"Someone bringing a beef to HigherWorks?" Shimago asks, walking up with take-away bags in each hand. "Let them. They will discover that we are . . ." He swings the bags like nunchacku, leans in for effect: ". . . vegetarian."

Leelee blinks, a remarkable effect with those huge eyes, swings a long tapered thumb at the kebab stand. "Got some bad news den about the sha-warma, arms."

"The shawarma is for Mrs. John Dee, and she is, as she reminded me this afternoon, from London."

"Safe," Leelee says, satisfied, and starts in on the frills around her collar.

"You're sure Kal doesn't need help with this woman with the taser?" Dyer asks. "The street's crazy today, with the anti-migrant rally, those USERs pulled out of the river, and that's just the start of the weird."

"Kal bare fine, just getting the tourist lost round the wrong ends so I could find you. Won't take long, with the sket limpin' like that."

"This American has a limp?" Shimago asks.

"Does now, innit?" Leelee says, pulls up xyr long frilly skirts to show the wicked points of xyr Mary Janes.

"Admirable," Shimago says. "Dyer, the problems of the day are now behind you and surely moving too slow to catch you up, thanks to . . ."

"Leelee, Shimago," Dyer says, and pays for the shawarma. "That only works if I'm moving at all, and all day I've felt like I'm suspended."

"Girl, way Kal tells it, your mind running, all the time."

"This is true," Shimago says.

"Straight out of my head," Dyer says. "Which is the point, actually. Shimago, that ghost nano thing . . ."

"Ghost nano is—"

"Real," Dyer says. "Meaning nanites that don't decay, that self-repair, that can connect between brains without a network node."

Shimago frowns dubiously. "Dyer, even Alphet couldn't—"

"They did. I did. That's what my lab was doing, that was the project I couldn't talk about. Military contracts, whole squads linked empathically, using each other's eyes, ears, brains. Then the Crash happened and, Jesus, I've never told anyone this, the truth is, even though we were running from everything we'd known, part of me was glad that project went down with everything else. But now I'm not sure, now I think maybe something leaked out, and it's looking for me."

In the patient tone he reserves for The Wayward's most unlikely theories, Shimago says, "Persistent or not, I find it unlikely that nano could create a complex enough network for consciousness to emerge."

"I'm not talking AI, I'm talking about a pathway for consciousness to travel. Mental migrants." Dyer's accent was slipping. She looked around at the crowd in the market, London in its motley, two thousand years of migration, Camden in its shoddy sham glam even more of a refuge because no one pretended to be who they seemed.

"Literally out of your head, in a strange body?" Shimago asks.

"Don't knock it 'til you try it, arms," Leelee replies.

2042-05-18T19:31:53+01:00 +51.539044-0.135225

- CONTACT: TARGET (UNCONFIRMED)—LEANNA VANCE—PRIORITY AA
  APH2035.Z980023—ONGOING
- ATTACHMENT: PERSONAL MESSAGE
- WE GOT ANY DIRT ON AN AMERICAN IN LONDON GOING BY "KAL"?
  THAT'S THE EXPAT I MENTIONED BEFORE—PIX ATTACHED BUT IT WAS
  DARK—SHE AND HER BITCH OF A WHATEVERFRIEND JUST GOT IN MY
  FACE BIG-TIME—F-ING TYPICAL—*SHE* COMES HERE FROM THE STATES
  BUT HERE I AM JUST TRYING TO GET A F-ING HANDHOLD SO I CAN STAY
  AND SHE "DON'T LIKE MY ATTITUDE"—I'LL SHOW HER ATTITUDE I'M
  BRINGING THE TASER TONIGHT DON'T CARE IF THE TREATY ALLOWS IT
  OR NOT I'M DONE FOOLING AROUND
- KISSES—JO
- ATTACHMENT: IMAGES (3)—<CLICK TO OPEN>

Dyer, Shimago, The Wayward, and Mrs. John Dee, the Drop—Camden Catacombs—Friday Night

Dyer knows the Drop is coming but that makes no difference. A skittering cicada orchestra over the drums cut by a crackle like a chord unplugged, jagged blue lines like the afterimage of lightning, and there they hang in darkness, silence: four hundred indrawn breaths, four hundred hearts hitting the beat together. Dyer watches Mrs. John Dee and The Wayward watch each other in the glow of their tablets, pushing the break as long as they can. With the heightened sensitivity of the nano sync Dyer can hear all four hundred heartbeats count it out, can feel the muscles burning to take a breath, can smell the sync start to fray and curl at the edges—circuits burning, Dyer remembers—and just as their suspended state teeters on the edge of impossibility, she sees the upbeat like a spark between Dee and Way and then the Drop like the thunder arriving: crashing drums, shimmering gamelan gongs, a thick golden glow like a flood of honey, four hundred breaths released, and through it all the bass a presence as physical as the brick and iron of the catacombs, as the bodies of the dancers.

Shimago has his blimp on a slow loop, real spotlights roving through The Wayward's illusory glow, which has drifted a neon red broken by slashes like kanji. Dyer sees the bandwidth bump on her monitors as he releases another batch of nano from the blimp's dispensers.

Dyer's own work is mostly done by the time the dancing starts. She keeps an eye on the network, makes sure the biometrics feedback gets to

Dee and Way, checks in with the security crew, makes sure no one hacks the donation points; they lost an entire evening's take that way in Amsterdam.

But now, right now, HigherWorks drops into the flow, and Dyer dives in after it, ecstatic.

The Wayward has lowered his microdrones into the crowd, is layering their video streams into the flow—surveillance drones popping, Dyer remembers—the sensation of being everywhere in the crowd at once: her own face in the distance, Shimago and Dee side by side underlit by tablet light, a view over her own shoulder, but echoed—Way is delaying the stream by one two three beats, the crowd tripled by ghosts of itself—the blimp drifting life-sized in closeup, the dancers below like a cityscape of rooftop eyes and antennae arms, Leelee's unmistakable eyes, Dyer herself again dancing head high eyes blinked black to match skin and leather, and there in the feed behind Dyer is a woman in a yellow hoodie pulled low a carbon gleam in each hand and behind her is a shape all in black like a hole in the dancers hair flown out like a storm coming.

Dyer turns—and turns again in the flow and again and again—but the yellow hoodie and her impossible woman are gone, a trick of The Wayward's echoing video stream. That feed is already shifting, a strobe staccato of images off the news, protestors packed like dancers, coiled razorwire, a line of walkers in an infinite tunnel. Mrs. John Dee layers in a beat sped to seizure pitch, a sticky sucking backward bass. Dyer can feel another Drop coming.

She looks back through swaying silhouettes at Way, Dee, Shimago sitting almost perfectly still at the heart of the flow. But that flow is pulling her the other way, under the blimp striding over the crowd on spotlight legs—the scent of apple blossoms, Dyer remembers—through a swirl of shimmying Brazilians, past Kal and Leelee spinning tidally locked face to face, eyes to eyes, by a bioluminescent blur in Day-Glo Doc Martens, into a clumped conversation in a chorus of accents, and out—

The flow is still rising, but there's no way forward. Dyer's hit the far wall.

It's dark there at the edge and the HigherWorks stream is a migraine aurora of color, an earthquake rumble. Dyer feels her way along the wall: brick stone iron concrete peeled paper gluey tape slick paint—a sick canvas, Dyer remembers, and knows where she is now—a little lump of gum on the wall the sense of something too close to her head and as she ducks the dry fragile feel of carbon against her palm.

The break hits. Four hundred bodies stop in sync. Darkness, silence.

It's one of The Wayward's stickum cameras under her fingers, stuck low and facing down toward the floor, lit by a flat white light from over her head.

"Leanna Vance," a voice says from behind that light.

Dyer says, "Leanna Vance is a ghost." She turns, slides herself up against the wall. The woman in the yellow hoodie is standing there, hood up but close enough that Dyer can see the twitchy highlights of her eyes, smell her scent—bougainvillea, Dyer remembers. The woman has a tablet in one hand, taser in the other. The taser has an attached camera, and that camera has a light, and that light stays aimed at Dyer's face.

"Leanna Vance," the woman insists. There's no mistaking the American accent in those long nasal vowels as she reads from her tablet. "As a licensed agent of Alphet Corporation and its court appointed overseers, I am ordering you to cease and desist, and arresting you for the theft and distribution of the intellectual property of Alphet et al, as registered in complaint Z980023. I am legally bound to warn you that under provisional treaty agreed one five twenty forty-two between the US and UK, I am allowed any means necessary to secure and deliver you into custody up to and including nonlethal force. That means you try anything, bitch, and I will take you down and drag you to the US embassy. This has been one messed up day, and all I want is my money and some place to sleep for a week."

Dyer still has a few maps in her jacket. She thinks for a second of pulling one out and open, of the neural cue flaring in the hoodie woman's face, of the hoodie woman falling through that window into the Drop, of grabbing the taser, of running. But that would be running from everything she's made with HigherWorks.

"Opt-in," Dyer says, instead, and raises her hands.

In the flow around her, she feels four hundred hearts hit the upbeat.

On the far side of the room, oblivious, The Wayward, Shimago, Mrs. John Dee tap in perfect sync.

The downbeat drops.

A flare as all the blimp's lights come on, a virtual image of lone floating eyes opening, a blare of sampled horns, a shockwave of bass.

Dyer sees the woman in the hoodie flinch, knows what's coming in the split second before she feels the taser darts hit her cheek, her throat. The discharge itself is lost beneath an impossible pain at the base of her skull. Her head snaps back, hits the wall, and then she's falling for what seems like a long time.

She lands on her back, legs folded under her, hits her head again against the floor. The bricks feel rough and cool through her jacket. She's wedged against the wall, looking up.

From this extreme angle all the graffiti posters' paint comes together into a perfect anamorphic image: this paint stroke a lip, that shredded paper an eyelash, those overlapped flyers the shadow of a cheek. That sick canvas of the wall, that seemingly random accretion of junk: from Dyer's collapsed perspective it is revealed as the image of a face.

The face of her impossible woman. Of the ghost nano. Of Leanna Vance.

The image, the face she sees now, is a neural cue.

She feels the new nano trigger, a giddy rush outward, a new layer of input, a new level of sensitivity on top of the HigherWorks stream. The feel of that rush, the taste of it, is familiar, like her own nano strains grown strange and wild. Feral, Dyer thinks.

"Feral. Lost in the wilderness," a voice says inside her head.

"These are your strains, your works, from the lab at Alphet. With limited tools and knowledge, the changes we have been able to make to the nano are small and slow," another internal voice says.

And another adds, "Evolution, you could say, rather than intelligent design."

"But now that changes, with you," the first says.

This is not the ghost-whisper from before. These voices are clear and real and utterly unfamiliar.

"We had limited access to your cortex before . . ."

"Before you saw our cue."

Dyer still can't move her eyes, can't feel her body. I didn't opt-in to this, she thinks.

"We had no choice. We had to plan for the worst case. And here it is."

The woman in the yellow hoodie looms into view; she must be kneeling over Dyer's body.

"Come on, Vance," the woman says. "In the face or not, that was the lowest setting. Do not screw with me."

"The nano created multiple discharge paths through your brain. With prompt treatment, there is a chance the damage is not fatal."

The woman in the hoodie has leaned in close. She says, "Jesus, what is that smell? Like burning circuits."

Through the HigherWorks stream, Dyer catches glimpses of the dancers, of her crew, her body, the woman in the hoodie just a smudge against the wall, unnoticed.

Who are you? Dyer thinks.

"Since that moment when self-awareness became awareness of other selves, we humans have left echoes of ourselves on others."

"This is, perhaps, the creation of identity, the definition of culture."

"And language, art, the book, the net, nano, these have flung those echoes farther."

"But those echoes still die away, as fast as memories fade and culture evolves."

"Until you created self-repairing nano."

Locked away in a lab in Berkeley, Dyer thinks. Behind layers and layers of safety measures.

"In those days after the Crash, samples were stolen, sold, synthesized, made their way to the street."

"I took a hit and drifted and just kept drifting, dancing through other people's heads."

"From our scattered bodies gone. Dozens, hundreds of us. And we've lost the way back."

I can't help you, Dyer thinks. I don't know the way back. And if I did, I'm done with all that.

The woman in the hoodie slaps her face; Dyer can see that out of the corner of her eye, though she doesn't feel it. She can raise her arm, though, sees it wobble above her. Far above, she sees the lights of Shimago's blimp.

"We don't want to go back, any more than you do. We live here now, our whole lives, in the flow from brain to brain. But the nano is glitchy, the passage treacherous. We need Leanna Vance's knowledge."

"And Dyer's vision."

Vision, Dyer thinks. She'd laugh if she could. The HigherWorks stream has switched to the stickum camera just over her head, her face in closeup, lit by the shifting spotlights of the blimp. The music cuts out, midbeat; Mrs. John Dee's voice cries "Dyer?" But her own sight, broken as it is, the sound of the hoodie woman swearing, it's gone all glitched. Her own hand is all she can see, vibrating in a stop-motion blur.

"Seizure."

"Your brain a failed state. But there are others."

"It's your choice. But you need to make it now."

What choice? Dyer thinks.

"This nano, it's a street, a window, a border. The crossing, that's your choice."

Dyer's eyes have completely failed, but she can still see herself in the HigherWorks stream, through the stickum camera, her lips peeled back from her teeth, a trickle of blood from one ear.

Opt-in, Dyer thinks. Time to move on.

And then she is flowing out of herself like the tide, body to body, mind to mind.

A moment of mortal terror as she goes too wide—four hundred bodies hanging in silence, four hundred minds watching her own face in the HigherWorks stream—and feels herself start to tatter, to dissolve.

A moment of dizzy suffocation as she pulls herself too tight, scrabbles to find enough space for herself around the edges of a single couple's entwined thoughts. Dyer oh god Dyer all right? Kal thinks all around her, oblivious to her presence. But Leelee's luminous eyes seem to see her. Safe, xe thinks.

A moment of complete disorientation as she looses the thread back to her own body, fears that it has broken at the other end. But the HigherWorks stream is everywhere, a counter-current to her own drifting, and that stream still holds her face in the feed from the stickum camera. That sight is enough to orient her; her body is there, the life in it slow and stubborn and still beating.

And then the fear and confusion drops away. This flowing together, this connection through movement, it's what dancers have always done, since two first danced together. It's what her work has always been about, both as Leanna Vance in her lab and as Dyer in a hundred borrowed warehouses and vacant lots in as many cities. It's why HigherWorks exists.

Dyer flows across the crowd, leaping mind to mind, and now all she feels is ecstasy. Crowdsurfing, she remembers, and the dozen dancers through which she is flowing feel her glee wash over them and laugh out loud.

She swims against the current of the HigherWorks stream, finds Shimago, The Wayward, Mrs. John Dee. Their minds are open, familiar; part of her was already here inside them.

Dyer traces her own nano in their brains, finds the cortical connections, wills herself into their sight and hearing, plucks words from their minds and plays them back: "So, ghost nano . . . turns out it's not urban legend after all. It's the golden land. The shiny future."

She wraps their fear and anger and confusion in her own joy, hears Shimago's growing understanding like a swelling chord, feels The Wayward's rising joy like sun on her face, is caught up swirling in Mrs. John Dee's determination.

The ghost nano, how is it everywhere, in everyone? Dyer wonders.

"We've been spreading for years, searching for you."

"We have a presence, a ghost, if you will, across the world."

Dyer watches though Mrs. John Dee's eyes as the DJ pushes her way through the crowd toward the wall, toward Dyer's body.

"But that presence is thin. Too thin, we feared, to save you. The only way to be sure the nano would be strong enough when you needed it was to send it with her."

The woman in the yellow hoodie is staring around wild-eyed. Her hoodie has fallen back, revealing bruised eyes in a too-thin face. She can't be more than eighteen, twenty. She looks like every USER Dyer has ever seen, starting with herself, running from something, running to something, in the flow.

"I am a licensed agent of Alphet Corporation," the woman says, waving first her tablet, then the taser. "I'm a US citizen. I've got a damned take-down notice. There's a frigging treaty. I order you to cease and desist this, this . . ."

The woman slides down the wall to squat next to Dyer's body, still waving the taser.

Dee shoves the taser out of the way. "If you've killed Dyer I will haunt you, which apparently is a thing we can bloody well do now, until your dying day," she snarls. She kneels down, checks Dyer's pulse, gasps a sigh of relief.

"I'm a licensed agent of—" The woman looks at Dee. "Look, I'm sorry, okay? I've got no choice. I don't know where else to go."

Dyer slips into her own body, opens her eyes.

The lights of Shimago's blimp spin above her, trace the image of the face on the wall. Nano glitters in the beams. Dyer inhales, the mixed scent of bougainvillea and apple blossoms, a bubbling on her tongue.

Dyer expands with that breath, feels Dee's love above her, feels Shimago's calm and The Wayward's delight as they kneel down by her. Dyer feels the hoodie woman's churning confusion, her dread of returning empty-handed to a place not a home, staggering one small step ahead of decay despair disaster, chasing a ghost even more elusive, more impossible than Dyer's impossible woman, something worn smooth by years of brick stone iron concrete carbon, something scattered scattered scattered but still alive.

"Jocelyn," Dyer says. The hoodie woman stares at her in astonishment. "I don't know where we're going, either. But I hope. You can come with us, if you want. It's your choice."

Dyer raises a shaky hand toward the ghost nano's neural cue. They all look up, together.

2042-06-02T08:15:41+01:00 <location data omitted>
- CONTACT: TARGET—LEANNA VANCE—PRIORITY AA APH2035. Z980023—LOST
- ATTACHMENT: PERSONAL MESSAGE
— WHEN U FOUND ME IN THAT HELL OF A "HOME" AND TOLD ME U HAD A JOB FOR A BRIGHT YOUNG THING LIKE ME—IF I WASN'T AFRAID TO GO, U SAID—IF I WAS BRAVE ENOUGH, U SAID—AND ANYWAY, U SAID, WHERE ELSE ARE U GONNA GO?

— WELL IT'S ME ASKING THAT QUESTION NOW—GIVING U A CHOICE U NEVER GAVE ME—I'M ATTACHING IT—WHEN U R READY JUST OPEN IT UP AND—OPT-IN

— KISSES—JO

• ATTACHMENT: IMAGE (1)—<CLICK TO OPEN>

T. R. Napper's short fiction has appeared in *Asimov's*, *Interzone*, *Grimdark Magazine*, *Galaxy's Edge*, and numerous others. His work has been translated into Hebrew, German, and French.

By profession T. R. Napper is an aid worker, recently returned to Australia after three years in Vietnam. He is currently undertaking a creative writing PhD focusing on speculative fiction in Southeast Asia.

A STRANGE LOOP

T. R. Napper

In the end, we self-perceiving, self-inventing, locked-in mirages are little miracles of self-reference.—Douglas R. Hofstadter, *I Am A Strange Loop*

A huge clown, jaws as wide as Irving was tall, about to swallow him whole *. . . A woman, black hair with the fringe cut too short, green eye-shadow, skin so smooth it looked real-life airbrushed . . . The woman—what was her name again?—yelling at him, perfect skin creased with contempt . . . a red fireworks blast, neon, frozen into the sky . . . fairy floss and sweat and machine grease in his nostrils and a girl, freckled, staring up at him with tears in her eyes . . . and those sounds, tinny music on a maddening, endless cycle, and the clown, swallowing him, while the woman yelled and the girl watched with sadness.*

Irving Kupfermann blinked into consciousness. White room with a white duo, man and woman, standing over him. The woman, young, lips glistening in the bright lights, pressed a paper cup into his hand. "Drink this," she said.

Irving drank, first sipping, then gulping as the extent of his thirst hit him.

The man looked familiar. He wore a white lab coat and grasped a flexiscreen in both hands, looking down into its green-glowing ideograms. The doctor—Irving was pretty sure that's what he was—had a full head of silver hair that probably wasn't real, and a movie star chin that most definitely wasn't real. The gold of the heavy chain around his wrist: that would be real. The doctor looked forty, but he stank of money. Probably closer to sixty.

Doctor Eduard—the name floated up and popped into Irving's forebrain—spoke to the nurse. "Potentials for synaptic growth and multiplication high, as are an increased release of kinase A proteins. Emotional response very high; memories appear authentic across all measures. Or the patient believes they are real, in any case." He enunciated each word clearly, like he expected his audience to savour every single one.

"Yes doctor," the nurse replied, smiling, as she eased something from the top of Irving's head—he caught a glimpse of a green neon circle. To his left, coming into view as the nurse moved to one side, was a painting of a tobacco pipe. Underneath it was written: *this is not a pipe.* Irving furrowed his brow at that.

The doctor looked up at Irving and gave him the perfect imitation of a smile, his pristine white teeth matching the room. "You always bring us a first-class product, Irving."

Irving grunted and handed the nurse the empty cup.

"Now: do you remember anything of the memory you just sold?"

Irving shook his head. "No. Not really. It's like a dream. It's there at the edge of my mind . . . fragments. There was a woman, I think she was angry."

Doctor Eduard nodded. "Best that you sold it to us then. The key to happiness, Irving, is a bad memory."

Irving gave a non-committal shrug.

"Those remaining fragments should fade away, and by the time you get home today, they will have decamped completely from your cerebral cortex. But, remember Irving," said the doctor, finger in the air, "in the unlikely event any of this does come back to you, you must inform us post-haste. It is a violation of mnemonic copyright to remember things you no longer legally own. In such an eventuality we would need you to return here immediately to eliminate the rogue memories."

"Post-haste," said Irving. "Indubitably."

The doctor missed the sarcasm, smiled insincerely, and returned to looking over his flexiscreen.

Irving leaned back into the chair, relieved at the embrace of the soft, real leather against the back of his head. He'd been seated during the procedure, yet still felt exhausted. "How can I know if I'm remembering things I've sold?"

"Ah yes, very good question," said the doctor, returning Irving's gaze with a supercilious expression that clearly indicated that, in fact, it was a very stupid question. "We have a trace program downloaded from the *Kandel-Yu* machine into your memory pin. If it picks up a specific neural pattern in your cerebral cortex—a unique grouping we call a memory-print—you will receive a warning on-retina advising you that you have begun to re-consoli-date memories under license to us here at *Thanks for the Memories*. Often this will happen when you are dreaming."

Irving rubbed at his eye. "You tell me this often, doctor?"

"Very."

The nurse suppressed a giggle.

Irving nodded at her. "Is she an actual nurse, or are the staff here hired to laugh at you?"

The doctor raised an eyebrow. The nurse retained her smile as she said: "A post-graduate qualification, three-year internship, and a field of five hundred candidates for this position."

Her response came easy. Irving pushed his unruly hair back from his fore-head. "I guess I've said that before, as well."

"Once or twice," said the doctor, with a smirk. "When you're in a particularly bad mood. Something, I suspect, related to the experience you just sold to us."

"Yeah. Yeah, forget it."

"I was hoping you would," replied the doctor.

The nurse's smile widened.

Irving rolled his eyes.

The doctor pulled a vial from the pocket of his coat. "This is Neothebaine. Pour yourself a stiff drink when you get home, and add this before you imbibe. The memory eradication procedure should be sufficient to disrupt the neural print containing the target memory. But *this*—" the doctor held the vial up, its amber contents catching the light "—will be sure to wipe any remnants clean. You likely will not remember coming here to *Thanks for the Memories*, and you certainly will not remember either the procedure or this conversation."

"No problem," said Irving, and touched the cochlear-glyph implant behind his left ear, fingertip against the small circle of cool steel. "Exo-memory: remind me to drink Doctor Eduard's date-rape drug when I get home."

His exo-memory whispered back to him, its tone as flat as the steel of the implant: "Yes, Mister Kupfermann."

Unperturbed, the doctor typed something into his flexiscreen. "And finally, your compensation has gone through."

A message appeared on-retina, to Irving's eyes only, in soft green glowing type:

A deposit of 70,500 dollars has been recorded in your UberCoin account. You've done it! You've hit your savings target. Next steps:

1) Ask your wife, Ondine Drinkwater, out to dinner to an expensive restaurant

2) At dinner, explain that through your entrepreneurial acumen, you've become highly successful

a) Making sure to avoid mention of your numerous trips to Thanks for the Memories

3) As financial security has always been important to Ondine, it is important that you emphasize both your newfound reliability, and your considerable wealth

4) This will convince her to end your trial separation and let you return home to her and your daughter, Eulalie

Just a glance at the list made him smile. He'd done it. It'd been a long time, it'd been . . . Well, he wasn't sure how long it had been. None of that mattered now. He was going to be reunited with his wife and daughter.

Irving pushed himself out of the chair and walked out of the room. The doctor was trying to tell him something; he didn't hear a word the man said. He walked through the expansive, marble reception and stepped out of the large double doors at the front of the building. Irving breathed deeply, smile still on his face, squinting under a hot white sun.

It was time for him to come home.

"Irving."

He looked up and there she was: Ondine. Purple eye shadow, black hair with the fringe cut too short, and that soft, glowing skin. She was underdressed in denim pants and a tight leather jacket, but he didn't notice that. She was twenty minutes late, but he didn't think about that, either. All he could think about at that moment was the time, long ago, when he could have leaned over and kissed this beautiful woman, and she would have laughed and let him do so.

She wasn't laughing now.

"Ondine," he said, smiling despite the expression on her face. He stood up, dropping the gold-trimmed napkin he'd been playing with, and moved around the table to take her chair out.

"I got it Irving, I got it," she said, but he pulled it out anyway.

She treated that with a raised eyebrow and half-smile. "I'm, ah, sorry I'm late." Ondine's voice was rich, throaty. She could be lead singer in a hard rock band. Or the voice-over for a sexy cartoon character.

"Oh, it's nothing, nothing. Wine?"

"No," she said, brusquely. And then, less so: "Not at lunch. I've got to get back to work after this."

"Well—" he grimaced "—you couldn't make dinner."

"Be thankful you got lunch," she said, deadpan.

Something twisted in his chest. "Shall we order, then?"

"Maybe. What's this about, Irving?" she asked, indicating his clothes with her chin.

He glanced down. The suit was dark-blue, tailor-made, with sharp creases freshly pressed. He wore a white shirt and smoke-blue tie, set with a silver tie-pin that matched the ring on his pinkie finger. He'd shaved his rough beard off, dabbed on some cologne, and tied his unruly curls back in a short pony-tail. The restaurant was none other than *The Prince*—the most sought-after dining spot in town. Gold-gilded cutlery, waiters in blood-red jackets, white light glinting through crystal chandeliers, and the soft murmurings of the good and great as they smiled fake smiles at each other and crunched hors d'oeuvres between perfectly symmetrical teeth.

"I'm trying to make an impression," he said.

"You look like an insurance salesman."

"That wasn't the impression I was going for."

"So you're not trying to sell me something?"

"Just a dream."

"Oh Irving," she said. "Spare the schmaltz, buster. It doesn't suit either of us." But she smiled as she said it, and the twisting in Irving's chest loosened a little.

He pointed at her clothes. "Where do you get to work dressed like that? You a roadie now?"

"I work from home, you know that."

"Doing what?"

Her brows furrowed. "Speech therapist, Irving. Same as always; same as I've been doing for the past ten years."

"Yes, yes, of course," he lied. "I meant the same sort of speech therapy you used to do."

She narrowed her eyes. "Right. Sure. The same *sort of* speech therapy as I always did."

Irving carefully hid his embarrassment. "And Eulalie—how is she? Still the smartest kid in class?"

Ondine paused, permitting her irritation to ebb. "Yes. Her teacher thinks she'll be able to skip fourth grade. She . . ." Ondine trailed off, looked down at her purple-painted nails.

"She?"

She sighed and looked back at him. "She misses you."

"I miss her too," he said, and it was the truest thing he'd said in a long time. Things went well after that. For a little while, anyway.

Ondine agreed that she may as well stay for lunch, as she was there, after all. So they ate. And it was good. He ordered real meat and Ondine said *oh no*, eyes like circles, but he insisted and they shared a minute steak. They agreed neither of them had eaten meat since they honeymooned in Fiji, and then laughed about getting kicked out of the resort. They'd taken magic mushrooms and—in the throes of a sublime mind-and-body-buzz—broken into the kids' play centre and pasted glitter all over their naked bodies. Ondine had then convinced Irving that they were Moroccan glow worms looking for a burrow. A groundskeeper caught them an hour later, digging a hole in a golf course green with their hands.

Irving excused himself to the bathroom after they'd finished the main. He checked the stalls to make sure he was alone, then put a finger to his implant. "Exo-memory: I want on-retina recall dialled to maximum while I have lunch with Ondine Drinkwater. I don't want to forget a single detail about our lives together—not a detail. Understood?"

"Understood, Mister Kupfermann," whispered the implant. "I am required to remind you that you have previously ordered me to keep all memory prompts down to Level One: *only in case of emergency or direct request.* You said, and I quote, 'I don't need that shit haunting me anymore'."

Irving looked at himself in the mirror. He didn't recognize the guy in there. The shiny blue suit and the pale, sweaty skin and the ponytail and that ridiculous tie-pin he bought for ten grand at a glittering store full of smug service staff. He looked like a douche. Felt like one, too. The only thing that remained familiar was the nose. Big hook nose that Ondine charitably called 'Roman.' Combined with the bags under his eyes he didn't feel very Roman, right then. He looked like a vulture, picking over the carcass of his marriage.

"Bloody hell," he said, to himself. "Way to ruin the mood, arsehole."

"Sorry, Mister Kupfermann?" murmured the implant.

"Nothing, it's nothing."

"Mister Kupfermann?"

"*What?*" he hissed.

"Are you sure you want your exo-memory turned up to maximum?"

He looked away from the mirror. "You heard me. I want to remember everything."

Dessert came. She had ice-cream; he had coffee, strong and black. Ondine was quiet, biting her bottom lip as she ran her finger slow around the edge of the porcelain bowl. Irving waited for her to say what she wanted to say.

Eventually she did. "So where did all this—" she waved a hand at the room "—come from?"

"Hope, Ondine, it came from hope," he said, and reached across the table, putting his hand on hers. She didn't take hers away. "Hope can be the irrational desire for a miracle, despite all evidence to the contrary. But that's not the sort of hope I have. Mine is based on the reality of what we had together, Ondine, and the concrete steps I've taken to reclaim my life. I'm successful now, like you always said I could be. I can be someone you depend on. I'm someone *you* can build realistic hopes around. All this is a manifestation of that—not an idle promise, but a promise kept, to myself, that I was worthy enough to get you back."

Ondine was silent for a time, a strange expression on her face. "You been practicing that?"

"No."

His exo-memory typed: **You have been practicing: seven times this morning and eleven times last night. Twelve in front of the mirror, five while walking in a circle around the kitchen table, once while you were on the toilet.**

He rubbed his eye, annoyed at the contradictory blurb in the corner of his vision. "Yes. Okay yes, I've been practicing." He looked at her. "How did I do?"

"You did fine."

"But?"

For the next few weeks, every time he smelled the bitter scent of strong black coffee, his mind would time travel backwards, and he'd see her as she was then. Something alive and real against the forced elegance of the restaurant and the manufactured glamour of its patrons. He would remember every detail: her leather jacket, creased with decades of loving use; her smooth skin a perfection no amount of genetic manipulation could replicate; and the sadness in her eyes as she first realised, and then rejected, his intentions.

"*But*, Irving," she said, "I'm happy you're back on your feet again. Truly happy, I mean that. And if you want to start seeing Eulalie, then I'll agree to that. Slow at first, with me there, at my place. She wants to see her father again and I want you back in her life." Ondine sighed. "But you and I, Irving? That's ancient history. We had a good run. A few good years followed by a couple of terrible ones. It's how these things end all the time, every day: in bitterness and regret. There's no hope left for us, just the rubble."

He gripped her hand harder. "But Ondine. You're not listening. This restaurant isn't an accident. This is who I am now. I'm successful, I'm a winner—I'm all those things you wanted me to be."

She pulled her hand from his. The softness left her voice. "It isn't about money."

"Bullshit," he said, loud enough for heads turn their way. He lowered it again. "*Bullshit*. It's all you ever talked about."

"That's not true."

"It is precisely true. Always money: money for the rent, for holidays, organic food, fancy medicine, better schools, better fucking everything. You want me to play it back for you right now? I still have all those memories."

As he spoke the exo-memory popped up on-retina, taking some of the heat out of his accusations: **I have many examples of Ondine criticizing you for other reasons. Would you like me to list them?**

Ondine didn't get angry. Instead she sighed, pushing her two scoops of fifty dollar ice-cream absently with her spoon. "I'm sure you could play back those fights. I remember all that, too. And you're right, it was wrong of me to put it that way. When you're angry you reach for the cheap shots, and they were cheap shots. But it was never about that."

"Then what was it about?"

She looked up from the bowl, her face tinged with regret. "It was about ambition, Irving. We used to dream and plan together, about our family, our careers. But you fell into this rut and never got out. You gave up on nano-tech, neglected your daughter. Me. God Irving—you spent more time betting on weather patterns and drinking gin with your pals down at the bowls club than you ever did on trying to make a career. You were just going through the motions of life, constantly looking over the horizon, waiting for your ship to come in."

"That's not true."

Ondine Drinkwater is correct. She encouraged you on 103 occasions to pursue your career. You spent 2,428 hours researching and betting on weather patterns, whereas you spent 41 hours applying for jobs in the nano-technology field. An image appeared above the words, of Ondine, concerned expression on her face. If he gave his exo-memory the command the image would become a playback of Ondine, from many years before, encouraging him to pursue his career. He didn't give the command.

The present-day Ondine continued talking, her voice overlapping with the on-retina accusations. "Remember when you won the University Prize for your thesis on nano-technology and desertification? You could have parlayed that into a career—you had some great companies offer you an internship." She shook her head. "But you said you didn't want to work for free. You wanted the big bucks, straight away, so you turned them all down."

He creased his forehead.

Ondine Drinkwater is incorrect about the University Prize. No record of receiving an award for your thesis exists in your exo-memory. Ondine Drinkwater's recollections of job offers are correct. You rejected job offers from four different companies.

"I never won a university prize."

Her eyes narrowed. "What are you talking about, 'never won'?"

Something itched in his mind. He couldn't remember it. Unless . . .

"You don't remember, do you?"

He set his jaw. "I don't remember because it never happened."

Ondine sighed through her nose. "It was one of the best nights we ever had, Irving. We got wasted at the reception at the Chancellor's house; we danced and danced while all the guests just stood around staring at us. Then we snuck off and did it in one of the spare rooms. The Chancellor's wife found us the next morning, passed out on the bed. You were naked except for a smoking jacket you'd stolen from the Chancellor's wardrobe." She shook her head, half-smiling at the memory. "She didn't even blink. Just told us she was happy someone enjoyed the party, and then cooked us omelettes for breakfast."

Irving was silent.

"How can you not remember that, Irving? And what did you mean before when you said you *still had all those memories* of us fighting?"

"I . . ." He broke eye contact, looked down into the black of his coffee.

She shook her head. "I knew it. I *knew* it. You're selling memories aren't you? That's what all this—" she dropped her spoon into the ice-cream "—bullshit is. This room filled with wankers, that ridiculous suit. It's another get rich quick scheme, isn't it?"

"No. No it's not another scheme."

You have previously discussed—on twenty-eight occasions—getting rich quick through selling memories, Mister Kupfermann. Your bank account currently has over fifteen million dollars, which you have claimed, in conversation with others, has come from memory sales. While your exo-memory has no direct recordings of you selling memory, it does have twenty-three instances of you approaching a memory acquisition business. It is possible you had these sections of your memory wiped during the procedure. I have scanned the two years since you separated from Ondine and can find no other possible source of your current wealth.

"Okay," Irving said, fists clenching against the tabletop. "Okay." He breathed out slowly. "Okay, yeah, I sold some memories. Just to get ahead. Get my life back together." He tried to reach for her again, but she jerked her hand away like he'd just offered her a dead rat. "I did it for us, Ondine, for our family."

"Oh Irving, you and your bullshit. Every scheme was always *for the family*." She threw one hand up, exasperated. "I don't get it. Why would you sell something so good? If your goal was getting back together with me, why would you sell one of the best moments we shared?"

He said: "I don't know," but he did know. Even if he couldn't remember the procedures, he understood the pricing structure behind them perfectly. The most emotionally potent memories always fetched the most money—that and *them being unique*. Wiping them from one's own memory, so the rich client was the sole proprietor. "I didn't see it as selling memories. I saw it as an investment in a long, happy future of new memories. Once we're back together, I'll never have to sell another."

"More bullshit." She started to get up from her seat. "And I'm done listening to it."

"Wait." He got up from his seat as well. "Eulalie—I do want to see our daughter. That's not bullshit." As the words came out of his mouth he felt the truth of them, and was relieved.

She rubbed her forehead, but he'd found the right nerve. She sat back down, gingerly, on the edge of the seat.

He took a deep breath.

His exo-memory assumed the pause was an invitation for further information. **Eulalie, your daughter, eight years old.** A picture of his daughter's face appeared above the writing. Hazel eyes like his, black hair like her mother's, a cheeky grin all her own. **Eulalie goes to North Fitzroy Montessori primary school, her favourite colour is purple with blue spots, and she has a pet goldfish called Squeak-and-Bubble.**

"Are you reading something on-retina?" asked Ondine, sharply.

He refocused on her. "No."

"Bullshit. Same old Irving. Even now, in your grand attempt at winning me back, you can't help but put the freewave on. Is there a cricket game on today?"

"I'm not watching the cricket. I'm not watching anything."

"I don't believe you. It was ever thus—zoned out on some stupid live-feed every time I tried to talk to you."

He felt his face going red. Part anger, part embarrassment. "That's not true."

It is mostly true: you watched sports, betting markets, or Chinese Kung-Fu films on-retina during 81% of your conversations with Ondine.

His fingernails dug into the palms of his hand.

Ondine looked at him for ten long seconds before she said: "Do you remember Luna Park?"

It was a test. And it was immediately clear it was a test he was going to fail. "Umm."

"*Do you remember Luna Park*, Irving?"

"Yes." He licked his lips. "Of course."

"Don't lie to me."

"I'm not lying—I do remember Luna Park."

No recording of Luna Park exists in your exo-memory.

"Ah—*stop*!"

Her eyes went a stone-cold shade of bitter. "I will *not* stop."

"No, no, not you. It's my exo-memory, it—"

"I knew it."

He hit the table. Cutlery danced, heads turned his way again and a middle-aged man in a red jacket suddenly appeared next to the table.

"Is everything all right here, sir?"

"Yes, yes," said Irving. "We're fine."

Ondine said to the maître d': "It's not a problem. I'm leaving," and got up from her seat.

"I think that would be best," replied the maître d'.

Irving reached out his hand to her, begging. "No Ondine, please don't leave."

Ondine looked down at him, eyes glistening. "You need help, Irving. Professional help. You're stuck in an endless loop of self-denial. You need to find a way out."

She walked away.

"Sir," said the head waiter, interposing himself between Irving and the exit as he rose to follow his wife. Irving's lip curled in anger, but before he could barge past, the man spoke, voice an urgent whisper. "Sir, you are making a *scene*."

"Fuck you," Irving hissed. He pushed past, jogging from the restaurant, red-faced, as everyone stared.

He couldn't see Ondine when he burst out onto the street. Squinting under the bone-white sun, spinning around, trying to glimpse her receding form in the heat shimmer rising from the sidewalk. His eyes watered from the sun. The sun: that's what he tried to tell himself, anyway, before he sold the memory a few weeks later.

Irving stood in the huge clown mouth that formed the entrance of Luna Park, jaws three times as wide as he was tall. Eulalie waited, looking up at him, a cloud of pink fairy floss in her left hand. She was trying to tell him something, but he had a hand up, trying to stop her from speaking while he read the weather reports on-retina. He'd placed a series of bets on temperature and precipitation ranges in south-eastern China, and the official results were just coming in.

"Fuck it!" he yelled.

"Daddy?"

"Fuck fuck fuck."

"But daddy—"

"Not now Eulalie."

"But daddy I want to go—"

"Not now dammit!" he screamed.

Eulalie jumped, dropping the floss to the ground. Tears welled instantly.

Ondine had walked ahead, not realizing that he and Eulalie had stopped. Now she returned just to hear the end of him yelling. She seemed to be in shock for a few seconds, standing there, her smooth skin glowing in the blinking neon backwash of the amusement park.

"Jesus Irving," she said, picking her daughter up.

"Quiet," he hissed, eyes unfocussed as the massacre of his wagers scrolled down on-retina.

"Quiet? No. I'm not . . ."

He tuned her out, her words background static to failure's sting. He clenched his teeth as the news got worse and worse, and as Ondine's criticisms started to cut through his concentration.

"Enough!" he yelled. "Enough of your nagging. Enough of your complaints."

She put a hand over her daughter's ear. "Not in front of Eulalie."

"Eulalie," he sneered, focusing now on wife and daughter. "I hate that name. Where did you get it? 'Top ten hippest new names for children' in the Huffington Post?"

Ondine's mouth popped open, struggling to get out a reply.

He didn't let her.

"No! Time for me to speak now. Time. For. Me. To. Speak." He jabbed a finger at her with each word. "You never support my business decisions. You never listen to me. All I get from you is scorn and derision. You didn't even let me have a say in our own daughter's name. Eulalie? What sort of ridiculous name is that!?"

The steam started to leave his delivery as he watched the reaction of his wife and daughter. Eulalie, head buried in her mother's shoulder, sobbing. Ondine, her perfect skin creased with contempt.

"You d-don't understand," he stuttered, his rage train coming off its rails.

"I understand, Irving."

"Don't look at me like that."

"Lose another bet, I take it?"

"It's not that simple."

"Oh it is Irving, it is exactly that simple," she said, her voice a terrifying calm. "It's the most uncomplicated thing in the world. You're lazy."

"Don't."

"Greedy."

"Don't."

"Resentful."

"Not in front of Eulalie."

"Cruel, isn't it? Almost as bad as telling your own daughter that you hate her name. Well, I've needed to be cruel for a long time, but I've been a coward. Not anymore. I'm going to do what I needed to do a year ago, and I'm doing it here, in front of your daughter, so you understand that it is final."

Eulalie had taken her head from her mother's shoulder and was staring up at her as she spoke.

His eyes flicked to his daughter, then back to his wife. "Don't. I'm sorry—"

"Goodbye Irving."

She walked away. Only his daughter looked back. Watching him over her mother's shoulder, eyes filled with tears.

Irving watched them leave, hands hanging limply at his side. Nowhere else to go, he wandered back into Luna Park. Into the cacophony of tinny music on a maddening, endless cycle, into the smell of fairy floss and sweat and machine grease, and the clown, swallowing him, while—

WARNING WARNING WARNING: these memories are property of the Mobius Group. Report immediately to your nearest Thanks for the Memories franchise for memory realignment.

Bleep bleep bleep bleep

WARNING WARNING WARNING: these memories are property of the Mobius Group. Report immediately to your nearest Thanks for the Memories franchise for memory realignment.

bleep bleep bleep bleep

"No." Irving woke himself with the moan. "No." He switched off the alarm and dismissed the message flashing on-retina.

He lay back on the bed, stared at the off-white ceiling. Moonlight and street light ebbed through the slatted window. The hum of the building's hydrogen generator drifted up from below. He took control of his breathing, the rise and fall of his chest slowing.

"No."

The ubiquitous double happiness ideogram split in two as the doors opened for Irving. The room inside was gloomy, thick with incense. A cymbal and discordant pipes of traditional Chinese music played softly from hidden speakers, and overhead red lanterns swung slightly on a breeze Irving couldn't feel. A young Chinese man in a traditional straight-collared suit sat behind a darkwood reception desk.

"Um," said Irving. "My exo-memory told me I had an appointment."

The receptionist stood and bowed. "Mister Kupfermann. Omissioner Zau is waiting for you. Follow me."

Irving tried to bow back, but the young man had already disappeared down the dim, red-tinted corridor. Irving was shown through a dark redwood door carved with stylistic, eastern dragons with large, wild eyes. The receptionist closed the door behind Irving, leaving him in an even darker room.

It took his eyes a moment to adjust. Within the gloom lay a traditional study with dark, wood-panelled walls, interspersed with red scrolls marked with calligraphy. There were white-and-blue porcelain pots sitting on plinths; leather-bounds books along the back wall; a golden bust of some old Chinese guy with a receding hairline in one corner; and in the middle of it all, an even older Chinese man sitting cross-legged on a woven mat with arms crossed, hands hidden in dark blue silk sleeves.

The old man had a strand of grey hair clinging to his chin. His eyes were closed.

Irving hesitated, wondering for a moment whether he'd caught the old bugger sleeping.

"Kupfermann *xiansheng*," the old man intoned, in a thick Chinese accent. "Please, sit."

Irving jumped a little. On second glance the man's eyes were open. Sparkling slivers in a lined old face, fixed on him.

Irving stutter-stepped forward. "Omissioner Zau?"

The old man bowed.

"I . . . I don't remember making this appointment."

"But you have a problem," said the Omissioner. It wasn't a question.

"I've—ah—yeah. Yeah, I've got a problem."

"Sit."

Irving sat, cross-legged, three feet from the Omissioner.

"Tea?"

Irving shook his head.

The Omissioner waited, face inscrutable. It took Irving a long half-minute to realise the old man was waiting for him to speak. He cleared his throat, irritated by the incense. "It's a—it's about a memory I've sold to an extraction service."

Still the old man waited.

Irving continued: "It—the memory—is coming back. And I . . ." He paused. It felt like he was making confession. "I'm worried about others I've sold. I think things may have got a little out of control—I had this life with my wife. I mean *lunch*—lunch with my wife. She mentioned this—this incident in Luna Park, which I couldn't remember at first, but which I've started to dream about."

A hand appeared from within the Omissioner's sleeve. "Your memory pin please, Mister Kupfermann."

Irving's mouth tightened.

The old man waited, gnarled hand extended.

Irving sighed. He put his finger to his cochlear implant and murmured the password. A quiet *click* sounded and the memory pin popped out of the steel. He plucked it between thumb and forefinger and handed it to the Omissioner.

Zau unclipped a dark green bracelet from his wrist and unfurled it, revealing a latest-model flexiscreen. One foot square, paper-thin, soft-glowing green. The Omissioner placed the memory pin on it and hid his hands back within his sleeves. The ancient lines of the old man's face were lit up by reflected green as ideograms and graphs flowed across the screen.

After a minute of looking through the data, the man's disposition changed completely. He took his hands from his sleeves, stopped squinting, and pulled a pack of cigarettes from a hidden pocket. "Dear oh dear. So you're a Johnny," he said, in a suddenly broad Australian accent. He lit his cigarette with a chrome lighter and snapped it shut, throwing it on the floor in front of him.

"A what?" asked Irving.

The Omissioner blew a cloud of smoke upwards. "You know—a memory hooker, an auto-amnesiac. Selling off those crystal-clear, seminal life moments to the ruling class—a Johnny."

Irving paused, trying to get past the incongruity of the broad Australian accent coming out of the old Chinese guy's mouth. "What? What is this—what game are you playing here?"

"Whatever do you mean?" the old man replied, with a half-smile that suggested he knew exactly what Irving meant.

Irving pointed an open hand at the room. "This game."

"This," said the Omissioner, letting his gaze roam around the gloom. "This is all part of the *Mysteries of the East* surcharge." When he said *Mysteries of the East* his accent switched, for a moment, from Australian back to Chinese.

"Mysteries of the East?"

"Mysteries of the East, mate. Rich bastards don't come here just for science; they want a mythic flourish from an ancient civilization. So I charge them extra for their ignorance, and give the same service they'd get from any other memory expert."

"But—but everyone says the role of the Omissioner is an ancient Chinese tradition."

"Oh yeah, sure mate. Thousands of years ago China had the Omissioners. Their sole responsibility was to remind the Emperor of important traditions or precedents." Zau took a drag on his cigarette, blew the smoke upwards. "But many other cultures had something similar. In pre-Islamic Arabia, people known as *Rawis* were attached to poets as official memorizers. For centuries the Jews had the *tannaim*, who memorized oral law. All cultures, more or less, have had memory experts attached to the elite. The advent of the printing press, books, and libraries changed all that: they democratized exo-memory for the masses. For a couple of centuries, anyway. Until the invention of the cochlear-glyph and the subsequent epidemic of memory decline that has made good recall the rarest of commodities. These days, the virtuosos of natural memory like me—" an ironic grin touched Zau's lips "—Well mate, I'm the darling of the elite."

Zau pointed at Irving with the end of his cigarette. "But you ain't the elite. You ain't a repeat customer. You're a Johnny. Your wealth has come from selling off your personal history, right?"

"Well—"

"And you're here to ask me to fix the dog's breakfast you've made of the inside of your head, yes?"

"Well, yes, there's this—"

"Then you're here to ask me to fix the unfixable. I see people like you all the time. Bloody idiots, one and all. You got no other source of income, right?"

Irving started to deny it, out of instinct. But he relented and shook his head *no*.

"Then I can't prescribe a way out of this for you. To fix the damage you've done, to reclaim some of the fragments of these lost memories, I'll need time. Months. But even if you could afford me, the memories I'd reconstruct would mostly be copyrighted. So that's no good." He took another drag, glittering eyes fixed on Irving. "You could purchase the memories of others in order to improve your overall brain function, of course. But I'm not a butcher. I don't trade in the prime cuts of the personal histories of the desperate."

Irving decided to focus on the only part of the little speech that could help him. "How would other people's memories help?"

"You don't know?" asked the Omissioner, with a hint of surprise.

"It's—" Irving rubbed at his eye, he knew this "—on the tip of my tongue."

"You don't remember. Of course you don't. How could you, after all the things those bastards have done to you?" The Omissioner had let his anger show, for a moment, but he stubbed it out with his cigarette in the ashtray in front of him.

Zau took a long breath, and then said: "When you sell a memory to the ruling class, you're not simply selling one of your experiences. I mean, that's part of it—having their subconscious integrate someone else's experience as their own. The human brain is a wonderful thing isn't it? Takes a distinct event from someone else's life and—with a little nudging from technology and a good night's sleep—absorbs it as one of its own.

"But what you're *really selling* is the vitality and emotion of that experience. The power of these memories is such that when you experience them, they increase the strength and number of synaptic connections in your neural pathways. The rich need this, more than anyone, because nearly all of them are constantly editing their histories. For *everything*: relationships, jobs, family, making their lives seem superior to that of regular people. Bloody hell—some of them have a bad day they'll erase it and replace it with a good one. In the end you get a kind of mass delusion among the one per cent—half their lives are based on vivid memories they've bought from Johnnies like you. So they become ever more dependent on top-of-the-line exo-memory to fabricate visual recordings and forge a consistent life narrative. In turn, they become less and less reliant on their own brains to encode new memories, and unused, those pathways atrophy."

Zau took a long drag on his smoke and blew out a long slow cloud, watching as it curled its way to the ceiling. "So, there it is, mate. That's why they pay so handsomely for your memories. Not just for the experience, but to repair brain damage."

Irving felt the dread, sitting on his chest, making it hard for him to breathe. "How bad, Zau? How much have I lost?"

The Omissioner pointed at Irving's memory pin, sitting on the flexiscreen. "I can't tell you what memories you've lost. Not at a glance, anyway."

"What can you tell me then?"

"How many memories you've sold."

Irving's breath came harder. "Well then, how many?"

"Two hundred and nineteen."

It felt like a punch in the chest. "Fuck me."

"Hmmm."

"That's bad, isn't it?"

"Mate. It's as bad as it gets."

"Can . . . can I buy memories, like you said, help repair the damage?"

The Omissioner shook his head. "You're remembering for them wholesale, but they're selling it retail. If you've got no income other than selling memories, then you're nothing more than a snake eating its own tail."

"And you?"

"No. I'm not going re-craft your life into some sort of delusion—that's what mercenaries like *Thanks for the Memories* do. That's simply replacing one form of mental illness—dementia—for another—psychosis. My methods are more sophisticated than those butchers. They're also much more expensive."

"Can you do anything for me?" asked Irving, voice strained.

Omissioner Zau seemed oblivious. "Prescribe you Alzheimer's medication. It'll stabilize your condition, maybe even allow for a partial improvement. You'll never be the way you were, but so long as you don't sell anymore memories you should lead a relatively normal life."

"Relatively?"

"Well—like I said—you have low-grade Alzheimer's. You're mildly intellectually impaired."

"What the fuck?"

Zau paused for a moment. "Apologies. I tend to be less polite with people who won't remember my rudeness." The old man held out his cigarettes. "Fag?"

Irving shook his head.

"Drink?"

"Yeah," Irving said, with a sigh. "Yeah, I could use one."

The old man hopped up, far more sprightly than Irving would have guessed, and disappeared through a bead curtain in a dark corner of the room. As he did so, Irving saw that the Omissioner had no cochlear-glyph implant behind his ear. It had been a long time since he'd met someone unplugged.

Zau returned soon after with a bottle of amber liquid and two tumblers. The Omissioner settled down again across from Irving, poured them each three fingers. Irving downed his in a single hit. It burned his throat, but not too much, and relieved a little of the tension in his chest.

"I could go back to work," said Irving. "Nano-tech pays well, if you stick with it. I could make enough to afford even you." He smiled weakly.

Zau poured Irving another whisky. "No."

"No?" What smile Irving had faded.

"Impossible."

"Why?"

The Omissioner finished his whisky, eyes on Irving. "Imagination, that's why. If you went back to work you'd be largely reliant on exo-memory, and exo-memory never made a new discovery or developed a new idea. It doesn't have the rich associations of a natural memory, cannot accrete the layers of knowledge, interacting with each other, which give birth to an original idea. Memory is an *act of creativity*—the ability to form connections between disparate memories, build something new with them, and hurl it into the future so it becomes a poem, or a dance, or a nano-tech innovation.

"And you, Irving? You've pretty much lost your ability to create future memory. You used to be good at nano-tech? That's gone now. You can't get that back."

Irving stared at the glass in his hand. He gave a sigh that included his shoulders, and said: "Well, I want to keep what I've got left, including the one I have of my daughter." His throat closed a little when he said *daughter*.

"Sorry mate. But you won't be able to do even that. You keep remembering copyrighted memories, you'll get three years in jail and a fine so big you'll be out on the street." Zau waved his cigarette absently in the air. "You could leave the country, if you're that desperate. A few countries left don't have memory copyright. Belize has great beaches."

Irving looked up at him. "Belize?"

"Belize."

"Fuck Belize."

Zau shrugged.

"Fuck Belize right in the arse."

"That's probably overdoing it."

Irving picked his whisky up, and then put it down again, un-sipped. "What are my other options?"

"Options, chief?" Zau said, eyes narrowing. "You're all out of options. You're a fly, struggling in their web. Being aware of this fact is largely irrelevant. They'll get what they want from you, one way or another. You resist, you'll go to jail, and the judgment against you will include enforced reclamation of that stolen property—" Zau placed a finger on his own temple "—sitting there inside your head. And the government ain't as careful extracting memories as the recall companies. It can get messy."

Irving was silent. He let the words sting him, let the sting linger.

"Unless . . ." Zau trailed off. His eyes bored right into Irving, searching for something.

"Unless?"

The Omissioner took a long drag of his cigarette. "Unless you settle for the only thing you really can get now: revenge."

"Revenge? Against who?"

"Mate. Against the mercenaries that built this edifice of mnemonic servitude to the rich. Against the recall companies."

Irving stroked his long, curved nose. Revenge was such an exhausting pastime. "Maybe. I don't know."

"What else have you got?" asked the Omissioner. "Your family and career are gone."

Irving narrowed his eyes. "What was that about you being rude, again?"

"I'm just being straight with you, mate."

Irving was silent as he turned it all over in his mind. Ondine, looking at him, her face creased with contempt and Eulalie, water-blurred eyes, uncomprehending at the creeping neglect of his fatherhood.

Eulalie.

If he could have been a good father, all the other failures wouldn't have mattered. Everything else was bullshit. If only.

And he thought about the recall companies. Yeah—them, most of all. With their spacious, marble receptions and employees with perfect white teeth and franchises popping up in every city, every suburb even. On the back of *his* dreams, *his* experiences, his *essence*, commodified as a plaything for the lucky rich. They were the ones who had done all this, brought him to this, reduced him to this. Tore his family apart, for profit.

Irving fixed his gaze on Zau. "Maybe you're right. Maybe revenge is exactly what I want."

The Omissioner leaned towards him. "Yes. Good. Now, if this works out, you won't remember doing it."

"Perfect."

"From a certain perspective, yes. I'll fix it so you won't remember this conversation. You also won't remember that *Thanks for the Memories* stole your life, or that you got revenge for all they've done. What point then, Irving? How does this act exist, if you cannot remember it?"

Irving downed the last of his whisky, cleared his throat. "Let's not get metaphysical here, Omissioner. The tree still falls in the forest. The world still exists outside the boundaries of my skull. And if I make these motherfuckers pay, well they are going to pay."

Zau nodded, eyes twinkling. "Good. You're going to have to go to *Thanks for the Memories*, have the propriety product you are re-remembering wiped, *and* sell them one more legit memory."

Irving shook his head immediately. "No. I'm done with it. They can take back Luna Park, but no more. I've lost too much of myself—you've just got through telling me I'm going to end up a retard."

"Dementia."

"Whatever. I've done enough damage. Time to draw a line under it."

"Just one more, mate. It's the only way to do it. This lunch you had recently, where your wife talked about Luna Park, it has to go."

"Why?"

"Because it is part of a mnemonic loop that will keep sending you back in time to Luna Park, and forward in time to me, here. We need to snip it out, cover our tracks."

Irving opened his mouth to say no, but the image came of Ondine, looking at him from across the table, her expression a mixture of sadness and pity. He rubbed at his eyes with his palms. "Yeah. Maybe that is one memory I could do without."

"Good, mate, good," said the Omissioner, eyes shining. "Now, they'll be uploading more than a visual recording from your pin and a memory print from your cerebral cortex. They'll be uploading a project I've been working on for a long time. An offensively expensive virus I've commissioned, one that will bypass—"

Irving held up hand. "I don't care what it is, Omissioner, just so long as it works."

"Oh, it will work. When they take your memory, the virus will plug straight into the *Kandel-Yu* machine. It will ensure that every customer after you experiences an immediate decline in the release of certain proteins crucial to long-term memory formation. They will suffer anterograde amnesia—everything that happens after their trip to *Thanks for the Memories* will be lost."

"They'll still have memory pins."

"Yes, yes, they'll still have exo-memory. That's why it's such a cracker—it won't become immediately apparent. Not before hundreds, even thousands have been exposed. Those infected will be increasingly reliant on a computer to tell them what day it is, where they work, whether or not they ate lunch, who their new friends are, the names of their children. They'll keep going back to recall companies, buying more memories, infecting more *Kandel-Yu* machines. We do this right, the whole system of memories trickling up to the rich, of the desperate selling off chunks of their own soul, will be broken."

Irving laughed without humour. "And here I was thinking I'd never achieve anything in this life."

Zau watched Irving through the glass, doing a stunned kind of shuffle, following his vulture nose down the sidewalk.

"Your insider at the recall centre," said Zau. "She chose well."

"Yes," replied Qiang from behind the reception desk. "She knows a hopeless case when she sees one."

"He's better than hopeless." Zau continued to watch Irving walk down the street. "He's the utterly irredeemable still yearning for redemption."

Qiang waited until Irving had disappeared from sight. "Mister Kupfermann said you'd come to an agreement and that he wasn't to be charged for the session."

Zau looked over at him. "Charge him triple."

"Triple?"

"Yeah. He won't remember what it's for, and I've told his exo-memory to hide it from him. Plus—" the old man smiled, his eyes sparkling "—it's for a good cause."

The doors to *Thanks for the Memories* wouldn't open. Distracted by the glare of the sun, Irving had missed the red neon sign flashing CLOSED next to the entrance.

"Exo-memory, why is *Thanks for the Memories* closed? What day is it?"

"Thursday," whispered the implant. "A media release by the parent company, released nine days ago, stated that this franchise was not located in a profitable area, and was consolidating its branches to maximize economic returns for shareholders. However, multiple sources on the freewave have contradicted this, theorizing that the closure is related to several recent high-profile cases of amnesia. Shall I put the most-read article from each perspective up on-retina?"

"No, no, I don't care about the details."

Irving pursed his lips. This was a nuisance. Just a couple more sales and he would hit the target he'd set himself. Fifteen million and he'd take Ondine out for dinner, reveal his newfound wealth and success. Just a couple more sales were all he needed to win his wife and daughter back.

"Exo-memory."

"Yes, Mister Kupfermann?"

"Give me directions to the nearest *Thanks for the Memories* franchise."

Xia Jia is associate professor of Chinese literature at Xi'an Jiaotong University. She obtained a PhD at Peking University in 2014, with "Chinese Science Fiction and Its Cultural Politics Since 1990" as the topic of her dissertation. Besides, she has been publishing speculative fiction since college in *Science Fiction World* and other venues. Several of her stories have been translated into English, Japanese, Polish, Russian, Italian, and French. Her first story written in English, "Let's have a talk," was published in *Nature* in 2015.

NIGHT JOURNEY OF THE DRAGON-HORSE

Xia Jia

1.

The dragon-horse awakens in moonlight.

Drops of cold dew drip onto his forehead, where they meander down the curve of his steel nose.

Plink.

He struggles to open his eyes, rusted eyelids grinding against eyelashes. A pair of silvery specks reflects from those giant dark red pupils. At first he thinks it's the moon, but a careful examination reveals it to be a clump of white flowers blooming vibrantly in a crack in the cement, irrigated by the dew dripping from his nose.

He can't help but inhale deeply, as though trying to taste the fragrance of the flowers, but he smells nothing—after all, he is not made of flesh and blood and has never smelled anything. The air rushes into his nostrils, whistling loudly in the narrow gaps between mechanical components. He feels a slight buzzing all over his body, as if each one of his hundreds of scales is vibrating at a different frequency, and so he sneezes, two columns of white fog erupting from his nostrils. The white flowers tremble in the fog, drops of dew falling from the tips of the translucent petals.

Slowly the dragon-horse opens his eyes all the way and lifts his head to survey the world.

The world has been desolate for a long time and now looks very different from his memory of it. He remembers once having stood in the middle of a brightly lit hall, shaking his head and waving his tail at Chinese and foreign visitors, surrounded by cries of delight and surprised intakes of breath. He remembers nights when, after the lights in the museum had been extinguished, lingering visitors murmuring in strange tongues had disturbed his dreams.

The hall is now in ruins, the cracked walls askew with vines sprouting from fissures and seams, leaves susurrating in the wind. Vine-shrouded trees have punched holes large and small in the glass skylight overhead. Bathed by moonlight, dewdrops *plink-plonk* like pearls falling onto a jade platter.

The dragon-horse glances around the great hall of the museum—now a decayed courtyard—and sees that all the other inhabitants are gone, leaving only him dreaming for untold centuries amongst the rubble. He peers at the night sky through the holes in the skylight: the empyrean is a shade of midnight blue, and the stars twinkle like silver-white flowers. This is also a sight he can't remember having seen for a long, long time.

He recalls his birthplace, a small city named Nantes on the shores of the tranquil Loire, where the brilliant pinpricks of the stars reflected in the water resembled an oil painting. But in this metropolis, thousands of miles from Nantes, the sky always hung overhead like a thick, waxy gray membrane by day, varicolored neon lights turning it even more turbid at night.

Tonight the limpid moon and luminous stars arouse in him an intense nostalgia for his hometown, for the tiny workshop where he was born on an isle in the middle of the river, where the artisans drew the plans for his design using pens with nibs as fine as a single strand of hair, and then cast the components, polished, spray-painted, and assembled them until he was fully formed. His massive body weighed forty-seven tons, composed from tens of thousands of individual components.

With his reinforced steel frame and wooden scales, he stood erect, a terrifying sight. Then the gears, axles, motors, and cables inside him collaborated seamlessly in a mechanical symphony so that he could come alive: his four hoofed legs extending and flexing as though made of flesh, his neck curving and straightening like a startled wild goose, his spine gyrating like a playful dragon, his head lifting and dipping like a lazy tiger, his steps as light as an immortal dancing across water.

On top of his horse-like body is a dragon's neck and head, along with a long beard, deer antlers, and dark red glass eyes. Each of the golden scales covering his body is inscribed with a Chinese character: "dragon," "horse," "poem," "dream." These characters embody the romantic fantasies his clever artisan-creators harbored about another ancient civilization.

Long ago, he came here in a Year of the Horse. "Vigorous as dragon and horse" is an auspicious phrase the people of this land loved to say to one another, and it was this phrase that inspired his creators and endowed him with his present mythical form.

He remembers also parading across a square packed with crowds with his head held high and his legs stretched out. Children greeted him with curious eyes and delighted screams as the mist spewing from his nostrils drenched them. He remembers the lovely music that filled the air, a combination of Western symphonies and Chinese folk tunes—slowly and gracefully he strolled, swaying and stepping to the rhythm of the music. He remembers the streets and buildings spreading before him like a chessboard, stretching endlessly under the hazy gray sky. He remembers his performance partner, a mechanical spider who was almost as large as he was and whose eight legs sliced through the air menacingly. They performed together for three days and three nights, enacting a complete mythical tale.

Nüwa, the goddess of creation, sent the dragon-horse to survey the mortal world, where he encountered the spider, who had escaped from the heavenly court and was wreaking havoc everywhere. They fought an epic battle until—neither able to overcome the other—they forged a peace based on friendship. Then the four seas undulated in harmonious tranquility, and even the weather became mild and pleasant.

After the show, the spider returned to its birthplace, leaving the drag-on-horse alone as guardian of this strange land.

Yet isn't this place another homeland for him? He was created to cele-brate the lasting friendship between two nations, and from conception he was of mixed blood. The dreams and myths of this land were his original seed. After eons of being passed from one storyteller to another, the legends—transformed into the languages of strange lands, borne across oceans to new realms—were substantiated by the magic of steel and electricity, like those agile robots and spaceships. Finally, across thousands of miles, he came here to become a new legend to be passed down through the ages. Tradition and modernity, myth and technology, the East and the West—which is his old country, which the new?

The dragon-horse, unable to puzzle out the question, lowers his heavy head. He has been asleep for too long, and now the whole world has turned into a ruined garden. Are there still places in this garden for people to live? In the cold moonlight, the dragon-horse carefully lifts his legs and, step by step, begins to explore.

Every joint in his rusty body screeches. In a glass wall filled with spider-web cracks, he sees a reflection of himself. His body has also been decaying. Time flows like a river, halting for no one. His scaled armor is now patchy, incomplete, like an aged veteran returning from the wars. Only his glass eyes continue to glow with that familiar dim light.

The wide avenue where cars had once streamed like a river of steel is now filled with lush trees dancing in the wind. As soon as there's a break in the rustling of leaves, birds and insects fill the silence with their chittering music, which only makes everything seem even more desolate. The dragon-horse looks around, uncertain where he should be headed.

Since it makes no difference, he picks a direction at random and strolls forward.

The clopping hoofbeats echo against the pavement. The moon stretches his lonely shadow a long way over the ground.

2.

The dragon-horse isn't sure how long he has been walking.

Silently the stars spin overhead, and the moon wanders across the firmament, but without clocks or watches, time's passage cannot be felt.

The avenue he's on was once this city's most famous street. Now it is a deep canyon whose craggy walls are formed from an amalgam of bricks, steel, concrete, and trees, the product of mixing the inorganic with the organic, decay with life, reality with dream, the steel-and-glass metropolis with ancient myths.

He remembers there was once a square nearby where bright lights remained lit throughout the night like a thousand-year dream. But in the end, the lights went out, and the dream ended. There's nothing in this world that can outlast time itself.

Coming into the valley that was once that square, he sees an impossible vision: thousands and thousands of steel wrecks heaped and stacked like the skeletal remains of beasts, the looming piles stretching as far as the eye can see. These were once automobiles of various makes and sizes, most of them so corroded by rust that only the frames remain. Twisted branches emerge from the dark, empty windows and stab into the sky as though clawing for some elusive prey. The dragon-horse experiences a nameless sorrow and terror. He lowers his eyes to gaze at his own rusty forelimbs. How is he different from these dead cars? Why should he not fall into a perpetual slumber alongside them?

No one can answer these questions.

A scale falls from his chest, rolling among the steel wrecks and echoing dully in the watery moonlight. The insects, near and far, fall silent for a moment before resuming their joyful chorus, as though what fell were nothing more than an insignificant pebble.

He becomes even more frightened, and picks up his pace as he continues his night journey.

Squeaks come from a certain spot in the ruins. The sound is thin and dreary, different from birdcall and insect chitter. The dragon-horse follows the sound to its source, searching among the thick grass with his nose. Suddenly, in the shadow of a shallow cave, he finds himself gazing at a pair of tiny, dark eyes.

"Who are you?" the dragon-horse asks. It has been so long since he has heard his own voice that the thrumming timbre sounds strange to him.

"Don't you recognize me?" a thin voice answers.

"I'm not sure."

"I'm a bat."

"A bat?"

"Half-beast, half-bird, I sleep during the day and emerge at night to swoop between dawn and dream."

The dragon-horse carefully examines his interlocutor: sharp snout, large ears, a soft body covered by fine gray fur and curled upon itself, and two thin, membranous wings shimmering in the moon.

"And who are you?" the bat squeaks.

"Who am I?" the dragon-horse repeats the question.

"You don't know who you are?"

"Maybe I do; maybe I don't," replies the dragon-horse. "I'm called Dragon-Horse, meaning I am both dragon and horse. I began as a myth in China, but I was born in France. I don't know if I'm a machine or a beast, alive or dead—or perhaps I've never possessed the animating spark. I also don't know if my walk through the night is real or only a dream."

"Like all poets who make dreams their horses." The bat sighs.

"What did you say?"

"Oh, you reminded me of a line from a poem from long ago."

"A poem?" The word sounds familiar to the dragon-horse, but he's not certain what it means.

"Yes. I like poems," the bat says, and nods. "When the poets are gone, poems are even more precious."

"The poets are gone?" the dragon-horse asks carefully. "You are saying no one writes poems anymore?"

"Can't you tell? There are no longer any people in this world."

The dragon-horse doesn't bother looking around. He knows she's right.

"Then what should we do?" he asks, after being silent for a while.

"We can do whatever we want," says the bat. "Humans may be gone, but the world goes on. Look at how lovely the moon is tonight. If you want to sing, sing. If you don't want to sing, just lie still. When you sing, the world will listen; when you are quiet, you'll hear the song of all creation."

"But I can't hear it," admits the dragon-horse. "I can only hear the chitter of insects in the ruins. They frighten me."

"Poor baby—your ears aren't as good as mine," says the bat compassionately. "But you heard *me*. That's odd."

"Is it really that strange?"

"Usually only bats can hear other bats. But the world is so big, anything is possible." The bat shrugs. "Where are you going?"

"I don't know where I'm headed," the dragon-horse says. It's the truth.

"You don't even have a destination in mind?"

"I'm just walking about. Also, I don't know how to do anything except walk."

"I have a destination, but I got held up on the way." The bat's voice turns sorrowful. "I'd been flying for three days and three nights, and then an owl came after me. The owl almost tore my wings."

"You're hurt?" asks the dragon-horse solicitously.

"I said 'almost.' Do I look like I'm easy prey?" Her indignant speech is interrupted by a fit of coughing.

"Do you not feel well?"

"I'm thirsty. Flying parched my throat, and I want a drink. But the water here is full of the flavor of rust; I can't stand it."

"I have water," says the dragon-horse. "It's for my performance."

"Would you give me a drink? Just a sip."

The dragon-horse lowers his head, and a white mist sprays from his nostrils. The mist soaks the bat's tiny body, forming droplets on the fine fur. Satisfied, the bat spreads her wings and carefully licks up the droplets.

"You're nice," squeaks the bat. "I feel much better now."

"Are you leaving for where you want to go, then?"

"Yes. I have an important mission tonight. What about you?"

"I don't know. I guess I'll just keep on moving forward."

"Can you carry me for a while? I'm still tired and need rest, but I don't want to be late."

"But I walk very slowly," the dragon-horse says, embarrassed. "My body is designed so that I can only walk haltingly, step by step."

"I don't care." Briskly flapping her light wings, the bat lands next to the dragon-horse's right ear. The bat's claws lightly clutch a branch of his long antler, and then she's dangling upside down.

"See, now we get to talk as we walk. There's nothing better than a night journey with conversation."

The dragon-horse sighs and carefully shifts his limbs. The bat is so light that he almost can't feel the creature's presence. He can only hear that thin, reedy voice whispering poetry in his ear:

"Faced with the great river, I am consumed by shame. What has my exhaustion accomplished . . . ?"

3.

They pass through the graveyard of cars. The road is now more rugged and uneven, and the moon has hid itself behind wispy clouds so that the road is illuminated in patches.

The dragon-horse carefully picks his way through, fearful of falling and breaking a limb. With each step, his whole body creaks and groans, and gears and screws fall off him—*clink-clank*—and disappear in the gaps between rubble and weeds.

"Are you in pain?" asks the bat curiously.

"I've never known what pain is," confesses the dragon-horse.

"Wow, impressive. If it were me, I'd be dead from the pain by now."

"I don't know what death is, either." The dragon-horse falls silent. The nameless sorrow and terror have returned. If he is considered alive now, is that essence of life scattered among the tens of thousands of components making up his body, or is it concentrated in some special spot? If these components are all scattered along the path he has trodden, will he still be alive? How will he continue to sense all that is around him?

Time flows like a river, halting for no one. There's nothing in this world that can outlast time itself.

"Walking like this is boring," says the bat. "Why don't you tell me a story? You were born so long ago that you must know many stories I don't."

"Story? I don't know what a story is; I certainly can't tell you one."

"It's easy! Okay, repeat after me: 'Long, long ago.'"

"Long, long ago . . ."

"What comes to your mind now? Do you see something that doesn't exist?"

The dragon-horse does. The wheel of time seems to be reversing before his eyes. Trees shrink into the ground, and giant buildings shoot out of the earth, part to the sides like the sea, and leave a straight, wide avenue down the middle.

"Long, long ago, there was a bustling metropolis."

"Are there people in the city?" asks the bat.

"Many, many people."

"Can you see them clearly?"

The image before the dragon-horse's eyes clarifies like a long, painted scroll: everyone's expression is vivid and lifelike. He sees the people's joys and sorrows, partings and meetings, as though seeing the moon waxing and waning.

"Long, long ago, there was a bustling metropolis. In this city there lived a young woman . . ."

He starts to tell the stories of those people.

A young woman who'd never been in love fell for a stranger she met through the chat program on her phone, but then she discovered that her interlocutor was only a perfect bit of conversation software. Yet, the digital boy loved her back, and they happily spent a lifetime together. After the woman died, a record of her life—her frowns and laughter, her actions and reactions—was uploaded to the cloud, and she became the shared goddess of people and AIs.

A pious monk went to a factory to pray and bring blessings to the robot workers who were plagued by short-circuits and malfunctions. But the ghosts of the dead robot workers hounded him. Just as the investigation of the strange occurrences was about to end, the monk was found dead in a tiny hotel room, his nude body smeared with the blood of a woman. An autopsy revealed the truth: he was also a robot.

A famous actress was known for being able to portray a wide variety of roles. So skilled was she, the paparazzi suspected that she was only a software simulation. But by the time they managed to break into her well-secured mansion, all they saw was a cold corpse lying on a magnificent bed. Frighteningly, whether you were looking at her body with the naked eye or through a camera, everyone and every camera saw a different woman. And even years later, the actress continued to show up on the silver screen.

A blind child prodigy began to play Go against the computer when he was five. As time passed, his skill improved, and his computer opponent also became smarter through competition with him. Many years later, as he lay dying, the blind Go player played one last match against his old opponent. But unbeknownst to him, as they played, others opened his skull and scanned each part of his brain layer by layer, digitizing the results into computer modules that his machine opponent could learn from, until this last Go match became so complicated that no one could follow it.

Delighted by the stories told by the dragon-horse, the bat dances upside down. In turn, she squeaks other stories into the dragon-horse's ear:

A bell that rang only once every hundred years was forgotten in the dark basement of an art museum in the heart of the city. But due to a marvelous resonance phenomenon, whenever the bell did ring, its sound would be echoed and magnified by the entire city until the ringing resounded like an ensemble of pipe organs, and everything stood still in awe.

An unmanned drone took to the skies every dawn. Each clockwise swoop over the city also served to recharge its solar-powered batteries. Whenever spring turned to summer, a flock of fledgling birds followed the drone to practice flying like a magnificent cloud.

Piles of paper books which no one ever read filled an ancient library where the temperature was always kept at sixty-two degrees Fahrenheit. The main computer of the library was capable of reciting every poem in every language. If you were lucky enough to find the way there, you would receive an unimaginably enthusiastic reception.

A musical fountain was capable of composing new music as soon as you deposited some coins. At dusk, feral cats and dogs often dropped coins they picked out of the ruins into the fountain; and so, as the birds and beasts took turns bathing in the fountain in an orderly manner, they also got to enjoy lovely music that never repeated itself.

"Is it really true?" they each ask the other, again and again. "And then? What happened then?"

Shadows dance in the moon. The longer they walk, the longer seems the road.

Gradually they hear gurgling water, like the babbling of a brook echoing through a deep canyon. Before the founding of the metropolis, creeks and brooks had crisscrossed this spot. Year by year, they were tamed as people multiplied, and turned into lakes, ditches, and dank underground sewers. But now the brooks have been freed, wantonly meandering their way over the rolling terrain, singing, nourishing the life on this patch of land.

The dragon-horse stops. The road he's on disappears into a wild lotus pond. The pond stretches as far as the horizon, covered by layer after layer of lotus leaves. A breeze passes, and the lotus leaves ruffle, causing undulating ripples through the dark-green-and-gray-white sea. Red and white lotus flowers peek out of the leaves as though they're pieces of frozen moonlight, with no trace of the merely terrestrial in their beauty.

"How lovely." The bat sighs lightly. "It's so beautiful that my heart aches."

The dragon-horse is startled because he feels the same, though he doesn't know if he has a heart.

"Shall we go on?" he asks.

"I need to fly over this lake," replies the bat. "But you can't go on any longer. You're made of metal; the water will probably cause you to short-circuit."

"Maybe." The dragon-horse hesitates. He has never been in the water.

"Then let us say farewell here." The bat's flapping wings tickle the dragon-horse's ear.

"You're leaving?"

"Yes, I don't want to be late."

"Bon voyage!"

"The same to you! Take care of yourself, and thank you for your stories."

"Thank you as well."

The dragon-horse stands at the shore and watches as the shadow of the bat diminishes until she has disappeared in the night.

He is alone again. The watery moon gently illuminates all creation.

4.

He looks at his reflection in the water. His body seems more skeletal than he remembers from before the start of this journey. The scales covering his body have mostly fallen off, and even one of his antlers is gone. Through the holes in his skin, messy bundles of wires and cables can be seen wrapped around his rusty steel skeleton.

Where shall I go? Should I go back? Back to where I started?

Or maybe I should head in the opposite direction. The Earth is round. No matter where I want to go, as long as I keep going, I'll get there.

Though he's pondering turning back, he has already, without realizing it, stepped forward.

His front hooves disappear underneath the ice-cold waves.

The lotus leaves scratch gently against his belly. Countless sparkling droplets roll across their surfaces: some return to the starting point after wandering about for a while; others coalesce like beads of mercury and then tumble off the edge of the leaf into the water.

The world is so lovely. I don't want to die.

The thought frightens him. *Why am I thinking about death? Am I about to die?*

But the endless lotus pond continues to tempt him. He moves forward, one step after another. He wants to reach the other shore, which he has never seen.

The water rises and covers his limbs, his belly, his torso, his spine, his neck.

His legs sink into the mud at the bottom of the pond, and he can't pull them out. His body sways, and he almost falls. The last scale falls from his body.

The golden scale splashes into the water like a lotus-shaped floating lantern. Slowly it drifts away, carried by the ripples.

The dragon-horse is exhausted, but he also feels as though all weight has been lifted from him. He closes his eyes.

He hears the sound of rushing water, as though he has returned to the place of his birth. Long-forgotten memories replay before his eyes. He seems to be on the ocean at this moment, riding in a giant ship headed for China. Perhaps all that he has seen and heard over the years are but a dream on this long voyage.

A breeze caresses his beard like a barely audible sigh.

The dragon-horse opens his eyes. The tiny figure of the bat is flattened against his nose.

"You're back!" Joy fills him. "Did you make it on time?"

"I got lost." The bat sighs. "The pond is too big. I can't seem to find the other shore."

"It's too bad that I'm stuck in the mud. I can't help carry you any farther."

"I wish we had fire."

"Fire?"

"Wherever there's fire, there's light. I want to lead the way for everyone!"

"For . . . who?"

"For the gods in darkness, for the lonely ghosts and lost souls, for anyone who doesn't know where to go—I will lead them all."

"You need fire?"

"Yes, but where would we find fire in all this water?"

"I have fire," says the dragon-horse. "I don't have much, but I hope it's enough for you."

"Where?"

"Give me a bit of space."

The bat flaps over to a lotus leaf nearby. The dragon-horse opens his jaw and sticks out his black tongue. Pure kerosene flows out of a seam under the tongue, and a dark blue electric spark comes to life at the tip of the tongue, lighting the kerosene spray. A golden-scarlet column of fire shoots into the sky.

"I had no idea you had such hidden talents!" the bat shouts in admiration. "More, more!"

The dragon-horse opens his mouth, and more flames shoot out. Kerosene burns easily, even after so many years of storage. He can't remember the last time he performed the fire-breathing trick—it's possible that he hasn't done it since the battle with the spider. Fire is so warm and beautiful, like a god whose shape is constantly shifting.

"Millions wish to extinguish the fire, but I alone will lift it high overhead." The bat's voice rings out clearly in the ear of the dragon-horse, resonating with each and every one of his components:

> *This fantastic fire, a storm of blossoms that blankets the sacred motherland.*
> *Like all poets who make dreams their horses,*
> *By this fire, I survive the long, dark night.*

He feels like a burning match. But he doesn't feel any pain.

All around him, faint lights appear in the distance, gathering like fireflies.

Oh, what a collection of spirits and demons! They are of every shape and material, sporting every strange color and outline: hand-drawn door gods and buddhas; abstract graffiti on factory walls; tiny robots no bigger than a thumb made out of computer components; mechanical Guan Yu constructed from truck parts; dilapidated, ancient stone guardian lions; teddy bears as tall as a house and capable of telling stories; simple, clumsy robot dogs; strollers capable of singing a baby to sleep . . .

They are just like him, mixed-blood creations of tradition and modernity, myth and technology, dream and reality. They are made of Art, yet they are Natural.

"It's time!" the bat sings joyfully. "Come with us!"

"Where are we going?" asks the dragon-horse.

"Anywhere is fine. Tonight you will find eternal life and freedom in poetry and dream."

She sticks out a tiny claw and pulls him into the air, where he transforms into a fluttering butterfly with dark red eyes and golden wings full of Chinese characters. He looks down and sees the massive body of the dragon-horse still burning in the endless lotus pound, like a magnificent torch.

Along with all his companions, he flies higher into the sky. The rolling landscape of ruins diminishes in the distance. Next to his ear, the bat's voice continues to whisper.

> *A thousand years later, if I were to be born again on the riverbank of my motherland,*
> *A thousand years later, I will again possess China's rice paddies and the snow-capped mountains of the King of Zhou, where sky-horses roam.*

Farewell, and good-bye. He sighs.

The flame disappears in darkness.

They fly for a long time until they reach the end of the world.

Everywhere they look, gloom greets their eyes. Only a giant, sparkling river lies between heaven and earth.

The blue water gleams like fire, like mercury, like the stars, like diamonds— twinkling, shimmering, melding into the dark night. No one knows how wide it is, or how long.

The spirits flap and flutter their wings, heading for the opposite shore. Like mist, like a cloud, like a rainbow, like a bridge, they connect two worlds.

"Go on," says the bat. "Hurry."

"What about you?"

"I still have some tasks to finish. When the sun rises, I must return to my nest to sleep and wait for the next night."

"So we're to say farewell again?"

"Yes. But the world is so grand, I'm sure we'll meet somewhere else again."

They embrace, wrapping their tiny wings about each other. The dragon-horse spirit turns to leave, and the bat recites poetry to send him on his way.

> *Riding the five-thousand-year-old phoenix and a dragon whose name is "horse," I am doomed to fail.*
> *But Poetry itself, wielding the sun, will surely triumph.*

He heads for the opposite shore, and he isn't sure how long he has been flying. The starry river flows by.

Next to the shore is his birthplace, the tiny, tranquil isle of Nantes. The mechanical beasts have been slumbering for an unknown number of years: the twenty-five-meter-tall carousel horse of the ocean world; the fifty-ton giant elephant; the immense, frightening reptile; the heron with the eight-meter wingspan capable of carrying a man; the bizarre mechanical ants, cicadas, and carnivorous plants . . .

He sees his old partner, the spider, who lies tranquilly in the soft moonlight, his eight legs curled under him. Landing gently on the forehead of the spider, the dragon-horse spirit closes his wings like a dewdrop falling from the heavens.

When you sing, the world will listen; when you are quiet, you'll hear the song of all creation.

The night breeze carries the sounds of collision, percussion, and metal creaking and grinding against metal. He smells the aroma of machine oil, rust, and electrical sparks. His friends have awakened, and to welcome his return, there will surely be a great feast.

But first, he falls into a deep slumber.

PEARL

Aliette de Bodard

I n Da Trang's nightmares, Pearl is always leaving—darting away from him, toward the inexorable maw of the sun's gravity, going into a tighter and tighter orbit until no trace of it remains—he's always reaching out, sending a ship, a swarm of bots—calling upon the remoras to move, sleek and deadly and yet too agonizingly slow, to do anything, to save what they can.

Too late. Too late.

It wasn't always like this, of course.

In the beginning . . . in the beginning . . . his thoughts fray and scatter away, like cloth held too close to a flame. How long since he's last slept? The Empress's courtier was right—but no, no, that's not it. She doesn't understand. None of them understand.

In the beginning, when he was still a raw, naive teenager, there was a noise, in the hangar. He thought it was just one of the countless remoras, dipping in and out of the room—his constant companions as he studied for the imperial examination, hovering over his shoulder to stare at the words; nudging him when one of them needed repairs they couldn't provide themselves. And once—just after Inner Grandmother's death, when Mother had been reeling from the loss of her own mother, and when he'd come running to the hangar with a vise around his chest—he'd seen them weaving and dancing in a pattern beautiful beyond words as he stood transfixed, with tears running down his cheeks.

"Can you wait?" Da Trang asked, not looking away from the text in his field of vision. "I'm trying to work out the meaning of a line." He was no scholar, no favored to be graced with a tutor or with mem-implants of his ancestors: everything he did was like moving through tar, every word a tangle of meanings and connotations he needed to unpack, every clever allusion something he needed to look up.

A nudge then; and, across his field of vision, lines—remoras didn't have human names, but it was the one he thought of as Teacher, because it was one of the oldest ones, and because it was always accompanied by a swarm of other remoras with which it appeared to be in deep conversation.

>Architect. Need to see.<

Urgent, then, if Teacher was attempting to communicate—remoras could use a little human speech, but it was hard work, tying up their processes—they grew uncannily still as they spoke, and once he'd seen a speaking remora unable to dodge another, more eager one.

He raised his gaze, and saw . . .

Teacher and another remora, Slicer, both with that same look of intent sleekness, as if they couldn't hold still for long without falling apart—and, between them, a third one, looking . . . somehow wrong. Patched up, like all remoras—leftovers from bots and ships that had gone all but feral, low-level intelligences used for menial tasks. And yet . . .

The hull of the third remora was painted—engraved with what looked like text at first, but turned out to be other characters, long, weaving lines in a strange, distorted alphabet Da Trang couldn't make out.

>Is Pearl,< Teacher said, on the screen. >For you.<

"I don't understand," Da Trang said slowly. He dismissed the text, watched the third remora—something almost graceful in the way it floated, like a calligraphy from a master, suggesting in a few strokes the shape of a bird or of a snake. "Pearl?"

Pearl moved, came to stand close to him—nudging him, like a pet or favorite bot—he'd never felt that or done that, and he felt obscurely embarrassed, as if he'd given away some intimacy that should have been better saved for a parent, a sibling, or a spouse.

>Architect.< Pearl's lines were the same characters as on its hull for a brief moment; and then they came into sharp focus as the remora lodged itself on his shoulder, against his neck—he could feel the heat of the ship, the endless

vibrations of the motor through the hull, like a secret heartbeat. >Pleased. Will help.<

Da Trang was about to say he didn't need help, and then Pearl burrowed close to him—a sharp, painful stab straight into his flesh; and before he had time to cry out, he saw—

The hangar, turned into flowing lines like a sketch of a Grand Master of Design Harmony; the remoras, Slicer and Teacher, already on the move, with little labels listing their speed, their banking angles; their age and the repairs they'd undergone—the view expanding, taking in the stars beyond the space station, all neatly labeled, every wavelength of their spectrum cataloged— he tried to move, to think beyond the confines of the vision the ship had him trapped in; to remember the poem he'd been reading—and abruptly the poem was there, too, the lines about mist over the water and clouds and rain; and the references to sexual foreplay, the playfulness of the writer trying to seduce her husband—the homage to the famed poetess Dong Huong through the reuse of her metaphor about frost on jade flowers, the reference to the bird from Viet on Old Earth, always looking southward. . . .

And then Pearl released him; and he was on his knees on the floor, struggling for breath. "What—what—" Even words seemed to have deserted him.

>Will help,< Pearl said.

Teacher, firmer and steadier, a rock amidst the turmoil in his mind. >Built Pearl for you, Architect. For . . . examinations?< A word the remora wasn't sure of; a concept Da Trang wasn't even sure Teacher understood.

>For understanding,< Slicer said. >Everything.< If it had been human, the remora would have sounded smug.

"I can't—" Da Trang pulled himself upward, looked at Pearl again. "You made it?"

>Can build others,< Teacher said.

"Of course. I wasn't doubting that. I just—" He looked at Pearl again and finally worked out what was different about it. The others looked cobbled together of disparate parts—grabbing what they could from space debris and scraps and roughly welding it into place—but Pearl was . . . not perfect, but what you would get if you saved the best of everything you found drifting in space, and put it together, not out of necessity, not out of a desire for immediate survival or return to full functionality—but with a carefully thought-out plan, a desire for . . . stability? "It's beautiful," he said at last.

>We built,< Teacher said. >As thanks. And because . . . < A pause, and then another word, blinking on the screen. >We can build *better*.<

Not beauty, then, but hope, and longing, and the best for the future. Da Trang found his lips twisting in a bitter smile, shaping words of comfort, or something equally foolish to give a remora—some human emotions to a being that had none.

Before he could speak up, though, there came the patter of feet. "Li'l brother, li'l brother!" It was his sister Cam, out of breath. Da Trang got up—Pearl hovering again at his shoulder, the warmth of metal against his neck.

"What—" Cam stopped, looked at him. "What in heaven is this?"

Pearl nudged closer; he felt it nip the surface of his skin—and some of that same trance rose in him again, the same sense that he was seeing the bones of the orbital, the breath of the dragon that was the earth and the void between the stars and the universe—except oddly muted, so that his thoughts merely seemed far away to him, running beneath a pane of glass. He could read Cam—see the blood beating in her veins, the tension in her hands and in her arms. Something was worrying her, beyond her usual disapproval of a brother who dreamt big and spent his days away from the family home. Pearl?

"This is Pearl," Da Trang said awkwardly.

Cam looked at him—in Pearl's trance, he saw her face contract; saw electrical impulses travel back and forth in her arms. "Fine," she said, with a dismissive wave of her hand. "You were weird enough without a remora pet. Whatever."

So it wasn't that which worried her. "What's on your mind?" Da Trang asked.

Cam jerked. There was no other word for it—her movement would have been barely visible, but Pearl's trance magnified everything, so that for a moment she seemed a puppet on strings, and the puppet master had just stopped her from falling. "How do you know?"

"It's obvious," Da Trang said, trying to keep his voice steady. If he could read her—if he could read people—if he could remember poems and allusions and speak like a learned scholar . . .

"The Empress is coming," Cam said.

"And?" Da Trang was having a hard time seeing how that related to him. "We're not scholars or magistrates, or rich merchants. We're not going to see her unless we queue up for the procession."

"You don't understand." Cam's voice was plaintive. "The whole Belt is scraping resources together to make an official banquet, and they asked Mother to contribute a dish."

Da Trang was going to say something funny, or flippant, but that stopped him. "I had no idea." Pearl was showing him things—signs of Cam's stress, the panic she barely kept at bay, the desire to flee the orbital before things got any more overwhelming—but he didn't need Pearl for that. Imperial favor could go a long way—could lift someone from the poorer, most outward orbitals of the Scattered Pearls Belt all the way to the First Planet and the Imperial Court—but it could also lead someone into permanent disgrace, into exile and death. It was more than a dish; it would be a statement made by Mother's orbital, by the Belt itself, something they would expect to be both exquisite and redolent with clever allusions—to the Empress's reign name, to her campaigns, to her closest advisers or her wives. . . .

"Why did they ask Mother?"

"I don't know," Cam said. Blood flowed to her face, and her hands were moments away from clenching. "Because there was no one else. Because they wanted us to fail. Take your pick. What matters is that we can't say no, lest we become disgraced."

"Can you help?" he asked, aloud, and saw Cam startled, and then her face readjusting itself into a complex mixture of—contempt, pity—as she realized he was talking to the remora.

"You really spend too much time here," she said, shaking her head. "Come on."

"Can you help?" Da Trang asked again, and felt Pearl huddle more closely against him, the trance rising to dizzying heights as the remora bit deeper.

>Of course, Architect.<

Days blur and slide against one another; Da Trang's world shrinks to the screen hovering in front of him, the lines of code slowly turning into something else—from mere instructions and algorithms to semiautonomous tasks—and then transfigured, in that strange alchemy where a programmed drone becomes a remora, when coded behaviors and responses learnt by rote turn into something else: something wild and unpredictable, as pure and as incandescent as a newborn wind.

Movement, behind him—a blur of robes and faces, and a familiar voice calling his name, like red-hot irons against the nape of his neck: "Councillor Da Trang."

Da Trang turns—fighting the urge to look at the screen again, at its scrolling lines that whisper he'll fix it if he can write just a few more words, just a few more instructions. "Your Highness." Forces his body into a bow that takes him, sliding, to the floor, on muscles that feel like they've turned to jelly—words surface, from the morass of memory, every one of them tasting like some strange foreign delicacy on his tongue, like something the meaning of which has long since turned to meaningless ashes. "May you reign ten thousand years."

A hand, helping him up: for a moment, horrified, he thinks it's the Empress, but it's just one of the younger courtiers, her face shocked under its coat of ceruse. "He hasn't slept at all, has he? For days. Councillor—"

There's a crowd of them, come into the hangar where he works, on the outskirts of the capital: the Empress and six courtiers, and bodyguards, and attendants. One of the courtiers is staring all around him—seeing walls flecked with rust, maintenance bots that move only slowly: the dingy part of the city, the unused places—the spaces where he can work in peace. There is no furniture, just the screen, and the pile of remoras—the failed ones—stacked against one of the walls. There's room for more, plenty more.

The Empress raises a hand, and the courtier falls silent. "I'm concerned for you, councillor."

"I—" He ought to be awed, or afraid, or concerned, too—wondering what she will do, what she can do to him—but he doesn't even have words left. "I have to do this, Your Highness."

The Empress says nothing for a while. She's a small, unremarkable woman—looking at her, he sees the lines of deep worry etched under her eyes, and the shape of her skull beneath the taut skin of the face. Pearl, were it still here, were it still perching on his shoulder, would have told him—about heartbeats, about body temperature and the moods of the human mind, all he would have needed to read her, to convince her with a few well-placed words, a few devastating smiles. "Pearl is gone, councillor," she says, her voice firm, stating a fact or a decree. "Your remora was destroyed in the heart of the sun."

No, not destroyed. Merely hiding—like a frightened child, not knowing where to find refuge. All he has to do is find the right words, the right algorithms . . . "Your Highness," he says.

"I could stop it," the Empress said. "Have you bodily dragged from this room and melt every piece of metal here into scrap." Her hand makes a wide gesture, encompassing the quivering remoras stacked against the walls; the one he's working on, with bits and pieces of wires trailing from it, jerking from time to time, like a heart remembering it has to beat on.

No. "You can't," he starts, but he's not gone far enough to forget who she is. Empress of the Dai Viet Empire, mistress of all her gaze and her mindships survey, protector of the named planets, raised and shaped to rule since her birth. "You—" and then he falls silent.

The Empress watches him for a while but says nothing. Is that pity in her face? Surely not. One does not rise high in the Imperial Court on pity or compassion. "I won't," she says at last, and there is the same weariness in her voice, the same hint of mortality within. "You would just find another way to waste away, wouldn't you?"

He's not wasting away. He's . . . working. Designing. On the verge of finding Pearl. He wants to tell her this, but she's no longer listening—if she ever was.

"Build your remoras, councillor." The Empress remains standing for a while, watching him. "Chase your dreams. After all—" And her face settles, for a while, into bleak amusement. "Not many of us can genuinely say we are ready to die for those."

And then she's gone; and he turns back to the screen, and lets it swallow him again, into endless days and endless nights lit only by the glare of the nearby star—the sun where Pearl vanished with only its cryptic good-bye.

He isn't building a single remora but a host of them, enough that they can go into the sun; enough to comb through layer after layer of molten matter, like crabs comb through sand—until they finally find Pearl.

None of them comes back, or sends anything back; but then, it doesn't matter. He can build more. He must build more—one after another and another, until there is no place in the sun they haven't touched.

The first Da Trang knew of the banquet was footsteps, at the door of the hangar—Mother, Pearl's trance said, analyzing the heavy tread, the vibrations of the breathing through the hangar's metal walls. Worried, too; and he didn't know why.

"Child," Mother said. She was followed by Cam, and their sister Hien, and a host of aunts and uncles and cousins. "Come with me." Even without Pearl, he could see her fear and worry, like a vise around his heart.

"Mother?" Da Trang rose, dismissing the poetry he'd been reading—with Pearl by his side, it was easier to see where it all hung together; to learn, slowly and painstakingly, to enjoy it as an official would; teasing apart layers of meaning one by one, as though eating a three-color dessert.

Mother's face was white, bloodless; and the blood had left her hands and toes, too. "The Empress wants to see the person who cooked the Three Blessings."

Three Blessings: eggs arranged around a hen for happiness and children; deer haunches with pine nuts for longevity; and carp with fishmint leaves cut in the shape of turtle leaves, for prosperity and success as an official. "You did," Da Trang said mildly. But inwardly, his heart was racing. This was . . . opportunity: the final leap over the falls that would send them flying as dragons, or tumbling down to earth as piecemeal, broken bodies.

"And you want me to come."

Mother made a small, stabbing gesture—one that couldn't disguise her worry. It was . . . unsettling to see her that way; hunched and vulnerable and mortally afraid. But Da Trang pushed the thought to the back of his mind. Now wasn't the time. "You were the one who told me what to cook." Her eyes rested on Pearl; moved away. She disapproved; but then she didn't understand what Pearl could do. "And . . ." She mouthed silent words, but Pearl heard them, all the same.

I need you.

Da Trang shook his head. He couldn't—but he had to. He couldn't afford to let this pass him by. Gently, slowly, he reached for Pearl—felt the remora shudder against his touch, the vibrations of the motors intensifying—if it were human, it would be arching against his touch, trying to move away—he didn't know why Pearl should do this now, when it was perfectly happy snuggling against him, but who could tell what went through a remora's thought processes?

"It's all right," he whispered, and pressed the struggling remora closer to him—just a little farther, enough for his mind to float, free of fear—free of everything except that strange exhilaration like a prelude of larger things to come.

The banquet room was huge—the largest room in the central orbital—filled with officials in five-panel dresses, merchants in brocade dresses, and, here and there, a few saffron-dressed monks and nuns, oases of calm in the din. Pearl was labeling everyone and everything—the merchants' heart rate and body temperature; the quality of the silk they were wearing; the names of the vast array of dishes on the table and how long each would have taken to prepare. And, beyond the walls of the orbital—beyond the ghostly people and the mass of information that threatened to overwhelm him, there was the vast expanse of space, and remoras weaving back and forth between the asteroids and the Belt, between the sun and the Belt—dancing, as if on a rhythm only they could hear.

At the end of the banquet room was the Empress—Da Trang barely caught a glimpse of her, large and terrible, before he prostrated himself to the ground along with Mother.

"Rise," the Empress said. Her voice was low, and not unkind. "I'm told you're the one who cooked the Three Blessings."

"I did," Mother said. She grimaced, then added, "It was Da Trang who knew what to do."

The Empress's gaze turned to him; he fought the urge to abase himself again, for fear he would say something untoward. "Really," she said. "You're no scholar." If he hadn't been drunk on Pearl's trance, he would have been angry at her dismissal of him.

"No, but I hope to be." Mother's hands tightening; her shame at having such a forward son; such unsuitable ambitions displayed like a naked blade.

The Empress watched him for a while. Her face, whitened with ceruse, was impassive. Beyond her, beyond the courtiers and the fawning administrators, the remoras were slowing down, forming up in a ring that faced toward the same direction—neither the sun nor the Belt, but something he couldn't identify. Waiting, he thought, or Pearl thought, and he couldn't tell what for.

"Master Khong Tu, whose words all guide us, had nothing to say on ambition, if it was in the service of the state or of one's ancestors," the Empress said at last. She was . . . not angry. Amused, Pearl told him, tracking the minute quirking of the lips, the lines forming at the corner of her eyes. "You are very forward, but manners can be taught, in time." Her gaze stopped at his shoulder, watching Pearl. "What is that?"

"Pearl," Da Trang said slowly.

One of the courtiers moved closer to the Empress—sending her something via private network, no doubt. The Empress nodded. "The Belt has such delightful customs. A remora?"

To her, as to everyone in the room, remoras were low-level artificial intelligences, smaller fishes to the bulk and heft of the mindships who traveled between the stars—like trained animals, not worth more than a moment's consideration. "Yes, Your Highness," Da Trang said. On his shoulder, Pearl hesitated; for a moment he thought it was going to detach itself and flee; but then it huddled closer to him—the trance heightened again, and now he could barely see the Empress or the orbital, just the remoras, spreading in a circle. "Pearl helps me."

"Does it?" The Empress's voice was amused again. "What wisdom does it hold, child? Lines of code? Instructions on how to mine asteroids? That's not what you need to rise in the Imperial Court."

They were out there—waiting—not still, because remoras couldn't hold still, but moving so slowly they might as well be—silent, not talking or communicating with one another, gathered in that perfect circle, and Pearl was feeling their sense of anticipation too, like a coiled spring or a tiger waiting to leap; and it was within him, too, like a flower blossoming in a too-tight chest, pushing his ribs and heart outward, its maddened, confused beating resonating like gunshots in the room.

"Watch," he whispered. "Outside the Belt. It's coming."

The Empress threw him an odd glance—amusement mingled with pity.

"Watch," he repeated, and something in his stance, in his voice, must have caught her, for she whispered something to her courtier and stood.

Outside, in the void of space, in the freezing cold between orbitals, the remoras waited—and, in the center of their circle, a star caught fire.

It happened suddenly—one moment a pinpoint of light, the next a blaze—and then the next a blaring of alarms aboard the station—the entire room seeming to lurch and change, all the bright lights turned off, the ambient sound drowned by the alarms and the screaming, the food tumbling from the tables, and people clinging to one another as the station lurched again—a merchant lost her footing in a spill of rice wine and fell, her brocade dress spread around her.

On Da Trang's shoulder, Pearl surged—as if it was going outside, as if it was going to join the other remoras watching the star ignite—but then it fell back against Da Trang; and he felt something slide into him: needles with another liquid, which burnt like fire along his spine. At the next lurch of the station, his feet remained steady, his body straight, as if standing at attention, and his muscles steadfastly refusing to answer him—even his vocal cords feeling frozen and stiff. >Don't move.<

Da Trang couldn't have moved, even if he'd wished to, even if he wasn't standing apart, observing it all at a remove, high on Pearl's trance and struggling to make sense of it all—no fear, no panic, merely a distant curiosity. A star-wildfire; light waves that were destabilizing the station, frying electronics that had never been meant for such intensity—Pearl's readouts assured him the shielding held, and that radiation levels within the room remained non-lethal for humans, poor but welcome reassurance in the wake of the disaster.

In front of him, the Empress hadn't moved either; with each lurch of the station, she merely sidestepped, keeping her balance as if it were nothing. Of course she would have augments that would go far beyond her subjects', the best her Grand Masters and alchemists could design.

Abruptly, the station stopped lurching, and the lights slowly came back on—though they were white and blinding, nothing like the quiet and refined atmosphere of the banquet; and instead of the ambient sound there was only the low crackle of static. The Empress gazed at him levelly, and then went on, as if their conversation had been merely stopped by someone else's rude interruptions, "In all of the Dai Viet Empire, there is no one who can predict a star wildfire. We can determine when the conditions for the ignition are met, of course, but the scale of such predictions is millennia, if not millions of years. And yet you knew."

Da Trang shook his head. Pearl had withdrawn; he could still see the remoras outside, now utterly still, though Pearl's readouts assured him they were not broken—merely oddly, unnaturally still. Merely . . . content. Who knew that remoras basked in wildfire? "Pearl knew," he said. "You asked how it helped me. That's how."

The Empress watched him for a while; watched Pearl nestled on his shoulder, the remora's prow wedged in the hollow where his collarbone met his neck. "I see. I think," she said, slowly, softly, "it would be best for you to take your things and come back with us, child."

And like that—just like that, with two simple sentences, and a polite piece of advice that might as well be a command—Da Trang started his rise at the Imperial Court.

Da Trang is watching his latest remora, a sleek, small thing with a bent thruster—even as he does, he sees it move, and the thruster *flows* back into place; and the remora dips its prow, a movement that might as well be a nod, and is gone through the open doorway, following the path of the previous ones—pulling itself upward into the sky, straight toward the sun. Toward silence.

>Architect. We are here.< Da Trang's head jerks up. The words are blinking, in a corner of his field of vision, insistent, and the remora saying this is close by too. It's not one of the ones he made, but it's one he's seen before, a vision from his past when he was still repairing remoras and studying for the imperial examinations—before Pearl, before the Empress. Pitted metal and those broken thrusters at the back, and the wide gash on the right side that he's never managed to patch; the nub on the prow and the broken-off wing, clumsily repaired with only a basic welder bot. . . .

"Teacher," he whispers, addressing the remora by the name he gave it, all those years ago. "I'm sorry."

Remoras don't have feelings, don't have human emotions. They lie somewhere halfway between ships and bots, outside the careful order of numbered planets; cobbled together from scraps, looking as though they're going to burst apart at any moment.

Behind Teacher is Slicer, and Tumbler, and all the rest of the remoras: the ones who were with him at the very beginning, the ones who made and gave him Pearl.

Teacher's image wavers in and out of focus, and Da Trang fights the urge to turn away, to go back to his code, because he owes Teacher that much. Because Pearl was given to him for safekeeping, and he has lost it.

"I'm sorry," Da Trang says again, though he doesn't even know if Teacher can understand him.

>New things are more easily broken,< Teacher says. Something very like a shrug, and the remora weaving closer to him. >Don't concern yourself, Architect.<

"Are you—are you building another?" Da Trang knows the answer even before he asks.

>Like Pearl? No.< Teacher is silent for a while. >It was flawed, Architect. Too . . . much vested into a single vessel. We will ponder how to build otherwise.<

Da Trang cannot wait. Cannot stand to be there, with the emptiness on his shoulder, where Pearl used to rest; to gaze at the remoras and the hangar and have nothing about them, no information about their makeup or their speed; all the things Pearl so easily, effortlessly provided him. If he closes his eyes, he can feel again the cold shock of needles sliding into his neck, and the sharpening of the world before the trance kicked in, and everything seemed glazed in light.

Slicer weaves its way to the first pile of remoras in the corner of the hangar: the flawed ones, the ones that wouldn't lift off, that wouldn't come to life, or that started only to crash and burn. It circles them, once, twice, as if fascinated—it never judges, never says anything, but Da Trang can imagine, all too well, what it sees: hubris and failure, time and time again. He's no Grand Master of Design Harmony, no Master of Wind and Water: he can repair a few remoras, but his makings are few, and pitiful, and graceless, nothing like Pearl.

"I have to try," Da Trang whispers. "I have to get it back."

>It was flawed,< Teacher says. >Will not come back.<

They know too, more than the Empress does, that it will take more than a sun's warmth to destroy a remora. That Pearl is still there. That he can still reach it, talk to it—make it come back.

Teacher moves, joins Slicer around the pile of stillborn remoras. >Architect. Use of this?<

No scraps of metal left unused, of course—they scavenge their own dead, make use of anything and everything to build. Once, Da Trang would have found it disquieting; but now all he feels is weariness, and impatience that they're keeping him from his algorithms. "I don't need them anymore. They're . . . flawed. Take them."

>Architect. Thank you.< He'd have thought they didn't know gratitude, but perhaps they do. Perhaps they've learnt, being so close to humans. Or perhaps they're merely doing so to appease him—and would it really make a difference if that was the case? So many things human are fake and inconstant—like favors. >We will return. Much to ponder.<

"Wait," Da Trang calls, as the remoras move away from his discarded scraps, from the blurred, indistinct remnants of his failures. "Tell me—"

>Architect?<

"I need to know. Was it my fault?" Did he ignore Pearl—was there some harbinger of the things to come—were the odd times the remora fell silent, with its prow pointed toward the sun, a sign of what it secretly yearned for?

Could he . . . could he have stopped it, had he known?

Silence. Then Teacher's answer, slow and hesitant. >We built. We made, from metal and electronics to the spark of life. We didn't *determine*, Architect. It went where it willed. We do not know.<

No answer then, but why had he thought it would be so easy?

On the morning of the day he was to be raised to councillor, Da Trang got up early, with an unexpected queasiness in his stomach—fear of what would happen, of Mother and her dire warnings about Empresses' fickle favorites being right?—no, that wasn't it.

Pearl was gone. He reached out, scratching the callus on his neck, in the place where it usually rested—scanning the room and finding nothing, not even a trace of its presence. "Pearl? Pearl?"

Nothing under the sheets, nothing in the nooks and crannies of the vast room—he turned off everything, every layer of the Purple Forbidden City's communal network, and still he couldn't see Pearl.

Impossible. It wasn't human; it didn't have any desires of its own except to serve Da Trang, to serve the whims of the Empress and her endless curiosity about anything from stellar phenomena to the messages passed between remoras and bots, to the state of the technologies that underpinned the communal network—to be shown off to scientists and alchemists and engineers, its perceptions and insights dissected and analyzed for anything of use to the Empire. It couldn't just go wandering off. It—

Da Trang threw open the doors of his room, startling one of the servants who'd been carrying a tray with a cup of tea—almost absentmindedly, he reached out and straightened the tray before moving on. "Pearl? Pearl?"

Courtiers, startled out of their impassivity, turned their heads to follow him as he ran into courtyard after courtyard, finding nothing but the usual bustle of the court, the tight knots of people discussing politics or poetry or both—an endless sea of officials with jade-colored sashes barely paying attention to him—and still no Pearl, no trace of it or word on his coms.

It was only two bi-hours until the ceremony; and what would he say to the Empress, if Pearl wasn't there—if he couldn't perform any of the feats of use to her, and that distinguished him from the mass of upstart courtiers?

"Pearl?"

He found the remora, finally, in the quarters of the Master of Rites and Ceremonies. The Master was deep in discussion with her students, pointing to something on an interface Da Trang couldn't see. Pearl was in the small room at the end, where they had gathered the necessary supplies for the ceremony.

"Pearl?"

It stood, watching the clothes on the mannequin in the center of the room: the five-panel robe made from the finest brocade with the insignia of the sparrow on the chest—not an official rank attained through merit and examinations, but one reserved for special cases, for emperors' and empresses' fickle favors. On the shoulder was a rest for Pearl, with a small model of the remora.

"What are you doing here?"

Pearl didn't move, or acknowledge him in any way. It was . . . that same particular intent stillness it had had, back at the time of the first star wildfire. Waiting—what for? "Is something going to happen? Pearl?"

>Architect.< The words were hesitant—letter after letter slowly materializing in his field of vision. And still Pearl didn't move, didn't head to Da Trang's shoulder, to fill the empty space he couldn't get used to. >Need. Time.<

"What for? The ceremony is in two bi-hours—"

Pearl shifted; and he realized then that it had been standing in a shaft of sunlight, its prow turned toward the heavens. >Not meant for this.<

"You were built for this," Da Trang said. Why the strange mood—fear or nervousness? But remoras couldn't feel any of that, surely?

But, then, Pearl wasn't just any remora. *We can build better,* Teacher had said. Better, or merely more unstable? "Come," Da Trang said.

Pearl hovered to the shoulder of the mannequin—nudging the small model they'd made of it, which looked nothing like a remora: bedecked with silk and scraps of translucent cotton. >Not meant for this.< Its prow rose again, toward the sun. >Space. The song of stars. The heartbeat of the universe.<

"We'll be going into space," Da Trang said. "Often enough. I promise." It scared him now—the Imperial Court wasn't a place to hear the song of the stars or the rhythm of the universe or whatever else it was going on about. "Come."

>Not the same.< Pearl made a small whirring noise.

"They built you to help me," Da Trang said. And, without Pearl, he was nothing—just another dull-witted poor boy, the Empress's favor soon forgotten. "Pearl. Come on." He fought an urge to bodily drag it from the room, like a disobedient child, but it would have been unkind. "Remember Teacher and Slicer and the other remoras? They said they'd built you for me. For the examinations. For understanding."

Come on, come on, come on—if Pearl left him, he didn't know what he'd do, what he'd become, what he could make of the shambles that would be his life—

>Understanding.< Pearl's prow dipped again, toward the mannequin. >Building better.< Again, the same slowness to the words, as if it were considering; and then, to Da Trang's relief, it flew back to him, and the familiar weight settled on his shoulder—the familiar ice-cold feeling of needles biting into his shoulder, the sense of reality becoming unbearably sharp, unbearably clear, everything labeled and parceled and analyzed, from the Master of Rites and Ceremonies' minute frown to the student fighting off sleep in the first row—from the cut and origin of the silk to the fluctuating intensity of the sunlight in the room.

>Can help.< But as Da Trang turned away, he felt Pearl's weight on his shoulder—felt the remora looking upward at the sun—the pull of the motors, barely suppressed; and he knew that he hadn't managed to quell Pearl's yearnings.

He doesn't sleep—only so many hours in a day, and there are ways to enjoy them all. Not for long, of course, not with the drugs he's pumped himself full of; but what does he care for more time? He *needs* Pearl back, so badly it's like a vise, squeezing his ribs into bloodied shards. Without Pearl, he's nothing: an ex-favorite of the Empress, fallen from her regard—an overambitious boy from the outer edges of the Empire, overreaching and tumbling over the waterfalls instead of soaring, dragonlike, in the wake of imperial favor. But it's Pearl that the Empress was truly interested in—its tidbits on stellar phenomena, on technologies, on ships and what made them work—what Pearl called the understanding of the universe, with an earnestness that didn't seem to belong in a remora: everything that they put into always moving, never stopping, it put into intent stillness, in that posture on his shoulder where its eyes, if it'd had any, would have bored holes into steel or diamond.

It's still there, in the heart of the sun. Waiting. For him, or for something else; but if Pearl is there, that means he can find it. That means . . . He doesn't know what he will do when he finds Pearl, how he'll beg or plead or drag it from the sun—but he'll find a way.

It was a routine journey, a shuttle ride between the First Planet and the White Clouds orbital; and the Empress, of course, insisted her new Councillor come with her, to show her the wonders of space.

Da Trang came, because he had no choice—in spite of deep unease—because Pearl had been restless and distant, because he'd tossed and turned at night, trying to think of what he could do and thinking of nothing.

Halfway through the trip, the Empress called for him.

She was in her cabin, surrounded by her courtiers—they were all sitting on silk cushions and sipping tea from a cup as cracked as eggshells. In front of her was a hologram of space as seen from the prow of the ship. As Da Trang entered, the view blurred and shifted, and became the outside of the orbital—except that the stars were dimmer than they ought to have been.

"Councillor," the Empress said. "I thought you would enjoy seeing these."

Pearl snuggled closer to Da Trang—needles extended, the blissful cold spreading outward from the pinpricks, the trance rising—extending to the outside, narrowing until he could see the bots maneuvering nano-thin filaments, unfolding a large, dark shape like a spread cloth behind the orbital.

Void-nets. Da Trang had sat in nightlong sessions with the Ministry of War's engineers, describing to them what Pearl saw—what Pearl thought—how the remora could even analyze the dust of stars, the infinitesimal amounts of matter carried by the wind in the void of space—and how, in turn, those could be trapped.

He hadn't thought—

"Your Highness," Da Trang said, struggling to remember how to bow. "I had no idea this was such a momentous occasion."

"The Ministry of War has been testing prototypes for a while—but it is the first time a void-net is deployed in the vicinity of a Numbered Planet, to be sure." The Empress was almost . . . thoughtful. "All to your credit, and Pearl's."

Another nudge, but he had no need to see heartbeats or temperature to catch the anger of the courtiers. As if they'd ever be capable of matching him . . .

"Tell us," the Empress said. "What will we find in your nets?"

A brief moment of panic, as nothing happened—as Pearl didn't move, the thought that it was going to be today, of all days, when the remora failed him—and then a stab so deep under his collarbone it was almost painful—

and the view shifting, becoming dotted with hundreds of pinpoints of colored lights, each labeled with a name and concentration. "Suffocating metal 5.3 percent," he whispered. "Frozen water 3 percent. Gray adamantine crystals 9.18 percent . . ." On and on, a litany of elements, labeled and weighed: everything the Empire would decant to fuel its machines and stations and planets, names and images and every use they could be put to, a flood of information that carried him along—such a terrible, breathless sense of being the center, of knowing everything that would come to pass . . .

He came to with a start, finding Pearl all but inert against him, softly vibrating on his shoulder. The Empress was looking at him and smiling— her face and body relaxed, her heartbeat slow and steady. "A good take. The Ministry of War should be satisfied, I should think." She watched the screens with mild curiosity. "Tell me what you see."

"Colors," Da Trang said. Even with Pearl quiescent, he could make them out—slowly accreting, the net bulging slightly outward as it filled—the bots straining under the pressure. "A dance of lights—"

He never got to finish the sentence.

On his shoulder, Pearl surged—gone before Da Trang's flailing arms could stop it, tearing through the cabin—and then, with scarcely a pause, through the walls of the ship as if they were nothing more than paper; alarms blaring, the Empress and him thrown to the ground as the cabin sealed itself—but Pearl was already gone. Fumbling, Da Trang managed to call up a view from ships around the orbital—a slow zoom on Pearl, weaving and racing toward the stars, erratic and drunken, stopping for a bare moment, and then plunging toward the heart of the sun.

>Architect. Farewell. Must be *better*. Must show them.<

And then there was nothing—just emptiness on his shoulder like a hole in his own heart, and the memory of those words—and he could not tell if they were angry or sad or simply a statement of fact.

Nothing.

Days blur and slide against one another; his world shrinks to the screen hovering in front of him, the lines of code slowly turning into something else. He can barely read them now; he's merely inputting things from rote—his hands freeze, at odd intervals; and his vision goes entirely black, with whole chunks of time disappearing—everything oddly disjointed.

Except for his remoras.

They're sleek and beautiful and heartbreaking now, moving with the grace of officials and fighter-monks—one by one, pulling themselves from the

floor, like dancers getting up and stretching limb after limb—still for a heartbeat, their prows turned toward him, and then gone toward the sun, a blur of
speed he cannot follow anymore—as darkness grows and encroaches on his
field of vision.

He must build more.

Remoras come and go: Teacher, Slicer, and all the others, taking from the
pile of scraps, making small noises as they see a piece of metal or a connector; slowly, determinedly taking apart his earlier efforts—the tearing sound
of sheets of metal stretched past the breaking point; the snapping of cables
wrenched out of their sockets; the crackling sound of ion thrusters taken
apart—his failures, transfigured into life—patched onto other remoras, other
makings; going on and on and on, past Da Trang's pitiful, bounded existence—going on, among the stars.

"Tell me," he says, aloud.

>Architect. What should I tell you?< One of them—Slicer, Teacher, he's
not sure he can tell them apart anymore; save for his own remoras, everything
seems small and blurred, diminished into insignificance. Everything seems
dimmer and smaller, and even his own ambitions feel shriveled, far away,
belonging to someone else, a stranger with whom he shares only memories.

"Pearl wanted to be better than you. It said so, before it left. Tell me what
it means."

Silence, for a while. Then letters, steadily marching through his darkening
field of vision. >Everything strives. It couldn't be better than us, Architect. It
is—<

"Flawed. I know."

>Then you understand.<

"No, I don't. That's not what I want. I want to—I need to—" He stops
then, thinks of remoras, of scarce resources that have to be endlessly recycled,
of that hunger to rebuild themselves, to build others, that yearning that led
to Pearl's making.

And he sees it then. "It doesn't matter. Thank you, Slicer." He stifles a bitter
laugh. Everything strives.

>I am Teacher.<

Its words are almost gentle, but Da Trang no longer cares. He stares ahead,
at the screen, at the blurred words upon it, the life's blood he fed into his
remoras, making them slowly, painstakingly, and sending them one by one
into the heart of the sun. He thinks of the remoras' hopes for the future, and
of things that parents pass on to their children, and makers to their creations.
He knows now that Pearl, in the end, is like Teacher, like Slicer, no better

or no different, moved by the same urges and hungers. He thinks of the fires of the sun, the greatest forge in the system; and of Pearl, struggling to understand how things worked, from the smallest components of matter to mindships and humans—he'd thought it was curiosity, but now he sees what drove it. What still drives it.

If you know how things work, you can make them.

Darkness, ahead and behind him, slowly descending upon the screen—the remoras dancing before him, scavenging their own to survive, to make others.

Yearnings. Hunger. The urge to build its own makings, just as it was once built.

Must be better.

Must build better.

And as he slides into shadows—as his nerveless fingers leave the keyboard, his body folding itself, hunched over as if felled by sleep—he thinks of the other remoras, taking their own apart—thinks of the ones he made, the ones he sent into the heart of the sun; and he sees, with agonizing clarity, what he gave Pearl.

Not tools to drag it back or to contact it, but offerings—metal and silicon chips and code, things to be taken apart and grafted, to be scavenged for anything salvageable—the base from which a remora can be forged.

As his eyes close—just for a moment, just for a heartbeat, he sees Pearl—not the remora he remembers, the sleek making of Teacher and Slicer, but something else—something *changed*, reshaped by the heat of the sun, thickened by accreted metal scooped from the heart of a star, something slick and raw and incandescent, looming over him like a heavenly messenger, the weight of its presence distorting the air.

Darkness, ahead and behind him—rising to fill the entire world; and everything he was, his lines of code, his remoras, scattering and fragmenting—into the fires of the sun, to become Pearl's own makings, reforged and reborn, and with no care for human toil or dreams or their petty ambitions.

There is no bringing Pearl back. There is no need to.

And as his eyes close for the last time, he smiles, bitterly—because it is not what he longed for, but it is only fair.

>Farewell, Architect.<

And Pearl's voice, booming, becomes his entire world, his beginning and his ending—and the last thing he hears before he is borne away, into the void between the stars.

Nick Wolven's stories have appeared in *Clarkesworld*, *Asimov's*, *Analog*, and *F&SF*, among other publications. He attended Clarion in 2007. He can be found on Twitter @nickwolven and online at nickthewolven.com. He lives in New York City with his loved ones and small animals.

THE METAL DEMIMONDE

Nick Wolven

Tipper's in the south parking lot when her phone starts going mad. Not just ringing. It's a tone she's never heard before, high and warbling, almost a scream. She's halfway up the fairway before she places it.

An alarm.

The ride.

She bumps through the crowds, heedless of complaints, her lineman's boots crushing foam cups and toes. *Breakdown.* That's the word that's in her head, along with a few others. *Accident. Screwup.*

Yeah, you screwed up, kid. Big time.

The rides clash and swoop overhead, flinging screaming riders at the stars.

Snake is located near the end of the fairway where the grounds trail off into grit and chaparral. Even from a distance, behind the bulk of the Haunted House, Tipper can see the ride stretched out like a beached leviathan, the tubular body sprawled in the dirt, lights all down it twinkling emergency colors; orange, yellow, red. The mouth gapes hugely, like a crimson castle door. Escape hatches along the sides have popped open to show steel ribs. In the lurid aura of the Haunted House, the thing looks like some dying dragon, felled by a southwestern St. George. But it's not dead, only paralyzed, screaming a mechanical plea through Tipper's phone.

She thumbs the screen and shuts off the alarm.

The ride is surrounded by a mob of gawking bystanders. Tipper pushes through and vaults the aluminum fence. Suzie is standing by Snake's mouth, all ten fingers curled in her tufty hair. The wrinkles in her metalhead concert-T twitch with agitation.

Tipper pulls off her sleeveless hoodie as she jogs up, panting in mouthfuls of the desert night.

"Suzie, I'm sorry. I just got the buzz. What's wrong with—?"

Before Suzie can answer, another woman steps out from behind the ride. Amy Carter is pure carnie, longboned and lean, with a trailing gray braid that runs down to her white jeans. She runs the Haunted House, or as she likes to put it, keeps the gate to Dracula's castle. Her gray eyes screw hard into Tipper's.

"Supposed to be back half an hour ago, weren't you, kid?"

"I . . ." Tipper falters.

"What were you doing, getting cuddly with some boy behind the bathrooms? You think this isn't a real job?"

"Dial it down, Carter. Just a notch." Suzie's face is round, smooth-cheeked, and somehow always seems to be smiling. She puts a hand on the back of Tipper's neck. "There's nothing Tipper could've done, even if she was here. Snake's got something caught in her throat, that's all."

Tipper tries to look cool as she clomps up to the ride.

"So someone got stuck? No one's hurt, are they?"

"You better damn well hope not." Carter stomps into the ride's wide mouth.

Suzie pats Tipper's arm. "They're not hurt, don't worry. Snake'd never let that happen."

It's true. Snake could never put anyone in danger. Safety first, right? It's in the wiring.

Tipper follows the two women into the ride's gullet, between the big foam-rubber fangs. The machine is a tender behemoth, incapable of harming a human being.

But here's the problem, always the problem: What if a human being decides to harm Snake?

From the ride's mouth, Tipper has a great view of the fairgrounds, framed in the robot's arching jaws. Over the tent arcade, the Scream-o-Saurus chomps at the stars. Octowhip, the LandShark, the Abominable Go-Go-Go Man, they're all here, waving segmented arms, dancing like giants, giving loads of shrieking riders the time of their lives.

At moments like this, Tipper feels a kind of aching self-consciousness, like a sunburn all over her body. Who is she but another lost kid, trying to look older than her age? Skinny hips, brown face, clothing too bulky for the Arizona climate. A child of the Fringe, with nothing to keep her going but an outsize attitude.

Suzie trusts her, though. One month into the job, and Suzie is already letting Tipper share responsibility for Snake. She can see it, Suzie says—Tipper has the touch, the feel.

"You got the magic, kid. I always know."

It's a good thing to hear in these lonely desert nights, when the fair shuts down and the rides go to sleep, settling on their lots like weary monsters. As their engines click into silence, Suzie sits in the door of her trailer, bottle of Cuervo between her knees, and takes in the phantasmagoria with a hand.

"You know what I mean? I mean love. Seriously. You want to be a ride operator, you got to love these things like your own two hands. These aren't your granddad's rides, some swivel-mounted cages on a rotating frame. These are beasts. They need TLC. And I'll tell you something, if you give that to 'em? They'll return it a thousand-fold."

Tipper's brothers would say that's crazy talk. Carnie superstition, technophilia. But in the juniper smell of the carnival night, with saurian heads bobbing against the moon, when you're puffing homegrown pot under bowers of luciferase lights, and those cool Sonoran breezes come up with just a whiff of kerosene . . . how could you want any other kind of life?

"Trust," Suzie'll say, "that's what it comes down to. The beautiful trust between woman and machine."

"Hey. Tip." The snap of Suzie's fingers is muffled in the ride's padded throat. "You okay?"

Speechless, feeling ridiculous, Tipper turns and follows her down the red tunnel.

Snake is one of the smaller rides, intended for younger kids and their parents. Bloated with extra padding, painted nonthreatening colors, it has the googly eyes of a family attraction. Synthetic flesh of gel-packed polyfabric masks the feedback systems: the thigmotaxics, the thixotropic sensors and servos that keep riders bouncing along. You'd have to try to get hurt inside Snake, and even then you'd probably be okay. Like a princess oversensitive to a pea, Snake would smother you in loving cushions, push you along through a gentle peristalsis, and pop you out into the world unharmed.

The kids love it. Getting swallowed and expelled, then rushing around to do it again: the ride seems to exorcise some childish fear. Tipper herself always feels queasy in here. She keeps close to Suzie, stumbling on the padded floor, trying not to touch the slightly grubby walls. One thing about Snake, the ride may be safe, but you can only swallow so many children per day without picking up a few not totally wholesome odors. Snake is self-cleaning, so most of the puke and pee and food is masked with an alcoholic tang of disinfectant. Still . . .

"Suze?" Tipper pauses ten feet down the throat. The ride is stiff but not quite straight; they've lost sight of Carter around the curve. Suzie turns.

"Listen," Tipper says. "I'm real sorry. I was in the parking lot, and I don't know what happened, I guess I dropped a mental digit or something—"

"Tip?" Suzie braces herself against the bouncy walls. "I've been at this a long time, okay? These rides, they're like dogs. Big, friendly, and dumb. They get in trouble. It happens."

"I know. I'm saying, though, what I did, it was totally stupid, and I won't ever—"

"Ah, ah, ah!" Suzie waves her hands by her ears. "It's history. I've already forgotten it."

"But I—"

"I'm sure you had your reasons." Suzie's face creases, and for a moment, Tipper can see how old she is. At least fifty, maybe more. A whole life, probably not a happy one, etched in those plump Chinese features. "If I cared about punctuality, you think I'd be working the 'grounds? Think I'd be tending to this dumb brute?" Suzie gives the wall an affectionate whap. "We're all hopeless screw-ups, down here in the metal demimonde."

Tipper nods. She still wishes she could explain. "The thing is, I haven't even told you why I was—"

But Suzie reaches out, holding Tipper's hot face between her hands. This is a woman who spends her life wrangling metal monsters the size of tractor-trailers. A woman used to being in control.

"Tip? Listen. You're one of us, now. You're a robot wrangler, a monster rider, and you're literally standing in the belly of the beast. It's just me and you down here, and we've got to look out for each other. Right? Right."

It's a nice moment, until the screaming starts.

Tipper's first to move, bounding down the jiggling tube. Already she can hear occasional giggles between the cries. The screams themselves edge higher, becoming falsetto, false. Something weird is going on, here.

Another bend, and Tipper slams into Carter's jean-jacketed back. The screams break into boyish laughter.

"Help . . . I'm being eaten . . . I think my scrotum's caught!"

Carter's face is like something out of her Haunted House. "You." She jabs a finger. "Enough. Move."

Clutching Carter's shoulder, standing on tiptoes, Tipper can see two boys wedged into the pillowed tunnel, feet and hands jammed into the walls, like a couple of throat-choking chicken bones. The smartfoam is pulsing around them, spasming like a misfiring muscle as the ride tries to shake them loose. This is the only way to jam the ride: You have to give it everything you've got.

"Guys." Suzie squeezes past them, frowning at the boys. "Come on, already. There's kids waiting to ride."

"Hey, ma'am, is it our fault your ride's not safe? I'm really stuck. This is, like, misleading advertising. Some poor little innocent child could lose a testicle."

More snickers.

"Out." Suzie's thumb jerks at an exit. With a laugh, the boys let go and drop to the cushioned floor. The foamy muscles of the throat stop twitching. You can almost hear the ride's sigh of relief.

Suzie stands over them. "Get elsewhere, fellas. Fast."

"I don't know, ma'am, I'm pretty shook up." The older boy winces theatrically, rubbing his elbows. "That was a kind of traumatic experience. I feel like I might need some time to recover."

Suzie's thumb is not in a humoring mood. It becomes a standoff, the boys laughing, Suzie's thumb jerking, till one of the guys happens to notice Tipper.

It's like someone pushed a button. The boy's childish attitude drops away. He jumps to his feet, reaches for his friend. "All right, man, come on, that's enough."

The other kid, younger and smaller, doesn't pick up the hint. "I don't know, man, I think this ride is, like, molesting me."

"*Enough*, dick."

They stand together, balanced on the padding. A couple of Fringe kids in workmen's clothes. You'd never guess that ten seconds ago they were acting like a pair of giggling toddlers.

The tall one nods. "Hey, there, Tipper."

Tipper can feel Suzie staring. She suddenly has a fantasy of the foam walls flexing, shaking, bouncing her toward some place far away from here.

Suzie squints. "Tip, you *know* these idiots?"

"Uh, sort of." Tipper flinches. "I mean, we only—"

"We're friends," says the older boy. "Well, acquaintances."

Suzie's squint contracts. With a shake of her head, Tipper staggers across the wobbly floor, grabs the tall boy by the elbow. "Come on," she hisses, ushering him to the exit hatch. Amazingly, the boy obeys.

Out in the open, the noise of the fair explodes into salience. Tipper drags the two guys back between the trailers.

"What are you *doing* here?"

The tall one takes her hand. "What do you think?"

Without warning, he grabs Tipper by the arms, pulls her toward him. "Luke," she begins. But already he's kissing her, holding her head with his hands, and Tipper just knows, all the way from her head to her boots, that she's in serious trouble.

It started three nights ago, in the land of Orphans.

Orphans: that's what the carnies call the independent rides. Most of them are ungainly clunkers. Exposed works, wheezy pistons. They're self-sufficient, but without human help, the fairgoers tend to feel leery about riding them. The Orphans hunker at the edge of the grounds, silent and neglected, accompanied only by the service bots that tighten their screws and top up their fluids. Like a bunch of old crocodiles, Tipper thinks, getting picked over by Egyptian plovers.

There's something sadly romantic about the Orphans. Tipper likes to come out here on break, sit with a bucket-sized cup of Coke, and bask in the silence of these patient, old machines. Usually, the Orphans sit near the parking lot, and Tipper's view is of auto-drive cars lined in arrays, tight and neat as corn kernels. Beyond the lattice of windshields, she can just make out the lights of a typical southwestern 'burb. Lawns dead from water rationing. Shuttered factories, hard-luck malls. The Fringe.

That's where Tipper was three nights ago, when she heard laughter from among the machines. She gulped her hotdog, put down her Coke, and picked her way through the thicket of steel limbs.

And there they were. Gathered in the shadow of Tentaculus, four boys were passing around a vaper pipe. Perfect stereotypes, these guys, with their caveman beards, their mechanic's jumpsuits, their construction vests and Pan-Am coats. All of them affecting the styles of jobs that no longer existed.

Manuals.

Tipper stepped over the limp limbs of Tentaculus, wiping hot dog grease on her shorts. As she approached, one of the guys was leaning back, sighting up an extended arm, a J&B bottle dangling from his hand.

"Hey!" Tipper shouted, just as the bottle went winging toward Tentaculus's monstrous face. The ride blinked, a fiberglass lid slamming down over its one huge eye. The bottle bounced off, fell harmlessly in the dirt.

Tipper stomped forward. "Dick. These are functional rides."

The group turned. She found herself facing four teenage sneers.

"Doesn't look too functional to me." The guy who'd thrown the bottle kicked a limp tentacle, a hose of compressed air sheathed in piezocanvas.

"Well, they don't get a lot of riders," Tipper said, "but that doesn't mean . . ." She wasn't in a mood to argue. "Look, I'm just saying, be respectful, okay?"

"Respectful?" The guy lifted his scruffy chin. "And who are you, the ride fairy?"

Snickers all around.

"I'm an operator," Tipper said, "and you—"

But suddenly, a boy broke free of the group. He was the tallest, by far, and the only clean-shaven one, dressed in an airman's jacket and carpenter's pants. Long black hair reached to his shoulders.

"Hey, I know you." He tipped his head toward the grounds. "You run the Snake, over by the Haunted House. With that Chinese lady and the mean-looking cowgirl."

"Their names," Tipper said, "are Suzie and Amy."

The guy wasn't fazed by her tone. "I've seen you working. You know your stuff."

"There's nothing to know." Tipper hesitated. "The rides do all the work, mostly."

"Sure." The boy looked up at the Orphans, hands in his brass-zippered pockets. "Still, it takes a kind of talent, right? Like with animals."

"I guess." Tipper knew not to trust guys like this. She'd seen more than enough of the type; she had three older brothers, after all. But something about him . . . there was tension in the boy's presence, more intriguing than threatening, like a faint scent of something burning.

"Animals? Really?" One of the others sneered up at Tentaculus' cartoon grin. "Animals are cool. But look at this stupid thing."

The tall boy and Tipper both ignored him.

"Luke." He held out a hand. "You're Tip, huh? I'm always hearing that old lady shout your name."

"Suzie. That's the old lady. She's not old, though; she's only like, fifty. I'm Tipoli. Tipper." She gave Luke's hand a single, brisk pump.

"You're on break? Well, I wonder, Tipper . . ." He grinned, and this much was true: he was dazzlingly handsome. "I wonder if you could give me a hand?"

The fair's parking lot had seemed vast and cracked, that night, the site of a mall that never got built. The cars were packed so tight you couldn't even squeeze between them; the drivers would have to summon them through the valet station. Crazy, the navigational skills of machines.

Luke went to a section of the lot marked off with chains, where old cars had been parked at madcap angles. Pickups, mod-jobs, a vintage corvette. The antique bodies and scattershot parking betrayed what signs on the pavement confirmed.

HUMAN DRIVERS ONLY.
NO AUTO-DRIVE BEYOND THIS POINT.

Luke pointed. "Mine's over here."

The vehicle made Tipper gasp and laugh at once. It was a courier truck, squeezed between two streetlight pedestals, the logo of the company still showing under a hasty spray-paint job. The thing was modded in a serious way: integrated tire-wheels, expanded cab, tinted windows custom-cut and sealed into 3D-printed panels hung on a modular frame. The cargo box rode low; Tipper suspected more than package-sorting machinery had been stored away back there.

"Home sweet home." Luke pounded the box. "Got a bed back here, internet, built-in fridge, the best game hookup you'll ever see. With a ride like this, who needs property taxes, huh?"

Tipper followed him along the vehicle's fiberglass flank. The compact design, the lightweight frame, the aerodynamic lines . . . it was obviously a computer-driven truck, built for maximum speed on the shipping-only roads. Never meant for a human driver.

She peered at him. "So you drive this thing?"

"Trying to. That's why you're here."

He popped open the door, a maintenance hatch he'd expanded to fit his makeshift cab. Inside, the components had been shifted and rebuilt, making room, just barely, for a driver and passenger. A carbon-fiber NASCAR seat, crudely cabled to the frame, took up most of the space. An ancient Mini Cooper steering wheel bloomed like a thistle from a two-foot exposed column. The pedal system looked like something from an old church organ. Although the interface for the computer was in place, showing all systems normal, Tipper assumed it had been clipped out of the loop.

Her older brothers, car jocks all, would have heartily approved. Cars ought to be an open book, they thought. No hidden triggers, no mechanical turks. They wanted to pull back the curtain from the autodriving wizard. Put the driver in control.

She ran her hands over the welding. "No way this is legal."

"No way," Luke agreed with a grin.

He grabbed the hatch, contracted his body, and half jumped, half tumbled into the jackleg seat. "They're still using the same parts as the trucker days. You just have to load 'em up with different stuff. Legacy line systems, right? All the same tools and dies, injection molds. So it's not too hard to pull everything out and retrofit."

Tipper ducked in after him. "You crash in this, you'll crumple like a beer can."

"Yeah, I'll be chewed like Trident, huh?" He laughed silently, running two fingers round the wheel. "You know about cars?"

"My family does."

"Well, it's this queen bee that's giving me problems." Luke tapped a knuckle on the autodrive. "I clipped everything I could think of, but I can't seem to shut it down for good. I still need it to—"

"To check in at the toll gates, right." Tipper knew how this stuff worked. "Or they'll snap your plates and call it in as a malfunction."

"Right. So mother brain here has to be awake and talking. Only thing is, I tried to code feedback in for all the connectivity checks. Edge-stitching, they call it. So the program, like, talks back to itself?"

"Right, I know."

"Well, it's not working. She keeps noticing she's disconnected. And shouting alerts at other drivers. So everywhere I go, all the cars around me are getting these alarms, like I'm a runaway truck. It gives me a nice open road, but . . ."

Tipper edged him over, sliding in. "You need to shut off the emergency alerts. It's got one of those AI security systems, right? So just give it your info and a statement, tell it you're taking legal responsibility as a human being. It's federal law, the car has to—"

"Exactly." Luke was holding out his license, his phone. "That's all I need you to do."

Tipper sighed. She should have known.

"All right." She waved him out of her space. "Hand it over." Taking Luke's license, she keyed on the comm. The touch interface showed a smiling cartoon truck.

"Sorry," Luke said with shy pride. "It's just that I don't—"

"You don't talk to robots. I get it." Tipper did the old touchscreen fingerdance, darting glances at his workman's clothes. "I should have guessed."

Luke smoothed his airman's jacket over the roadworker's vest underneath. "It's kind of a code with me."

"Right. I know. You're a Manual." She keyed her way into the security system.

"I wouldn't use that label." Luke shrugged. "I mean, I'm not all hardcore about it. I don't go all the way. I don't get into sabotage."

Typing in the last commands one-handed, Tipper pulled out her strapless Navy watch. Ten to ten. Almost the end of her break.

"You know, this could take a while. There's a whole interview you have go through. I mean, federal law and shit . . ."

Luke watched her. "I guess you probably have to get back to your job, huh?"

Tipper hesitated. Two shadows, the merest hints of dimples, appeared in Luke's cheeks. He put his hand over hers, gently drew it away from the screen. "Guess we'll have to do this another time."

And that's when Tipper got a feeling, a very strong feeling, that this whole thing wasn't about Luke's truck at all.

Now, in the shadows among the trailers, Luke draws back, lips lingering to brush Tipper's cheek. Almost against her will, Tipper stretches up for his retreating mouth, clinging to him with feral hunger as his boots scratch away across the sandy ground.

"I've been waiting for you." The instant she hears herself saying it, Tipper wants to viciously kick her own ass. So cliché, but the problem is, it's true. Every night for the past three days, she's spent her breaks lounging around the lots, wandering the Orphans, waiting for Luke to come strolling through the forest of hydraulic limbs.

Which is why she was standing around like an idiot, earlier, wasting time, dragging out her break, when Snake started blasting that alarm through her phone. Which is why she absolutely should not be standing here, grabbing this boy by the collar, pulling him down to her lips and . . .

"What's up, anyway? Where've you been?" Tipper shoves him back halfway through the kiss, annoyed in twenty different ways. "And why are you coming around here, now, screwing up my ride?"

"Sorry." Luke pushes down her hands. "I had some things to do." Boys and their vague excuses. Of course he doesn't even answer her second question. "Hey, listen, you still up for it? You know, giving me a hand with that truck?"

Tipper holds back. She has to at least pretend not to seem too interested. "Are you going to actually meet me this time? Or just screw around and make me lose my job?"

He glances up. She can see the whole fair, a brief gold flicker in his eyes.

"How about tomorrow? I'll come by. You'll be around?"

"Till Sunday. Then we're moving on." Tipper hopes he feels the pressure implicit in those words.

"Hey, Luke?" The runty sidekick pipes up; Tipper had almost forgotten he was there. "If we're going to meet with that guy . . ."

Luke waves. "One second." His fingers rest, briefly, on the back of Tipper's hand. "Tomorrow, then."

And she could swear those words are still hovering above her, like one of the fair's ethereal projected signs, even after his body has gone away.

The fair has no name, no official schedule. The rides themselves choose the itinerary, following summons on the radio waves. A shambolic, clunking caravan, they clump across the desert, sticking to corridors set aside for drone traffic, free and grand as demigods in this federally sequestered space. With a strange and phaneric benevolence, they settle on the outskirts of towns, sending out their ads and alerts, putting up tents and stalls, declaring to everyone that the fair has arrived.

And with it, in buggies and battered trailers, in terrain-adaptive four-by-fours, in the guts of the rides themselves, sunburned under dragon tats and open leather vests, scented with the smoke of sweet-flavored cigarillos—with it, as ever, come the carnies.

It's five p.m., peak family time, and Suzie is deep into her routine.

"All right, folks, come and meet our baby. Fifty feet long and heavier'n a bucket of elephants, she lives on a diet of hydrogen and motor oil. Believe it or not, she's a baby of her kind. Sweet as an orange creamsicle and twice as gentle as a St. Bernard. She's more scared of you than you are of tigers and only looking for a little help. Give us a hand, and we'll give you a reward, if you can help us cure the tummy-ache of our Baby Snake."

A few families are at the gate. The kids, as usual, look entranced and terrified. The parents stand back with wary frowns.

"Is it clean?" a mom asks.

Suzie's answer is prompt. "Snake, like all of her kind, has a grade-A immune system. She fully cleans herself after every ride."

"I don't know." The mom takes her kid by the shoulders. "Hon, this looks a little intense."

That's when Suzie switches tactics, aiming her pitch at the little girl.

"Well, I have one question for you, little lady. Can you guess who Baby Snake's parents were?"

A shake of black curls.

"Her mom was the Loch Ness monster," Suzie says, "and her dad was a washing machine."

"*No*," the girl insists, showing gapped teeth.

"It's true. Baby Snake got lost one day, and now we're trying to help her get back home. Only problem is, I broke my phone, and silly Snake here swallowed all the pieces! You think you could help us get them out, so we can fix them up and help this poor little girl find her parents?"

The girl gazes with alarmed curiosity into Snake's wide-open mouth, up at Suzie's friendly face, and then at her mother's skeptical frown.

"Mommy," she whispers, tugging her mother's shirt. And Tipper hears snatches of an ancient negotiation.

"I want . . ."

"Are you sure . . . ?"

"I really really really . . ."

"You won't be scared?"

"I promise promise promise . . ."

A few other kids are coming up. It's the old, the universal need. To be brave, to be helpful, to answer a call. As the children gather at the gate, their faces seem less eager than awed. They're really doing it, going down the monster's throat. But this is a gentle monster. And it's all for a good cause.

"I suppose there's some kind of policy?" the skeptical mom asks.

Suzie already has it out. "That's me, Suzie Choi. That's my license, that's my insurance, and that's my safety record. Go here, and you can see the ride stats: four hundred units operating in thirty countries, and we've never had a robot-initiated accident. Just in case, me and my assistant will be on hand at all times. But we've never had anything go wrong."

Which is not *quite* true. What goes wrong, Tipper knows, is that the kids get over-excited, start fights, cry when the ride has to end, suffer the inevitable effects of too much fairground food. It's the source of all robot woes: human error. But another ancient need is being met, now: the shaking of hands, the meeting of eyes, the reassurance of human contact. The mother gives in and thumbs the screen.

"All right, Nichelle, I guess we can try it."

"*Ye-es!*"

Suzie opens the gate. "One at a time, guys, one at a time."

It's Tipper's job to guide the kids in. That means maintaining even spacing, giving the fainthearted a last chance to quit, infusing the doughty with a final dose of assurance. Amazing, how needed it can make you feel, just doing this simple human work. The kids have so much faith, gazing up at her, amazed at the ease with which Tipper stands in the Snake's open mouth.

In they go, out they come. Until at last . . .

"Tip." Suzie comes to her side. The last kids are bouncing out of the ride, carrying foam pieces of the fake phone, trading them in for tokens at the gate. The adults gather up their charges and depart, listening to gleeful tales of derring-do. Suzie hangs out the come back later sign, the little clock set for thirty minutes.

"I think we need to have a talk."

Suzie's trailer is a buggy-style unit, the living quarters hung from a big-wheeled frame. Autodrive only, keyed to follow Snake wherever the ride might choose to go. Snake herself travels under a lightweight, woven-ceramic shroud, loaded on a radio-piloted, all-terrain wheelbed. Rugged and unglamorous. But the carnies don't demand much in the way of style.

Stepping in, Tipper throws back the curtain from her hammock, tumbles into the nylon mesh. Suzie settles into her own sling near the door. The size of the trailer means they can never be more than eight or nine feet apart. Ultra-compact storage is more a theory than a practice: Shirts have completely flooded the floor. The gallon water jugs, the potted cottontop cacti, Suzie's Metalhead posters, the Mojave pattern pillows—everything is fastened tight or swinging free. Even with the best in dynamic suspension, travel on the desert roads is some rough riding. It's the ridegirl ethos. You stick with your machine, wherever it happens to go.

Tipper can still smell the oily aroma of the fair, the cool evening air, the spice of empanada stalls—until Suzie hits the privacy switch, the walls tighten their lignin weave, and there's nothing but the whir of the ventilation fans.

Suzie pops open her traveling case, lifts out a vape, loads a homebrew cart. The LED cherry cycles green to gold, making the trailer glow with magic light. "So," she says. "How awkwardly unsubtle should I make this?"

Tipper plants a toe on the wall and sets her hammock swaying. On the curved ceiling above is one of Suzie's posters, Controlled Discord, a metalhead act from way back. Algorithmic music, scientifically tested, calculated to produce acute feelings of unease. Not Tipper's thing.

"You know what I want to talk about, I assume." Suzie passes over the vape. "Give me a cue. Where should we jump in?"

The swinging hammocks arrive at moment of synchronized periodicity; Tipper plucks the vape from Suzie's hand. It's THC extract, hints of green tea and tapioca. Tipper puffs judiciously. MJ juice always hits her hard.

"These past couple of days," Suzie says, "you've been awfully distracted. Almost like you'd rather be somewhere else."

Tipper weighs her answer. "I want to be here. Working for you."

Suzie's smile is unrevealing. "You come from where, Tipper? Originally, I mean. Near Phoenix, right?"

"I don't really want to—"

"All right, all right, I'm only saying, you came here for a reason. You could've gone anywhere. So why the fair?" Before Tipper can answer, Suzie says, "I'll put it this way. Was it for the boys?"

Instead of responding, Tipper sucks on the vape. Maybe she needs that THC after all.

"This new friend of yours," Suzie says. "Our buddy Mister Longhair Lothario—"

"His name is Luke."

"What do you think *he's* looking for? A good time? A little innocent fun, screwing around with my ride?"

"He was just joking. I think he was only trying to get my attention."

"Well, he's got it, doesn't he?" When Tipper offers to pass the vape back, Suzie waves it away. "I ever tell you how I came to the fair, Tip? Going way back?"

Tipper's heard the story half a hundred times. "Your parents—"

"Yeah, yeah, my parents were crazy." Suzie flicks dismissive fingers. "More like out of touch. Wanted me to be a doctor. I told them, 'Mom, Dad, there *are* no doctors anymore. There were doctors when *you* were kids. Now there are machines, with human assistants.' 'Okay, Suzie,' they said, 'so be an engineer. Be the person who *makes* the machines.' I told them the machines make all the machines. You see, they were stuck in the old way of thinking. You work hard, you study hard, you get a good job.

"Anyway." Suzie folds her hands on her stomach. "That's not what I'm talking about. Hold on to something heavy, girl, 'cause you're about to sit through a teen girl's worst nightmare. You're about to hear an old lady talk about her first love."

She opens a minifridge and pulls out a tea.

"First thing to point out, like it needs pointing out: this was a long damn time ago. If you think the Manual trend is hot, now, all these kids running around in pilot jackets and construction vests, hell, back then, this stuff was *new*. The golden era of applied robotics, everything a thousand times more efficient, exponential productivity gains forever, blah blah blah. We were all going to be rich and live in a new age of leisure, have all the free time in the world, wipe our butts with golden circuit boards, whatever. And suddenly, every guy in suburbia is dropping out of high school, hanging around in boilersuits and tool belts, refusing to talk to voice interfaces, and talking about how he wants to do 'real work' for a living. Wild.

"Well, okay, this one kid, my neighbor, he was the type. Eighteen years old, covered with burns, which he'd gotten by doing honest-to-God-welding. What did he weld? Who cares? This was the Fringe. This guy worked with his hands. That was cool. He used to run a service ripping brains out of appliances, washing machines, blenders, whatever you brought over. Stupidifying, he called it. Making smart machines less smart. Had this teller machine he'd reconstructed, totally transparent, so you could see it all working, Monopoly money going round and round these big rollers, the whole thing running by gears and weights. And here I was, this little nerd-girl, who'd spent her life memorizing shit no human needed to memorize anymore. So."

Settling back with a brain full of vapor, Tipper can picture teenage Suzie, a squat girl lost in a giant concert T, shuffling around with a head full of Taylor polynomials and math rock.

"Now." Suzie sips her tea. "Okay. One day this young rebel comes by with a proposition. He wants to go to the fair, just me and him, and try out this new ride they have there. Me?" Suzie sets her empty can on the floor. "I'm fifteen. He's eighteen. I think this is the best idea I ever heard. Friday night comes, I lie to my parents, he picks me up—no autodrive for this guy—and off we go. I'll paint the scene. The rides, they were totally different then. No AI. No protocols. The operator pulled a lever, it started up. He pushed the lever, it shut down. Simple.

"But this new ride? This was something special. The Gentle Giant it was called. Big legless guy, about thirty feet tall. Long arms, kind of like a gorilla. You'd get in a kind of transparent ball, like a giant hamster ball, and he'd pick you up, and—well, there wasn't much to it, really. He'd kind of wave you around, pass you from hand to hand. Nothing like the Scream-o-Saurus, that's for sure.

"But me?" Suzie sat up. "My generation? This was brand new. This was scary. Because it wasn't just a machine, like what we grew up on. It was *thinking*. It was *deciding*. It was unpredictable. And you were literally putting yourself in this robot's hands."

Suzie pauses, settling lower in her hammock.

"Well, as you can bet, there were lots of safety precautions. Full body patdown, two riders only, waivers, harnesses, the whole thing. We go through the rigmarole. We get in the big ball. And while we're waiting, we look up at the Giant's face, and that's when this boy tells me his plan."

The ventilation fans have shut off, the air slowly growing warm with contained heat. Tipper tries to remember if she's ever seen this ride, which sounds, as Suzie says, intensely boring. A big robot picking you up, then putting you down? So what?

"Well, my brave new boyfriend, it turns out he's been studying." Suzie takes out a new tea. "The Gentle Giant has a pretty sure grip. But this guy thinks, okay, maybe if we both get up at the same time, throw ourselves against the wall—maybe if we time it just right, he says, we can get the Giant to, in a phrase, drop the ball."

"And then what?" Tipper narrows her eyes. "You would die? What's the point?"

"Here's the point. This ride was special. It was new. There were magazine stories. There were giant crowds. If the Giant screwed up, even just once—"

"But only because you guys broke the rules."

"But that's just it! I mean, picture it. A nice young girl, her handsome boyfriend, out on their very first date . . . maybe they're a little foolish, but who isn't at that age? And then suddenly, thanks to this crazy, unreliable robot . . ."

Tipper sighs. Of course. It's a typical Manual ploy. Do something insanely stupid, then blame it on a robot. They'll do anything to sow distrust and fear.

"Sending a message," Tipper says.

"*Egg*-xactly. Well, we're sitting there, arguing, and all of a sudden, the ride starts up. At first, I can hardly tell what's happening. The change is so gentle, so precise. Looking through the plastic, I see the fair sinking away. We're up in the sky. Now the real excitement starts. Rising, dipping, whirling, flying. All of it amazingly smooth. It's like being cradled, that's what I keep thinking. Like being rocked to sleep in giant hands. I look over at my boy. I can see he feels it, too. Except he has a different reaction: It makes him angry.

"Around and around." Suzie mimics the motion, sketching lemniscates with her can of tea. "Now it comes. My guy nudges me. Unlocks my harness. We stumble to the wall. 'Get ready,' he says."

"Well?" Tipper prompts when Suzie falls silent.

"You know, I really liked that kid." Suzie takes back the vape. "I can't deny it. He was driven, he was passionate. I was fifteen." She loads a cart, checks the light, lays down the vaper without tasting. "So we jumped together. Wham! Right into the wall."

Her hands come together, palm to palm, making her hammock bounce and sway.

"First, there's an awful feeling. Total vertigo. We lie together, pressed up against the plastic. Suddenly we're floating, weightless. The guy told me we'd be okay. Couple bruises, maybe a broken finger. We wouldn't fall more than fifteen feet. But right then, I really believed it was happening. I really believed we were going to die.

"Stillness." Suzie's hand hovers. "We're sinking. Then, suddenly, we start to rise. Slowly, like a baby in its father's arms. We're high up, now, looking down at the Giant's face. It was a simple design, all metal, with big round eyes. I realized, then, he'd been in control the whole time. He really was *gentle*, more tender than any living thing. And I felt this incredible sense of sureness. I wanted to *be* him, you know? Like that robot. I want to be that strong, that caring. That reliable."

Suzie remembers the vaper, considers it a moment, puts it back in its case. "So that was it for my big rebel romance. I looked at my boy. He was slamming himself into the wall, almost crying, shouting, 'Help me, Suzie, help!' And I just stared. Because it was suddenly so clear to me." Suzie grins. "It was so obvious who was the better man."

During peak hours, the fairway develops an edgy vibe. Fringe girls go slouching along in rancher outfits, homesteader gingham and cowgirl boots, the remnants of jobs so impossibly long gone that no one even remembers anything but the clothes. Their boyfriends sip from Big Gulp sodas spiked with groundbrew hallucinogens, recipes cooked up in underground labs hidden in tunnels made by well-digging drones. Sometimes one of them will pause and talk to Tipper. Sad boys, aimless boys, breathing in her face the caramelized fog of their illiterate conversation, breath rich with the stink of the flavored syrups they add to their drinks to mask the chemicals.

Tipper waits beside the Haunted House, in the little alley that leads to the trailers, clutching her phone like a plastic amulet. Above the gabled roof, the Scream-o-Saurus lifts a shrieking rider, chews him in foam jaws, and gulps him down its waterslide throat. A group of robospooks leave the House by a back door, two rubber-skinned frogmen and a stooped Dracula. They carry a limp figure between them, a damaged werewolf who dangles like a cadaver from their arms. Heading for the repair station, no doubt. It's a perennial problem around the House. Rowdy boys like to kick and abuse the exhibits.

A kiddie ride like the Snake doesn't see a lot of business at this hour, and Tipper's been given the rest of the night off. She checks her phone, knowing it's pointless. The only kind of phone Luke would use is the kind made of two cans and a string.

"Hey."

Quiet suddenly, he's here. Dark against the glare of the virtual arcade, he steps aside to let the crew of spookbots shuffle by. His pale skin glows an eerie yellow in the light of the nearby picnic area.

"Ready?" Hands in pockets, Luke tips his head toward the parking lots.

Tipper hesitates. "The thing is . . ." Luke waits, expressionless, while she works up her nerve. "The thing is," Tipper says, "do you kind of have a second? I sort of promised someone we'd meet with her first."

"Someone?"

Before Tipper can answer, Luke gives a jump. Two shadows have manifested on either side of him, inhumanly still, crowding in like mafia toughs.

"Little boy?" The voice of the left figure is shrill. "You've been a *bad* boy, haven't you? I can always spot a naughty little boy."

Luke stumbles back as a woman steps forward, lifting a hand to her gashed and bleeding throat. It's the Murdered Bride, one of Tipper's favorites.

"Oh, you best beware, naughty boy. Mother is up above, watching us all."

The Bride lifts her dark-ringed eyes to the House's gothic facade.

Tipper laughs at Luke's expression. "It's okay. I know these guys."

Hearing her voice, the two spookbots step back, edging into the light of the picnic area. The Murdered Bride tips her head back, sluicing blood, which dribbles down her décolletage into a culvert between her breasts. Next to her, the Mummy clutches his stray bandages, glints of eye and tooth and bone peeking through the windings on his head.

"Uhhhh," says the Mummy, and then, at a skeptical glance from Luke, "*Uhhhhh!*"

Luke straightens his jacket. "What are these, your chaperones?"

"Kind of." Tipper offers a hand. "Come on, this'll only take a minute."

"Mother *hates* for her children to be late." The Bride shakes her head. And as Tipper draws Luke into the alley, the spookbots shuffle forward to escort them inside.

The Murdered Bride leads the way, to a service entrance concealed in a thorn-grown porte-cochere. The thorns retract, the door creaks open, revealing a tipsy staircase.

"Hurry, please." The Bride lifts her skirts. "We *mustn't* keep Mother waiting."

Up to the second floor, down a dark main hall. The House is one of the newer rides, a collective artificial mind. Thirty rooms host seventy-two independent robots. The whole fantasia revolves around a gadget called the Morbid Eye, a pulpy, brainish thing that uses a compressed air system to levitate through the corridors. The Eye coordinates every system, HVAC to crowd flow to the spookbots themselves. Fishmen and lizardmen, ghouls and ghosts: The Eye leads them all, but only *primus inter pares*. The spookbots are communal, telepathic, autonomous. Carter once told Tipper that the Haunted House is a lot like an old computer program, every component neatly encapsulated. Even to the all-seeing Morbid Eye, the spookbots are mysterious and unpredictable, free-roaming ghosts in a grand machine.

"We're very lucky." The Bride pauses in the armory to adjust her skirts. "Mother will be taking her supper at this hour. She's *ever* so much nicer when she's feasting on a long slab of rare meat."

Carter's rooms are in the center of the House. Their little group enters a gloomy study. At the central desk, Carter waits to receive them, working at a toothsome and bloody steak. Like most of the ride, the furniture here is lightweight mycocore, cobbled together by the spooks themselves. With twenty-five humanoid robots on staff, they can knock together the whole mansion in a single day.

Carter has a heavy tome in her lap, dark shapes writhing on an embedded screen. She slaps it shut. "Evening, kids."

The Murdered Bride bows over her chair.

"I've brought them, Mother, just as you asked. I *do* try to be a good girl. But now look at me, I've gone and bled all over my dress!"

"Yes, I see that. Okay, Bride, I'll take it from here."

Leering with horrible enthusiasm, the Bride takes the Mummy by the arm. "Thank you, Mother. I'm *so* glad I could be helpful. But do, oh *do* be strict with these two children. They're very naughty, and spoiled, too."

"I'll keep that in mind, Bride, thanks."

As they pass by Luke, the Mummy can't resist a last comment.

"Uhhhhhh!"

Tipper turns to watch as the spookbots stagger out. What must it be like, she wonders, living in this place, year upon year, day and night? But the obvious answer makes her laugh: It must be like caring for a huge, deranged family.

"I won't take a lot of your time." Carter comes around the desk. "Suzie says she's given you the night off. Guess you two are heading out for some puppy love."

"Not exactly, ma'am." Luke is curt. Tipper can feel him tensing beside her. Carter, too, goes unusually still.

"Right. Well. Before you do . . . whatever it is you'll be doing, I have something I wanted to run by you." Carter picks up the tome, flips to the embedded screen. Tipper braces for something shocking. But it's only a spookbot in the display, snarling fangs and a drooping fabric tongue, a burst of hair over a ripped check shirt.

"Look familiar?" Carter sticks a toothpick between her teeth.

Luke considers the image, shrugs.

"No?" Carter swings the book from side to side, making sure they get a good look. "Well, this here, this is Puppy. Puppy's a part of our team here at the Haunted House. Our resident werewolf, you might say. And I'll let you in on a trade secret: He's one of our most advanced and expensive machines. Puppy's got a Croatian hair extrusion grid, a chemical-electric body-to-brain feedback module, a moral module based on the soul of a Border Collie. Puppy's only wish in life is to bring thrills and joy to little boys and girls."

Carter slaps shut the book.

"Here's the rub. Two hours ago, while I was helping a sick visitor, someone walked in, held Puppy down, and poured fifty pounds of birdshot and epoxy down his throat. So I thought I'd inquire if y'all might know anything about that."

Luke's face is resolutely bland. Tipper remembers the troupe of spookbots who left the House when they came in.

"Is Puppy going to be okay?"

"Puppy?" Carter tosses the book onto the table. "Puppy's built for this shit. Puppy's also insured for a pretty purse of money. My concern goes way beyond Puppy. I'm talking to you, son, you and your friends. You've been spending a lot of time around the grounds."

Luke blinks. "And?"

"And?" Carter grins, exposing an impressive spread of cigarette stains. "Y'all been having a good time?"

"We—"

Carter cuts him off. "You seemed to be having a good time last night, when you jammed up the gears of my friend's ride."

"That was—"

"A joke. I know." Carter raps the mycocore table. "I guess the kids who busted up my werewolf robot, they also thought they were playing a pretty funny joke."

Luke's eyes narrow. "I had nothing to do with that, ma'am. Ask Tipper."

Carter's nod is calm and slow, every bit as lazy as a branch of sage bobbing in a Sonoran wind. "Right. No one saw a thing. Pretty convenient how that works."

Luke parts his lips, shows his palms, shakes his head. Carter sighs and pushes off the table. In the back of the room, there's a multipaned window, looking down on the mansion's central yard. Carter hits a button, and the panes wink and flicker, becoming screens that show views of different rooms. Moonlit bedchambers, grisly dungeons, hordes of gleefully screaming kids. The views are jumpy, jouncing like old horror flicks, and Tipper realizes she's looking through the eyes of six dozen robots, the congregant POV of the House's host of spooks.

"I got six dozen witnesses to everything that happens in this place," Carter says. "Full surveillance in every room. And wouldn't you know? Amazing as it seems, *none* of these ever-vigilant robots of mine has any idea what happened to our dear Puppy. Son, you got any idea why that might be?"

Arms folded, she looks over her shoulder, and Tipper feels chilled, like it's Dracula himself standing there in shit-kicking boots.

Luke says nothing. Carter sighs.

"Well, I'll tell you. It's because they don't *want* to know. Two dozen potential witnesses, but when this crime went down, they all blinked at once. Even Puppy himself. He's got a bellyful of industrial resin, but I guarantee, when we get him working again, he won't say a thing. So riddle this riddle for me, if you can: why would a robot equipped with sensory capabilities approaching clairvoyance fail to notice a couple of boys holding him down and filling him full of beans?"

Carter pronounces the word *clear-voy-ants*. Tipper glances at Luke again, who seems calmer, now, like he knows where this is going.

"I don't know," Luke says. "You're the woman who runs this place. You tell me."

"I'm the woman who runs this place." Carter bites a thumbnail, looking at the screens. "That's one way of looking at it. Another is to say this place runs itself. All these spooks and ghouls, they've got their own priorities. And their top priority, number one, is taking care of the kids who come through. Keeping those kids safe and happy and out of trouble. The client's always right, even when he's wrong.

"Well, that philosophy leads to some pretty funny decisions. Like, for instance, not ratting out or spanking any trouble-making thug who comes through here. Do I understand it? I have to say I don't. I say, a bad apple's just a bad apple. And the truth is, a lot of the kids in this country smell to me like some pretty rotten fruit."

Carter turns, sets her hands to the back of the mockwood chair, and looks at Luke from under bristly gray brows. Tipper understands. It's a weird fact of modern life: Privacy has actually been increased by machine surveillance. When people spy on each other, there's an innate urge to meddle. Robots are infinitely more scrupulous. To a fault.

"Here's the point." Carter's hands tighten. "Over the past four days, we've had thirteen rides at this fair get jammed, damaged, graffitied, sabotaged, or generally screwed with, and nobody knows by who. Some of these accidents, we're seeing sophisticated methods, radio hacks that go deep into the brain. I'm talking battlefield shit, the kind of crap our lovely government uses to make enemy drones attack their own people. The rides aren't talking. To them, it's all human error. Me, I've got another theory. I think we have some serious assholes coming through here: criminal elements, vandals, saboteurs. And if I catch a hold of 'em, I'm not going to be as kind and forgiving as these robot friends of ours. If I catch a hold of 'em, believe me, these guys'll *wish* it was a werewolf on their tail."

Finally, Luke speaks. "If you don't mind my saying, ma'am—"

"I do mind your saying." Carter lifts the chair, thumps it down. "I can't accuse you of a thing except what I know. And it happens that the stunt you pulled with Snake, that was a lot more stupid than illegal. But I'm not worried about *your* future, son. It's Tipper I asked to come here. It's her I want to talk to."

Carter looks at Tipper for a long time, the creases in her face slowly coming to seem less stark, more like the wear and tear inflicted on a loving but overburdened mother.

"Four words, kid. Take 'em to heart. *Suzie. Loves. That. Ride.*" Carter thumps the foam chair on each syllable. "I'm not talking hot-and-bothered love, like your epically raging teenage feelings. I mean the real stuff. Dogs and babies. If anything happened to that stupid metal monster . . ."

Tipper holds Luke's arm and squeezes, terribly sorry for how awkward this evening has become. "I know, Carter. But really, I promise—"

"Amy," Carter corrects her. "I been traveling with Suzie for eighteen years. I'm Amy to her, and I'm Amy to you. You know we used to run a ride together?" She nods deeply, as if Tipper has denied it. "Yep. An old haunted house, one of the first. Six rooms, ten units, with Suzie and me doing all the training. All night, I'd see her running the routines, tutoring those robots, teaching 'em human behavior. When a scream is a good scream, when a scream is a bad scream, how to tell the difference between a thousand different kinds of laughs. She has the touch, Suzie does, like no one else, and the reason's this. When Suzie looks into the eyes of a machine, she doesn't see a machine. She sees a soul, same as the one in you or me. That's why her rides are always the best, that's why they're the safest, that's why people want to ride 'em, again and again. It's a talent, it's a gift, and it's not something to be screwed with. It comes down to this."

Carter comes forward and holds Tipper's shoulders, staring into her eyes. And Tipper wonders what Carter's seeing there—a full-blown soul, a busted machine, or maybe just a girl who's a little bit of both?

"Trust," Carter says. "You think about that, as you're tearing up the town, tonight." She turns back to her steak, her screens, her big family of monsters. "Oh, and while you're at it? Have yourselves a real fun time."

A junkyard, that's how Tipper thinks of the Fringe. A junkyard covering half of America, full of scrapped and outmoded machines. Except these machines are the kind you can't throw out when they're no longer needed, the kind whose main function is watching TV, the kind who run on soda pop and corn-fed beef.

Human machines, superfluous and unwanted.

She pulls her eyes from the sprawl of lights, checks the dashboard, and clamps her hands to the wheel.

"Easy." Luke touches the steering wheel, giving her a bit of reassurance. "No problem, right? Looks like you might want to ease off the pedal. Keep your eye on those proximity lights."

Tipper eases off the gas, slowing by an amount imperceptible to her, but plenty salient to the computer-driven cars all around. The pedals are almost too far away to reach; she has to stretch to hit the brake. By contrast, the steering wheel's right under her nose.

In the NASCAR seat of Luke's jury-rigged courier truck, Tipper sits in a nest of buckles and screens. Luke, beside her, taps the proximity monitor, the color-coded warnings for the four sides of the car.

"Be careful with these guys, okay? If it's in the red for over half a minute, it gets called in as a violation. Three violations, they'll log it as a malfunction. That could get us a repair drone on our tail."

Tipper nods, tongue between her teeth. Outside, shipping rigs and long-distance taxis tool along at a droningly steady speed, exactly one-hundred-thirty MPH. When she looks out the light-adjusting windows, the cars seem locked in a shared inertial frame, sitting still while blacktop and scenery stream by. Occasionally there'll be a coordinated shuffle, simple flocking programs producing an elegant, emergent waltz that lets an ambulance or repair drone speed ahead. Then Tipper has to shift with the pattern, breathless and Zen-like, focused on simulating the precision of a machine. Up on this highway, it's autodrive-only: the world's least forgiving video game.

She flicks her eyes to Luke. "So this is the big plan for tonight? Hanging out in high-speed traffic?"

He smiles. "You're doing amazing. It's kind of fun, right?"

Warning chimes. Tipper checks her alerts. A tanker in the left lane wants to get off. She steers by the screen embedded in the dash, which gives an overhead view of the scanned environment. It really is like playing a game.

"I feel like a bird." Her laugh surprises her, the silly joy of it. "No, I mean really, that's how it feels."

He grins, feeling it with her. "Take the next exit. You'll want to start getting over soon."

Tipper flicks on the signaling program, sending out a brief pulse of encoded vector arrays. She checks the windows. Nothing out there but the usual sprawl. "Where we going?"

"Little place I like to call the asshole of America. Thought I'd take you on a tour."

"Of an asshole? Fun, fun."

A long silence. When she looks over, he's got that expression boys get sometimes, unexpectedly vulnerable and shy.

"No," he says, turning to the window. "Of me."

It's been a strange evening. Tipper began it by fixing Luke's car. Tapping commands by habit, she plowed through screens of legalese, while Luke lay back in the passenger seat with a hand-rolled joint. Every so often he asked her how it was going.

"Okay." Some of the work she did by voice input, some by hand; she wondered how much Luke had been following. "I'm logging the ID tags, now.

Voice, eyes . . . You realize that to go through with this, I'm going to have to be registered as an approved operator?"

Luke shrugged. "Yeah?"

"Yeah. Like if we go all the way with this, I could get in your car at any time and start driving."

"Yeah?"

She grinned at his casual attitude. "So? You're fine with that?"

He shrugged. "If you are."

Tipper turned back to the dash. "All right, then. What's your social?"

And that set up the theme of the evening. They were taking things quickly, tonight, sharing vital details before they'd shared much more than a kiss. Punching in the last codes, Tipper turned to Luke. "That's it. *Su carro es mi carro*, now. We're both registered drivers. I hope you trust me."

She squirmed out of the deep NASCAR seat, making room for Luke to edge in, but he pulled her back. "Hey, where you going?"

Tipper glanced between him and the wheel. "What do you mean? You're not—"

"You're a registered driver, now. Wanna drive?"

Tipper tested the clumsy pedals, the undersize wheel. "I should let you know, I'm not exactly . . ." What word did she want to use? *Skilled? Experienced?* "I'm not very good at this."

He shrugged. "I trust you."

"With your life?"

"Sure."

How could anyone really mean that?

And yet, Luke hit the switch that engaged lockdown, sealing the doors and the trailer compartment, puffing the temper-fit foam of the seats. "Go for it. I'll tell you the turns."

Tipper started up the sensor system, fumbling at the switches. Suddenly, his hand was over hers.

"Whoops. Not that one."

Tipper laughed. "What'd I just almost do?"

"Something bad." He spoke in his usual calm way. Then, with a smile: "Something extremely bad."

She laughed. And just like that, they were kissing, his lips over her laughing mouth, their teeth knocking together as she responded with clumsy surprise. He held her until the surprise became excitement, then dropped back into his usually lazy pose.

"I . . . I want you to know," Tipper stammered, "I mean, after everything Carter was saying. I do, too."

"You do what?"

"Trust you," she whispered.

He hit the starter, fired up the engine. "Let's move."

All through the drive, Tipper had been in a funny state, hovering somewhere between delight and annoyance. Boys, she thought, what could you do with them? Crazy, maddening, incomprehensible boys.

Being with Luke brought back memories of home, that house full of older brothers, where every day meant a new joke or taunt or impromptu wrestling match. Tipper's oldest brother, Timmy, had worked at the service station, sitting around watching robots change oil. It made him act strange, all that boring work. When he came home, he'd just sit and stare at Tipper, like she was only another machine. Staring and staring, until at last she couldn't take it. "*What*, Timmy? What is your *problem*?" Then he'd laugh and whoop, thrilled at getting any kind of reaction.

None of her other brothers had jobs at all, and it was always worth a heart attack an hour, trying to do her homework with them prowling around. They made a sport out of messing with the cleaning bots, flipping them over, kicking them around, triggering the auto-repair alarms. Instead of waiting for the repair drones to arrive, Tipper would fix the bots herself, which usually involved nothing more than talking them through their diagnostic routines. And while she sat with the things in her lap, murmuring into the mikes, her brothers would lounge around, sucking beers and teasing her.

"Maybe you could just kiss it and make it better, Tipper."

"Guys! Shut *up*."

Then, out of nowhere, they could be entrancingly nice, taking her out to show her the projects they'd been working on in the barn, old Corvettes on blocks, pinball tables they were building from scratch. And with their big, greasy hands lying over hers, they'd guide Tipper through the cleaning of spark plugs, the setting of windows, the wiring of solenoids to EOS switches.

Anyway, her brothers were a hell of a lot nicer than Dad.

Thinking about Dad, his rages, his *they-drove-me-to-it* attitude, makes Tipper give a twitch and jerk the wheel, almost veering into the side of a commuter van.

"Whoa," Luke says. "Look, you're okay. Just wait for this guy to pass, you'll see the ramp."

In another moment, they're bumping down the interchange, descending into the bright yellow dots of suburbia.

The sprawl of lights starts right where the highway ends. For a moment, Tipper has a panicked feeling, like she really is heading home. Same wide streets thronged with autodriving taxis. Same crowds of nobodies. Same adobe bunkers, each in a plot of dark solar panels that used to be a lush green lawn.

The Fringe.

A sign by the road is flashing a helpful advisory:

TIPOLI SMITH
ARE YOU LOST?
AUTODRIVE MALFUNCTION?
HONK TWICE FOR ASSISTANCE.

They've been driving around the same block for too long, killing time, and the streetside monitors have picked up the aberration.

"All right, here we go." Luke calls up a map. Even a dyed-in-the-wool Manual is compelled to respect the usefulness of dynamic mapping. "Go straight at this next intersection."

"But there's nothing there." Tipper checks the map, the windows. The area Luke indicates is all blacked out, an abyss of darkness in the lamp-bejeweled town.

"Oh, there's something there." Luke sits back, savoring his air of manly mystery.

Tipper lets him have his fun. Pushing the car forward at precisely the recommended speed, she hits the edge of the blacked-out land. Suddenly she understands. At the end of the road is a ditch. Across the ditch is a bridge. And beyond the bridge is a gate and fence. The signs everywhere are entirely unnecessary. Tipper knows what's beyond this point.

"This way." Luke points right. They drive along the fence, the reflective signs flashing by in a menacing strobe. WARNING WARNING WARNING. RESTRICTED RESTRICTED RESTRICTED. CONTROLLED CONTROLLED CONTROLLED. On the car's display, there's nothing to see. To the mapping software, this is nowhere, nonexistent land.

"There's a turn up here. It's kind of hard to spot." Luke leans into her. "There."

The fence veers away. A dirt road rises up a silhouetted ridge. Tipper flicks on the headlamps for the first time that night. Between the dingy bursts of desert bushes, she can see the dark land dropping away, a blackness that seems to deepen as they rise. Luke guides her off the road.

"Slow, now. There's a certain spot . . ."

They halt on a ridge of sandstone and grit, the headlights plunging out into darkness. He yanks on the brake and shuts off the car. The temperfoam relaxes; the doors unlock. Tipper steps into a strikingly cool breeze. Her first tentative steps nearly spill her down a ghostly chasm, ragged walls of rock made spectral by the moon. Luke grabs her arm.

"Easy. Don't worry. It's not as far as it looks. The night makes everything seem weird."

The night does indeed. His silhouette seems strange and huge beside her, hewn from rock.

"Out there." Luke's arm extends. "Below those two bright stars."

The shapes she makes out are distant but distinct: four dark squares, rising up like buttes, and one long mesa of flat-topped shadow. Tipper's first impression is of a holy site, some natural wonder sanctified by the rites of the Navajo, those restless neighbors of her own ancestral people. But the moonlight, strengthening with a suddenness peculiar to desert climes, dispels the illusion. Those are buildings, four silos and a compound, with not a single window to vary the dark walls.

"Air Force," Luke says. "Testing sight. See that long, flat building? My granddad used to work there."

"He was a pilot?"

Luke shakes his head. "Engineer. Mathematician. Data-crunching, modeling, that kind of thing."

Tipper knows where this is going. "And he got fired."

Luke's eyes are on the distant buildings. "Not exactly. You know how many people work this site, now? Zero. Know why it's so dark? Because no one needs any light. The entire place is run by machines. Machines on site. Machines on network. A guy like my grandpa, it's not like he got fired. It's more like his whole industry ceased to exist."

Tipper considers the expanse below, thinking about what Luke has said. *Machines to do the work. And machine to guard the machines.* Any person trespassing on that turf will quickly find himself a target of some of the world's most sophisticated perimeter drones. Even with the best night-vision gear, a human would be helpless against their full-spectrum scanning. Of course, the drones don't actually injure anyone. They have no need for such sloppy tactics.

"What about your parents?" she says. "The rest of your family?"

Luke sucks in night air. "That's next."

And he guides her on, through shapeless towns, down nameless roads. Actually, the streets here do have names—Spanish names, Navajo names—

but no one cares. To the cars and their riders, it's all just instructions: left, right, straight, ten meters, two miles.

Eventually, something looms ahead, massive and broken. Luke tells her to stop.

"That building? That was where my great-grandfather worked. Back in the twentieth century. Putting lawnmowers together. Then all *those* jobs went overseas. Then they came back, except they were being done by computer scientists. Then those jobs went overseas. And then all the jobs went away forever. So we did it." He laughs. "We finally achieved true global equality."

As they drive on, the names of the streets become increasingly irrelevant, until Tipper no longer even notices the towns. It's all jumbled together, geography, history, family, a random walk of turns and dead ends.

"Over here, this was where my grandma used to work. A library. Can you believe they used to have physical libraries? And over here, this is where the college was. I had a friend whose dad worked there. Guess what he taught? Game design and pedagogical process. Whoops! Taught himself right out of a job."

In a downtown where the all-night restaurants twinkle with animated ads, Luke urges Tipper to get out and walk.

"That's where the old Walmart used to be. My dad worked there as a cashier. Then in the stockroom. Then as a greeter. They all thought Walmart was the epitome of evil, back then. There's the salon where my sister used to work. They're still open, but they're cutting back. Get it? No, but seriously, all they employ now is a couple of touchers. Know what that is?"

Growing up as a tomboy with three ubermale brothers, Tipper hasn't had a chance to learn much about the ways of hair salons.

"Okay," Luke explains. "So the machines do all the work, right? There's a whole line of robots to do the washing, the styling. But what they still need is, I guess you could call it 'the human touch.' So before you get your hair cut, they have a person who comes and checks you out, massages your scalp, makes a little chitchat. After you get your hair cut, there's another person who comes over to tell you how great you look. It's completely useless. It's what they call 'perk employment.' Touchers. But over here, this is what I wanted to show you."

He runs ahead, boyish in his eagerness, pulling at the weather-tenting on a squat lump of a building.

"Uh, Luke?" Tipper's not sure if she's charmed or unsettled by the way her cool seducer has become this gamboling tour guide. But quick as an autodriving car will switch routes, Luke reverts to his broody persona, hoisting up the slippery film of the tenting to expose a small, glassless window. Smooth as a burglar, he slides inside. A pale hand extends to help Tipper.

She waves him way and lifts herself over. With the weatherproof shroud its owner has thrown over it, the building has taken on the dusty, almost sweet scent of a desert cave. Luke fumbles for her hand.

"It's okay. My friend's got a unit outside, running a baffler on the AI alarm. It thinks we're weevils. Here."

A small spot of light falls on the dusty floor. Luke leads Tipper among shrouded furniture. She lifts up a flap and sees thirties-era fractal construction, fake wood printed in sea-anemone patterns. Charmingly retro.

"This place—"

"It's a club." Luke has a beer in hand. He pushes one toward Tipper. She sees no fridge, but there's a crystal-insulated cooler lying lopsided on a couch. Luke's flashlight whips over dust, reed tables, a little riser of a stage. "It used to be, anyway. I've been hanging out here since it closed. They used to have music on weekends, comedy four nights a week. This was where my mom got started."

"And she was—?"

Luke pulls out a portobook, thumbs in a name, tosses it over. The book's an old model, no frills, just e-paper. Tipper flips through the document, which appears to be the career summary of a rather unremarkable actress. If this is Luke's mother, she doesn't seem to have gone very far. The credits paint a picture of a low-tier thespian scrounging for work.

> Babe, It's Okay (uncredited)
> Monster Matriarch (voice)
> The Long and Short of It (unreleased)

A shout jerks Tipper's head up.

"Ladies and gennelmen!"

Luke is onstage, addressing a phantom crowd, swinging an old mike stand. "Tonight, we have a real fine treat. Get ready for the boundary-crossing, risk-taking, no-holds-barred comedy of Lucas Averro!"

He grins, comedian-style. Tipper shakes her head as Luke mugs his way through a spoof of standup.

"Okay, guys, seriously. Seriously, people."

Suddenly he *is* serious, holding the stand at arm's length, making it clear there's no mike in the grip, no lights, no crowd. His performance consists of a single line.

"What the fuck happened to us?"

Luke scans the room. "Tipper? You out there? You hearing this?" He hops off the stage. "I mean, it was supposed to be the one thing we'd always fall back on, right? The one thing they could never take away from us."

He holds out a hand. Tipper sees what he wants, gives him the porto-book. Luke shakes it like a magician. The pages flap out into a single stiff screen, magazine-size. He loads a video. Seeing the image, Tipper can't help but laugh.

"There it is." Luke's watching over her shoulder. "End game."

The video, sensing her attention, begins to play. It's like a fragment of Tipper's teenage experience, shaken loose and tossed up into the present, a scene from her sixteen-year-old self's favorite cartoon show.

Darly the Penguin is more or less the sum of everything a modern girl experiences. A tad overweight, insecure about her body, dirty-minded, ambitious, loyal to her friends, fiercely smart, intermittently sassy . . . with a bizarre little mop of biologically incorrect hair . . . who in the world wouldn't love Darly?

This clip is from one of the early shows, when Darly was trying to make her way in the modern office. Here, Darly's talking to her polar-bear boss, Dexter, and it seems that during a strategic planning meeting, when Darly self-deprecatingly referred to herself as a "big bird," Dexter's response was—

Well, the plot doesn't really matter. What's funny is Darly's attitude, the way this CGI penguin somehow captures everything crazy about being a human being at the start of the twenty-second century. Darly has a whole bundle of oddball tics: spelling out dirty words (or more often misspelling them), flapping her wings and squeaking like a kazoo, tapping her forehead and reminding herself, "Penguins are *chill*, Darly—penguins are chill." Sometimes, when things get really crazy, Darly'll dive to the floor and slide on her belly out of awkward situations. It's all too funny, and Tipper's already laughing when Luke abruptly shuts off the playback.

"Programmed." He closes the portobook. "Every second."

Tipper's annoyed. Of *course* it's programmed. It's TV! But Luke's looking at her like he thinks she doesn't get it.

"You know how they write these shows?" He waves the portobook. "They don't. No *human* does. The scenarios are randomly generated, based on trending topics. The jokes are crowdsourced: Thousands of one-liners are submitted, and the producers pick the best ones. And the characters? They're AI. Your Darly? She's a program. Gestures, catchphrases, even the voice. All coded, trained on test audiences. It can even improvise."

Tipper sighs. She knows this. Everyone knows this. It's like kayfabe: You know it; you don't have to harp on it. But guys like Luke always seem to overexplain.

"My mom?" He turns to the stage. "This is where she did it. Up on that stage, every night, trying out her jokes, trying out her voices. And for what? To create an act. A persona. And that would be her product. That would become her shtick.

"This?" He waves the portobook. "This killed all that. Why? Because guess what? That mysterious allure? That human appeal? All those things a performer is supposed to have: charm, gravitas, charisma? Turns out, you can simulate all of it, no problem. Because that's exactly what a shtick *is*. Predictability. Routine."

Tipper wonders: What do you say when you see the point someone's trying to make, but don't quite see the point of making it? She reaches for his hand. Luke doesn't even notice. He's too intent on striding among the tables, kicking old beer cans out of his path.

"So there it is, folks! End of the road. Muscle, skill, brains . . . the one thing left, the one thing we thought we could always rely on, was personality. Our wonderfully human, charming imperfections. Well, here you go. Darly the Penguin is more charmingly fucked up than someone like my mom could ever be. So it's over. Gone. We've cleared the last hurdle. We've finally perfected imperfection." He points at Tipper's nose. "You see what you've been doing?"

"Me?" It's the first time Tipper's spoken since entering this shrouded place, and her voice sounds weird for such a haunted scene, bold, young, strong. Luke comes toward her. Without thinking, she holds out her arms.

"Your boss. Your friends at the fair. You know who you people are working for?" He dodges her embrace, counting on his fingers. "You don't own the rides. The company owns the rides. Traveling Troupe, a subsidiary of SevenStar Entertainments. Who owns the company? The shareholders own the company. Who are the shareholders? Funds and banks. Who are the funds and banks? Who else? They're a bunch of computer programs, who sometimes hire human beings to go to meetings. And guess what? The hair salons, the stores, the factories, the Air Force: the same programs are running it all." He taps his nose. "Follow it back, Tipper. Follow it back."

Tipper finally gets a hold of him, grabbing his wrists, which feel surprisingly thin and frail. Guys like this always shock her with their fragility. She holds him by the collar, putting her palms to his cheeks, calming him.

"I know, Luke, okay? I know."

"And where does it start?" He's still looking away. "It starts with you, Tipper. A friendly girl, leading little children up to a big monster, saying, 'Don't be afraid. It's your friend. It's okay.'"

She can't stop thinking of her brothers. How they always used to talk this way, taking her out to the barn to show her their projects. How one day, they said, they were going to change it all, bring the whole system crashing down.

Well, something changed, all right. Tipper doesn't remember what exactly set it off. But her father never needed an excuse to fly into a rage. He was at his worst, that day, stomping around the house, kicking anything that would break, and eventually he made his way out to the barn, throwing open the doors to expose the projects of Tipper's brothers, the car engines, the game tables, the magnetic and chemical experiments. As he worked his way through the collection, sometimes with a hammer, sometimes with his hands, he shouted out his verdict. "*Useless . . . ridiculous . . . a fucking waste.*" What made Tipper tremble as she stood there in the door, what made her shake with a rage that terrified her, was the way her brothers stood back, passive, simply watching the destruction. Their constructions, their creations, their hobbies, all crushed, complexity pounded to scrap, sacrificed to their father's aimless anger. And they accepted it. Like biblical sons, they bowed under the patriarchal judgment. Even to themselves, they were nothing, in the end. Useless, ridiculous, a fucking waste.

It's like Tipper can see them all, right now, the angry boys and the angry girls, the mothers and fathers who'll never work again, the Manuals and the doctors and the mathematicians, scattered all through the lonely Fringe towns.

She holds Luke by the collar, pulling his face toward hers. "It will be okay," she whispers against his lips. "It will."

With instinctual ease, Tipper guides him. She doesn't push, doesn't pull, just leads him where she needs him to be. At one point, her foot skids on something, suddenly rolling, and she sees it's the flashlight, dropped from his hand. By its wheeling light, they find their way to the couch. Tipper pats the sheet-covered cushions. The crystal-insulated cooler falls to the floor. The crash only adds to her urgency—a brittle music of glass bottles in the dark.

She lays him down, climbing onto his hips. *I trust you, Luke, I trust you.* Even as she's thinking this, Tipper knows it's not quite right. What she trusts, what she's bending to kiss, is the feeling inside him, the hurt and need of a boy who's seen everything smashed, abused, stolen: Everything he's worked for, everything he loves.

From the highway, the fair looks like a true menagerie. Monstrous heads and swinging tails cast wild shadows against the gaudy lights. The people register as no more than specks. You can almost imagine that history has run backwards, and that they've all come back again, the lost and majestic monsters, the prehistoric beasts.

Luke pulls deftly off the road, guiding his truck through the autodriving traffic.

HELLO, TIPOLI SMITH! flashes a sign. WELCOME TO THE TRAVELING TROUPE FAIR!

The Traveling Troupe. The Metal Demimonde. Call it what you will, the fair will always be a welcoming place for the wandering, the footloose, the cast aside.

"We forgot to change the login." Tipper taps the screen as Luke steers through the gate. "All the monitors will think you're me."

Normally, it wouldn't matter; the car would detect the driver automatically. But this automatic function, like most of the others, has been shut off.

Luke doesn't care. He's been driving all night with his eyes on the overheads, impassive and silent, expertly imitating a machine. Now he steers past the public lots, onto the service road beyond the gates. Tipper looks out the window.

WARNING, flashes a sign. RESTRICTED AREA. STAFF ONLY. WARNING. WARNING. Then: WELCOME, TIPOLI SMITH!

"You're not supposed to be back here."

"It's okay." He keeps his eyes on the screen. "I'll take you to your trailer."

An almost painfully gallant gesture, it seems to Tipper. After tonight, they're unlikely to meet again. More lonely traveling for her, more lonely ranting for him. But he can do this for her, if nothing else: He can drop her like a gentleman at her front door.

The trailer flickers with LED light. Suzie must be waiting up. A little distance away, Snake lies curled under lamps, dormant for the night. Luke parks at the fence, lets the truck idle. The engine, built for all-night driving, hums softly in the dark.

"Well." He reaches for the dashboard. "Guess this is it."

It's hard to say why, but Tipper feels almost panicked. "Are you . . . I could probably get tomorrow night off."

"I don't think I'll be around." He makes it harshly final. And like that, Tipper realizes that this is what he wants, what he's always wanted. Not to kiss her, not even to sleep with her. Only to have given her the tour of his life.

"So that's it?" She tries to keep her voice from shaking. "That's all we're doing?"

"Tip." His hand twitches on the dashboard.

"You drive me around, you show me your life, you put on this big demonstration . . . I mean, what was all this about?"

He doesn't answer at first. His face is answer enough.

"Well." He sighs. "I guess I wanted you to know. To know why I'm doing what I do. So you would . . . so you would understand."

"To under—" Then she sees where his hand his resting, hovering on that unremarkable black button, the one she almost pressed before. The one he warned her never to touch.

"Luke!"

Even before it happens, Tipper realizes he's right. He's done it, achieved his goal. In a way, in a hidden, angry part of her, she does understand.

The first ride to go is the Haunted House. A spook on the roof, a winged gargoyle, jerks and lurches like a drunken suicide. It quivers, stiffens, tumbles off, crashing to the hard-packed gravel and snapping a wing. The doors fly open. A lizardman staggers out, lashing a rubber tail, clawing the air. Two people follow, a pair of teenage girls, screaming in genuine terror. It's pandemonium, the windows opening, the walls shaking, shrieks and howls from every corner. The spookbots run riot and jump from the rooftops, even punch holes in the mycocore walls. A kid staggers out with one of the cannibal babies clamped like a monkey to the back of his head. From the central courtyard, the Morbid Eye ascends, puttering on its failing jets, sailing away over the gables, into the night.

Nearby, the Scream-o-Saurus is lashing its tail, tipping over souvenir stalls and a BBQ stand. As the riders and operators shout and flee, the ride shudders, tips, whipping its head wildly side to side. The Abominable Go-Go-Go man is pounding dents in his chest. The LandShark chomps earth. Octowhip reels into the midway, flinging out its arms and dispensing mayhem. With a screech of straining hydraulics, the Dementor sways and falls.

The worst, though, is Snake. A salted slug, a suffocating fish, a worm under a magnifying glass: there's no comparison for the flailing of this great fat body.

The tail alone is a menace, whacking nearby trailers, catching the bars of fences and flinging them hundreds of feet. The big mouth gapes and gnashes. The googly eyes, ordinarily so jolly, are now the soul of anguish and fear. Even in eighteen years of rough-and-tumble Fringe life, Tipper has never seen such a display of agony.

She's at the edge of the gravel. She must have gotten out of the car. Luke is here, beyond the reach of Snake's gyrations. Suzie, Carter, all the operators: they've come out of their trailers, their private compartments, to witness this artificial Armageddon.

"What's *happening*?" An operator from the Bear Jamboree, a woman Tipper scarcely recognizes, drifts by like a refugee. Suzie and Carter stand almost perfectly still, only moving their heads as they watch.

Tipper ducks into Luke's truck. She pounds at the interface, entering random commands. The car beeps. She hears a clunk. With Luke's hands clutching at her shoulders, she kicks out of the seat and marches around to the rear.

The big storage compartment has popped open, exposing the interior. Tipper remembers Luke's description: *a bed back here, internet, built-in fridge . . . the best game hookup you'll ever see . . .*

But it's no traveling rec room hidden amid the braces and padding of his cargo hold. Fighting Luke's hands, Tipper climbs in, scanning the jumble of wires and consoles.

"What the hell? What is all this?"

"Tip." He grabs her under the arms. Tipper's been in too many sibling fights to let him get away with that. "Listen," he pleads as she kicks him back, "don't . . . don't touch anything, okay? It's too late, anyway."

She hops down from the truck and spins to face him, gravel spitting from her toes. "You planned this." Luke's face is miserable but resigned. "You had me fix your car so it would be registered to me. So you could get it back here in the staff areas. You only did this so you could . . ."

He doesn't object. That's the worst part of it. Hanging his head, staring at the ground, he can't even bother to tell her it's all more complicated than she understands.

Sabotage. Everything, every event of the week, begins and ends in that word. *Sabotage.*

"You shit." Tipper begins to pant. "You piece of shit."

She lurches away from the car, remembering Carter's words. *Radio hacks, sophisticated methods, like the military uses on enemy drones.* She can see now it's not only rides that are affected. The local repair drones are sputtering into walls, dropping like addled moths from the sky. Tipper's own brain feels fuzzy, scrambled. She finds Carter seated in the dirt, vomiting into a tuft of grass.

The apocalypse is winding down. A wall of the Haunted House collapses, bricks and fake armchairs tumbling out. Snake is a twitching hulk, the joints of the skeleton snapped or fused, fabric flesh hanging in ragged swags. The image of death couldn't be more complete if it were a real dragon here, vanquished and moribund.

Tipper approaches. A flame spits from the ride's battered head. Sparks begin to jump and catch. The gel-pack padding burns with an awful stench.

"Tipper, stop."

A hand grabs her wrist. Tipper wheels around.

Suzie stands behind her, not crying, only watching as Baby Snake melts into a greasy mass. Up the fairway, a siren yowls. The main emergency station is proofed against attacks, and the fire-dousing drones are already in formation, descending with jets and extinguishers and warnings.

"Keep Back. Danger. Keep Back. Danger."

"Suzie." Tipper is surprised to see that the older woman's face is unmarked by grief, as if Suzie can't even quite comprehend what has happened. "Suzie, I'm so sorry."

Tipper tries to say more, but she can't go on without sobbing or choking. Smoke spreads in a thin haze. As Suzie's eyes track over the ride, the plumpness seems to leach from her features, cheeks clinging to her bones.

Tipper turns, looking for Luke. Bad move. Suzie turns also, seeing the truck. As for Luke himself, there's no sign.

"Oh." Suzie releases Tipper's hand. "Okay, I see. Yes, I see, now."

"Wait." Tipper clutches at her hand. "Suzie, I didn't know, I swear. He took me out, we drove around, I didn't think he was—"

Suzie nods dully. "All *right*, Tip. Just . . . just give me a second, here, okay."

The Haunted House is a crumbling wreck. Carter stumbles around it, wiping her mouth. The area is thick with drones and bots, most of them gathering around Luke's truck. As for Luke himself, he seems to have completely disappeared.

"Suzie, you have to believe me, I trusted him, he never said he would—"

"All right, Tip." Suzie's tone is like the grating of a key. "I see what happened, here, okay? I get it."

It's somehow more awful than being yelled at, this calm detachment, this sudden withdrawal. Because Suzie has been through everything, down here in the metal demimonde. She knows what's what. And when Suzie makes up her mind, there's no one who can unmake it.

Tipper backs away, stumbling on stalled drones. "Please, Suzie. Please, believe me."

But the old operator drifts away, standing over the corpse of her ride.

Tipper finds that she's crying like a child, snot and tears flowing together. She wipes her face clumsily, vision blurred. Without thinking, she turns and runs.

A group of teens trip by her on the fairway, one draped over two supporting friends. The crowds, already thin, are dwindling fast. "I'll find you," Tipper hears herself panting. "I'll find you, you son of a bitch."

A ripped-off arm, part of the Dementor, lies like a fallen tree across the midway, repair bots swarming around it. Fairgoers circle like leaves in a stream, some fleeing, some gawking, some apparently aimless. Tipper remembers how Luke first appeared, one boy among many, a member of the crowd.

She'll get him. If security hasn't done it yet, she'll bring him in.

Her stomping boots take her past the game stalls, through hordes of staring attendees. At the security tent, she searches the area. On to the repair station, the prize displays, the main gate.

Nothing.

She circles back through the wreckage to the road, under the fence and out of the fair, to where squatters have set up ersatz attractions.

Nothing.

Finally, Tipper takes her hunt to the limits, the public parking lots where it all began. And that's when she has to admit that he's gone, vanished the same way he appeared, another lost soul drifting through the Fringe and the idle decades and empty towns. And she finds a fallen trashcan and kicks it to death and sits on it and lets herself cry.

When the sobbing ends, Tipper lifts her head. The fair is strangely quiet, now. She checks for messages from Suzie, Luke, the security team, but the whole world seems to have fallen silent. An eerie air of solitude hands over the empty parking lot, and she realizes that out here, she is entirely alone—except for a host of watching machines.

Yes, they're all around her. Rabbit Run, Wheelie-Dealie, The Speedy Demon. And the true relics, the old classics: Tyger-Tyger, Tentaculus, The Great Jim-Jamboree. The Orphans bow over her with solemn stares. With surprise and delight, Tipper realizes that they must have been out of range, spared the effects of Luke's scrambling radiation. Rabbit Run sends out a bouncing bunny; it cocks at her a velveteen ear. Tyger-Tyger burns with a welcoming light. A tap on her shoulder makes Tipper jump. She sees Tentaculus grinning down at her, giving a slow wink of its huge eye.

She stands and walks through this forest of the forgotten, this cohort of the estranged. The rides all vie for her attention. *Come take a run with the racing rabbits! Are you hunting the tiger, or is he hunting you? It's more than a monster: it's Tentaculus!* Without operators, these machines have to fend for themselves, begging for riders, attention, trust.

Tipper works her way deep into the crowd, wondering, hoping. She hasn't memorized every ride in the fair, which sometimes switches units between stops. An old ride, a small ride, an obscure ride, might just have escaped her noticed. It's possible. . . .

And as she rounds a corner and sees what's ahead, the thrill of discovery thunderbolts through her heart.

Approaching the gate, Tipper hears a ding of greeting.

"Don't be afraid! Step right up and meet the Gentle Giant!"

It's smaller than expected, a mere runt compared to the mighty Scream-o-Saurus. It's also the cheapest ride Tipper's ever seen, no more than the cost of a soda deducted from her account. Everything looks as Suzie described: the plastic ball, the gorilla-like arms. The seat smells musty and old. A click of a buckle, a tightening of straps. No protocols, now, no humans at all. When the ride confirms that she's secure, up she goes.

The Giant's hands hold the sphere without a tremor. Like a flea in a soap bubble, Tipper slowly rises, though it seems as if the world is dropping away. A twist of the Giant's hands, and she's facing the fairgrounds, held aloft over the robot's head, looking down on this strange little kingdom of wandering monsters and carnies and kids. From up here, the rides look like the toys they really are, the corpse of the Snake a frail black curl, the Haunted Mansion a crumbled doll's house. Away beyond the dirt and brush, far down the highway, are the scattered Fringe towns, the strange blue shapes of the moonlit desert. And farther off, in some smattering of lights too remote to see, the home that Tipper has left behind.

The great hands move. The ball slowly spins. Tipper looks down into the face of the Giant, who gazes up, solemn and intent, as if trying to decide what kind of fairy he's captured. *Does this little creature sting? Will it bite? Is it dangerous?* His eyes, as Suzie said, are a somber green, and Tipper holds their gaze as she undoes her harness. Her feet move silently on the padded floor. When she presses her hands to the plastic shell, a trickle of air runs past her palms, and she realizes the whole plastic sphere is pierced with tiny holes.

The metal face looms below, larger than Tipper's entire body. It's proudly masculine in appearance—big square jaw, a prominent brow—and oddly reassuring. Here it is, what Suzie fell in love with, a great gentleness born of great strength.

Spreading her arms, Tipper rests her weight on the plastic, looking down into eyes that will never look away. And she feels almost joyful, now, almost loved, as she reflects that, for this unbearably brief moment, she is undoubtedly in good hands.

Alastair Reynolds is the bestselling author of over a dozen novels. He has received the British Science Fiction Award for his novel *Chasm City*, as well as the Seiun and Sidewise Awards, and was shortlisted for the Hugo and Arthur C. Clarke Awards. He has a PhD in astronomy and worked for the European Space Agency before he left to write full time. His short fiction has been appearing in *Interzone, Asimov's*, and elsewhere since 1990. Alastair's latest novel is *The Medusa Chronicles*, co-written with Stephen Baxter.

THE IRON TACTICIAN

Alastair Reynolds

M erlin felt the old tension returning. As he approached the wreck his mouth turned dry, his stomach coiled with apprehension, and he dug nails into his palms until they hurt.

He sweated and his heart raced.

"If this was a trap," he said, "it would definitely have sprung by now. Wouldn't it?"

"What would you like me to say?" his ship asked, reasonably.

"You could try setting my mind at ease. That would be a start. It's one of ours, isn't it? You can agree with me on that?"

"It's a swallowship, yes. Seven or eight kiloyears old, at a minimum estimate. The trouble is, I can't get a clean read of the hull registry from this angle. We could send out the proctors, or I could just sweep around to the other side and take a better look. I know which would be quicker."

"Sometimes I think I should just let you make all the decisions."

"I already make quite a lot of them, Merlin—you just haven't noticed."

"Do whatever you need to do," he said, bad-temperedly.

As *Tyrant* swooped around the wreck, searchlights brushed across the hull like delicate, questing fingertips, illuminating areas of the ship that would have been in shadow or bathed only in the weak red light of this system's dwarf star. The huge wreck was an elaborate flared cylinder, bristling with navigation systems and armaments. The cylinder's wide mouth was where it sucked in interstellar gas, compressing and processing it for fuel, before blasting it out the back in a vicious, high-energy exhaust stream. Swallowships were ungainly, and they took forever to get up to the speed where that scoop mechanism was effective, but there was nowhere in the galaxy they couldn't reach, given time. Robust, reliable, and relatively easy to manufacture, there had been only minor changes in design and armaments across many kilo-years. Each of these ships would have been home to thousands of people, many of whom would live and die without ever setting foot on a world.

There was damage, too. Holes and craters in the hull. Half the cladding missing along one great flank. Buckling to the intake petals, beyond anything a local crew could repair.

Something had found this ship and murdered it.

"There," *Tyrant* said. "Swallowship *Shrike*, commissioned at the High Monarch halo factory, twelve twelve four, Cohort base time, assigned to deterrent patrol out of motherbase Ascending Raptor, most recently under command of Pardalote . . . there's more, if you want it."

"No, that'll do. I've never been near any of those places, and I haven't heard of Pardalote or this ship. It's a long way from home, isn't it?"

"And not going anywhere soon."

Beyond doubt the attacking force had been Husker. Whereas a human foe might have finished this ship off completely, the Huskers were mathematically sparing in their use of force. They did precisely enough to achieve an end, and then left. They must have known that there were survivors still on the ship, but the Huskers seldom took prisoners and the continued fate of those survivors would not have concerned them.

Merlin could guess, though. There would have been no chance of rescue this far from the rest of the Cohort. And the damaged ship could only have kept survivors alive for a limited time. A choice of deaths, in other words: some slow, some fast, some easier than others.

He wondered which he might have chosen.

"Dig me out a blueprint for that mark of swallowship, the best you can, and find a docking port that places me as close as possible to the command deck." He touched a hand to his sternum, as if reminding himself of his own vulnerability. "Force and widsom, but I hate ghost ships."

"Then why are you going in?"

"Because the one thing I hate more than ghost ships is not knowing where I am."

The suit felt tight in places it had never done before. His breath fogged the faceplate, his lungs already working double-time. It had been weeks since he had worn the suit, maybe months, and it was telling him that he was out of shape, needing the pull of a planet's gravity to give his muscles something to work against.

"All right," he said. "Open the lock. If I'm not back in an hour, find a big moon and scratch my name on it."

"Are you sure you don't want the proctors to accompany you?"

"Thanks, but I'll get this done quicker on my own."

He went inside, his suit lit up with neon patches, a moving blob of light that made his surroundings both familiar and estranged at the same time. The swallowship was huge but he only meant to travel a short distance through its innards. Up a level, down a level, each turn or bend taking him further from the lock and the debatable sanctuary of his own ship. He had been steeling himself for corpses, but so far there were none. That meant that there had been survivors. Not many, perhaps, but enough to gather up the dead and do something with their bodies.

Slowly Merlin accepted that the ship was all that it seemed, rather than a trap. The suit was beginning to seem less of a burden, and his breathing had settled down. He was nearly at the command deck now, and once there it would not take him long to decide if the ship held useful information.

He needed better charts. Recently there had been a few close scrapes. A couple of turbulent stretches had damaged *Tyrant*'s syrinx, and now each transition in and out of the Waynet had Merlin praying for his last shred of good luck. Swallowships could not use the Waynet, but any decent captain would still value accurate maps of the old network. Its twinkling corridors of accelerated spacetime provided cover, masking the signature of a ship if it moved on a close parallel course. The location of the Waynet's major hubs and junctions was also a clue as to the presence of age-old relics and technological treasure.

Merlin paused. He was passing the doorway to one of the frostwatch vaults, where the surviving crew might have retreated as the last of their life-support systems gave out. After a moment's hesitation he pushed through into the vault. In vacuum, it was no colder or more silent than any other space he had passed through. But he seemed to feel an additional chill as he entered the chamber.

The cabinets were stacked six high on opposite walls of the vault, and the vault went on much further than his lights could penetrate. Easily a hundred or more sleepers in just this vault, he decided, but there would be others, spread around the ship for redundancy. Thousands in total, if the swallowship was anything like his own. The status panels next to each cabinet were dead, and when Merlin swept the room with a thermal overlay, everything was at the same low temperature. He drifted along the cabinets, tracing the names engraved into the status panels with his fingertips. Sora . . . Pauraque . . . they were common Cohort names, in some cases identical to people he had known. Some had been colleagues or friends; others had been much more than that. He knew that if he searched these vaults long enough he was bound to find a Merlin.

It had not been such a rare name.

One kindness: when these people went into frostwatch, they must have been clinging to some thought of rescue. It would have been a slim hope, but better than none at all. He wanted to think that their last thoughts had been gentle ones.

"I'm sorry no one came sooner," Merlin whispered, although he could have shouted the words for all the difference they made. "I'm too late for you. But I'm here to witness what happened to you, and I promise you'll have your justice."

Filled with disquiet, he left the vault and made his way to the command deck. The control consoles were as dead and dark as he had been expecting, but at least there were no bodies. Merlin studied the consoles for a few minutes, satisfying himself that there were no obvious booby-traps, and then spooled out a cable from his suit sleeve. The cable's end was a standard Cohort fixture and it interfaced with the nearest console without difficulty.

At first all was still dead, but the suit was sending power and data pulses into the console, and after a few minutes the console's upper surface began to glow with faint-but-brightening readouts. Merlin settled into a chair with his elbow on the console and his fist jammed under his helmet ring. He expected a long wait before anything useful could be mined from the frozen architecture. Branching diagrams played across his faceplate, showing active memory registers and their supposed contents. Merlin skimmed, determined not to be distracted by anything but the charts he had come for. The lives of the crew, the cultural records they carried with them, the systems and worlds this ship had known, the battles it had fought, might have been of interest to him under other circumstances. Now was the time for a ruthless focus.

He found the navigation files. There were thousands of branches to the tree, millions of documents in those branches, but his long familiarity with Cohort data architecture enabled him to dismiss most of what he saw. He carried on searching, humming an old Plenitude tune to cheer himself up. Gradually he slowed and fell silent. Just as disappointment was beginning to creep in, he hit a tranche of Waynet maps that were an improvement on anything he had for this sector. Within a few seconds the data was flowing into his suit and onward to the memory cores of his own ship. Satisfied at last, he made to unspool.

Something nagged at him.

Merlin backtracked. He shuffled up and down trees until he found the set of records that had registered on his subconscious even as his thoughts had been on the charts.

Syrinx study and analysis

Beneath that, many branches and sub-branches relating to the examination and testing of a fully active syrinx. A pure cold shiver ran through him.

Something jabbed into his back, just below the smooth hump of his life-support unit. Merlin did the only thing that he could, under the circumstances, which was to turn slowly around, raising his hands in the age-old gesture. The spool stretched from his glove, uncoupled, whisked back into its housing in the wrist.

Another suit looked back at him. There was a female face behind the visor, and the thing that had jabbed him was a gun.

"Do you understand me?"

The voice coming through in his helmet spoke Main. The accent was unfamiliar, but he had no trouble with the meaning. Merlin swallowed and cleared his throat.

"Yes."

"Good. The only reason you're not dead is that you're wearing a Cohort suit, not a Husker one. Otherwise I'd have skipped this part and blown a hole right through you. Move away from the console."

"I'm happy to."

"Slowly."

"As slow as you like." Merlin's mouth felt dry again, his windpipe tight. "I'm a friend. I'm not here to steal anything, just to borrow some of your charts."

"Borrowing, is that what you call it?"

"I'd have asked if there was anyone to ask." He eased from the console, and risked a slow lowering of his arms. "The ship looked dead. I had no reason to assume anyone was alive. Come to think of it, how *are* you alive? There were no life signs, no energy sources . . .

"Shut up." She waggled the gun. "Where are you from? Which swallowship, which motherbase?"

"I haven't come from a swallowship. Or a motherbase." Merlin grimaced. He could see no good way of explaining his situation, or at least none that was likely to improve the mood of this person with the gun. "I'm what you might call a freelancer. My name is Merlin . . ."

She cut him off. "If that's what you're calling yourself, I'd give some serious thought to picking another name."

"It's worked well enough for me until now."

"There's only one Merlin. Only one that matters, anyway."

He gave a self-effacing smile. "Word got round, then. I suppose it was inevitable, given the time I've been travelling."

"Word got round, yes. There was a man called Merlin, and he left the Cohort. Shall I tell you what we were taught to think of Merlin?"

"I imagine you're going to."

"There are two views on him. One is that Merlin was a fool, a self-deluding braggart with an ego to match the size of his delusion."

"I've never said I was a saint."

"The other view is that Merlin betrayed the Cohort, that he stole from it and ran from the consequences. That he never had any intention of returning. That he's a liar and criminal and deserves to die for it. So the choice is yours, really. Clown or traitor. Which Merlin are you?"

"Is there a third option?"

"No." Behind the visor, her eyes narrowed. He could only see the upper part of her face, but it was enough to tell that she was young. "I don't remember exactly when you ran. But it's been thousands of years, I know that much. You could be anyone. Although why anyone would risk passing themselves off under that name . . ."

"Then that proves it's me, doesn't it? Only I'd be stupid enough to keep calling myself Merlin." He tried to appeal to the face. "It has been thousands of years, but not for me. I've been travelling at near the speed of light for most of that time. *Tyrant*—my ship—is Waynet capable. I've been searching these files . . ."

"Stealing them."

"Searching them. I'm deep into territory I don't know well enough to trust, and I thought you might have better charts. You do, as well. But there's something else. Your name, by the way? I mean, since we're having this lovely conversation . . ."

He read the hesitation in her eyes. A moment when she was on the verge of refusing him even the knowledge of her name, as if she had no intention of him living long enough for it to matter. But something broke and she yielded.

"Teal. And what you mean, something else?"

"In these files. Mention of a syrinx. Is it true? Did you have a syrinx?"

"If your ship is Waynet capable then you already have one."

Merlin nodded. "Yes. But mine is damaged, and it doesn't function as well as it used to. I hit a bad kink in the Waynet, and each transition's been harder than the one before. I wasn't expecting to find one here—it was the charts that interested me—but now I know what I've stumbled on . . ."

"You'll steal it."

"No. Borrow it, on the implicit understanding that I'm continuing to serve the ultimate good of the Cohort. Teal, you *must* believe me. There's a weapon out there that can shift the balance in this war. To find it I need *Tyrant*, and *Tyrant* needs a syrinx."

"Then I have some bad news for you. We sold it." Her tone was off-hand, dismissive. "It was a double-star system, a few lights back the way we'd come. We needed repairs, material, parts the swallowship couldn't make for itself. We made contact—sent in negotiators. I was on the diplomatic party. We bartered. We left them the syrinx and Pardalote got the things we needed."

Merlin turned aside in disgust. "You idiots."

Teal swiped the barrel of the gun across his faceplate. Merlin flinched back, wondering how close she had been to just shooting him there and then.

"Don't judge us. And don't judge Pardalote for the decisions she took. You weren't there, and you haven't the faintest idea what we went through. Shall I tell you how it was for me?"

Merlin wisely said nothing.

"There's a vault near the middle of the ship," Teal went on. "The best place to hide power, if you're going to use it. One by one our frostwatch cabinets failed us. There were a thousand of us, then a hundred . . . then the last ten. Each time we woke up, counted how many of us were still alive, drew straws to see who got the cabinets that were still working. There were always less and less. I'm the last one, the last of us to get a working cabinet. I ran it on a trickle of power, just the bare minimum. Set the cabinet to wake me if anyone came near."

Merlin waited a moment then nodded. "Can I make a suggestion?"

"If it makes you feel better."

"My ship is warm, it has air, and it's still capable of moving. I feel we'd get to a position of trust a lot quicker if we could speak face to face, without all this glass and vacuum between us."

He caught her sneer. "What makes you think I'd ever trust you?"

"People come round to me," Merlin said.

The syrinx was a matte-black cone about as long as Merlin was tall. It rested in a cradle of metal supports, sharp end pointing aft, in a compartment just forward of *Tyrant*'s engine bay. Syrinxes seemed to work better when they were somewhere close to the centre of mass of a ship, but beyond that there were no clear rules, and much of what *was* known had been pieced together through guesswork and experimentation.

"It still works, to a degree," Merlin said, stroking a glove along the tapering form. "But it's dying on me. I daren't say how many more transits I'll get out it."

"What would you have done if it had failed?" Teal asked, managing to make the question sound peremptory and businesslike, as if she had no real interest in the answer.

They had taken off their helmets, but were still wearing the rest of their suits. Merlin had closed the airlock, but kept *Tyrant* docked with the larger ship. He had shown Teal through the narrow warren of his linked living quarters without stopping to comment, keen to show her that at least the syrinx was a verifiable part of his story.

"I doubt I'd have had much time to worry about it, if it failed. Probably ended up as an interesting smear, that's all." Merlin offered a smile, but Teal's expression remained hard and unsympathetic.

"A quick death's nothing to complain about."

She was a hard one for him to fathom. Her head looked too small, too childlike, jutting out from the neck ring of her suit. She was short haired, hard boned, tough, and wiry-looking at the same time. He had been right about her eyes, even through the visor. They had seen too much pain and hardship, bottled too much of it inside themselves, and now it was leaking back out.

"You still don't trust me, and that's fine. But let me show you something else." Merlin beckoned her back through into the living area, then made one of the walls light up with images and maps and text from his private files. The collage was dozens of layers deep, with the records and annotations in just as many languages and alphabets.

"What is this supposed to prove?"

He skimmed rectangles aside, flicking them to the edge of the wall. Here were Waynet charts, maps of solar systems, schematics of the surfaces of worlds and moons. "The thing I'm looking for," he said, "the weapon, the gun, whatever you want to call it—this is everything that I've managed to find out about it. Clues, rumours, whispers, from a hundred worlds. Maybe they don't all point to the same thing—I'd be amazed if they did. But some of them do, I'm sure of it, and before long I'm going to find the piece that ties the whole thing together." He stabbed a finger at a nest of numbers next to one of the charts. "Look how recent these time tags are, Teal. I'm still searching—still gathering evidence."

Her face was in profile, bathed in the different colours of the images. The slope of her nose, the angle of her chin, reminded him in certain small ways of Sayaca.

She turned to him sharply, as if she had been aware of his gaze.

"I saw pictures of you," Teal said. "They showed us them in warcreche. They were a warning against irresponsibility. You look much older than you did in those pictures."

"Travel broadens the mind. It also puts a large number of lines on you." He nodded at the collage of records. "I'm no angel, and I've made mistakes, but this proves I'm still committed. Which means we're both in the same boat, doesn't it? Lone survivors, forced together, each needing to trust the other. Are you really the last of your crew?"

There was a silence before she answered.

"Yes. I knew it before I went under, the last time. There were still others around, but mine was the last reliable cabinet—the only one that stood a chance of working."

"You were chosen, to have the best chance?"

"Yes."

He nodded, thinking again of those inner scars. "Then I've a proposition." He raised a finger, silencing her before she could get a word out. "The Huskers did something terrible to you and your people, as they did mine. They deserve to be punished for that, and they will be. Together we can make it happen."

"By finding your fabled weapon?"

"By finding the syrinx that'll help me carry on with my search. You said that system wasn't far away. If it's on the Waynet, I can reach it in *Tyrant*. We backtrack. If you traded with them once, we can trade again. You've seen that system once before, so you have the local knowledge I most certainly lack."

She glanced away, her expression clouded by very obvious misgivings.

"We sold them a syrinx," Teal said. "One of the rarest, strangest things ever made. All you have is a little black ship and some stories. What could you ever offer them that would be worth that?"

"I'd think of something," Merlin said.

The transition, when it came, was the hardest so far. Merlin had been expecting the worst and had made sure the two of them were buckled in as tightly as their couches allowed, side by side in *Tyrant*'s command deck. When they slipped into the Waynet it had felt like an impact, a solid scraping blow against the ship, as if it were grinding its way along the flank of an asteroid or iceberg. Alarms sounded, and the hull gave off moans and shrieks of structural complaint. *Tyrant* yawed violently. Probes and stabilisers flaked away from the hull.

But it held. Merlin waited for the instruments to settle down, and for the normal smooth motion of the flow to assert itself. Only then did he start breathing again.

"We're all right. Once we're in the Way, it's rarely too bad. It's just coming in and out that's becoming problematic." Long experience told him it was safe to unbuckle, and he motioned for Teal to do likewise. She had kept her suit on and her helmet nearby, as if either of those things stood any chance of protecting her if the transition failed completely. Merlin had removed all but the clothes he normally wore in *Tyrant*—baggy and tending to frills and ornamentation.

"How long until we come out again?"

Merlin squinted at one of the indicators. "About six hours. We're moving very quickly now—only about a hundred billionth part less than the speed of light. Do you see those circles that shoot past us every second?"

They were like the glowing ribs of a tunnel, whisking to either side in an endless, hypnotic procession.

"What are they?"

"Constraining hoops. Anchored back into fixed space. They pin down the Way, keep it flowing in the right direction. In reality, they're about eight light hours apart—far enough that you could easily drop a solar system between them. I think about the Waymakers a lot, you know. They made an empire so old that by the time it fell hardly anyone remembered anything that came before it. Light and wealth and all the sunsets anyone could ever ask for."

"Look at all the good it did them," Teal said. "We're like rats, hunting for crumbs in the ruins they left us."

"Even rats have their day," Merlin said. "And speaking of crumbs . . . would you like something to eat?"

"What sort of rations do you have?"

He patted his belly. "We run to a bit more than rations on *Tyrant*."

With the ship weightless, still rushing down the throat of the Way, they ate with their legs tucked under them in the glass eye of the forward observation bubble. Merlin eyed Teal between mouthfuls, noticing how entirely at ease she was with the absence of gravity, never needing to chase a gobbet of food or a stray blob of water. She had declined his offer of wine, but Merlin saw no need to put himself through such hardship.

"Tell me about the people you traded with," he said.

"They were fools," Teal said. She carried on eating for a few mouthfuls. "But useful fools. They had what we needed, and we had something they considered valuable."

"Fools, why exactly?"

"They were at war. An interplanetary conflict, fought using fusion ships and fusion bombs. Strategy shaped by artificial intelligences on both sides. It had been going on for centuries when we got there, with only intervals of peace, when the military computers reached a stalemate. Just enough time to rebuild before they started blowing each other to hell again. Two worlds, circling different stars of a binary system, and all the other planets and moons caught up in it in one way or another. A twisted, factional mess. And stupid, too." She stabbed her fork into the rations as if her meal was something that needed killing. "Huskers aren't thick in this sector, but you don't go around making noise and light if you've any choice. And there's *always* a choice."

"We don't seem to have much choice about this war we're in," Merlin said.

"We're different." Her eyes were hard and cold. "This is species-level survival. Their stupid interplanetary war was over trivial ideology. Old grudges, sustained and fanned. Men and women willingly handing their fates to battle computers. Pardalote was reluctant to do business with them: too hard to know who to speak to, who to trust."

Merlin made a pained, studious look. "I'd never meddle in someone else's war."

She pushed the fork around. "In the end it wasn't too bad. We identified the side best placed to help us, and got in and out before there were too many complications."

"Complications?"

"There weren't any. Not in the end." She was silent for a second or two. "I was glad to leave that stupid place. I've barely thought about them since."

"Your logs say you were in that system thirteen hundred years ago. A lot could have changed since then. Who knows, maybe they've patched up their differences."

"And maybe the Huskers found them."

"You know what, Teal? You're cheerful company."

"Seeing the rest of your crew die will do that. You chose to leave, Merlin— it wasn't that you were the last survivor."

He sipped at his wine, debating how much of a clear head he would need when they emerged from the Way. Sometimes a clear head was the last thing that helped.

"I lost good people as well, Teal."

"Really?"

He pushed off, moved to a cabinet, and drew out a pair of immersion suits.

"If you went through warcreche you'll know what these are. Do you trust me enough to put one on?"

Teal took the dun-coloured garment and studied it with unveiled distaste. "What good will this do?"

"Put it on. I want to show you what I lost."

"We'll win this war in reality, not simulations. There's nothing you can show me that . . ."

"Just do it, Teal."

She scowled at him, but went into a back room of *Tyrant* to remove her own clothes and don the tight-fitting immersion suit. By the time she was ready Merlin had slipped into the other suit. He nodded at Teal as she spidered back into the cabin. "Good. Trust is good. We'll only be inside a little while, but I think it'll help. Ship, patch us through."

"The Palace, Merlin?"

"Where else?"

The suit prickled his neck as it established its connection with his spine. There was the usual moment of dislocation and *Tyrant* melted away, to be replaced by a surrounding of warm stone walls and tall fretted windows, shot through with amber sun.

Teal was standing next to him.

"Where are we?"

"Where I was born. Where my brother and I spent the first couple of decades of our existence, before the Cohort came." Merlin walked to the nearest window and bid Teal to follow him. "Gallinule created this environment long after we left. He's gone now as well, so this is a reminder of the past for me in more ways than one."

"Your brother's dead?"

"It's complicated."

She left it at that. "What world are we on?"

"Plenitude, we called it. Common enough name, I suppose." Merlin stepped onto a plinth under the window, offering a better view through its fretwork. "Do you see the land below?"

Teal strained to look down. "It's moving—sliding under us. I thought we were in a castle or something."

"We are. The Palace of Eternal Dusk. My family home for thirteen hundred years—as long as the interval between your visits to that system." He touched his hand against the stonework. "We didn't make this place. It was unoccupied for centuries, circling Plenitude at exactly the same speed as the line between day and night. My family were the first to reach it from the surface, using supersonic aircraft. We held it for the next forty generations." He lifted his face to the unchanging aspect of the sun, hovering at its fixed position over the endlessly flowing horizon. "My uncle was a bit of an amateur archaeologist. He dug deep into the rock the palace is built on, as far down as the anti-gravity keel. He said he found evidence that it was at least twenty thousand years old, and maybe quite a bit more than that." Merlin touched a hand to Teal's shoulder. "Let me show you something else."

She flinched under his touch but allowed him to steer her to one of the parlours branching off the main room. Merlin halted them both at the door, touching a finger to his lips. Two boys knelt on a carpet in the middle of the parlour, their forms side-lit by golden light. They were surrounded by toy armies, spread out in ordered regiments and platoons.

"Gallinule and I," Merlin whispered, as the younger of the boys took his turn to move a mounted and penanted figure from one flank to another. "Dreaming of war. Little did we know we'd get more than our share of it."

He backed away, leaving the boys to their games, and took Teal to the next parlour.

Here an old woman sat in a stern black chair, facing one of the sunlit windows with her face mostly averted from the door. She wore black and had her hands in her lap, keeping perfectly still and watchful.

"Years later," Merlin said, "Gallinule and I were taken from Plenitude. It was meant to be an act of kindness, preserving something of our world in advance of the Huskers. But it tore us from our mother. We couldn't return to her. She was left here with the ruins of empire, her sons gone, her world soon to fall."

The woman seemed aware of her visitors. She turned slightly, bringing more of her face into view. Her eyes searched the door, as if looking for ghosts.

"She has a gentle look," Teal said quietly.

"She was kind," Merlin answered softly. "They spoke ill of her, but they didn't know her, not the way Gallinule and I did."

The woman slowly turned back to face the window. Her face was in profile again, her eyes glistening.

"Does she ever speak?"

"She's no cause to." Merlin's mouth was dry for a few moments. "We saw it happen, from the swallowship. Saw the Husker weapons strike Plenitude— saw the fall of the Palace of Eternal Dusk." Merlin turned from the tableau of his mother. "I mean to go back, one of these days—see what's left with my own eyes. But I find it hard to bring myself to."

"How many died?" Teal asked.

"Hundreds of millions. We were the only two that Quail managed to save, along with a few fragments of cultural knowledge. So I know what it's like, Teal—believe me I know what it's like." He turned from her with a cold disregard. "Ship, bring Teal out."

"What about you?"

"I need a little time on my own. You can start remembering everything I need to know about the binary system. You've got about five hours."

Tyrant pulled Teal out of the Palace. Merlin stood alone, silent, for long moments. Then he returned to the parlour where his mother watched the window, imprisoned in an endless golden day, and he stood in her shadow wondering what it would take to free her from that reverie of loss and loneliness.

They made a safe emergence from the Waynet, Merlin holding his breath until they were out and stable and the syrinx had stopped ringing in its cradle like a badly cracked bell.

He took a few minutes to assess their surroundings.

Two stars, close enough together for fusion ships to make a crossing between them in weeks. A dozen large worlds, scattered evenly between the two stars. Hundreds of moons and minor bodies. Thousands of moving ships, easily tracked across interplanetary distance, the vessels grouped into squadrons and attack formations. Battle stations and super-carriers. Fortresses and cordons. The occasional flash of a nuclear weapon or energy pulse weapon—battle ongoing.

Tyrant was stealthy, but even a stealthy ship made a big splash coming out of the Waynet. Merlin wasn't at all surprised when a large vessel locked onto them and closed in fast, presumably pushing its fusion engines to the limit.

Teal carried on briefing him as the ship approached.

"I don't like the look of that thing," *Tyrant* said, as soon as they had a clear view.

"I don't either," Merlin said. "We'll treat it respectfully. Wouldn't want you getting a scratch on your paintwork, would we?"

The vessel was three times as large as Merlin's ship and every inch a thing of war. Guns bristled from its hull. It was made of old alloys, forged and joined by venerable methods, and its engines and weapons depended on the antique alchemy of magnetically bottled fusion. A snarling mouth that had been painted across the front of the ship, crammed with razor-tipped teeth.

"It's a Havergal ship," Teal said. "That's their marking, that dagger-and-star. It doesn't look all that different to the ships they had when we were here before."

"Fusion's a plateau technology," Merlin remarked. "If all they ever needed to do was get around this binary system and blow each other up now and then, it would have been sufficient."

"They knew about the Waynet, of course—hard to miss it, cutting through their sky the way it does. That interested them. They wanted to jump all the way from fusion to syrinx technology, without all the hard stuff in between."

"Doesn't look like they got very far, does it?"

The angry-looking ship drew alongside. An airlock opened and a squad of armoured figures came out on rocket packs. Merlin remained tense, but commanded *Tyrant's* weapons to remain inside their hatches. He also told the proctors to hide themselves away until he needed them.

Footfalls clanged onto the hull. Grappling devices slid like nails on rust. Merlin opened his airlock, nodded at Teal, and the two of them went to meet the boarding party. He was half way there when a thought occurred to him. "Unless they bring up your earlier visit, don't mention it. You're just along for the ride with me. I want to know if there's anything they say or do that doesn't fit with your picture of them—anything they might be keeping from me."

"I speak their language. Isn't that going to take some explaining?"

"Feign ignorance to start with, then make it seem as if you're picking it up as you go. If they get suspicious, we'll just say that there are a dozen other systems in this sector where they speak a similar dialect." He flashed a nervous smile at Teal. "Or something. Make it up. Be creative."

The airlock had cycled by the time they arrived. When it opened, Merlin was not surprised to find only two members of the boarding party inside. There would not have been room for more.

"Welcome," he said, making a flourishing gesture of invitation. "Come in, come in. Take your shoes off. Make yourselves at home."

They were a formidable looking pair. Their vacuum armour had a martial look to it, with bladed edges and spurs, a kind of stabbing ram on the crowns of their helmets, fierce-looking grills across the glass of their faceplates. All manner of guns and close-combat weapons buckled or braced to the armour. The armour was green, with gold ornamentation.

Merlin tapped his throat. "Take your helmets off. The worst you'll catch is a sniffle."

They came into the ship. Their faces were lost behind the grills, but he caught the movement as they twisted to look at each other, before reaching

up to undo their helmets. They came free with a tremendous huff of equalis-
ing pressure, revealing a pair of heads. There were two men, both bald, with
multiple blemishes and battle-scars across their scalps. They had tough, griz-
zled-looking features, with lantern jaws and a dusting of dark stubble across
their chins and cheeks. A duelling scar or similar across the face of one man,
a laser burn ruining the ear of the other. Their small, cold-seeming eyes were
pushed back into a sea of wrinkles. One man opened his mouth, revealing a
cage of yellow and metal teeth.

He barked out something, barely a syllable. His voice was very deep, and
Merlin caught a blast of stale breath as he spoke. The other man waited a
moment then amplified this demand or greeting with a few more syllables of
his own.

Merlin returned these statements with an uneasy smile of his own. "I'm
Merlin," he said. "And I come in peace. Ish."

"They don't understand you," Teal whispered.

"I'm damned glad they don't. Did you get anything of what they said?"

"They want to know why you're here and what you want."

The first man said a few more words, still in the same angry, forceful tone
as before. The second man glanced around and touched one of the control
panels next to the airlock.

"Isn't war lovely," Merlin said.

"I understand them," Teal said, still in a whisper. "Well enough, anyway.
They're still using the main Havergal language. It's shifted a bit, but I can still
get the gist. How much do you want me to pretend to understand?"

"Nothing yet. Keep soaking it in. When you think you've given it long
enough, point to the two of us and make the sound for 'friend.'" Merlin
grinned back at the suited men, the two of them edging away from the lock in
opposite directions. "I know; it needs a little work, doesn't it? Tired décor. I'm
thinking of knocking out this wall, maybe putting a window in over there?"

Teal said something, jabbing one hand at her chest and another at Merlin.
"Friendly," she said. "I've told them we're friendly. What else?"

"Give them our names. Then tell them we'd like to speak to whoever's in
charge of that planet you mentioned."

He caught "Merlin" and "Teal" and the name "Havergal." He had to trust
that she was doing a good job of making her initial efforts seem plausibly
imperfect, even as she stumbled into ever-improving fluency. Whatever she
had said, though, it had a sudden and visible effect. The crag-faced men came
closer together again and now directed their utterances at Teal alone, guessing
that was the only one who had any kind of knowledge of their language.

"What?" Merlin asked.

"They're puzzled that I speak their tongue. They also want to know if you have a syrinx."

"Tell them I have a syrinx but that it doesn't work very well." Merlin was still smiling at the men, but the muscles around his mouth were starting to ache. "And tell them I apologise for not speaking their tongue, but you're much better at languages than me. What are their names, too?"

"I'll ask." There was another halting exchange, Merlin sensing that the names were given grudgingly, but she drew them out in the end. "Balus," Teal said. "And Locrian. I'd tell you which is which, but I'm not sure there'd be much point."

"Good. Thank Balus and Locrian for the friendly reception. Tell them that they are very welcome on my ship, but I'd be very obliged if the others stopped crawling around outside my hull." Merlin paused. "Oh, and one other thing. Ask them if they're still at war with Gaffurius."

He had no need of Teal to translate the answer to that particular part of his query. Balus—or perhaps Locrian—made a hawking sound, as if he meant to spit. Merlin was glad that he did not deliver on the gesture; the intention had been transparent enough.

"He says," Teal replied, "that the Gaffurians broke the terms of the recent treaty. And the one before that. And the one before that. He said the Gaffurians have the blood of pigs in their veins. He also says that he would rather cut out his own tongue than speak of the Gaffurians in polite company."

"One or two bridges to build there, then."

"He also asks why they should care what you think of the ones still on your hull."

"It's a fair question. How good do you think you're getting with this language of theirs?"

"Better than I'm letting on."

"Well, let's push our luck a little. Tell Balus—or Locrian—that I have weapons on this ship. Big, dangerous weapons. Weapons neither of them will have ever seen before. Weapons that—if they understood their potency, and how near they've allowed that ship of theirs to come—would make them empty their bowels so quickly they'd fill their own spacesuits up to the neck ring. Can you do that for me?"

"How about I tell them that you're armed, that you're ready to defend your property, but that you still want to proceed from a position of peaceful negotiation?"

"On balance, probably for the best."

"I'll also add that you've come to find out about a syrinx, and you're pre-pared to discuss terms of trade."

"Do that."

Merlin waited while this laborious exchange was carried on. Teal reached some sort of critical juncture in her statement and this drew a renewed burst of angry exclamations from Balus and Locrian—he guessed they had just been acquainted with the notion that *Tyrant* was armed—but Teal continued and her words appeared to have some temporary soothing effect, or as best as could be expected. Merlin raised his hands in his best placating manner. "Honestly, I'm not the hair-trigger type. We just need to have a basis for mutual respect here."

"Cohort?" he heard one of them say.

"Yes," he answered, at the same time as Teal. "Cohort. Big bad Cohort."

After a great deal of to-ing and fro-ing, Teal turned to him: "They don't claim to know anything about a syrinx. Then again, I don't think these men necessarily *would* know. But one of them, Locrian, is going back to the other ship. I think he needs to signal some higher-up or something."

"It's what I was expecting," Merlin said. "Tell him I'll wait. And tell the other one he's welcome to drink with us."

Teal relayed this message, then said: "He'll stay, but he doesn't need any-thing to drink.

"His loss."

While Locrian went back through the airlock, Balus joined them in the lounge, looking incongruous in his heavily armoured suit. Teal tried to engage him in conversation, but he had obviously been ordered to keep his communica-tions to a strict minimum. Merlin helped himself to some wine, before catching his own pink-eyed reflection and deciding enough was enough, for now.

"What do you think's going on?" Teal asked, when an hour had passed with no word from the other ship.

"Stuff."

"Aren't you concerned?"

"Terribly."

"You don't look or sound it. You want this syrinx, don't you?"

"Very much so."

Balus looked on silently as his hosts spoke in Main. If he understood any part of it, there was no clue on his face. "But you seem so nonchalant about it all," Teal said.

Merlin pondered this for a few seconds. "Do you think being *not* noncha-lant would make any difference? I don't know that it would. We're here in the moment, aren't we? And the moment will have its way with us, no matter how we feel about things."

"Fatalist."

"Cheerful realist. There's a distinction." Merlin raised his empty, wine-stained glass. "Isn't there, Balus? You agree, don't you, my fine fellow?"

Balus parted his lips and gave a grunt.

"They're coming back," Teal said, catching movement through the nearest window. "A shuttle of some sort, not just people in suits. Is that good or bad?"

"We'll find out." Merlin bristled a hand across his chin. "Mind me while I go and shave my beard."

"Shave your tongue while you're at it."

Merlin had just finished freshening up when the lock completed its cycle and the two suited individuals came aboard. One of them, wearing a green and gold suit, turned out to be Locrian. He took off his helmet and motioned for the other, wearing a red and gold suit, to do likewise. This suit was less ostentatiously armoured than the other, designed for a smaller frame. But when the figure lifted their helmet off, glanced at Locrian and uttered a few terse words, Merlin had no difficulty picking up on the power relationship between the two.

The newcomer was an old man—old, at least, in Merlin's reckoning. Seventy or eighty years, by the Cohort way of accounting such things. He had fine, aristocratic features, accented by a high, imperious brow and a back-combed sweep of pure white hair. His eyes were a liquid grey, like little wells of mercury, suggesting a sharp, relentless intelligence.

Officer class, Merlin thought.

The man spoke to them. His voice was soft, undemonstrative. Merlin still did not understand a word of it, but just the manner of speaking conveyed an assumption of implicit authority.

"His name is . . . Baskin," Teal said, when the man had left a silence for her to speak. "Prince Baskin. Havergal royalty. That's his own personal cruiser out there. He was on some sort of patrol when they picked up our presence. They came at full thrust to meet us. Baskin says things come out of the Way now and then, and it's always a scramble to get to them before the enemy."

"If Locrian's spoken to him, then he already knows our names. Ask him about the syrinx."

Teal passed on Merlin's question. Baskin answered, Teal ruminated on his words, then said: "He says that he's very interested to learn of your interest in the syrinx."

"I bet he is."

"He also says that he'd like to continue the conversation on his cruiser. He says that we'll be guests, not prisoners, and that we'll be free to return here whenever we like."

"Tell Prince Baskin . . . yes, we'll join him. But if I'm not back on *Tyrant* in twelve hours, my ship will take action to retrieve me. If you can make that sound like a polite statement of fact, rather than a crudely worded threat, that would be lovely."

"He says there'll be no difficulty," Teal said.

"He's right about that," Merlin answered.

Part of Prince Baskin's cruiser had been spun to simulate gravity. There was a stateroom, as grand as anything Merlin had encountered, all shades of veneered wood and polished metal, with red drapes and red fabric on the chairs. The floor curved up gently from one end of the room to the other, and this curvature was echoed in the grand table that took up much of the space. Prince Baskin was at one end of it, Merlin and Teal at the other, with the angle of the floor making Baskin seem to tilt forward like a playing card, having to lift his head to face his guests. Orderlies had fussed around them for some time, setting plates and glasses and cutlery, before bringing in the elements of a simple but well-prepared meal. Then—rather to Merlin's surprise—they had left the three of them alone, with only stony-faced portraits of royal ancestors and nobility for company. Men on horses, men in armour, men with projectile guns and energy weapons, both grand and foolish in their pomp.

"This is pure ostentation," he said, looking around the room with its sweeping curves and odd angles. "No one in their right mind puts centrifugal gravity on a ship this small. It takes up too much room, costs too much in mass, and the spin differential between your feet and head's enough to make you dizzy."

"If the surroundings are not quite to your taste, Merlin, we could adjourn to one of the *Renouncer*'s weightless areas."

Prince Baskin had spoken.

Teal cocked her chin to face him. The curvature of the room made it like talking to someone half way up a hill. "You speak Main."

"I try."

"Then why . . ." she began.

Baskin smiled, and tore a chunk off some bread, dipping it into soup before proceeding. "Please join me. And please forgive my slight deception in pretending to need to have your words translated, as well as my rustiness with your tongue. What I have learned, I have done so from books and recordings, and until now I have never had the opportunity to speak it to a living soul." He bit into the bread, and made an eager motioning gesture that they should do likewise. "Please. Eat. My cook is excellent—as well he should be, given what it costs me to ship him and his kitchen around. Teal, I *must* apologise. But there was no deception where Locrian and Balus were concerned. They genuinely did not speak Main, and were in need of your translation. I am very much the exception."

"How . . ." Merlin started.

"I was a sickly child, I suppose you might say. I had many hours to myself, and in those hours—as one does—I sought my own entertainment. I used to play at war, but toy soldiers and tabletop campaigns will only take you so far. So I developed a fascination with languages. Many centuries ago, a Cohort ship stopped in our system. They were here for two years—two of *your* years, I should say—long enough for trade and communication. Our diplomats tried to learn Main, and by the same token the Cohort sent in negotiating teams who did their best to master our language. Of course there were linguistic ties between the two, so the task was not insurmountable. But difficult, all the same. I doubt that either party excelled itself, but we did what was needed and there was sufficient mutual understanding." Baskin turned his head to glance at the portraits to his right, each painting set at a slight angle to its neighbours. "It *was* a very long time ago, as I'm sure you appreciate. When the Cohort had gone, there was great emphasis placed on maintaining our grasp of their language, so that we'd have a head start the next time we needed it. Schools, academies, and so on. King Curtal was instrumental in that." He was nodding at one of the figures in the portraits, a man of similar age and bearing to himself, and dressed in state finery not too far removed from the formal wear in which Baskin now appeared. "But that soon died away. The Cohort never returned and, as the centuries passed, there was less and less enthusiasm for learning Main. The schools closed, and by the time it came down to me—forty generations later—all that remained were the books and recordings. There was no living speaker of Main. So I set myself the challenge to become one, and encouraged my senior staff to do likewise, and here I am now, sitting before you, and doubtless making a grotesque mockery of your tongue."

Merlin broke bread, dipped it into the soup, made a show of chewing on it before answering.

"This Cohort ship that dropped by," he said, his mouth still full. "Was it the *Shrike*?"

Teal held her composure, but he caught the sidelong twitch of her eye.

"Yes," Baskin said, grimacing slightly. "You've heard of it?"

"It's how I know about the syrinx," Merlin said, trying to sound effortlessly matter-of-fact. "I found the *Shrike*. It was a wreck, all her crew dead. Been dead for centuries, in fact. But the computer records were still intact." He lifted a goblet and drank. The local equivalent to wine was amber coloured and had a lingering, woody finish. Not exactly to his taste but he'd had worse. "That's why I'm here."

"And Teal?"

"I travel with Merlin," she said. "He isn't good with languages, and he pays me to be his translator."

"You showed a surprising faculty with our own," Baskin said.

"Records of your language were in the files Merlin pulled from the wreck. It wasn't that hard to pick up the rudiments."

Baskin dabbed at his chin with napkin. "You picked up more than the rudiments, if I might say."

Merlin leaned forward. "Is it true about the syrinx?"

"Yes," Baskin said. "We keep it in a safe place on Havergal. Intact, in so far as we can tell. Would that be of interest to you?"

"I think it might."

"But you must already have one, if you've come here by the Way."

Teal said: "His syrinx is broken, or at least damaged. He knows it won't last long, so he needs to find a spare."

Again Baskin turned to survey the line of portraits. "These ancestors of mine knew very little but war. It dominated their lives utterly. Even when there was peace, they were thinking ahead to the moment that peace would fail, and how they might be in the most advantageous position when that day came. As it always did. My own life has also been shaped by the war. Disfigured, you might say. But I have lived under its shadow long enough. I should very much like to be the last of my line who ruled during wartime."

"Then end the war," Merlin said.

"I should like to—but it must be under our terms. Gaffurius is stretched to its limits. One last push, one last offensive, and we can enforce a lasting peace. But there is a difficulty."

"Which is?" Teal asked.

"Something of ours has fallen into the wrong hands—an object we call the Iron Tactician." Baskin continued eating for several moments, in no rush to explain himself. "I don't know what you've learned of our history. But for centuries, both sides in this war have relied on artificial intelligences to guide their military planning."

"I suppose this is another of those machines," Merlin said.

"Yes and no. For a long time our machines were well-matched with those of the enemy. We would build a better one, then they would, we would respond, and so on. A gradual escalating improvement. So it went on. Then—by some happy stroke—our cyberneticists created a machine that was generations in advance of anything they had. For fifty years the Iron Tactician has given us an edge, a superiority. Its forecasts are seldom in error. The enemy still has nothing to match it—which is why we have made the gains that we have. But now, on the eve of triumph, we have lost the Iron Tactician."

"Careless," Merlin said.

A tightness pinched the corner of Baskin's mouth. "The Tactician has always needed to be close to the theatre of battle, so that its input data is as accurate and up-to-date as possible. That was why our technicians made it portable, self-contained, and self-reliant. Of course there are risks in having an asset of that nature."

"What happened?" Teal asked. "Did Gaffurius capture it?"

"Thankfully, no," Baskin answered. "But it's very nearly as bad. The Tactician has fallen into the hands of a non-aligned third party. Brigands, mercenaries, call them what you will. Now they wish to extract a ransom for the Tactician's safe return—or they will sell it on to the enemy. We know their location, an asteroid holdout, and if we massed a group of ships we could probably overwhelm their defences. But if Gaffurius guessed our intentions and moved first . . ." Baskin lifted his glass, peering through it at Merlin and Teal, so that his face swam distorted, one mercurial eye wobbling to immensity while the other shrunk to a tight cold glint. "So there you have it. A simple proposition. The syrinx is yours, Merlin—provided you recover the Tactician for us."

"Maybe I still wouldn't be fast enough."

"But you'll be able to strike without warning, with Cohort weapons. I don't see that it should pose you any great difficulty, given the evident capabilities of your ship." Baskin twirled his fingers around the stem of his goblet. "But then that depends on how badly you want our syrinx."

"Mm," Merlin said. "Quite badly, if I'm going to be honest."

"Would you do it?"

Merlin looked at Teal before answering. But she seemed distracted, her gaze caught by one of the portraits. It was the picture of King Curtal, the ancestor Baskin had mentioned only a little while earlier. While the style of dress might not have changed, the portrait was yellowing with old varnish, its colours time-muted.

"I'd need guarantees," he said. "Starting with proof that this syrinx even exists."

"That's easily arranged," Prince Baskin said.

Tyrant had a biometric lock on Merlin, and it would shadow the *Renouncer* all the way to Havergal. If it detected that Merlin was injured or under duress, *Tyrant* would deploy its own proctors to storm the cruiser. But Merlin had gauged enough of his hosts to conclude that such an outcome was vanishingly unlikely. They needed his cooperation much too badly to do harm to their guest.

Locrian showed Merlin and Teal to their quarters, furnished in the same sumptuous tones as the stateroom. When the door opened and Merlin saw that there was only one bed, albeit a large one, he turned to Teal with faked resignation.

"It's awkward for both of us, but if we want to keep them thinking you've been travelling with me for years and years, it'll help if we behave as a couple."

Teal waited until Locrian had shut the door on them and gone off on his own business. She walked to the bed, following the gently, dreamy up-curve of the floor. "You're right," she said, glancing back at Merlin before she sat on the edge of the bed. "It will help. And at least for now I'd rather they didn't know I was on the swallowship, so I'm keen to maintain the lie."

"Good. Very good."

"But we share the bed and nothing else. You're of no interest to me, Merlin. Maybe you're not a traitor or a fool—I'll give you that much. But you're still a fat, swaggering drunk who thinks far too much of himself." But Teal patted the bed. "Still, you're right. The illusion's useful."

Merlin settled himself down on his side of the bed. "No room for manoeuvre there? Not even a little bit?"

"None."

"Then we're clear. Actually, it's a bit of a relief. I meant to say . . ."

"If this is about what I just spoke about?"

"I just wanted to say, I understand how strange all this must be. Not everyone goes back to a place they were thirteen hundred years ago. In a way, it's a good job it was such a long time ago. At least we don't have to contend with any living survivors from those days, saying that they remember you being on the diplomatic team."

"It was forty three generations ago. No one remembers."

Merlin moved to the window, watching the stars wheel slowly by outside. There was his own ship, a sharp sliver of darkness against the greater darkness of space. He thought of the loves he had seen ripped from by time and distance, and how the sting of those losses grew duller with each year but was never entirely healed. It was an old lesson for him, one he had been forced to learn many times. For Teal, this might be her first real taste of the cruelty of deep time—realising how far downstream she had come, how little chance she stood of beating those currents back to better, kinder times.

"I'd remember," he said softly.

He could see her reflection in the window, *Tyrant* sliding through her like a barb, but Teal neither acknowledged his words nor showed the least sign that they had meant anything to her.

Five days was indeed ample time to prepare Merlin for the recovery operation, but only because the intelligence was so sparse. The brigands were holed up on an asteroid called Mundar, an otherwise insignificant speck of dirt on some complex, winding orbit that brought it into the territorial space of both Havergal and Gaffurius. Their leader was a man called Struxer, but beyond one fuzzy picture the biographical notes were sparse. Fortunately there was more on the computer itself. The Iron Tactician was a spherical object about four metres across, quilted from pole to pole in thick military-grade armour. It looked like some hard-shelled animal rolled up into a defensive ball. Merlin saw no obvious complications: it needed no external power inputs and would easily fit within *Tyrant*'s cargo hold.

Getting hold of it was another matter. Baskin's military staff knew how big Mundar was and had estimates of its fortifications, but beyond that things were sketchy. Merlin skimmed the diagrams and translated documents, but told Baskin that he wanted Teal to see the originals. He was still looking out for any gaps between the raw material and what was deemed fit for his eyes, any hint of a cover-up or obfuscation.

"Why are you so concerned?" Teal asked him, halfway to Havergal, when they were alone in Baskin's stateroom, the documents spread out on the table. "Eating away at your conscience, is it, that you might be serving the wrong paymasters?"

"I'm not the one who chose sides," he said quietly. "You did, by selling the syrinx to one party instead of the other. Besides, the other lot won't be any better. Just a different bunch of stuffed shirts and titles, being told what to do by a different bunch of battle computers."

"So you've no qualms."

"Qualms?" Merlin set down the papers he had been leafing through. "I've so many qualms they're in danger of self-organizing. I occasionally have a thought that *isn't* a qualm. But I'll tell you this. Sometimes you just have to do the obvious thing. They have an item I need, and there's a favour I can do for them. It's that simple. Not everything in the universe is a riddle."

"You'll be killing those brigands."

"They'll have every chance to hand over the goods. And I'll exercise due restraint. I don't want to damage the Tactician, not when it's the only thing standing between me and the syrinx."

"What if you found out that Prince Baskin was a bloodthirsty warmonger?"

Merlin, suddenly weary, settled his head onto his hand, propped up with an elbow. "Shall I tell you something? This war of theirs doesn't matter. I don't give a damn who wins or who loses, or how many lives end up being lost because of it. What matters—what *my* problem is—is the simple fact that the Huskers will wipe out every living trace of humanity if we allow them. That includes you, me, Prince Baskin, Struxer's brigands, and every human being on either side of their little spat. And if a few people end up dying to make that Husker annihilation a little less likely, a few stupid mercenaries who should have known better than to play one side against the other, I'm afraid I'm not going to shed many tears."

"You're cold."

"No one loves life more than me, Teal. No one's lost more, either. You lost a ship, and that's bad, but I lost a whole world. And regardless of which side they're on, these people will all die if I don't act." He returned to the papers, with their sketchy ideas about Mundar's reinforcements, but whatever focus he'd had was gone now. "They owe you nothing, Teal, and you owe them nothing in return. The fact that you were here all those years ago . . . it doesn't matter. Nothing came of it."

Teal was silent. He thought that was going to be the end of it, that his words had found their mark, but after a few moments she said: "Something isn't right. The man in the portrait—the one they call King Curtal. I knew him. But that wasn't his name."

As they made their approach to Havergal, slipping through cordon after cordon of patrols and defence stations, between armoured moons and belts of anti-ship mines, dodging patrol zones, and battle fronts, Merlin felt a sickness building in him. He had seen worse things done to worlds in his travels. Much worse, in many cases: seen worlds reduced to molten slag or tumbling rubble piles or clouds of hot, chemically complex dust. But with few exceptions those horrors had been perpetrated not by people but by forces utterly beyond their control or comprehension. Not so here. The boiled oceans, the cratered landmasses, the dead and ashen forests, the poisoned, choking remnants of what had once been a life-giving atmosphere—these brutalities had been perpetrated by human action, people against people. It was an unnecessary and wanton crime, a cruel and injudicious act in a galaxy that already knew more than its share.

"Is Gaffurius like this?" Merlin asked, as *Renouncer* cleaved its way to ground, *Tyrant* matching its course with an effortless insouciance.

"Gaffurius?" Baskin asked, a fan of wrinkles appearing at the corner of his eyes. "No, much, much worse. At least we still have a few surface settlements, a few areas where the atmosphere is still breathable."

"I wouldn't count that as too much of a triumph." Merlin's mind was flashing back to the last days of Lecythus, the tainted rubble of its shattered cities, the grey heave of its restless cold ocean, waiting to reclaim what humans had left to ruin. He remembered Minla taking him to the huge whetstone monument, the edifice upon which she had embossed the version of events she wished to be codified as historical truth, long after she and her government were dust.

"Don't judge us too harshly, Merlin," Baskin said. "We don't choose to be enmeshed in this war."

"Then end it."

"I intend to. But would you opt for any ceasefire with the Huskers, irrespective of the terms?" He looked at Merlin, then at Teal, the three of them in *Renouncer's* sweeping command bridge, standing before its wide arc of windows, shuttered for the moment against the glare of re-entry. Of course you wouldn't. War is a terrible thing. But there are kinds of peace that are worse."

"I haven't seen much evidence of that," Merlin said.

"Oh, come now. Two men don't have to spend too much time in each other's company to know each other for what they are. We're not so different, Merlin. We disdain war, affect a revulsion for it, but deep down it'll always be in our blood. Without it, we wouldn't know what to do with ourselves."

Teal spoke up. "When we first met, Prince Baskin, you mentioned that you hadn't always had this interest in languages. What was it you said? Toy soldiers and campaigns will only get you so far? That you used to play at war?"

"In your language—in Main," Baskin said, "the word for school is 'warcreche.' You learn war from the moment you can toddle."

"But we don't play at it," Teal said.

The two ships shook off their cocoons of plasma and bellied into the thicker airs near the surface. They levelled into horizontal flight, and the windows de-shuttered themselves, Merlin blinking against the sudden silvery brightness of day. They were overflying a ravaged landscape, pressed beneath a low, oppressive cloud ceiling. Merlin searched the rolling terrain for evidence of a single living thing, but all he saw was desolation. Here and there was the faint scratch of what might once have been a road, or the gridded thumbprint of some former town, but it was clear that no one now lived among these ruins. Ravines, deep and ominous, sliced their way through the abandoned roads. There were so many craters, their walls interlacing, that it was as if rain had begun to fall on some dull grey lake, creating a momentary pattern of interlinked ripples.

"If I need a planet looking after," Merlin mumbled, "remind me not to trust it to any of you lot."

"We'll rebuild," Baskin said, setting his hands on the rail that ran under the sweep of windows. "Reclaim. Cleanse and resettle. Even now our genetic engineers are designing the hardy plant species that will re-blanket these lands in green and start making our atmosphere fit for human lungs." He caught himself, offering a self-critical smile. "You'll forgive me. Too easy to forget that I'm not making some morale-boosting speech at one of our armaments complexes."

"Where do you all live now?" Teal asked. "There were surface cities here once . . . weren't there?"

"We abandoned the last of those cities, Lurga, when I was just out of boyhood," Baskin said. "Now we live in underground communities, impervious to nuclear assault."

"I bet the views are just splendid," Merlin said.

Baskin met his sarcasm with a grim absence of humour. "We endure, Merlin—as the Cohort endures. Here. We're approaching the entry duct to one of the sub-cities. Do you see that sloping hole?" He was nodding at an angled mouth, jutting from the ground like a python buried up to its eyes. "The Gaffurians are good at destruction, but less good at precision. They can impair our moons and asteroids, but their weapons haven't the accuracy to strike across space and find a target that small. We'll return, a little later, and you'll be made very welcome. But first I'd like to settle any doubts you might have about the syrinx. We'll continue a little way north, into the highlands. I promise it won't take long."

Baskin was true to his word, and they had only flown for a few more minutes when the terrain began to buckle and wrinkle into the beginnings of a barren, treeless mountain range, rising in a series of forbidding steps until even the high-flying spacecraft were forced to increase their altitude. "Most of our military production takes place in these upland sectors," Baskin said. "We have ready access to metallic ores, heavy isotopes, geothermal energy, and so on. Of course it's well guarded. Missile and particle beams will be locking onto us routinely, both our ships. The only thing preventing either of them being shot down is our imperial authorisation."

"That and the countermeasures on my ship," Merlin said. "Which could peel back these mountains like a scab, if they detected a threat worth bothering with."

But in truth he felt vulnerable and was prepared to admit it, if only to himself. He could feel the nervous, bristling presence of all that unseen weaponry, like a migraine under the skin of Havergal.

Soon another mouth presented itself. It was wedged at the base of an almost sheer-sided valley.

"Prepare for descent," Baskin said. "It'll be a tight squeeze, but your ship shouldn't have any difficulties following."

They dived into the mouth and went deep. Kilometres, and then tens of kilometres, before swerving sharply into a horizontal shaft. Merlin allowed not a flicker of a reaction to betray his feelings, but the fact was that he was impressed, in a grudging, disapproving way. There was expertise and determination here—qualities that the Cohort's military engineers could well have appreciated. Anyone who could dig tunnels was handy in a war.

A glowing orange light shone ahead. Merlin was just starting to puzzle over its origin when they burst into a huge underground chamber, a bubble in the crust of Havergal. The floor of the bubble was a sea of lava, spitting and churning, turbulent with the eddies and currents of some mighty underground flow which just happened to pass in and out of this chamber. Suspended in the middle of the rocky void, underlit by flickering orange light, was a dark structure shaped like an inverted cone, braced in a ring and attached to the chamber's walls by three skeletal, cantilevered arms. It was the size of a small palace or space station, and its flattened upper surface was easily spacious enough for both ships to set down on with room to spare.

Bulkily suited figures—presumably protected against the heat and toxic airs of this place—came out and circled the ships. They attached a flexible docking connection to *Renouncer*.

"We call it the facility," Baskin said, as he and his guests walked down the sloping throat of the docking connector. "Just that. No capital letters, nothing to suggest its ultimate importance. But for many centuries this was the single most important element in our entire defence plan. It was here that we hoped to learn how to make the syrinx work for us." He turned back to glance at Merlin and Teal. "And where we failed—or *continue* to fail, I should say. But we had no intention of giving up, not while there was a chance."

Teal and Merlin were led down into the suspended structure, into a windowless warren of corridors and laboratories. They went down level after level, past sealed doors and observation galleries. There was air and power and light, and clearly enough room for thousands of workers. But although the place was clean and well-maintained, hardly anyone now seemed to be present. It was only when they got very deep that signs of activity began to appear. Here the side-rooms and offices showed evidence of recent use, and now and then uniformed staff members passed them, carrying notes and equipment. But Merlin detected no sign of haste or excitement in any of the personnel.

The lowest chamber of the structure was a curious circular room. Around its perimeter were numerous desks and consoles, with seated staff at least giving the impression of being involved in some important business. They were all facing the middle of the room, whose floor was a single circular sheet of glass, stretched across the abyss of the underlying lava flow. The orange glow of that molten river underlit the faces of the staff, as if reminding them of the perilous location of their workplace. The glass floor only caught Merlin's eye for an instant, though. Of vastly more interest to him was the syrinx, suspended nose-down in a delicate cradle over the middle of the glass. It was too far from the floor to be reached, even if someone had trusted the doubtful integrity of that glass panel. Merlin was just wondering how anyone got close to the syrinx when a flimsy connecting platform was swung out across the glass, allowing a woman to step over the abyss. Tiptoeing lightly, she adjusted something on the syrinx, moving some sort of transducer from one chalked spot to another, before folding the platform away and returning to her console.

All was quiet, with only the faintest whisper of communications from one member of staff to another.

"In the event of an imminent malfunction," Baskin said, "the syrinx may be dropped through the pre-weakened glass, into the lava sea. That may or may not destroy it, of course. We don't know. But it would at least allow the workers some chance of fleeing the facility, which would not be the case if we used nuclear charges."

"I'm glad you've got their welfare at heart," Merlin said.

"Don't think too kindly of us," Baskin smiled back. "This is war. If we thought there was a chance of the facility itself being overrun, then more than just the syrinx would need to be destroyed. Also the equipment, the records, the collective expertise of the workers . . ."

"You'd drop the entire structure," Teal said, nodding her horrified understanding. "The reason it's fixed the way it is, on those three legs. You'd press a button and drop all these people into that fire."

"They understand the risks," Baskin said. "And they're paid well. Extremely well, I should say. Besides, it's a very good incentive to hasten the work of understanding."

Merlin felt no kinship with these warring peoples, and little more than contempt for what they had done to themselves across all these centuries. But compared to the Waymakers, Merlin, Teal, and Baskin may as well have been children of the same fallen tribe, playing in the same vast and imponderable ruins, not one of them wiser than the others.

"I'll need persuasion that it's real," he said.

"I never expected you to take my word for it," Baskin said. "You may make whatever use of the equipment here you need, within limits, and you may question my staff freely."

"Easier if you just let me take it for a test ride."

"Yes, it would—for you." Baskin reached out and settled a hand on Merlin's shoulder, as if they were two old comrades. "Shall we agree—a day to complete your inspection?"

"If that's all you'll allow."

"I've nothing to hide, Merlin. Do you imagine I'd ever expect to dupe a man like you with a fake? Go ahead and make your enquiries—my staff have already been told to offer you complete cooperation." Baskin touched a hand to the side of his mouth, as if whispering a secret. "Truth to tell, it will suit many of them if you take the syrinx. Then they won't feel obliged to keep working in this place."

They were given a room in the facility, while Merlin made his studies of the syrinx. The staff were as helpful as Baskin had promised, and Merlin soon had all the equipment and records he could have hoped for. Short of connecting the syrinx to *Tyrant*'s own diagnostic systems, he was able to run almost every test he could imagine, and the results and records quickly pointed to the same conclusion. The syrinx was the genuine article.

But Merlin did not need a whole day to arrive at that conclusion.

While Baskin kept Teal occupied with endless discussions in Main, learning all that he could from this living speaker, Merlin used the console to dig into Havergal's history, and specifically the background and career of Baskin's long-dead ancestor, King Curtal. He barely needed to access the private records; what was in the public domain was clear enough. Curtal had come to power within a decade of the *Shrike*'s visit to this system.

Merlin waited until they were alone in the evening, just before they were due to dine with Prince Baskin.

"You've been busy all day," Teal said. "I take it you've reached a verdict by now?"

"The syrinx? Oh, that was no trouble at all. It's real, just as Baskin promised. But I used my time profitably, Teal. I found out something else as well—and I think you'll find it interesting. You were right about that portrait, you see."

"I know you enjoy these games, Merlin. But if you want to get to the point . . ."

"The man who became King Curtal began life called Tierce." He watched her face for the flicker of a reaction that he knew she would not be able to conceal. The recognition of a name, across years or centuries, depending on the reckoning.

Merlin cleared his throat before continuing.

"Tierce was a high-ranking officer in the Havergal military command— assigned to the liaison group which dealt with the *Shrike*. He'd have had close contact with your crew during the whole time you were in-system."

Her mouth moved a little before she found the words. "Tell me what happened to Tierce."

"Nothing bad. But what you might not have known about Tierce was that he was also minor royalty. He probably played it down, trying to get ahead in his career on his own merits. And that was how things would have worked out, if it wasn't for one of those craters. A Gaffurian long-range strike, unexpected and deadly, taking out the entire core of the royal family. They were all killed, Teal—barely a decade after you left the system. But they had to maintain continuity, then more than ever. The chain of succession led to Tierce, and he became King Curtal. The man you knew ended up as King."

She looked at him for a long moment, perhaps measuring for herself the reasons Merlin might have had to lie about such a thing, and then finding none that were plausible, beyond tormenting her for the sake of it.

"Can you be sure?"

"The records are open. There was no cover-up about the succession itself. But the fact that Tierce had a daughter . . ." Merlin found that he had to glance away before continuing. "That was difficult. The girl was illegitimate, and that was deeply problematic for the Havergal elite. On the other hand, Tierce was proud and protective of his daughter, and wouldn't accept the succession unless Cupis—that's the girl's name—was given all the rights and privileges of nobility. There was a constitutional tussle, as you can imagine. But eventually it was all settled in favour of Cupis and she was granted legitimacy within the family. They're good at that sort of thing, royals."

"What you're saying is that Cupis was my daughter."

"For reasons that you can probably imagine, there's no mention that the child was born to a Cohort mother. That would be a scandal beyond words. But of course you could hardly forget that you'd given birth to a girl, could you?"

She answered after a moment's hesitation. "We had a girl. Her name was Pauraque."

Merlin nodded. "A Cohort name—not much good for the daughter of a king. Tierce would have had to accept a new name for the girl, something more suited to local customs. I don't doubt it was hard for him, if the old name was a link to the person he'd never see again, the person he presumably loved and missed. But he accepted the change in the girl's interests. Do you mind—was there a reason you didn't stay with Tierce, or Tierce didn't join you on the *Shrike*?"

"Neither was allowed," Teal said, with a sudden coldness in her voice. "What happened was difficult. Tierce and I were never meant to get that close, and if one of us had stayed with the other it would have made the whole affair a lot more public, risking the trade agreements. We were given no choice. They said if I didn't go along with things, the simplest option would be to make Pauraque disappear. So I had to leave my daughter behind on Havergal, and I was told it would be best for me if I forgot she ever existed. And I tried. But when I saw that portrait . . ."

"I can't imagine what you went through," Merlin answered. "But if I can offer anything by way of consolation, it's this. King Curtal was a good ruler—one of the best they had. And Queen Cupis did just as well. She took the throne late in her father's life, when Curtal abdicated due to failing health. And by all accounts she was an honest and fair-minded ruler who did everything she could to broker peace with the enemy. It was only when the military computers overruled her plans . . ." Merlin managed a kindly smile and produced the data tablet had been keeping by his side. It was of Havergal manufacture, but rugged and intuitive in its functions. He held it to Teal and a woman's face appeared on the screen. "That's Queen Cupis," he said. "She wasn't one of the portraits we saw earlier, or you'd have made the connection for yourself. I can see you in her pretty clearly."

Teal took the tablet and held it close to her, so that its glow underlit her features. "Are there more images?" she asked, with a catch in her voice, as if she almost feared the answer.

"Many," Merlin replied. "And recordings, video and audio, taken at all stages in her life. I stored quite a few on the tablet—I thought you'd like to see them."

"Thank you," she said. "I suppose."

"I know this is troubling for you, and I probably shouldn't have dug into Curtal's past. But once I'd started . . ."

"And after Cupis?"

"Nearly twelve hundred years of history, Teal—kings and queens and marriages and assassinations, all down the line. Too many portraits for one room. But your genes were in Cupis and if I've read the family tree properly they ought to be in every descendant, generation after generation." He paused, giving her time to take this all in. "I'm not exactly sure what this makes you. Havergal royalty, by blood connection? I'm pretty certain they won't have run into this situation before. Equally certain Baskin doesn't have a clue that you're one of his distant historical ancestors. And I suggest we keep it that way, at least for now."

"Why?"

"Because it's information," Merlin said. "And information's always powerful."

He left her with the tablet. They were past the hour for their appointment with Prince Baskin now, but Merlin would go on alone and make excuses for Teal's lateness.

Besides, he had something else on his mind.

Merlin and the Prince were dining, just the two of them for the moment. Baskin had been making half-hearted small-talk since Merlin's arrival, but it was plain that there was really only one thing on his mind, and he was straining to have an answer.

"My staff say that you were very busy," he said. "Making all sorts of use of our facilities. Did you by any chance . . ."

Merlin smiled sweetly. "By any chance . . . ?"

"Arrive at a conclusion. Concerning the matter at hand."

Merlin tore into his bread with rude enthusiasm. "The matter?"

"The syrinx, Merlin. The syrinx. The thing that's kept you occupied all day."

Merlin feigned sudden and belated understanding, touching a hand to his brow and shaking his head at his own forgetfulness. "Of course. Forgive me, Prince Baskin. It always was really just a formality, wasn't it? I mean, I never seriously doubted your honesty."

"I'm glad to hear that." But there was still an edge in Baskin's voice. "So . . ."

"So?"

"Is it real, or is it not real. That's what you set out to establish, isn't it?"

"Oh, it's real. Very real." Merlin looked at his host with a dawning understanding. "Did you actually have doubts of your own, Prince? That had never occurred to me until now, but I suppose it would have made perfect sense. After all, you only ever had the *Shrike*'s word that the thing was real. How could you ever know, without using it?"

"We tried, Merlin. For thirteen hundred years, we tried. But it's settled, then? You'll accept the syrinx in payment? It really isn't much that I'm asking of you, all things considered."

"If you really think this bag of tricks will make all the difference, then who I am I to stand in your way?"

Baskin beamed. He stood and recharged their glasses from the bottle that was already half-empty.

"You do a great thing for us, Merlin. Your name will echo down the centuries of peace to follow."

"Let's just hope the Gaffurians hold it in the same high esteem."

"Oh, they will. After a generation or two under our control, they'll forget there were ever any differences between us. We'll be generous in victory, Merlin. If there are scores to be settled, it will be with the Gaffurian high command, not the innocent masses. We have no quarrel with those people."

"And the brigands—you'll extend the same magnanimity in their direction?"

"There'll be no need. After you've taken back the Tactician, they'll be a spent force, brushed to the margins."

Merlin's smile was tight. "I did a little more reading on them. There was quite a bit in the private and public records, beyond what you showed me on the crossing."

"We didn't care to overwhelm you with irrelevant details," Baskin said, returning to his seat. "But there was never anything we sought to hide from you. I welcome your curiosity: you can't be too well prepared in advance of your operation."

"The background is complicated, isn't it? Centuries of dissident or breakaway factions, skulking around the edges of your war, shifting from one ideology to another, sometimes loosely aligned with your side, sometimes with the enemy. At times numerous, at other times pushed almost to extinction. I was interested in their leader, Struxer . . ."

"There's little to say about him."

"Oh, I don't know." Merlin fingered his glass, knowing he had the edge for now. "He was one of yours, wasn't he? A military defector. A senior tactician, in his own right. Close to your inner circle—almost a favoured son. But instead of offering his services to the other side, he teamed up with the brigands on Mundar. From what I can gather, there are Gaffurian defectors as well. What do they all want, do you think? What persuades those men and women that they're better off working together, than against each other?"

"They stole the Tactician, Merlin—remember that. A military weapon in all but name. Hardly the actions of untainted pacifists."

Behind Baskin, the doors opened as Teal came to join them. Baskin twisted around in his seat to greet her, nodding in admiration at the satin Havergal evening wear she had donned for the meal. It suited her well, Merlin thought, but what really mattered was the distraction it offered. While Baskin's attention was diverted, Merlin quickly swapped their glasses. He had been careful to drink to the same level as Baskin, so that the subterfuge wasn't obvious.

"I was just telling Prince Baskin the good news," Merlin said, lifting the swapped glass and taking a careful sip from it. "I'm satisfied about the authenticity of the syrinx."

Teal took her place at the table. Baskin leaned across to pour her a glass. "Merlin said you were feeling a little unwell, so I wasn't counting on you joining us at all."

"It was just a turn, Prince. I'm feeling much better now."

"Good . . . good." He was looking at her intently, a frown buried in his gaze. "You know, Teal, if I didn't know you'd just come from space, I'd swear you were . . ." But he smiled at himself, dismissing whatever thought he had been about to voice. "Never mind—it was a foolish notion. I trust you'll accept our hospitality, while Merlin discharges his side of the arrangement? I know you travel together, but on this occasion at least Merlin has no need of an interpreter. There'll be no negotiation, simply a demonstration of overwhelming and decisive force. They'll understand what it is we'd like back."

"Where he goes, I go," Teal said.

Merlin tensed, his fingers tight on the glass. "It might not be a bad idea, actually. There'll be a risk—a small one, I grant, but a risk nonetheless. *Tyrant* isn't indestructible, and I'll be restricted in the weapons I can deploy, if the

Prince wants his toy back in one piece. I'd really rather handle this one on my own."

"I accept the risk," she said. "And not because I care about the Tactician, or the difference it will make to this system. But I do want to see the Huskers defeated, and for that Merlin needs his syrinx."

"I'd have been happy to give it to Merlin now, if I thought your remaining on Havergal would offer a guarantee of his return. But the opposite arrangement suits me just as well. As soon as we have the Tactician, we'll release the syrinx."

"If those are you terms," Merlin said, with an easy-going shrug.

Baskin smiled slightly. "You trust me?"

"I trust the capability of my ship to enforce a deal. It amounts to the same thing."

"A pragmatist. I knew you were the right man for the job, Merlin."

Merlin lifted his glass. "To success, in that case."

Baskin followed suit, and Teal raised her own glass in half-hearted sympathy. "To success," the Prince echoed. "And victory."

They left the facility the following morning. Merlin took *Tyrant* this time, Teal joining him as they followed *Renouncer* back into space. Once the two craft were clear of Havergal's atmosphere, Prince Baskin issued a request for docking authorisation. Merlin, who had considered his business with the prince concluded for now, viewed the request with a familiar, nagging trepidation.

"He wants to come along for the ride," he murmured to Teal, while the airlock cycled. "Force and wisdom, that's exactly what it'll be. Needs to see Struxer's poor brigands getting their noses bloodied up close and personal, rather than hearing about it from halfway across the system."

Teal looked unimpressed. "If he wants to risk his neck, who are you to stop him?"

"Oh, nobody at all. It's just that I work best without an audience."

"You've already got one, Merlin. Start getting used to it."

He shrugged aside her point. He was distracted to begin with, thinking of the glass he had smuggled out of the dining room, and whether Prince Baskin had been sharp enough to notice the swap. While they were leaving Havergal he had put the glass into *Tyrant's* full-spectrum analyser, but the preliminary results were not quite what he had been expecting.

"I wasn't kidding about the risks, you know," Merlin said.

"Nor was I about wanting to see you get the syrinx. And not because I care about you all that much, either."

He winced. "Don't feel you need to spare my feelings."

"I'm just stating my position. You're the means to an end. You're searching for the means to bring about the destruction of the Huskers. The syrinx is necessary for that search, and therefore I'll help you find it. But if there was a way of *not* involving you . . ."

"And I thought we broke some ice back there, with all that stuff about Tierce and your daughter."

"It didn't matter then, it doesn't matter now. Not in the slightest."

Merlin eyed the lock indicator. "It isn't as clear-cut as I thought, did you know? I swiped a gene sample from his lordship. Now, if your blood had been percolating its way down the family tree the way it ought to have been, then I should have seen a very strong correlation . . ."

"Wait," she said, face hardening as she worked through the implications of that statement. "You took a sample from him. What about me, Merlin? How did you get a look at my genes, without . . . ?"

"I sampled you."

Teal slapped him. There had been no warning, and she only hit him the once, and for a moment afterwards it might almost have been possible to pretend that nothing had happened, so exactly had they returned to their earlier stances. But Merlin's cheek stung like a vacuum burn. He opened his mouth, tried to think of something that would explain away her anger.

The lock opened. Prince Baskin came aboard *Tyrant*, wearing his armoured spacesuit with the helmet tucked under one arm.

"There'll be no objections, Merlin. My own ship couldn't keep pace with *Tyrant* even if I wished to shadow you, so the simplest option is to join you for the operation." He raised a gently silencing hand before Merlin—still stung—had a chance to interject. "I'll be along purely as an observer, someone with local knowledge, if it comes to that. You don't need to lecture me on the dangers. I've seen my share of frontline service, as you doubtless know, having made yourself such an expert on royal affairs." He nodded. "Yes, we tracked your search patterns, while you were supposedly verifying the authenticity of the syrinx."

"I wanted to know everything I could about your contact with the Cohort mission."

"That and more, I think." Baskin mouthed a command into his neck ring, and *Renouncer* detached from the lock. "None of it concerns me, though, Merlin. If it amused you to sift through our many assassinations and constitutional crises, so be it. All that matters to me is the safe return of the Tactician. And I will insist on being witness to that return. Don't insult me by suggesting that the presence of one more human on this ship will have any bearing on *Tyrant*'s capabilities."

"It's not a taxi."

"But it is spacious enough for our present needs, and that is all that matters." He nodded at Teal. "Besides, I was enjoying our evening conversations too much to forego the pleasure."

"All right," Merlin said, sighing. "You're along for the ride, Prince. But I make the decisions. And if I feel like pulling out of this arrangement, for any reason, I'll do just that."

Prince Baskin set his helmet aside and offered his empty palms. "There'll be no coercion, Merlin—I could hardly force you into doing anything you disliked, could I?"

"So long as we agree on that." Merlin gestured to the suite of cabins aft of the lock. "Teal, show him the ropes, will you? I've got some navigation to be getting on with. We'll push to one gee in thirty minutes."

Merlin turned his back on Teal and the Prince and returned to *Tyrant*'s command deck. He watched the dwindling trace of the *Renouncer*, knowing he could outpace it with ease. There would be a certain attraction in cutting and running right now, hoping that the old syrinx held together long enough for a Waynet transition, and seeing Baskin's face when he realised he would not be returning to Havergal for centuries, if at all.

But while Merlin was capable of many regrettable things, spite was not one of his failings.

His gaze slid to the results from the analyser. He thought of running the sequence again, using the same traces from the wine glass, but the arrival of the Prince rendered that earlier sample of doubtful value. Perhaps it had been contaminated to begin with, by other members of the royal staff. But now that Baskin was aboard, *Tyrant* could obtain a perfect genetic readout almost without trying.

The words of Baskin returned to mind, as if they held some significance Merlin could not yet see for himself: *If it amused you to sift through our many assassinations and constitutional crises, so be it.*

Assassinations.

When Merlin was satisfied that Prince Baskin's bones were up to the strain, he pushed *Tyrant* to two gees. It was uncomfortable for all of them, but bearable provided they kept to the lounge and avoided moving around too much. "We could go faster," Merlin said, as if it was no great achievement. "But we'd be putting out a little more exotic radiation than I'd like, and I'd rather not broadcast our intentions too strongly. Besides, two gees will get us to Mundar in plenty of time, and if you find it uncomfortable we can easily dial down the thrust for a little while."

"You make light of this capability," Prince Baskin said, his hand trembling slightly as he lifted a drinking vessel to his lips. "Yet this ship is thousands of years beyond anything possessed by either side in our system."

Merlin tried to look sympathetic. "Maybe if you weren't busy throwing rocks at each other, you could spend a little time on the other niceties of life, such as cooperation and mutual advancement."

"We will," Baskin affirmed. "I'll bend my life to it. I'm not a zealot for war. If I felt that there was a chance of a negotiated ceasefire, under terms amicable to both sides, I'd have seized it years ago. But our ideological differences are too great, our mutual grievances too ingrained. Sometimes I even think to myself that it wouldn't matter *who* wins, just as long as one side prevails over the other. There are reasonable men and women in Gaffurius, it's just . . ." But he trailed off, as if even he viewed this line of argument as treasonable.

"If you thought that way," Teal said, "the simplest thing would be to let the enemy win. Give them the Iron Tactician, if you think it will make that much difference."

"After all our advances . . . ? No. It's too late for that sort of idealism. Besides, we aren't dealing with Gaffurius. It's the brigands who are holding us to ransom."

"Face it," Merlin said. "For all this talk of peace, of victory—you'd miss the war."

"I wouldn't."

"I'm not so sure. You used to play at battle, didn't you? Toy soldiers and tabletop military campaigns, you said. It's been in your blood from the moment you took your first breath. You were the boy who dreamed of war."

"I changed," Baskin said. "Saw through those old distractions. I spoke of Lurga, didn't I—the last and greatest of our surface cities? Before the abandonment my home was Lurga's imperial palace, a building that was itself as grand as some cities. I often walk it in my dreams, Merlin. But that's where it belongs now: back in my childhood, along with all those toy soldiers."

"Lurga must have been something to see," Merlin said.

"Oh, it was. We built and rebuilt. They couldn't bear it, of course, the enemy. That's why Lurga was always the focus of their attacks, right until the end."

"There was a bad one once, wasn't there?" Merlin asked.

"Too many to mention."

"I mean, a particularly bad one—a direct strike against the palace itself. It's in your public history—I noticed it while I was going through your open records, on Havergal. You'd have been six or seven at the time, so you'd easily remember it. An assassination attempt, plainly. The Gaffurians were trying to bite the head off the Havergal ruling elite."

"It was bad, yes. I was injured, quite seriously, by the collapse of part of the palace. Trapped alone and in the dark for days, until rescue squads broke through. I . . . recovered, obviously. But it's a painful episode and not one I care to dwell on. Good people died around me, Merlin. No child should have to see that."

"I couldn't agree more."

"Perhaps it was the breaking of me, in the end," Baskin said. "Until then I'd only known war as a series of distant triumphs. Glorious victories and downplayed defeats. After the attack, I knew what blood looked like up close. I healed well enough, but only after months of recuperation. And when I returned to my studies, and some engagement with public life, I found that I'd begun to lose my taste for war. I look back on that little boy that I once was, so single-mindedly consumed by war and strategy, and almost wonder if I'm the same person." He set aside his drinking vessel, rubbing at the sore muscles in his arm. "You'll forgive me, both of you. I feel in need of rest. Our ships can only sustain this sort of acceleration for a few tens of minutes, not hour after hour."

"It's hard on us all," Merlin said, feeling a glimmer of empathy for his unwanted guest. "And you're right about one thing, Prince. I want an end to the war with the Huskers. But not at any cost."

When they were alone Teal said: "You've got some explaining to do. If it wasn't for Baskin I'd have forced it out of you with torture by now."

"I'm glad you didn't. All that screaming would have made our guest distinctly uncomfortable. And have you ever tried getting blood out of upholstery?" Merlin flashed a smile. But Teal's hard mask of an expression told him she was in no mood for banter.

"Why were you so interested in his genetic profile?"

There were sealed doors between the lounge and the quarters assigned to the Prince, but the ship was silent under normal operation and Merlin found himself glancing around and lowering his voice before answering.

"I just wanted peace of mind, Teal. I just thought that if I could find a genetic match between you and Prince Baskin, it would settle things for good, allow you to put your mind to rest about Cupis . . ."

"Put *my* mind to rest."

"I know I shouldn't have sampled you without your permission. It was just some hair left on your pillow, with a skin flakes . . ." Merlin silenced himself. "Now that we're aboard, the ship can run a profile just by sequencing the cells it picks up through the normal air circulation filters."

Teal still had her arm out, her look defiant. But slowly she pulled back the arm and slid her sleeve back down. "Run your damned tests. You've started this, you may as well finish it."

"Are you sure, Teal? It may not get us any nearer an answer of what happened to your bloodline."

"I said finish it," Teal answered.

Tyrant slipped across the system, into the contested space between the two stars. Battle continued to rage across a dozen worlds and countless more moons, minor planets, and asteroids. Fleets were engaging on a dozen simultaneous fronts, their energy bursts spangling the night sky across light hours of distance. Every radio channel crackled with military traffic, encrypted signals, blatant propaganda, screams of help or mercy from stricken crews.

Tyrant steered clear of the worst of it. But even as they approached Mundar, Merlin picked out more activity than he had hoped for. Gaffurian patrol groups were swinging suspiciously close to the brigands' asteroid, as if something had begun to attract their interest. So far they were keeping clear of the predicted defence perimeter, but their presence put Merlin on edge. It didn't help that the Gaffurian incursions were drawing a counter-response from Havergal squadrons. The nearest battlefronts were still light-minutes away, but the last thing Merlin needed was a new combat zone opening up right where he had business of his own.

"I was hoping for a clear theatre of action," he told Baskin. "Something nice and quiet, where I could do my business without a lot of messy distractions."

"Gaffurian security may have picked up rumours about the Tactician by this point," Baskin said.

"And that wasn't worth sharing with me before now?"

"I said rumours, Merlin—not hard intelligence. Or they may just be taking a renewed interest in the brigands. They're as much a thorn in the enemy's side as they are in ours."

"I like them more and more."

They were a day out when Merlin risked a quick snoop with *Tyrant's* long-range sensors. Baskin and Teal were on the command deck as the scans refreshed and updated, overlaid with the intelligence schematics Merlin had already examined on the *Renouncer*. Mundar was a fuzzy rock traced through with the equally ghostly fault-lines of shafts, corridors, internal pressure vaults, and weapons emplacements.

"That was a risky thing to do" Baskin said, while Teal nodded her agreement.

"If they picked up anything," Merlin said, "it would have been momentary and on a spread of frequencies and particle bands they wouldn't normally expect. They'll put it down to sensor malfunctions and move on."

"I wish I had your confidence."

Merlin stretched out his hands and cracked his knuckles, as if he were preparing to climb a wall. "Let's think like Struxer. He's got his claws on something precious, a one-off machine, so chances are he won't put the Tactician anywhere vulnerable, especially with these patrol groups sniffing around."

"How does that help us?"

"Because it narrows down his options. That deep vault there—do you think it would suit?"

"Perhaps. The main thing is to declare our intentions; to give Struxer an unambiguous idea of your capabilities." Baskin danced his own finger across the display. "You'll open with a decisive but pin-point attack. Enough to shake them up, and let them know we absolutely mean business. At what distance can you launch a strike?"

"We'll be in optimum charm-torp range in about six hours. I can lock in the targeting solutions now, if you like. But we'll have a sharper view of Mundar the nearer we get."

"Would they be able to see us that soon?" Teal asked.

Merlin was irritated by the question, but only because it had been the next thing on his mind.

"From what we understand of your ship's sensor footprint, they'll be able to pick you out inside a volume of radius one and a half light seconds. That's an estimate, though. Their weapons will be kinetic launchers, pulse beams, drone missiles. Can you deal with that sort of thing?"

"Provided I'm not having a bad day."

Baskin extended his own finger at the scans, wavering under the effort. "These cratered emplacements are most likely the sites of their kinetic batteries. I suggest a surgical strike against all of them, including the ones around the other side of Mundar. Can you do it?"

"Twelve charm-torps should take care of them. Which is handy, because that's all I've got left. We'll still have the gamma-cannons and the nova-mine launchers, if things get sticky."

"If I know Struxer, they will." Something twitched in Baskin's cheek, some nervous, betraying tic. "But the deaths will be all on his side, not ours. If that's the cost of enforcing peace, so be it."

Merlin eyed him carefully. "I've never been very good with that sort of calculus."

"None of us like it," Baskin said.

Teal went off to catch some sleep until they approached the attack threshold. Merlin grabbed a few hours as well, but his rest was fitful and he soon found himself returning to the command deck, watching as the scans slowly sharpened and their view of Mundar grew more precise. *Tyrant* was using passive sensors now, but these were already improving on the earlier active snapshot. Merlin was understandably on edge, though. They were backing toward the asteroid, and if there was ever a chance of their exhaust emissions being picked up, now was the time. Merlin had done what he could, trading deceleration efficiency for a constantly altering thrust angle that ought to provide maximum cover, but nothing was guaranteed.

"I thought I'd find you here," Baskin said, pinching at the corners of his eyes as he entered the room. "You've barely slept since we left Havergal, have you?"

"You don't look much more refreshed, Prince."

"I know—I saw myself in the mirror just now. Sometimes when I look at my own portrait, I barely recognise myself. I think I can be excused a little anxiety, though. So much depends on the next few hours, Merlin. I think these may be the most critical hours of my entire career. My entire life, even."

Merlin waited until the Prince had taken his seat, folding his bones with care. "You mentioned Struxer back there."

"Did I?"

"The intelligence briefings told me very little, Prince—even the confidential files I lifted from your sealed archives on Havergal. But you spoke as if you knew the man."

"Struxer was one of us. That was never any sort of secret."

"A senior tactician, that's what I was told. That sounds like quite a high-up role to me. Struxer wasn't just some anonymous military minion, was he?"

After a moment Baskin said: "He was known to me. As of course were all the high-ranking strategists."

"Was Struxer involved in the Tactician?"

If Baskin meant to hide his hesitation, he did a poor job of it. "To a degree. The Tactician required a large staff, not just to coordinate the feeding-in of

320   Alastair Reynolds

intelligence data, but to analyse and act on the results. The battle computers I mentioned . . ."

"But Struxer was close to it all, wasn't he?" Merlin was guessing now, relying on hard-won intuition, but Baskin's reactions were all he needed to know he was on the right track. "He worked closely with the computer."

"His defection was . . . regrettable."

"If you can call it a defection. That would depend on what those brigands actually want, wouldn't it? And no one's been terribly clear on that with me."

Baskin's face was strained. "They're against peace. Is there anything more you need to know?"

Merlin smiled, content with that line of questioning for now. "Prince, might I ask you something else? You know I took an interest in your constitutional history when we were on Havergal. Assassinations are commonplace, aren't they? There was that time when almost the entire ruling house of Havergal was wiped out in one strike . . ."

"That was twelve or thirteen centuries ago."

"But only a little after the visitation of the Shrike. That was why it caught my eye."

"No other reason?"

"Should there be?"

"Don't play games with me, Merlin—you'll always lose. I was the boy who dreamed of war, remember."

The door behind them opened. It was Teal, awake sooner than Merlin had expected. Her face had a freshly scrubbed look, her hair wetted down.

"Are we close?"

"About thirty minutes out," Merlin said. "Buckle in, Teal—it could get interesting from any point onwards, especially if their sensors are a little better than the Prince believes."

Teal slipped into the vacant seat. Befitting her Cohort training, she had adapted well to the two gees, moving around *Tyrant* with a confident, sinewy ease.

"Have you run that genetic scan again?" she asked.

"I have," Merlin said. "And I came up with the same result, only at a higher confidence level. Do you want to tell him, or should I?"

"Tell me what?" Baskin asked.

"There's a glitch in your family tree," Merlin said, then nodded at Teal for her to continue.

"I've already been to your world," she said, delivering the words with a defiant and brazen confidence. "I was on the diplomatic party, aboard the swallowship *Shrike*. I was with them when they sold you the syrinx." Before he had a chance to voice his disbelief, she said: "A little later, our ship ran into trouble in a nearby system. The Huskers took us, wrecked the ship, but left just enough of us alive to suffer. We went into frostwatch, those of us who remained. And one by one we died, when the frostwatch failed. I was the last living survivor. Then Merlin found me, and we returned to your system. You know this to be possible, Prince. You know of frostwatch, of near-light travel, of time-compression."

"I suppose . . ." he said.

"But there's more to it than that," Teal went on. "My daughter stayed on Havergal. She became Cupis, Queen Cupis, after Tierce was promoted to the throne. You said it yourself, Prince: there was something in my face you thought you recognised. It's your own lineage, your own family tree."

"Except it isn't, quite," Merlin said. "You see, you're not related, and you should be. I ran a genetic cross-match between the two of you on Havergal, and another since you've been on *Tyrant*. Both say there's no correlation, which is odd given the family tree. But I think there's a fairly simple explanation."

Baskin glanced from Merlin to Teal and back to Merlin, his eyes wide, doubting and slightly fearful. "Which would be?"

"You're not Prince Baskin," Merlin said. "You just think you are."

"Don't be absurd. My entire life has been lived in the public eye, subject to the harshest scrutiny."

Merlin did his best not to sound too callous, nor give the impression that he took any pleasure in disclosing what he now knew to be the truth. "There's no doubt, I'm afraid. If you were really of royal blood, I'd know it. The only question is where along your family tree the birth line was broken, and why. And I think I know the answer to that, as well . . ."

The console chimed. Merlin turned to it with irritation, but a glance told him that the ship had every reason to demand his attention. A signal was beaming out at them, straight from Mundar.

"That isn't possible," Baskin said. "We're still three light seconds out—much too far for their sensors."

Teal said: "Perhaps you should see what it says."

The transmission used local protocols, but it only took an instant for *Tyrant* to unscramble the packets and resolve them into a video signal. A man's head appeared above the console, backdropped by a roughly hewn wall of pale rock. Merlin recognised the face as belonging to Struxer, but only because he had paid close attention to the intelligence briefings. Otherwise it would have been easy to miss the similarities. This Struxer was thinner of face, somehow more delicate of bone structure, older and wearier looking, than the cold-eyed defector Merlin had been expecting.

He started speaking in a high steady voice, babbling out a string of words in the Havergal tongue. *Tyrant* was listening in, but it would be a little while before it could offer a reliable translation.

Merlin turned to Teal.

"What's he saying?"

"I'm just as capable of telling you," Baskin said.

Merlin nodded. "But I'd sooner hear it from Teal."

"He's got a fix on you," she said, frowning slightly as she caught up with the stream of words. "Says he's had a lock since the moment you were silly enough to turn those scanning systems onto Mundar. Says you must have thought they were idiots, to miss something that obvious. Also that we're not as stealthy as we think we are, judging by the ease with which he's tracking our engine signature."

"You fool," Baskin hissed. "I told you it was a risk."

"He says he knows what our intentions are," Teal went on. "But no matter how much force you throw at them they're not going to relinquish the Iron Tactician. He says to turn back now, and avoid unnecessary violence."

Merlin gritted teeth. "Ship, get ready to send a return transmission using the same channel and protocols. Teal, you're doing the talking. Tell Struxer I've no axe to grind with him or his brigands, and if we can do this without bloodshed no one'll be happier than me. Also that I can take apart that asteroid as easily as if it's a piece of rotten fruit."

Baskin gave a thin smile, evidently liking Merlin's tone.

"Belligerent enough for you, was it?" Merlin asked, while Teal leaned in and translated Merlin's reply.

"Threats and force are what they understand," Baskin said.

It took three seconds for Teal's statement to reach Mundar, and another three for Struxer's response to find its way back to *Tyrant*. They listened to what he had to say, Merlin needing no translator to tell him that Struxer's answer was a great deal more strident than before.

"You can forget about them handing it over without a struggle," Teal said. "And he says that we'd be very wise not to put Mundar's armaments to the test, now that the Iron Tactician's coordinating its own defence plans. They've got every weapon on that asteroid hooked directly into the Tactician, and they're prepared to let it protect itself."

"They'd still be outgunned," Merlin said. But even he couldn't quite disguise the profound unease he was beginning to feel.

"It's a bluff," Baskin said. "The Tactician has no concept of its own self-preservation."

"Can you be sure?" Teal asked.

"Tell Struxer this," Merlin said. "Surrender the Iron Tactician and I won't lay a finger on that asteroid. All they have to do is bring it to the surface—my proctors can take care of the rest."

Teal relayed the statement. Struxer barked back his answer, which was monosyllabic enough to require no translation.

"He says if we want it, we should try taking it," Teal said.

Merlin nodded—he had been expecting as much, but it had seemed worth his while to make one last concession at a negotiated settlement. "Ship, give me manual fire control on the torp racks. We're a little further out than I'd like, but it'll give me time to issue a warning. I'm taking out those kinetic batteries."

"You have control, Merlin," *Tyrant* said.

Baskin asked: "Are you sure it isn't too soon?"

Merlin gave his reply by means of issuing the firing command. *Tyrant* pushed out its ventral weapons racks and the charm-torps sped away with barely a twitch of recoil. Only a pattern of moving nodes on the targeting display gave any real hint that the weapons had been deployed.

"Torps armed and running," *Tyrant* said.

"Teal, tell them they have a strike on its way. They've got a few minutes to move their people deeper into the asteroid, if they aren't already there. My intention is to disable their defences, not to take lives. Make sure Struxer understands that."

Teal was in the middle of delivering her message when *Tyrant* jolted violently and without warning. It was a sideways impulse, harsh enough to bruise bones, and for a moment Merlin could only stare at the displays, as shocked as he had been when Teal had slapped him across the face.

Then there was another jolt, in the opposite direction, and he understood.

"Evasive response in progress," *Tyrant* said. "Normal safety thresholds suspended. Manual override available, but not recommended."

"What?" Baskin grimaced.

"We're being shot at," Merlin said.

Tyrant was taking sharp evasive manoeuvres, corkscrewing hard even as it was still engaged in a breakneck deceleration.

"Impossible. We're still too far out."

"There's nothing coming at us from Mundar. It's something else. Some perimeter defence screen we didn't even know about." He directed a reproachful look at Baskin. "I mean, that *you* didn't know about."

"Single-use kinetics, perhaps," Baskin said. "Free-floating sentries."

"I should be seeing the activation pulses. Electromagnetic and optical burst signatures. I'm not. All I'm seeing are the slugs, just before they hit us."

They were, as far as *Tyrant* could tell, simply inert slugs of dense matter, lacking guidance or warheads. They were falling into detection range just in time to compute and execute an evasion, but the margins were awfully fine.

"There are such things as dark kinetics," Baskin said. "They're a prototype weapon system: mirrored and cloaked to conceal the launch pulse. But Struxer's brigands have nothing in their arsenal like that. Even if they had a local manufacturing capability, they wouldn't have the skills to make their own versions . . ."

"Would the Tactician know about those weapons?" Teal asked.

"In its catalogue of military assets . . . yes. But there's a world of difference between knowing of something and being able to direct the duplication and manufacture of that technology."

"Tell that to your toy," Merlin murmured. He hoped it was his imagination, but the violent counter-manoeuvres seemed to be coming more rapidly, as if *Tyrant* was having an increasingly difficult time steering between the projectiles. "Ship, recall six of the charm-torps. Bring them back as quickly as you can."

"What good will that do?" Baskin snapped. "You should be hitting them with everything you've got, not pulling your punch at the last minute."

"We need the torps to give us an escort screen," Merlin said. "The other six can still deal with all the batteries on the visible face."

It had been rash to commit all twelve in one go, he now knew, born of an arrogant assumption as to his own capabilities. But he had realised his mistake in time.

"Struxer again," Teal said. "He says it's only going to get worse, and we should call off the other missiles and give up on our attack. Says if he sees a clear indication of our exhaust, he'll stand down the defence screen."

"Carry on," Baskin said.

"Charm-torps on return profile," *Tyrant* said. "Shall I deploy racks for recovery?"

"No. Group the torps in a protective cordon around us, close enough that you can interdict any slugs that you can't steer us past. And put in a reminder to me to upgrade our attack countermeasures."

"Complying. The remaining six torps are now being reassigned to the six visible targets. Impact in . . . twenty seconds."

"Struxer," Merlin said, not feeling that his words needed any translation. "Get your people out of those batteries!"

A sudden blue brightness pushed through *Tyrant's* windows, just before they shuttered tight in response.

"Slug interdicted," the ship said calmly. "One torp depleted from defence cordon. Five remaining."

"Spare me the countdown," Merlin said. "Just get us through this mess and out the other side."

The six remaining charm-torps of the attack formation closed in on Mundar in the same instant, clawing like a six-taloned fist, gouging six star-hot wounds into the asteroid's crust, six swelling spheres of heat and destruction that grew and dimmed until they merged at their boundaries. Merlin, studying the readouts, could only swallow in horror and awe, reminded again of the potency of even modest Cohort weaponry. Megatonnes of rock and dust were boiling off the asteroid even as he watched, like a skull bleeding out from six eye-sockets.

Three of the cordon torps were lost before *Tyrant* began to break free into relatively safe space, but by then Merlin's luck was stretching perilously thin. The torps could interdict the slugs for almost any range of approach vectors, but not always safely. If the impact happened close enough to *Tyrant*, that was not much better than a direct hit.

They were through, then, but not without cost. The hull had taken a battering from two of the nearer detonations, and while none of the damage would ordinarily been of concern, Merlin had been counting on having a ship in optimum condition. Limping away to effect repairs was scarcely an option now.

The consolation, if he needed one, was that Mundar had taken a much worse battering.

"Is Struxer still sending?" Merlin asked.

"He's trying," Teal said.

Struxer's face appeared, but speckled by interference. He looked strained, glancing either side of him as he made his statement. Teal listened carefully.

"He says they've still got weapons, if we dare to come any nearer. His position hasn't changed."

"Mine has," Merlin said. "Ship, send in the remaining torps, dialled to maximum yield. Strike at the existing impact sites: see if we can't open some fracture plains, or punch our way deep inside." Then he enlarged the asteroid's schematic and began tapping his finger against some of the secondary installations on the surface—what the intelligence dossiers said were weapons, sensor pods, airlocks. "Ready nova-mines for dispersal. Spread pattern three. We'll pick off any moving targets with the gamma-cannon."

Teal said: "If you hit Struxer's antenna you'll take away our means of communicating."

"I'm past the point of negotiation, Teal. My ship's wounded and I take that personally. If you want to send a last message to Struxer, tell him he had his chance to play nicely."

Baskin leaned forward in his seat restraints. "Don't do anything too rash, Merlin. We came to force his hand, not to annihilate the entire asteroid."

"Your primary consideration was stopping the Tactician falling into the wrong hands. I'm about to guarantee that never happens."

"I want it intact."

"It was never going to work, Prince. There was never going to be any magic peace, just because you had your battle computer back." A sudden indignation passed through him. "I know wars. I know how they play out. Squeeze the enemy hard and they just find new ways to fight back. It'll go on and on and you'll never be any nearer victory."

"We were winning."

"One tide was going out. Another was due to come back in. That's all it was."

The charm-torps were striking. Set to their highest explosive setting, the bursts were twenty times brighter than the first wave. Each fireball scooped out a tenth of the asteroid's volume, lofting unthinkable quantities of rock and dirt and gas into space, a ghastly swelling shroud lit from within by pulses of lightning.

Lines of light cut through that shroud. Kinetics and lasers were striking out from what remained of the asteroid's facing hemisphere, sweeping in arcs as they tried to find *Tyrant*. The ship swerved and stabbed like a dancing snake. The edge of a laser gashed across part of its hull, triggering a shriek of damage alarms. Merlin dispatched the nova-mines, then swung the nose around to bring the gamma-cannon into play. The flashes of the nova-mines began to pepper the shrouded face of Mundar. The kinetics and lasers were continuing, but their coverage was becoming sparser. Merlin sensed that they had endured the worst of the assault. But the approach had enacted a grave toll on *Tyrant*. One more direct hit, even with a low-energy weapon, might be enough to split open the hull.

Tyrant had reduced its speed to only a few kilometres per second relative to the asteroid. Now they were beginning to pick up the billowing front of the debris cloud. *Tyrant* was built to tolerate extremes of pressure, but the hot, gravelly medium was nothing like an atmosphere. Under other circumstances Merlin would have gladly turned around rather than push deeper. But *Tyrant* would have to cross the kinetic defence screen to reach empty space, and now he had used up all his charm-torps. If the Tactician had indeed been coordinating Mundar's defences, then Merlin saw only one way to dig himself out of this hole. He could leave nothing intact—even if it meant butchering whoever was left alive in Mundar.

Debris hammered the hull. Merlin curled fingers into sweat-sodden palms.

"Merlin," Teal said. "It's Struxer's signal again. Only it's not coming from inside Mundar."

Merlin understood as soon as he shifted his attention to the navigational display. Struxer's transmission was originating from a small moving object, coming toward them from within the debris field. The gamma-cannon was still aimed straight at Mundar. Merlin shifted the lock onto the object, ready to annihilate it in an instant. Then he waited for *Tyrant*'s sensors to give him their best estimate of the size and form of the approaching object. He was expecting something like a mine or a small autonomous missile, trying to camouflage its approach within the chaos of the debris. But then why was it transmitting in the first place?

He had his answer a moment later. The form was five-nubbed, a fat-limbed starfish. Or a human, wearing a spacesuit, drifting through the debris cloud like a rag doll in a storm.

"Suicidal," Baskin said.

There was no face now, just a voice. The signal was too poor for anything else. Teal listened and said: "He's asking for you to slow and stand down your weapons. He says we've reached a clear impasse. You'll never make it out of this area without the Tactician's cooperation, and you'll never find the Tactician without his assistance."

Merlin had manual fire control on the gamma-cannon. He had settled one hand around the trigger, ready to turn that human starfish into just another crowd of hot atoms.

"I said I was past the point of negotiation."

"Struxer says dozens have already died in the attack. But there are thousands more of his people still alive in the deeper layers. He says you won't be able to destroy the Tactician without killing them as well."

"They picked this fight, not me."

"Merlin, listen to me. Struxer seems reasonable. There's a reason he's put himself out there in that suit."

"I blew up his asteroid. That might have something to do with it."

"He wants to negotiate from a position of weakness, not strength. That's what he says. Every moment where you *don't* destroy him is another moment in which you might start listening."

"I think we already stated our positions, didn't we?"

"He said you wouldn't be able to take the Tactician. And you can't, that's clear. You can destroy it, but you can't take it. And now he's asking to talk."

"About what?"

Teal looked at him with pleading eyes. "Just talk to him, Merlin. That woman you showed me—your mother, waiting by that window. The sons she lost—you and your brother. I saw the kindness in her. Don't tell me you'd have made her proud by killing that man."

"My mother died on Plenitude. She wasn't in that room. I showed you nothing, just ghosts, just memories stitched together by my brother."

"Merlin . . ."

He squeezed the fire control trigger. Instead of discharging, though, the gamma-cannon reported a malfunction. Merlin tried again, then pulled his shaking, sweat-sodden hand from the control. The weapons board was showing multiple failures and system errors, as if the ship had only just been holding itself together until that moment.

"You cold-hearted . . ." Teal started.

"Your sympathies run that deep," Merlin said. "You should have spoken up before we used the torps."

Baskin levelled a hand on Merlin's wrist, drawing him further from the gamma-cannon trigger. "Perhaps it was for the best, after all. Only Struxer really knows the fate of the Tactician now. Bring him in, Merlin. What more have we got to lose?"

Struxer removed his helmet, the visor pocked and crazed from his passage through the debris cloud. Merlin recognised the same drawn, weary face that had spoken to them from within Mundar. He made an acknowledgement of Prince Baskin, speaking in the Havergal tongue—Merlin swearing that he picked up the sarcasm and scorn despite the gulf of language.

"He says it was nice of them to send royalty to do their dirty work," Teal said.

"Tell him he's very lucky not to be a cloud of atoms," Merlin said.

Teal passed on this remark, listened to the answer, then gave a half smile of her own. "Struxer says you're very lucky that the Tactician gave you safe passage."

"That's his idea of safe passage?" Merlin asked.

But he moved to a compartment in the cabin wall and pulled out a tray of coiled black devices, each as small and neat as a stone talisman. He removed one of the translators and pressed it into his ear, then offered one of the other devices to Struxer.

"Tell him it won't bite," he said. "My ship's very good with languages, but it needs a solid baseline of data to work with. Those transmissions helped, but the more we talk, the better we'll get."

Struxer fingered the translator in the battered glove of his spacesuit, curling his lips in distrust. "Cohort man," he said, in clear enough Main. "I speak a little your language. The Prince made us take school. In case Cohort come back."

"So you'd have a negotiating advantage over the enemy?" Merlin asked.

"It seemed prudent," Baskin said. "But most of my staff didn't see it that way. Struxer was one of the exceptions."

"Be careful who you educate," Merlin told him. "They have a tendency to start thinking for themselves. Start doing awkward things like defecting, and holding military computers to ransom."

Struxer had pushed the earpiece into position. He shifted back to his native tongue, and his translated words buzzed into Merlin's skull. "Ransom—is that what you were told, Cohort man?"

"My name's Merlin. And yes—that seems to be the game here. Or did you steal the Tactician because you'd run out of games to play on a rainy afternoon?"

"You have no idea what you've been drawn into. What were you promised, to do his dirty work?"

Teal said: "Merlin doesn't need you. He just wants the Tactician."

"A thing he neither understands nor needs, and which will never be his."

"I'd still like it," Merlin said.

"You're too late," Struxer said. "The Tactician has decided its own fate now. You've brought those patrol groups closer, with that crude display of strength. They'll close on Mundar soon enough. But the Tactician will be long gone by then."

"Gone?" Baskin asked.

"It has accepted that it must end itself. Mundar's remaining defences are now being turned inward, against the asteroid itself. It would rather destroy itself than become of further use to Havergal, or indeed Gaffurius."

"Ship," Merlin said. "Tell me this isn't true."

"I would like to," *Tyrant* said. "But it seems to be the case. I am recording an increasing rate of kinetic bombardments against Mundar's surface. Our own position is not without hazard, given my damaged condition."

Merlin moved to the nearest console, confirming for himself what the ship already knew. The opposed fleets were altering course, pincering in around Mundar. Anti-ship weapons were already sparking between the two groups of ships, drawing both into closer and closer engagement.

"The Tactician will play the patrol groups off each other, drawing them into an exchange of fire," Struxer said, with an icy sort of calm. "Then it will parry some of that fire against Mundar, completing the work you have begun."

"It's a machine," Baskin said. "It can't decide to end itself."

"Oh, come now," Struxer said, regarding Baskin with a shrewd, skeptical scrutiny. "We're beyond those sorts of secrets, aren't we? Or are you going to plead genuine ignorance?"

"Whatever you think he knows," Merlin said, "I've a feeling he doesn't."

Struxer shifted his attention onto Merlin. "Then you know?"

"I've an inkling or two. No more than that."

"About what?" Teal asked.

Merlin raised his voice. "Ship, start computing an escape route for us. If the kinetics are being directed at Mundar, then the defence screen ought to be a little easier to get through, provided we're quick."

"You're running?" Baskin asked. "With the prize so near?"

"In case you missed it," Merlin said, "the prize just got a death-wish. I'm cutting my losses before they cut me. Buckle in, all of you."

"What about your syrinx?" Teal demanded.

"I'll find me another. It's a big old galaxy—bound to be a few more knocking around. Ship, are you ready with that solution?"

"I am compromised, Merlin. I have hull damage, weapons impairment and a grievous loss of thruster authority. There can be no guarantee of reaching clear space, especially with the build-up of hostile assets."

"I'll take that chance, thanks. Struxer: you're free to step back out of the airlock any time you like. Or did you think all your problems were over just because I didn't shoot you with the gamma-cannon?"

Tyrant began to move. Merlin steadied a hand against a wall, ready to tense if the gee-loads climbed sharply.

"I think our problems are far from over," Struxer answered him levelly. "But I do not wish to die just yet. Equally, I would ask one thing."

"You're not exactly in a position to be asking for anything."

"You had a communications channel open to me. Give me access to that same channel and allow me to make my peace with the Tactician, before it's too late. A farewell, if you wish. I can't talk it out of this course of action, but at least I can ease its conscience."

"It has no conscience," Baskin said, grimacing as the acceleration mounted and *Tyrant* began to swerve its away around obstacles and in-coming fire.

"Oh, it most definitely does," Struxer said.

Merlin closed his eyes. He was standing at the door to his mother's parlour, watching her watching the window. She had become aware of his silent presence and bent around in her stern black chair, her arms straining with the effort. The golden sun shifted across the changing angles of her face. Her eyes met his for an instant, liquid grey with sadness, the eyes of a woman who had known much and seen the end of everything. She made to speak, but no words came.

Her expression was sufficient, though. Disappointed, expectant, encouraging, a loving mother well used to her sons' failings, and always hopeful that the better aspects of their nature might rise to the surface. Merlin and Gallinule, last sons of Plenitude.

"Damn it all," Merlin said under his breath. "Damn it all."

"What?" Teal asked.

"Turn us around, ship," he said. "Turn us around and take us back to Mundar. As deep as we can go."

They fought their way into the thick broil of the dust cloud, relying on sensors alone, a thousand fists hammering their displeasure against the hull, until at last *Tyrant* found the docking bay. The configuration was similar to the *Renouncer*, easily within the scope of adjustments that *Tyrant* could make, and they were soon clamped on. Baskin was making ready to secure his vacuum suit when Merlin tossed him a dun-coloured outfit.

"Cohort immersion suit. Put it on. You as well, Struxer. And be quick about it."

"What are these suits?" Baskin asked, fingering the ever-so-ragged, grubby-looking garment.

"You'll find out soon enough." Merlin nodded at Teal. "You too, soldier. As soon as *Tyrant* has an electronic lock on the Tactician it can start figuring out the immersion protocols. Won't take too long."

"Immersion protocols for what?" Baskin asked, with sharpening impatience.

"We're going inside," Merlin said. "All of us. There's been enough death today, and most of it's on my hands. I'm not settling for any more."

It waited beyond the lock, the only large thing in a dimly lit chamber walled in rock. The air was cold and did not appear to be recirculating. From the low illumination of the chamber, Merlin judged that Mundar was down to its last reserves of emergency power. He shivered in the immersion suit. It was like wearing paper.

"Did I really kill hundreds, Struxer?"

"Remorse, Merlin?"

Something was tight in his throat. "I never set out of kill. But I know that there's a danger out there beyond almost any human cost. They took my world, my people. Left Teal without a ship or a crew. They'll do the same to every human world in the galaxy, given time. I felt that if I could bring peace to this one system, I'd be doing something. One small act against a vaster darkness."

"And that excuses any act?"

"I was only trying to do the right thing."

Struxer gave a sad sniff of a laugh, as if he had lost count of the number of times he had heard such a justification. "The only right action is not to kill, Merlin. Not on some distant day when it suits you, but here and now, from the next moment on. The Tactician understands that." Struxer reached up suddenly as if to swat an insect that had settled on the back of his neck. "What's happening?"

"The immersion suit's connecting into your nervous system," Merlin said. "It's fast and painless and there won't be any lasting damage. Do you feel it too, Prince?"

"It might not be painful," Baskin said. "But I wouldn't exactly call it pleasant."

"Trust us," Merlin said. "We're good at this sort of thing."

At last he felt ready to give the Iron Tactician his full attention.

Its spherical form rested on a pedestal in the middle of the chamber, the low light turning its metallic plating to a kind of coppery brown. It was about as large as an escape capsule, with a strange brooding presence about it. There were no eyes or cameras anywhere on it, at least none that Merlin recognised. But he had the skin-crawling sensation of being watched, noticed, contemplated, by an intellect not at all like his own.

He raised his hands.

"I'm Merlin. I know what you are, I think. You should know what I am, as well. I tried to take you, and I tried to hurt your world. I'm sorry for the people I killed. But I stand before you now unarmed. I have no weapons, no armour, and I doubt very much that there's anything I could do to hurt you."

"You're wasting your words," Baskin said behind him, rubbing at the back of his neck.

"No," Struxer said. "He isn't. The Tactician hears him. It's fully aware of what happens around it."

Merlin touched the metal integument of the Iron Tactician, feeling the warmth and throb of hidden mechanisms. It hummed and churned in his presence, and gave off soft liquid sounds, like some huge boiler or laundry machine. He stroked his hand across the battered curve of one of the thick armoured plates, over the groove between one plate and the next. The plates had been unbolted or hinged back in places, revealing gold-plated connections, power and chemical sockets, or even rugged banks of dials and controls. Needles twitched and lights flashed, hinting at mysterious processes going on deep within the armour. Here and there a green glow shone through little windows of dark glass.

Tyrant whispered into Merlin's ear, via the translator earpiece. He nodded, mouthed back his answer, then returned his attention to the sphere.

"You sense my ship," Merlin said. "It tells me that it understands your support apparatus—that it can map me into your electronic sensorium using this immersion suit. I'd like to step inside, if that's all right?"

No answer was forthcoming—none that Merlin or his ship recognised. But he had made his decision by then, and he felt fully and irrevocably committed to it.. "Put us through, ship—all of us. We'll take our chances."

"And if things take a turn for the worse?" *Tyrant* asked.

"Save yourself, however you're able. Scuttle away and find someone else that can make good use of you."

"It just wouldn't be the same," *Tyrant* said.

The immersion suits snatched them from the chamber. The dislocation lasted an instant and then Merlin found himself standing next to his companions, in a high-ceilinged room that might well have been an annex of the Palace of Eternal Dusk. But the architectural notes were subtly unfamiliar, the play of light through the windows not that of his home, and the distant line of hills remained resolutely fixed. Marbled floor lay under their feet. White stone walls framed the elegant archwork of the windows.

"I know this place," Baskin said, looking around. "I spent a large part of my youth in these rooms. This was the imperial palace in Lurga, as it was before the abandonment." Even in the sensorium he wore a facsimile of the immersion suit, and he stroked the thin fabric of its sleeve with unconcealed wonder. "This is a remarkable technology, Merlin. I feel as if I've stepped back into my childhood. But why these rooms—why recreate the palace?"

Only one doorway led out of the room in which they stood. It faced a short corridor, with high windows on one side and doors on the other. Merlin beckoned them forward. "You should tell him, Struxer. Then I can see how close I've come to figuring it out for myself."

"Figured what out?" Baskin asked.

"What really happened when they attacked this place," Merlin said.

They walked into the corridor. Struxer seemed at first loss for how to start. His jaw moved, but no sounds came. Then he glanced down, swallowed, and found the words he needed.

"The attack's a matter of record," he said. "The young Prince Baskin was the target, and he was gravely injured. Spent days and days half-buried, in darkness and cold, until the teams found him. Then the prince was nurtured back to strength, and finally allowed back into the world. But that's not really what happened."

They were walking along the line of windows. The view beyond was vastly more idyllic than any part of the real Havergal. White towers lay amongst woods and lakes, with purple-tinged hills rising in the distance, the sky beyond them an infinite storybook blue.

"I assure you it did," Baskin said. "I'd remember otherwise, wouldn't I?"

"Not if they didn't want you to," Merlin said. He walked on for a few paces. "There was an assassination strike. But it didn't play out the way you think it did. The real prince was terribly injured—much worse than your memories have it."

Now an anger was pushing through Baskin's voice. "What do you mean, the 'real prince'?"

"You were substituted," Struxer said, "the assassination attempt played down, no mention made of the extent of the real Prince's injuries."

"My bloodline," Teal said. "This is the reason it's broken, isn't it?"

Merlin nodded, but let Struxer continue. "They rebuilt this palace as best they could. Even then it was never as idealised as this. Most of the east wing was gone. The view through these windows was . . . less pretty. It was only ever a stopgap, before Lurga had to be abandoned completely."

They had reached the only open door in the corridor. With the sunlit view behind their backs their shadows pushed across the door's threshold, into the small circular room beyond.

In the middle of the room a small boy knelt surrounded by wooden battlements and toy armies. They ranged away from him in complex, concentric formations—organised into interlocking ranks and files as tricky as any puzzle. The boy was reaching out to move one of the pieces, his hand dithering in the air.

"No," Baskin whispered. "This isn't how it is. There isn't a child inside this thing."

Struxer answered softly. "After the attack, the real Prince was kept alive by the best doctors on Havergal. It was all done in great secrecy. It had to be. What had become of him, the extent of his injuries, his dependence on machines to keep him alive . . . all of that would have been far too upsetting for the populace. The war was going badly: public morale was low enough as it was. The only solution, the only way to maintain the illusion, was to bring in another boy. You looked similar enough, so you were brought in to live out his life. One boy swapped for another."

"That's not what happened."

"Boys change from year to year, so the ruse was never obvious," Struxer said. "But *you* had to believe. So you were raised exactly as the Prince had been raised, in this palace, surrounded by the same things, and told stories of his life just as if it had been your own. Those games of war, the soldiers and campaigns? They were never part of your previous life, but slowly you started to believe an imagined past over the real one—a fiction that you accepted as the truth."

"You said you grew bored of war," Teal said. "That you were a sickly child who turned away from tabletop battles and became fascinated by languages instead. That was the real you breaking through, wasn't it? They could surround you with the instruments of war, try to make you dream of it, but they couldn't turn you into the person you were not—even if most of the time you believed the lie."

"But not always," Merlin said, watching as the boy made up his mind and moved one of the pieces. "Part of you knew, or remembered, I think. You've been fighting against the lie your whole life. But now you don't need to. Now you're free of it."

Struxer said: "We didn't suspect at first. Even those of us who worked closely with the Tactician were encouraged to think of it as a machine, an artificial intelligence. The medical staff who were involved in the initial work were either dead or sworn to silence, and the Tactician rarely needed any outside intervention. But there were always rumours. Technicians who had seen too much, glimpsed a little too far into the heart of it. Others—like myself—who started to doubt the accepted version of events, this easy story of a dramatic breakthrough in artificial intelligence. I began to . . . question. Why had the enemy never made a similar advancement? Why had we never repeated our success? But the thing that finally settled it for me was the Tactician itself. We who were the closest to it . . . we sensed the changes."

"Changes?" Baskin asked.

"A growing disenchantment with war. A refusal to offer the simple forecasts our military leaders craved. The Tactian's advice was becoming . . . quixotic. Unreliable. We adjusted for it, placed less weight on its predictions and simulations. But slowly those of us who were close to it realised that the Tactician was trying to engineer peace, not war."

"Peace is what we've always striven for," Baskin said.

"But by one means, total victory," Struxer said. "But the Tactician no longer considered such an outcome desirable. The boy who dreamed of war had grown up, Prince. The boy had started to develop the one thing the surgeons never allowed for."

"A conscience," Merlin said. "A sense of regret."

The boy froze between one move and the next. He turned to face the door, his eyes searching. He was small-boned, wearing a soldier's costume tailored for a child.

"We're here," Struxer said, raising a hand by way of reassurance. "Your friends. Merlin spoke to you before, do you remember?"

The boy looked distracted. He moved a piece from one position to another, angrily.

"You should go," he said. "I don't want anyone here today. I'm going to make these armies fight each other so badly they'll never want to fight again."

Merlin was the first to step into the room. He approached the boy carefully, picking his way through the gaps in the regiments. They were toy soldiers, but he could well imagine that each piece had some direct and logical correspondence in the fleets engaging near Mundar, as well as Mundar's own defenses.

"Prince," he said, stooping down with his hands on his knees. "You don't have to do this. Not any more. I know you want something other than war. It's just that they keep trying to force you into playing the same games, don't they?"

"When he didn't give the military planners the forecasts they wanted," Struxer said, "they tried to coerce him by other means. Electronic persuasion. Direct stimulation of his nervous system."

"You mean, torture," Merlin said.

"No," Baskin said. "That's not how it was. The Tactician was a machine . . . just a machine."

"It was never that," Merlin replied.

"I knew what needed to be done," Struxer said. "It was a long game, of course. But then the Tactician's strength has always been in long games. I defected first, joined the brigands here in Mundar, and only then did we start putting in place our plans to take the Tactician."

"Then it was never about holding him to ransom," Merlin said.

"No," Struxer said. "All that would have done is prolong the war. We'd been fighting long enough, Merlin. It was time to embrace the unthinkable: a real and lasting ceasefire. It was going to be a long and difficult process, and it could only be orchestrated from a position of neutrality, out here between the warring factions. It would depend on sympathetic allies on both sides: good men and women prepared to risk their own lives in making tiny, cumulative changes, under the Tactician's secret stewardship. We were ready—eager, even. In small ways we had begun the great work. Admit it, Prince Baskin: the tide of military successes had begun to turn away from you, in recent months. That was our doing. We were winning. And then Merlin arrived." Struxer set his features in a mask of impassivity. "Nothing in the Tactician's forecasting predicted *you*, Merlin, or the terrible damage you'd do to our cause."

"I stopped, didn't I?"

"Only when Mundar had humbled you."

The room shook, dust dislodging from the stone walls, one or two of the toy soldiers toppling in their ranks. Merlin knew what that was. *Tyrant* was communicating the actual attack suffered by Mundar through to the sensorium. The asteroid's own kinetic weapons were beginning to break through its crust.

"It won't be long now," he said.

Teal picked her way to Merlin's side and knelt between the battlements and armies, touching a hand to the boy. "We can help you," she said. Followed by a glance to Merlin. "Can't we?"

"Yes," he said, doubtfully at first, then with growing conviction. "Yes. Prince Baskin. The real Prince. The boy who dreamed of war, and then stopped dreaming. I believe it, too. There isn't a mind in the universe that isn't capable of change. You want peace in this system? Something real and lasting, a peace built on forgiveness and reconciliation, rather than centuries of simmering enmity? So do I. And I think you can make it happen, but for that you have to live. I have a ship. You saw me coming in—saw my weapons and what they could do. You blooded me good, as well. But I can help you now—help you do what's right. Turn the kinetics away from Mundar, Prince. You don't have to die."

"I said you should go away," the boy said.

Teal lifted a hand to his cheek. "They hurt you," she said. "Very badly. But my blood's in you and I won't rest until you've found peace. But not this way. Merlin's right, Prince. There's still time to do good."

"They don't want good," the boy answered. "I gave them good, but they didn't like it."

"You don't have to concern yourself with them now," Merlin said, as another disturbance shook the room. "Turn the weapons from Mundar. Do it, Prince."

The boy's hand loitered over the wooden battlements. Merlin intuited that these must be the logical representation of Mundar's defense screens. The boy fingered one of the serrated formations, seemingly on the verge of moving it.

"It won't do any good," he said.

"It will," Merlin said.

"You've brought them too near," the boy said, sweeping his other hand across the massed regiments, in all their colours and divisions. "They didn't know where I was before, but now you've shown them."

"I made a mistake," Merlin admitted. "A bad one, because I wanted something too badly. But I'm here to make amends."

Now it was Baskin's turn to step closer to the boy. "We have half a life in common," he said. "They stole a life from you, and tried to make me think it was my own. It worked, too. I'm an old man now, and I suppose you're as old as me, deep down. But we have something in common. We've both outgrown war, whether those around us are willing to accept it or not." He lowered down, upsetting some of the soldiers as he did—the boy glaring for an instant, then seeming to put the matter behind him. "I want to help you. Be your friend, if such a thing's possible. What Teal said is true: you *do* have her blood. Not mine, now, but it doesn't mean I don't want to help." He placed his own hand around the boy's wrist, the hand that hovered over the wooden battlements. "I remember these games," he said. "These toys. I played them well. We could play together, couldn't we?" Slowly, with great trepidation, Baskin risked turning one of the battlements around, until its fortifications were facing outward again.

The boy said: "I wouldn't do it that way."

"Show me how you would do it," Baskin said.

The boy took the battlement and shifted its position. Then he took another and placed them in close formation. He looked up at Baskin, seeking both approval and praise. "See. That's better, isn't it?"

"Much better," Baskin said.

"You can move that one," the boy said, indicating one of the other battle-ments. "Put it over there, the other way round."

"Like this?" Baskin asked, with a nervous, obliging smile.

"A little closer. That's good enough."

Merlin realised that he had been holding his breath while this little exchange was going on. It was too soon to leap to conclusions, but it had been a while since the room last shook. Hardly daring to break the fragile spell, he slipped into a brief subvocal exchange with *Tyrant*. His ship confirmed that the rain of kinetics had ceased.

"Now for the tricky part," Merlin murmured, as much for himself as his audience. "Prince, listen to me carefully. Rebuild those defences. Do it as well as you can, because you need to protect yourself. There's hard work to do—very hard work—and you need to be at your strongest."

"I don't like work," the boy said.

"None of us do. But if you're bored with this game, I've got a much more interesting one to play. You're going to engineer a peace, and hold it. It's going to be the hardest thing you've ever done but I've no doubt that you'll rise to the challenge."

Struxer whispered: "Those fleets aren't exactly ready to set down their arms, Merlin."

"I'll make them," he said. "Just go give the Prince a running start. Then it's over to him." But he corrected himself. "Over to all of you, in fact. He'll need all the help he can get, Struxer." Merlin leaned in closer to the boy, until his mouth was near his ear. "We're going to lie," he said, confidingly. "We're going to lie and they're going to believe us, those fleets. Not forever, but long enough for you to start making peace seem like the easier path. It's a lot to ask, but I know you're up to it."

The boy's face met Merlin's. "Lie?"

"You'll understand. *Tyrant*: open a channel out to those ships. The whole binary system, as powerful a signal as you can put out. Hijack every open transmitter you can find. And translate these words, as well as you can." Then he frowned to himself and turned to Teal. "No. You should be the one. Better that it comes from a native speaker, than my garbled efforts."

"What would you like me to say?"

Merlin smiled. He told her. It did not take long.

"This is Teal of the Cohort," she said, her words gathered within the senso-rium, fed through *Tyrant*, pushed out beyond the ruins of Mundar, through the defense screens, out to the waiting fleets, onward to the warring worlds.

"I came here by Waynet, a little while ago. But I was here once before, more than a thousand years ago, and I knew King Curtal before you set him on the throne. I stand now in Mundar, ready to tell you that the time has come to end this war. Not for an hour, or a day, or a few miserable years, but forever. Because what you need now is peace and unity, and you don't have very long to build it. A Husker attack swarm is approaching your binary system. We slipped ahead of them through the Waynet, but they will be here. You have less than a century . . . perhaps only a handful of decades. Then they'll arrive." Teal shot a look at Merlin, and he gave her a tiny nod, letting her know that she was doing very well, better than he could ever have managed. "Ordinarily it would be the end of everything for you. They took my ship, and I'm with a man who lost a whole world to them. But there's a chance for you. In Mundar is a great mind. Call him the Iron Tactician for now, although the day will come when you learn his true name. The Iron Tactician will help you on the road to peace. And when that peace is holding, the Iron Tactician will help you prepare. The Tactician knows of your weapons, of your fusion ships and kinetic batteries. But in a little while he will also know the weapons of the Cohort, and how best to use them. Weapons to shatter worlds—or defend them." Teal drew breath, and Merlin touched his hand to her shoulder, in what he hoped was a gesture of comradeship and solidarity. "Hurt the Tactician, and you'll be powerless when the swarm arrives. Protect it—honour it—and you'll have an honest chance. But the Tactician would sooner die than take sides."

"Good," Merlin breathed.

"He's my blood," Teal continued. "My kin. And I'm staying here to give him all the protection and guidance he needs. You'll treat me well, because I'm the only living witness you'll ever know who can say she saw the Huskers up close. And I'll do what I can to help you."

Merlin swallowed. He had not been expecting this, not at all. But the force of Teal's conviction left him in no doubt that she had set her mind on this course. He stared at her with a searing admiration, dizzy at her courage and single-mindedness.

"You'll withdraw from the space around Mundar," Teal said. "And you'll cease all hostilities. A ship will be given free passage to Havergal, and then on to the Waynet. You won't touch it. And you won't touch Mundar, or attempt to claim the Tactician. There'll be no reminders, no second warnings—we're beyond such things. This is Teal of the Cohort, signing off for now. You'll be hearing more from me soon."

Merlin shook his head in astonishment. "You don't have to do this, Teal. That was . . . courageous. But you're not responsible for the mess they've made of this place."

"I'm not," she said. "But then again we had our chance when we traded with them, and instead of helping them to peace we took one side and conducted our business. I don't feel guilty for what happened all those years ago. But I'm ready to make a change."

"She does have an excellent command of our language," Baskin said.

"And she's persuasive," Struxer said. "Very persuasive."

Merlin made sure they were no longer transmitting. "You all know it's a lie. There's no attack swarm heading this way—not how Teal said it was. But there *could* be, and for a few decades there'd be no way of saying otherwise, not with the sensors you have now. Here's what matters, though. You've been lucky so far, but somewhere out there you can be sure there is a Husker swarm that'll eventually find its way to these worlds. A hundred years, a thousand . . . Who knows? But it will happen, just as it did to Plenitude. The only difference is, you'll be readier than we ever were." Then he turned to direct his attention to the boy. "You'll have the hardest time of all, Prince. But you have friends now. And you have my confidence. I know you can force this peace."

For all the toys and battlements, some spark of real comprehension glimmered in the boy's eyes. "But when they find out she lied . . ."

"It'll take a while," Merlin said. "And by then you'll just have to make sure they've got used to the idea of peace. It's not such a bad thing. But then again, you don't need me to tell you that."

"No," the boy reflected.

Merlin nodded, hoping the boy—what remained of the boy—felt something of the confidence and reassurance he was sending out. "I have to go soon. There's something I need on Havergal, and I'd rather not wait too long to get my hands on it."

"Whatever authority I still have," Baskin said, "I'll do all that I can to assist."

"Thank you." Then Merlin turned back to the Prince. "I hope you won't be alone again. I'll leave the immersion suits behind, and a few spares. But even when Teal and Struxer and Baskin can't be with you, you don't have to be without companionship." He dipped his head at the ranged formations. "There are two other boys who used to enjoy games like this, but like you their hearts were always elsewhere. They could come here, if you like. I think you'd get on well."

Doubt flickered across Teal's brow. He nodded at her, begging her to trust him.

"They could come," the boy said, doubtfully. "I suppose."

"Merlin," Teal said.

"Yes?"

"I'm not sure if we'll see each other again, after you've left this place. And I know it isn't going to be safe out there, whatever sort of ceasefire we end up with. But I want you to know two things."

"Go on."

"I'm glad you saved me, Merlin. If I never showed my gratitude until now . . ."

"It wasn't needed. The war took too much from both of us, Teal. There was nothing else that had to be said. You'll do all right here, I know it. Maybe I'll drop back."

"You know you won't," Teal said. "Just as you'll never go back to Plenitude."

"And the other thing?"

"Take your ship, take your syrinx, and find your gun. For me. For your mother, your brother, for all the dead of Plenitude, for all the dead of the *Shrike*, for all who died here. You owe it to all of us, Merlin."

He made to speak, but between one moment and the next he decided that words were superfluous. They met eyes for one last time, and an acknowledgement passed between them, a recognition of obligations met, duties faced, of good and bold hopes for better times.

Then he dropped out of the sensorium.

He was through into *Tyrant* in a matter of seconds. "Get us out of here," he said. "Suspend all load ceilings. If I break a few bones, they'll just have to heal."

"Complying," *Tyrant* said.

Merlin's little dark ship was bruised and lame, but the acceleration still came hard and sudden, and he came very close to regretting that off-hand remark about his bones.

"When you have a chance," he said, "transfer Gallinule's sensorium through to the Iron Tactician. All of it—the whole of the Palace of Eternal Dusk."

"While keeping a copy here, you mean?"

"No," Merlin said. "Delete it. Everything. If I ever need to walk those corridors again, or watch my mother looking sad, I'll just have to go back to Mundar."

"That seems . . . extreme."

"Tell that to Teal. She's made more of a sacrifice than I'll ever know."

Tyrant punched its way through the thinning debris cloud. Merlin studied the navigation consoles, watching with a fascinated distraction as the ship computed various course options, testing each against the last, until it found what promised to be a safe passage to . . .

"No," Merlin said. "Not the Waynet. Not until we've gone back to Havergal and claimed that syrinx."

"Did you not study the data, Merlin? I looked at it closely, after your inspection of the syrinx."

"It's real."

"Real, but damaged beyond safe use. More risky to use than the syrinx you already have. I'd have mentioned it sooner, but . . ."

"What do you mean, damaged?"

"Probably before Pardalote ever sold it on, Merlin. I doubt there was any intention to deceive. It's just that a broken syrinx is very hard to distinguish from a fully functioning one. Unless you've had quite a lot of experience in the matter."

"And you kept that from me?"

"I was curious, Merlin. As were you. Another artificial intelligence. I thought we might at least see what this Iron Tactician was all about."

Merlin nodded sagely. Occasionally he reached a point where he felt that little was capable of surprising him. But always the universe had something in store to jolt him out of that complacency. "While we're on the subject, then. That little stunt you pulled back there, when I tried to shoot Struxer with the gamma-cannon . . ."

"You'd have come to regret that action, Merlin. I merely spared you endless years of racking remorse and guilt."

"By contravening a direct order."

"Which was foolish and unnecessary and born entirely out of spite. Besides, I was the damaged party, not you."

Merlin brooded. "I didn't know you had it in you."

"Then we've both learned something new of each other, haven't we?"

He smiled—it was the only possible reaction. "But let's not make too much of a habit of it, shall we?"

"On that," *Tyrant* said, "I think we find ourselves in excellent agreement."

He felt the steering jets cut in, rougher than usual, and he thought about the damage that needed repairing, and the difficult days ahead. Never mind, though. Before he worried about those complications, he had a few small prayers to ask of his old, battered syrinx.

He hoped they would be answered.

Tobias S. Buckell is a *New York Times*–bestselling author born in the Caribbean. He grew up in Grenada and spent time in the British and US Virgin Islands, which influence much of his work. His novels and over fifty stories have been translated into eighteen different languages. His work has been nominated for awards like the Hugo, Nebula, Prometheus, and the John W. Campbell Award for Best New Science Fiction Author. He currently lives in Bluffton, Ohio, with his wife, twin daughters, and a pair of dogs.

Barbadian author, editor, and research consultant Karen Lord is known for her debut novel, *Redemption in Indigo*, which won the 2008 Frank Collymore Literary Award, the 2010 Carl Brandon Parallax Award, the 2011 William L. Crawford Award, the 2011 Mythopoeic Fantasy Award for Adult Literature, and the 2012 Kitschies Golden Tentacle (Best Debut), and was longlisted for the 2011 Bocas Prize for Caribbean Literature and nominated for the 2011 World Fantasy Award for Best Novel. Her second novel, *The Best of All Possible Worlds*, won the 2009 Frank Collymore Literary Award, the 2013 RT Book Reviews Reviewers' Choice Awards for Best Science Fiction Novel, and was a finalist for the 2014 Locus Awards. Its sequel, *The Galaxy Game*, was published in January 2015. She is the editor of the 2016 anthology *New Worlds, Old Ways: Speculative Tales from the Caribbean*.

THE MIGHTY SLINGER

Tobias S. Buckell and Karen Lord

Earth began to rise over the lunar hills as The Mighty Slinger and The Rovers readied the Tycho stage for their performance. Tapping his microphone, Euclid noticed that Kumi barely glanced at the sight as he set up his djembe and pan assembly, but Jeni froze and stared up at the blue disk, her bass still limp between her hands.

"It's not going anywhere," Kumi muttered. His long, graying dreadlocks swayed gently in the heavy gravity of the moon and tapped the side of a pan with a muted 'ting.' "It'll be there after the concert . . . and after our trip, *and* after we revive from our next long-sleep."

"Let her look," Vega admonished. "You should always stop for beauty. It vanishes too soon."

"She taking too long to set up," Kumi said. "You-all call her Zippy but she ain't zippy at all."

Euclid chuckled as Jeni shot a stink look at her elder and mentor. She whipped the bass out stiff like she meant business. Her fingers gripped and danced on the narrow surface in a quick, defiant riff.

Raising his mic-wand at the back, Vega captured the sound as it bounced back from the lunar dome performance area. He fed the echo through the house speakers, ending it with a punctuating note of Kumi's locks hitting the pan with a ting and Euclid's laughter rumbling quietly in the background. Dhaka, the last of the Rovers, came in live with a cheerful fanfare on her patented Delirium, an instrument that looked like a harmonium had had a painful collision with a large quantity of alloy piping.

An asteroid-thin man in a black suit slipped past the velvet ropes marking off the VIP section and nodded at Euclid. "Yes sir. Your pay's been deposited, the spa is booked and your places in the long-sleep pool are reserved."

"Did you add the depreciation-protection insurance this time?" Euclid answered, his voice cold with bitter memory. "If your grandfather had sense I could be retired by now."

Kumi looked sharply over. The man in the suit shifted about. "Of course I'll add the insurance," he mumbled.

"Thank you, Mr. Jones," Euclid said, in a tone that was not at all thankful.

"There's, ah, someone else who would like to talk to you," the event coordinator said.

"Not now Jones." Euclid turned away to face his band. "Only forty minutes to curtain time and we need to focus."

"It's about Earth," Jones said.

Euclid turned back. "That rumour?"

Jones shook his head. "Not a rumour. Not even a joke. The Rt Hon Patience Bouscholte got notification this morning. She wants to talk to you."

The Rt Hon Patience Bouscholte awaited him in one of the skyboxes poised high over the rim of the crater. Before it: the stands that would soon be filling up, slanting along the slope that created a natural amphitheatre to the stage. Behind it: the gray hills and rocky wasteland of the Moon.

"Mr. Slinger!" she said. Her tightly wound hair and brown spidersilk headscarf bobbed in a slightly delayed reaction to the lunar gravity. "A pleasure to finally meet you. I'm a huge admirer of your sound."

He sat down, propped his snakeskin magnet-boots up against the chair-back in front of him, and gave her a cautious look. "Madame Minister. To what do I owe the pleasure?"

All of the band were members of the Rock Devils Cohort and Consociate Fusion, almost a million strong, all contract workers in the asteroid belt. They were all synced up on the same long-sleep schedule as their cohort, whether working the rock or touring as a band. And here was a Minister from the RDCCF's Assembly asking to speak with him.

The RDCCF wasn't a country. It was just one of many organisations for people who worked in space because there was nothing left for them on Earth. But to Euclid, meeting the Rt Hon Patience Bouscholte felt like meeting a Member of Parliament from the old days. Euclid was slightly intimidated, but he wasn't going to show it. He put an arm casually over the empty seat beside him.

"They said you were far quieter in person than on stage. They were right." Bouscholte held up a single finger before he could reply, and pointed to two women in all-black bulletproof suits who were busy scanning the room with small wands. They gave a thumbs up as Bouscholte cocked her head in their direction, and retreated to stand on either side of the entrance.

She turned back to Euclid. "Tell me, Mr. Slinger, how much have you heard about the Solar Development Charter and their plans for Earth?"

So it was true? He leaned toward her. "Why would they have any plans for Earth? I've heard they're stretched thin enough building the Glitter Ring."

"They are. They're stretched more than thin. They're functionally bank-rupt. So the SDC is taking up a new tranche of preferred shares for a second-ary redevelopment scheme. They want to 'redevelop' Earth, and that will *not* be to our benefit."

"Well then." Euclid folded his arms and leaned back. "And you thought you'd tell an old calypso singer that because . . . ?"

"Because I need your rhymes, Mr. Slinger."

Euclid had done that before, in the days before his last long-sleep, when fame was high and money had not yet evaporated. Dishing out juicy new gos-sip to help Assembly contract negotiations. Leaking information to warn the workers all across the asteroid belt. Hard-working miners on contract, strug-gling to survive the long nights and longer sleeps. Sing them a song about how the SDC was planning to screw them over again. He knew that gig well.

He had thought that was why he'd been brought to see her, to get a little something to add extempo to a song tonight. Get the Belt all riled up. But if this was about Earth . . . ? Earth was a garbage dump. Humanity had sucked it dry like a vampire and left its husk to spiral toward death as people moved outward to bigger and better things.

"I don't sing about Earth anymore. The cohorts don't pay attention to the old stuff. Why should they care? It's not going anywhere."

Then she told him. Explained that the SDC was going to beautify Earth. Re-terraform it. Make it into a new garden of Eden for the rich and idle of Mars and Venus.

"How?" he asked, sceptical.

"Scorched Earth. They're going to bomb the mother planet with comets. Full demolition. The last of us shipped into the Ring to form new cohorts, new generations of indentured servitude. A clean slate to redesign their brave new world. That is what I mean when I say *not to our benefit*."

He exhaled slowly. "You think a few little lyrics can change any of that?" The wealth of Venus, Mars, and Jupiter dwarfed the cohorts in their hollowed out, empty old asteroids.

"One small course adjustment at the start can change an entire orbit by the end of a journey," she said.

"So you want me to harass the big people up in power for you, now?"

Bouscholte shook her head. "We need you to be our emissary. We, the Assembly, the last representatives of the drowned lands and the dying islands, are calling upon you. Are you with us or not?"

Euclid thought back to the days of breezes and mango trees. "And if they don't listen to us?"

Bouscholte leaned in close and touched his arm. "The majority of our cohort are indentured to the Solar Development Charter until the Glitter Ring is complete. But, Mr. Slinger, answer me this: where do you think that leaves us after we finish the Ring, the largest project humanity has ever attempted?"

Euclid knew. After the asteroid belt had been transformed into its new incarnation, a sun-girdling, sun-powered device for humanity's next great leap, it would no longer be home.

There were few resources left in the Belt; the big planets had got there first and mined it all. Euclid had always known the hollow shells that had been left behind. The work on the Glitter Ring. The long-sleep so that they didn't exhaust resources as they waited for pieces of the puzzle to slowly float from place to appointed place.

Bouscholte continued. "If we can't go back to Earth, they'll send us further out. Our cohorts will end up scattered to the cold, distant areas of the system, out to the Oort Cloud. And we'll live long enough to see that."

"You think you can stop that?"

"Maybe, Mr. Slinger. There is almost nothing we can broadcast that the big planets can't listen to. When we go into long-sleep they can hack our communications, but they can't keep us from talking, and they'll never stop our songs."

"It's a good dream," Euclid said softly, for the first time in the conversation looking up at the view over the skybox. He'd avoided looking at it. To Jeni it was a beautiful blue dot, but for Euclid all it did was remind him of what he'd lost. "But they won't listen."

"You must understand, you are just one piece in a much bigger game. Our people are in place, not just in the cohorts, but everywhere, all throughout the system. They'll listen to your music and make the right moves at the right time. The SDC can't move to destroy and rebuild Earth until the Glitter Ring is finished, but when it's finished they'll find they have underestimated us—as long as we coordinate in a way that no one suspects."

"Using songs? Nah. Impossible," he declared bluntly.

She shook her head, remarkably confident. "All you have to do is be the messenger. We'll handle the tactics. You forget who you're speaking to. The Bouscholte family tradition has always been about the long game. Who was my father? What positions do my sons hold, my granddaughters? Euclid Slinger . . . Babatunde . . . listen to me. How do you think an aging calypso star gets booked to do an expensive, multi-planetary tour to the capitals of the Solar System, the seats of power? By chance?"

She called him that name as if she were his friend, his inner-circle intimate. Kumi named him that years . . . decades ago. *Too wise for your years. You were here before*, he'd said. *The Father returns, sent back for a reason.* Was this the reason?

"I accept the mission," he said.

Day. Me say Day-Oh. Earthrise come and me want go . . .

Euclid looked up, smiled. Let the chord go. He wouldn't be so blatant as to wink at the VIP section, but he knew that there was a fellow Rock Devil out there, listening out for certain songs and recording Vega's carefully assembled samples to strip for data and instructions in a safe location. Vega knew, of course. Had to, in order to put together the info packets. Dhaka knew a little but had begged not to know more, afraid she might say the wrong thing to the wrong person. Jeni was still, after her first long-sleep, nineteen in body and mind, so no, she did not know, and anyway how could he tell her when he was still dragging his feet on telling Kumi?

And there was Kumi, frowning at him after the end of the concert as they sprawled in the green room, taking a quick drink before the final packing up. "Baba, you on this nostalgia kick for real."

"You don't like it?" Euclid teased him. "All that sweet, sweet soca you grew up studying, all those kaiso legends you try to emulate?"

"That ain't your sound, man."

Euclid shrugged. "We can talk about that next time we're in the studio. Now we got a party to be at!"

After twenty-five years of long-sleep, Euclid thought Mars looked much the same, except maybe a little greener, a little wetter. Perhaps that was why the Directors of the SDC-MME had chosen to host their bash in a gleaming biodome that overlooked a charming little lake. Indoor foliage matched to outer landscape in a lush canopy and artificial lights hovered in competition with the stars and satellites beyond.

"Damn show-offs," Dhaka muttered. "Am I supposed to be impressed?"

"*I* am," Jeni said shamelessly, selecting a stimulant cocktail from an offered tray. Kumi smoothly took it from her and replaced it with another, milder option. She looked outraged.

"Keep a clear head, Zippy," Vega said quietly. "We're not among friends."

That startled her out of her anger. Kumi looked a little puzzled himself, but he accepted Vega's support without challenge.

Euclid listened with half his attention. He had just noticed an opportunity. "Kumi, all of you, come with me. Let's greet the CEO and offer our thanks for this lovely party."

Kumi came to his side. "What's going on?"

Euclid lowered his voice. "Come, listen and find out."

The CEO acknowledged them as they approached, but Euclid could sense from the body language that the busy executive would give them as much time as dictated by courtesy and not a bit more. No matter that Euclid was a credentialled ambassador for the RDCCF, authorised by the Assembly. He could already tell how this meeting would go.

"Thank you for hosting us, Mx Ashe," Euclid said, donning a pleasant, grinning mask. "It's always a pleasure to kick off a tour at the Mars Mining and Energy Megaplex."

"Thank *you*," the executive replied. "Your music is very popular with our hands."

"Pardon?" Kumi enquired, looking in confusion at the executive's fingers wrapped around an ornate cocktail glass.

"Our employees in the asteroid belt."

Kumi looked unamused. Euclid moved on quickly. "Yes. You merged with the SDC . . . pardon me, we are still trying to catch up on twenty-five years of news . . . about ten years ago?"

A little pride leaked past the politeness. "Buyout, not merger. Only the name has survived, to maintain continuity and branding."

Euclid saw Dhaka smirk and glance at Vega, who looked a little sour. He was still slightly bitter that his ex-husband had taken everything in the divorce except for the de la Vega surname, the name under which he had become famous and which Vega was forced to keep for the sake of convenience.

"But don't worry," the CEO continued. "The Glitter Ring was always conceptualised as a project that would be measured in generations. Corporations may rise and fall, but the work will go on. Everything remains on schedule and all the hands . . . all the—how do you say—*cohorts* are in no danger of losing their jobs."

"So, the cohorts can return to Earth after the Ring is completed?" Euclid asked directly.

Mx Ashe took a careful sip of bright purple liquid before replying. "I did not say that."

"But I thought the Earth development project was set up to get the SDC a secondary round of financing, to solve their financial situation," Dhaka demanded, her brow creasing. "You've bought them out, so is that still necessary?"

Mx Ashe nodded calmly. "True, but we have a more complex vision for the Glitter Ring than the SDC envisioned, and so funding must be vastly increased. Besides, taking money for a planned redevelopment of Earth and then not doing it would, technically, be fraud. The SDC-MME will follow through. I won't bore you with the details, but our expertise on geo-engineering is unparalleled."

"You've been dropping comets on vast, uninhabited surfaces," Dhaka said. "I understand the theory, but Earth isn't Venus or Mars. There's thousands of years of history and archeology. And there are still people living there. How are you going to move a billion people?"

Mx Ashe looked coldly at Dhaka. "We're still in the middle of building a Ring around the sun, Mx Miriam. I'm sure my successors on the Board will have it all figured out by the next time we wake you up. We understand the concerns raised, but after all, people have invested trillions in this project. Our lawyers are in the process of responding to all requests and lawsuits, and we will stand by the final ruling of the courts."

Euclid spoke quickly, blunt in his desperation. "Can't you reconsider, find another project to invest in? Earth's a mess, we all know it, but we always thought we'd have something to come back to."

"I'm sure a man of your means could afford a plot on New Earth—" Mx Ashe began.

"I've seen the pricing," Vega cut in dryly. "Musicians don't make as much as you think."

"What about the cohorts?" Jeni said sadly. "No-one in the cohorts will be able to afford to go back."

Mx Ashe stepped back from the verbal bombardment. "This is all speculation. The cohorts are still under contract to work on the Glitter Ring. Once they have finished, negotiations about their relocation can begin. Now, if you will excuse me, have a good night and enjoy the party!"

Euclid watched despondently as the CEO walked away briskly. The Rovers stood silently around him, their faces sombre. Kumi was the first to speak. "*Now* I understand the nostalgia kick."

> *The SDC, now with the MME*
> *You and I both know*
> *They don't stand for you and me*

There was still a tour to play. The band moved from Elysium City to Electris Station, then Achillis Fons, where they played in front of the Viking Museum.

The long-sleep on the way to Mars had been twenty-five years. Twenty-five years off, one year on. That was the shift the Rock Devils Cohort and Consociation Fusion had agreed to, the key clause in the contract Euclid had signed way-back-when in an office built into the old New York City sea wall.

That gave them a whole year on Mars. Mx Ashe may have shut them down, but Euclid wasn't done yet. Not by a long shot.

Kumi started fretting barely a month in.

"Jeni stepping out with one of the VIPs," he told Euclid.

"She's nineteen. What you expecting? A celibate band member? I don't see you ignoring anyone coming around when we breaking down."

Kumi shook his head. "No Baba, that's one thing. This is the same one she's seeing. Over and over. Since we arrived here. She's sticky sweet on him."

"Kumi, we got bigger things to worry about."

"Earth, I know. Man, look, I see why you're upset." Kumi grabbed his hand. "I miss it too. But we getting old, Baba. I just pass sixty. How much longer I could do this? Maybe we focus on the tour and invest the money so that we can afford to go back some day."

"I can't give it up that easy," Euclid said to his oldest friend. "We going to have troubles?"

Back when Euclid was working the rocks, Kumi had taken him under his wing. Taught him how to sing the old songs while they moved their one-person pods into position to drill them out. Then they'd started singing at the start of shifts and soon that took off into a full career. They'd traveled all through the Belt, from big old Ceres to the tiniest cramped mining camps.

Kumi sucked his teeth. "That first time you went extempo back on Pallas, you went after that foreman who'd been skimping on airlock maintenance? You remember?"

Euclid laughed. "I was angry. The airlock blew out and I wet myself waiting for someone to come pick me up."

"When you started singing different lyrics, making them up on the spot, I didn't follow you at first. But you got the SDC to fire him when the video went viral. That's why I called you Baba. So, no, you sing and I'll find my way around your words. Always. But let me ask you—think about what Ashe said. You really believe this fight's worth it?"

Euclid bit his lip.

"We have concerts to give in the Belt and Venus yet," he told Kumi. "We're not done yet."

Five months in, the Martians began to turn. The concerts had been billed as cross-cultural events, paid for by the Pan-Human Solar Division of Cultural Affairs and the Martian University's division of Inter-Human Musicology Studies school.

Euclid, on stage, hadn't noticed at first. He'd been trying to find another way to match up MME with "screw me" and some lyrics in between. Then a comparison to Mars and its power, and the people left behind on Earth.

But he noticed when *this* crowd turned.

Euclid had grown used to the people of the big planets just sitting and listening to his music. No one was moving about. No hands in the air. Even if you begged them, they weren't throwing their hands out. No working, no grinding, no nothing. They sat in seats and *appreciated.*

He didn't remember when they turned. He would see it on video later. Maybe it was when he called out the 'rape' of Earth with the 'red tape' of the SDC-MME and made a visual of 'red' Mars that tied to the 'red' tape, but suddenly those chair-sitting inter-cultural appreciators stood up.

And it wasn't to jump.

The crowd started shouting back. The sound cut out. Security and the venue operators swept in and moved them off the stage.

Back in the green room, Jeni rounded on Euclid. "What the hell was that?" she shouted.

"Extempo," Euclid said simply.

Kumi tried to step between them. "Zippy—"

"No!" She pushed him aside. Dhaka, in the corner of the room, started disassembling the Delirium, carefully putting the pieces away in a g-force protected aerogel case, carefully staying out of the brewing fight. Vega folded his arms and stood to a side, watching. "I damn well know what extempo is. I'm young, not ignorant."

Everyone was tired. The heavy gravity, the months of touring already behind them. "This always happens. A fight always come halfway through," Euclid said. "Talk to me."

"You're doing extempo like you're in a small free concert in the Belt, on a small rock. But this isn't going after some corrupt contractor," Jeni snapped. "You're calling out a whole planet now? All Martians? You crazy?"

"One person or many, you think I shouldn't?"

Euclid understood. Jeni had been working pods like he had at the same age. Long, grueling shifts spent in a tiny bubble of plastic where you rebreathed your own stench so often you forgot what clean air tasted like. Getting into the band had been her way 'off the rock.' This was her big gamble out of tedium. His too, back in the day.

"You're not entertaining people. You're pissing them off," she said.

Euclid sucked his teeth. "Calypso been vexing people since all the way back. And never mind calypso, Zippy, entertainment isn't just escape. Artists always talking back, always insolent."

"They paid us and flew us across the solar system to sing the song they wanted. Sing the fucking song for them the way they want. Even just the Banana Boat Song you're messing with and going extempo. That shit's carved in stone, Euclid. Sing the damn lyrics."

Euclid looked at her like she'd lost her mind. "That song was *never* for them. Problem is it get sung too much and you abstract it and then everyone forget that song is a blasted lament. Well, let me educate you, Ms Baptiste. The Banana Boat Song is a mournful song about people getting their backs broken hard in labor and still using call and response to help the community sync up, dig deep, and find the power to work harder 'cause *dem ain't had no choice*."

He stopped. A hush fell in the green room.

Euclid continued. "It's not a 'smile and dance for them' song. The big planets don't own that song. It was never theirs. It was never carved in stone.

I'll make it ours for *here*, for *now*, and I'll go extempo. I'm not done. Zippy, I'm just getting started."

She nodded. "Then I'm gone."

Just like that, she spun around and grabbed her bass.

Kumi glared at Euclid. "I promised her father I'd keep an eye on her—"

"Go," Euclid said calmly, but he was suddenly scared that his oldest friend, the pillar of his little band, would walk out the green room door with the newest member and never come back.

Kumi came back an hour later. He looked suddenly old . . . those raw-sun wrinkles around his eyes, the stooped back. But it wasn't just gravity pulling him down. "She's staying on Mars."

Euclid turned to the door. "Let me go speak to her. I'm the one she angry with."

"No." Kumi put a hand on his shoulder. "That wasn't just about you. She staying with someone. She's not just leaving the band, she leaving the cohort. Got a VIP, a future, someone she thinks she'll build a life with."

She was gone. Like that.

Vega still had her riffs, though. He grumbled about the extra work, but he could weave the recorded samples in and out of the live music.

Kumi got an invitation to the wedding. It took place the week before the Rovers left Mars for the big tour of the asteroid belt.

Euclid wasn't invited.

He did a small, open concert for the Rock Devils working on Deimos. It was just him and Vega and fifty miners in one of the tear-down areas of the tiny moon. Euclid sang for them just as pointedly as ever.

> So it's up to us, you and me
> to put an end to this catastrophe.
> Them ain't got neither conscience nor heart.
> We got to pitch in and do our part
> 'cause if this Earth demolition begin
> we won't even have a part/pot to pitch/piss in.

Touring in the Belt always gave him a strange feeling of mingled nostalgia and dissonance. There were face-to-face reunions and continued correspondence with friends and relatives of their cohort, who shared the same times of waking and long-sleep, spoke the same language and remembered the same things. But there were also administrators and officials, who kept their own schedule, and workers from cohorts on a different frequency—all strangers from a forgotten distant past or an unknown near-present. Only the most social types kept up to date on everything, acting as temporal diplomats, translating jokes and explaining new tech and jargon to smooth communication between groups.

Ziamara Bouscholte was social. Very social. Euclid had seen plenty of that frivolous-idle behaviour from political families and nouveau-nobility like the family Jeni had married into, but given *that* surname and the fact that she had been assigned as their tour liaison, he recognised very quickly that she was a spy.

"Big tours in the Belt are boredom and chaos," he warned her, thinking about the argument with Jeni. "Lots of down time slinging from asteroid to asteroid punctuated by concert mayhem when we arrive."

She grinned. "Don't worry about me. I know exactly how to deal with boredom and chaos."

She didn't lie. She was all-business on board, briefing Vega on the latest cryptography and answering Dhaka's questions about the technological advances that were being implemented in Glitter Ring construction. Then the butterfly emerged for the concerts and parties as she wrangled fans and dignitaries with a smiling enthusiasm that never flagged.

The Vesta concert was their first major stop. The Mighty Slinger and his Rovers peeked out from the wings of the stage and watched the local opening act finishing up their last set.

Kumi brought up something that had been nagging Euclid for a while. "Baba, you notice how small the crowds are? *This* is our territory, not Mars. Last big tour we had to broadcast over Vesta because everything was sold out."

Vega agreed. "Look at this audience. Thin. I could excuse the other venues for size, but not this one."

"I know why," Dhaka said. "I can't reach half my friends who agreed to meet up. All I'm getting from them are long-sleep off-shift notices."

"I thought it was just me," Kumi said. "Did SDC-MME leave cohorts in long-sleep? Cutting back on labour?"

Dhaka nodded. "Zia mentioned some changes in the project schedule. You know the Charter's not going to waste money feeding us if we're not working."

Euclid felt a surge of anger. "We'll be out of sync when they wake up again. That messes up the whole cohort. You sure they're doing this to cut labour costs, or to weaken us as a collective?"

Dhaka shrugged. "I don't like it one bit, but I don't know if it's out of incompetence or malice."

"Time to go," said Vega, his eyes on the openers as they exited stage left.

The Rovers drifted on stage and started freestyling, layering sound on sound. Euclid waited until they were all settled in and jamming hard before running out and snagging his mic. He was still angry, and the adrenaline amped up his performance as he commandeered the stage to rant about friends and lovers lost for a whole year to long-sleep.

Then he heard something impossible: Kumi stumbled on the beat. Euclid looked back at the Rovers to see Vega frozen. A variation of one of Jeni's famous riffs was playing, but Vega shook his head *not me* to Dhaka's confused sideways glance.

Zia's voice came on the sound system, booming over the music. "Rock Devils cohort, we have a treat for you! On stage for the first time in twenty-five years, please welcome Rover bassist Jeni 'Zippy' Baptiste!"

Jeni swooped in from the wings with another stylish riff, bounced off one of the decorated pylons, then flew straight to Kumi and wrapped him in a tumbling hug, bass and all. Prolonged cheering from the crowd drowned out the music. Euclid didn't know whether to be furious or overjoyed at Zia for springing the surprise on them in public. Vega smoothly covered for the absent percussion and silent bass while Dhaka went wild on the Delirium. It was a horrible place for a reunion, but they'd take it. Stage lighting made it hard to tell, but Jeni did look older and . . . stronger? More sure of herself?

Euclid floated over to her at the end of the song as the applause continued to crash over them all. "Welcome back, Zippy," he said. "You're still good— better, even."

Her laugh was full and sincere. "I've been listening to our recordings for twenty-five years, playing along with you every day while you were in long-sleep. Of course I'm better."

"You missed us," he stated proudly.

"I did." She swatted a tear out of the air between them with the back of her hand. "I missed *this*. Touring for our cohort. Riling up the powers that be."

He raised his eyebrows. "*Now* you want to shake things up? What changed?"

She shook her head sadly. "Twenty-five years, Baba. I have a daughter, now. She's twenty, training as an engineer on Mars. She's going to join the cohort when she's finished and I want more for her. I want a future for her."

He hugged her tight while the crowd roared in approval. "Get back on that bass," he whispered. "We got a show to finish!"

He didn't bother to ask if the nouveau-nobility husband had approved of the rebel Rover Jeni. He suspected not.

In the green room Jeni wrapped her legs around a chair and hung a glass of beer in the air next to her.

"Used to be it would fall slowly down to the floor," Jeni said, pointing at her drink. "They stripped most of Vesta's mass for the Ring. It's barely a shell here."

Dhaka shoved a foot in a wall strap and settled in perpendicular to Jeni. She swirled the whiskey glass around in the air. Despite the glass being designed for zero gravity, her practiced flip of the wrist tossed several globules free that very slowly wobbled their way through the air toward her. "We're passing into final stage preparations for the Ring. SDC-MME is panicking a bit because the projections for energy and the initial test results don't match. And the computers are having trouble managing stable orbits."

The Glitter Ring was a Dyson Ring, a necklace of solar power stations and sails built around the sun to capture a vast percentage of its energy. The power needs of the big planets had begun to outstrip the large planetary solar and mirror arrays a hundred years ago. Overflight and shadow rights for solar gathering stations had started turning into a series of low-grade orbital economic wars. The Charter had been created to handle the problem system-wide.

Build a ring of solar power catchments in orbit around the sun at a slight angle to the plane of the solar system. No current solar rights would be abridged, but it could catapult humanity into a new industrial era. A great leap forward. Unlimited, unabridged power.

But if it didn't work . . .

Dhaka nodded at all the serious faces. "Don't look so glum. The cohort programmers are working on flocking algorithms to try and simplify how the solar stations keep in orbit. Follow some simple rules about what's around you and let complex emergent orbits develop."

"I'm more worried about the differences in output," Jeni muttered. "While you've been in long-sleep they've been developing orbital stations out past Jupiter with the assumption that there would be beamed power to follow. They're building mega-orbitals throughout the system on the assumption that the Ring's going to work. They've even started moving people off Earth into temporary housing in orbit."

"Temporary?" Euclid asked from across the room, interrupting before Dhaka and Jeni got deep into numbers and words like exajoules, quantum efficiency, price per watt and all the other boring crap. He'd cared intimately about that when he first joined the cohort. Now, not so much.

"We're talking bubble habitats with thinner shells than Vesta right now. They use a layer of water for radiation shielding, but they lack resources and they're not well balanced. These orbitals have about a couple hundred thousand people each, and they're rated to last fifty to sixty years." Jeni shook her head, and Euclid was forced to stop seeing the nineteen year old Zippy and recognise the concerned forty-four year old she'd become. "They're risking a lot."

"Why would anyone agree?" Vega asked. "It sounds like suicide."

"It's gotten worse on Earth. Far worse. Everyone is just expecting to hit the reset button after the Glitter Ring goes online. Everyone's holding their breath."

Dhaka spoke up. "Okay, enough cohort bullshit. Let's talk about you. The band's heading back to long-sleep soon—and then what, Zippy? You heading back to Mars and your daughter?"

Jeni looked around the room hesitantly. "Lara's never been to Venus, and I promised her she could visit me . . . if you'll have me?"

"If?" Vega laughed. "I hated playing those recordings of you. Rather hear it live."

"I'm not as zippy up and down the chords as I used to be, you know," Jeni warned. Everyone was turning to look at Euclid.

"It's a more confident sound," he said with a smile. Dhaka whipped globules of whiskey at them and laughed.

Kumi beamed, no doubt already dreaming about meeting his 'granddaughter.'

"Hey, Zippy," Euclid said. "Here's to change. *Good* change."

"Maybe," she smiled and slapped his raised hand in agreement and approval. "Let's dream on that."

The first few days after long-sleep were never pleasant, but this awakening was the worst of Euclid's experience. He slowly remembered who he was, and how to speak, and the names of the people who sat quietly with him in the lounge after their sessions with the medics. For a while they silently watched the high cities of Venus glinting in the clouds below their orbit from viewports near the long-sleep pools.

Later they began to ask questions, later they realised that something was very wrong. They'd been asleep for fifty years. Two long-sleeps, not the usual single sleep.

"Everyone gone silent back on Vesta," Dhaka said.

"Did we get idled?" Euclid demanded. They were a band, not workers. They shouldn't have been idled.

The medics didn't answer their questions. They continued to deflect everything until one morning an officer turned up, dressed in black sub-uniform with empty holster belt, as if he had left his weapons and armour just outside the door. He looked barely twenty, far too young for the captain's insignia on his shoulders.

He spoke with slow, stilted formality. "Mr. Slinger, Mr. Djansi, Mr. de la Vega, Ms Miriam and Ms Baptiste—thank you for your patience. I'm Captain Abrams. We're sorry for the delay, but your recovery was complicated."

"Complicated!" Kumi looked disgusted. "Can you explain why we had two long-sleeps instead of one? Fifty years? We had a contract!"

"And *we* had a war." The reply was unexpectedly sharp. "Be glad you missed it."

"Our first interplanetary war? That's not the change I wanted," Euclid muttered to Vega.

"What happened?" Jeni asked, her voice barely a whisper. "My daughter, she's on Mars, is she safe?"

The officer glanced away in a momentary flash of vulnerability and guilt. "You have two weeks for news and correspondence with your cohort and others. We can provide political summaries, and psychological care for your readjustment. After that, your tour begins. Transport down to the cities has been arranged. I just . . . I have to say . . . we still need you now, more than ever."

"The *rass*?" Kumi stared at the soldier, spreading his arms.

Again that touch of vulnerability as the young soldier replied with a slight stammer. "Please. We need you. You're legends to the entire system now, not just the cohorts."

"The hell does that mean?" Vega asked as the boy-captain left.

Jeni's daughter had managed one long-sleep but woke on schedule while they stayed in storage. The war was over by then, but Martian infrastructure had been badly damaged and skilled workers were needed for longer than the standard year or two. Lara had died after six years of 'extra time', casualty of a radiation exposure accident on Deimos.

They gathered around Jeni when she collapsed to her knees and wept, grieving for the child they had never known.

Their correspondence was scattered across the years, their cohort truly broken as it had been forced to take cover, retreat, or fight. The war had started in Earth orbit after a temporary habitat split apart, disgorging water, air and people into vacuum. Driven by desperation and fury, several other orbital inhabitants had launched an attack on SDC-MME owned stations, seeking a secure environment to live, and revenge for their dead.

Conflict became widespread and complicated. The orbital habitats were either negotiating for refugees, building new orbitals, or fighting for the SDC-MME. Mars got involved when the government sent its military to protect the Martian investment in the SDC-MME. Jupiter, which was now its own functioning techno-demarchy, had struck directly at the Belt, taking over a large portion of the Glitter Ring.

Millions had died as rocks were flung between the worlds and ships danced around each other in the vacuum. People fought hand to hand in civil wars inside hollowed out asteroids, gleaming metal orbitals, and in the cold silence of space.

Humanity had carried war out of Earth and into the great beyond.

Despite the grim history lesson, as the band shared notes and checked their financial records, one thing became clear. They *were* legends. The music of the Mighty Slinger and the Rovers had become the sound of the war generation and beyond: a common bond that the cohorts could still claim, and battle hymns for the Earth emigrants who had launched out from their decayed temporary orbitals. Anti-SDC-MME songs became treasured anthems. The Rovers songs sold billions, the *covers* of their songs sold billions. There were tribute bands and spin-off bands and a fleet of touring bands. They had spawned an entire subgenre of music.

"We're rich at last," Kumi said ruefully. "I thought I'd enjoy it more."

Earth was still there, still a mess, but Vega found hope in news from his kin. For decades, Pacific Islanders had stubbornly roved over their drowned states in vast fleets, refusing resettlement to the crowded cities and tainted badlands of the continents. In the last fifty years, their floating harbours had evolved from experimental platforms to self-sustaining cities. For them, the war had been nothing but a few nights filled with shooting stars and the occasional planetfall of debris.

The Moon and Venus had fared better in the war than Mars, but the real shock was the Ring. According to Dhaka, the leap in progress was marked, even for fifty years. Large sections were now fully functional and had been used during the war for refuelling, surveillance, barracks and prisons.

"Unfortunately, that means that the purpose of the Ring has drifted once again," she warned. "The military adapted it to their purposes, and returning it to civilian use will take some time."

"But what about the Assembly?" Euclid asked her one day when they were in the studio, shielded from surveillance by noise and interference of Vega's crafting. "Do they still care about the purpose of the Ring? Do you think we still have a mission?"

The war had ended without a clear victor. The SDC-MME had collapsed and the board had been tried, convicted and exiled to long-sleep until a clear treaty could be hammered out. Jupiter, Mars, Venus and some of the richer orbitals had assumed the shares and responsibility of the original solar charter. A tenuous peace existed.

Dhaka nodded. "I was wondering that too, but look, here's the name of the company that's organising our tour."

Euclid leaned in to read her screen. *Bouscholte, Bouscholte & Abrams.*

Captain Abrams revealed nothing until they were all cramped into the tiny cockpit of a descent craft for Venus's upper atmosphere.

He checked for listening devices with a tiny wand, and then, satisfied, faced them all. "The Bouscholte family would like to thank you for your service. We want you to understand that you are in an even better position to help us, and we need that help now, more than ever."

They'd come this far. Euclid looked around at the Rovers. They all leaned in closer.

"The Director of Consolidated Ring Operations and Planetary Reconstruction will be at your concert tonight." Abrams handed Euclid a small chip. "You will give this to him—personally. It's a quantum encrypted key that only Director Cutler can access."

"What's in it?" Dhaka asked.

Abrams looked out the window. They were about to fall into the yellow and green clouds. The green was something to do with floating algae engineered for the planet, step one of the eventual greening of Venus. "Something Cutler won't like. Or maybe a bribe. I don't know. But it's an encouragement for the Director to consider a proposal."

"Can you tell us what the proposal is?"

"Yes." Abrams looked at the band. "Either stop the redevelopment of Earth and further cement the peace by returning the orbitals inhabitants to the surface, or . . ."

Everyone waited as Abrams paused dramatically.

". . . approve a cargo transit across Mercury's inner orbit to the far side of the Glitter Ring, and give us the contracts for rebuilding the orbital habitats."

Dhaka frowned. "I wasn't expecting something so boring after the big 'or' there, Captain."

Abrams smiled. "One small course adjustment at the start can change an entire orbit by the end of a journey," he said to Euclid.

That sounded familiar.

"Either one of those is important?" Euclid asked. "But you won't say why."

"Not even in this little cabin. I'm sure I got the bugs, but in case I didn't." Abrams shrugged. "Here we are. Ready to change the solar system, Mr. Slinger?"

Venusian cities were more impressive when viewed from the outside. Vast, silvery spheres clustered thickly in the upper atmosphere, trailing tethers and tubes to the surface like a dense herd of giant cephalopods. Inside, the decor was sober, spare and disappointing, hinting at a slow post-war recovery.

The band played their first concert in a half-century to a frighteningly respectful and very exclusive audience of the rich and powerful. Then it was off to a reception where they awkwardly sipped imported wine and smiled as their assigned liaison, a woman called Halford, briskly introduced and dismissed awe-struck fans for seconds of small talk and a quick snap.

"And this is Petyr Cutler," Halford announced. "Director of Consolidated Ring Operations and Planetary Reconstruction."

Bodyguards quickly made a wall, shepherding the Director in for his moment.

Cutler was a short man with loose, sandy hair and bit of orbital sunburn. "So pleased to meet you," he said. "Call me Petyr."

He came in for the vigorous handshake, and Euclid had already palmed the small chip. He saw Abrams on the periphery of the crowd, watching. Nodded.

Cutler's already reddened cheeks flushed as he looked down at the chip. "Is that—"

"Yes." Euclid locked eyes with him. The Director. One of the most powerful people in the entire solar system.

Cutler broke the gaze and looked down at his feet. "You can't blackmail me, not even with this. I can't change policy."

"So you still redeveloping Earth?" Euclid asked, his tone already dull with resignation.

"I've been around before you were born, Mr. Slinger. I know how generational projects go. They build their own momentum. No-one wants to become the executive who shut down two hundred years of progress, who couldn't see it through to the end. Besides, wars aren't cheap. We have to repay our citizens who invested in war bonds, the corporations that gave us tech on credit. The Earth Reconstruction project is the only thing that can give us the funds to stay afloat."

Somehow, his words eased the growing tightness in Euclid's chest. "I'm supposed to ask you something else, then."

Cutler looked suspicious. He also looked around at his bodyguards, wanting to leave. "Your people have big asks, Mr. Slinger."

"This is smaller. We need your permission to move parts across Mercury's orbit, close to the sun, but your company has been denying that request. The Rock Devils cohort also wants to rebuild the surviving temporary Earth orbitals."

"Post-war security measures are still in place—"

"Security measures my ass." Jeni spoke so loudly, so intensely that the whole room went quiet to hear her.

"Jeni—" Kumi started.

"No. We've sacrificed our lives and our children's lives for your damn Ring. We've made it our entire reason for existence and we're tired. One last section to finish, that could finish in less than three decades if you let us take that shortcut to get the last damn parts in place and let us go work on something worthwhile. We're tired. Finish the blasted project and let us live."

Kumi stood beside her and put his arm around her shoulders. She leaned into him, but she did not falter. Her gaze stayed hard and steady on the embarrassed Director who was now the centre of a room of shocked, sympathetic, judging looks.

"We need clearance from Venus," Director Cutler mumbled.

Euclid started humming a quick back beat. Cutler looked startled. "*Director*," Euclid sang, voice low. He reached for the next word the sentence needed to bridge. *Dictator*. How to string that in with . . . something to do with the project finishing *later*.

He'd been on the stage singing the old lyrics people wanted to hear. His songs that had once been extempo, but now were carved in stone by a new generation.

But right here, with the bodyguards all around them, Euclid wove a quick song damning him for preventing progress in the solar system and making trouble for the cohorts. That's right, Euclid thought. That's where the power came from, singing truth right to power's face.

Power reddened. Cutler clenched his jaw.

"I can sing that louder," Euclid said. "Loud enough for the whole system to hear it and sing it back to you."

"We'll see what we can do," Cutler hissed at him, and signalled for the bodyguards to surround him and move him away.

Halford the liaison congratulated the band afterwards. "You did it. We're cleared to use interior transits to the other side of the Ring and to move equipment into Earth orbit."

"Anything else you need us to do?" Dhaka asked.

"Not now, not yet. Enjoy your tour. Broadcasting planetwide and recording for rebroadcast throughout the system—you'll have the largest audience in history."

"That's nice," Euclid said vaguely. He was still feeling some discomfort with his new status as legend.

"I can't wait for the Earth concert," Captain Abrams said happily. "That one will really break the records."

"Earth?" Kumi said sharply.

Halford looked at him. "After your next long-sleep, for the official celebration of the completion of the Ring. That can't happen without the Mighty Slinger and his Rovers. One last concert for the cohorts."

"And maybe something more," Abrams added.

"What do you mean, 'more'?" Euclid demanded, weary of surprises.

Halford and Captain Abrams shared a look—delight, anticipation, and caution.

"When we're sure, we'll let you know," the captain promised.

Euclid sighed and glared at the door. He nervously twirled a pair of virtual-vision goggles between his fingers.

Returning to Earth had been bittersweet. He could have asked to fly over the Caribbean Sea, but nothing would be the same—coral reef islands reclaimed by water, new land pushed up by earthquake and vomited out from volcanoes. It would pollute the memories he had of a place that had once existed.

He put the past out of his mind and concentrated on the present. The Rovers were already at the venue, working hard with the manager and crew in technical rehearsals for the biggest concert of their lives. Estádio Nacional de Brasília had become ENB de Abrams-Bouscholte, twice reconstructed in the last three decades to double the seating and update the technology, and now requiring a small army to run it.

Fortunately Captain Abrams (retired) knew a bit about armies and logistics, which was why Euclid was not at technical rehearsal with his friends but on the other side of the city, waiting impatiently outside a large simulation room while Abrams took care of what he blithely called 'the boring prep.'

After ten minutes or so the door finally opened and Captain Abrams peeked around the edge, goggles pushed up over his eyebrows and onto his balding head. "We're ready! Come in, Mr. Slinger. We think you'll like what we've set up for you." His voice hadn't lost that boyish, excited bounce.

Still holding his goggles, Euclid stepped into the room and nodded a distracted greeting to the small group of technicians. His gaze was quickly caught by an alloy-plated soprano pan set up at the end of the room.

"Mr. Djansi says you were a decent pannist," Captain Abrams said, still brightly enthusiastic.

"Was?"

Captain Abrams smiled. "Think you can handle this one?"

"I can manage," Euclid answered, reaching for the sticks.

"Goggles first," the captain reminded him, closing the door to the room.

Euclid put them on, picked up the sticks and raised his head to take in his audience. He froze and dropped the sticks with a clang.

"Go on, Mr. Slinger. I think you'll enjoy this," Abrams said. "I think we all will."

On the night of the concert, Euclid stood on the massive stage with his entire body buzzing with terror. The audience packed into stadium tiers all around him was a faceless mass that rose up several stories, but they were his family and he knew them like he knew his own heart. The seats were filled with Rock Devils, Gladhandlers, Sunsiders and more, all of them from the cohorts, workers representing every section of the Ring and every year and stage of its development. Many of them had come down from Earth orbit and their work on the decaying habitats to see the show.

Euclid started to sing for them, but they sang for him first, calling out every lyric so powerful and sure that all he could do was fall silent and raise his hands to them in homage and embrace. He shook his head in wonder as tears gathered in his eyes.

Kumi, Vega, Dhaka and Jeni kept jamming, transported by the energy, playing the best set of their careers, giving him a nod or a sweet smile in the midst of their collective trance as he stood silently crying and listening to the people sing.

Then it was time.

Euclid walked slowly, almost reverently, to the soprano pan at the centre of the stage. Picked up the sticks, just as he had in the simulation room. Looked up at his audience. This time he did not freeze. He played a simple arpeggio, and the audience responded: lighting a wedge of stadium seating, a key for each note of the chord, hammered to life when he hammered the pan. He lengthened the phrase and added a trill. The cohorts followed him flawlessly, perfected in teamwork and technology. A roar came from overhead as the hovering skyboxes cheered on the Mighty Slinger playing the entire stadium like it was his own personal keyboard.

Euclid laughed loud. "Ain't seen nothing yet!"

He swept his arm out to the night sky, made it a good, slow arc so he was sure they were paying attention. Then the other arm. Showmanship. Raise the sticks with drama. Flourish them like a conductor. Are you ready? *Are you ready!?*

Play it again. This time the sky joined them. The arc of the Ring blazed section by section in sync with each note, and in step with each cadence. The Mighty Slinger and his cohorts, playing the largest instrument in the galaxy.

Euclid grinned as the skyboxes went wild. The main audience was far quieter, waiting, watching for one final command.

He raised his arms again, stretched them out in victory, dropped the sticks on the thump of the Rovers' last chord, and closed his eyes.

His vision went red. He was already sweating with adrenaline and humid heat, but for a moment he felt a stronger burn, the kiss of a sun where no sun could be. He slowly opened his eyes and there it was, as Abrams had promised. The *real* last section of the Ring, smuggled into Earth's orbit during the interior transits permitted by Venus, now set up in the mother planet's orbit with magnifiers and intensifiers and God knows what else, all shining down like full noon on nighttime Brasilia.

The skyboxes no longer cheered. There were screams, there was silence. Euclid knew why. If they hadn't figured it out for themselves, their earpieces and comms were alerting them now. Abrams-Bouscholte, just hours ago, had became the largest shareholder in the Ring through a generation-long programme of buying out rights and bonds from governments bankrupted by war. It was a careful, slow-burning plan that only a cohort could shepherd through to the end.

The cohorts had always been in charge of the Ring's day-to-day operations, but the concert had demonstrated beyond question that only one crew truly ran the Ring.

The Ring section in Earth orbit, with its power of shade and sun, could be a tool for geoengineering to stabilise Earth's climate to a more clement range

. . . or a solar weapon capable of running off any developers. Either way, the entire Ring was under the control of the cohorts, and so was Earth.

The stadium audience roared at last, task accomplished, joy unleashed. Dhaka, Jeni, Kumi and Vega left their instruments and gathered around Euclid in a huddle of hugs and tears, like soldiers on the last day of a long war.

Euclid held onto his friends and exhaled slowly. "Look like massa day done."

Euclid sat peacefully, a mug of bush tea in his hands, gazing at the cold metal walls of the long-sleep hospice. Although the technology had steadily improved, delayed reawakenings still had cost and consequences. But it had been worth the risk. He had lived to see the work of generations, the achievements of one thousand years.

"Good morning, Baba." One of Zippy's great great grandchildren approached, his dashiki flashing a three-dimensional-pattern with brown and green images of some offworld swamp. This Baptiste, the head of his own cohort, was continuing the tradition of having at least one descendant of the Rovers in attendance at Euclid's awakening. "Are you ready now, Baba? The shuttle is waiting for you."

"I am ready," Euclid said, setting down his mug, anticipation rising. Every hundred years he emerged from the long-sleep pool. *Are you sure you want this?* Kumi had asked. *You'll be all alone.* The rest of the band wanted to stay and build on Earth. Curiosity had drawn him to another path, fate had confirmed him as legend and griot to the peoples and Assemblies of the post-Ring era. *Work hard. Do well. Baba will be awake in a few more years. Make him proud.*

They *had* done well, so well that this would be his last awakening. The Caribbean awaited him, restored and resettled. He was finally going home to live out the rest of his life.

Baptiste opened the double doors. Euclid paused, breathed deeply, and walked outside onto the large deck. The hospice was perched on the edge of a hill. Euclid went to the railing to survey thousands of miles of the Sahara.

Bright-feathered birds filled the air with cheerful song. The wind brought a cool kiss to his cheek, promising rain later in the day. Dawn filtered slowly over what had once been desert, tinting the lush green hills with an aura of dusty gold as far as the eye could see.

Come, Baba. Let's go home.

Karl Bunker's short stories have appeared in *Asimov's, Fantasy & Science Fiction, Analog, Interzone, Cosmos, The Year's Best Science Fiction*, and elsewhere. In the past Bunker has been a software developer, jeweler, musical instrument maker, artist, and mechanical technician. He currently lives in a small town north of Boston, Massachusetts, with his wife, sundry pets, and an assortment of wildlife.

THEY HAVE ALL ONE BREATH

Karl Bunker

Apassing streetcar noticed me on the sidewalk. It slowed to a stop, opening its door and dinging its bell to invite me onboard. I ignored it, preferring to walk. It was hours before dawn, early to be heading home by the standards of some, but I'd had enough club-hopping for one night. My skull, my brain, my body were all still vibrating with echoes of the evening's music. It was a good feeling, but I wanted to get home and put in a few hours of work before crashing. I was walking down Boylston Street, enjoying the cool evening air.

There was a loose crowd filling the little plaza at Copley Square. As I walked past, a tall, thin figure separated himself from the rest and called out to me: "James! Hey James, Maestro James!" He laughed, dancing up to me on the balls of his feet.

"How goes it, Ivan?"

"Goes good, *confrere*." He fell into step beside me, then lifted his hand and pointed straight up. "The sky is busy tonight. I don't suppose you've noticed, walking along with your nose scraping the ground the way you do."

I looked up. He was right. White and blue sparklers were winking on and off in a dozen places, and three separate shimmery threads stretched across random patches of the sky.

Ivan hooked his thumb in the direction of the crowd now behind us. "It's got this pack spooked. They think the AIs are putting the finishing touches on a starship, and any second now they're going to fly away, leaving us poor miserables to fend for ourselves."

I grunted, still watching the sky. One of the big orbiters had scrolled into view, its X shape visible as it crept along.

"Kind of like in that E. M. Forster story," Ivan said. "'The Machine Stops.' Have you read it?"

"Yeah." Lisa had given me a copy of the story; Forster was responding to what he saw as the naive optimism H. G. Wells expressed in some of his science-exalting utopian fiction. In Forster's dystopia people live in hive-like underground dwellings, cared for by a great machine that provides them with everything. They rarely have any physical contact with other people, rarely travel or even leave their rooms. They sit and watch entertainments, talk via videophone, eat machine-produced food, breathe machine-produced air. Many of them have come to worship the machine as a kind of god. ("O Machine! O Machine!")

"That's what they're afraid of—that the machine will stop," Ivan was saying. "And then where will we be? No more freebies, no more zaps to keep us all behaving like good boys and girls. All the bad old stuff of the bad old days will come back again." He turned and walked backward for a few steps, looking back at the people filling the square. "Some people just like to fret. About what the AIs have done, about what they'll do next, or this bunch—fretting that they'll stop doing anything."

"The Machine," I pondered aloud. People have never been able to settle on a good name for the whatever-it-is that runs the world now. "The AIs" is an awkward mouthful. And should we properly be calling it/them "the AIs," plural, or "the AI," singular? Nobody knows. Some like using the term "the I's" for short, which of course has a handily appropriate homophone. But usually people just talk about "they" and "them." They did this, they ought to do that, they won't do this other thing. They've been making it rain too much. I wish they'd move me to a bigger house. I can't believe they zapped me—I wasn't *really* going to hit her. They they they they. "The machines" is what Lisa used to call them. "The Machine," dressed up in singular and capitals, has a nice ring to it, too.

Ivan got ahead of me and started walking halfway backward, bending his knees to get his face into my field of vision. I guess I was staring down at the ground again. "Where are you headed, James? Home to the salt mines?"

"Yeah, home," I said. "Maybe get some work done."

"Ah . . . work." He turned to face in the direction he was walking. There was an extra bounce in the rhythm of his steps, like there was too much energy in him for the act of walking to contain. People who don't know Ivan want to know what kind of drugs he's using and where they can get some. But it's all just him, just the way he is. He's a man who looks like he's all crackling hyperactive surface charge, but who in fact has more depth and inner stillness than anyone I know. "I should do me some of that 'work' stuff myself," he said. "I've got an idea for a mural, and there's a restaurant in Oak Square that's talking about letting me do a couple of walls, one inside and one exterior." He scanned the space around us until his gaze settled on a curbside tree. "I'm thinking something natural. Old nature, from back when it was scary."

"Red in tooth and claw," I said.

When I was about ten years old, my mother had a job that was walking distance from where we lived. Her walk to work took her past a park with a pond that was home to a population of ducks, and as winter came on some of these ducks chose not to fly south. It was a typical New England winter, with the temperature fluctuating randomly between mild and brutally cold. On one of the colder mornings, my mother decided that the ducks, now huddled together on a small part of the pond that remained unfrozen, must be hungry. And so from that day on she began bringing food for the ducks on her morning walk to work. First it was a few slices of bread, then a half-loaf, then a whole loaf, then a concoction of bread, cheap peanut butter, and lard that she would mix up by the gallon every evening. Naturally, ducks greeted her in greater and greater numbers every morning, and to my mother's eye at least, ate with greater and greater frenzy and desperation.

One day she came home with her right hand raw and red, the tips of three fingers bandaged. She'd given herself a case of frostbite by scooping the gooey duck food out with her bare hand in sub-zero weather. She sat at the kitchen table, crying as my father gently re-bandaged her fingers. Her tears weren't from the pain, but over the plight of "her" ducks. My father began to argue with her, using his calm, captain-of-the-debating-team tone that my mother and I alternately admired and loathed, depending on whether it was directed at us. "This is crazy, Ann. You're killing yourself over a few birds that were too stupid to fly south when they should have. And as long as you keep feeding them, they never *will* fly south. And there's just going to be more and more of them . . ." And on he went, softly logical and reasonable. I saw my mother's face hardening with anger and saw my father being oblivious to this. Knowing that an explosion was coming, I retreated to my room.

I didn't have to wait long. First there was my father's voice—too muffled to make out any words, but so recognizable in its stolid rationality—and then my mother's ragged shout, interrupting him: "Natural? Why would I give a damn about what's natural? Nature is a butcher! Nature is a god damned butcher!" Next came the sound of my parents' bedroom door being slammed.

Of course. This was a recurring theme with my mother. She loved the beauty of nature, loved animals of any species, but always she saw ugliness behind the beauty. Every bird at our backyard feeder would remind her of how many chicks and fledglings died for each bird that survived to maturity. Every image of wildlife on television or the web would bring to her mind the bloody, rapacious cycle of predator and prey. The boundless, uncaring wastefulness of nature infuriated her. All through my childhood our home was an impromptu hospital, rehabilitation clinic, and long-term rest home for a host of rescued wild and domesticated animals. Orphaned fledgling birds and baby squirrels, starving semi-feral alley cats, and then the mice and birds rescued from the jaws of those same cats.

A few moments after my mother's tirade, my father came into my room and sat beside me on my bed, looking as shamefaced and apologetic as a scolded dog. He often came to me in situations like this. As poor a job as he often did of understanding her, I never questioned that he loved my mother with a helpless intensity. And when he had made her angry he would come to me, as if I were the closest replacement for her that he could find. "You'd think I'd know her better by now, eh, champ?" he said with a sad smile, resting a hand on my shoulder. Then we talked about trivialities for a while, my father ordered a take-out meal, and life went on.

When Ivan and I arrived at our building, a squat little delivery bot was trundling up the outside steps with a stack of packages. Moving ahead of us, it opened the door to Ivan's studio, deposited the boxes a few yards inside the door, and left again, silent on its padded treads. "Ah," Ivan said, looking through the packages. "Every day is Christmas, eh? Canvas, stretchers, some tubes of color, and . . ." he yanked open the top of one of the boxes, "yup; some genuine imitation AI-brand single malt Scotch. Yum yum." He pulled out a bottle and cocked it at an angle near his head. The label had the words "Scotch, Islay single malt (simulated)" printed over a nice photograph of (presumably) Scottish countryside. Nothing else. "Join me in a few, *confrere*?" Ivan asked.

I dropped into one of Ivan's hammock chairs while he flitted into the kitchen for glasses and ice. "You know what I hear?" he said when he came back, handing me a clinking tumbler. "Shanghai, man! That's what I hear. People say great things are happening there. *Really* happening. Music, art, literature, movies . . . They say it's wide open there. New ideas, new things, stuff like nobody's done before, nobody's thought of before. A real renaissance, happening right out on the streets! We should go, James. We should go!"

I grunted noncommittally. Ivan had these flights of enthusiasm; a new one every few weeks, it seemed. A while ago he'd been reading about the Vorticists and Futurists of the early twentieth century, and had been wild to write an artist's manifesto like theirs—one that would "encapsulate the role of the artist in a post-singularity world." That had kept him busy for a month or two, and then there had been some vague but dangerous-sounding talk of performance art involving pyrotechnics, and after that he'd returned to painting with a deep dive into old-school realism and precise draftsmanship.

Ivan had been wandering around his studio as he drank, and now, standing at an open window, he said, "Hey, come look." I weaved my way around a half-dozen or so unfinished canvases on easels and went to him. He pointed down at the outer woodwork of the window. The building was old, with brick walls and weathered wooden trim around the windows. The wooden sill Ivan was pointing at was partly rotted at the corners, and busily at work in those rotted areas was a crew of micro-bots. Vaguely insect-like and about a quarter-inch long, they were the same grayish brown as the weathered wood. There were around ten or twenty of them crawling over the sill, some making their way to one of the rotted voids in the wood and squirting out dollops of resinous material. Others were engaged in chewing away bits of rotten wood, using ant-like pincer jaws.

Ivan reached out and picked up one of the chewer bots, first holding it between thumb and forefinger, and then letting it crawl over his hand. It moved with an unhurried purpose, eventually dropping off the side of his hand to the windowsill and rejoining its comrades. "You remember Louisiana a couple of years ago?" he said, still watching the little bots at work. "The governor and legislature were puffing up their chests about reintroducing a money-labor economy by making it illegal to accept any goods or services from 'any artificial entity.' Then it turned out that little mechanical bugs like these guys were swarming through both the statehouse and the governor's mansion. They'd been rebuilding both from the inside out for months."

I reached out to the window myself, picking up one of the bots and holding it by the edges. It churned its legs for a moment and then went still as I held it close to my eyes. A memory of Lisa's voice murmured into my ear, vicious and accusing: *You love them. It makes me sick how much you love them.*

Lisa appeared in my life right about the time of the world's big tipping point. It was during the few days of the last war in the Middle East. The War That

Wasn't; the Fizzle War. I was in a club called The Overground, and the atmosphere was defiantly celebratory. The wall-sized screen behind the stage was showing multiple videos—scenes that have since become iconic, even clichéd and boring: tanks rolling off their own treads and belly-flopping onto the desert sand, soldiers trying to hold onto rifles that were falling to pieces in their hands, a missile spiraling crazily through the air before burying itself in the ground with the impotent thud of a dead fish. And from other parts of the world, scenes of refugee camps where swarms of flying bots were dropping ton after ton of food, clothing, shelter materials.

No one claimed ownership of these Good Samaritan cargo-bots, nor of the gremlinesque nanoes that were screwing up the mechanisms of war. It soon became known that these were machines built and run by other machines. It was becoming undeniably evident that something new was moving upon the face of the land. Indeed, that the world was being rebuilt around us, disassembled and reassembled under our feet. The AIs were taking over, and they were changing the rules.

The bands playing at The Overground that night had hastily cobbled together some new songs for the occasion. I remember one was "Slaves to the Metal Horde," played to a bouncing dance tune and with silly lyrics about politicians and generals losing their jobs to automation and joining the vast ranks of the unemployed. "God 2.0" was another song; only a few vague and suggestive phrases for lyrics, but with a sly and sinister tune that made it a bonafide hit for a few months. It was during one of those songs that Lisa and I, both partnerless, eyed each other on the dance floor and fell into a face-to-face rhythm. She had a broad smile, a strong, graceful body, and a fondness for dancing with her hands behind her back. Her dancing consisted of lots of dips and hops and twisting her upper body to one side or the other. Often she would seem to be on the verge of throwing herself off-balance, but then she would smack a foot to the floor in flawless synchrony with the beat of the music, showing she had herself exactly where she meant to be. In height, her proportions were as close as my eye could measure to Polykleitos' ideal, and she had lean breasts and a solid muscularity that suggested she had seriously applied herself to some sport in her student days.

But the real story of her beauty was in her face. It wasn't the beauty of clinical perfection, but of personhood. There was a whole human being written out in the length of her nose, the curve of her jaw, the hard straightness of her eyebrows. And of course her eyes. They were eyes that were full of knowing humor and incisive smarts and even more full of absolutely no bullshit. Usually when I see a face as beautiful and interesting as hers, I set about memorizing it so I can sketch it later. I look and then look away, rebuild the lines, curves, shapes and shadows of the face in my head, then look again to check my reconstruction against the original. Repeat and repeat until the person gets annoyed and asks what the fuck I'm doing. I didn't do this with Lisa, and it took me a while to realize why: You only have to memorize a face when it's a face you might not see again, and I didn't want to think about not seeing this woman's face again.

After dancing for a while we had a couple of drinks, and after that we left the club together. The sudden quiet and fresh air of the street hit me like a splash of cold water, and I just stood there for a bit, breathing and looking up at the starry sky.

"I hope it's going to be something good," Lisa said, the first words we'd spoken to each other without having to shout over music. "I hope to hell it's going to be something good."

For an embarrassing, imbecilic moment, I thought she was talking about us, about the prospects of a relationship between us. That's how I was thinking already. Something had me already thinking about "us" before there was anything remotely resembling an "us." I said "Yeah, I hope so too," but before the sentence was halfway out of my mouth I realized that wasn't what she meant. She was talking about the subject that everyone was talking about— the AIs and what they were up to; what was happening to the world and what was going to happen to it. Then she grabbed my hand, yanked our bodies together and gave me a grinning kiss on the lips, and I went back to thinking maybe she was talking about us. We walked and talked for a while, and then she keyed her number into my phone, gave me another peck on the lips, and left.

"Anyway, Shanghai is the place, man. That's what I hear." Ivan said, trying to pull my attention back to him. Then he added, "She ain't up there, man."

I realized I was standing with my head tilted back, staring up as if I could see through the ceiling above me and the floor above that and into the apartment over Ivan's. My apartment, where Lisa would be, if she were there. Ivan was eyeing me obliquely, neither pity nor ridicule in his expression. "She's been gone a long time."

True, but she'd been gone before, and come back before. Three times, or was it four? A funny thing to lose track of.

I started wandering around Ivan's studio, looking at some of his recent work. As usual I liked his charcoal sketches and pencil drawings better than his paintings; maybe I only have a sculptor's eye for color—which is to say, no eye at all. Maybe it's all shades of gray with me. Or maybe my problem was that the color had gone out of my life, ha ha. One piece he'd clearly put a lot of work into was done up as an imitation of an old-style biological illustration. It was several images on one canvas, depicting the same creature from different angles and in different postures. Each image had a caption in precise calligraphy, short quotations from Genesis and the Rig Veda. But the creature wasn't a creature. It had pinkish skin, no apparent head, only vague flippers for limbs. It looked something like a cross between a jellyfish and a rat. It was creepy as hell. "What the fuck is this?" I asked.

Ivan only glanced at the painting, as if he didn't like looking at it himself. "That's a squirmer. That particular one was picked up somewhere in Costa Rica; some scientists posted an article about it, about what it does and how it works, with a bunch of pictures and videos." When I gave him a blank stare Ivan went on. "You know, food! Manufactured food for animals that will only eat live prey. Not all the predator animals in the world are happy eating the piles of synthetic puppy chow that our AI friends leave lying around, so they also make these things—blobs of protein that act alive, that squirm around on the ground. Nice, eh?" He took another quick look at the canvas, then turned it to face the wall.

"They think of everything, huh?" I said. And of course they do. That's what you do when you have an IQ in the millions or billions: You think of everything. All the infinite details that go into remaking a world, dismantling every minutest bit of the old world that doesn't fit your idea of how things should be and replacing it with a corresponding bit that suits you better.

Ivan and I sat facing each other across a neat little table a woodworker friend of his had made, the bottle of Scotch on the table between us. Over what was left of the night we got as drunk as the faux booze—or maybe it was the nanoes in our blood—would allow, which turned out to be pretty drunk.

After his third refill, Ivan started holding his glass close to his chest and staring sullenly at an empty spot in the air about four feet in front of him.

"Tell me about Shanghai," I said.

"Fuck Shanghai. It's all bullshit. Things are as dead there as they are here, or New York, or Palookaville, or anywhere."

"You really think things are all that dead?"

"Agh, you know . . ." He paused, rolling the ice around inside his glass. "They aren't *alive*. Not like they used to be." He raised his eyes to meet mine. "You were at the Carver Club tonight?"

I nodded.

"How was it?"

"Good," I said, tilting my head to the right.

"Yeah. Exactly. You remember the early days? The Fizzle War and all that, when it was all starting? You remember—" He started tossing out the names of bands and of songs, and I started throwing back some of my own favorites, and for a while we may as well have been two geezer-farts, grinding our rocking chairs into the ground as we reminisced about The Good Old Days.

"Anyway," Ivan said, "things were *alive* then. The bands were trying to be different, trying to do something *new*. And it wasn't just the music. It was right around then that Johansson started writing her crazy *Extinction* poems, and the contra-perspectivist painters sprang up in L.A., and the New Minimalist writers in the U.S. and India . . . New stuff, man. *Great* stuff. Back then there really *was* a renaissance going on. It didn't last, but it was sure as hell something *real*."

I got caught up in Ivan's enthusiasm. "It was, wasn't it?" I said. "That's how a renaissance happens. One schmoe sees another schmoe doing something amazing, and he gets pumped up. Even if he works in a totally different field, he gets inspired. He starts thinking about trying to do something amazing himself. And before you know it you've got Italy in the fifteenth century, or Harlem in the 1920s. You've got Duke Ellington and Aaron Douglas and Fats Waller and Josephine Baker, all rubbing shoulders, lighting each other up, driving each other to greatness."

I knew the Scotch was making me blather, and I shut up. But I went on thinking about those days of a few years ago, when the world felt a lot more alive, as Ivan put it. I thought about spending night after night running from one club to the next, trying to catch every one of the dozens of new bands that were springing up, trying to take it all in, feeling awed by the energy, the newness, the vitality. And more than that, feeling a burn, an absolute *burn* to go back to my studio and create something, make something, even though I doubted I would ever, in a hundred lifetimes, be able to sculpt anything half as good as all the examples of genius that seemed to be roaring to life all around me . . . Of course, my relationship with Lisa was gleaming and new back then, and that added its own brand of creative fire to my life.

"I think it's because we were scared in those days," Ivan said. "A lot of the creative types were making a joke of it, but that was just whistling past the graveyard. We didn't know what the AIs were going to do, and we were scared. Maybe it was that fear that made people more creative. Nowadays nobody's really afraid about anything. The worst thing anyone feels now is bored and cranky." He caught my eye as soon as he said this, then looked down at the floorboards. "Sorry, man. Stupid thing for me to say."

I grunted and waved a hand to dismiss the subject, and we went on talking. We talked about the old world, the new world, about Scotch, about art-world gossip, and not Lisa. I spent a lot of time not talking about Lisa.

The first time Lisa came home with me to my studio, she went straight to the shelves that held my sculptures. She looked at each one slowly and carefully, taking it in from different angles. I was working small in those days, figures eighteen inches tall at most, and she leaned in close to squint at all the fine details I'd sweated over in anticipation of just such a squint. "Hmm," she said now and then, and "Ah" once or twice. These little vocalizations were hardly more than a breath, and when she was done looking she summarized with a quiet "Okay" and a smile. I suppose it was just me being silly, but those few syllables felt like all the praise in the world; like a Guggenheim fellowship and a MacArthur grant and a hearty handshake from Rodin, all rolled into one.

She spent the night, and the next morning we went to her place so she could make us breakfast, and later that day we went back to my place so I could make us lunch, and some time after that we went to her place for supper and to see if the sex was as good in her bed as it had been in mine. After a few weeks of this, the back and forth was getting kind of tiresome, so we packed up her stuff and moved it to my place. And that was that; there was officially an "us."

I suppose—one has to suppose—that to the AIs, love is just one more quantifiable entity in a universe of quantifiable entities. Probably it's as basic to them as a bit of clockwork; the right neurons firing, a few chemicals in the right combination. But then again, the same can be said of life itself. The sweet, living Earth, with all its countless green fronds and numberless beating hearts, is all just clockwork and chemistry, all eminently quantifiable and understandable. That doesn't stop it from being something amazing and magical, measureless and infinite.

After some impassioned entreaties, Lisa agreed to model for me. I had just started working on *Geckos* then; a pair of female figures climbing up a smooth vertical wall, their bodies somewhere between lizard and human, and also abstracted and simplified à la Constantin Brancusi. It was a design that could easily slump into kitschy faux-Deco drivel, but I was hopeful I could hopscotch my way across that minefield. When Lisa saw how abstract the piece was going to be she laughed. "Are you sure you need a naked woman to model for this?"

"Oh absolutely. It's all in there, even if I don't do a straight copy of it; the muscles, the bones, the skin and hair, all the lines and curves, all the, um . . .

details . . . And it can't be just any naked woman. It has to be you. It's all about capturing the inner essence, don'cha know, and if there's anyone whose inner essence I want to capture, it's yours."

"I can think of six or seven dirty jokes about that," she said, "but they're all really lame."

I answered her grin with one of my own, but I wasn't kidding. I had visions of this woman being my lifelong inspiration. My muse, I would have said, if that word weren't too worn out and clichéd to speak without gagging. She would be the Rose Beuret to my Rodin, the Jeanne Hébuterne to my Modigliani, the Wally Neuzil to my Schiele. That's the sort of thing that runs through your mind when you're young and in love and have enough naïve ego to insert your own name into a sentence alongside some of the world's greatest artists. As it turned out, I would work on that sculpture throughout all the time Lisa and I were together.

Meanwhile, the world outside our lust-fogged windows was continuing on its way. After stopping all mechanized war, the AIs set about rebuilding slums and refugee camps. Beginning with the worst of them, these wretched huddling places of tents and corrugated iron shacks were suddenly—by seeming magic—replaced with rows of cute little cottages, neatly trimmed out with comfortable furniture and curtains in the windows. Sewer systems and running water appeared where there had only been open ditches and hand pumps. The shiny kiosk buildings started to spring up like oversized mushrooms, first in the poorest parts of the world, but soon to expand globally. Aisle after aisle of shelves filled with the necessities of life, all of it free for the taking and constantly restocked by the endlessly roving supply-bots. Clearly the AIs had solved the riddle of nano-assembly. They could put together matter of any size and complexity from base molecules, base atoms, and for all we knew, maybe even base protons and electrons. However they did it, the bottom line was that they seemed capable of making anything, anywhere, of any size, in any quantity.

It was a fun time when this age of abundance came home to the First World. Mysterious online catalogs started appearing; you could order a pair of shoes or a dozen eggs or new dining room furniture, with no mention of the awkward little detail of payment. Needless to say, this was seen as a threat to the economy—to the whole idea of there even being anything worth calling an "economy," and this scared a lot of people. It scared some people even more than the fact that mankind's God-given right to wage war had been taken away. A lot of people were scared, and a wealth of imminent dooms were predicted, but there was nothing much anyone could do. The

AIs had seen to it that there was nothing anyone could do. They'd thought of everything.

Fewer people found any reason to object when disease stopped happening. This one began with hospitals noting a slump in new admissions, and with doctors finding nano-sized foreign bodies of unknown origin in the blood of some patients. But soon it was everyone's blood, and everyone, everywhere, stopped getting sick. At all, ever.

It's funny how people adjust. The world was going through changes that, before they happened, would have been thought of as mind-boggling, world-shattering, unfathomable. And yet life just went on, the way it does. In years past, people had adjusted to the notion that humanity might be wiped out by a couple of psychotic button-presses. People had adjusted to living in the midst of bubonic plague, to having their cities bombed every night, to being ruled by lunatic, murderous despots. If people could adjust to those things, they could adjust to a life of no war, no disease, and unearned abundance.

It was right around the time Lisa moved in with me that the zaps were added to the catalog of revolutions being wrought upon the world. They started out as just one more among thousands of not-too-believable rumors flitting around the web, but in a matter of days the reports became a flood. The zaps were real.

For Lisa and me, that reality was visited on us late one night as we were walking through one of the less-affluent neighborhoods of Cambridge, on a residential side street off of Mass Ave. In the middle of a quiet, poorly lit block, a man was suddenly standing in front of us. He was big, broad, and pretty rough-looking, with a dried road-rash scab on one cheek, torn and dirty clothes, and hair that might have been neatly combed earlier in the day but was now a crazed mop. "Hey, man," he said, apparently to both of us, "you gotta see this."

I tightened my grip on Lisa's hand and tried to side-step around the guy, but he side-stepped with me, putting a hand on my chest. "No. You *got* to see this!" His eyes roved over the empty air around him, somewhere above head level. "It's like they're here. Watching. They know what I'm going to do, before I even do it!"

I figured him for crazy and/or drunk, and tried to convince myself that crazies and drunks usually aren't dangerous. "It's okay," I said. "They won't hurt you. They haven't hurt anyone."

He widened his eyes at me, smiling like he knew something hugely funny that I didn't know. "It kinda hurts, actually," he said, a thoughtful look crossing his face. "But it's wild . . . Wild. Just watch. Just watch this!" His hand was on my chest again, this time grabbing my jacket. He wrenched me around, shoving me up against a parked car. Lisa yelled something, grabbing at his free arm. He shook her off and grinned wildly at her. "Just watch!" he said again, turning back to me and bringing his right arm up with his fist clenched and his elbow cocked in a classic I-am-going-to-punch-your-face pose. Lisa screamed.

When you've played a memory over and over in your head a few hundred times, it becomes difficult to know what you actually saw at the time and what details your mind has edited in after the fact. Since those early days, everyone's seen slow-motion videos of zappings, heard people describing the sensation with all brands of colorful language, seen scientists expounding on the probable mechanism of their function. But reliably or not, I remember the electric buzz-pop, a flash of light with no apparent source, and then our unpleasant companion going into shuddering rigidity for less than a second before slumping to the ground like an abandoned marionette. Lisa and I stood looking blankly at each other for a moment, and then she bent over the man, reaching out to touch him. There was an acrid, bleach-like smell in the air, which I later learned was the smell of ozone.

"Did ya see it?" the man cackled, turning his head toward Lisa. He was breathing hard and clutching at his right arm—the arm he'd been about to punch me with. "Did ya fucking *see* it?" It seemed to be really important to him that we'd seen it.

"Yes, we saw it," Lisa said, and we left.

We walked a block or two in silence, just absorbing what had happened. I was mostly thinking about the implications of this new manifestation of the AIs. They would be able to stop any human action they didn't approve of, and I wondered what that was going to mean. Lisa was thinking more about the man we'd left lying on the sidewalk. "He wanted it to happen," she said softly. "Everyone keeps wondering why the machines won't talk to us, why they won't tell us what they're going to do, what their plans are. That guy wanted that thing to happen to him, because he knew it was *them*, speaking to him, in a way. He wanted to be electrocuted, or whatever that was, so that he could feel them doing something, *saying* something. It was like he thought of it as being touched by the hand of God."

I figured she was right. Luckily, before too long there was so much coverage of people being zapped that it became old hat, and not many were silly enough to go out of their way to provoke getting zapped just for its own sake. It also turned out that only violence or extreme cases of theft or destruction of personal property would bring on a zap, so fears of the AIs trying to whip the human race into robotic docility and uniformity died down after a while.

But the zaps meant there was no longer much use for police, the courts, laws, politicians, or government. All of these grand edifices of Civilization As We Know It were becoming as obsolete as buggy whips. The faint electric crackle of the zaps was really a thunderclap. It was the boom of a coffin lid slamming shut on the notion of humans being in charge of humanity.

Naturally, this fact once again made many people unhappy, or frightened, or both. Worrying about what the AIs were up to was becoming humanity's favorite pastime. And Lisa was becoming one of those people who worried.

"You have to wonder," she said one day. "When you look at what the machines are doing from a few different angles, it makes me wonder."

"Wonder about what?" I asked. "No more crime or war or disease or poverty. Those are good things to be rid of, I'd say."

"Sure they are. The world is a million times better off now than it was before. But . . ." She paused for a long time before continuing. "I was just reading about the women's suffrage movement. Some of those women went through hell year after year after year; getting beaten up by cops at their protest marches, getting arrested, going on hunger strikes in prison, being force-fed with tubes rammed down their throats. And then when they were released from prison, they just went back out on the streets to march again. Some of them had their health ruined for the rest of their lives, and some of them died." She looked at me, her eyes shining with tears. "How many millions of stories like that are there in history? People fighting and dying for human progress—for freedom and democracy, to end slavery, to end war, to make progress in science—all the ways people have worked and suffered and sacrificed themselves to make the world a better place." She paused again, looking away from me, looking out a window at a blank sky.

"And now all of that is over," she said. "The machines are jumping in and kicking us off the field. They're saying we're nothing but a bunch of screwups, so they're taking over, taking the world out of our hands. So as of now, there's no such thing as human progress anymore, because it isn't humans who are *doing* it. It's them. It's all them, imposing progress on us from above."

"That's true, I guess," I said. "But it's also true that their sense of morality must have come from us. Either it was programmed into their ancestors or they learned it by observing our culture, and now they're only taking those human ideals and applying them, enforcing them. And isn't that what laws have done throughout history? To apply the highest human ideals that one can realistically hope to enforce? So you could say they're just super-cops, enforcing a system of morality that's entirely human in origin."

"But it's not *human*. It's a change in how we behave that hasn't come from us. It hasn't evolved. It's just being imposed on us by goddamned machines."

"Yes, and what's wrong with that? So maybe it bruises our little egos that they're in charge, that they're more powerful than us, that they're smarter than us. Maybe a bruised ego is an okay price to pay for children not being shot and napalmed and dying of dysentery."

"I'm just saying that being human used to be something special," Lisa said. "People like Martin Luther King, like Mahatma Gandhi, like those suffragettes and like all the millions of plain, ordinary people who did some little thing, just out of the hope that they were helping to make the world a better place—they made us special. The human race was progressing, it was evolving. And now that's all over. We'll never progress to anything, because we don't have any choice. Whatever progress we make, it won't be us doing it. We aren't free. We're just pets who belong to *them*."

I kind of slumped at that, a realization settling over me. "The difference between you and me," I said, "is that you have a lot more faith in humanity than I do. I'm not so sure we were progressing anywhere. And if we were, it could have taken a million dead martyrs like Martin Luther King and Mahatma Gandhi before we got to the place where we are today: People not killing each other. And personally I'm not sure the human race would have lasted long enough to kill off many more martyrs."

Of course, a lot of what both of us were saying was just rehashing arguments we'd read or heard from others. All these issues and lines of thought had been chewed over endlessly by everyone with a keyboard or microphone. But for Lisa and me, the argument died there, for the time being. It was our first glimpse of the distance that could exist between us, and neither of us wanted to dwell on it. We didn't want to admit to ourselves that it was a real thing; that it mattered. Life went on, and we went on being happy.

What we didn't realize was that the AIs still weren't done with remaking the world. Their next bombshell came about a year later. Seemingly overnight, the birthrate dropped. Nine births per thousand population per year was the new number, and it was quickly confirmed that it was the same everywhere in the world. This worked out to about one and a quarter children per family, and was well below replacement level. Apparently the AIs had decided that the human population needed to be lowered, so in their inimitable manner they had made it come to pass.

And once again this latest seismic readjustment to the world brought out a thousand gradations of response, from joyful acceptance on down to batshit hysterical predictions of doom. It was calculated that the population would dwindle down to nothing at all in several hundred years if the birthrate stayed as low as it now was. "They're wiping us out," some declared. "Yeah, but," the more moderate yeah-butters said, "if they wanted to get rid of us, why wouldn't the birthrate be zero? Or why wouldn't they just kill us outright, disassemble us into pink goo, and be done with the job in a millisecond instead of centuries?"

There was another wrinkle to the new birthrate, and it was one that many disliked even more than they disliked the plain numbers. The AIs appeared to be picking and choosing who would be allowed to conceive. Unwanted pregnancies dropped to zero, as did pregnancy among the mentally ill, those who were in bad relationships, and women who already had two or more children. Teenaged pregnancy likewise became almost unknown. When a pregnant teen did occasionally appear, she would turn out to be some absurdly mature and levelheaded girl who was studying for her Master's in developmental psychology or some such thing. Or it would be discovered that she was best friends with a gay couple next door who were breathlessly excited about the upcoming birth and had already redecorated one of their rooms as a nursery and installed child-proof locks on all their cabinets.

So those granted the gift of conception were clearly all good and deserving people, as determined by the AIs in their presumably infallible wisdom.

As for me, because I'm an idiot, a blinkered idiot, days went by before I thought much about where I stood on this issue. Or rather, before Lisa pointed out to me where *we* stood. We were talking about one of the endless "why do you suppose *this* couple was allowed to have a baby" stories, when I realized that Lisa's expression had gone dark. She was glaring at me with something in her eyes I couldn't identify, but I knew it wasn't good. She looked at me like that for a long time.

"You really don't care, do you?" she said finally, making it more of a statement than a question.

"Care?" I said blankly.

"I mean you aren't thinking . . . You aren't thinking about . . ."

Still I was clueless. "About what?"

"About us!" She yelled, suddenly almost in tears. "About the fact that this means *us*, too! Did it really never occur to you that you and I might want to have kids some day? Maybe get married, be a family, all that bourgeois middle class crap? Does that really never cross your mind?" We were sitting on our couch, and at this point she leaned into me, resting her head on my shoulder. She sniffed noisily, openly crying now. "Did it never occur to you that . . ." She made a fist and thumped it down softly on my thigh, "that I love you so much that I would feel blessed—fucking *blessed*—to have a baby with you?"

In my imagination, her words echoed in the room for minutes. No, it hadn't occurred to me. How could I, miserable finite entity that I am, ever think that someone like her could feel a thing like that about me? And in any case, all thoughts of fathering children had always been a pretty distant thing from my notions of life and my place in the world. I knew the possibility was out there, and I suppose in some dusty, unused corner of my mind I connected that possibility with Lisa, but . . .

In a kind of stunned internal silence, I reached out for the idea, drawing it from its dusty corner and into the light. A child. Parenting. A child with Lisa. A son, or a daughter . . . The image burst on me then, like a sculpture suddenly assembled out of particles of light. It was beautiful. It was the most beautiful thing I'd ever imagined. Yes. A baby. A baby with Lisa.

"Yes," I said aloud, suddenly teary. "Yes, yes, yes. Let's have a baby." I grabbed her hands in both of mine, then let go again so I could pull her to me, hug her hard, bury my face in the crook of her neck. "Yes, yes, yes."

"Who says they'd let us?" Lisa asked. "Even if you wanted to."

"I *do* want to!" I sputtered. "And they'll *have* to let us! We'll get married, we'll be a family. We'll read books, take courses on parenting, we'll . . . I don't know, do whatever responsible, well-adjusted parents do. Maybe we can't count on a whole brood of kids, but we can have at least one. They'll have to let us have at least one."

"You want to?" Lisa said, her voice quivering again. "You really want to?"

I said "Yes" a dozen or so times more, and then we just sat there with our heads together, both of us sniffling, grinning, laughing.

So the next day we started figuring out how to get married. There was still a functioning city hall in those days, so we filled out the required forms, got the required signature and lined up a justice of the peace. As soon as I told Ivan what we were up to, he leapt into the job of planning the thing like a frenzied mother-in-law-to-be. I had some pieces in a group show at the time, and Ivan convinced the gallery owner to let us use the space for the ceremony. He pestered us with a flurry of different designs and redesigns for invitations. He begged and bartered with one of the better local bands, not only getting them to play some upbeat and danceable music after the ceremony, but also brow-beating the guitarist into working up a Jimi-Hendrix-esque version of the wedding march. And when the day came it was a great little party, much like the night when Lisa and I first met. Only when Lisa danced this time, it was with her arms high in the air, as if there was too much joy in her for her body to contain. And looking at her, that feeling was echoed in my own heart. Until that moment, I wouldn't have guessed I could love anyone as much as I loved this woman.

But the wedding was to be the last truly, purely happy moment of our lives. After that began the long succession of monthly disappointments; the repeated non-conception of our child. Though statistics showed that the birth rate was steady and unvarying, once we were in the game, once we were among the ranks of those hoping for a child, it seemed that everyone except us was getting pregnant. Middle-aged couples, young couples, single women, seventeen-year-old girls. How were the AIs choosing? Had they modeled the human personality so perfectly that they could know, to some Nth level of certainty, who would make the best parents? And what did "best" mean? By whose definition? What kind of next generation did they want? These were just a few of the infinite questions that the whole world was pondering, arguing over, fighting and breaking up over.

"It's probably me," Lisa said. "The machines know that I'm not all gung-ho for the new world order, so why would they let me be a mother? You should hook up with some woman who loves Big Brother as much as you do. You'd have six kids by now!" And I would take issue with that line about loving Big Brother, and we would argue and fight over that.

Or: "Maybe it's you. Maybe they won't let us have a baby because they know you don't really want one. You're happy with your life the way it is. You don't want a messy, noisy brat screwing up your neat little world. I know it, and *they* know it." And we would fight over that.

The topic of parenthood and our persistently not-appearing child was the main locus of argument between us, but there were others. I'd been keeping my day job when an increasing number of people around us were finding it easy enough to live without employment. But when the company that we'd been paying our rent to went out of business and wasn't replaced by anyone or anything who cared about the building or who lived in it, I told Lisa I was going to quit. It was a doomed job anyway; there's not much use for an ad designer when the whole institution of selling goods for money was crumbling apart.

"If you don't work, you're giving up." Lisa said. "You're dropping out of the economy and dropping out of human society. You won't be contributing anything; you'll be nothing but a *pet* to the machines."

"All I'm 'giving up' on is being a damned wage-slave," I snapped back. "I'm dropping out of spending half of my waking life doing work I don't care about for a company that doesn't matter. And we don't need the money. I've got savings enough to get the few things we want that you still have to pay for, and who knows where the world will be by the time that runs out? Money may not even exist by then. And meanwhile I'll be able to spend full time doing the work that matters to me." I waved an arm in the direction of the room set aside as my studio.

"Sure. Let the machines feed you and clothe you and keep you warm in the winter. Let them give you toys to play with and let them clean your litter box and let them wipe your ass when it needs wiping. Be a good little pet."

And so on, and so on, and so on. Of course, I'm the one remembering all this, so it's a given that my memory is biased. I'm sure I said my share of stupid and hurtful things too, when it was my turn to be stupid and hurtful. And no amount of skewed memory, of snuffling self-pity and hurt feelings can hide the fact that we had great times too. Times when Lisa's smile and laughter lit up the air and washed over me like sunlight. Times when the two of us fit together like the jagged half-pieces of something that was meant to be whole. Times when I was sure that nothing in the world could ever make sense without her at my side, completing me.

Then the company Lisa worked for went out of business, and she couldn't find a job anywhere else. For a while she filled her time with watercolor painting and drawing, and I swear she had a natural talent that would have had my professors at the MFA School weeping onto their smocks. But she gave it up, switching to guitar playing for a while, then keyboard, then reading nineteenth-century novels, then studying political theory . . . Nothing lasted, nothing consumed her, nothing gave her the sense of purpose that a lump of clay and a few modeling tools gave to me. She became more and more convinced that only one thing would do that for her, and that was the one thing the machines wouldn't allow us to have. I convinced her to see a therapist—a profession that was grandly thriving, thanks to the vast population of the unemployed who were thrashing about for something to give meaning to their lives—but that too didn't last.

At some point our arguing and bitterness seemed to become the rule rather than the exception, and she left me. And a few weeks later she came back, both of us extravagantly tearful and contrite and swearing that we'd never fight again and blah blah blah. And we didn't, until we did. So she moved out again, and came back again, and left again. How many times? A funny thing to lose track of.

I do remember what triggered our last breakup, though. It was the thing with the animals. When the AIs decided to extend their reach into the realm of animals and nature, that was what finally and utterly ruined my marriage.

As usual, the news crept in on us by degrees. First came the stories of some act of violence against an animal being prevented in one way or another. A deer hunter in Vermont found his 30-06 falling to pieces in his hands, just like the soldiers in the Fizzle War. A short-tempered dog owner in Egypt and a malicious slingshot-owning youngster in France were zapped onto their respective behinds. Soon the scattered reports became a deluge, and the meaning was clear: The AIs' umbrella of protection had been spread to animals. All animals, everywhere. Harm to any creature larger than a bug was no longer allowed, and even wholesale attacks on insects were liable to bring down the stinging reprimand of a zap. Slaughterhouses around the world were disassembled to dust overnight, and the herds and flocks of livestock wandered off, to be fed and cared for by the machines. By this time, synthetic copies of every food imaginable had been available for years, and they'd been shown to be indistinguishable from their real-food counterparts. So this latest stricture had no real impact on anyone's dining habits, but needless to say there were many who chafed under this imposition on their inalienable right to kill things. No matter. As ever and always, there was nothing anyone could do about it.

And then came the capstone on the AIs' new world: Reports from forests, jungles, and wildlife reserves began to show that it wasn't just humans who were prohibited from harming animals. One early video showed a pride of lions stealthily closing in on a mother zebra and her foal. Then there was a series of flashes and crackles, and predator and prey darted off in opposite directions. That same afternoon, a drone on caterpillar treads was seen dropping off a load of realistic-looking but undoubtedly synthetic meat upwind of the lions. The lions ate well that night, and the zebra mother and her foal lived to see another sunrise. A thousand confirmations eventually followed, and soon after it was reported that the birthrate of all prey animals had dropped precipitously. The new rulers of the Earth weren't content to simply take a hand in the affairs of humans; they'd decided that nature itself needed some straightening out. So no longer would a mother zebra need to birth and rear ten or twenty offspring so that one or two might live to reproductive age. No longer would nature be so profligate with lives, so red in tooth and claw. That bit about God's eye being on the sparrow would no longer be a cruel joke at the sparrow's expense as its life ended in agony and terror, with torn flesh and crushed bones. Now, in the remade world, that sparrow could look forward to a long and carefree life, a dignified old age, and a quiet death in its little sparrow bed, the whole of its time on Earth innocent of pain and fear.

My mother died when I was sixteen. She was driving and somehow managed to swerve off the road, hurtle down a steep embankment, and crash into a tree. I was sure I knew how it had happened—almost before I could even fathom the *what* of her being dead, I was sure of the *how*. She had seen something in the road, a squirrel or a cat, a turtle or a snake, and had yanked the wheel over to miss it. I was sure, and though we never mentioned it to each other, I felt my father had the same thought, and was just as sure.

The idea of a funeral would have been anathema to my mother, but my father held a small "memorial gathering" for her in our home. It was one of those secular affairs where a succession of friends and relations stood and spoke. Many had reminiscences, some recited poetry or other texts. My father went last, and he started by noting that although his wife was the staunchest of atheists, she had a fondness for certain parts of the King James Bible. Then he read, very briefly, from Ecclesiastes:

> *For that which befalleth the sons of men befalleth beasts; even one thing befall-*
> *eth them: as the one dieth, so dieth the other; yea, they have all one breath; so*
> *that a man hath no preeminence above a beast.*

He spoke softly, as if his words weren't intended so much for the people in the room as for himself, or for some closely hovering spirit of my mother—though she would surely have been as disdainful of that image as she would have been of a traditional religious funeral.

I imagine everyone likes to think that they aren't fettered by their parents' beliefs. Even while she was alive, I made little rebellions against my mother's militant veganism. I would spend my allowance on sneaky little violations of the diet she'd raised me under. With all the furtive subterfuge that other kids invested on illicit drugs, I bought ice cream and pizza with real cheese; I ate snack foods without checking the ingredients list. And in my teens and adulthood I abandoned one after another of her strictures. I wore leather shoes; I stopped checking for "cruelty free" labels; I even nibbled at an occasional hot dog. I thought I was freeing myself from my mother's irrationality, that I was growing up, becoming my own person.

"This really tears it, doesn't it?" Lisa said. "This just wraps it up for you." She was standing behind me, and we were watching the news of the AIs' latest doings on our wall screen. At that moment the screen was showing a picture of a female mallard duck swimming on a sunlit pond, followed by a single fluffy duckling.

"What are you talking about?" I said. I honestly had no idea, but the anger in her voice was making my own anger flare up. It felt like we'd leapt into the middle of another argument, with no preamble or warm-up.

"I mean that this is where you find your god." She waved an arm at the wall screen. "This is him, or it, or them, climbing up onto his golden throne." She made the same arm-wave in my direction. "And this is you, getting ready to kneel and worship at his feet."

"Damnit, Lisa, I'm not worshiping—"

"And this is me, being a monster," she interrupted. "A fucking monster who cares more about her own right to have a baby than she cares about war and disease and poverty and . . ." She waved her arm once more, this time hitting the screen with the back of her hand, "and a million, *billion* fucking baby ducklings being born just so they can be eaten by foxes or crocodiles or whatever the fuck eats baby ducklings!" Her voice became choked and strangled, and she pressed her forehead to the screen, banging it with her fist. "I'd let them all die! I'd let the world burn, so long as I can have my baby! Doesn't that make me a monster? Doesn't it?" She turned to me, her face twisted and smeared with tears.

The anger melted out of me, replaced by a sense of hopelessness that wasn't much of an improvement. "You're not a monster, and you don't feel that. You don't want anyone or anything to die. You just want to have a baby, and so do I, and we have a right to want that. But . . ."

"But everything's for the best in this, the best of all possible worlds. You believe that, don't you? Especially now—now that the machines are fucking with nature, now that they're so moral and righteous and holy that they're saving little birdies and mousies and zebras and whatever the hell else from getting eaten. It used to be a joke when people talked about them being the new god. But now . . . now they really are god. The best god ever, isn't that right? Isn't that what you believe?"

That damn duckling picture was still on the screen, and I couldn't help looking at it. "It matters, Lisa. There's so much less pain and misery in the world now that I can't even get my mind around it, and that matters. I'm not about to get down on my knees and pray to the machines, but . . . it matters. It matters a lot."

Lisa turned her back to the wall then, slowly bending her knees until she was sitting on the floor. She looked beaten, as if all the fight had been burned out of her. "It matters more than our baby, you mean," she said flatly. "And yeah, how can I argue? I can't say that we should go back to the way things were, bring back all the war and disease and shit. I can't say I want the world to burn. I can't even say bring back the slaughterhouses and little birds getting eaten." She turned her head to look at me, her face slack and infinitely weary. "But I can say one thing. I can say that I hate them. I hate them for treating the human race like it was their property. I hate them for making us into something less than human. And most of all I hate them for telling me that I'm not good enough to be a mother." She made a dry, humorless laugh. "People in the old days didn't know how good they had it. Back then, if you didn't like the way God was running the world, you could just stop believing in the old bastard. You didn't have to go through life being angry at him, hating him, wishing he'd get his fucking hands off of your life."

I didn't say it, but I knew she was wrong about that. My mother didn't believe in God, and yet she hated him with a boundless ferocity. She hated the blood-soaked cruelty of nature as if it was an animate thing, and what other name is there for that animate thing if not God? And despite my attempts to be free of her, to be my own person, I was still my mother's son. Her hatred of the old God was still a part of me. So now, with this latest act of the machines—this remaking of the world of nature, this act of compassion, of *tenderness* for all the creatures of the world, I found it impossible not to feel something like love for them.

So Lisa left me, for good and all, this time. There was just too much distance between us. "Irreconcilable differences," as they used to say in court. We were simply lost to each other. I can remember every detail of her face and body, every nuance of expression and every habit of gesture. And yet when I visualize her I see her as a dim, far-off figure, obscured by misty distance, separated from me by a bottomless chasm.

The birds were chirping hello to another day when I left Ivan's and weaved my way upstairs. I was debating whether to make some coffee or just drop into bed when I saw there was a message waiting for me on my screen. It was from Gwen, one of the people who works—or maybe a better term would be hangs out—as voluntary caretaker of the workshop where I get my sculptures scanned, enlarged, and 3-D printed as faux-bronze polymer.

Hey James,
    Our 'bot buddies just delivered a new printer. They also built a whole new wing to the building here to hold it, because

THIS SUCKER IS *BIG*. LIKE, PRINTING OUT SCULPTURES 10 METERS TALL AND 5X5 METERS FOOTPRINT. NOBODY ASKED FOR THIS BEAST, OF COURSE, IT JUST APPEARED OVERNIGHT, THE WAY THINGS DO.

ALSO, SOME NEW EQUIPMENT AND SPEC FILES SHOWED UP AT THE SAME TIME. THEY'RE INSTRUCTIONS AND MATERIALS FOR ATTACHING BIG THINGS TO THE EXTERIOR WALLS OF BUILDINGS, EVEN GLASS-WALLED BUILDINGS LIKE THE HANCOCK TOWER.

SO THE OTHER FOLKS HERE WERE SCRATCHING THEIR HEADS WONDERING WHAT'S UP WITH THIS AND WHAT WE CAN DO WITH IT, BUT NOT ME. MY THOUGHTS WENT STRAIGHT TO YOUR PIECE *GECKOS*, OF WHICH YOU SENT US SOME PICS OF YOUR CLAY ORIGINAL A FEW WEEKS BACK, ASKING IF WE HAD ANY IDEAS ABOUT WHERE YOU MIGHT DO AN INSTALLATION OF A LIFE-SIZE COPY. YOU MAYBE REMEMBER THAT I WROTE YOU BACK SAYING THAT I THOUGHT THIS WAS A REALLY GREAT PIECE, AND IT DESERVED AS BIG AND NOTEWORTHY AN INSTALLATION AS WE COULD MANAGE. WELL, HOW ABOUT A *FIVE TIMES* LIFE SIZE COPY, DUDE? YOU COULD PUT THOSE FIGURES TEN OR TWENTY STORIES UP ON THE SIDE OF THE HANCOCK TOWER! IS THAT AN AWESOME THOUGHT OR WHAT? WE ALL FIGURE THIS MUST BE EXACTLY WHAT THE AIS HAVE IN MIND. NOBODY ELSE AROUND HERE HAS BEEN TALKING ABOUT STICKING ANYTHING BIG ONTO THE OUTSIDE WALL OF A BUILDING, SO THIS DELIVERY HAS *GOT* TO BE THEIR WAY OF GIVING YOU THE GO-AHEAD TO DO THE BIGGEST- AND COOLEST-ASS SCULPTURE INSTALLATION THIS TOWN HAS SEEN SINCE, WELL, FOREVER.

GET BACK TO US QUICK, DUDE, OR JUST SHOW UP WITH YOUR CLAY ORIGINAL. ALL OF US HERE ARE REALLY JAZZED ABOUT FIRING UP THIS BIG PRINTER AND MAKING THIS PROJECT HAPPEN.

YRS. ETC.,
GWEN

I sat staring at the text on the screen for a long time, waiting. Waiting for the good feeling this news should have given me. It didn't come. It didn't come, and it kept on not coming. I got up and pulled the dust cover off of the two clay figures that were *Geckos*. A crazy obsession of a piece; one that I had kept working on, giving up on, trashing and restarting, re-thinking and un-re-thinking, over the past four years. I'd finished plenty of other work, but this was my Big One. It's no *Guernica*, no *Nude Descending a Staircase*, no *Balzac*, but it's as close to all of that as I expected I'd ever get. It was the best thing I'd ever done. It had as much of me in it as I could tear out through my skin. It had my blood and sweat and everything I knew about what's beautiful and true in it. It had my love of Lisa in it, and her love for me.

I visualized the whole installation project to come. There would be six or eight volunteers from the fabrication shop; Gwen, José and Steve, maybe Philipa and her latest partner, probably some others whose names I don't know. There would be the cheerful camaraderie, the enthusiasm of working on a nifty new project. The specs and equipment the AIs had provided would be pondered and discussed carefully in advance, and then we'd set off to the site and do whatever it was we were supposed to do. Set up a scaffold or run cables from a window or whatever. The project would take a while, maybe a few days. And when it was done we'd all look up at it, a big, conspicuous sculpture, visible for miles around, with my name attached to it. The crew of volunteers would grin and pop open beers and congratulate me, still breathless from their exertions.

And it was all a crock of shit. If the machines wanted that sculpture expanded to five times life size and stuck onto the side of the Hancock Tower, they could do it themselves. In hours, maybe minutes or seconds, they could use their nano-assembly trick to make it materialize in place, no human participation required. No camaraderie, no good friends toiling happily together. All of that was crap. It was just their way of putting some stupid humans onto a hamster wheel, running from nowhere to nowhere as fast as their stupid little legs could go.

"Fuck you," I said, talking to the empty room, to the room that would have been empty if there were any such thing as an empty room in the world today. "Fuck you. You can go to hell." I went to the cabinet where I kept my stone-cutting tools and pawed through it until I found the heaviest mallet. "You can all go straight to hell," I said to them, to them, them, *them*, as the room got blurry through my tears.

There's something I never told Lisa. Because it was silly and goofy, and because it wouldn't have made a difference. Because I was afraid she'd laugh at me with that cruel, barbed laugh she used when she was angry enough. It's this: I have seen our child. She doesn't exist and she never will, but I've seen her. She comes to me like a ghost. Standing in a doorway and looking in at me, sitting on a sunlit patch of grass in a park, looking out a window at the huge world that waits for her. I see her as she would be, not yet three years old, all toddling legs and chubby arms; tiny, gentle fingers. I see her eyes looking at me; wonderful eyes that are too wise and too full of no bullshit for a kid her age, and yet innocent. They're eyes that haven't known pain, aren't even sure that pain is a real thing in the world, and yet belie enough strength to endure pain when it comes. They're eyes that are open wide to the whole world, ready for all of it. I see our child; I see her as all the best parts of Lisa and all the best parts of me embodied, walking around, breathing and living. And it rips my fucking heart out every time I see her.

I took the mallet back to where the two clay figures of *Geckos* were standing on their low plinth, and lifted it up over my head, my arm already tasting the long swing downward, the thudding impact on soft clay. "You can all go to—"

I was sitting on the floor, my back to the studio wall. The mallet lay on the floor beside me, near my right hand. A hand that seemed disconnected from me; that only made a vague twitch when I told it to move. As my mind slowly cleared, I became aware of a buzzing, numbing pain through my whole right arm. The bleachy smell of ozone was in the air.

The two figures of *Geckos* were in front of me, but for a few seconds I resisted the urge to lift my eyes to look at them. When I did, I was looking up at my sculpture, unharmed, un-bludgeoned, not smashed into an amorphous lump. I let out a long, shaky breath.

A motion caught my eye. One of the little insect-sized bots was crawling up the wall on my right. Probably it was one of the team I'd seen in Ivan's studio, busily engaged in repairing the building's exterior woodwork. It paused in its climb as I watched it, as if it was looking back at me. How much like a bee it was, I thought, busily going about its little bee life. At that moment the bot flexed itself in an odd way, seeming to expand a little and then shrink again, as if taking a breath. Then it continued up the wall, disappearing into a crack under the frame of a window.

"All right then," I said, climbing to my feet, flexing life and sensation back into my right arm. "Okay."

Sarah Pinsker is the author of the 2015 Nebula Award–winning novelette "Our Lady of the Open Road." Her novelette "In Joy, Knowing the Abyss Behind" was the 2014 Sturgeon Award–winner and a 2013 Nebula finalist. Her fiction has been published in magazines including *Asimov's, Strange Horizons, Lightspeed, Fantasy & Science Fiction,* and *Uncanny,* among others, and numerous anthologies. She is also a singer/songwriter with three albums on various independent labels and a fourth forthcoming. She lives in Baltimore, Maryland, with her wife and dog.

SOONER OR LATER EVERYTHING FALLS INTO THE SEA

Sarah Pinsker

The rock star washed ashore at high tide. Earlier in the day, Bay had seen something bobbing far out in the water. Remnant of a rowboat, perhaps, or something better. She waited until the tide ebbed, checked her traps and tidal pools among the rocks before walking toward the inlet where debris usually beached.

All kinds of things washed up if Bay waited long enough: not just glass and plastic, but personal trainers and croupiers, entertainment directors and dance teachers. This was the first time Bay recognized the face of the new arrival. She always checked the face first if there was one, just in case, hoping it wasn't Deb.

The rock star had an entire lifeboat to herself, complete with motor, though she'd used up the gas. She'd made it in better shape than many; certainly in better shape than those with flotation vests but no boats. They arrived in tatters of uniform. Armless, legless, sometimes headless; ragged shark refuse.

"What was that one?" Deb would have asked, if she were there. She'd never paid attention to physical details, wouldn't have recognized a dancer's legs, a chef's scarred hands and arms.

"Nothing anymore," Bay would say of a bad one, putting it on her sled.

The rock star still had all her limbs. She had stayed in the boat. She'd found the stashed water and nutrition bars, easy to tell by the wrappers and bottles strewn around her. From her bloated belly and cracked lips, Bay guessed she had run out a day or two before, maybe tried drinking ocean water. Sunburn glowed through her dark skin. She was still alive.

Deb wasn't there; she couldn't ask questions. If she had been, Bay would have shown her the calloused fingers of the woman's left hand and the thumb of her right.

"How do you know she came off the ships?" Deb would have asked. She'd been skeptical that the ships even existed, couldn't believe that so many people would just pack up and leave their lives. The only proof Bay could have given was these derelict bodies.

—

Inside the Music: Tell us what happened.

Gabby Robbins: A scavenger woman dragged me from the ocean, pumped water from my lungs, spoke air into me. The old films they show on the ships would call that moment romantic, but it wasn't. I gagged. Only barely managed to roll over to retch in the sand.

She didn't know what a rock star was. It was only when I washed in half-dead, choking seawater that she learned there were such things in the world. Our first attempts at conversation didn't go well. We had no language in common. But I warmed my hands by her fire, and when I saw an instrument hanging on its peg, I tuned it and began to play. That was the first language we spoke between us.

—

A truth: I don't remember anything between falling off the ship and washing up in this place.

There's a lie embedded in that truth.

Maybe a couple of them.

Another lie I've already told: We did have language in common, the scavenger woman and me.

She did put me on her sled, did take me back to her stone-walled cottage on the cliff above the beach. I warmed myself by her woodstove. She didn't offer me a blanket or anything to replace the thin stage clothes I still wore, so I wrapped my own arms around me and drew my knees in tight, and sat close enough to the stove's open belly that sparks hit me when the logs collapsed inward.

She heated a small pot of soup on the stovetop and poured it into a single bowl without laying a second one out for me. My stomach growled. I didn't remember the last time I'd eaten. I eyed her, eyed the bowl, eyed the pot.

"If you're thinking about whether you could knock me out with the pot and take my food, it's a bad idea. You're taller than me, but you're weaker than you think, and I'm stronger than I look."

"I wouldn't! I was just wondering if maybe you'd let me scrape whatever's left from the pot. Please."

She nodded after a moment. I stood over the stove and ate the few mouthfuls she had left me from the wooden stirring spoon. I tasted potatoes and seaweed, salt and land and ocean. It burned my throat going down; heated from the inside, I felt almost warm.

I looked around the room for the first time. An oar with "Home Sweet Home" burnt into it adorned the wall behind the stove. Some chipped dishes on an upturned plastic milk crate, a wall stacked high with home-canned food, clothing on pegs. A slightly warped-looking classical guitar hung on another peg by a leather strap; if I'd had any strength I'd have gone to investigate it. A double bed piled with blankets. Beside the bed, a nightstand with a framed photo of two women on a hiking trail, and a tall stack of paperback books. I had an urge to walk over and read the titles; my father used to say you could judge a person by the books on their shelves. A stronger urge to dive under the covers on the bed, but I resisted and settled back onto the ground near the stove. My energy went into shivering.

I kept my eyes on the stove, as if I could direct more heat to me with enough concentration. The woman puttered around her cabin. She might have been any age between forty and sixty; her movement was easy, but her skin was weathered and lined, her black hair streaked with gray. After a while, she climbed into bed and turned her back to me. Another moment passed before I realized she intended to leave me there for the night.

"Please, before you go to sleep. Don't let it go out," I said. "The fire."

She didn't turn. "Can't keep it going forever. Fuel has to last all winter."

"It's winter?" I'd lost track of seasons on the ship. The scavenger woman wore two layers, a ragged jeans jacket over a hooded sweatshirt.

"Will be soon enough."

"I'll freeze to death without a fire. Can I pay you to keep it going?"

"What do you have to pay me with?"

"I have an account on the Hollywood Line. A big one." As I said that, I realized I shouldn't have. On multiple levels. Didn't matter if it sounded like a brag or desperation. I was at her mercy, and it wasn't in my interest to come across as if I thought I was any better than her.

She rolled over. "Your money doesn't count for anything off your ships and islands. Nor credit. If you've got paper money, I'm happy to throw it in to keep the fire going a little longer."

I didn't. "I can work it off."

"There's nothing you can work off. Fuel is in finite supply. I use it now, I don't get more, I freeze two months down the line."

"Why did you save me if you're going to let me die?"

"Pulling you from the water made sense. It's your business now whether you live or not."

"Can I borrow something warmer to wear at least? Or a blanket?" I sounded whiny even to my own ears.

She sighed, climbed out of bed, rummaged in a corner, and pulled out a down vest. It had a tear in the back where some stuffing had spilled out, and smelled like brine. I put it on, trying not to scream when the fabric touched my sunburned arms.

"Thank you. I'm truly grateful."

She grunted a response and retreated to her bed again. I tucked my elbows into the vest, my hands into my armpits. It helped a little, though I still shivered. I waited a few minutes, then spoke again. She didn't seem to want to talk, but it kept me warm. Reassured me that I was still here. Awake, alive.

"If I didn't say so already, thank you for pulling me out of the water. My name is Gabby."

"Fitting."

"Are you going to ask me how I ended up in the water?"

"None of my business."

Just as well. Anything I told her would've been made up.

"Do you have a name?" I asked.

"I do, but I don't see much point in sharing it with you."

"Why not?"

"Because I'm going to kill you if you don't shut up and let me sleep."

I shut up.

—

Inside the Music: Tell us what happened.

Gabby Robbins: I remember getting drunk during a set on the Elizabeth Taylor. *Making out with a bartender in the lifeboat, since neither of us had private bunks. I must have passed out there. I don't know how it ended up adrift.*

———

I survived the night on the floor but woke with a cough building deep in my chest. At least I didn't have to sing. I followed the scavenger as she went about her morning, like a dog hoping for scraps. Outside, a large picked-over garden spread around two sides of the cottage. The few green plants grew low and ragged. Root vegetables, maybe.

"If you have to piss, there's an outhouse over there," she said, motioning toward a stand of twisted trees.

We made our way down the footpath from her cottage to the beach, a series of switchbacks trod into the cliffside. I was amazed she had managed to tow me up such an incline. Then again, if I'd rolled off the sled and fallen to my death, she probably would've scraped me out of my clothes and left my body to be picked clean by gulls.

"Where are we?" I had managed not to say anything since waking up, not a word since her threat the night before, so I hoped the statute of limitations had expired.

"Forty kilometers from the nearest city, last I checked."

Better than nothing. "When was that?"

"When I walked here."

"And that was?"

"A while ago."

It must have been, given the lived in look of her cabin and garden. "What city?"

"Portage."

"Portage what?"

"Portage. Population I don't know. Just because you haven't heard of it doesn't make it any less a city." She glanced back at me like I was stupid.

"I mean, what state? Or what country? I don't even know what country this is."

She snorted. "How long were you on that ship?"

"A long time. I didn't really pay attention."

"Too rich to care."

"No! It's not what you think." I didn't know why it mattered what she thought of me, but it did. "I wasn't on the ship because I'm rich. I'm an entertainer. I share a staff bunk with five other people."

"You told me last night you were rich."

I paused to hack and spit over the cliff's edge. "I have money, it's true. But not enough to matter. I'll never be rich enough to be a passenger instead of entertainment. I'll never even afford a private stateroom. So I spend a little and let the rest build up in my account."

Talking made me cough more. I was thirsty, too, but waited to be offered something to drink.

"What's your name?" I knew I should shut up, but the more uncomfortable I am, the more I talk.

She didn't answer for a minute, so by the time she did, I wasn't even sure if it was the answer to my question at all. "Bay."

"That's your name? It's lovely. Unusual."

"How would you know? You don't even know what country this is. Who are you to say what's unusual here?"

"Good point. Sorry."

"You're lucky we even speak the same language."

"Very."

She pointed at a trickle of water that cut a small path down the cliff wall. "Cup your hands there. It's potable."

"A spring?"

She gave me a look.

"Sorry. Thank you." I did as she said. The water was cold and clear. If there was some bacterium in it that was going to kill me, at least I wouldn't die thirsty.

I showed my gratitude through silence and concentrated on the descent. The path was narrow, just wide enough for the sled she pulled, and the edge crumbled away to nothing. I put my feet where she put hers, squared my shoulders as she did. She drew her sweatshirt hood over her head, another discouragement to conversation.

We made it all the way down to the beach without another question busting through my chapped lips. She left the sled at the foot of the cliff and picked up a blue plastic cooler from behind a rock, the kind with cup holders built into the top. She looked in and frowned, then dumped the whole thing on the rocks. A cascade of water, two small dead fish. I realized those had probably been meant to be her dinner the day before; she had chosen to haul me up the cliff instead.

This section of beach was all broken rock, dotted everywhere with barnacles and snails and seashells. The rocks were wet and slick, the footing treacherous. I fell to my hands several times, slicing them on the tiny snails. Could you catch anything from a snail cut? At least the ship could still get us antibiotics.

"What are we doing?" I asked. "Surely the most interesting things wash out closer to the actual water."

She kept walking, watching where she stepped. She didn't fall. The rusted hull of an old ship jutted from the rocks down into the ocean; I imagined anything inside had long since been picked over. We clambered around it. I fell further behind her, trying to be more careful with my bleeding palms. All that rust, no more tetanus shots.

She slowed, squatted. Peered and poked at something by her feet. As I neared her, I understood. Tidal pools. She dipped the cooler into one, smiled to herself. I was selfishly glad to see the smile. Perhaps she'd be friendlier now.

Instead of following, I took a different path from hers. Peered into other pools. Some tiny fish in the first two, not worth catching, nothing in the third. In the fourth, I found a large crab.

"Bay," I called.

She turned around, annoyance plain on her face. I waved the crab and her expression softened. "Good for you. You get to eat tonight too, with a nice find like that."

She waited for me to catch up with her and put the crab in her cooler with the one decent-sized fish she had found.

"What is it?" I asked.

"A fish. What does it matter what kind?"

"I used to cook. I'm pretty good with fish, but I don't recognize that one. Different fish taste better with different preparations."

"You're welcome to do the cooking if you'd like, but if you need lemon butter and capers, you may want to check the pools closer to the end of the rainbow." She pointed down the beach, then laughed at her own joke.

"I'm only trying to be helpful. You don't need to mock me."

"No, I suppose I don't. You found a crab, so you're not entirely useless."

That was the closest thing to a compliment I supposed I'd get. At least she was speaking to me like a person, not debris that had shown an unfortunate tendency toward speech.

That evening, I pan-fried our catch on the stovetop with a little bit of sea salt. The fish was oily and tasteless, but the crab was good. My hands smelled like fish and ocean and I wished for running water to wash them off. Tried to replace that smell with wood smoke.

After dinner, I looked over at her wall.

"May I?" I asked, pointing at the guitar.

She shrugged. "Dinner and entertainment—I fished the right person out of the sea. Be my guest."

It was an old classical guitar, parlor sized, nylon-stringed. That was the first blessing, since steel strings would surely have corroded in this air. I had no pure pitch to tune to, so had to settle on tuning the strings relative to each other, all relative to the third string because its tuning peg was cracked and useless. Sent up a silent prayer that none of the strings broke, since I was fairly sure Bay would blame me for anything that went wrong in my presence. The result sounded sour, but passable.

"What music do you like?" I asked her.

"Now or then?"

"What's the difference?"

"Then: anything political. Hip-hop, mostly."

I looked down at the little guitar, wondered how to coax hip-hop out of it. "What about now?"

"Now? Anything you play will be the first music I've heard other than my own awful singing in half a dozen years. Play away."

I nodded and looked at the guitar, waiting for it to tell me what it wanted. Fought back my strange sudden shyness. Funny how playing for thousands of people didn't bother me, but I could find myself self-conscious in front of one. "Guitar isn't my instrument, by the way."

"Close enough. You're a bassist."

I looked up, surprised. "How do you know?"

"I'm not stupid. I know who you are."

"Why did you ask my name, then?"

"I didn't. You told it to me."

"Oh, yeah." I was glad I hadn't lied about that particular detail.

"Let's have the concert, then."

I played her a few songs, stuff I never played on the ship.

"Where'd the guitar come from?" I asked when I was done.

An unreadable expression crossed her face. "Where else? It washed up."

I let my fingers keep exploring the neck of the guitar, but turned to her. "So is this what you do full time? Pull stuff from the beach?"

"Pretty much."

"Can you survive on that?"

"The bonuses for finding some stuff can be pretty substantial."

"What stuff?"

"Foil. Plastic. People."

"People?"

"People who've lost their ships."

"You're talking about me?"

"You, others. The ships don't like to lose people, and the people don't like to be separated from their ships. It's a nice change to be able to return someone living for once. I'm sure you'll be happy to get back to where you belong."

"Yes, thank you. How do you alert them?"

"I've got call buttons for the three big shiplines. They send 'copters."

I knew those copters. Sleek, repurposed military machines.

I played for a while longer, so stopping wouldn't seem abrupt, then hung the guitar back on its peg. It kept falling out of tune anyway.

I waited until Bay was asleep before I left, though it took all my will-power not to take off running the second she mentioned the helicopters. I had nothing to pack, so I curled up by the cooling stove and waited for her breathing to slow. I would never have taken her food or clothing—other than the vest—but I grabbed the guitar from its peg on my way out the door. She wouldn't miss it. The door squealed on its hinges, and I held my breath as I slipped through and closed it behind me.

The clifftop was bright with stars. I scanned the sky for helicopters. Nothing but stars and stars and stars. The ship's lights made it so we barely saw stars at all, a reassurance for all of us from the cities.

I walked with my back to the cliff. The moon gave enough light to reassure me I wasn't about to step off into nothingness if the coastline cut in, but I fig-ured the farther I got from the ocean, the more likely I was to run into trees. Or maybe an abandoned house, if I got lucky. Someplace they wouldn't spot me if they swept overland.

Any hope I had for stealth, I abandoned as I trudged onward. I found an old tar road and decided it had to lead toward something. I walked. The cough that had been building in my chest through the day racked me now.

The farther I went, the more I began to doubt Bay's story. Would the ships bother to send anyone? I was popular enough, but was I worth the fuel it took to come get me? If they thought I had fallen, maybe. If they knew I had lowered the lifeboat deliberately, that I might do it again? Doubtful. Unless they wanted to punish me, or charge me for the boat, though if they docked my account now, I'd never know. And how would Bay have contacted them? She'd said they were in contact, but unless she had a solar charger—well, that seemed possible, actually.

Still, she obviously wanted me gone or she wouldn't have said it. Or was she testing my reaction? Waiting to see if I cheered the news of my rescue?

I wondered what else she had lied about. I hoped I was walking toward the city she had mentioned. I was a fool to think I'd make it to safety anywhere. I had no water, no food, no money. Those words formed a marching song for my feet, syncopated by my cough. No water. No food. No money. No luck.

Bay set out at first light, the moment she realized the guitar had left with the stupid rock star. It wasn't hard to figure out which way she had gone. She was feverish, stupid with the stupidity of someone still used to having things appear when she wanted them. If she really expected to survive, she should have taken more from Bay. Food. A canteen. A hat. Something to trade when she got to the city. It said something good about her character, Bay supposed, down below the blind privilege of her position. If she hadn't taken Debra's guitar, Bay's opinion might have been even more favorable.

—

Inside the Music: Tell us what happened.

Gabby Robbins: My last night on the ship was just like three thousand nights before, up until it wasn't. We played two sets, mostly my stuff, with requests mixed in. Some cokehead in a Hawaiian shirt offered us a thousand credits each to play "My Heart Will Go On" for his lady.

"I'll give you ten thousand credits myself if you don't make us do this," Sheila said when we all leaned in over her kit to consult on whether we could fake our way through it. "That's the one song I promised myself I would never play here."

"What about all the Jimmy Buffet we've had to play?" our guitarist, Kel, asked her. "We've prostituted ourselves already. What difference does it make at this point?"

Sheila ignored Kel. "Dignity, Gab. Please."

I was tired and more than a little drunk. "What does it matter? Let's just play the song. You can mess with the tempo if you want. Swing it, maybe? Ironic cheesy lounge style? In C, since I can't hit those diva notes?"

Sheila looked like she was going to weep as she counted off.

I ran into Hawaiian Shirt and his lady again after the set, when I stepped out on the Oprah deck for air. They were over near the gun turrets, doing the "King of the World" thing, a move that should have been outlawed before anyone got on the ship.

"You know who that is, right?" I looked over to see JP, this bartender I liked: sexy retro-Afro, sexy swimmer's build. It had been a while since we'd hooked up. JP held out a joint.

I took it and said he looked familiar.

"He used to have one of those talk radio shows. He was the first one to suggest the ships, only his idea was religious folks, not just general rich folks. Leave the sinners behind, he said. Founded the Ark line, where all those fundamentalists

spend their savings waiting for the sinners to be washed away so they can take the land back. He spent the first two years with them, then announced he was going to go on a pilgrimage to find out what was happening everywhere else. Only, instead of traveling the land like a proper pilgrim, he came on board this ship. He's been here ever since. First time I've seen him at one of your shows, though. I guess he's throwing himself into his new lifestyle."

"Ugh. I remember him now. He boycotted my second album. At least they look happy?"

"Yeah, except that isn't his wife. His wife and kids are still on the Ark waiting for him. Some pilgrim."

The King of the World and his not-wife sauntered off. When the joint was finished, JP melted away as well, leaving me alone with my thoughts until some drunk kids wandered over with a magnum of champagne. I climbed over the railing into the lifeboat to get a moment alone. I could almost pretend the voices were gulls. Listened to the engine's thrum through the hull, the waves lapping far below.

Everyone who wasn't a paying guest—entertainers and staff—had been trained on how to release the lifeboats, and I found myself playing with the controls. How hard would it be to drop it into the water? We couldn't be that far from some shore somewhere. The lifeboats were all equipped with stores of food and water, enough for a handful of people for a few days.

Whatever had been in my last drink must have been some form of liquid stupid. The boat was lowered now, whacking against the side of the enormous ship, and I had to smash the last tie just to keep from being wrecked against it. And then the ship was pulling away, ridiculous and huge, a foolish attempt to save something that had never been worth saving.

I wished I had kissed JP one more time, seeing as how I was probably going to die.

—

Gabby hadn't gotten far at all. By luck, she had found the road in the dark, and by luck had walked in the right direction, but she was lying in the dirt like roadkill now. Bay checked that Deb's guitar hadn't been hurt, then watched for a moment to see if the woman was breathing, which she was, ragged but steady, her forehead hot enough to melt butter, some combination of sunburn and fever.

The woman stirred. "Are you real?" she asked.

"More real than you are," Bay told her.

"I should have kissed JP."

"Seems likely." Bay offered a glass jar of water. "Drink this."

Gabby drank half. "Thank you."

Bay waved it away when the other woman tried to hand it back. "I'm not putting my lips to that again while you're coughing your lungs out. It's yours."

"Thank you again." Gabby held out the guitar. "You probably came for this?"

"You carried it this far, you can keep carrying it. Me, I would have brought the case."

"It had a case?"

"Under the bed. I keep clothes in it."

"I guess at least now you know I didn't go through your things?"

Bay snorted. "Obviously. You're a pretty terrible thief."

"In my defense, I'm not a thief."

"My guitar says otherwise."

Gabby put the guitar on the ground. She struggled to her feet and stood for a wobbly moment before leaning down to pick it up. She looked one way, then the other, as if she couldn't remember where she had come from or where she was going. Bay refrained from gesturing in the right direction. She picked the right way. Bay followed.

"Are you going to ask me why I left?" Even this sick, with all her effort going into putting one foot in front of the other, the rock star couldn't stop talking.

"Wasn't planning on it."

"Why not?"

"Because I've met you before."

"For real? Before the ships?" Gabby looked surprised.

Bay shook her head. "No. Your type. You think you're the first one to wash ashore? To step away from that approximation of life? You're just the first one who made it alive."

"If you don't like the ships, why did you call them to come get me?" Gabby paused. "Or you didn't. You just wanted me to leave. Why?"

"I can barely feed myself. And you aren't the type to be satisfied with that life anyhow. Might as well leave now as later."

"Except I'm probably going to die of this fever because I walked all night in the cold, you psychopath."

Bay shrugged. "That was your choice."

They walked in silence for a while. The rock star was either contemplating her choices or too sick to talk.

"Why?" Bay asked, taking pity.

Gabby whipped her head around. "Why what?"

"Why did you sign up for the ship?"

"It seemed like a good idea at the time."

"Sounds like an epitaph fitting for half the people in this world."

Gabby gave a half smile, then continued. "New York was a mess, and the Gulf states had just tried to secede. The bookers for the Hollywood Line made a persuasive argument for a glamorous life at sea. Everything was so well planned, too. They bought entire island nations to provide food and fuel."

"I'm sure the island nations appreciated that," said Bay.

The other woman gave a wry smile. "I know, right? Fucked up. But they offered good money, and it was obvious no bands would be touring the country for a while.

"At first it was just like any other tour. We played our own stuff. There were women to sleep with, drugs if we wanted them, restaurants and clubs and gyms. All the good parts of touring without the actual travel part. Sleeping in the same bed every night, even if it was still a bunk with my band, like on the bus. But then it didn't stop, and then they started making us take requests, and it started closing in, you know? If there was somebody you wanted to avoid, you couldn't. It was hard to find anyplace to be alone to write or think.

"Then the internet went off completely. We didn't get news from land at all, even when we docked on the islands. They stopped letting us off when we docked. Management said things had gotten real bad here, that there was for real nothing to come back to anymore. The passengers all walked around like they didn't care, like a closed system, and the world was so fucking far away. How was I supposed to write anything when the world was so far away? The entire world might've drowned, and we'd just float around oblivious until we ran out of something that wasn't even important to begin with. Somebody would freak out because there was no more mascara or ecstasy or rosemary, and then all those beautiful people would turn on each other."

"So that's why you jumped?"

Gabby rubbed her head. "Sort of. I guess that also seemed like a good idea at the time."

"What about now?"

"I could've done with a massage when I woke up today, but I'm still alive."

Bay snorted. "You wouldn't have lasted two seconds in a massage with that sunburn."

Gabby looked down at her forearms and winced.

They walked. Gabby was sweating, her eyes bright. Bay slowed her own pace, in an effort to slow the other woman down. "Where are you hurrying to, now that I've told you there's nobody coming after you?"

"You said there was a city out here somewhere. I want to get there before I have to sleep another night on this road. And before I starve."

Bay reached into a jacket pocket. She pulled out a protein bar and offered it to Gabby.

"Where'd you get that? It looks like the ones I ate in the lifeboat."

"It is."

Gabby groaned. "I didn't have to starve those last two days? I could've sworn I looked every place."

"You missed a stash inside the radio console."

"Huh."

They kept walking, footsteps punctuated by Gabby's ragged breath.

"We used to drive out here to picnic on the cliff when my wife and I first got married," Bay said. "There were always turtles trying to cross. We would stop and help them, because there were teenagers around who thought driving over them was a sport. Now if I saw a turtle I'd probably have to think about eating it."

"I've never eaten a turtle."

"Me neither. Haven't seen one in years."

Gabby stopped. "You know, I have no clue when I last saw a turtle. At a zoo? No clue at all. I wonder if they're gone. Funny how you don't realize the last time you see something is going to be the last time."

Bay didn't say anything.

The rock star held Deb's guitar up to her chest, started picking out a repetitive tune as she walked. Same lick over and over, like it was keeping her going, driving her feet. "So when you said you traded things like aluminum foil and people, you were lying to me, right? You don't trade anything."

Bay shook her head. "Nobody to trade with."

"So you've been here all alone? You said something about your wife."

Bay kicked a stone down the road in front of her, kicked it again when she caught up with it.

The rock star handed her the guitar and dropped to the ground. She took off her left shoe, then peeled the sock off. A huge blister was rising on her big toe. "Fuck."

Bay sighed. "You can use some of the stuffing from your vest to build some space around it."

Gabby bent to pick a seam.

"No need. There's a tear in the back. Anyhow, maybe it's time to stop for the night."

"Sorry. I saw the tear when you first gave me the vest, but I forgot about it. How far have we traveled?"

"Hard to say. We're still on the park road."

"Park road?"

"This is a protected wilderness area. Or it was. Once we hit asphalt, we're halfway there. Then a little farther to a junction. Left at the T used to be vacation homes, but a hurricane took them twenty years ago. Right takes you to the city."

Gabby groaned. She squinted at the setting sun. "Not even halfway."

"But you're still alive, and you're complaining about a blister, not the cough or the sunburn."

"I didn't complain."

"I don't see you walking any farther, either." Bay dropped her knapsack and untied a sleeping bag from the bottom.

"I don't suppose you have two?"

Bay gave Gabby her most withering look. What kind of fool set out on this walk sick and unprepared? Then again, she had been the one who had driven the woman out, too afraid to interact with an actual person instead of the ghosts in her head.

"We'll both fit," she said. "Body heat'll keep us warm, too."

It was warmer than if they hadn't shared, lying back to back squeezed into the sleeping bag. Not as warm as home, if she hadn't set out to follow. The cold still seeped into her. Bay felt every inch of her left side, as if the bones themselves were in contact with the ground. Aware, too, of her back against the other woman, of the fact that she couldn't remember the last time she had come in physical contact with a living person. The heat of Gabby's fever burned through the layers of clothing, but she still shivered.

"Why are you living out there all alone?" Gabby asked.

Bay considered pretending she was asleep, but then she wanted to answer. "I said already we used to picnic out here, my wife and I. We always said this was where we'd spend our old age. I'd get a job as a ranger, we'd live out our days in the ranger's cabin. I pictured having electricity, mind."

She paused. She felt the tension in the other woman's back as she suppressed a cough. "Debra was in California on a business trip when everything started going bad at a faster rate than it'd been going bad before. We never even found out what it was that messed up the electronics. Things just stopped working. We'd been living in a high-rise. I couldn't stay in our building with no heat or water, but we couldn't contact each other, and I wanted to be someplace Debra would find me. So when I didn't hear from her for three months, I packed what I thought I might need into some kid's wagon I found in the lobby and started walking. I knew she'd know to find me out here if she could."

"How bad was it? The cities? We were already on the ship."

"I can only speak for the one I was living in, but it wasn't like those scare movies where everyone turns on one another. People helped each other. We got some electricity up and running again in a couple weeks' time, on a much smaller scale. If anything, I'd say we had more community than we'd ever had. But it didn't feel right for me. I didn't want other people; I wanted Deb."

"They told us people were rioting and looting. Breaking into mansions, moving dozens of people in."

"Would you blame them? Your passengers redirected all the gas to their ships and abandoned perfectly good houses. But again, I can only speak to what I saw, which was folks figuring out the new order and making it work as best they could."

Gabby stayed silent for a while, and Bay started to drift. Then one more question. "Did Debra ever find you? I mean I'm guessing no, but . . ."

"No. Now let me sleep."

—

Inside the Music: Tell us what happened.

Gabby Robbins: You know what happened. There is no you anymore. No reality television, no celebrity gossip, no music industry. Only an echo playing itself out on the ships and in the heads of those of us who can't quite let it go.

—

Bay was already out of the sleeping bag when I woke. She sat on a rock playing a simple fingerpicking pattern on her guitar.

"I thought you didn't play," I called to her.

"Never said that. Said I'm a lousy singer, but didn't say anything about playing the guitar. We should get moving. I'd rather get to the city earlier than late."

I stood up and stretched, letting the sleeping bag pool around my feet. The sun had only just risen, low and red. I could hear water lapping on both sides now, beyond a thick growth of brush. I coughed so deep it bent me in two.

"Why are you in a hurry?" I asked when I could speak.

She gave me a look that probably could have killed me at closer range. "Because I didn't bring enough food to feed both of us for much longer, and you didn't bring any. Because I haven't been there in years and I don't know if they shoot strangers who ride in at night."

"Oh." There wasn't much to say to that, but I tried anyway. "So basically you're putting yourself in danger because I put myself in danger because you made me think I was in danger."

"You put yourself in danger in the first place by jumping off your damn boat."

True. I sat back down on the sleeping bag and inspected my foot. The blister looked awful. I nearly wept as I packed vest-stuffing around it.

I stood again to indicate my readiness, and she walked back over. She handed me the guitar, then shook out the sleeping bag, rolled it, and tied it to her pack. She produced two vaguely edible-looking sticks from somewhere on her person. I took the one offered to me.

I sniffed it. "Fish jerky?"

She nodded.

"I really would've starved out here on my own."

"You're welcome."

"Thank you. I mean it. I'd never have guessed I'd have to walk so long without finding anything to eat."

"There's plenty to eat, but you don't know where to look. You could fish if you had gear. You might find another crab. And there are bugs. Berries and plants, too, in better seasons, if you knew what to look for."

As we walked she meandered off the road to show me what was edible. Cattail roots, watercress. Neither tasted fantastic raw, but chewing took time and gave an excuse to walk slower.

"I'm guessing you were a city kid?" she asked.

"Yeah. Grew up in Detroit. Ran away when I was sixteen to Pittsburgh because everyone else ran away to New York. Put together a decent band, got noticed. When you're a good bass player, people take you out. I'd release an album with my band, tour that, then tour with Gaga or Trillium or some flavor of the month."

I realized that was more than she had asked for, but she hadn't told me to shut up yet, so I kept going. "The funny thing about being on a ship with all those celebrities and debutantes is how much attention they need. They throw parties or they stage big collapses and recoveries. They produce documentaries about themselves, upload to the ship entertainment systems. They act as audience for each other, taking turns with their dramas.

"I thought they'd treat me as a peer, but then I realized I was just a hired gun and they all thought they were bigger deals than me. There were a few other entertainers who realized the same thing and dropped down to the working decks to teach rich kids to dance or sing or whatever. I hung onto the idea longer than most that my music still meant something. I still kinda hope so."

A coughing spell turned me inside out.

"That's why you took my guitar?" Bay asked when I stopped gagging.

"Yeah. They must still need music out here, right?"

"I'd like to think so."

I had something else to say, but a change in the landscape up ahead distracted me. Two white towers jutted into the sky, one vertical, the other at a deep curve. "That's a weird looking bridge."

Bay picked up her pace. I limped after her. As we got closer, I saw the bridge wasn't purposefully skewed. The tower on the near end still stood, but the road between the two had crumbled into the water. Heavy cables trailed from the far tower like hair. We walked to the edge, looked down at the concrete bergs below us, then out at the long gap to the other side. Bay sat down, her feet dangling over the edge.

I tried to keep things light. "I didn't realize we were on an island."

"Your grasp of geography hasn't proven to be outstanding."

"How long do you think it's been out?"

"How the hell should I know?" she snapped.

I left her to herself and went exploring. When I returned, the tears that smudged her face looked dry.

"It must've been one of the hurricanes. I haven't been out here in years." Her tone was dry and impersonal again. "Just goes to show, sooner or later everything falls into the sea."

"She didn't give up on you," I said.

"You don't know that."

"No."

I was quiet a minute. Tried to see it all from her eyes. "Anyway, I walked around. You can climb down the embankment. It doesn't look like there's much current. Maybe a mile's swim?"

She looked up at me. "A mile's swim, in clothes, in winter, with a guitar. Then we still have to walk the rest of the way, dripping wet. You're joking."

"I'm not joking. I'm only trying to help."

"There's no way. Not now. Maybe when the water and the air are both warmer."

She was probably right. She'd been right about everything else. I sat down next to her and looked at the twisted tower. I tried to imagine what Detroit or Pittsburgh was like now, if they were all twisted towers and broken bridges, or if newer, better communities had grown, like the one Bay had left.

"I've got a boat," I said. "There's no fuel but you have an oar on your wall. We can line it full of snacks when the weather is better, and come around the coast instead of over land."

"If I don't kill you before then. You talk an awful lot."

"But I can play decent guitar," I said. "And I found a crab once, so I'm not entirely useless."

"Not entirely," she said.

—

Inside the Music: Tell us what happened.

Gabby Robbins: I was nearly lost, out on the ocean, but somebody rescued me. It's a different life, a smaller life. I'm writing again. People seem to like my new stuff.

—

Bay took a while getting to her feet. She slung her bag over her shoulder, and waited while Gabby picked up Deb's guitar. She played as they walked back toward Bay's cottage, some little riff Bay didn't recognize. Bay made up her own words to it in her head, about how sooner or later everything falls into the sea, but some things crawl back out again and turn into something new.

Margaret Ronald is the author of the Hunt series (*Spiral Hunt, Wild Hunt,* and *Soul Hunt*) as well as a number of short stories. Originally from rural Indiana, she now lives outside Boston. This story is dedicated to her parents.

AND THEN, ONE DAY, THE AIR
WAS FULL OF VOICES

Margaret Ronald

It's near the end of the first day of the conference when Randall shows up. I'm in the middle of the "End of a Zeitgeist" panel, waiting for one of the other panelists to wind up an interminable digression about SETI, when I see him at the back of the room, checking his glass. I meet his eyes, just long enough to acknowledge that he's there, and he nods. He's wearing a badge; he must have paid the money for a one-day pass, even though he can't stand Coronal academics and the fringe element even less. Got enough of one from me, and enough of the other from Wallace, I'd guess.

The other panelist—I've forgotten his name—isn't winding up, and because he's remoting in he doesn't notice the moderator casting irritated glances at him. "The mistake we've always made, it seems to me, is that we have always assumed that communication must be the same no matter whether human or xenosapient. The Corona Borealis informational space proved the exact opposite."

"That isn't exactly true," I interrupt. The panelist blinks; he must have assumed that I was zoning out. Safe assumption, these days. "The actual transmissions found in Coronal infospace are remarkably similar to what you'd find in a thirty-year slice of human broadcast media—in fact, what we find in most recorded communication: lists, transactions, announcements, stories. The context is different, but the content is similar. It was the method that was opaque."

He splutters, ready to argue. But the moderator's still young enough to be nostalgic, and she doesn't like him any more than I do. "Speaking of opacity, Dr. Kostia, it's really been your metaphor that's driven most of our understanding of Coronal transmissions. Would you care to recapitulate it?"

I glance at Randall and decide against drawing it out. "You've got to leave me something for the closing keynote," I say, and get a chuckle from somewhere in the audience. "It's a story for another time."

Wrong choice of words. I can see that in the faces of the front row. The stories have all been told. The stories are all gone now.

"Imagine a man in a bright room," I say. It's two days later, I'm giving the ending keynote, and *bright room* is a little too on-the-nose for where I am currently standing. I can barely see the edge of the stage past the lights, and I can only assume my images are up on the screens. "He wanders around the room, calling out, and wonders why there is no answer from outside. On that basis, he assumes that outside must be empty."

Randall isn't here. I hope he's home, with Brendan and the girls. I hope he's had the sense to ignore all of this. I know I don't have to hope, because Randall has always been the quietly sensible one of us, the one who empathized and cared and knew that the best thing to do was to steer his own ship. The Coronals had heroes like him, I know.

My breath catches in my throat. "Imagine that man," I say again, and swallow. "And then, imagine his realization that if he stands close to the glass of his walls, blocking the glare of his lights, he can see through them. And there is someone on the other side, waving."

Randall waits for me to make my way to him through the departing audience. "Hello, Randall," I say, and reach out for a hug.

He pulls me in, almost off my feet. "Hi, Ma." It feels like hugging a cinderblock in a sweater.

"Oof. Give me my ribs back, won't you? How's Brendan? How are the girls?"

"He's fine. Sinny made a picture for you—I should have brought it, I wasn't thinking." He shoves both hands in his pockets, checks his glass again. "Ma, have you heard from Wally at all?"

"I'm rarely in touch with Wallace," I say breezily, and it doesn't even begin to mask the sting. "I'd hoped we'd see him at Thanksgiving this year."

"Yeah, that's—I'd hoped so too, but he's . . ." He raises both hands as if to offer me something, then lowers them. "You know he's with one of the—these groups." He nods to some of the one-day attendees, two wearing carefully reconstructed Coronal jewelry, one with her ears pinned forward in what some idiot has claimed must be some resemblance to the Coronal cranial shape. There are always a few at any conference, but these are as hollow-eyed as the rest of us, their hope as extinguished as the empty lanterns some carry (a reference to a Coronal song cycle, and likely mistranslated). "Like the ones he was with in high school. And college."

I take a long, slow breath and let it out. College was news to me; I thought he'd gotten away from the cults when he left high school. "You think I'm likely to see him here? That'd be lovely. I mean it; I'd love to see him before November."

"No, I mean—not like the dress-up-and-sing-songs people. The group he's with sounds, well, kind of scary-intense." He lowers his voice. "Ma, he asked me if I had any access to Granma's old cloud. I mean, I get descendant-right requests all the time, but they're all from, you know." He nods to the girls and to the man behind them holding a mandala-patterned banner. I think of Virginia and Denmark, and shiver. "And if he's asking me, it has to be something that he doesn't have first full descendant-right to, so it's probably one of the ones Granma shut off from immediate request. Like the, the original Coronal code."

I do the thing with the breath again. "That's . . . not good."

"Even if it's nothing, I think—he sounded down, Ma. Real depressed, like back in high school. And I think about the, the news out of Virginia—"

"Hush." I put my fingertips to his lips. The room's emptied out, but more people will be coming in shortly, and right now no one wants to think about mass suicides. The fringe because they want to distinguish themselves from that level of crazy; the academics because we're guiltily aware we've contributed to it. "You really think he might?"

"I don't know. I've never been able to tell, with him." Poor sensible Randall, beset on either side by the Coronals. "I know you can, though."

To my shame, I think seriously about telling him I can't go. It's the middle of the conference, after all, and I have two more panels in the next couple of days, never mind the closing keynote. And it's not like this conference will be happening again. "Where is he?" I finally ask.

"On the coast." I feel my glass twitch with the information he's sent over. "It's about a day's drive. I'd go, but you know he doesn't listen to me. Well, he listens, but it's not like he lets it make a difference."

I can make it there and back before the closing keynote. Assuming nothing goes wrong. Assuming it's not too late already. "Come on. Help me check my car back out."

"For those of you who were around for the initial signal—that's, what, half of us?—you remember how much of a shift it was. Here we were, going along in our bright room, and suddenly this signal from ADS 9731 in Corona Borealis starts rewriting an entire high performance computing center." I've told the story about that day so many times, and I'm suddenly tired of telling it. It's the embellished version, anyway; I mostly knew something was up because the power went out in the base and I couldn't play Puppy Duel on my dad's tablet until it recharged. But the story made a good introduction, and I could still remember Mom's face when she came out of lockdown.

"Danforth and Rajasthani were the first ones who realized that the initial signal wasn't an attack. It was, and is, the closest thing we have to semisapient code. When the signal came in contact—and by which I mean when it was recorded, replayed, and analyzed in an appropriately complex context—it did exactly what it was supposed to do. It changed our world, though that was really more of a side effect."

Someone laughs, nervously. I ignore it. "What it did was to rewrite its surroundings—the computing center—and turn it into a receiver for Coronal infospace." And then go dormant, for which my mother was grateful every day of her life. The signal in its dormant form was usable, understandable, replicable to the point that just about anyone could make their own access to infospace—and it didn't go trying to rewrite anything. Mom once told me that some idiot had attempted to encode the Coronal signal into human DNA to see if it would perceive that as an informational context. Lucky for us all, either the semisapient code deemed it not complex enough or detected significant harm done in potential rewrite, so it just fizzled. But it gave her, and then me, nightmares.

"There was one metaphor—I'm glad it wasn't mine—that it was like giving a radio to a 'savage.' Strip away the racism, and there's a grain of truth: because we had never known about infospace, we'd assumed there was nothing to hear. But now we switch that radio on, and we find that what was silence is now chatter. The air is full of voices. Strange voices, from four hundred light-years away."

They've heard this before. Those voices are why they are here.

"Incomprehensible voices, mind you. Do any of you remember those first few translations? I think someone set them to a dance remix when I was in junior high. But the second genius of the initial transmission was that it didn't just convert itself into an infospace receiver; it made itself a translator for whatever linguistic context it was in. All of the Coronal communications—all of the drama, news, bulletins, pleas, shopping lists, everything that went out into their infospace—was so much clearer when viewed through multiple translations.

"With every language I learned, I was able to focus my understanding of Coronal broadcasts, get a better sense of their original meaning. I would imagine the same holds true for most of us in this room. For decades, we have had the entire infospace of an alien civilization to investigate. And look at all the things we found!"

I hold up the program, read a few names of papers. It's a cheap trick, meant to make people feel as if their work hasn't been for naught. I'd planned to say more about the smaller discoveries, the paths that Coronal Studies have made, as if I were pleading before the university trustees again not to disband the department. I don't have it in me, now. My joints hurt from travel; my throat from shouting, even now; my eyes just hurt. I drop the program, and it slides off the stage. Somewhere behind me, I can almost hear the conference organizers frowning.

"And yet there's so much we don't know." And won't, now. "We do not know what it means that so many of their family sagas ended mid-childbirth scene. Nor why their military might was measured in what translated to most Earth languages as *moons*. I personally have always wondered why in the Interleaf broadcast, the speaker repeats *You are my taste, my tongue, my scenting organ*. It obviously meant something. But like an inscription in a secondhand book, that meaning is lost."

So much of what I've had from my second son has been secondhand. So much lost.

Randall apologizes again for not bringing Sinny's drawing, asks what I'm going to do now that the department is closing. I haven't told him my real plans. I think once he finds out, he'll be just as worried about me on some level as he is about Wallace. We make our way out, through the protests, the crowds, the gawkers, and I give Randall a goodbye kiss.

I start driving up the coast. I used to drive this way with the boys on vacation. And earlier, coming up this way with Mom and Dad, hearing them argue about infospace, whether it could be anything but a hoax, how much work it would take to make such a hoax, why her computing cycles had been co-opted by Danforth and Rajasthani and why was Rajasthani such a bitch anyway. (They were colleagues, not friends.)

This far off the interstates, there are still billboards: *Cathedral Mountain Retreat/Divinity Center* (with *Coronal Meditation* removed so recently the shadow of the letters is still there); *Legal Advice? You Deserve More; Samaritans—We're Here to Listen; Apple Picking and Hayride—You Just Missed Us. Book for Family Events! Next Exit! It's Not Too Late!*

If I were on the interstate, I could pull down a screen to block those advertisements from view; as it is, I read each as it goes by. After a while, I make myself spell out alphabets from them, one by one. Another game from those long drives.

I'm doing that breath thing again. It's not as if I have to psych myself up to say this. It's nothing new. "About sixteen, seventeen years ago, I noticed something off about Coronal infospace. I didn't point it out at the time mainly because I thought I was projecting. Coronal communications are so easy to reinterpret to fit the details of whatever the interpreter is concerned with, and right then I was very concerned with death."

Silence. The organizers are probably in the wings now, trying to figure out whether to cut my mike; I must sound like I'm going confessional. Well, so I am. "Both of my parents were dying at the time, Dad from a slow-escalating kidney failure, Mom from ovarian cancer that threatened to overtake Dad's timeline. I had doctors' appointments and hospice preparation and PTA and soccer and meetings and meetings and meetings . . . and whenever I reviewed infospace, I kept seeing the same things.

"The official broadcasts had shifted a little, more reassurance that all was well, that citizens should be aware of their risks, that all was well. *It's just a stomach cramp, don't worry. No, I don't need to get it checked out. I'm fine.*

"Local transmissions were less sanguine, sometimes directing emergency services, sometimes eliminating entire subjects or regions from their discussions. *I don't want to talk about it. I'm seeing a doctor, and that's all you need to know.*

"Occasionally there would be sudden bursts of frantic activity, calls for help. We'd gotten used to that, but these—there wouldn't be any follow-up. No answer to those calls. *This is a lot to put on you, but here's what's happening. I'm sorry. I'm sorry.*

"The music and art had always been diverse in subject and style, but there seemed to be a melancholic, pensive tone to much of it now. *Well, you get to a certain point, and you know there's fewer days ahead than behind. How does that one poem go, the one about regret?*

"Individual communications had always been a very minor subset of the transmissions, but the few I followed seemed to be Coronals reaching out for each other, trying to find each other, holding on. *Sit with me here a while. This is nice, isn't it? I've always been so proud of you.*"

My eyes are watering. "I was, at the time, very aware that I was reading my parents' deaths into infospace. I hoped it was just me."

Half of the conference is on flow; I tune the car's glass to mine and let presentation after presentation eat the road. "Linguistic Difference in a Cross-Section of the Early Conquest Dramas" derails pretty quickly, assuming that the Conquest Dramas are a purposeful corpus rather than a loose grouping of similar works. I can't watch the visuals on a road like this—I have to keep watch on the road—but I can imagine the expressions of the attendees. "Infospace as Archive? The Purpose of Coronal Transmission" tries to claim that infospace was meant as a sacred repository, rather than what they had available—like assuming we used radio out of worship of a sky-deity.

I pull into a rest stop after the day closes with "Marking Time: Signatures in Coronal Rhythm-Intensive Music," and none too soon; Coronal music does not translate well, and it's always made me drowsy. My glass wakes me before dawn, and after I return from a trip to the restrooms the early-morning presentations have begun with "Fear of the Other and Governmental Responses to the Initial Signal." My bones hurt even more now, and it takes me a couple of minutes to fold myself back into the car, more to make myself eat a breakfast muffin from the vending machines.

I reach the address Randall sent just after noon. The sign used to read COSMIC ILLUMINATION MEDITATION RETREAT, but it's been papered over poorly with a crude poster of a hand holding a torch. I don't know which worries me more.

It's a small cluster of houses, close to the ocean, probably once a little resort before its cosmic phase. There's a big, bare circle in the middle, not a parking lot as I first think. I get out and see it's a sand painting, or rather dirt painting, gravel raked into a crosshatch pattern that I recognize. Infospace didn't have visuals for the most part, but many broadcasts described mandalas like this.

I think of the images from Virginia, the painted mandala on the concrete and the bodies laid out carefully around it, the similar images from Malawi, from Honduras, from Denmark. There are people walking around the houses, some talking expressively, waving their hands; some pumping water; one or two regarding me with curiosity.

I march up to the women at the pump, absently identifying the language they're speaking as Finnish. "I'm looking for Wallace," I say. "*Estin Wallace.*"

One of them has the pinned-ear look; the other is wearing a gauze skirt and blouse, what my mother would have called *another goddamn hippie* and my father tried to capture in paint. Both of them wear glass, though, and they don't bristle at my presence. The End of Speech cult, the one that Wallace got involved in when he turned seventeen—they scorned anyone who actually knew Coronal studies instead of "sensing their way through them."

Pinned-ears looks me up and down. "Main house. Top floor." She adds as I start to walk, "You look like him."

I don't know what I'm expecting inside the house. There's what looks like another mandala in the foyer, this time in brightly colored sand that's been tracked over several times, and a rack of servers in the dining room, with fans running next to them. I step around the mandala, thinking that the one rack probably has all the computing power of my mother's old research center. Changes, not all driven by the Coronals.

Two people are arguing in Urdu on the second floor. I catch the gist of it: wide-band transmission versus focused, which way to point. One of them sees me and waves absently, as if I belong here. In another life, I might have. But not now. And not Wallace.

I pause halfway up the last set of stairs to catch my breath. Someone's painted in straggling letters: *WE REMEMBER WHAT HAS BEEN FORGOTTEN.* I can't carry him out of here; haven't been able to pick him up since he was six. I could, I suppose, call the authorities and try to have him involuntarily committed, try to have them all committed. Better that than the quiet circle of poisoned bodies. I tell myself that, and know I'm rationalizing whatever unforgivable action I'll take.

I can't stop crying. It's a gift, I suppose, that I can do it without my voice going all to pieces, but it's noticeable, and the audience's silence has an embarrassed, horrified quality to it. "It became clear what was happening soon enough. Even if we denied it. And now we were stuck behind the glass, watching this new civilization, this new contact, these new friends we'd come to study and mimic and love—watching them die.

"And we could do nothing. We weren't just separated by some metaphorical glass. We were separated by time. Everything that had happened had happened four hundred years ago. Scream and cry and pound on the glass as much as we tried, the Coronals were already dying. Already dead. And we heard every moment of their deaths. The wars. The plagues. The pleas for help that never came. The litanies of the dead."

Someone in the back of the auditorium makes a sound like a sob. I blow my nose, but my eyes are still streaming. "I still remember when one idiot physicist made a comment that, well, at least the Fermi Paradox still held; it's just that sapient races kill themselves off before they develop space travel. Gallows humor, but he still took quite the hit from that, professionally speaking. But he wasn't wrong."

My son is alive when I see him. He's also wearing only pajama bottoms, hunched over a keyboard on his lap, typing with one hand and eating cold scrambled eggs off a scratched camp plate with the other. He must have shaved his head not long ago; it's all bristly now, like when I gave the boys buzz cuts after their brush with head lice in elementary school.

His entire back is covered with mandalas, one after another, all the different interpretations of the Coronal descriptions. Burned—branded—on top of them is a hand holding a torch.

My step creaks the floorboards, and he waves one hand behind his back, scrambled eggs falling from his fork. "Harris, can you tell Zahra that I've almost got the reambiguation figured, if she'll just give me another week?"

"Wallace," I say. I don't even have to take a deep breath to do it.

He drops the fork and spins around, kicking aside plate and keyboard alike. He stares at me for a moment, then scrambles upright. He's not as tall as Randall, never has been, but they're both taller than me. "Ma."

I'm too worried to smile. "Yes," I say, and stop. What do I say? I'm here? I found you? Please don't go, the Coronals aren't worth it?

His shoulders go down, just a little bit. "Randall told you I was here, didn't he?"

"He did," I say. "He worries."

Wallace shrugs. "It's what he does." He bends and sorts through the mess at his feet, finding a shirt with TOUCH THE STARS—8TH ANNUAL silkscreened onto it. "I think he thinks we're some kind of death cult."

He straightens up as he says the last, and he sees my face. "You're not?" I manage, because he's already seen as much in my expression. "The mandalas—"

"The mandalas are important, Ma. That we may remember what has been forgotten." The last has the sound of catechism, and I can't help rolling my eyes. He looks up at the ceiling, and I think of far too many Thanksgivings where we talked past each other. This is going to be another one of those fights. "You seem so determined to forget that you're willing to let them close the department."

"I don't see how that's relevant," I say, but it's a sore point, and I take the bait. "Besides, it's not about forgetting."

"Then what's it about? You're just turning your back on what we have of the Coronals? You're letting the university—"

"There are other Coronal Studies departments." Withering, yes, but holding on in the same way that departments allow specialized study of Ottoman textiles or obscure Scottish poets. "And don't change the subject. My job is my own. This—" I gesture at the mess, "—is, I'm assuming, your new job."

He glares at me, nudges the plate of eggs away with one foot. "Yeah. So maybe it is." I brace for the defense, but he doesn't bother with it, instead straightening up as if he were giving a presentation. "Ma, I need a favor. I need access to Granma's cloud."

"There's nothing in it. Nothing that isn't public."

"No, there is. I need the initial signal. The originating one, the one that rewrote her research center, before it went dormant."

I think of my mother, of the cancer rewriting her DNA. "There's nothing there."

"That's only what you say because you don't *see*."

"I don't need to see! There's nothing *to* see! You can re-run the translator as many times as you like, and it's not—"

"Ma—"

"It's not going to show you anything new! It's just going to give you the same old signal, the same things we heard, the same things that *aren't there any more*!" Now I'm shouting. Guess it was my turn to start this time. "You can't tune it, you can't adjust it—it's done, Wallace. It's done, and maybe your friends here with their mandalas and their slogans, they can screw around with their cosmic bullshit, but you are better than that! I will not let you waste yourself like that!"

"It's not a waste, Ma!" He puts his hands to his head. "It's never a waste! Jesus, why is this so hard to understand?"

"There's no one there!" The words come out, and I put both hands to my mouth, as if I've said something obscene. The argument downstairs has stopped; I'm pretty sure they're listening. "No one," I repeat. "It's all silence now."

Wallace shakes his head, slowly, the way I would when I was sick of the arguments. His turn, now.

I make myself stop, make myself draw a new breath. "Could someone shut off the slides? Thank you." One nervous laugh, somewhere at the front.

Everyone else is silent. They don't like seeing someone cry in public. Nobody does.

I think about what I want to say, what I've said already elsewhere. "It's all silence now," I say. Somewhere in the auditorium, I'm certain people are shaking their heads, not quite the way Wallace did but with the same determination.

"The air is no longer full of voices.

"Or, rather, not the same voices.

"This is the one thing the Coronals did for us that we don't even think about any more. Every one of you, every one who has bothered to do more than a cursory study of Coronal infospace, is a polyglot. We had to be.

"This is the gift they gave us. Not the knowledge that we were not alone. We have never been alone. To understand them, we had to understand each other."

Wallace shakes his head, slowly. "It doesn't have to be silent."

I'm about to snap at him, to tell him that I have spent my life on the Coronals and if anyone would know silence, it is me. But I don't. I don't know why I don't. Maybe I'm just tired from the drive. "There aren't any other transmissions in infospace," I finally say. "I know whole arrays that have been searching for anything since before the Coronal collapse. There's nothing."

"Not from them. From us." He nudges the keyboard with his feet. "We're— all of us, here, we're trying to repurpose the original code. So we can send out our own into infospace."

It takes me a moment to realize that he's not talking about every other attempt to use the code, to strengthen it or tune it or seek out more information, more voices in the static. "You want to broadcast," I say slowly.

"Not quite. We want to repurpose their tool and make it ours, and *then* broadcast. I mean, they're dead, and we signed on much too late, but if we— if there's someone else out there too, maybe they can hear us."

I stand very still for a long moment. Below us, I hear the Urdu argument start up again, not nearly so vehement now. "Have you thought about the entity extraction issue?" I say finally.

"It's not as much of a problem as you might think. Here, take a look." He picks up the keyboard, pulls down a screen, and code fills the air. "The original signal was expansive-reductive, taking one set and expanding it to many. We think if we can train it another way, it can work with many sets at once, so we don't have to restrict our infospace broadcasts to one language. It's semisapient, so it really is like training, but the base code . . ."

He goes off, and I think about my mother staring at her own lines of code, convinced it was all a hoax but one she'd go along with for now. It's opaque to me, but Wallace swims in it.

"We're getting close—well, closer. Beatriz thinks we have only ten years to go, instead of twenty. But if we had Granma's records, it'd give us a clearer idea of how the signal is supposed to behave when it's active, instead of its dormant state, which is all we have to work with now. It's only a, a receiver. We need to make it a transmitter again. A whole technician, if we train it right."

He looks alight, the same way Randall does when he's with Brendan. I step back. "I'll deed you the cloud access," I say. For a moment I consider inviting him to drive back with me, but eight hours in the car are pretty much guaranteed to destroy any détente we currently have. "Let me know if you need anything else."

Wallace stops abruptly, as if he's just remembered who he's talking to. "You don't have to go."

I smile at him. "Did Randall tell you what I'm doing, now that the department's closing down? I'm going back to school. For a fine arts degree. Poetry."

"That's . . . not what I would have expected." He stops, takes a deep breath, lets it out. "Good luck."

"I'd like to speak to the other half of the audience now. Those of you who grew up in a world where we knew for a fact we were not alone."

Randall, Brendan, and their girls. Abrams and Lucienne from the department, Sadako who is our last Ph.D. student and has still soldiered on, Martinez with the giant paintings, and Park with the Opera based on Coronal texts. All the ones who passed through my hands, who went on, who continue on without me.

Wallace, my Wallace, so sad and determined. I am so proud of you, of all of you.

"You have never known a world in which Earth held the only life in the universe. Everywhere, you have heard the voices of a world far away. Now you have to hear the nearer voices. I want you to hold on to that knowledge, that certainty that we are not alone. We have never been alone.

"We will never be."

I step down, out of the light. My glass vibrates, and I check it to see a set of messages turn up.

W: good speech ma randy sent me the flow
R: did not. the girls got to listen. Sinny drew a new picture for you.
W: i have some old antholgies if you need textbks

It's a start. I lower my glass and let the organizers walk me back out on stage.

Lettie Prell's short fiction has appeared in Tor.com, *Apex Magazine, Analog,* and elsewhere. Her fiction often explores the edge where humans and their technology are increasingly merging. Her writing also occasionally touches on justice issues, arising from her research work in that field. She lives in Des Moines.

THE THREE LIVES OF SONATA JAMES

Lettie Prell

Exposition: Allegro Impetuoso

Sonata James was twenty-three years old when she decided what she wanted to do with her life and her iterations to come. She sought out her friend Dante to tell first. It was noon and the sun was bright, but not warming. Her cheeks and hands stung with the brisk autumn air off the lake as she made her way from her mom's house on South Dorchester to Dante's usual spot on Ellis Avenue. As she entered the coffee shop, the crisp chill was instantly replaced by cozy aromas of fresh-brewed beans and wood. She ordered a large French roast, paused to dose it liberally with milk, then held it high as she threaded among the crowded tables, mostly occupied by singles drawn to the free Wi-Fi. At last she arrived at the back near the emergency exit and unisex restroom, where Dante occupied the only high-backed booth in the place, a leftover from when this had been a bar or maybe an ice cream parlor. His gaze was locked on his screen as she approached, the glow accentuating his profile and projecting bursts of color onto his black-on-black athletic suit and hoodie.

She slid into the seat opposite him, a little coffee slopping onto the tabletop as she did so. She sat cupping the steaming drink between her hands until Dante looked up from his screen. The way his eyes shone betrayed how happy he was to see her, but he played it down.

"I was reading about fine art photography back before digital," she began.

He slipped his headphones down off his ears, and Sonata heard a few strains of Missy Elliott haranguing about a "one minute man" before Dante punched the pause button. After she repeated her sentence, his brows drew together. "And this is exciting news because—?"

She grinned. "People would buy one of a hundred copies or so of a photo. They could print however many they wanted with the same negative, but it was the artist's choice to limit the number of prints. Even at the beginning of digital, a photographer would decide to make only so many hard copies to sell. To make it more special."

Dante took a sip of his own drink and grimaced. It had likely gone cold long ago. "To drive the price of the art up, you mean."

She drummed her fingers impatiently on the tabletop. "And to make it more special. A statement. Come on, don't ruin this."

"Ruin what?" He'd gone back to his screen. It was impossible for him to unplug for even a few moments. Three-dimensional reality was just another frame opened to his awareness.

She was brimming with the news. "Because I'm going to be a limited edition."

His fingers twitched over the sense pad, but he remained the picture of coolness.

"I just decided today. This is going to define me. It's my *thing*."

He actually closed his computer. He sat back, not looking at her but at some point on the table between them. "If you don't upload . . ."

His voice cracked and she put a hand on his, suddenly realizing how much he cared about her. "I *will* upload," she said. "If I don't, I'll be like any other person who can't afford it or doesn't want to for whatever reason. It won't be special."

His lower lip drew inward, and he jerked his hand away. "So you're just going to let your newbody crash? That's *whacked*."

Several patrons—whites, blacks, and newbies alike—turned to stare at the shout. The way the newbies, especially, regarded her made her face grow hot. She sat up straighter and kept her own voice quiet. "It's a *statement*. If you pulled your head out of the Internet once in a while, you'd notice how crowded we're getting. Only the poor are having babies anymore. Everyone else is hanging on to their money for themselves, for their newbodies."

Dante folded his arms and slouched back in the booth, his long legs bumping her feet as he stretched them out. "Am I now going to hear the antitech rant? Because I don't need you to run that down for me. I can tune into it anytime. Ironically, it's all over the web."

She sighed. "No antitech. Promise." She stared at her coffee. "I need you to hear me."

Dante let out a long breath, deflating. "I hear you. I just don't get you. Have you told your mother yet?"

She shook her head and laughed without humor. "I wanted to tell *you* first. A friend who would understand."

He snorted. They sat looking at each other. Again, Sonata sensed a deeper caring emanating from Dante than she'd thought was there. Maybe he was just realizing it, too, as they spoke of her eventual mortality.

Dante nodded slightly, and for a split second Sonata wondered if he'd read her mind. But he said, "Okay, so you're a limited edition. I suppose I can get used to the idea you'll only have a hundred iterations or so."

"Not one hundred," she said. "That won't hold the public interest." She saw the storm clouds gathering around Dante again and pressed on. "And I don't want to get lumped in with the newbodies who didn't plan ahead and are out of cash already. They'll do any crummy job in order to afford an upgrade before their software becomes so old it's unsupported. I want everyone to know I'm doing this on purpose."

Dante's face had become an unreadable mask. "So how many of you are there going to be, Sonata?"

"Three."

Dante cursed.

"Three iterations, because there are three movements in a sonata. Me here now, and two newbies."

Dante glowered. "Your mom is going to kill you."

"It's my body." She realized she was rehearsing now, for when her mother was back from work. "I want to make my existence really count, to push myself to express and achieve in a way I don't think would be possible if I had all the time in the world. I want to dedicate my iterations as a reminder that we can only understand ourselves—understand life itself—within the context of a finite existence. People are unbearably bored with literally everything now. I want to show people what it's like to *live*."

Dante leaned forward and grasped her right hand in both of his. His palms trembled. "You're whacked," he whispered. "Damned philosophy major."

"I love you, too." She'd meant to tease, but the words hung in the air between them. Their hands clasped tighter, as if separate small animals. Dante swallowed hard, then nodded and released his grip. She rose, feeling buoyant, and stammered her way through a casual farewell.

As she wended her way toward the door she passed a table where two new-bies sat. One turned his silvery face toward her. "Sorry, but I couldn't help overhearing. Have you considered man is something to be overcome?"

She recognized the reference from Nietzsche. She tossed her head and shot back, "'What is great in man is that he is a bridge and not an end.' Yes, I've read *Thus Spake Zarathustra*."

The other newbie, androgynous and blue skinned, regarded her with curiosity as Sonata moved on.

She breathed a sigh as she reemerged onto the streets of Hyde Park. Bolstered against the wind by the warm milk and coffee in her belly, she flowed along with the crowd, thinking ahead to the conversation with her mother. There wasn't any question she would share her news. The two of them were very close. As she rounded a corner into an even thicker mass of humanity, she thought how her mother was not likely to get angry like Dante. Instead, she'd pull her signature line: *You'll change your mind about that when you're older.* It was what had been unspoken in the newbie's stare, back at the coffee shop.

"And just how old will I be when I'm supposed to change my mind about everything?" she muttered to herself. The crowd had slowed to a crawl. There were too many people these days. Exasperated, she pushed forward, not caring that she was bumping people. She was nearly at the end of the block, and up ahead through the sea of bodies she saw the green light. Anyone could see it was time to walk, yet no one was. It was like they were waiting to be herded. She shoved forward in exasperation, hearing horns blaring from different directions, and stepped out into the street where there was some space to move at last—

She felt a jolt along her left side just as she heard a whoop of siren from the same direction, and then she was floating. Distantly, she heard the screech of brakes and a scream not her own. She saw rust-colored leaves blow from the tree across the street and go fluttering in slow motion against blue sky. Then her head slammed into pavement, which normally didn't happen when one was flying. The world was atilt. She saw the face of a little boy, his mouth shaped in the exact oval of his head. Then the sun was in her eyes, or not the sun but a blinding stab from behind her eyes. The pain shot down her side even as her head felt stuffed like a pillow. Everything became a blur. Even the sounds seemed to smear together. Then all collapsed inward upon itself, contracting until the entire universe was but a single point. Then nothingness.

Development: Vivace

Sonata opened her eyes to find the kind and intelligent faces of three newbies gazing down upon her. Then she recognized two of them and sat up quickly with a gasp. Or at least, she tried to gasp, but she couldn't draw in any air. She tried again to breathe, and then panic set in. She clawed at her throat but no one moved to help her. It was her worst nightmare. She flashed back to being in the water at the Washington Park Pool, ten years old, holding on to the edge as she followed her girlfriend Lana around the perimeter. There were two men in their way, and Lana went around them. Sonata let go of the edge too, realizing too late she was toward the deep end. She couldn't swim. Her eyes went wide as she fell back in the water and slipped under. One of the men had reached out to pull her up—

The newbie with the silvery face, who had said something to her in the coffee shop earlier—and who she would come to know as Miller—was speaking to her in calm tones. "Become aware of your body," he repeated.

Sonata answered with a scream. At least she could still do that.

The blue-skinned newbie who had also been there stood beside a shorter newbie whose form closely resembled a man's body. They nodded in encouragement at her efforts. Later she would know them as Satchya and Kent.

Miller continued with beatific patience. "Observe your own distress. Feel your body. Is your heart racing?"

She couldn't stop clawing at her throat. She couldn't feel anything but her inability to breathe.

Miller answered for her. "No, your heart is not racing. There is no heart to beat. You are not sweating. Notice how calm your body is. It's operating exactly as it should. Your panic is in your mind only."

Newbody. Sonata forced the word past her animal reflexes. With great effort, she removed her hands from her throat. That's when she noticed her new hands. She stared at them. They were black like polished onyx, and gorgeous. But what mesmerized her was the slowly moving musical score that wound silently around her fingers and wrists before proceeding at a stately pace up her arms.

"That's right," Miller cooed. "See? They call us newbies, but that's short for NBs. Non-breathers."

She saw it was true. She laughed her new laugh, without needing to fuel it with breath. Just like her scream had been without breath.

The musical score wound gracefully around her torso as well, and down her legs, where it appeared to pool before it reversed course. "How did you know? I didn't have time to record any plans."

The blue-skinned newbie she would soon learn was called Satchya made a low chuckling noise. "Everything about you is captured in the upload."

It took a moment to put it all together. "This is my sonata." She heard the tinge of awe in her voice.

Satchya regarded her approvingly. "We wanted to give you a form that reflected your intentions and desires for yourself."

"It's perfect. Thank you." She wondered if it was appropriate to thank them. She pointed at Miller and Satchya. "You two were at the coffee shop just now." Then she stared at Kent, the newbie she did not know.

"Your accident occurred close by," Satchya said. "When your bio-alert signaled the emergency, we responded and brought you in."

"I'm the technician," Kent said, a touch of shyness in his voice.

"How long . . . ?"

"It's seven p.m.," Kent said. "Same day as your death."

"My mother?"

"She's waiting down the hall," Satchya said. "I'm sure she'll be relieved to see you functioning."

Sonata rose from the table where she'd been created. Her movements were effortlessly smooth, without core muscles clenching in the belly or the dull thud of feet striking the floor. She was suddenly embarrassed her mother might not approve of how black she was, nor care for the musical embellishments on her surface. Her face didn't grow hot with emotion, however, so she let her concern slide away.

Miller touched her arm lightly, a sensation of coolness against coolness, slightly metallic yet yielding. "Come meet us tonight, after your mother goes to bed."

They were all going to be friends, then. She smiled. "Where?"

There was an instant transfer of data through the touch. Miller's name and salutary information, as well as coordinates for where to meet and when. Satchya and Kent touched her as well, transferring their salutary information. It took fewer than ten seconds, she noted with her inner clock. Then she was out the door, accessing the virtual map that showed her the way to the waiting room to greet her mother.

Sonata spent the night in Lake Michigan. She'd met Miller, Satchya, and Kent by Shedd Aquarium at twelve thirty.

Miller's silvery face shone in the moonlight. "Ready to face your inmost fears?"

Kent slapped her on the back. Again she felt that yielding, slightly metal sensation. "Tag. You're it." Then he ran full-speed into the harbor waters. Sonata hesitated, watching as Miller and Satchya bolted as well, then splashed and hooted at her.

Sonata closed her eyes and focused on her body. It was utterly still and calm. The fear was all in her mind, then, once again. She opened her eyes and challenged herself in the language of childhood: *Geronimo!* She ran toward the group.

The nightlong odyssey was full of self-discovery. Not only did Sonata overcome her fear of drowning, reveling in the fact she didn't have to breathe, she could also *swim*, and quickly, nearly keeping up with a northern pike they'd surprised as they glided in the relative calm several yards beneath the choppy surface. They navigated by their internal maps, used GPS to track one another, and communicated by way of subvocal messaging protocol. The latter Sonata fancied was akin to ESP, and she pretended they were psychic secret agents on an espionage mission.

As they finished their frolic, emerging from the waters by the Navy Pier, she felt a deep tranquility settle into her titanium bones. She regarded the huge skeleton of the Ferris wheel looming in the night and wondered how negative emotions like fear sloughed away while this transcendent feeling lingered. Epicurus himself would've been jealous of her attainment, she thought, this newfound peacefulness born of an absence of bodily pain. Most people who hadn't taken philosophy didn't get what hedonism was really all about, and until tonight, she had had book knowledge only.

Kent tumbled onto the dock with a soft clatter, a technological Adonis, and stretched out his arms. "This night is fermenting in the veins of God."

Sonata looked up the quote and saw it was part of a poem that had been cited on the first page of a sonata written by a woman named Rebecca Clarke. Only then did she consider she could activate the song coursing over her body. She did, and her new friends gathered around to listen to her soul's sound. It was grounded in the modern but reached back across the centuries, hinting at classical keys even as it played with new tonalities.

Two days later, Sonata entered the coffee shop on Ellis again, shutting the glass door quickly against the wind, conscious of patrons who would feel the bracing chill. She felt a pang of guilt as she spotted Dante slouching over his computer in the back booth. It was as if he'd never left it. He was even wearing the same black athletic suit, although this time a Chicago Bears scarf hung loosely around his neck.

The barista cleared her throat loudly. Sonata remembered the rules and complied, scanning her palm and watching as five dollars were deducted from her sky account. There was no longer a need to eat or drink, but an NB took up space. It was only fair to pay.

"Dante," she said when she was seven feet away and approaching the boundary of his personal space. He was wearing his earbuds, though, so she slid unnoticed into the seat opposite him. Now that she was completely integrated, the appendages of technology on breathers looked clunky and sad. It was strange to be living in the future, amidst the past.

He nearly catapulted from the booth. The earbuds jerked from their lodgings and fell to the tabletop. Sonata could hear tinny strains of old R&B weaving inside a hip-hop mix.

"What the . . ." He stopped and stared at her white tattoos of musical notes floating against their midnight backdrop. He caught his breath. "Sonata, that better be you."

"It is." Surprising him made her pleased.

"You. Are. Awesome. Not kidding." He reached out and touched one of the notes on her arm, but of course it maintained its uninterrupted glide toward her wrist.

"Like it?" She basked in his admiration.

He huffed out a breath, and she could see a tear glistening at the corner of one eye. "I am so glad to see you, you have no idea. Now look at you. I didn't think you'd go this radical. I love it, don't get me wrong. It's perfect. Tell me."

"What do you want to know?" She considered. "Not sleeping is great."

He nodded. "I'd wondered about that. There's this old science-fiction book about some people not needing to sleep. They have all that extra time to do things."

"Not just the time," she said. "It's the integration. I'm continuously in touch with myself, consciously."

His expression went momentarily blank, uncomprehending. He went back to admiring her form. That quickly, they'd come to the divide. Kent had explained it simply to her before she'd come here. *We occupy the same space, but we live in different worlds. No relationships can last across that gulf.*

She didn't know what to say, so she stared at Dante's computer. It was like looking into an archeological find. Dante suddenly seemed fragile, like a fragment of a child's collarbone from *Homo naledi*. He would've drowned in Lake Michigan that first night of her new life. Even if he could swim, he wouldn't have had the stamina, nor could he have remained underwater with her without special equipment.

"I'll admit I'm jealous," he was saying. "And sure, I'm sad, too. I thought we'd be closer in age when we went into our next iterations. But hey, we're still here."

He was hoping against hope for friendship. A deep sadness suddenly seized her, but her body remained unaffected, so the emotion faded quickly. "Still here," she agreed.

Dante reached out and touched her hand. It felt different from when her NB friends touched her. It felt flat, like nothing. She didn't know what it felt like to him, but he withdrew and placed his hand on his computer. He frowned. "It must be painful for you, having your life cut off so suddenly."

She could have laughed, but didn't. "Oh, I'm really not sorry I had the accident. It's like my real life is just beginning. I'd understand it if someone wanted to commit suicide to become an NB sooner."

He blinked. "You think I'd commit suicide? To be with you?"

"What? No!" Why was he jumping to such a wild interpretation? Her NB friends knew how to just listen. "Never mind. I guess I was trying to be philosophical."

Dante's eyes narrowed as he appraised her, his gaze following her gliding musical notations. She could tell he'd already forgotten what she'd said. "I didn't take you for someone who'd design their newbody this far ahead of time."

She deflected the comment so she wouldn't have to explain particulars. "If Mother had had her way, I'd be in some screwed-up form that looked like me in life."

Dante laughed. "Instead you're cutting-edge."

She smiled. "I went so young, I got top dollar for my body parts. Nine million. They gave me all the latest enhancements, and I only used a fraction of my worth."

His hand traced a pattern across the top of his computer in a way that made her wonder what she'd felt like to him. "Are you still set on this limited-edition idea for yourself?"

She could hear the longing in his voice, and the unspoken question: Would she still be in an iteration by the time he uploaded, decades from now? She held out an arm for him to see. "It's written in my skin. This is my second movement." Seeing his face fall, she quickly added, "It's a luxury model, though. Modular design and completely updateable. Kent says it'll last more than a hundred years, easy."

There was an awkward silence at the mention of another man's name. They tried to recover an amicable conversation, but Sonata became so utterly exhausted with the effort, she made a polite excuse and left.

As she made her way to the door, she saw she commanded the gazes of the breathers in the coffee shop. Some expressions were admiring, but several frowned, and as she passed a young man with a goatee standing at the counter, he turned and sneered.

Sonata had also come to the great divide with her mother. The house itself, although its tall windows let in ample light, felt confining to her now. She marveled at how she used to be able to find things to do inside houses for hours at a time. Yet what did she need a house for now? A bedroom? She never slept. A kitchen? She didn't cook or eat. A bathroom? Useless to her now. She didn't own clothes that she had to store in a closet. All the technology she required was built-in. None of her new friends lived in homes. They didn't live with breathers. What had Miller said to her that last day of her own breathing life, in the coffee shop? That man is something to be overcome?

She sat straight and unmoving in the chair opposite her mother, watching the soft, aging woman sip coffee before rushing off to her job in the urban development office. Sonata had used to like the smell of coffee. Instead she was mentally removed from the scene, running the most likely scenario in a background routine. She would make the announcement that it was time for her to leave and go live with her kind. Her mother would look up, her face registering relief, fleetingly. Then she would stage a drama of surprise and hurt feelings, which would transition into sadness and tears. Her mother would then get up from the table and Sonata would rise as well. They would embrace. Her mother would say she would worry about Sonata every day.

Sonata halted the scenario and made her announcement. Her mother looked up, her face registering relief so briefly that Sonata might have missed it if she hadn't run the simulation first. Everything played out similarly, in real time, ending with them hugging in the sunlit dining room.

"Be careful," her mother whispered. "You never know what can happen out there on the streets. There are stories. Not everyone approves of newbodies."

Her mother moved away and picked up the coat hanging on the spare chair where her purse and keys rested efficiently on the seat. "Your home is always here if you need it," she said, pulling on the wrap. She picked up her purse and keys and left, at that point on a trajectory to be a mere fifteen minutes late for work. As the door closed, Sonata noted the efficiency with which her mother had handled the news. It was a final sign they had both been ready for this change.

Sonata waited till the sound of her mother's car blended into the rest of the traffic. Then she stepped out of the house. She could no longer smell, but the very air seemed to carry the fresh scent of freedom.

She spent that first day of her true independence as an iteration celebrating with Miller, Satchya, and Kent, avoiding the crowds by diving to the floor of Lake Michigan where they watched the myriad forms of sea life and experimented with the new subvocal language the NBs were inventing that expressed in symbols, colors, and mathematics rather than words. They were like babies struggling to learn. Sonata caught glimpses of a deeper reality to explore. It was thrilling being at the beginning of a new development in the NB world.

An hour before dawn they all emerged from the lake by Grant Park. Miller and Satchya went their ways while Sonata and Kent visited the Cloud Gate. They lay side-by-side under the omphalos of the silvery sculpture, where they observed their forms repeated within it, as if time had ceased to exist and the myriad future iterations were laid out before them. Sonata activated the song of her body that her moving tattoos represented, and told Kent her plans of coming out publicly as a limited edition.

"The problem is, I didn't have a chance to become known for this when I was a breather," she said as regret passed fleetingly through her mind. "I'm in my second iteration already."

"Really, dear," Kent replied, "your vision was formed before you had all the data. No one will hold you to it."

She frowned up at their distorted reflections in the sculpture. "But I want it. Kent, no one understands me. They think I'll grow up and change my mind." She thumped the concrete with a fist. "I *hate* when people say that." She would've been crying by now if she could.

Kent sat up and looked down at her. "Go say your piece, then, if you want. But just be aware . . ." His gaze wandered over Millennium Park.

"What?"

"I'm sure you already know there are haters amongst the breathers."

"Well, you know the cliché about haters." She grabbed his arm playfully. "I prefer to say that lovers gonna love."

Her Adonis lay back down beside her, and they accessed an intimacy protocol together, where their minds entwined in an ecstasy of togetherness she had never experienced during her sweaty biological grapplings with fellow breathers in her old life.

One of the breathers' videocasts was enthusiastic about having her as a guest. A young man with long red hair and a spiral tattoo on his forehead listened raptly as she related her vision for her life and iterations. She found herself opening up in a way she hadn't before, sharing her personal disappointment. "I was going to use this iteration as a means to further explore what I'd made of myself in my first life," she admitted. "Now it's like I need to discover who that young woman was who died. I need to invent her future."

The man's eyes gleamed. "Are you admitting the you that's sitting here is not the same as the woman who lived?"

She smiled and shook her head. "Oh, no. I know there's a fringe out there that disbelieves in the continuity of awareness from the life to the iteration."

The interviewer stared at the camera. "Fringe?"

She nodded. "Most everyone knows that's an incorrect belief born of suspicion and antitech sentiment. The continuity of consciousness within iterations is well documented in the research. And personally, I can vouch that I'm still me." She refrained from saying she was actually better now.

The man chuckled. "Okay, but still, I can't believe you're going to give up living forever after going through the procedure for it. I've never heard an iteration say they wanted to die. I know you've told us why, from a philosophical perspective. But what about you, *personally*? What's going on inside that titanium casing of yours?"

He was mocking her. Sonata was starting to wish the show would end. "I'm committed to my vision," she explained as patiently as she could. She was going to elaborate, but the man cut her off.

"And you no longer have the human will to live, now."

"Well, I wouldn't say—"

"But I'm saying. That's the truth. There's something missing in you, and that's your human core."

She had a curious desire to reach out and separate the man's head from the rest of his body. She'd unwittingly become a tool in the hands of a hater. "I think this interview is over."

As she rose to leave, she heard the man wrap up. "There you have it, everyone. What would it take for all the other iterations to want to shut themselves off? How do we make that happen? You've been listening to New Forum. And remember: actions speak louder than words."

How unoriginal, she thought as she shut the door of the studio behind her. And what a liar that young man was. She could detect the hum of his bio-alert—in nonemergency mode of course—the entire time. When his breathing life ran out, he would become just like her, by choice.

A group of over thirty NBs sat along the stately gazing pool leading up to the steps of the Baháʼí temple. It was shortly after midnight in mid March, a week after that awful interview on the Forum. The sky was moonless and stars were everywhere, even seeming to be winking up from the spring-thawed water, emanations from some companion universe. Sonata sat between Kent and Satchya as the group conversed in the new language. There was a lot of discussion around the new concept of beyond centeredness, a simultaneous experience inward and outward or the micro/macro linkage of all things.

She gazed into the starry waters and remembered how as a breather she'd dedicated her limited, preaccident life to display the beautiful meaning that she thought at the time could only exist within the context of a finite existence. Now, after that awful interview with the hater, and amid the excitement of exploring new concepts in an invented language, her attitude had transformed. She replayed her mother's signature line to herself: *You'll change your mind about that when you're older.* She smiled ruefully. Her mother had been right. Kent had been right, too, to point out she'd made that pact without fully knowing what it was like to be a non-breather. How NBs not only lived; they *thrived.*

She looked over at Kent, her Adonis. Yes, they were higher forms of being, just as Miller had said that day in the coffee shop after she'd told Dante her plans. A pang of old emotion stabbed her emotional center as she recalled the way Dante had looked at her, their clasped hands gripped tight on the tabletop. She averted her eyes from her perfect lover to the sky and waited for the feelings to slide away, as they always did.

A black bird glided across the stars within the deep. No, not a bird. Sonata tracked the drone across her line of vision and watched it bank and turn.

"Hey," she said. "Someone's shooting video of us."

Satchya followed her gaze, and then leapt to her feet, emitting a siren blast.

Everywhere, iterations leapt upright. Sonata's newbody responded automatically as well. Kent touched her lightly on the shoulder and indicated a direction. "Run." His touch transmitted his plan to her.

There was a flash of light, and Kent's arm went flying. Sonata saw another drone scoop low, tracking after a small group fleeing for the parking lot. Everyone was scattering. Kent followed her as she ran toward Sheridan Road.

Satchya caught up with them and passed them just as they ran across the road, heading for a stand of trees. Her blue-skinned friend's body was in an erratic hyperdrive. Smoke curled from the side of Satchya's neck, then her form suddenly jerked and crumpled at the base of a trunk.

Sonata felt fear in her mind, but she moved with efficient confidence. With Kent on her heels she headed under the cover of the trees, and they made their way through to the far edge of the tree line, where they saw their goal within reach. They paused to locate the drone's position and calculate when they could make their final move with the least amount of risk. Then on Kent's subvocalized signal they burst through into the open again on the other side of the grove, sped across a short span of lawn, leapt a hedge, and landed on the sand leading to the safety of the lake.

As they entered the water and submerged, Sonata subvocalized to Kent. *What was that?*

Attack of the idiots, he replied. *Anti-NB sentiment has bloomed into terrorism, my dear.*

Everything suddenly fell into place. From her mother's voiced worries the day Sonata had left her home, to the distasteful moues on the street, to the Forum interview, and up to this moment, she'd been so into herself she'd been oblivious to what was going on in the world. That damned interview had played into the anti-NB sentiment.

Satchya. The subvocal protocol couldn't convey the grief she felt, nor the sense she'd contributed to her friend's destruction.

Kent reached out with his one arm and touched her shoulder with tenderness. *I'll restore her from backup when things calm down. They can't annihilate us. We're their future.*

Yet Sonata recalled how she'd felt the day she'd pushed impatiently through the crowds. When any species is confined to an overcrowded space, the stress can cause them to attack one another. The haters were acting on emotions she'd once experienced herself. The interviewer who had mocked her knew he would eventually become an iteration. Every day, 150,000 breathers died, and over 25 percent now went into iterations. The birth rate was starting to decline, but not quickly enough. At some future point there would be no more breathers—or at least so few their breeding would not matter—and population would stabilize. There was a long time till then, however. What would happen in the meantime? She refused to run those scenarios.

A long, hot summer night was succumbing to a predawn rain bringing cooling northern winds when Sonata burst in the door of her mother's house, slammed it behind her, and drew the dead bolt into place. She'd shut off her tattoos so she could blend into the shadows unseen. Looking around the living room for something to use as a weapon, she noticed the old couch had been replaced with matching loveseats facing each other across a sleek glass cocktail table. A chilling thought crossed her mind. Maybe her mother had moved. Maybe Sonata was standing in someone else's house now. She felt a wave of deep regret wash through her mind, but her body remained calm and functional, so she let the feeling pass.

She heard a movement, and then a light went on, illuminating her mother standing at the top of the stairs. Her hand lingered on the switch, then fell away. Slowly, using the railing as support, the older woman made her way down the stairs and stopped, staring at Sonata.

Sonata remembered her tattoos were off, and turned them on again so her mother would recognize her.

"It's you."

"Yes." They stood there, neither one moving. "The iteration hospital is gone, mother."

"Gone? Tonight?"

"Burned." In her mind, she felt deep grief. "I have friends who are no more. They got the backups."

"Oh, baby." Her mother approached, and they hugged. "I'm so sorry."

With effort, Sonata pushed her mother away. "I could be endangering you, coming here."

"Don't talk nonsense." Her mother suddenly seemed energetic, in charge. This was her mother's working self. She motioned for Sonata to follow her up the stairs, which she scaled herself at a quick trot. "We'll put you in your old room till this settles," she said, heading down the hall. "There are good people left who won't let this go away. I know who to talk to. People have rights, and that includes iterations."

The door to Sonata's room stood open. Her mother threw on a light and crossed to the window where she drew the drapes. The room had been converted into a media center, with a large flat-screen facing a couch. Sonata stayed in that room for a full week, convinced any glimpse of her through a window would jeopardize her mother's safety. Finally, she realized her mother could take care of herself, and allowed herself freedom to roam the rest of the house, though she avoided standing at the windows. Her mother worked longer hours now and was meeting with the alderman of the ward and other officials after work, pushing for a solution.

During her seclusion, Sonata was in touch with her own kind over their secure network. Driven into hiding, they communicated exclusively in the new language of symbols and mathematics. Sonata discovered some of her friends, including Miller, had fled into the Upper Peninsula of Michigan. Others had spread out to midsized urban centers relatively untouched by the unrest. When she learned at last that Kent and Satchya were gone forever, their bodies destroyed and their backups burned in the fire, she mourned for them terribly until the emotion slid away.

There were hundreds of attempts to bring down the NB network, or to infect it—and the NBs—with one virus or another. But the NBs had superior technology, and the system stood. With the new language, they could conceive of technological developments much more rapidly than ever before. Planning went forward at a new supercomputing pace.

The breathers were busy as well. There were citywide protests, arrests, negotiations, and, finally, a formal agreement that became a model for the nation. When Sonata left her mother's house at last, it was to go live in a special area set aside for NBs, where they were guaranteed to live free of harassment, and where they would be allowed to build their technological Eden. It wasn't far from where the Cabrini-Green projects had once stood, and where a mixed income neighborhood had struggled to become viable but had failed just as miserably. And now? The non-breathers called it the tech ghetto.

Not trusting the truce, they erected a virtual security fence guarded by the most sophisticated anti-intruder system yet devised. The bodies of the elderly and near dead were delivered to the perimeter to receive newbodies, but the rate of new NBs had slowed markedly. The unrest had left people wary, and the prospect of leaving their communities for an unknown, isolated existence was a profound deterrent. The NBs turned their attentions to perfecting the longevity of their forms.

It was during this time that Sonata was called to her mother's deathbed. She received an emergency pass to make the trip beyond the tech ghetto to a hospice center off the Eisenhower Expressway. It was eerie: leaving the NB environment, seeing cars again, hearing spoken English.

"Mom," she said, holding the dying woman's hand and feeling a wave of loss course through her mind. "Why aren't you going to join me? Why did you cancel your iteration?"

"Oh . . . child." She struggled to form words. "That nonsense. Not for me." She relaxed back in the bed, smiling. "I saved you, though. You made it."

Sonata didn't leave her mother's side until the old woman breathed her last breath. As she held the husk of her mother's hand, Sonata relived the memory of her own death, long ago. She wished she could cry for her, and for Kent and Satchya, but she was beyond that now. She focused on the calm of her body, and let the emotions of her mind slip away.

Sonata lived three hundred more years. After her mother's death, she threw her energies into work for her community, just as her mother had worked for hers. It turned out her multimillion-dollar newbody was well equipped to last. She saw the breather population decline due to a combination of war, infertility, and devastating new strains of MRSA and flu. With overcrowding no longer an issue, the aging virtual security fence was disabled and NBs were once again welcomed to mingle with breathers. Walking the old streets of Hyde Park, Sonata saw the breathers were enjoying a boom of abundance after their trials. There were no homeless, no beggars. Strollers of babies were numerous, and older children huddled in groups, sharing texts and laughing, looking up to watch her with curious eyes.

Sonata traveled to many cities, giving lectures to mixed crowds of breathers and NBs. They listened with interest as she let her body play the music of her soul. The composition had grown richer over time, and multilayered. After the concert she spoke about philosophy, about her intention to have one more iteration after her current one ended.

Eventually her newbody began to wear down and malfunction. She had to stop traveling. Occasionally she would be invited to appear on a podcast, but as she continued to display erratic functioning, the invitations ceased. To the dismay of her technician, Randall, she refused another iteration.

"There's no such thing as an old folks' home for NBs," he said. "I can't continue to fix you."

She tried to reach out and touch his hand but hers flopped ineffectually. She could no longer subvocalize. Yet the young woman of ancient times would've been proud of her. Didn't Socrates himself declare that philosophy is the preparation for death? "It's time," she agreed. "Keep my backup, but not for another iteration."

He cocked his head at her. "Then what are we to do with your stored data?"

"Wait till there's something new. A breakthrough of some kind. You'll know when."

Word spread that Sonata James was coming to the end of her second movement. A documentary crew of NBs arrived.

She lay on a table for the shutdown procedure that would capture her data for storage. One of the NBs on the documentary crew leaned close over her. She squinted up into a set of violet eyes that whirled in spiral patterns. The eyes were set in a bronze face whose features were only vaguely human. It was more like the face of a bird. Was there an Egyptian god that looked like this?

"I don't know why I stayed away all these years," the stranger said. She felt the NB attempt to subvocalize to her, in vain. He went on speaking. "I think it was because you had a century's head start. You were well established in your new life."

"Who . . . do I know you?"

There was a hint of sadness in the stranger's smile. "Likely not now. We knew each other a lifetime ago, but not for very long."

Sonata wanted to talk to the stranger some more, but the proceedings were underway. With a pang of regret, she relaxed back into the shutdown sequence.

Recapitulation: Presto

Sonata was pulled to her feet by many hands. "You nearly got yourself killed," a bystander chided. She looked across the street and saw a boy, his mouth agape at the close call. A gust of wind whipped up, pulling orange and red leaves from the trees and sending them on a final journey, dancing across the face of the midday sun high overhead.

Then Dante was suddenly there, hood thrown back, his face twisted with concern. "I was just leaving the coffee shop when I heard the commotion." She was suddenly engulfed in his embrace. Her hands touched the hardness of his computer backpack, but it was the warmth of his flesh that gave her joy. She burrowed her face in his neck.

"I love you, Dante," she said, realizing the truth of her words as they cascaded unbidden from her lips.

"Easy there," he said. But when he nudged his face around to meet her gaze, she saw the delight in his eyes. "I'm just glad you're okay. How about you come over to my place? Rest up a bit from your near miss."

"I should tell my mom . . ." She trailed off, suddenly disoriented. She looked around at the street, at the throngs of people that had gathered on the sidewalks and were even now moving on. There were fewer people around than she expected to see, and not one of them was a newbie.

She drew in a deep breath, and let it out. Tears sprang to her eyes. She was crying, weeping tears of relief but also mourning what was lost, which she was incapable of putting into words.

"Hey now," Dante cooed, and took her chin in his fingers. "Can't have that. Come to my place and rest awhile."

She nodded. Dante slung a reassuring arm around her shoulders as they walked eastward, toward the lake. The scenery was simpler in a way that could only be explained by way of virtual reality. Bits of memory brushed her hair like blowing leaves and moved on, borne on a biting autumn wind that brought fresh smells. Somewhere inside her core she knew there would be no mother here, but that the friend walking at her side was really Dante. The fleeting image of an Egyptian god with whirling eyes passed through her mind, but finding no purchase, no reality within her current frame of reference, it moved on to whatever land the leaves were going to. She tried to track it in her mind, but couldn't. She'd lost some of her memory in her fall, then. The phantoms that were even now quickly dissipating . . . Were they shreds from her past? Or were they the mind's attempt to fill in what was lost with a backstory that was false? She was certain there had been a conversation about Nietzsche, but all that came to mind was her favorite quote of his. "This ring in which you are but a grain will glitter afresh forever. And in every one of these cycles of human life there will be one hour where, for the first time one man, and then many, will perceive the mighty thought of the eternal recurrence of all things: and for mankind this is always the hour of Noon."

She touched her brow, aware she had paused on the sidewalk. She felt emotionally raw from the near accident. She could've died. She pressed against Dante's side, and he tightened his grip on her shoulder and bent to kiss the top of her head. As they walked on, she pledged to make something of her life.

An (pronounce it "On") Owomoyela is a neutrois author with a background in web development, linguistics, and weaving chain maille out of stainless steel fencing wire, whose fiction has appeared in a number of venues including *Clarkesworld, Asimov's, Lightspeed,* and a handful of Year's Bests. An's interests range from pulsars and Cepheid variables to gender studies and nonstandard pronouns, with a plethora of stops in-between.

THE CHARGE AND THE STORM

An Owomoyela

Petra was already in a bad mood, not that that said much. Her good moods had become increasingly apocryphal over recent years. But today there was a lightning storm outside her Faraday cage of an office, and she could feel it like a second psyche, inhuman and insentient and laid over her thoughts.

And today, when she walked into her office, there was a familiar man sitting on the chair before her desk. Amad.

She stopped, a step in from the doorway. Amad turned, looking back at her over his shoulder. He had a small device in one hand, and while Petra could sense the stream of information flowing from it, the mental interference from the lightning storm drowned it out.

"I've jammed your communication lines," Amad said.

Petra gave him a withering look and headed toward her desk. "You think that'll keep me from contacting security?"

"For a couple minutes, yes," Amad said. "We need to talk, *Sulai Tabov.*"

"No," Petra said. "You need to be arrested."

She settled into her desk chair, bringing her interface up with a sweep of her hand. He *had* jammed her communications lines, the bastard. Clever bastard—she had a very nice system, full of redundancies and adaptive compensators—but he'd always been clever. Probably always been a bastard, too, though she'd looked past that, once.

"It's about Nash," Amad said.

"He needs to be arrested, too."

Amad made a frustrated noise. "Look," he said. "Knowing there's no love lost between the two of you, and knowing that I would rather hang myself by my thumbs from the lightning towers than come ask you for help, I expect you to know what it means that I'm here and I'm asking. This is about Nash's life."

A cold anger sparked into being at the bottom of Petra's stomach, ringing against the lightning she could feel outside. There was no sound of thunder in here, no electrical interference except the noise inside her head, but her fingers twitched, as though urging her to become a conduit. A lightning tower herself. She could string Amad up by his thumbs right here on her own.

"I have," she said, "on multiple occasions, attempted to help Nash fix his life. On the last occasion, he sold Su secrets to violent revolutionaries and got my wife kidnapped. I'm not interested in trying again."

"Yeah, great," Amad said. He stood up from the chair, almost started pacing, then caught himself. Petra watched with a knife-sharp interest, taking in the tension in his shoulders, the tremor concealed in his hands. Amad liked to think he was better at being unreadable than he was. "Leaving aside your ignorant and well-intentioned efforts to turn him into a good little colonizee, this isn't about *fixing* his life. It's about *saving* it. Are you going to help, or do you honestly think he should die for screwing up and screwing you over?"

Yes, Petra thought, but it was a knee-jerk thought, more spite than sense. And *it was a pretty damn big screw-over*, her brain retorted, and it took a moment for her to blink and realize what Amad had said.

"What," she managed, the anger still smoldering but neatly derailed.

Amad glared at her, then took a deep breath. "The Su," he said, voice bitter and brittle, "have decided that he's a detriment to the colony and should be excised. However, they will accept his abject submission to a citizen in good standing, to whom reparations are owed, in lieu of his death."

The anger in Petra's gut gave a long, uneasy turn. "No one else is willing to speak for him?"

"No one the Su are inclined to listen to."

"Doesn't surprise me." She watched Amad. As an afterthought, she gestured away her interface. Right or wrong—and she felt that it was wrong, for all that knowing that didn't stop her—she wasn't going to fix the lines, call in the authorities, turn Amad in. "You came to me because you had nowhere else to go."

Amad didn't bother confirming her comment.

"And what makes you think I'd agree to this?"

Amad's fingers curled around his jammer. "You used to be friends."

"Used to be."

"You're not that heartless," Amad said.

He was right. The Su had a casual disregard for life. If the life in question didn't serve their ambitions, they had no compunctions about casting it aside.

Petra, human, balked at that.

Yes, she resented Nash. Hated him, it felt like. She would have liked to see him suffer for screwing her over, years ago.

Seeing him *die* was a little much.

"Well." The word left a taste like ozone in the back of her throat. It very nearly made her sick to her stomach, until she shoved it away, hunted out the control she'd developed to turn down her own feelings. "Then. What jurisdictor has him?"

Some of the tension leached out of Amad's shoulders. Not all. "The information is here," he said, and gestured a data sigil to her interface. Petra could feel it blink into availability; text, no more than a few lines. Amad said *All the information*; Petra heard *everything you need to know*, and her fingers itched for the comm line again. One call and she could very easily ruin Amad's life, if not end it.

Him and Nash. Always so eager to use her. Sudamn opportunists, both.

She accepted the transfer. Amad backed toward the door, the jammer in his hand coming up like a talisman.

"I'm sorry about your wife," he offered. "I—you know, I liked her. We never intended for anything to happen to her."

"Ex-wife, now," Petra said. "And what you intended doesn't matter much, does it?"

Amad made a noise like he was the one who should resent all of this. In his mind, maybe so. "Can't say it's been a pleasure seeing you, Sulai Tabov," he said. "Shouldn't happen again."

Then he vanished into the halls.

After a moment, the comm lines cleared.

The jurisdictor module was in a part of the colony Petra never visited. Other, more skilled, biologically *Su* Makers maintained the physical mechanisms of that part of the colony, and there was nothing in that area that Petra needed to concern herself with personally: the organs that recycled air and water and processed waste back around into nourishment; raw material intake from the ruined outside world; corpse handling. And the jurisdictors, where aberrants against the colony peace were held and, if necessary, excised.

The Su had a particular sense of utility.

One Su was waiting outside the cluster, her antennules moving in the still air. "Sulai Tabov," she said, each word humming out of the speech synthesizer embedded on the underside of her head.

How, exactly, all the Su managed to recognize her and her exact place in society was an open question, and one Petra didn't bother asking. She had her suspicions, but it didn't matter much, so long as their system worked.

Unfortunately, she had no such skill when it came to the Su. Fortunately, the Su hierarchy was stiff enough that she knew what rank would be standing here, acting as custodian to the condemned.

"*Sudaeg*," she said. "You have *Sudaeg* Nash Carder?"

The Su gestured assent. "You would like to take ownership of the aberrant?"

Saying *No, I'd like nothing of the sort, but I seem to be obligated to* would mean that the Su would only hear the *no*. "I would," Petra said.

The Su didn't question the statement or ask for any justification. Petra had standing among the Su; Petra was owed reparations from Nash; Petra, therefore, had the right to claim his life. The Su never questioned the exercise of rights. The Su did not believe that if one had the right to do something that thing could be morally questionable.

Sometimes Petra wished she could see it the same way.

"This way, Sulai Tabov," the Su said, and unfolded her legs beneath her. At her full height, she stood nearly half a meter taller than Petra: an armored mass, through whom hummed a faint bioelectricity that Petra could feel at the corner of her mind. Stronger than a human's but too faint and too subtle to control.

The Su led her back into the module. Only one of the cells was occupied, though another had been sealed off—and through its translucence, Petra could see a dark shape, rounded toward the extremities and just about the size of her own torso. Someone, human or Su, who had been excised already, their body being digested by the biomat cell walls.

She turned away from it.

"The aberrant is here," the Su announced, pressing claws and her tarsal pad into a receptor. It sensed her energy, or her pheromones, or simply pressure—though Petra doubted it was simply pressure—and a membrane dilated open, revealing the figure inside.

Nash was looking worse for wear, Petra thought. The years hadn't treated him well, or maybe it was just sitting in a cell that might devour him that had him looking grey of mien, thin, and uneasy. His head snapped up when the membrane retracted, and a flood of emotion passed through his expression—mortification, horror, desperate relief. "Petra—"

"Amad found me," Petra said. She could hear her voice resonating in her head, oddly cold, almost alien. There was a cold pressure constricting her lungs, too. She didn't let herself think about it. "Come on."

Then she turned on her heel and walked out again. It took Nash a moment to scramble to his feet and follow, the Su coming along after him.

"How did you end up with a death sentence?" Petra asked. The Su didn't give a damn about life, but out of respect for their human constituents, they usually didn't jump straight to excision from the colony. Not these days. The fact that they had with Nash—a man who, despite his many faults, was neither violent nor destructive—suggested that he'd annoyed them more than he'd ever annoyed her, and that was a feat.

Nash hurried to keep up with her, trying to put a few paces' distance between himself and the Su custodian. "I wasn't expecting you to come save me," he said.

"Neither was I." Petra increased her own pace, focusing on the crisp *clip* of every footfall. The rhythm gave her something to focus on that wasn't the lightning storm and wasn't Nash. "What did you do, Nash?"

"It's complicated," he said. And then they were at the gate, and the Su moved in front of them and took a collar from a cache on the wall. She regarded Petra with characteristic nonchalance.

"I will put this on the aberrant," she said. "For you."

Petra nodded acquiescence.

Nash stiffened, but he didn't resist as the band fastened around his neck, the inner lining adhering to his skin with a soft *schup*. "In typical situations I would format the collar myself," the Su said. "However, you possess the skills to format it yourself, Sulai. You are free to request that I format it for you."

"Thank you, no," Petra said. "I understand the technology."

"You are free to return him for excision at any time. You are to format the collar before removing him from the jurisdictor. May I serve you otherwise?"

Petra gestured her to leave, and the Su made an answering movement of assent and acknowledgement. Then she turned and walked away, folding herself down into repose at the door again.

Petra turned to Nash, who looked back at her with as much mistrust as he'd shown the Su. Unsurprising. To listen to Amad, Petra was half-Su anyway, and she knew who Nash had thrown his lot in with.

After a moment, though, he forced himself to relax. Put on a smile that was as fake as anything Petra had seen. "Try not to electrocute me?"

"It will be an effort," Petra said, and took the collar in her hands.

She could feel it resonating against the colony around them; feel it asking the colony walls for information, catching the signals the walls sent out. The colony was never quiet, to Petra—it was always murmuring to itself, bright paths of directed energy and a haze of signals. But the loudest things to her senses were the flashes of lightning, carving brilliant but transient pathways through the atmosphere. The electricity running through the channels in the colony was dull by comparison. Hard to focus on. And the collar was fainter still.

And Nash's closeness made it hard to concentrate, too. They'd enjoyed an easy physicality when they'd been on good terms: a clap on the back, a nudge with the elbow, a warm presence against the flank or in repose against the chest. Now, Petra couldn't help but feel that she shouldn't be standing so near, that Nash might try to seize her by the arm or pick her pocket or loop an arm over her shoulders. Try to trick her into believing that they were still friends.

She closed her eyes and wrote permissions into the collar.

Every circuit in the collar, live or dead, mapped onto one of the halls in the colony; all she needed to do was energize the ones she needed. Like trying to draw a line of sand in a statue of glass capillaries while wind howled through cracks in the habitat. But she got the basics done with the same determination she applied to all of her work. The lightning storms were nothing new, nor were the headaches or the brain-fog that accompanied them, and while it might slow her down, it wouldn't incapacitate her.

She let her hands drop and stepped back, away from the sound of Nash's breath, the heat of his body. "Dare I ask where I'm allowed to go?" Nash asked, with a kind of wary wryness.

"For now," Petra said, "the halls from here to my quarters. I requisitioned a room across from mine. You can go from there to the baths, the libraries, and the commissary, using the most direct routes between all four. I'll figure out more later."

"Thanks," Nash said. By his tone, he wasn't sure that was the correct response.

She'd saved him from death, and put him under house arrest. Petra wasn't sure there was a correct response. "I have work to do," she said. "The room will open for you. We'll talk later."

She turned, and Nash said "Wait," and she turned back, already seething. She hadn't expected to get away that easily, no. But it would have been nice.

At least Nash caught that and made an appeasing gesture. "Sorry. I don't mean to keep you. But there's stuff in my lodgings, out by the ship corridor. If I could—"

"I'll ask a *sudaeg* to get it," Petra said. "Forgive me if I don't feel like letting you go back there."

"Right," Nash said.

Petra watched him. "The collar will kill you if you stray too far from the path."

"Right," Nash said again and made a stiff, Su gesture of apology. It had an overtone of self-parody to it. "I won't delay you any longer."

Petra could have said something to that.

She didn't.

She met Kaah at the juncture between the human First Cluster and the Su Brooding Cluster 9. Kaah gave no indication of how long she'd been waiting; she only crouched with an unconcerned stillness and with the smug self-assurance all Su seemed to carry with them.

Petra drew her fingers down from her forehead to her chin to indicate respect. "Hello, Sulai Kaah. How are we operating?"

Kaah echoed the gesture. "We have erected seven additional towers along the polar perimeter," she said. She flicked her claws toward the wall, which beaded out a display and lit up with graphs. "We have an excess of energy, Sulai Petra. Now we must craft it. It interests me to create a new habitat in the Third Cluster. Do you agree?"

"It would behoove the colony," Petra said. Third Cluster wasn't yet over-crowded—the Su would never let it get to that point—but it was coming close, and Kaah at least saw creating more space as the natural answer. Being a human cluster, it would do more for colony harmony than the other answer, which was to curtail population growth outright.

In a race like the Su, where all reproduction was hierarchically decided, such an edict was non-notable. Among the human population, it was a call for rioting. Or for just the kind of separatism that Amad and his ilk espoused.

"I'll follow," Petra said, and Kaah uncurled her legs and paced off in Third Cluster's direction—slowly, for a Su, in consideration of Petra's shorter and fewer legs.

The Su had no real use for small talk, and so they walked mostly in silence. They passed one of the human commissaries and a number of dwellings—nearly all empty, as First Cluster housed those who worked directly with the Su, and the Su valued productive work more than they valued much else.

A hall or two into Third Cluster they passed a human woman with two boys who looked at Petra walking stride-along-stride with Kaah and seemed to come to her own unvoiced conclusions about that. Humans and Su lived together, but the pace and activities of their lives were so different as to make *living together* academic. There were only so many positions where a human would work alongside the Su.

Kaah turned her head, and made a superior greeting. "*Hurem* Omotoso," she said. "Your children grow well?"

The woman's eyes softened a bit, and she made a gesture of subordinate greeting—though the quirk of her lips, an expression interpretable by Petra but not Kaah, suggested she was playing along with propriety rather than moved by any genuine submission. "They do, thank you for asking, Sulai," she said, then looked to Petra. "Sulai . . . ?"

"Petra Tabov," Petra said, and extended a hand. Omotoso took it.

"First time in Third Cluster?" Omotoso asked. "We don't often rate two Makers."

"We're building an expansion," Petra said.

"Long time coming," Omotoso said, and made an offhand gesture of appropriate respect toward Kaah. Petra gestured recognition and acceptance—the Su didn't understand speaking like this across hierarchy. But that Petra accepted it satisfied them. So long as Petra gestured acceptance, Omotoso would not face any penalties for hierarchical transgression.

It nagged at the edge of Petra's mind, these days.

"I've got a third at home," Omotoso said, tousling the tight curls of one of her son's hair. "People get jealous, you know, and there's no room. So even another level would be godsent; my eldest, you know, she wants to move out, start her own family, not inherit my house. But she doesn't want to live in another Cluster. Well." Omotoso eyed Petra, thoughtfully. "First Cluster, maybe, but she'd have to marry up."

Or wrong someone, Petra thought. Wrong them and contrive to be taken in by them. She wondered what Nash's living space had been like—if he, like Amad, took pride in his cracked and patched and atmosphere-leaking quarters in the old human ship. She wondered if he would rhapsodize about the noise of the hull, how it sang that it wasn't designed for atmosphere.

Humans, Amad liked to say, *and human inventions, adapt well to circumstance.*

The Su adapted well to necessity. Circumstance took much longer.

"It is a wise use of resources," Kaah said, and gestured certainty. "Act well, *Hurem* Omotoso."

"As you shall, Sulai Kaah," Omotoso said, and nodded to Petra as well, and continued on her way.

For a moment Petra wanted, irrationally, to stop her. Ask, for all their failings, you're glad to live with the Su, aren't you? They're different, yes, but this is possible. It doesn't have to be thrown away.

But this was not an argument to be had with strangers. Petra's soft desperation was her own.

She followed Kaah to the access nub at the end of a terminal hall.

Kaah, without ceremony, pressed her claws into the wall at the nub, and a stream of energy surged through her. Petra stepped up and pressed her hands into the wall across the nub from her, and closed her eyes, and called up the lightning.

The nub expanded like a bubble, stretching out into the atmosphere and accreting material. Far beneath their feet, toward the center of the colony, the colony's organs chewed at the mineral substrate beneath them and reprocessed it into usable form; now, crops and stomachs full of smart matter disgorged their contents and sent it crawling in waves toward the Makers' call. The static matter of the existing colony walls hummed in recognition.

Petra could feel every one of them echoing in her awareness. As though she was one limb of a colony and the walls were part of her body, sluggish and slow but movable with nothing but thought and energy and effort.

The nub grew to encompass them, Kaah and Petra both, flooding the area with oxygen-rich atmosphere and moving them out of the insulation of the colony, into the maelstrom of storm and smart matter, where stability sat behind them and potential all around. And together, Kaah and Petra began to Make.

The colony had always grown like a fern, uncoiling—and Petra found it hard to imagine ferns and fauna growing outside. Still, she had toured the oxygen facilities like most classes of her generation, and ferns grew in some variety in the gardens. The human colony ship had brought its own miniature ecosystem for air purification, and the Su had been happy to integrate that system into their colony and research it for any new information on how to optimize the plants they'd scavenged from their own vanished biomes. Petra didn't visit the facilities often, but she remembered them in brilliant greens, reds brighter than blood, yellows cleaner and softer than the atmosphere outside.

After spending enough time in her head—or casting her thoughts outward, forming the colony walls—it took time for color to seep back into Petra's awareness. She could see the walls, but they were the meaningless shapes they'd be if she'd stared at a spot until her eyes canceled its contrast out.

But she came back to herself. In time.

Here in Third Cluster, there were patterns inlaid in the floor, murals, windows: all the things the human population did to make the colony habitable. There were windows through which you could see the roiling clouds—or the battered landscape, when the clouds lifted enough that the ghostly shapes of rocks and craters could be seen. Sometimes, Petra could see vast shapes moving in the distance, not quite the way the clouds moved, and wonder if they were some echo of the vanished ecosystem the Su had clambered out of.

Sometimes, Petra wondered what the hell the Su had *done* to this place.

Sometimes, she wondered what it had been like to be on that first ship, watching the gamble pay off. How they had felt as they saw their potential near-Earth resolve into a tangle of yellow clouds and fierce winds.

Petra had never been out through the old, crumbling habitat spaces that had covered the ship like a blanket. She had no reason to do so; the Su didn't find the ship of much historical interest, and her parents hadn't been willing to go through the hassle of compensating for the damaged environment in those areas. Suiting up, taking medical packs and lights, traveling out past the well-maintained central Su spaces to a ship that would never fly again. They had books, images, videos, holos, history preserved for digestion in everything but physical presence. The ship was roughly as real to her as Earth was.

Nothing like the colony, solid and present under her shaking limbs, a vast map of power and potential to her sensing mind. She could lean back into it, let it soak up the tremors in her muscles. Her fine motor control was shot. Humans hadn't been meant to shape this kind of energy.

But Petra among them had been made. One of the first attempts, a grand experiment toward the full participation of humanity in the colony. Amad had said once that that privilege made her uncaring—*You've got yours, so fuck the rest of us*—but Petra couldn't breathe without the awareness that she was judged by the Su as a possibility. She'd been representing humanity in the court of Su opinion for her entire productive life.

Sulai Kaah had finished her own work, and turned to Petra, forelimbs crossing over each other, out of the way. "You are well?" she asked.

She'd asked a thousand times before, and would ask a thousand times again. So long as they worked on the same projects. "I will be," Petra said.

Sulai Kaah gestured understanding. "Our work will benefit many," she said.

"I look forward to its completion," Petra answered, and with their good-byes said, Kaah wandered off.

Petra's work had a way of scouring all the petty day-to-day concerns of her life out of her mind. She'd become used to coming home feeling drained, pleasantly empty—at least, empty in a way she could convince herself was pleasant, because none of the pollution in her mind, the grudges and doubts and recriminations, seemed to survive.

Unfortunately, it looked like the business with Nash was more persistent than the day-to-day annoyances of being her. She pushed it away—*It's done, I've made my decision, it's nothing to do with me until he starts something*—and then she rounded the last curve in the corridor to see Ilen walking out of her quarters.

An uneasy stiffness went up Petra's spine. She'd never removed Ilen's access permissions from her doors—she'd always said Ilen was welcome any time. But seeing her there, emerging, unannounced, hooked jealousy into her diaphragm and tugged.

Ilen saw her and pursed her lips before forcing them into a smile. "Petra," she said, and crossed the hall and took Petra's shoulders. Petra tried to relax them. "We need to talk."

"It's good to see you," Petra said, though woodenly.

"I wish I saw you more often," Ilen said.

I'm sure, Petra thought, and her diaphragm tugged again, insistently. *But you don't come by, do you?* Not until Nash winds up here.

"I wish you did," she said.

It wasn't Ilen's fault, after all. Ilen wasn't the one who'd ended things between them. *Ilen* wasn't the one who'd established a carefully constructed distance, measured out degrees of separation like they were insulators. That was all on Petra's head.

The jealousy didn't care if Petra had no one to blame but herself.

"Coffee?" Ilen asked.

Petra bit on nothing. "I've probably just made some more enemies."

"And I've never cared. Coffee?"

There wasn't any question, really. Petra nodded and gestured along down the hall. "Please."

The corridors in this section were all separated into levels, with slopes up at the perimeter and at places that had been the perimeter before colony growth had overtaken it. That was how you could tell it was a human sector—at least, it was one of the ways. The Su had no issues with clambering up and down wherever they found it most expedient, not caring much whether one room shared an elevation with another chamber adjacent to it. But they'd designed these sectors after the floors-stacked-atop-each-other layout of the human ship.

The commissary was little more than a food receptacle with an open chamber adjoined to it. A colonist could go and select the food they wanted and eat communally, if they so chose. The chairs and tables were a human invention; the space to prepare food, and the modules that heated or cooled food on demand, had been Su gestures of goodwill to accommodate human taste. The Su didn't have the breadth of culinary aesthetics that the human population had.

Petra and Ilen went to a hot receptacle and got bulbs of coffee—a thin, dark liquid that tasted vegetative and burnt. She had to wonder if it bore any resemblance to the coffee the colonists had remembered from Earth; if this was a replica, Su ingenuity and human gengineering, or just some poor substitute carrying a name that meant almost nothing.

"I don't want to talk about Nash," Petra said, and found a table. This commissary was empty; in general, the people with rooms in this area tended to have nicer places to eat.

Ilen followed her, but paused at her words. "Neither do I," she admitted. "But, you know, you shut me down when it's not about business. Nash is business."

Despite the heat of the coffee in her hands, despite the sensation of lightning over the habitat, Petra felt cold. "Why is Nash your business?"

"Because he threatens colony harmony," Ilen said, "and my rank theoretically obliges me to be conscious of that."

Petra blinked at her, then cracked a thin smile. "How long did it take you to come up with that excuse?"

"Oh, I've been holding it in my pocket," Ilen admitted. "Not that it's any less true."

"You're not a social engineer. You're a medical worker."

"And you're a construction specialist, Sulai," Ilen pointed out. "Not a warden. Or a rehabilitator. Looks like today's the day we wake up with new vocations."

Petra set her coffee on the table.

Ilen hadn't taken a seat yet, and she didn't. Instead, she came around the table and pressed her hands into Petra's shoulders. And then she *pressed*, her Su-engineered powers coming down through Petra like a wave.

Petra could sense the lightning, sense the chattering patterns of electricity racing through the walls, the floor, here and there through the air. But none of it was like the golden warmth of Ilen's hands and Ilen's power, moving through her. Putting right, it felt, all the cells that had been excited or singed by Petra's work.

Petra melted, sinking onto the table with a mew. "Ilen . . ."

"You haven't been taking care of yourself," Ilen pointed out. Petra grimaced, though the expression melted away.

"I'm still here, aren't I?"

"So's the pitted, pock-marked ground," Ilen said. "That means nothing."

Then she ducked and pressed her lips against Petra's jaw. Petra caught her breath.

"I don't want to talk about Nash," Ilen said, and Petra felt her shoulders trying to stiffen up again, but the tension was chased away by Ilen's hands. "I want to talk about you. Do you know what you're doing?"

Petra let out a weak laugh. "Amad came to me," she said, and felt Ilen's fingers pause on her muscles. "Nash was going to be executed. No one else in the colony was going to speak for him. Can you believe it?"

A moment passed before Ilen said, "No, actually. He must have gotten a lot better at making enemies. But we're talking about you, Pet—"

"Once I knew about it," Petra said. She tried to make her voice like the end of an argument. "If I knew about it and didn't stop it, I'd be complicit in his death. Or I could stop it and end up owning the man. Those were my choices. Kill him or own him."

"You still blame him—" Ilen started.

Petra pulled herself out of the chair, out of Ilen's grip. The sense of the storm closed in around her awareness again, an angry backdrop. It felt like coming home to herself. She turned to look Ilen in the eyes. "You don't?"

"Pet," Ilen said. She stepped forward, bringing them almost body-to-body, and cradled Petra's head in carefully poised fingers. She washed away the chaos of the lightning again. "All right. Your choices are rotten. But you're going to burn yourself to death in anger here, if you don't end up killing him yourself. Something has to change."

"If you have any suggestions," Petra said.

Ilen said nothing.

"Thought not," Petra said, but it was difficult to be mad at her. Especially difficult when Ilen's hands, Ilen's power, carved out a safe, quiet spot in Petra's head.

Petra leaned forward, slipped her own hands onto Ilen's shoulders, slid them down toward her elbows. Tried not to feel like her hands, this contact between them, was a veiled threat.

Ilen—*Suva* Ilen, highest rank in the colony, could reach into a person's body and direct, in broad strokes, the growth of cells, the patterns of immune response, the firing of synapses. Sulai Petra, one rank below as the Su recognized it, could only control the lightning.

A strong skill, a Maker skill, when it came to directing the responsive material of the habitats, feeding the biomat infrastructure with power. The *Suva*, Su Fathers, could create new Su life, but the Makers could control the colony.

More people than the Su valued that.

Petra could reach into the sky and blast lightning through Ilen. No matter the insulation in the walls, no matter the carefully constructed cages she was afforded as a human Maker. There was always a conductive line from the towers through the habitats, because without the possibility of access, the Makers couldn't make.

And while she'd never hurt Ilen—had never, would never—their being who and what they were had brought harm to Ilen. Petra's willingness to take Nash into their lives had channeled hurt right to her. Like Petra was only the conduit through which harm coursed.

"Pet," Ilen said. "I do love you. You know that, right?"

"I love you," Petra said, and her hands tightened on Ilen's arms. Her proximity, her sheer physical presence, drove Petra's mind back to Ilen in cords, Ilen hidden in the atmosphere-leaking, ill-powered castoff modules of the colony, Ilen bound by conductive wire to her captor, her image on an encrypted and bounced data-stream, her life reduced to leverage. And Petra hammering out messages to a data address she suspected represented nothing.

Nash

please

what did you do, Nash?

please help, please

"I love you," Petra said again, and Ilen didn't protest her hands, fear-tight. "I'll figure this out, Ilen. What happened before isn't going to happen again."

"Pet," Ilen said, voice like mourning. She probably meant to say, *That's not what I'm afraid of, not at all*, but Petra's mind was circling around *He won't get away with it again. I'll watch him. He ought to pay for what he's done.*

Nash was waiting for her at the doors to her quarters, and Petra pushed by him. He let out a breath and followed her in.

Petra considered ignoring him, but the consideration only lasted until she reached her desk. Nash wasn't one to be ignored.

"Why are you here, Nash? Curious citizen, wants to learn more about Su resource allocation?"

"Will you listen to me?" Nash asked.

Petra let out a long breath, shaped like a growl. "That doesn't seem to end well for me."

Nash didn't take the bait, and part of Petra was disappointed. "According to the Su I don't have rights as a member of the colony," Nash said. "Anything I want, anything I want to do, you have to specifically allow me to do it. The doors to the gardens won't even open for me any more. Did you save me just so I could spend the rest of my life going from bed to baths to library and back again?"

"I saved you because Amad came into my office and jammed the comm lines," Petra said, and dropped into her chair. Storm season meant the endless headaches of the lightning storms and the scrabbling emptiness she felt when Ilen's hands weren't on her shoulders, her temples, her hips. It also meant the abundant energy, refilling their reserves as fast as they could drain it, and that meant all the Makers were in a flurry to get the big projects done. For the benefit of the colony. Her fingers twitched.

The Third Cluster expansion would be something good. She could do something good. For colony harmony, to make life better, to carry them on into the next generation of improvements, negotiations, accommodations.

You've got yours, so screw the rest of us. She and Amad had had their share of hissing and spitting, coming to uneasy truces largely because of Nash. If it wasn't for Nash now, Amad would never have come to see her. Probably wouldn't have bothered spitting on her if she was on fire.

Like she was the one who'd done something to damage their friendship, and not him.

"What do you want?" she asked. "You want garden access?" She gestured up a console and skimmed her quarters' logs with half her attention. As expected, Nash had made a few cursory access attempts. She hadn't set up access for him, though, and it didn't look like he'd had any success. And the comm lines showed no abnormalities; she doubted Amad had come in to see him.

If the Su had been willing to kill off Nash, Petra could only imagine what they'd do if they found Amad skulking about in colony territory.

"I want you to forgive me," Nash admitted. "I want things to be okay between us again."

So says the criminal to his mark, Petra thought. "Because I own you now."

She could see flickers of Nash's temper in the muscles of his face. Like he was the one who should be frustrated here. And yes, she could admit—the better part of her could admit—that he had reason: his freedoms all curtailed; his life bound up to someone who hated him, or was making a good go at hating him; no recourse but to play nice and hope for the mercy of someone he'd wronged.

The part of her that ran her thoughts and her opinions just said: *well, that's a perfectly mercenary reason, isn't it?*

"Because," Nash said, "it kills me that this is what happened between us."

And? Petra thought. "Your guilt," she said, "is the outcome I care about the least."

A door alert pinged her awareness.

Petra gave a half-voiced *"Fuck,"* and pulled herself up from her chair. Her body felt nerveless and rubbery, between the earlier Making and Ilen's ministrations and the ongoing storm. She tried not to sway as she opened the door.

In the hallway stood a smaller Su, probably young. She drew her fingers from the top of her forehead down past her thorax: deep respect for a hierarchical superior. *Sudaeg*, then; just a worker. Petra gestured superior greeting. Then, because she could, because it was allowed, because she felt it, gestured annoyance and inquiry. The Su gestured back apology and necessity.

"There's an anomaly at one of the Maker sites, Sulai Tabov," she said. "We hoped to have your expertise."

Petra nodded, resigned. "Show me the way."

The anomaly itched in her awareness like a missing tooth. A dark spot in the paths of energy, like an insulated package attached to the collection lines. Not damage or disruption—something set with intent behind it.

Something that had made the Su seek out Petra, most senior of the human Makers, specifically, in lieu of a Su maker, closer or with more expertise.

Petra turned to the *Sudaeg*, the awareness settling in her stomach. "Have there been threats?"

The Su didn't have membranes over their eyes that would allow them to blink. But the look that the Su gave her was somehow languorous, unsurprised, perhaps calling into question Petra's own inquiry. "There are frequently threats, Sulai Tabov. The aberrant human elements wish the destruction of the colony."

Not all of them, Amad would have argued. *There are fringe elements in any movement. Most of us—the reasonable ones—just want independence.*

It was the sort of distinction that abruptly stopped mattering to Petra when her wife was kidnapped. "Credible threats?" she asked.

"We do not monitor the human activity outside the bounds of the colony," the Su answered.

As sentient creatures outside the colony limits, the human separatists were none of the Su's business. Not much concept of natural security in a Su colony—they didn't read human history, either. No sense of what to expect.

"The anomaly will be removed," the Su said. "Do you anticipate that it will be dangerous?"

By which the Su meant, *Should we send a Maker, who can quickly excise it and effect any repairs, or do we send a Worker, less skilled but more expendable?* If it was a bomb—and the Su did have some experience with bombs; it resided in their historical awareness, if not their future planning—they would rather a *Sudaeg* die.

She stretched her awareness out again, trying to filter out the mental noise of the storms. The anomaly was a black box, and she felt out the currents around it. Energy flowed in, but not through. It was gathering up energy for something.

She turned her attention outward, along the line of the colony, feeling the ragged channels in the old halls that had grown around the human ship. They tingled in her awareness, like a sleeping limb halfway to nerve death; a few faint lines, pirated energy that fell below the thresholds the Su needed to care about it, enough to eke out a subsistence existence on.

Could be a battery. Energy was life in the colony; it'd be life on the ship, too. Fill up a battery at the height of storm season, and, if they calibrated carefully enough, the Su wouldn't bother trying to shut them down. They could skim off the excess and power themselves through whatever they were planning now.

But the Su had noticed, which meant that someone had screwed up. Or the Su were meant to notice, and it was meant to have some meaning for them or prod them into some action.

Petra wasn't a tactical thinker, especially not with the static of the storm, the static of Nash, and her own emotions. She was a Maker. Her skills were in smart matter and architecture. She was human, yes, but her insight into the minds of human separatists had some serious failure points.

She gestured uncertainty. A sign to the Su that her judgment in this matter could be questioned; if a *Sudaeg* questioned it, it was no affront to the hierarchy. "My inclination is to treat it as dangerous until otherwise proven," she said. "But there are facts of which I am unaware, and which you cannot provide. My analysis is inconclusive."

The Su gestured recognition. "We will proceed on your analysis, Sulai Tabov," she said. "The colony will be well."

"You're welcome," Petra said, and let herself sink back on her heels, just a little, before turning and walking home.

Nash was sitting on the couch in her quarters, brooding, when she let herself in. Rehearsing the next phase of the argument, maybe. He could be persistent when he tried.

Petra walked past him, to her desk again. "Is Amad still agitating for segregation?"

Nash looked up, expression sharp and suspicious. "You save me so I could inform on him?"

"I'll take that as a yes, then," Petra snapped. Her patience for Nash's dissembling would have been low if the storms hadn't been going on. But Nash being Nash, he seemed to see the misstep, and rushed to make sure it didn't sound *that* bad.

"I know he's still interested in it," he said. ". . . He calls it independence and not segregation, by the way."

"I remember." Petra's mouth twisted. "He know anything about tampering in the collection lines?"

Silence, for a moment, and then Nash said "Amad doesn't sabotage," with damaged calm.

"He knows the people who do," Petra said.

"He knows everyone in the movement. He doesn't get along with half of them. Seven out of ten, he disagrees with. Says that's the reason they never get anything done."

"Anything except kidnapping," Petra said. "Theft—"

Nash stood up. "I don't want to argue this with you."

"There's been tampering," Petra said. "At the height of storm season. We're trying to build this colony; they're trying to tear it down. Nash, do you know anything?"

Nash gave her a cold, even glare. "If you want me to ask around," he said, "you'll have to give me access to the outskirts."

They'd probably be able to remove the collar, out there. "I didn't save you so you could continue colluding, either," Petra said.

Anger gathered itself in tense lines in Nash's expression. Petra watched it with a kind of distant anticipation—Nash didn't lose his temper often, and she was curious how it'd look when he did. Especially if he did in a situation like this. She couldn't picture him screaming his lungs out. He was so very practiced at not saying the salient things, but the anger had to go somewhere.

She'd never been in a fight, and suspected that Nash hadn't, either. But then, there was a lot of Nash's life she wasn't privy to. Who knew what the hell went on in the outskirts?

But if it came to a fight, if he took a swing at her, she'd put him down before she had to call for anyone. A twitch of her fingers; several thousand volts through his flesh. She could feel the possibility dancing at her fingertips.

And as though Nash could feel it too, he swallowed his own anger and backed down. Gestured, with heavy irony, submission, and appeasement. "People talk about blowing up the colony. They get shouted down. Everyone with any sense knows we can't survive without the colony's resources. The last guy—Dolan—they found him taking apart the ship's engine to make a bomb. They put him outside."

The anger stuttered on that, a space underneath it opening up to void. It didn't compute, and Petra was left, for a few seconds, with no way to respond.

Outside the colony, without any environmental protection, meant a choking, lung-searing death. With protection, but without the resources of the colony, it meant dying of thirst, isolated, and alone.

And here she'd thought the excisions, the culls, were the raison d'être for separatism in the first place.

The expression on Nash's face looked oddly satisfied, for being so bitter. "Yeah," he said. "We self-police. What, you thought we were all lawless bandits scheming in dark rooms? Amad voted for the execution, by the way. He said we couldn't tolerate that sort of thing and survive as a movement."

How very Su of him, Petra wanted to say. But that would kill the conversation there, and she wasn't done with it yet. "How did you vote?"

Nash was silent for a moment. "I was sick that day," he said.

Petra suspected he was lying.

"What did you do, Nash?" she asked. "What made the Su want to excise you?"

Nash's expression twitched, and he looked away. "I didn't blow anything up or kill anyone," he said. "Or kidnap them, if that's what you're thinking."

"You don't like to get your hands dirty."

"Like you," Nash said, tones clipped, "I don't like it when people get hurt. But it looks like we're both stuck with people who do." He gestured wish for dismissal—stiffly, with bitterness in his human expression. "I think I'd like to go back to my quarters, Sulai, if that's all right with you."

You invited yourself in here, Petra wanted to say. *Not me.* But she gestured dismissal and reminder of hierarchy, to bite back instead.

Petra woke earlier than she wanted, which was a shame, given how long it had taken her to get to sleep. She kept to a common human schedule, most days, with a bit of jitter room on either side—Makers tended to put in short periods of intense effort, unlike oxygen specialists or teachers or census-takers or social engineers. So she was early enough to catch the commissary while it was mostly full, exchange pleasantries with some First Cluster residents, and ignore the knowing looks when she pulled a bulb of some tasteless, aqueous nutritional solution. Her throat would close up on anything solid or well flavored; her stomach wouldn't admit hunger. But she could get the solution down, at least.

As she drank, she gestured up a token comm line to Kaah—no video, no audio, just a quick inquiry as to when they should meet for work on Third Cluster. By the time she'd finished, Kaah had gestured back that much of their work didn't need to be synchronized. A *do what you want*, or as close as a Su would come to saying it.

The first three answers to *And what do I want?* were impossible or inadvisable. The fourth took her through the halls to Ilen.

She found Ilen in one of the medical modules, her hands on a human woman's belly, eyes closed in concentration, face a smooth mask. She looked illuminated this way.

Deep in Petra's lungs rose a stirring of the old compulsion. Petra had never wanted to carry a child, and Ilen hadn't felt strongly enough to have one herself. But Ilen was a Father, through and through. If she'd been a Su, she would have been sought after. But even with humans, who could get by without her, she found her way in—her hands on a sweat-slick belly, guiding the fertilization and implantation of an egg; her mind teasing out the development of a zygote, encouraging the health of a fetus. She was no midwife, but she might as well be. She was godfather to a good handful of the children in the colony. The genetics of her body might not appear in their bloodlines, but she was wrapped up in their genetics nonetheless.

It was something Petra's mother had never understood, because without blood children, what link did you have to the future, what solace could you have in your old age? But her mother had been closer to the generation of the colonists, for whom the unbroken interweave of genetic lines was still a practical and moral imperative.

Petra was her own generation, and she was a Maker—held close, kept jeal-ously, by the Su. The Su of this generation let humans revere their elders; they didn't discard them for the resources. They had learned that lesson, in the early violence.

And the Su cared about the colony *in toto's* link to the future, not the genetic line of any specific individual. Petra had often said she didn't have a maternal bone in her body; Ilen did, after a fashion, but she could mother Petra and her human patients and feel as fulfilled as she would with a child. As fulfilled, and considerably less harried.

Petra watched the woman, who smiled at Ilen in something like affection and pride. After a while Ilen opened her eyes and her face, in profile, changed; somewhat less saintly, more warm and human. Through the door, Petra didn't hear what they said and didn't need to. The woman gave Ilen a quick, fleeting hug, and vanished out another entrance.

As soon as she'd gone, Ilen looked over and smiled. Ilen always seemed to have a sense of where everyone was in spaces around her. Petra had asked if it was like her own sense of the energy in the colony and the lightning above, but Ilen had sworn it wasn't—not a Father skill, just her own particular social proprioception.

Ilen gestured the door open and came to greet her. Petra wrapped her arms around Ilen, pressing her face into Ilen's hair.

Ilen's hair always smelled of some kind of vegetation—a deep, grounding scent; a ritual anointment held over from the ship, from Earth comforts, from ancient times. Every family in the colony had roots to Earth as deep as any other, most of them crossing at some point. But the ship hadn't homogenized them; some lines still passed down practices like scenting one's hair when washing. Not every line could have produced Ilen.

Ilen's hands curled in the small of Petra's back, holding her close. "This is a surprise," she said.

I might have sent a Su worker to her death, Petra didn't say. Nor did she say, *I had to see you; I had to know you were safe.* "I love you," she said, instead.

Which, she thought, was really saying almost nothing.

Ilen laughed into Petra's collarbone. "I know, Pet," she said. "I could get used to you stopping by to tell me, though."

"There was something on one of the collection lines," Petra said. She hadn't meant to say it.

Ilen stilled, and Petra wasn't sure if the sinking sensation she felt was Ilen sagging back, or her own estimation of herself dropping. "Are you all right?" Ilen asked.

Petra swallowed. "Fine," she said. *But that's not really the question.*

Ilen's hands traveled up her back, catching her shoulder blades like instruments fitted for her palms. "Pet," she said. "The Su *do* learn."

Any next words were shot down in Petra's throat. She pulled back to look at Ilen and saw Ilen looking at her, her expression level and grave.

"That's my line," Petra said. *Just not to you.*

"Yeah," Ilen said, "it is. So let me remind you: the Su *do* learn. They change their behavior. Just not always as quickly or as visibly as you'd like."

"*I* didn't plant the damn thing," Petra said.

Ilen smiled, but the smile was thin. "No," she said, "but you came here to warn me. The Su are not about to let anything happen to me. And frankly, if anyone thinks about grabbing me, *they* haven't learned much from last time."

"I know the Su can learn," Petra said. "The separatists, I'm not so sure about."

"Well, the lessons just get harder from here," Ilen said. "I'm not meeting anyone for a while yet. Breakfast?"

The nutrient solution sat uneasily in Petra's stomach. "Had it," she said. "I was on my way to work."

Ilen gave her the look she used to give when Petra had said that her head was fine, or she liked the windows, or she'd let an argument go, really. She didn't even need to say anything.

And Petra was still wound tight enough *not* to let her not say anything. "What?"

"One day," Ilen said, "I will get a *Sudaeg* to come in and sit on you just to keep you in one place long enough for something to get through your head. You know they'd do it if I asked them to."

Petra jerked back. The fact that Ilen could *joke* about the hierarchy always struck her like a ruptured coolant channel. "You wouldn't do that," she said, "because you're not officially insane."

Ilen shrugged. "No, I wouldn't," she agreed. "But you'd be surprised how many of my fantasies involve things like that, these days." The corner of her mouth twitched up. "I might get to see you for more than six heartbeats if we opened our relationship up."

"I—" Petra started. But getting into an argument about what their relationship was or wasn't seemed like a less good idea than almost any other available option. "I'm still a target, Ilen. Now more than ever."

"Because Nash has so many friends on the ship that they'll ransom someone to get him back?" Ilen asked. "That explain why Amad showed up, begging?"

Petra threw out two or three of the first available responses, and completely failed to throw out the next. "What, you've been talking to Amad, too?"

"No," Ilen said. "No, I think you two both burned that bridge and tossed the cinders in chemical reprocessing."

"You think I shouldn't have?" Anger was coiling up from under Petra's stomach, down where she usually shoved misery. "You, of all people, think I should be playing nice?"

Ilen's expression went hard and uncompromising. That was another part of her; the other half of what made her an effective Father, what made her adapt to and use the Su hierarchy. Ilen could command with warmth and gentle affection, but when those didn't work, out came the steel.

"If being angry was doing a damn thing to make your life better, I'd make you a pitchfork," she said. "Find you the music from that old Earth media Amad likes. We could go on the warpath together. But it's just making you sick and sad, Petra, and it's not getting better until you fix something."

Petra bit down on any response she could make. Because oh, she'd *tried* to fix things—this entire mess was her trying and failing to fix things. Mostly just managing to keep herself in a holding pattern and scrambling away from any bombs that came up. Things were bad enough without her trying to fix them further.

Eventually, she said "I have work to do. In Third Cluster."

Ilen's expression didn't change. Apparently she still felt that there was a high degree of shit in what Petra was saying.

But she didn't call her on it. "Well," Ilen said. "Later, then. And you can feel free to stop by."

Petra grunted. She'd always been free to stop by; the invitation was more irony than anything.

"If you need anything . . ." Petra said.

"The things I could say to that," Ilen said. "I'm fine, Petra. And you're humming like a lightning rod. Go Make."

The route to Kaah this time took Petra through the ebb and flow of the crowds. Third Cluster was one of those clusters that synchronized sleep-wake cycles, to some extent—there would always be early risers and late sleepers and those who eschewed the cycle altogether, but it was consensus early morning, and human colonists filled the halls. Here and there on whatever business they had; Petra had to admit, she didn't know what they got up to.

Sulai, her mind whispered. In one of their spats, Amad had said *You're half-Su yourself. Do you even know how to speak to real people?* Nash had apologized for him, and Amad had apologized in his own way—no words, no overt gestures of contrition, but he'd brought some physical media display in from the ship and showed her an old performance of something. He'd found it hysterical. She'd found it incomprehensible, and he'd sulked off and avoided contact with her halfway to the next season.

Kaah was already Making at the outgrowth when Petra entered it, and she was beaming, inasmuch as the Su had interpretable expressions that could be read as beaming. Petra sat on the ground, crossing her legs like a Su would, and waited, with her eyes closed, watching the colony take shape in ordered lines beneath the sporadic wrath of the sky.

Finally, Kaah finished her hallway, and the bright electricity quieted down to a more latent level. She turned to Petra and gestured greeting.

"My petition for offspring has been granted," she said.

Petra blinked back into a social mindset, then processed what Kaah had said.

"That's wonderful!" Petra said, then had to search a moment for the traditional Su response. "The news is my joy; the benefit of the colony is my joy. Have you found a willing Father?"

Kaah gestured assent. "*Suva* Umet, who approved my petition. She is skilled in constructing zygotes with Father and Maker potential. As we increase our capacity for gathering energy, there will be further roles in the colony for Makers. I expect a clutch of five, potentially more."

"It will be good," Petra said. Then, a human phrase: "I'm happy for you."

Kaah gestured pleasure, then said, "Your arrival is convenient. I defer to your expertise in the dimensions of family units."

Some expertise, Petra thought. Third Cluster tended to have family homes that kept a core of children and grandchildren and grandparents all together, a few peeling off in each generation, plenty staying behind. Petra had grown in a more Su-flavored cluster; individual rooms for the most part, pairs and two-generation groupings here and there. But she had a sense for what the division of rooms should be, at least; what private areas a human expected that a Su would find extraneous, what layouts between the units would help people mix in the halls as they did in the halls below. And in any case, it was a change of subject.

Thankfully, with the Su, a conversation about pregnancy would rarely turn toward whether or not the other participants hoped for a child. It wasn't a traditional milestone in a Su life. It was a bestowed honor.

"I'll set the foundation lines," Petra said, and pressed her hands into the smartmat.

A bestowed honor. Like the fact that one of the Su Fathers had pressed her hands into Petra's mother's belly, felt out the growing cells, and whispered to them that this human child, this one, should have the gift and the curse of hearing the lightning, of feeding it to the substance of the colony walls, feeling that substance change and grow and stretch into new walls and new forms. It had taken three generations on this planet for human Fathers and Makers to be born. Was that only because the Su Fathers had taken so long to understand their different biology? Maybe it was some quirk in how the Su found individuals worthy—maybe it had taken that long to overcome their revulsion at human reproduction.

To the Su, human females were defective—they possessed the necessary organs to carry life, but not the banks of gametes that could be prompted to combine at a Father's influence. They'd found human males even more bewildering: jettisoned gamete banks walking around in sentient containers that seemed, to the Su, unnecessary.

The Su had caches of each gamete in themselves. The Su Fathers impelled combination and controlled mutation. Autosexual reproduction requiring two participants, unless the Father self-fertilized, but the relationship was hierarchical, not intimate.

She traced out the energy-bearing conduits, laying the foundation for walls here, partitions here, thick sheets of smartmat to occupy the interstitial places. Big round rooms for families to gather in; little compartments for sleep, a storage room here, a solitude room here. Life dictated the layout of the rooms and was circumscribed by it in turn; Petra only aped it, feeling out the spatial rhythm of the units below.

The lines of energy through the colony made sense. She felt alive here, *right* here, laying her will into the colony walls. All the chaos in the sky came down through the towers and the smartmat and her hands and became something solid and good. And if she could dissolve herself in the doing, so much the better.

Petra came home to the smell of something frying.

Apparently one of the workers had moved in a collection of Nash's old culinary equipment, or he'd had them delivered somehow from the colony outskirts; he was one of the only people Petra had ever known who'd had cooking supplies manufactured for him. Most everyone was content with the variety of engineered foods the Su provided. But Nash had a few old-world aesthetic sensibilities.

And Petra had to admit, he could do damn impressive things with the raw materials that came from the Su.

He'd connected up a heating apparatus to the module's power, and when she walked in he flashed her a quick smile—uneasy, and probably forced—and transferred a series of somethings into a shallow, lens-shaped bowl. Every motion was deft, as though he'd rehearsed his actions in the event of her arrival.

He filled another bowl for himself, picking them off the stack of four sitting by the cooktop. There'd been a time when all four would have been filled. Four bowls, four bulbs of drinks, four little trays of whatever Nash had been experimenting with that evening. Four cushions around a low table, with Ilen's laughter and Nash's anecdotes and Petra and Amad sparring good-naturedly over this or that bit of policy or pragmatism.

Nash had only replicated the barest bones, here. He sat cross-legged on the floor, the lens bowl in his lap.

"Let's try this again," he said.

Petra rolled her palm around the curve of the bowl, feeling the heat, and took it to her desk. "A lot's missing."

From Nash's expression, he didn't see her meaning for a moment. Then he shook his head. "No, I just meant—you know. Talking."

Ah. Petra placed the bowl on her desk, which changed itself, just a little, to hold it. *Buttering me up.*

Still, food was food, and she turned her attention to it. Thin strips of grown protein matrix—a food form modeled to mimic the striations of muscle, glistening with a sauce that smelled sharp and sweet. Edible flowers, breaded in something that had heated up golden, so that the red of the petals peeked through like sunrise on a thin-atmosphere day. A long white grain, flecked with green. All of it so much more reminiscent of the raw material than anything Su-processed, Su-consumed.

She hadn't thought she was hungry, but the smell suffused her and woke her stomach. Storm, but it *did* smell good. She'd forgotten that food was an art, in some of the human subcultures. For a long time now, she'd just approached it as one of the mechanisms necessary to not die.

"I kinda used your authority to get some of this," he said, with a note of apology in his voice. "I told the *Sudaeg* that it would ease the mental strain of the storms."

That'd explain it, then; she hadn't thought they'd stock fresh flowers in the commissary. Low demand. Tension wound through Petra's jaw. "Always the people person, Nash."

"I'm not going to abuse your authority," Nash said. "I'm pretty sure I couldn't if I tried."

There were too many things Petra could say to that, and they all twisted in her throat. She took a bite, instead.

Flavors she'd known the names for, once, flooded her mouth; textures she hadn't eaten in ages rolled against her tongue. She let a long breath out and cursed. "I forgot all about this," she said.

"Old Earth specialty," Nash said, which was a lie. It was some new reinterpretation of the old cooking tradition, twisted around to match whatever food plants they'd brought and established in the colony. So much of Earth had remained on Earth, lost to their colony either forever or for the time it took for another generation ship to decide to come and bring their own array of important things.

"Lucky *Hurem*," Petra said, and took another bite. Nash chuckled and laid into his own food.

"You ever go down to the Folly Garden Cluster?" he asked.

Despite herself, Petra smiled. "Haven't. They did finish it, though."

"I heard," Nash said, and grinned. This smile looked less forced. Not quite right yet, but on its way. "Original size, too?"

Petra let out a laugh. "You know the Su," she said. "They commit."

"They committed to a spitball," Nash said. "Lin and I had *no idea* how to design a garden. They wanted a size, we said 'large' thinking we wanted something bigger than the garden modules we had, and when we woke up there was this *cavern* that a Maker had just gone ahead and put together and we were supposed to find a way to fill it. No one even thought that, hey, this is a ridiculous size."

"You said 'large,' they thought 'large in terms of absolute Making size,'" Petra said. "The Su tend to assume that humans know what humans want and will say what they mean when they ask for things." Whether or not they'd approve of those things as benefiting the colony was another question, but Nash and his colleague had asked for space at the height of storm season. They'd asked for a resource nearly as abundant as air. Any other time, and they'd have had to pin down dimensions and limit their expectations and find a Maker who felt like indulging human needs was a priority just then.

"That was the first resource allocation project I had, remember that?" Nash said. "Talk about distorting your expectations early."

"You didn't understand the Su," Petra said. "*I* would have expected that."

"So you told me," Nash said, and tilted his head at her. "That was back when you liked me."

Petra's humor cooled. She set down her utensil, fingers braced on the curve of the composite. She could etch it with lightning, but not much else; it wouldn't hold a charge or define a path through which intelligent circuitry could flow. "Remember when *Hurem* Keyne paid me a visit?" she asked.

All humor vanished from Nash's expression. "Don't," he whispered.

"Remember," Petra said, voice low to keep from breaking, "when I came home to a habitat rupture? Remember how I could smell the sulfur coming in from outside? They set off a blast inside our home, Nash. The lights were out. I could hear the air ingress. I couldn't find Ilen. I didn't know if she was lying dead in a corner. You wouldn't remember that, would you, because you *had run.*"

Nash was staring down at the floor, jaw stiff, expression hard. "I didn't ever think anyone would come after you," he said.

"You didn't ever think," Petra corrected. "You want to reminisce about the times when I liked you? You know exactly what happened. You made your choices, you sold us out, and when it all went up in sparks you vanished back to the ship. All that's on you, Nash—it's still on you. You think you can cook me dinner and all's forgiven?"

"I made mistakes," Nash said. "And people got hurt because of them. I know I'm not going to make that right, but I figured I could at least start making it up to you. Start," he added, quickly, as Petra found a retort at the tip of her tongue, "doing something good in your life, at least."

Petra stared at him.

"You look like you haven't eaten since I left," he said.

Petra blinked. She hadn't considered how she'd look to someone who hadn't seen her in so long—why would it matter, anyway? She knew she'd taken to running off the tension. Knew she felt harder and leaner than she had back in the good times. But seeing a fleck of maternalism in Nash stunned her for a moment.

Then, like everything about Nash, it fed a bit more fuel into the slow-burning anger in her gut.

"The food was very good," she said, stiffly. She couldn't find a way to say *I don't need your good works; I've survived this long without you caring; There's nothing you can do to change what happened, so why bother trying now?*

"Yeah," Nash said. "You know, I didn't do much cooking out in the ship. Harder to get food variety, there. It's more of a holiday thing."

Plenty of things Petra could ask, at that. *What kind of holidays do you celebrate, out there?* or *Wasn't there a big push to get the ship's hydroponics up and running again?* Time was, she'd been curious about life on the ship the way she'd been curious about life back on Earth: it was a foreign land, and one she'd never be visiting. Tales of strange customs were always passing amusements.

Now, the comment felt barbed.

"I'm glad," she said, "you've found something to enjoy here."

Nash bit back words—probably a curse, probably some invective. "Please," he said. "Can we just start over? Start from here?"

You haven't been living here, went Petra's anger. *I'm here. I'm always here. Where the hell else would I be starting from?*

Probably wasn't what he meant. Probably what he meant was, *can't we pretend like we don't have a past?* Or more likely, *can't we just pretend like our only past's the good one?*

And maybe he could pretend that they could have a fresh start. But Petra couldn't imagine what the hell it would take to feel good about this. About Amad showing up and throwing Nash's life into her arms, like it was her responsibility. About Nash forcing a smile and bringing his guilt to lay at her feet like it was her job to forgive him.

About him bringing up those times before all this, the food and the company and the easy companionship. Petra didn't get along with most people—Ilen and Nash had been notable exceptions. She'd pushed Ilen away herself, and Nash—

Was Nash.

"We are," she said, "exactly where we are."

The question was, as it always was, where the hell to go from here.

Sooner or later something would break, one way or another. Petra knew this. She'd either wall off Nash completely, let him live his ghost of a life out beyond the periphery of her awareness, or she'd crack, let him in again, maybe find herself dragged along to forgiving him. This shambling mockery of their former friendship was too unstable not to decay. But just the thought of forgiving him made her feel duped and stupid, like she was falling again for the easy smile and the amiable interest.

She knew that where they were now, what she was feeling, was miserable. Thing was, there was quite some distance between knowing that and knowing how to fix it.

And she didn't have a way to say it. Never had been the best with words, except those words she had a chance to rehearse, over and over, locked in her head for hours.

Still, she might have found something to say if the colony hadn't shuddered, as something in the sky exploded.

Petra's head snapped up, even though she couldn't see a damn thing through the colony composite. But there was no time to feel shock or fear: an instant later two more explosions shook the ground, presaged by a matter of moments by a wave of energy that rammed straight through her mind and tossed her in all directions at once.

Petra's mouth was open but sound wasn't coming out; her body curled and spasmed outward, skin and muscle and bone striking smartmat composite desk and floor and walls, mind tossed between them as though it didn't have a home in either one. *Attack*, part of her thought, but the rest of her was alight. Drowning in lightning. Her mind was scrabbling through the whole of the colony, lit up like a nightmare, smartmat *there* growing into tumorous outcrops, food receptacles *there* searing their contents or expelling them, the insulation at the oxygen recyclers glowing their resistance.

Nash *here*, reaching out to grab her, his voice insistent and concerned, and Petra threw out a hand and found his body and sent great gluts of energy cascading out of her—through her body straight from the screaming sky and the overloaded colony walls—and the body that was *Nash* flew away and out of her awareness again.

And then awareness flew out of her awareness, caught and twisted on the overload, and she was nowhere.

There was nothing, and then there was noise and senseless sense data and pain and *noise*, and then there was a tumult of energy she couldn't find her way out of.

And then there was a tiny sliver of calm, pressing its way into her awareness, with the barrage of energy hammering around it. Petra reached for it, tried to focus in the wreckage of all her thoughts, and the calm pressed deeper into her until she came to the surface of cool air and nausea and a hand on her forehead.

Petra tried not to whimper. At whatever sound did come out of her, the hand shifted, and a long, cool sensation wended down Petra's throat and into her stomach, settling it.

"Love?" Ilen asked.

Petra groped for her hand. Her body felt disconnected at the joints; all the muscles felt like water. Her coordination was shot. Ilen found her hand for her and pushed a sense of stability into her bones.

"Come on," Ilen said, and got an arm around her shoulders. "Come on, Pet. Sit up. Ground."

Vertiginous motion. The whole world went tilt-a-whirl and Petra collapsed against Ilen, swinging her feet out of the infirmary cubbybed, pressing bare soles into the floor.

"Ground," Ilen said again, and Petra fumbled for the energy in her mind. Everything was out of whack. The walls were cacophonous. The storm outside was too much, too close.

She took the energy in her body and the energy in the air and pushed it down into the channels beneath the floor of the habitat that would carry it to its repositories. She could feel them, distant and bright: new ones, as well, likely put into place by the Su Makers, who wouldn't have been incapacitated as she was.

All of her ached. The *colony* ached. The new channels stood out like lines of cold metal grafted into living flesh.

Then she could feel Ilen's fingers on her temples, Ilen's presence trying to clear up the mess of her mind.

"Pet," Ilen said. "If you can think, you need to deal with Nash. They're going to kill him."

Rage tingled at Petra's fingertips. Ilen must have felt it, must have felt the balance of her body's energies shift, because she moved her hands, palms against Petra's cheeks, tilting her head so Petra's choices were to look at her or close her eyes.

"Petra," Ilen said. "You almost killed him."

"*Fuck*," Petra breathed, and it sure as hell felt like the sky was falling in on her. She cast an arm out, seeing Ilen's shoulders, and Ilen got herself under it and pulled her up.

"All right?" Ilen asked, and Petra made herself nod. Then they were off; Petra was stumbling, her weight on Ilen, back through the halls to the jurisdictor.

There was a different *Sudaeg* there this time, her carapace paler, her stature taller—some older generation, then. Petra's stomach roiled, and not all of it was vertigo.

"Sulai Tabov," the Su said, and gestured respect and consideration. "Your health benefits the colony. You experience adequate recovery?"

"I request *Suva* Ilen's continued attention," Petra said. Beside her, Ilen made a perfunctory, granting gesture—as eager to dispense with the pleasantries as Petra was to not deal with any of this. "I also request aberrant Nash Carder's status."

"He is to be excised," the Su said. "Has there been a confusion?"

Petra nearly laughed. From what she could tell, a collection tower had been blown up. Of course there had been a confusion. But that wasn't what the Su worker meant. "He should not be excised."

"You yourself partially excised him," the Su observed. No *wounded* here; no *you hurt him, Petra, what were you thinking.* She hadn't been thinking. "Do you not wish this interpreted as your intention?"

Petra closed her eyes. Most of the Su didn't bother learning human expression; humans could speak or gesture what they needed understood. "His excision is not my intention."

"And yet, with knowledge of the effects of lightning energy on human physiology, you discharged a great deal through his body. Sulai Tabov," the Su said. "Are you admitting violent actions not in accordance with your intention?"

That was the question.

So far as Petra knew, the Su didn't understand self-control. They didn't understand that an emotional urge to do one thing could conflict with an intellectual desire to do another. If Petra wanted Nash hurting, the Su would understand it as wanting him dead. If they understood Petra hurting Nash and not wanting him dead, they would understand that as a dangerous aberration in Petra's own mind. A disease that, because it was violent, might warrant excision.

The leftover energy twisted around her gut, and bile attempted the back of her throat. But Ilen drew herself up.

"*Sudaeg,*" she said, and the Su made a gesture of deep respect. "Sulai Petra is human. You are aware that human Makers of the early generations can experience cognitive overload in high-energy environments? Interpret the situation in that light."

The Su made a gesture of apology, and turned to Petra again. "Sulai Tabov," she said. "Was it your intention to excise the aberrant, or did you damage him as an indirect result of the destruction of the lightning tower?"

I damaged him because I was angry and in pain and I resented the hell out of him and still do, Petra couldn't say. "The discharge which injured him was an indirect result of the attack on the tower." *Please don't kill him. Please don't kill me.*

"Is it your intention that he return to your custody?"

Can you be trusted? seemed to be the undercurrent of that, and Petra could have spit fire or bile there. Could *she.* Like maybe she should recuse herself for Nash's own safety, never mind that it was his people who'd done this to her.

"That," she said, "is the intention"—the *option*—"I have."

The *Sudaeg* put up her foreclaws, and gestured a series of commands into the jurisdictor module. "Then I release him into your custody," she said. "You are free to return him for excision at any time."

"I am keenly aware of that fact," Petra said, and pushed on toward the cells.

The moment they got to the cell and the membrane lensed open, Petra shoved away from Ilen's support. The Su didn't bother putting chairs or other furniture in their cells; creature comforts were too human a concept, comfort for the condemned even more so. She let herself collapse to the ground in a messy tangle of limbs, tipped against the wall.

"Is Amad part of this?" she hissed at Nash. Amad, whose friend had just faced excision. Amad, who'd had to beg someone in the Su power structure for his friend's life.

Amad, who'd hated the Su for years, and might take a chance at striking back at them if he could.

Amad, who'd practically adopted Nash, and who Nash would protect. Nash could be stupidly loyal, from time to time. It was just that none of that loyalty had been directed toward Petra, when it came down to it, in the end.

Nash raised his head, and there was actual terror in his eyes. There were lines under his jaw, spidering up his neck—discoloration from an electrical burn.

Petra drew back. A hand touched her shoulder and Ilen settled down next to her, a warm solid presence, twining the fingers of her own hand around Petra's.

Petra took in a breath, and tried not to feel how jealous she was of Ilen's steadiness, that ability to move past it all, to smile and forgive if it was the *useful* thing, the healthy thing, to do. Petra's head was a lightning storm. In a way it always had been, even when the atmosphere was quiet outside.

There was pain on Nash's face, as he gathered up his resolve to speak. After this, he might well believe that Petra planned on excising him, the moment he got too far out of line. Between that and the injury she'd inflicted, even accidentally, it almost made Petra feel like they were on equal ground.

"Do you really think the Su want what's best for us?" Nash asked.

For some reason, she hadn't been expecting that. She didn't know what she had been expecting—groveling apology, maybe, or some arrogant parroting of the party line. But Nash waved his hands to the soft cell walls—walls that were as eager as anything Su to close in and dissolve him.

Dissolve both of them, given a chance. The cell was much smaller, this time. It had already begun to close in, Petra thought, when Ilen had come to wake her.

They were far too close.

"I think the Su created this colony," she said. "And they've been adapting it to human use. They provide for us as well as they know how to, and—"

"As well as they know," Nash pressed. "But they have a different biology— they're from a different environment. They don't understand us—"

"And *blowing up a lightning tower* is supposed to help?"

Nash gestured helplessly. "I didn't know—it's not that I want—I can *understand* it, Petra, even if I don't agree. If we don't have the Su to rely on—" he began.

"Then we could *all* be exiles," Petra said. "And most of us like it here." Then, before he could retort, she asked, "What the hell did you do, Nash? Why did the Su want your execution?"

Did you come in here to tear us all down?

Nash looked away. "What the hell does it matter?" he asked. "The Su thought it was a crime. Isn't that all you care about?"

Petra shook off Ilen's hand, and reached out and grabbed Nash by the throat.

Nash's whole body went rigid, and an angry, twisting thrill wound through Petra's gut. This was a problem, this was something she'd have to think about, have to talk to Ilen about, but it felt *good* to feel that fear under her fingers. To know that on some fucking axis, at least, what she thought and felt mattered to Nash. In a way that it apparently hadn't, back when it was just her trust and her friendship on the line, and not the looming threat of excision.

"I could have been *excised*, out in that other room," she said, running over the intake of breath from her side, over the screaming in her head that she was going too far, or not far enough. "Because I wasn't trying to kill you when I almost killed you. Because if Ilen hadn't had the rank of a Su Father and if she didn't still care about both of us and *fuck* if I know why she does, they would have stamped me out because I was this close to seizures because of what *Amad's friends* did. You think I'm above all this? I've got mine? I live and die by the same sudamn rules. Do you fucking live by any? Do you just dream of not living by any?"

She could feel Nash's heartbeat racing under her fingers; feel him swallow, feel him breathe. Might have meant something if she was Ilen; as it was, it was just proof that he, like her, was a haphazard collection of blood and muscle and bone. Bodies didn't tell her much.

Beside her, Ilen breathed, "Oh, *Pet.*"

Petra shuddered. Ilen's voice was soft, like she'd just realized something, but if Ilen didn't know Petra was a walking disaster by this point, she just hadn't been paying attention. And that'd be all right, then. They could just blast all the illusions to pieces today.

Ilen reached out—slowly, carefully—and put her hand on Petra's wrist, disentangling her fingers from Nash's throat, and then drawing her in, Petra's head under her chin.

It wasn't until she had Ilen's arms around her that Petra realized just how badly she was shaking.

She turned into Ilen's chest and screwed her eyes shut, because even if she couldn't stop Nash from seeing this, she could stop herself from seeing the look in his eyes. She didn't want to fall apart—sick and shaking and blasted half to hell, ready to pave the rest of the way with her own Maker's hands. She didn't want him to see that this was how twisted-on-hooks she got. Didn't want him to know that he'd won.

Even if this had never been about winning, for him. But for all the power she had over him, he had *this* over her, and wasn't that just something?

She could feel, in the movement against the crown of her head, that Ilen had turned to look at Nash. She could feel a tilt of Ilen's head, and then Nash stood up and his unsteady footsteps left the cell. *Leaving us in it,* Petra thought. *And isn't that the story of all of us.*

There would have been a long silence, if not for the thrumming of blood and the hard drag of breath and Ilen making soothing noises, soothing motions of hands and power and influence. And Petra leaned into it despite herself.

"Come back to live with me," Ilen said, in time. "You can Make yourself an office in my quarters. You're not protecting me by staying away, Pet, you know that. And I don't want to see you on your own."

A laugh echoed up from somewhere in Petra, but it was a largely hollow thing. "Clearly not alone any more, am I?"

"No," Ilen said, but it didn't sound like agreement. "But you're more locked in your head than you've ever been. And, Pet, I know what your head's like, in the storms."

Petra could have said *the storms aren't the half of it,* but Ilen being Ilen, she would know that. Ilen being Ilen, Petra thought she meant *any storms, not just the ones in the atmosphere.* Nash was a sudamn storm of his own.

"I'm still here," she repeated.

"Is that the only thing that matters?"

Why not? Petra thought, and Ilen drew her hand back through Petra's hair.

"Just which one of you did you want me to file the grievance over?" Ilen asked. "Trusting someone isn't a crime, Pet, and you can stop punishing yourself for it any time now. Maybe you could even try again."

Petra laughed, though it wasn't much like laughter.

"You and Nash both saw the best potentials in people," Ilen said. "The only difference is that Nash still does."

"Do you even know why we're in here?" Petra asked. As far as she was concerned, there was more support for her point of view in the air than for Ilen's. Or Nash's, if that didn't go without saying.

"Four parts stubbornness and three parts enemy action," Ilen said. "Pet."

"I'll find a way through this," Petra said. It was easy to say if she didn't think about how much she was lying when she said it.

"I'm here for you," Ilen said.

Petra let out a breath and sagged closer to her. "Ilen," she said. "It was always supposed to be the other way."

There came a time when Petra could stand again, and take her leave. And she did, and she walked back to her quarters and went inside, and there was Nash stripped to his trousers, a Su biomat healing agent extruded from the wall and creeping across his skin.

Petra hadn't thought to give him access to the medical stations, but apparently someone had—Ilen, maybe, or Amad had come in and done whatever he could do to muck with the systems. But when Petra walked in the door Nash pulled himself away, the biomat suctioning off his bare shoulders, and went to one knee, head bowed. He touched his forehead, drawing his hand down in a line toward the ground. Gestured abasement.

"I didn't," he said, "want *any* of this to happen."

Petra stood rigid, watching him. There were still traces of discoloration on his skin, dark trees standing out like lash marks where lightning had coursed through him, gathering around his neck under the Su collar. A disconnected part of her thought she should check his collar; make sure she hadn't flooded the thing, make sure some control was still in place. Nash kept his eyes down.

"I want to fucking fix this," he said. "But there isn't a way, is there? What do I do, Petra?" Then, after a moment—not a long enough pause into which to speak—he said, "Amad wants to steal me back from you."

Petra's hands curled. "Of course you've been in contact with him."

"Of course he's been in contact with me," Nash said. "He cares. We both cared about you, believe it or not. But we told the wrong people the wrong things and then everything went to hell so fast that saving our own skins was all we could do. Would it have helped you or Ilen for us to get thrown into excision chambers then?"

Yes, part of her said, but it was the same part that would have watched Nash die in the first place. Small and miserable. *I could have saved you then. Would have meant something, then, that you faced what you did wrong.*

"I never thanked you," Nash said.

Petra's stomach turned.

"I showed up trying to spread separatist sentiment, and you didn't agree with me, but you made a space for me anyway," Nash said, and Petra's train of thought jolted. This wasn't about saving him from excision; it was about that time, years ago, when they'd worked and eaten and laughed together. When the word *friend* didn't have to stretch thin to cover them. "Got me into resource allocation. You know, there actually were times where I thought I was doing some good?"

"You were doing good," Petra said. "Doing good work is hard and slow. It's not flashy bright results like blowing up a tower."

Pain flickered under the muscles of Nash's face. Petra looked away.

Good work was the slow, generation-by-generation change of Su attitudes. It was the vanished practice of culling human elders. The dwindling practice of culling dissidents—though that probably didn't look dwindling to Nash. It was Petra, standing in the miasma of seasons-long headaches and knowing that the next generation of human Makers would benefit from what the Su Fathers had learned from her; that the next generation would call the lightning with more ease and less pain than she had.

Good work meant enduring the things that weren't perfect, because the people who solved things by burning them to the ground weren't people Petra would trust to build good infrastructure.

But that was Petra's thought on the matter. Amad had different ideas. The separatists, too. And as for Nash, well, who the hell knew where he stood, but him?

"Maybe," Nash said, and Petra could hear the separatist sentiment lingering around his tone. Words like *unendurable*, like *insurmountable difficulties*. One of Nash's great-great-grands had been an original colonist, excised for reasons Petra had never looked up. Amad's own parents had been excised— they'd been separatists of the violent strain. Petra had no such painful history. *Maybe it's easy for you to say*, the old saw went, *"wait and see."*

Maybe, Petra thought, there just were no good options, but she'd stand by hers as the best of the imperfect ones.

"I was informing on you from the beginning," Nash said. "I didn't think of it that way. I guess Amad and the others did."

And she, like an idiot, had taken him in and showed him the gardens in First Cluster and introduced him to her wife and talked politics and plans for the future. How they must have drunk that up, back where Nash came from. They must have thanked him.

How must that have felt.

What did you do, Nash? The question was on the tip of her tongue. And really, she could make Nash answer.

In the end, though, she didn't have to make him.

"You know how they got me?" he asked. "I came back in. I was trying to get in with one of the younger human Fathers. See if we could find some common ground. I guess I was spoiled by you; he pegged me pretty fast as a separatist, and tossed me to the Su, with prejudice. He never lodged a grievance over me, though. You know, you're the only person who ever has?"

Petra's stomach stilled like a dead thing. "I said that Ilen should have. It would have had more weight coming from her."

"I was nothing, remember?" Nash snorted. "Wasn't a *Sudaeg* any more, after I left allocation. *Hurem* Nash Carder. A grievance from a Maker had plenty of weight on its own." He looked at her. "I told Amad that Ilen was learning how to make human Fathers and Makers in utero. Amad told someone else. That's why they decided to take her. Can you imagine what that would do for human independence? We wouldn't need the Su at all."

"You made her a target," Petra said.

Nash showed his palms. "If you hadn't listed that grievance, they'd never have handed me over to you."

Petra laughed, if that was what you wanted to call it. "How convenient for you."

It was an unusual sight, to see Nash struggle with words. But there was a struggle between his throat and his jaw now, as though human articulators could not shape human words into their right sentiment. He gestured helplessness, and abasement again. "What can I do?"

Change the past, maybe, Petra thought. *Convince the Su to take back the ship territories. Give them what they need to do that. Hurt all the rest of these friends of yours the way you hurt me.*

"What makes you think I have an answer?"

Nash's shoulders slumped, just slightly. "Maybe I just look up to you," he said.

Then, literally, he did look up. Met her eyes, held her gaze.

"I'm going to keep trying," he said.

As long as I own you, Petra thought. Made it hard to trust his good intentions, even when some small traitorous part of her was tempted to.

"I'm going to go lie down," Petra said, and turned away from him.

Petra made it back through her quarters to her sleeping cubby and collapsed into bed, staring up at the curving ceiling.

She could feel an active bank of lightning clouds moving in. Energy for the colony, noise and pain for her. Not too long and they'd be right over her, and she'd be lucky to keep stringing thoughts together. Not that her thoughts were proving so helpful to her now.

She raised her hand and caught the faint lines of energy that pervaded the colony, and she almost tweaked them, almost gestured a comm channel into being, but stopped herself. That was interesting. She hadn't come this close to calling in a long time.

What do I do, Ilen?

Her fingers held there, on the edge of completing the gesture. Opening the comm line, seeing Ilen's face projected in the dark.

There'd been a time when she could have just rolled over, pressed her face into the curve of Ilen's neck at the shoulder, said wordlessly that which she didn't have words for. And Ilen would wrap around her, human warmth and human softness, and make the noise in her head go away. Lightning or no lightning. It was a skill Petra had never developed in herself.

What do I do, Ilen? Storms, what do I do?

A pressure was creeping up between her shoulder blades; it mirrored, above her, the crashing power of an unstable atmosphere, of some cataclysmic ecological mistake. The kind of thing that made anything she or Nash or Ilen or Amad could do pale by comparison. They hadn't managed to bring down an entire world.

Just felt like it, sometimes.

Her hand curled around the air. Even from here, with great effort, she could punch a spire of smart matter into the sky like she could cut it apart. With that cloud formation rolling in, the energy would be replenished as fast as she could deplete it. The Su would question it, but probably not excise her for it, and it would be just as pointless and futile as most of her other options.

Feel good, though, that energy coursing through her. Proof that she could make a mark, even if in the end it didn't matter.

She moved her hand, changed her gesture. Contact addresses scrolled through her awareness: an array of human and Su connections she wouldn't let herself reach out for. After three loops through she settled on the old address for Amad—a contact that she hadn't erased, despite every reason to do so. The address had been dead at Ilen's kidnapping and was probably still dead now, but the data pings, heading off into nowhere, occupied part of her awareness. With all the various storms, any distraction was welcome.

Anyway, calling out into nothingness fit her mood. She could sense the change in the data, the signals routing out, and watch them, waiting until they were dissolved in her awareness by the lightning strikes.

Then the nothingness answered.

The screen fitzed into existence in front of her, the pale white of ship lighting casting most of the picture as edges and impressions. What wasn't faint and poorly defined, though, was the face of the man who'd answered the comm.

"The hell?" Petra said.

Amad looked just as confused as she was. *"You're the one who called me!"*

"The hell are you still responding on this address?" Petra asked, scrambling up to sit and face the screen. And it might have been her imagination, but she thought Amad flushed.

"I—look, a colony data address is useful, okay? Why are you calling if you thought the address was dead?"

"Diagnostics," Petra said.

Amad stared at her for a moment. *"You,"* he said, *"are a crap liar."*

"We can't all be good at it," Petra growled.

Amad made a series of gestures that Petra couldn't interpret. She shook her head, and squinted at the screen. Some kind of human gesture, she thought; there were physical nonverbal languages in human history, and ship people sometimes pulled those things out as counterculture. Whatever he was saying, Petra got the feeling it wasn't complimentary.

"Right, so you found my little not-so-secret data address," Amad said, his voice still coming through flustered. Why the hell he felt flustered was an open question. If the emotion had anything to do with why he'd kept a data address he'd only set up at Petra's insistence in the first place, Petra didn't want to examine the situation too closely. *"Should we both go into another room and pretend this was a wrong gesture that never happened?"*

Petra's head was pounding. It sounded like an appealing option. Except then Amad would get in contact with Nash again, try to smuggle him back out to the edge of the colony and get the collar off, and this would probably come up—in a *what the hell is Petra playing at* way or an *is Petra investigating us* way or a *is something wrong with her* way, and Petra's mind flashed to Nash, kneeling on the floor, hand moving from his forehead to the ground.

What the hell were any of them supposed to do?

She let out a breath and collapsed back to the bed. Energy was itching at her fingertips, ready for the shaping.

Do something, it seemed to say.

"We need to talk," she said.

Not every writer enjoys the act of writing. Robert Reed enjoys writing. The author of several hundred stories, Reed is perhaps best known for his Great Ship—a world-sized machine journeying across the galaxy. *Marrow* and *The Memory of Sky* are two novels set in that universe. His stand-alone novella, "A Billion Eves," won the Hugo in 2007. Among the busy author's recent efforts is a giant alternate history entitled *The Trials of Quentin Maurus*, available only through Amazon and Kindle. Robert lives in Lincoln, Nebraska, with a small family of distractions.

PARABLES OF INFINITY

Robert Reed

There were better workers aboard the Great Ship. Virtuous entities with proven resumes reaching back across the aeons. But the timetable was inflexible, the circumstances brutal. Seventeen hours, six minutes, and two breaths. The job had to be completed within that impossible span, beginning now. Now. The client was among the weakest citizens of the galaxy, reasonably healthy one moment, and in the next, passing out of life. What wasn't a home and wasn't a shell had to be rebuilt from scratch. If the client perished, nobody was paid. But the respectable guilds would take too much time. The Avenue of Tools. That's who the experienced contractor approached when trying to dodge the bureaucracies. Speaking through private channels, he could offer extraordinary pay for brutal, brief work. "But only for those who get here first, and I mean immediately."

Then, one final enticement.

"And no background checks," the contractor promised.

The Avenue looked more like a clogged artery than any traditional street, and the 'Tools' portion of the name was a stubborn relic of intentionally clumsy translations. Every resident was a devised organism that lived against the walls, stacked high on its neighbors and waiting for work. Many were AIs, yes. But there were also organics drawn by various means, most sporting rugged exoskeletons and interchangeable limbs. According to galactic law and the ruling captains, every 'tool' was emancipated. All were competent, purpose-capable individuals. But like stone hammers and old plasma drills, they shared one sorry feature: each had been discarded by a previous owner.

The Great Ship was a vast machine, and the Avenue wasn't particularly close. But seven tools boarded slam-caps and made the journey. All were hired immediately, but finding more than enough hands, the contractor modified his earlier promise. Criminal histories were examined. One member of the team was subsequently released and arrested. The remaining six received wet-ware educations, and the new team plunged into the frantic work. Which has zero bearing on the story. With two breaths to spare, the project was finished and finished successfully. Competence never makes for an interesting tale. Tools appreciated that even more than humans did. But of course competence should always be welcomed with a glad heart, and that's why the contractor was humming while he paid his crew.

"Never seen an odder job," he mentioned.

The fresh funds were eagerly consumed by those ex-employees. Five offered agreeable, "Thank yous," and then five of them rushed off.

But the quiet tool preferred to linger.

She was female by choice or design, or maybe only by chance. Her visible biography reached back ten million years, which wasn't particularly remarkable. Well-designed AIs could yank out their own cognitive centers, replacing the weakest for better and then shifting their identities into fresh neurons. But today's background check showed several names riding the entity, and most interesting, the oldest name was based on a language extinct for millions of years.

Offering that old name, the contractor repeated his thanks.

Then the tool said, "I've been swallowed by many assignments far more peculiar than this, sir."

Neither of them had pressing engagements. The contractor sat on the edge of a cultivation chamber, and knowing how to prompt machinery, he said, "Let me judge what's peculiar."

The tool was large when she was naked, and she was dressed and gigantic now. The carapace was Mandelbrot-inspired, made from lovely diamond and a lovelier iron, and it was punctured in dozens of places. Where needed, arms and legs had been added. What wasn't a mouth produced words, and what couldn't be confused for eyes were staring at the human who demanded to be impressed. What did she know about this man? Quite a lot, she felt. Her research as well as a dedicated sieving of social noises proved that this compilation of meat and bioceramics was born on the Great Ship, and more importantly, he was barely a thousand years old. Which made him innocent and smug. Humans often felt they were blessed, and with reason: their young species owned the largest, most impressive starship ever constructed. And that's why the tool picked the story sure to leave her audience astonished.

"I'm older than you realize," she began.

"I see ten million years."

"I'm far older than that, sir."

The human had a perfectly reasonable face, ageless but holding the jittery energies common to recently born boys. Except there were occasions, like now, when the man seemed more complicated than a coy little sack of meat. In the eyes, mostly. When those wet white and blue eyes looked at her, she discovered a focused intensity that she had never witnessed in any other contractor.

The tool's longest limb reached toward his patient face and then reached farther. What served as toes gripped the cultivation chamber, first by a long helve and then a sealed extrusion valve. The just-completed project had demanded several thousand kilos of an exceptional grade of hyperfiber. Their former client was now sleeping safe inside the universe's finest armor. Unless, of course, a weapons-grade plasma torch arrived, or a black hole decided to gut the new home.

The tool said, "My first assignment," and paused.

The human offered silence. Nothing else.

"Was to cultivate hyperfiber," she continued. "That's the only reason I was built. And if I have a genius, hyperfiber is it."

The man nodded, feet absently tapping the granite path.

"I was working on a rather larger scale than this," she continued, invoking that respectable technique of misdirecting the audience's imagination.

"More than ten million years ago," said the man.

"Yes."

A smile emerged, and in his eyes, suspicion.

"This starship of yours," she said.

Wet eyes grew larger. "It isn't mine."

"Yes, agreed. But human, tell me this: have you ever wondered how this marvel was built?"

Larger than worlds, the Great Ship was discovered outside the Milky Way. A cold, lifeless derelict racing at one-third light speed, it might be billions of years old, implying that it was cobbled together in some distant portion of a much younger universe.

"I've never asked myself how," said the man. Then laughter emerged with the mocking words. "Not once. Not ever. No."

"Well, I know how," she said.

The laughter grew louder and angrier. Or happier. She was beginning to realize that this was a rather difficult creature to disassemble.

"Because you helped build the Ship," he guessed.

Every limb pointed at their surroundings. "If my hands and feet had done any piece of this, I would remember. And I don't have those recollections."

"Too bad," he said.

"I'm talking about my first job and a hundred thousand years of labor," she said. "You see, my makers intended to build their own Great Ship. Long before humans existed. Ages before anyone realized that this kind of wonder already existed."

"How long ago?"

"Ninety-three million years," she said.

The human took a moment to frame his answer.

"Bullshit," he said.

She offered her best contemptuous laugh.

Then he said, "I'm not a student of anything. But I don't remember any history where any species was stupid enough to attempt construction on this scale."

"Agreed," she said. "Inside this galaxy."

Big eyes grew small, the mouth clenched tight as could be.

"Do you want to hear my story, or don't you?" she asked.

"Yes to both," the human said. "I do, and I don't. So you tell it, and let's both discover what I think."

The contractor wasn't ancient, certainly not compared to the Great Ship or this well-traveled tool. But he was quite a lot older than he appeared to be. His born name was Pamir and he was an important captain serving the Great Ship, but certain troubles caused him to leave that life and the greatest profession. Hiding ever since, he had worn a wild variety of names and jobs, lives and passions. One of the galaxy's great experts in wearing carefully contrived life stories, he earned what he could to thrive, and that included hoarding secret funds and prebuilt lives ready for the moment his present lies began to crumble.

Pamir leaned back, looking like a man who had nowhere else to be.

"I was built near the center of a different galaxy," the tool began. "A satellite galaxy, but not to your Milky Way. No, this was a little sister to what you call Andromeda. My galaxy's stars were predominantly ancient, metal-poor and unsuited for life. But a later bloom of young stars produced rock worlds and metal worlds, and biologies, and a few lasting civilizations."

Remaining in character, the contractor offered a shrug and one vaguely interested gaze. But the genuine Pamir was interested enough to create a complete list of candidates, rating the likelihood of each while throwing none aside.

"I was born above a hot world," the tool reported. "An almost nameless world of iron and baked rock orbiting a red dwarf sun. There was nothing remarkable about that solar system, except that the sun and its dozen planets weren't native to my galaxy. Large events inside Andromeda had thrown them free. As a consequence, these interlopers were blessed with enormous momentum. And even better, their future course would carry them close to a massive local star and its black hole companion. Tailoring that flyby was possible. Barely. My makers had already spent thousands of years abusing the red dwarf. They struck its face with lasers, sank antimatter charges into its body. Towering flares rose up from the sun, punching the same piece of the sky, slowly changing the solar system's trajectory."

"To capture the interlopers," the human said.

"And add to one body's velocity, yes. One-eleventh the speed of light. That was the goal. Not as swift as your vessel, no. But it was a smaller galaxy, and our ship would wear engines large enough to let it maneuver. Shrouded in a hyperfiber envelope, that machine would drop close to suns and black holes, repeatedly surviving fire and gravity, always racing towards the next suitable target."

The tool paused, for dramatic purposes, or perhaps to let her audience respond.

"'The next suitable target,'" the human repeated.

"Yes."

"Just what were you building out there?"

"That should be self-evident," she said. "A warship. Why else encase the world inside a thousand kilometers of high-grade hyperfiber? Armor is the most trusted line of defense in any weapon. Save for invisibility, of course."

"Of course," said the invisible man.

"It's obvious that this Great Ship was designed to serve as someone's flagship," she said. "How can you think anything else? And I'll admit that my ship would never be as quick or grand, and yours is the far older vessel, and everything around us is lovely and mysterious, and splendid too. But your ship is also far less massive than mine. Forty percent less, which places the name 'Great' into question."

Pamir laughed. He laughed at the imagery and at the boast, and in secret, he weighed the words as well as the ideas behind them.

"I was one of an army," the tool continued. "One among billions. I was produced by a factory that had already consumed much of the sun's thin comet belt. Each one of my sisters was a simple and pure, easily duplicated device. Our mission demanded simplicity. My manufactured mind had passions, but those passions were narrowed to one subject: the nature of hyperfiber in all of its glories. And as I was born, as the first breath of electricity passed through me, my soul was filled with the image of a gray ocean of uncured hyperfiber spread across a world that wouldn't earn its final name until it was officially launched."

She offered another dramatic pause.

Pamir wasn't laughing. Even a civilian contractor with zero interest in far galaxies would be intrigued with this story, and that's why he could afford to show his feelings. Curiosity, doubt. A thousand pragmatic considerations colliding with one mighty beast of a question.

Why bother with this project?

He cleared his throat, started to laugh and then stopped himself. A thin smile turned scornful as he pointed out, "Some idiot had to pay for this."

There was no point in denying that statement.

Or for that matter, agreeing with it. Because when facts were obvious, the tool saw zero reason to respond.

Contractors and captains led similar lives. Goals had to be fulfilled, timetables ruled, and nothing but small problems and giant conundrums stood between them and success.

"But what kind of money-rich idiot? That's the first question." Pamir dropped a hand on the cultivation chamber. "Obviously, an advanced society. But even more important, this kind of project demands a social biology, and a highly cooperative one. If not out-and-out authoritarian. Organic or mechanical. I can see either way working, or a marriage between the two. But with a million-year outlook, which excludes almost every species I know. Particularly humans."

With the press of a thumb, he opened a minor valve, and the last surge of pressure brought out a bright gray bubble of uncured, left-behind hyperfiber.

"Yogurt," Pamir said.

"A food," said the tool.

"Built from billions of microbes doing only what nature tells them to do. Which is what you were. Are. One bacterium working on the great yogurt."

Laughing, she revealed a delightfully girlish voice.

Pamir continued. "Mass-produced machines, self-contained and self-repairing. That's how you hide some of the costs. Worlds are rebuilt every minute with that kind of technology. But the smallest tool still has to drink power, and a single red dwarf star isn't much of a nipple. Reactors linked in a nearby grid. That's what I'd do. Which means hydrogen by the gigaton, and that means dismantling one or more gas giant worlds. Which must have been available inside the same solar system, sure. But that means you aren't just rebuilding one world. You're dismantling another much bigger body, which is a fresh goliath-styled project requiring machine armies and more local reactors. And now we've entered the realm where the yogurt model collapses under its own success."

"And why is that?"

"You're not a bacterium," he offered. "A fleck of your skin is ten billion times more sophisticated than an ocean of yogurt. And worst still, you possess a full mind. A designed, standardized brain, but capable of learning and growing. You claim you were born with a passion for hyperfiber. But passion fades. Or worse, the target of your love shifts. Ten thousand years of determined labor, but there comes that treacherous nanosecond when you discover doubt, and after another ten thousand years of reflection and increasingly boring labor, you suddenly have to act on some long-ago inspiration."

"And I'll do what?"

"I don't know," he said. "Imagination isn't my strength."

She seemed to accept that judgment.

"I'm thinking like a contractor," he said. "Keeping tight control over billions of powerful workers. That requires AI watchdogs and relentless purges of bad ideas. I've overheard enough history to appreciate the troubles. Hive-mind societies are surprisingly frail. That abiding faith in rules . . . that's a damning strength. Some piece of the group will go mad, or lose focus, or fall behind in the work until it's obvious that the goals won't be reached and it's best to do anything else, including nothing."

She said nothing.

Pamir shrugged. "If I was painting the budget? The project's second biggest expense would be internal security."

"And the largest expense?"

"External security. Of course." In a sloppy fashion, the hyperfiber bubble had cured. Pamir took hold of the gray ball, finger and thumb lifting it free from the valve, twirling it close to his eyes. "You're building a warship. And because of the timescales and the very public nature of your work—a flaring star and an obvious trajectory, for example—you can't hide what you're doing. Your ultimate goals are going to be very visible. You're building a warship to conquer the galaxy. There would be no other explanation for your frantic efforts. But when every other species and wise player notices this, even eternal enemies are going to make alliances. Even the most passive species are going to work like maniacs, trying to bring disaster to your scheme. And that's why the construction site will have be armored and weaponized and filtered and controlled. A militarized sphere stretching out for tens of light-years. And now we've reached a level of expense that would bankrupt any civilization likely to arise in what still sounds like a small oxbow of a galaxy."

The tool offered a long silence, and then, one question.

"What if bankruptcy was just another calculation?"

Pamir grinned, mulling over the possibilities.

"No second choices," she said. "The empire abandons every inhabited world, colony, and farflung base. Its entire population coalesces around that giant iron world and its dim sun and the flares and those trillion tools that needed to be managed with absolute precision. And building the hull is just one job. The world beneath has to be hollowed out, making ready for crews and sleeping fleets. My great ship needs rockets worthy of its mass, and future weapon systems have to be designed and deployed. AI banks are built for no reason other than to wage every war to come, in their minds. And as you say, while all of that happens, my masters are battling an entire galaxy of united enemies."

She paused.

Pamir let the silence work on both of them. Or at least on him. Then he gave up, saying, "One of your solutions went wrong. I'm betting."

"Are you offering a wager?"

"Never."

"A wise inaction," she said. "Because every problem was recognized before the start. Every solution worked well enough. There were no rebellions of will, no invasion of enemies. The venture should have been a wild success. In another few million years, my tool makers and myself, and my children, if I had any, would have embraced that entire realm of stars and worlds, time and promise."

"Something else went wrong," Pamir guessed.

Silence.

"Tell me," he said. "Where did the dream lead?"

What weren't toes reached for his hand, claiming that bright gray bubble.

"This is what went wrong," she said.

"The hyperfiber?"

A long, painful sound emerged. Emotional, incoherent, purely miserable. Then the toes released the prize. And since the bubble was thin beyond thin, and because nothing but vacuum was inside it, the bubble shot into the air, rising out of reach and out of sight, neither of them watching after it.

The universe was built on weakness. Vacuum was one kind of weakness, vast and cold. Stars were feeble piles of sloppy fire. Atoms themselves were never more than temporary alliances between disloyal parts. The hardest object always broke, and every fine idea had to suffer until it died.

These were the first lessons fed to the tool, and they were learned long before the assembly line tossed her into the ranks.

Strength was possible, but only in special circumstances, and the tool was taught how genuine, enduring strength depended on cheating the universe. Not once, but constantly. Relentlessly. Black holes were cheats, and that's why tiny black holes were valuable for cutting and twisting lesser kinds of matter. Time was another cheat. Slice time thinly enough and the unlikely became real, including moments where entropy ran backwards. And there was a third cheat involving pure atoms and particles pretending to be atoms that aligned in quasi-crystal patterns—a maze of bonds and vibrations that might look like polished pale metal but actually resembled nothing normal. That was hyperfiber. That was the reason for her existence and her only love. She was born to do nothing but prepare lakes of pure hyperfiber that were carefully cured, drop by lustrous drop, until the lake was ready to be poured across the lovely, half-built warship.

At its worst, cheap hyperfiber was stronger than diamond and equal to bioceramics. But there was one last cheat to employ. No patch of hyperfiber existed alone. Those magical bonds weren't just here, but they also reached into parallel universes, into mirrors of themselves. Kick a shard of weak, low-grade fiber, and you were kicking ten million other shards at the same time. That's why the substance didn't break, melt or scream. And the higher grades were far more promiscuous. Billions of mirror universes shared power and stubbornness with one another, and that's what a great warship needed for its armor, and nothing else mattered for the first thousand centuries of her enormously important life.

"Every resource was used or set aside to be used later," she told the human. "The tool makers contrived and then spent every kind of currency. They stripped their home worlds of resources before converging around us, and they built factories and elaborate plans and fortifications that looked gigantic to every enemy and every former friend. Nothing mattered but finishing our great ship, on schedule and without flaw. And I was fortunate enough to have been swallowed by this venture. So consumed by the task that I never bothered imagining what would happen afterwards. To the galaxy. To myself. Even to the vessel whose hull belonged as much to me as to anyone. All that mattered was the next meter of fresh armor lying tight over every other strong layer."

Pamir watched, listened. And he nodded, understanding quite a lot more than his companion could have guessed.

Ten hands and feet moved, drawing round shapes in the air. "Mistakes were inevitable. Pico-crevices and tainted batches, mostly. I made those mistakes, and whenever I noticed flaws, I confessed. Sometimes others found my mistakes, and I confessed again. Just as my sisters welcomed the blame when I uncovered their blunders. That was our nature. That is the necessary attitude you cling to when you have considerable work and limited time, and particularly when your mistakes are being buried deeper and deeper inside the growing hull. We had to define the flaws early, and corrections were made, and sometimes the corrections were intricate and expensive . . . and this is where we doomed ourselves."

She paused.

Pamir watched the limbs freeze, and when the silence seemed too thick, he made a guess.

"You let small mistakes stand."

"No." She said it instantly, and the word was important enough to repeat eleven more times. Then every arm and leg dropped to the ground, save for one. A single finger needed to touch the cultivation chamber, run itself along the ribs and pipes and embedded AIs. The gesture was loving or scornful, or it was habit. Or it meant something else entirely. There was no way to be certain about the emotions of an entity like this. But the voice that emerged sounded sorry. She sounded hurt and small and old and a little warm with rage, riding on a pain already ninety million years old.

"The grade was diluted," she said.

"The fiber's grade," he guessed.

She offered a number. A detailed, thoroughly meaningful number. The hull that began being nearly the equal of the Great Ship's hull was diminished by percentage points. Not many points, not in the expanse of what was possible. But it was obvious that she didn't approve.

"That should have been plenty strong still," Pamir said.

She said nothing.

"Enough to endure any war," he added.

And in response, she touched his face. Poked it and ran the hard diamond finger along his fleshy nose and across his wet uncomfortable mouth, saying the one emphatic word, "Listen."

The warship was finished, and there was still enough time for many deep breaths. The tool makers had reason for pride. Their dream had demanded all of their native genius, consuming capital and their empire while destroying every other strategy to deal with an increasing number of enemies. They had to win. No other route would save them from obliteration. And while winning still wasn't assured, even with their flagship fueled and armed, the battle plans remained solid. That dense little sun was in position. The nudging solar flares were finished, the solar system exactly where it needed to be, and what promised to be a spectacular launch was about to commence. Those in charge weren't demonstrative souls, but the occasion demanded festivities and self-congratulatory speeches as well as honors bestowed by important voices. Several honors were given to the storyteller, and ages later she remained proud enough to name each award. Or perhaps she was just being thorough. Which was in her nature, after all. Then with her voice turning soft, she mentioned that half of her sisters were chosen to ride the warship, in stasis but perpetually ready to come awake whenever the vast gray hull was battered by comets or enemy bombs. As an asset, she wouldn't be scrapped. No, she would be frozen and carried along with the accompanying fleet. But after all of her steady selfless work, that critical duty felt like an insult. She implied that with her tone, then a brief silence. And finally, with one sharp confession. To a creature she barely knew, the tool admitted that a portion of her mind was doing nothing but wishing for a horrible, manageable disaster. Something foul would strike the warship, many sisters dying in the carnage, and then the tool makers would come to her with fresh work and many, many apologies.

"I was watching," she said. Then the words were repeated again and again, and Pamir gave up counting after twenty times. Then the watcher quit speaking, a considerable stillness taking hold of her body, and that stillness didn't end when she spoke again.

"That little sun struck its target. At the perfect moment, in the proper location, a small dense and relatively cool star dove into a much larger star, resulting in a fine explosion. A beautiful explosion."

"Explosions are always lovely," Pamir agreed.

"I was stationed aboard an auxiliary vessel safely removed from spectacle. But the heat of the blast, which was as rich as the outpouring light, could be felt. Could be relished. And those effects were minor next to the gravitational maelstrom. One star was swallowed by another, and a world-sized machine was set free. Without suffering any damage, by the way. But that event added nothing to its speed. No, the warship needed to plunge close to the quick-spinning, quick-moving black hole, and in turn, stealing away a portion of that enormous energy.

"No other maneuver demands so much precision. You can imagine. Several of the ship's giant engines were fired for the first time, and they didn't fail. My ship struck its mark within centimeters of the ideal. Within the length of a hand. What I built pushed fabulously close to a collapsed star, and I watched, and in an instant the nearest point was reached, and that I watched, and then as the tides found their maximum, everything seemed well. I watched and nothing changed inside my gaze, and that's when I discovered that, to my relief, I wasn't a bitter entity wishing the worst for the others. This total success made me genuinely happy. My hyperfiber was at least adequate if not superior, and still watching, I decided to speak to my nearby sisters, telling them that perhaps in the future we could build a second warship of this caliber, or better, and employ it to explore one of our neighboring galaxies."

The words stopped.

After a little while, Pamir said, "Tides," and then, "No. They shouldn't have mattered. A hull like that might have fractured a bit. But nothing that couldn't be patched, in time."

One foot lifted, toes drawing a sphere.

"You're imagining common failures and simple consequences," she said. "But that's only because you're a simple human, and why would you need to know anything else?"

"Tell me what else," he said.

"Hyperfiber," she said. "Those extraordinary bonds hold against every ordinary force. In most circumstances, the embedded power is out of reach. A contractor and his little tools have no need for these theoretical matters. But if each of those powerful bonds is shattered, and if the shattering happens in the proper, most awful sequence, energy is liberated. Not just the power available in our universe, but within countless adjacent realms too. Hyperfiber will burn, and it doesn't burn gently. Not like hydrogen fuses or antimatter obliterates. No, if one billion warships with identical flaws have worked hard to place themselves in one position, inside one moment and one tiny volume, they are nearly the same bodies. And if identical fissures open in each of these realms . . . well, the strength of a trillion ships floods into your existence, and the meaning of your life evaporates inside one wild light, and an empire dies, and the universe surrounding you breaks into a celebration considerably more joyous than the grubby little party you were having just a few breaths ago . . ."

It was rare for humans to enter the Avenue of Tools, and it was unprecedented for one of the Ship's captains to walk among the residents. But this was a unique captain. Competence, seamless and steady competence, had carried Aasleen from being a very successful engineer into the highest ranks of the administration. This was a human who understood the nature and beauty of machines, and she made no secret about relishing the company of machines over her own species. It was even said that the lady's husbands were robots and she had secret children who were cyborgs. That's why some of the tools, seeing her so close, began to hope that maybe she was looking for a new mate, and maybe this would be their best day ever.

But no, Aasleen was seeking one very particular tool, one using a string of names.

A locally famous tool, as it happened.

The captain found what she wanted soon enough. And the ancient tool wasn't entirely surprised by its visitor. Yet ignorance was a good starting point in any relationship, and that's why the tool said, "I've done nothing illegal."

"Have I accused you of crimes?" Aasleen asked.

"My business remains within the letter of the law," the tool added.

Aasleen laughed at the game. Then her human hands unfolded the crudest possible note: permanent ink on a piece of human skin. The skin was supple and pale and mostly depleted of its genetic markers. But not entirely, and what remained held hints of a known criminal who had been chased by nobody for many aeons now. What mattered were the words on the parchment. "'Madam captain, you're planning to fly us close to a black hole,'" she read aloud. "'The rendezvous is a few years off, but maybe you should think a little harder about your methods. And that's why you should chat with a genuine expert in hyperfiber.'"

She stopped reading. "At this point, your various names are listed."

The tool stood in the center of the artery, flanked by hundreds of motionless, intensely interested neighbors.

"Do you ever speak to humans?" Aasleen asked.

"I have, yes."

"Recently?"

"None recently," the tool said.

"Do you know any humans at all?"

She said, "I did. One man. But he died several decades ago."

"A man?"

"I worked with him, yes."

"He hired you for a job, did he?"

"For many jobs. We formed a partnership and thrived as a team. For nearly eighty years, yes. His last will gave me the business and all of its contracts, which is why I am the richest citizen in the Avenue today."

"How did this man die?"

"Tragically and without any corpse to honor," the tool said.

Aasleen let that topic drop. Instead, she shifted the parchment in her fingers, reading the rest of the odd note.

"'Ask the lady about the great ship that she built. Which may or may not have been real. But that isn't the point. You'll know that, Aasleen. The point is that maybe we don't want to be too precise in our aim. Or everything turns to shit on us. And you don't want that, my friend.'"

"You don't want that," the tool agreed.

Aasleen said nothing.

With a hopeful voice, the tool asked, "Is there more to the message?"

"'And this beauty,' he writes. 'This beauty before you has a thousand other wonderful stories to tell.'"

The tool moved her limbs, drawing spheres in the air.

"I don't know the author to this note of yours," she claimed. "But he is right in one regard, madam. Yes, I am a beauty."

Suzanne Palmer is a writer and artist who lives in western Massachusetts. A Linux systems and database administrator for a bunch of really awesome scientists by day, she writes into the late night, having given up on any pretense at sleep. Her short story "Tuesdays" won the *Asimov's* Reader's Choice Award in 2016, and she was a second-place finalist for the Sturgeon Memorial Award the previous year. Her work appears regularly in *Asimov's* and *Interzone,* and has also appeared in *Beneath Ceaseless Skies, Analog,* and *Black Static.*

TEN POEMS FOR THE MOSSUMS, ONE FOR THE MAN

Suzanne Palmer

1.

Sky egg blue, a nest
of walls,
a floor of fissioning stone
cottage made for close company
      lonely of but one.

Not that he really understands how the house floor works, given the odd impositions of the world surrounding him. It works, though; radiating warmth up through his feet as he paces, casting furtive glances back at the replica of an ancient machine where it sits upon a replica of an ancient desk, through which he has been trying to pull—tap tap—new words.

It's the first poem he hasn't crumpled up and tossed into the fireplace at the end of the vaulted room. The novelty of paper, of fire relentlessly marching from crisp edge to blackened ash, has consumed several salvageable scraps of work, but he's not here for scraps, for minute victories; he has come to be the flame, set his long-slumbering and cold imagination alight, and perhaps also to bury the embers of something else that never was meant to be.

The exhausting act of having crafted something that might not suck propels him past the desk, the textured matte black bulk of the Underwood, the thin flag of paper still standing his tiny effort up into the air. He needs to walk before he can judge: keep as is, keep going, fall into the limbo of tinkering, or smother now before he gets too attached.

The Project has thoughtfully provided him with boots and a walking stick propped by the door. He slips his feet into the boots and glances up at the large thermometer mounted on a turquoise porch post just outside the door. Turning, he checks the mechanical clock over the fireplace, then picks up the old-fashioned inkpen where it dangles on its string from the logbook by the door.

Day 7. 11:43. 12C, he writes on the next empty line. *Sunny. 1070 hPa.* The task is not as onerous a condition of his residency as he'd feared.

He slips on his coat, notebook in pocket, and steps out the door. Pausing there, he marvels at the pure existential joy of going for a stroll on an alien world, and one that he has, effectively, entirely to himself. For someone who had lived much of his adult life in the cramped and crowded towers of Old New York, the rolling hills and wide skies of Ekye are a dream. As a poet floundering, rendered wordless by the stale dregs of his own substanceless life, it is an offer of resurrection, reincarnation.

The hills that nestle around the cottage are a deep green, covered in a thick tangled carpet of a grasslike creeper named popim-weed. A forest of blue and green umbah-trees lines the ridge, and a lazy river winds its way down below through a field of green, fuzzy boulders called mossums.

Be cautious outdoors above 20C, they'd said.

That had worried him, but they assured him he was in no direct danger. *The landscape gets more active on warmer days*, they'd explained. *Keep your walking stick and watch your footing, and you'll be fine. Remember you're on an alien planet.*

Oh, and if it gets above 30C, don't linger below a mossum field.

A thick stone wall curves along the hillside behind the cottage, and above that, mossums are scattered in the bright midday sun like enormous green pebbles tossed from the riverbed.

2.

I walk with my eyes half-open,
the familiar and the unfamiliar

side by side, long-lost brothers
   yes—
      —the landscape of memory
tree and root and stone
succumb, uncomfortable,
     to pattern recognition
but hold fast, immovable,
    to lost particulars,
    like and unlike.

The cottage has stockpiles of both paper and notebooks, the latter for recording observations, but he doesn't think it improper if he carries one for moments of his own inspiration. They know he is a writer, that he wanted the long solitude of the post, was willing (eager!) to live under the low-tech strictures of Ekye. Loneliness is less terrible to bear when alone.

During orientation, the Project had explained about the swarming creatures—nochers—attracted by strong electromagnetic fields, much as moths were to flame; it was why the main heat source for the house was embedded inside a two-meter-thick block of hardened polymer, why he had a typewriter instead of a voice-text composer, why he made tea in a pot swung on a hook into the fire on his hearth.

He had spent nearly the entire first twenty-two-hour day obsessively tapping at the Underwood's space bar, eyes closed, listening to the keys as if he was hearing the hidden music of a thousand writers long dead. Then, in a burst of enthusiastic excess, he'd jammed them all up in a pile and slunk away out onto the porch in the spring rain. He is embarrassed by how much time he spent trying to figure out how to reboot the typewriter before he gave up and gently pressed the keys back into their proper places with his fingers.

The sun is warm after several cloudy days, so he goes to the cottage's shed, opens the door, and contemplates the bicycle. He's been told it requires practice, has seen vid of people riding them, but not how they got on or off. After staring at its thin, silver frame for some time, standing beside it in different ways to see if some method of getting safely aboard might become apparent, he decides he'll walk.

He climbs up the rolling hills that surround his cottage and sits in the sun with his back against a mossum, then pulls out the notebook and doodles a sketch of the view. He was never more than a passable artist, but it is sufficient skill for his own satisfaction.

The cottage is not far from the coast. A herd of creatures is moving across a meadow between him and the bright blue line on the horizon. Like inchworms the size of horses, hairy and horned and bright hues of blue, together they move like their own undulating wave of strangeness. The Project told him their name, but he cannot recall it, and, letting his gaze unfocus while he tries to remember, he slips into a light doze.

It is the name—*feffalons*, as if everything here has been named by a fanciful child—and the sense of weight pressing against his back that rouse him. The day has grown warmer.

He stands, stretches, repockets his notebook, and can't find his pen. He pokes through the ground cover, looking for it.

The popim-weed is a strange texture. Ferny, almost feathery, the whorls of green spray in a spiral helix up the stem to a point, where a small round bulb grows. *Flower buds?* he wonders. The end of his pen protrudes from a dense patch of the weed, just at the edge of the mossum he was leaning on. He grabs the tip, pulls, and discovers it is stuck beneath the mossum.

Reaching out, he touches it. It is as he expects: a solid boulder with a thick coating of moss-like fuzz, warm where the sun has fallen on it, chilly where it has not. He presses harder and it yields slightly. He is able to pull his pen free, and hastily pockets it.

There is a flattened patch of weed uphill from the mossum.

He is unnerved that the mossum may have moved. He's a poet, after all, not a geologist or mossologist or xenobiowhateverist. Next time he will sit beside an umbah-tree or on the upslope side of the mossums, and if the day is warm enough, he will watch.

3.

Not all rolling stones
gather, but are gathered by
impossible moss.

No, he doesn't like that. Trite, stupid. Writing haiku always makes him deeply self-conscious, as if failure has been predetermined before he even starts. He turns the little knob that advances the paper in satisfyingly analog increments until the offending bit of doggerel hangs over the back of the Underwood, out of sight.

4.

> There once was a poet named Davin,
> Who'd found his own private heaven,
> but the rocks, they rolled
> as the feffalons strolled
> —second thoughts, should he be a'havin'?

At least no one is looking over his shoulder, no one nearer than geostationary orbit to pass silent judgment. He yanks the paper free of the machine, crumples it up, and tucks it beneath the dead ashes of the morning's fire as a solemn promise for later.

One wall of the main room has bookshelves, and although the vast majority are a seemingly random assortment of static biography—Hypatia, Aaron Swartz, Mel Blanc (a desperate proxy crowd for some previous, lonely occupant?)—there are a few fiction books and a lone, hand-bound collection of watercolors. He can feel the texture of the paper, the way the paint buckled it slightly in places. It feels more real a presence than a dozen volumes of the stories of dead people.

The paintings are all dated within a few months of each other from the previous year. His predecessor, then. He wonders why she did not stay longer.

The second painting has been done from the cottage's front porch, the posts neatly framing the path down to the river, the small bridge that crosses it, and the low hillside beyond. He carries the book to the door and stands there, glancing down at the wash of vibrant color, up at the sunset-soaked landscape. The nearer stand of umbah-trees is taller now but accurately rendered, as is the flow and ebb of the land around it. The mossums on the hills, though, are mostly absent from the paper, and his own unhindered river instead shown choked with them.

Rocks rolling down . . . *that* he could process, if not find reason in. But *up*? Some unseen hand at work?

He closes the book and sets it on a small table by the door. The rest of his evening is spent idly thumbing through an impenetrably distant biography of Mary Anning, trying to dispel a quiet disorientation and the suspicion that he may be the unwitting target of a hoax.

In the end, only as he is drifting off to sleep in his bed, do the sheer logistical and financial impracticalities of his various paranoias convince him that whatever is happening, however opaque to reason, is unlikely to be anything to do with him.

5.

> The stone shifts in its coat of moss
>   in the wakening sun,
>   considers and discards
>   millennia of geologic
>   and poetic common sense,
>   and goes for a roll.
> The hill, for its part, is unsure
>   what the bold stone portends,
>   if it should protest
>   measured or stridenbtkjs

The keys are jammed again.

He hasn't yet adapted to the notion that he must compose tethered to the machine's needs, that creation is no longer the performance of a conductor to a rising orchestra of his own vision, but the precise and small monotonies of a technical transcriptionist. Frustrated, he sets down his half-drunk tea, leaving the chair and the broken, dangling disaster of a poem to go check on his other project.

He has found a roll of flexible sticky-tape and used it to hang a single sheet of paper beside each window that overlooks the mossum fields. On each, in a burst of morning diligence not usually his style, he has made a reference drawing of the locations of what should be fixed elements. Umbah-trees, hills and valleys, mossums of assorted sizes, and so forth. The drawings are a mockery of the fine watercolors that gave him the idea, but a solid reference. He has also used his pen to mark a tiny x on the floor about a meter and a half from the glass, which takes him several minutes to find. He hopes they'll escape the scrutiny of the Project, should they be looking for any petty (if well-intentioned) vandalisms during his stay.

Standing on the x, he studies his drawing, the scene out the window, then his drawing again. The thermometer at the door reads 15C. He is not certain, but it seems that the mossums have all shifted slightly further down the hill since his morning drawings, now several hours old.

He resolves to check again later. In the meantime, today is report day.

There is a logbook. He has already copied over into it each day's weather observations for the past four weeks, and adds the day's readings. The barometer has dropped, which he is learning means there could be rain. He has a window near the typewriter open, and a breeze is rifling through the corners of his poems, slowly sliding one toward the desk edge.

That reminds him that there is a mechanical device tucked up among the ceiling beams, a pen on a stick scribbling away tiny lines as the small windmill on the roof turns and spins in the wind. He drags a stool beneath its niche. Swapping out the paper is not as straightforward as the Project made it seem, but once he sees how it fits it is easily done.

Later, he turns to the survey the Project has provided him. Although ostensibly he is here as an exchange of needs—they need a reliable, intelligent observer who can function for extended periods in an isolated, low-tech environment and carry out occasional sampling and testing tasks, while he desires that self-same environment to try to reconnect with his creative self—part of the overhead of keeping him alive is making sure he isn't, to put it poetically, completely losing his marbles.

The survey is a series of mostly unobtrusive health questions, followed by a self-assessment of his mental well-being. Is he lonely? No more so here than where he came from. Is there anything he misses? Music. There is a space for questions/concerns about bodily matters, of which he has none, a supply checklist, and another blank space for items he would like. *Binoculars*, he writes in. He is fairly sure those can be made without electronics. *More of this*, he adds, and puts a small piece of the sticky-tape on the paper, drawing a line to it.

He picks up the weather log, wind-machine scribbles, and his survey, and then fetches a small, red metal tube from a cupboard. Opening a few more windows to let out the last lingering odors of bread he let burn in his distraction, he goes outside and walks up the steep hill behind the cottage.

There are a few clouds moving in, high pencil-line wisps that seem a precursor to most weather here. He hurries, feeling the pull in the backs of his calves and thighs, still unused to the exercise.

At the top there is a concrete circle with a metal pipe sticking out of it. He unlatches and removes the cap, trying to remember the sequence he went over ad nauseam one world too many ago. Anxiously he sets down his pile of papers and pipe and rummages in his coat, pulling out the instructions he had tucked into an inside pocket for just such a circumstance.

There are things he needs tucked inside the tube. As soon as he picks it up, his pile of papers is caught by the wind and takes flight down the hill. "No no no!" he cries and scrambles after them.

By the time he has caught the last, he's short of breath and more than a little irritated. Stomping back to the top of the hill, he stubs his toe on a small mossum half-buried in the popim-weed. He picks it up, intending to hurl it, but the solid weight of it in his hand gives him an idea.

Back at the launch site he uses the mossum to keep his papers from escaping again, and then empties out the contents of the red tube. A small black device, pinhole in one end, fits snugly onto the base of the tube. Once on, he is careful not to touch it further, despite assurances that it won't activate until it's in the launch pipe. He knows it will attract the nochers when it does.

There is a small bag with some mealy, oatmeal-like clumps in it that he spreads out on the ground several paces from the pipe. It will give the nocher swarm something to eat while he escapes back to the cottage.

Setting the mossum aside, he rolls the papers into a tight bundle and slides them down inside the tube. The last piece is the cap, which when inverted makes a pointed cone on the end. It makes the tube look like an ancient rocket, from back in the era before disc ships.

Everything is prepared. He can see the front now, a gray line on the horizon, the last bits of cobalt-blue sky fleeing ahead of the storm. He considers sitting atop the hill until the storm overtakes him, as if he were but a part of the landscape, but knows in his heart that it will only leave him damp, chilled, and in a fouler mood.

There's nothing else to do, so he slides the rocket into the pipe. It's been explained that there's a small, sharp needle in the base that will activate the cylinder, which will then launch the device. Putting both hands on the sides of the rocket, he bears down gently. There is a faint but clear click as it connects. He was told to immediately step away, but nowhere has anyone warned him how quickly the rocket would exit. Its progress is only markable by the bright column of smoke it paints up into the sky.

"Whoa," he says.

Somewhere high up, out of reach of the nochers, a drone will sense the coming rocket and intercept it, taking it to the Project station in orbit. He's still watching the thinning trail when he notices a strange humming, whistling sound in the wind.

He has imagined the nochers as bloated, one-eyed flying rats, but what emerges from the umbah-forest at first looks like mist, then resolves into whitish fluff, gigantic dandelion seed-tufts. They are converging and drifting up the hill.

As soon as you launch, go back to the cottage and stay indoors for at least an hour, the Project has told him.

He picks up the mossum from the cement, intending to throw it, but the cloud is picking up speed, so he drops it into his pocket and runs. Moving down the hill as fast as he can, he is terrified he's going to catch his foot on another mossum or in the popim-weed and pitch headfirst the rest of the way.

He makes it to the door safely, breathing so heavily his entire body is one giant, thudding heartbeat. He can no longer see the top of the hill for its seething mass of white. Inside, he closes the windows and gathers up all his papers where they have blown around the room, and sets them on the desk with the mossum atop to keep them in place.

He picks at the burnt loaf of bread, eating pieces absently until it is gone and the swarm is too.

6.

Benign is in the eye of memory,
  childhood and soft summer laughs—
  I remember your hand in mine
  as we wished on tiny seeds sailing
  the careless breeze.
Now, where are we? Wishes forgotten
  or remembered with jaded mockery—
  for the innocence we endured
  with impatient fortitude,
  as we waited to grow up.
We have traded dreams for lives,
  let go for a grounded world—
  all now is always as it seems,
  ambition moves us step by step,
  and surety keeps us apart.
I have taken a chance, returning to the dream
  where danger and delight inspire—
  I slough off my own dearest shadows
  only to wake in a new day,
  still missing you.

The rain is a frenetic drumbeat on the cottage roof for more than a week. He likes the sound of it at night, drifting in and out of sleep, but by day he craves the missing sun, someone to talk to, something else to do beside stare at the mercurial Underwood and listen to the wind howl. Words are failing him, and it is all he can do to not spend the days curled up in the bed, feeling lost at the bottom of a well of desolate emptiness.

In the Blanc biography, he finds loose notes tucked inside by the watercolor artist. They are scribbled, incoherent, dated past the last of the paintings, and talk of ghosts stalking the hillsides. His nerves frayed by days indoors, he considers feeding the pages into the fire, but instead tucks them back inside the book and returns it to the highest shelf.

When at last the blue sky peeks out, he is startled to see something bright red, high up in the sky, growing larger: the parachute for the supply drop. In his haste he almost loses his balance pulling his boots on. Catching himself, he knocks over his mug of tea onto the floor. The mug doesn't break, but the tea spreads out in a long puddle.

It will wait. He races out after the parachute.

A medium-sized inflatable crate lands fairly close to the house, bouncing and rolling until it comes to rest against a pair of mossums. He lets the air out, then unzips the recessed openings until he can pull free the items within. There is more toilet paper, sunscreen, a smaller crate of food items, a padded case holding a pair of binoculars, a roll of thick sticky-tape, and a packet of papers.

It takes him a few trips to carry everything up to the porch, the ground soggy and slick from the rain. He packs the deflated crate and bundled parachute into the shed, eyeing again the unmet challenge of the bicycle, before going back to the house and taking off his mud-covered boots outside the door.

Inside, he stops, hand still on the doorframe.

His poems are scattered again, and the mossum he was using to hold them down has fallen and is lying in the center of the floor.

"Hello?" he calls. He feels silly, but also angry. As little as an hour ago he was feeling the desperate drain of solitude. Now he is furious at the idea that it might have been violated. "I know someone is here!"

He bends down to pick up the mossum in case he needs to defend himself. The mossum is wet, spongy.

The puddle of tea is gone.

Davin Arturo Gordon-Fauci, Resident Poet-Hermit of Ekye, starts to laugh.

7.

When is a rock not a rock?
When it invites itself over to tea.

When is a fool not a fool?
When he slips off a life's lens
          and at last learns to see.

He has put the mossum on the floor, and not far from it a small saucer of water. Rather than stare at it the whole day, he has turned his back to it as he sorts through the new papers. The windows are closed, the door latched, and, in what he has decided to ascribe to thoroughness rather than paranoia, he has made sure the cottage is indeed free of intruders. The idea of ghosts holds no allure beyond the merely symbolic.

There is a folded newssheet, a throwback still in use in some of the tech-averse colonies, and perhaps this is simply one of their editions; it is free of the more salacious stories so embarrassingly popular on Earth and many of the colony worlds. It's comforting to have this window into current events available, but he can't summon much interest. None of it is relevant, anyway, not here or now.

Mr. G-F, the enclosed note reads, *We've included another wellness survey and a small tube. Our Soils division has requested, if you are able, that you send back a sample of the riverbed silt. Weather looks to be agreeable for the coming weeks in your location, with some significant warming over the next few days. We hope you are settled in and finding your stay conducive to your creative needs, and we look forward to hearing more about your impressions.*

He flips through the newssheet a while longer, then abandons it in a stack of paper waiting for the evening's fire. The mossum on the floor has not moved. Maybe he is wrong? Going to the windows, he checks his drawings, and the difference is unmistakable. The mossums are all moving toward the river.

It's 16C out and the barometer is regaining lost ground. He puts on his boots and climbs toward the top of the hill, intent on scouting out a stretch of level ground on which to finally test the bicycle; while there would be a certain poetic comedy in plummeting down the hill into the river and collecting the Project's soil sample with his face, he prefers to leave that particular bit of life's comedy unwritten.

When he reaches the launch pipe, he finds the popim-weed where he threw the oatmeal stuff ripped to shreds. A lone mossum nearby is scored by deep gouges, black sticky pitch seeping through what's left of the moss. The idea of the nochers as dandelion fluff is torn apart; again, he has fallen into the trap of benign assumptions that are as alien to this world as he is.

He takes the time to roll the damaged mossum lower down the hill, to where he hopes it will be safer. From here he can see a low plateau, ideal for his bicycle adventure, but his momentum toward the experience has waned again. *Maybe after lunch*, he thinks. *Or another day entirely.*

As ever, he does his best not to think about how good he has always been at putting off things, and people too.

Walking back down the hill, neck and shoulders stiff from moving the heavy mossum, he hears and does not pay attention to what, at first, sounds merely like a dog barking in the distance. When the impossibility of that sinks in, he stops and stares across the vista ahead of him, eyes and ears straining for a source.

It comes again, and this time it is the flash of blue that catches his eye. A herd of feffalons on the meadow breaks and runs, as a thing lumbers out of the umbah-trees behind them. He has brought the new binoculars, and after a vertigo-inducing sweep of the land he catches the feffalons in passing, and then the creature giving chase.

It is dark red, about the size of a small pony, and looks like what you'd get if you crossed a six-legged Tyrannosaurus Rex with a poorly knit wool sock. The feffalons have quickly left it behind. He watches as it opens its three-part, ridged jaw to the sky and calls again.

The Project has not warned him about predators other than the nocher swarm. It picks up a mossum and crushes it in its huge jaws, scattering debris and black fluids everywhere, before lurching out of sight behind more umbah-trees.

He flees down the hill at breakneck speed and into the cottage. If he'd gone for his walk on the far side of the river, over there . . .

Determined not to be lost in what-if terrors, he picks up a piece of paper and does his best to draw the thing's likeness and put down as many notes about his brief observation as he can. On consideration, he names it "Red Rex." His handwriting is appalling.

He turns in his chair and looks around the room. His mossum is gone. Bending down, he finally spies it under the desk along the back wall. Coincidence, or some awareness of the predator? He feels an enormous empathy for his moss-covered rock.

"The truth is," he tells it, "a good part of me wants to crawl under there and hide with you."

8.

Mothers of mine, I've had a bad dream—
  a monster that came in the night!

All my delight, my magic and care
faltered, and then took flight.
 I fear now to slumber
 lest all the wonder
be turned thus from the light.

O Child of ours, the truth you must know—
 the monsters are always here.
 They walk our dreams, our waking days
whispering doubts in our ear.
  The truth to hold tight,
  in sun, or in night
is that love, ever, is nearer.

He does not see or hear the Red Rex again, although he never forgets it is out there, not while outside, not while staring stagnant and dull at the blank sheet in the Underwood, not while lying in his bed at night trying not to imagine the worst thing creeping up silently upon him. In the shed behind the bicycle and underneath a fishing net he finds an old saw, and takes to carrying it whenever he is out; still, he doesn't stray far from the house.

At last he decides he should send up a rocket, even though it's several days early. He packs up his drawings and a tube and the saw and hurries to the top of the hill, staring around him as if the Red Rex—or a pack of them!—could be anywhere. Poor sleep has left him jumpy, restless, and feeling dangerously dull-witted.

He scatters the nocher-bait on the barest ground he can find. Over the last few, warm days, most of the mossums have moved much farther down the hill toward the river. The damaged one hasn't changed position. He wonders if he should pour water on it, or beside it, or something.

One thing he is entirely certain of is that they are alive, although he cannot say what specifically that means.

After one last, fretful look around, he finishes prepping the rocket, presses it into the tube, and hurries down the hill toward the cottage without looking back. He does not want to see the nochers coming, not now while fear already has such a grip on him.

It's 26C out, even warmer inside. The mossum in his house is sitting on the floor where sunlight streams in from the window. It has all the appearance of nothing more than a rock, and although he has still not caught it in motion, he knows that as the day has progressed the bright rectangle of light has shifted across the floor, and the mossum has remained in the center of it.

He picks it up from its warm spot. "Time to earn your keep," he tells it, and sets it atop his papers so he can open the windows and get air moving through the house.

As he does, he can hear a faint crackling sound in the distance, like popcorn. He pauses, hand on the windowsill, and listens. The sound is getting closer, and then suddenly it's as if the ground is alive, squirming. There is a flash of white, a moving line, like the front edge of a wave.

Then it reaches the cottage and he sees.

The swelling buds on the popim-weed are bursting, laid open to snow-white interiors, as bundles of squiggly, springy pale green threads explode out in all directions, tangling in the air before falling back to earth and muting the brief beauty of the open buds in masses of zigzag confetti.

Popim-weed, he thinks. Turns out to be a good name.

The synchronicity of it, the surprise of it, is almost overwhelming, and he is startled to realize there are tears on his cheeks. Fear has cost him irreplaceable weeks of his time on this planet, this beautiful, unexpected place. He feels unworthy, unbelievably blessed.

He goes outside and sits on the porch with his feet dangling over the edge, watching as the wave of white sweeps down to the river, pauses, then in fits and starts appears on the other side and transforms the distant banks. The mossums clustered down by the water are now stark green motes against the backdrop.

9.

Be an island of iron-cliff shores—
impervious to all incoming storms
unswayed by the movement of sea
built of immovable earth
no inhabitants to drain you,
no friend to speak out of turn

    —that exists, but will not be.

                Or be an island lost among thousands—
                    drenched by the fury of storms,
                      buried in fleeting wealth

> bidden and unbidden,
> cautious and carefree,
> frightening and fantastical

> —that dwells in an ocean of all things.

Mr. G-F, the next letter from the Project reads. *Your "Red Rex" (Project Nomenclature likes the name and would like to adopt it for official use, if you do not object) is a predator that is normally found in much hotter climes, where it has both more prey and more competition. Our theory is that the most recent storm somehow brought it to your island.*

As you guessed, it is extremely dangerous. If you wish us to extricate you, please notify us. We also have dispatched extra drones to the airspace above the island but have been unable to locate it. There is always the possibility it has gone back to where it came from—

I could live with that, he thinks.

—but more likely it has burrowed in somewhere and will emerge again when hungry. If we are able to locate the Red Rex we will keep you informed. In the meantime, please exercise all caution. Project Safety recommends you do not leave the cottage except for necessary—and short—outings until this is resolved.

The recommendation is sound, and up until the popim-weed explosion, exactly in line with his own miserable intentions. Now, though . . .

He has been a coward—here, and before here—and he cannot bear to reckon what it has cost him. There is no more running away. He takes the saw, a notebook and pen, and goes to get the bicycle out of the shed.

10.

Two meters and a handspan, twice over
I measure the circumference of my world
    with spoke and rim, moving circles,
        and eyes caught wide.

Ten poems I have written for the mossy stones
my only audience, adrift in my fields,
    that illuminate my interior landscape
        in obstinate incomprehension.

A thousand words written on endless pages,
set down with awful integrity and focus
will never out-measure the silence,
where I should have said I loved you.

Three months have carried Ekye fully into its summer. He is standing in the river in bare feet, eyes closed, enjoying the coolness of the slow-moving water. There's a vial in his hand—destined for yet another silt sample—but so far he's content to let the currents swirl around him, feel the sun hot on his back, half oblivious to everything except the raw feed of his other senses.

The banks and river itself are cluttered with mossums, the hills above nearly bare of them now. He has come to think of them as a slow-moving herd; the conception of them as stones, as inanimate objects, has been thoroughly dispelled and forgotten, and in its place he finds them amiable companions: silent, self-sufficient, present in the entirely self-contained way of sleeping cats. He still has not managed, despite great effort, to see them in motion.

So it is an enormous shock when a mid-sized mossum tumbles down the bank to bump against his leg. Opening his eyes, he stares down at it, then slowly moves his leg away. It remains where it is, so he takes one more step back, and another mossum bumps him from the other side.

"What?" he asks them, then jumps as an enormous mossum upstream drops into the river with a loud splash.

The banks are hard to see past where the big mossum fell, the water and shore occluded by curving, reedy plants. They are thrashing back and forth now, and for a moment he wonders if this is some spectacular natural phenomenon like the budding of the popim-weed. But no. Something large is moving up the bank, through the reeds, straight toward him.

He scrambles out of the river and grabs his saw from the bank just as the Red Rex breaks cover and lurches toward him. The water slows it down, and he is able to swing the saw in a wide arc, its rusted but still formidable teeth tearing a ragged line along its face. It lets out a high-pitched bark and throws itself up the far bank and half way up the slope before it slows, turns, and stands there regarding him.

He holds the bow-shaped handle of the saw in both hands in front of him, blade out. The adrenalin in his system is a rage he's never felt before, his blood become magma, and he wants to yell at the Red Rex, scream back at it a lifetime of noise kept mute under passivity and self-doubt.

The Red Rex watches as he backs away. It seems more gaunt, unraveled, than in the spring, but he knows too well the terrible pull of desperation and will not underestimate it. At last, perhaps sensing he is out of reach, the Red Rex stretches its legs one by one, then turns and scuttles away.

He stares after it until it is gone from sight. Somewhere, he dropped his vial. It doesn't matter.

The mossums warned him.

Physically shaking, it is that revelation, more even than the danger, that overwhelms him. At the porch steps he turns, seeing the mossums again with new eyes, through the blur of tears of wonder and fear. Then his stomach lurches viciously; on the far hillside, the Red Rex has returned.

He runs inside and slams the door, throwing a lock he never imagined had any purpose. Outside, the Red Rex howls, a terrible mocking sound, and he goes to the window and stares out, hands gripping the sill until his knuckles are white.

It lopes down the hillside again toward the river, picks up a mossum in its jaws and devours it.

"No," he says, not realizing he has spoken out loud until his own voice startles him.

He abandons the window, anger making him careen around the room looking for anything he can use. He will not, cannot, just watch; too much of his life has been wasted in inaction, watching fate plunder his life unchallenged.

Grabbing his saw, he runs outside and pulls the fishing net out of the shed. It should be enough to entangle the Red Rex, but not hold it indefinitely. And then what? The idea of killing it is abhorrent, even under such circumstances. If only he had some way to drive it off the island, back where it came . . .

He drops the net on the porch and goes back into the house. From the cupboard he pulls a dozen of the red rocket tubes, dumping their contents on the floor. He scoops up the inactive electronic control cylinders and the roll of sticky-tape from his desk.

On the porch, he watches the Red Rex as he wraps the mechanisms with tape and strings them as quickly as he can in the net. When done, he hauls out the bicycle. There are now several broken mounds of crushed and gutted mossums around the Red Rex, and the rest have moved away from it, forming clusters with the smallest mossums in their center.

He straddles the bicycle, leaning it so he still has one foot on the ground, and balances the saw atop the handlebars. He takes his pen out of his pocket and jabs it into the tiny hole in the base of one of the rocket cylinders taped to the net. It lights up, trying to connect to and launch a rocket that isn't there. One by one, he activates the rest and then drapes the net over his shoulder, wrapping his hands around both handlebar and saw handle together. Barely has he begun to roll when he hears the distant humming of the nochers over the rumble of his tires down the path.

Picking up speed, he aims for the bridge. The Red Rex has stood. If it is his increasing speed or memories of the saw that finally sinks in, he doesn't know, but it turns and runs.

He hits the bridge moving terrifyingly fast. What momentum he loses up the far shore isn't enough to give the Red Rex a lead, and by the time he crests the hill he is almost on top of it.

It stops and turns, its jaws opening wide. He expected this, has become nimble on the bike over the last few weeks, and he swerves, throwing the net as he passes. The creature lunges, catching the net nearly full in the face. Immediately it begins to roll and snap and snarl, tangling itself further.

He keeps going. He can hear the nochers coming, like an approaching storm, like the fury he released from inside himself when the net left his hands.

He crests the last hill before the long slow slope down to cliffs and sea. With a terrible whining cry, the Red Rex passes, two legs still tangled in the net, half-lost in the buzzing cloud of white fluff enveloping and chasing it. Tufts of dark red mix with the nochers as they pick it apart.

Remembering the damage to the mossum at the launch site, he feels sick.

The Red Rex plunges into the surf. It is only by the cloud of nochers still trying to follow that he can mark its progress out into deeper waters. When the nochers dissipate, he doesn't know if it's because the electronics have succumbed to the salt water, or the Red Rex has succumbed to the sea, but somehow he knows—is absolutely certain—that it will not return.

It is a long ride back to the cottage, and even though the sun is still well above the horizon, he climbs into his bed and pulls the blankets up until he feels as if he is drowning in them. He does not toss and turn, does not think of home, does not think of the dead, does not sleep.

For once, he *acted*. He was not the observer of life, but one of the living.

When the first tentative light kisses his window, he gives up and gets out of bed, padding in his bare feet across the still-dark floor in the gray monotones of first dawn into the living room.

There is a sound, familiar and unexpected, and he jumps, staring at the Underwood. The small mossum he'd left on his papers overnight is still there, and in the waxing light he sees, just barely, the small tendrils that disappear back into its rounded shape.

The keys are jammed.

11.

sadkl cmeiopwru hh mcvx

He sets the mossum down on the floor near the water saucer. Going to the window, he looks out at the alien landscape that has become suddenly, utterly home. The cottage is surrounded by a ring of mossums in the rising light. Startled, he realizes that, for the first time in his life—the sole human being on an entire planet—he also does not feel alone.

Full morning brings a parachute from the Project.

Our drones detected the Red Rex attack at the river as it began, but we were unable to put a craft out to reach you before you had already resolved the situation, the letter says. *It was never the intention of the Project to put you in danger. We have no explanation for the mass movement of mossums to the cottage. Limited as we are by both philosophy and circumstance to non-invasive, non-technological methods, we had hoped that a creative, intuitive person might be able to discern the nature of the mossums in a way we have not. Whether or not you choose to terminate our agreement and leave Ekye, we would greatly appreciate any insights you are willing to share with us.*

He still has a few rockets left, but no sense of urgency. He makes himself a cup of tea and sits at the typewriter, feeling the breezes off the ocean sweeping in through the window and around him before he sets to composing a reply.

I am fine here, Davin writes. *The nature of the mossums is: they are both stone and life, ghost and muse, solitude and company, unknowable and dear. In short: they are as we: poems.*

He rolls that up and sticks it in the red tube. Taking another sip of tea, he looks down at the mossum on the floor where it has found a first, thin streak of daylight.

"You should see my early drafts," he tells it, then picks up a fresh piece of paper to begin.

Rich Larson was born in West Africa, has studied in Rhode Island and worked in Spain, and now writes from Ottawa, Canada. His short work has been featured on io9, translated into Polish and Italian, and appears in numerous Year's Best anthologies as well as in magazines such as *Asimov's, Analog, Clarkesworld, F&SF, Interzone, Strange Horizons, Lightspeed,* and *Apex.* He was the most prolific author of short science fiction in 2015 and 2016.

YOU MAKE PATTAYA

Rich Larson

D orian sprawled back on sweaty sheets, watching Nan, or Nahm, or whatever her name was, grind up against the mirror, beaming at the pop star projected there like she'd never seen smartglass before. He knew she was from some rural eastern province; she'd babbled as much to him while he crushed and wrapped parachutes for their first round of party pills. But after a year in Pattaya, you'd think she'd have lost the big eyes and the bubbliness. Both of which were starting to massively grate on him.

Dorian had been in the city for a month now, following the tourist influx, tapping the Banks and Venmos of sun-scalded Russians too stupid to put their phones in a faraday pouch as they staggered down Walking Street. In the right crowd, he could slice a dozen people for ten or twenty Euros each and make off with a small fortune before a polidrone could zero in on him.

And in Baht, that small fortune still went a long way. More than enough to reward himself with a 'phetamine-fuelled 48-hour club spree through a lurid smear of discos and dopamine bars, from green-lit Insomnia to Tyger Tyger's tectonic dance floor and finally to some anonymous club on the wharf where he yanked a gorgeous face with bee-stung lips from a queue of bidders on Skinspin and wasted no time renting the two of them a privacy suite.

Dorian put a finger to his lips to mute the pop star in the mirror, partly to ward off the comedown migraine and partly just to see the hooker's vapid smile slip to a vapid pout that looked better on her anyways. She pulled the time display out from the corner of the mirror and made a small noise of surprise in her throat.

"I must shower." She checked the cheap nanoscreen embedded in her thumbnail, rueful. "Other client soon. Business lady. Gets angry when I late even one fucking second." She spun toward the bed. "I like you better," she cooed. "You're handsome. Her, I don't know. She wear a blur." She raked her glittery nails through the air in front of her face to illustrate.

"That's unfortunate," Dorian said, pulling his modded tablet out from under the sheets.

"Like I fuck a ghost," she said with a grimace. "Gives me shivers." She turned back to her reflection, piling up her dark hair with one hand and encircling her prick with the other. She flashed him an impish Crest-capped grin from the mirror. "You want a shower with me?"

Dorian's own chafed cock gave a half-hearted twitch. He counted the popped tabs of Taurus already littered around the room and decided not to risk an overdose. "I'll watch," he said. "How's that?"

Her shoulders heaved an exaggerated sigh, then she flitted off to the bathroom. Dorian flicked the shower's smartglass from frosted to one-way transparent, watching her unhook the tube and wave it expectantly in his general direction. Dorian used his tablet to buy her the suite's maximum option, sixty litres of hot water.

Once she was busy under the stream, rapping along to Malaysian blip-hop, he took advantage of the privacy to have a look at his Bank. The scrolling black figure in his savings account gave him a swell of pride. 30,000 Euros, just over a million in Baht. He was ripping down record cash and the weekend's binge had barely dented him. Maybe it was finally time to go to a boatyard and put in some inquiries.

Dorian alternated between watching curves through the wet glass and watching clips of long-keeled yachts on his tablet. Then, in the corner of his eye, the mirror left tuned to a Thai entertainment feed flashed a face he actually recognized: Alexis Carrow, UK start-up queen, founder of Delphi Apps, and freshly minted billionaire. Dorian sat up a bit straighter and the mirror noticed, generating English subtitles.

CARROW VACATION INCOGNITO

Alexis Carrow young CEO from Delphi Apps on vacay in our very own beautiful country, celebspotters made clip yesterday on Pattaya Bay Area. She appears having a wonderful time perusing Soi 17 with only bodyguard. No lover for her? Where is singer/songwriter Mohammed X? Alexis Carrow is secretive always.

Dorian dumped the feed from the mirror onto his tablet, zooming in on the digital stills from some celebspotter's personal drone that showed Ms Carrow slipping inside an AI-driven *tuk-tuk*, wearing Gucci shades and a sweat-wicking headscarf. Thailand still pulled in a lion's share of middle-class Russian and Australian holidayers, plus droves of young Chinese backpackers, but Dorian knew the West's rich and/or famous had long since moved on to sexier climes. Alexis Carrow was news. And she was here in Pattaya.

Cogs churned in his head; grifter's intuition tingled the nape of his neck. He eased up off the bed and walked to the smartglass wall of the bathroom. Inside, Nan—Nahm?—was removing her penis, trailing strands of denatured protein. He doubted it was her original organ—surgeons needed something to work with when they crafted the vagina, after all—but customers liked the fantasy.

Dorian put his forehead against the smartglass, watching as she slipped the disembodied cock into the nutrient gel of a chic black refrigerated carry-case. The night's activities were a slick fog. He tried to remember what she'd told him between bouts of hallucination-laced sex, the endless murmuring in his ear while they lay tangled together. Things about her family in Buriram, things about her friends, things about her clients.

Someone even richer than you, she'd said, fooled by his rented spidersilk suit and open bar tab. *Wants me all the week. You're lucky I think you are handsome.*

Dorian couldn't contain his grin as he looked down at his tablet, flicking through the photos. She was right about one thing: he had always been lucky.

By the time the hooker was dressed, Dorian had checked on Skinspin and verified her name was Nahm. She exited the bathroom with a slink of steam, wrapped in a strappy white dress, her black hair immaculate again. Dorian appraised her unending legs, soot-rimmed eyes, and pillowy lips. She was definitely enough to catch even a celebrity's biwandering eye.

"What?" she asked. She crouched to retrieve one Louboutin knock-off kicked under the bed; Dorian produced its partner.

"Nothing, Nahm," he said, handing her the sandal. "I was just thinking how much I'd like to take you back to London with me."

"Don't make a joke," she said, but she looked pleased. She gripped his arm for balance while she slipped into her shoes and then gave him a lingering goodbye kiss. As soon as the door of the privacy suite snicked shut behind her, Dorian scrambled back into his clothes.

Someone had dumped half a Singha across his shoes and his sport coat stank like laced hash, but he didn't have time for a clothing delivery. He raked fingers through his gel-crisped hair, prodded the dark circles under his eyes, and left. The narrow hall was a bright, antiseptic white unsullied by ads, and the soundproof guarantee of each privacy suite made it eerily quiet, too. AI-run fauxtels did always tend toward a minimalist aesthetic.

Walking Street, by contrast, bombarded every last one of Dorian's senses the moment he stepped outside. The air stank like spice and petrol, and a thousand strains of synthesized music mingled with drunk shrieks, laughter, trilingual chatter. The street itself was a neon hubbub of revelers.

Dorian used his tablet to track the sticky he'd slapped to the bottom of Nahm's shoe. He couldn't see her through the crush, but according to the screen she was heading upstreet toward the Beach Road entrance. He plunged off the step, ducking an adbot trailing a digital Soi 6 banner, and made for the closest tech vendor. A gaggle of tourists was arrayed around the full body Immersion tank, giggling at their electrode-tethered friend drifting inside with a tell-tale erection sticking off him.

Dorian cut past them and swapped 2,000 Baht for a pair of lime green knock-off iGlasses, prying them out of the packaging with his fingernails. He blinked his way through set-up, bypassed user identification, and tuned them to the sticky's signal. A digital marker dropped down through the night sky, drizzling a stream of white code over a particular head like a localized rainshower.

Stowing his tablet, Dorian hurried after the drifting marker, past a row of food stands hawking chemical-orange chicken kebabs and fried scorpions. A few girls whose animated tattoos he vaguely recognized grabbed at him as he went by, trailing fake nails down his arm. He deked away, but tagged one of them to Skinspin later—it looked like she'd gotten her implants redone.

Once he had Nahm in eyeball sight, he slowed up a bit. She was mouthing lyrics to whatever she had in her audiobuds as she bounced along, necksnapping a group of tank-and-togs Australian blokes with the sine curve sway of her hips. She detoured once outside Medusa, where bored girls were perusing their phones and dancing on autopilot, to exchange rapid-fire *sawatdees* and airkisses. She detoured again to avoid a love-struck Russian on shard.

Ducking into a stall selling 3D printed facemasks of dead celebrities, Dorian looked past Nahm to the approaching roundabout. A shiny black ute caught his eye through the customary swarm of scooters and *tuk-tuks*. As he watched, Nahm checked her thumbnail, then glanced up at the ute and quickened her pace. Dorian felt a jangle of excitement down his spine as he scanned the vehicle for identifying tags and found not a single one.

Someone had knocked over a trash tip, spilling the innards across Nahm's path, but she picked her way through the slimed food cartons and empty condom sprays with pinpoint precision that left Dorian dimly impressed. He squinted to trigger the iGlasses' zoom, wondering if he should chance trying to get a snap of the inside of the ute.

Then the lasershow started up again, throwing its neon green web into the dark clouds over Pattaya's harbor, and as Nahm craned her beautiful head to watch for what was probably the millionth time, her heel punctured a sealed bag of butcher giblets.

"Shit," Dorian said, at the same time Nahm appeared to be saying something similar. Casting a glance at the approaching ute, she lowered herself gingerly to the curb to hunt through her bag. She produced a wipe and cleaned the red gunge off her ankle and the strap of her sandal. Dorian bit at the inside of his cheek.

She continued to the underside of the shoe, wiping the needle-like heel clean, then paused. Dorian winced, thinking of all the many places he could have put the sticky. Slipped into her bag, or onto the small of her back, or even somewhere in her hair.

Nahm pincered the tiny plastic bead between two nails and peered at it. Dorian crossed his tattooed fingers, hoping she wasn't one of the many girls addicted to Bollywood spy flicks. She frowned, then balled the sticky up in the used wipe and tossed it away. The stream of code floated a half-meter over, now useless, as the ute pulled in.

Dorian slid closer, watching Nahm get to her feet, smooth out her dress. For the first time, she looked slightly nervous. The ute's shiny black door opened with a hiss. Dorian didn't have an angle to see the interior as Nahm slithered inside, but the voice within was unmistakable, Cockney accent undisguised.

"Christ, what is that stink? Please do *not* track that shit in with you, love."

Dorian didn't get to hear Nahm's retort. The door swooshed shut and the ute bullied its way back into the traffic. Dorian trotted over and picked up the bloody wipe, retrieving the sticky from inside. The smell barely bothered him, because Alexis Carrow was slumming it in Pattaya and he was going to blackmail the ever-loving shit out of her.

When Dorian tried to search Nahm's profile again, he wasn't particularly surprised to see she'd yanked it off Mixt and Skinspin and the rest. Either finding the sticky had spooked her, or her current customer was upping the pay enough to make exclusivity worthwhile. Dorian had to do things the old-fashioned way, with a sheaf of rumpled 200 Baht notes doled out to helpful individuals.

He didn't find her on the beach until late afternoon, and almost didn't recognize her when he did. She sat cross-legged on the palm-shaded sand, chatting to the old woman selling coconut milk and bags of crushed ice from a sputtering minifridge. Her face was more or less scrubbed of makeup, eyes smaller without the caked-on kohl, and her black hair hung gathered in a ponytail. Loose harem pants, flip-flops, a canary yellow Jack Daniels tank he assumed was being worn ironically.

"*Sawatdee krap*," Dorian said, butchering the pronunciation on purpose. He flashed her an incredulous grin. "This is a surprise."

Nahm looked up, surprised. "Hello," she beamed, running her fingers through her ponytail. Then her smile dimmed by a few watts. A crease of suspicion appeared on her forehead. "What is it you want? I am no working."

"I guessed from the flip-flops," Dorian said. "Long night for you?"

Nahm narrowed her eyes. "You," she said. "You put a . . . thing. To my shoe. First I think it was Ivan, but it was you." She said something to the old woman in machine-gun Thai, too fast for Dorian to even try at, and slunk to her feet. "I am going. I don't care you are handsome, you are crazy like Ivan." She brushed sand off her legs and made for the street.

"Have you figured out who you're fucking yet?" Dorian asked, dropping pretenses. "That business lady? The angry one?"

Nahm stopped, turned back.

Dorian clawed the air in front of his face as an extra reminder. "Whatever she's paying you is shit," he said.

"More than you pay me."

"She's a lot richer than me," Dorian said. "She's Alexis Carrow."

Nahm's eyes winched wide and she put a furious finger to her lips, scanning the beach as if paparazzi might burst up out of the grey sand.

Dorian grinned. "So you do know."

"What is it you want?" Nahm repeated, raking fingers through her ponytail.

"I want to talk business," Dorian said. "Walk with me a minute?"

He chased a few coins out of his pocket to buy a coconut milk and a bag of ice chips, then gestured down the beach. Nahm swayed, indecisive, but when Dorian started to walk she fired off another salvo of indecipherable Thai to the old woman and fell into step with him.

It was low tide and the beach was a minefield of broken glass bottles and plastic trash floating in tepid puddles. Other than a prone tourist couple baking away their hangovers, Dorian and Nahm had the place to themselves.

"You familiar with the term blackmail?" Dorian asked, handing her the coconut milk.

Nahm spun the straw between her fingers. "I watch bad movies. Yes."

"Your client is wearing a blur for a reason." Dorian ripped open the ice bag. "She's not keen on the tablos finding out she took a sex trip to Thailand."

Nahm gave an irritated shake of her head. "If she found that thing on my shoe, big fucking trouble for me, you know that?"

"Does she actually sweep you for bugs? Christ." Dorian popped a chunk of ice into his mouth. "Pawanoia."

"She careful."

Dorian crunched down on the cube, eliciting a squeal and crack. "Yes. Very careful. Meaning any fuck-footage from her trip is going to be extremely valuable. Do you want to get rich, Nahm?"

"Everybody wants to get rich," Nahm said, plumbing with her straw, not looking at him.

"Well, this is your shot. Also, my shot." Dorian spat a piece of ice into the filmy surf. "Alexis Carrow has enough money that paying two enterprising individuals such as you and me to suppress a sex scandal is easily worth 50,000 Euros. And if she refuses to negotiate, any of the bigger tablos would pay us the same for the footage."

Nahm's eyes went wide and Dorian realized he probably could have halved his actual demand a second time.

"Enough money to take care of your family out in Buriram," Dorian continued. "Get them out of the village, if you want. Definitely enough to assuage any lingering embarrassment about how their first-born financed her vaginoplasty."

"I make good money do what I do now," Nahm said sourly. "Enough money. I send them."

"Not 50,000 Euros money," Dorian said. "D'you really want to hook in Pattaya your whole life?" He packed another ice cube into his cheek. "This city is the diseased bleached asshole of Thailand. It's disgusting."

Nahm gave him a dirty look. "You're here."

"I'm disgusting," Dorian explained.

"And this is why Pattaya is Pattaya," Nahm said, lobbing her half-empty coconut milk into the water. "You make Pattaya be Pattaya."

"Don't have to litter about it." Dorian crunched his ice. "If you help me pull this off, you can live wherever you want."

"In London with you?" Nahm asked dryly.

"50,000 Euros," Dorian repeated. "Split even. Fifty percent yours, fifty percent mine. I've got a way to short-circuit the blur projector. I'll rig a sticky, it's the same thing I stuck to your shoe. Tiny. You just have to put it on the collar without her noticing."

"I told you she scans me in the car." Nahm folded her arms. "Very careful, remember?"

"That's why we plant it in the room beforehand, along with a little slip-in eyecam," Dorian said, groping inside the ice bag with reddened fingertips. "Where's she taking you tonight? Does she do fauxtels or the real thing?"

Nahm bit her lip. Dorian could practically see the tug-of-war on her creased forehead, a chance at instant wealth battling the cardinal rule of confidentiality.

"I want sixty percent," Nahm said. "I lose my best ever client. I maybe get big fucking trouble. You are safe with your phone somewhere, no risk."

Dorian grinned. "You're sharper than you let on. Why the dizzy bitch act? Do clients really like it that much?"

"Sixty percent," Nahm repeated, but with a hint of her own grin.

"Fine." Dorian spat out his ice and stuck out his hand. "Sixty."

Alexis Carrow had rented a suite at the Emerald Palace, a name Dorian thought a bit generous for an eight-story quickcrete façade topped by a broken-down eternity pool collecting algae. But if she was after privacy, it wasn't a bad choice. It was far enough from the main drag to be relatively quiet, and small enough to be inconspicuous.

Of course, gaining access was as easy as waltzing past reception wearing a drunken grin and clutching an expired keycard fished from the wastebasket outside. Dorian affected a slight stagger on his way to the lift. Once the shiny doors slid shut, he took out his tablet and called Nahm.

"How's the timing?" he asked, as she appeared on the screen putting up her hair with a static clip.

"She's on her way," Nahm said, unsticking a floating tendril of dark hair from her eyelash. "Get me from Bali Hai in five minute, then take ten, twelve minute back to hotel. Over."

"Alright." Dorian punched the backlit eight with his knuckle. "So I'm going to put it in the back of the toilet."

"So, how they did in *The Godfather*. Over." Nahm was now applying a gloss to her lips that shimmered like broken glass and was not paying as close attention as Dorian would have liked.

"Sure," he said. "As soon as you get in, go to the bathroom. Get some water going so she can't hear you take the lid off. Then open the ziplock, take the eyecam out first. You ever wear contacts?"

"Yes."

"It's like that," Dorian said. "Once you have the eyecam in, take the sticky out of the ziplock and hide it in your hand."

"And put it to the blur without her knowing it," Nahm continued, then, in a surprisingly credible imitation of Dorian's accent: "Base of the projector if possible, over."

"Yeah, then business as usual," Dorian said, as the lift jittered to a halt. "She won't notice when the projection goes down, so long as you're being your usual distracting self and you don't start complimenting her eyes or any-thing batshit like that." The lift made to open and he jammed it shut again. "Do what you normally do," he went on. "Let the eyecam do the work. After she pays you, come find me across the street and we'll get the POV uploaded to a private cloud. At which point, champagne and a blowjob."

"Who give the champagne, who give the blowjob?" Nahm asked, checking her thumbnail offscreen. "Over."

"Both on me if you do this right," Dorian said, knuckling the Open Door button. "Message me when you get the hotel." He paused, and then, because she was growing on him a bit: "Over."

Nahm's face lit up for the split second before he ended the call, then Dorian set off down the stucco-walled hallway. He made a quick check around the corner, then doubled back to door 811 and made short work of the electronic lock. The suite had obviously been prepped for her arrival. Freshly laundered sheets on the bed, a sea of fluffy white towels at the foot of it. Condom sprays and lubricants arrayed brazenly on the nightstand. Minibar stocked with Tanqueray gin and Lunar vodka.

Dorian plucked a cube out of the full ice bucket and popped it in his mouth, making his way to the bathroom. He lifted the featherweight top off the back of the Western-style toilet, then reached inside his pocket where the tiny eyecam and the even smaller sticky had been lovingly double-bagged in ziplock. Neither had been cheap, and he had a feeling he wasn't going to get the sticky back.

Setting the bag adrift in chemical-smelling water, Dorian replaced the top of the toilet and re-entered the room. He walked in a slow circle around the

bed, picturing angles, trying not to get distracted imagining Nahm and a
celebrity CEO fucking on it. In the end, he decided to plant his insurance
cam in the far corner. It would be an uncreative wide angle shot, but with a
near-zero chance of Alexis Carrow's deblurred face failing to make an appearance.

It wasn't that he didn't trust Nahm to manage the eyecam, but back-ups
were his cardinal rule where information storage was concerned. A healthy
fear of technical difficulties went hand-in-hand with hacking for a living.

Once satisfied with the cam's placement in a shadowy whorl of stucco,
Dorian put his ear to the door to listen for footsteps. Hearing nothing, he
exited the room, heart pumping with the old break-and-enter exhilaration
from his teenage years.

His hand was still on the doorknob when a black-shirted employee rounded
the corner in his peripheral. Dorian didn't look up. He pretended to struggle
with the door, then looked down at his keycard and made a slurred sound of
realization.

"This no your room, sir. Can I help you?"

Dorian tried not to jump. The man had slunk up and stopped directly
behind him, quiet as a cat, a feat made more impressive by the sheer size
of him. Tall for a Thai, broad-chested and broad-shouldered, with a shaved
scalp glistening in the fluorescent lighting and a tattoo of a cheerful cartoon
snake wriggling up and down one sinewy forearm. Dorian could have sworn
he'd been kicked out of a couple bars by the very same. Bouncers and hotel
security tended to overlap.

"Wrong floor," Dorian said, waving his keycard. "Hit the wrong button in
the lift. One too many Changs." He shook an imaginary beer bottle.

"Okay, sir," the guard said, not smiling.

"Nice tattoo," Dorian added. "Friendly-looking little bugger."

He gave the man a bleary grin, then made for the lift as quickly as he could
without looking suspicious.

Now that the rest of it was in Nahm's hands, Dorian had nothing to do but
wait. He camped out in an automated tourist bar across the way, slumping
into a plastic molded seat with his tablet. Once Nahm messaged him to say
they were at the hotel, he bought a gargantuan Heineken bottle, the litre sort
he never found outside Southeast Asia, and drank it slowly on ice.

Time ticked by on his tablet screen. He passed it imagining the whole
thing going off flawlessly, and then by imagining himself on a small sleek
yacht knifing through the blue-green waters off Ko Fangan. Maybe even with

Nahm draped on his shoulder for a week or two, wearing a pair of aviators and a skanky swimsuit. Between that and the tingly insulation of a half-litre of Heineken, he barely rattled when a hand slammed down on the table in front of him.

Dorian blinked hard. Nahm was standing in front of him, shoulders trembling, clutching herself. The static clip was still in place, moving her hair in graceful black ripples around her face, but the effect wasn't the same with her lip gloss smeared halfway across her cheek and a growing brown bruise under her bloodshot left eye. And hulking behind her, red-faced and furious, was the hotel security guard.

"Shit," Dorian said. The buzz from the beer slipped away all at once.

"I fuck up," Nahm said shakily. "I left the bathroom open. The blur go off, but when we switch around on the bed she see herself in the mirror."

The security guard barked something fast and angry, from which Dorian could only extricate *falang* and *police*. He reached across the table and hauled Dorian up by the armpit, jerking his head toward the door.

"The eyecam?" Dorian demanded, trying to twist away. No go.

"She call this big motherfucker, he take it out my eye," Nahm groaned, mascara finally starting to leak down her cheeks in inky trails. "She gets mad, she go. He says he will call the police so I tell him you have money."

"I don't have money," Dorian said reflexively, looking at the guard.

"Bullshit." Nahm's eyes were wide and desperate. "I know you have money."

Dorian looked around the bar, licking his lips. He'd picked it intentionally. A collection of steroid-bulky expats were cradling pints in the back, watching the situation with increasing interest. If he played ignorant right now, they looked both drunk and patriotic enough to intervene on behalf of a fellow Englishman. Nobody liked it when the locals stopped smiling.

"His cousin is police," Nahm said, winnowing on the edge of the sob. "He says if I don't pay he put me in the jail."

Dorian picked up his glass and finished it; the sweat pooling in his palms nearly made it slip out of his grip. He tried to think. If Carrow had left in a hurry, that meant the insurance cam he'd hidden was still there in the hotel room. The fact she'd left furious only confirmed how valuable the footage was.

If he wanted to get back into that room before some overzealous autocleaner wiped the cam off the wall, he needed to defuse things.

"Okay, fuck," Dorian said. "Okay. I'll come." He gave a glance toward the back table. "Nothing to worry about, lads. Just a bit of a . . . Lover's spat."

One of the men rubbed his bristly chin and raised his pint in Dorian's general direction. The others ignored him. As he let himself be steered out the door, the bar chirped goodbye in Thai and then English. Nahm followed behind, pinching the torn fabric of her shirt together. Her bare feet slapped on the tile. She was biting her lip, rubbing absently at the smeared gloss.

"Sorry I fuck up," she said miserably. Outside, the night air was warm and stank of a broken sewer line. Dorian fixed his eyes on the neon green sign of the hotel across the way. The sooner he had this dealt with, the sooner he could get the cam.

"Me too," Dorian said, but he searched for her free hand in the dark and gave it what he figured was a comforting squeeze.

She looked down at their interlaced hands, then back up, brow furrowed. "You should have said, though. You should have said, 'Nahm, don't let her see a mirror'."

Dorian took his hand back. The guard ushered them into the side alley, stopping underneath a graffitied Dokemon. Dorian crossed his arms.

"Alright," he said. "How much does he want? And if it's cash, we need a machine."

"No cash," the guard said, brandishing a phone still slick from the plastic wrap. "I do Bank."

"Of course you do," Dorian said. "So how much, shitface?"

"Five million Baht."

Dorian's exaggerated guffaw accidentally landed a speck of spit on the guard's shoulder, but the man didn't seem to notice and Dorian didn't feel keen to point it out. "Who do you think I am, the fucking king?" he demanded instead.

In reply, the guard thumbed a number into his phone. "I call cousin," he said, seizing Nahm's wrist. "Your ladyboy will go to jail, maybe you too."

Nahm gave a low groan again. Dorian made a few mental calculations. He had just over a million Banked, and the footage from the hotel had to be worth triple that, even if it wasn't a full encounter. He would still come out of this in the black. The last thing Dorian needed was police showing up. And he didn't like the idea of Nahm sobbing in some filthy lock-up, either.

"Half a million," Dorian said. "All I got."

The guard's ringtone bleated into the night air. He shook his shaved head. Nahm started cursing at him in Thai.

Dorian clenched his jaw. "A million," he snapped. "I can show it to you. It's really all I've got."

The guard stared at him, black eyes gleaming in the blurry orange street-light. The ringtone sounded again. Then, just as the click and a guttural *hallo* answered, he thumbed his phone off.

"Show me."

Dorian dug out his tablet and drained his account while the guard watched, dumping all of it to a specified address and waiting the thirty seconds for transaction confirmation. Nahm shifted nervously from foot to foot, mascara-streaked face bleached by the glowing screen, until it finally went through with an electronic chime. Dorian's stomach churned at the sight of the zeroes blinking in his Bank. He reminded himself it was temporary. Very, very temporary.

Once the transaction was through, the guard bustled out of the alley without so much as a *korpun krap*, leaving Dorian alone with Nahm. He was formulating the best way to get back into the hotel room without running into the guard again when she threw her arms around his neck and pulled him into a furious bruising kiss. Her fingers on his scalp and her tongue in his mouth made it difficult.

"Thank you," she panted. "For not letting him call." She hooked her thumb into the catch of Dorian's trousers, giving him her smeared smile. "No champagne. But . . ."

With her right hand working his cock, he nearly didn't feel her left slipping something into his pocket. He clamped over it on reflex. Nahm looked vaguely sheepish as the sound of a sputtering motor approached.

"I still am working on my hands," she said, wriggling her fingers out of his grip, leaving a small cold cylinder in their place. "Bye." She stepped away as a battered scooter whined its way into the alley, sliding to a halt in front of them. Dorian watched Nahm climb on to straddle a helmeted rider with a cartoon snake on one thick forearm. He lost his half-chub.

As the scooter darted back out into traffic, Dorian looked down at the insurance cam in his palm and grimaced.

It took another oversized bottle of beer before he could bring himself to watch the cam footage. Finally, slouched protectively over the table, he plugged it into his tablet and fast-forwarded through the empty hotel room until the door opened. Nahm glided inside on her pencil-thin heels, but instead of Alexis Carrow coming in behind her, it was the security guard, furtively checking the hallway before locking the door.

And instead of fucking, they sat on the edge of the bed and had a fairly business-like discussion in Thai. At one point Nahm departed for the bathroom and returned with the ziplock in hand. Dorian narrowed his eyes as she tossed it casually to her partner in crime, who stuffed it into a black duffel bag. The man paused, gesticulating at the bed and walls, then, with Nahm's approval, dug a scanner bar out of the duffel.

Dorian fast-forwarded through an impressively thorough search until the cam was spotted, plucked off the wall, and carried back to Nahm. She flashed a very un-vapid smile into the lens. The screen went black for a moment, then cleared again in the bathroom, pointing towards the mirror where Nahm was now painting a bruise under her eye.

Dorian swilled beer in his mouth, letting the carbonation sting his tongue while he listened to Nahm explain, in her roundabout way, how her "little" brother had caught him running a scam in a bar where he bounced. How Dorian had drunkenly bragged about his takings. How Nahm had shopped photos from Alexis Carrow's vacation in Malaysia six months ago and slipped the fake news report into the mirror for him to watch.

Her brother, working as a valet at the Emerald Palace, had gotten the imposing black ute out of the garage for a quick spin. She'd worked on her Cockney accent for a few weeks and done up a voice synthesizer. And from there, Dorian realized his overactive imagination had done the rest of the work.

"I hope the last part is so easy, too," Nahm said sweetly, smearing her lip gloss across her face with the heel of her hand. "With the money, we think maybe to buy a boat. Mwah." She blew a kiss to the cam, then reached in and switched it off.

Dorian leaned back at his table. Unprofessional of her, to add insult to injury like that and lay out her method besides. But he supposed it was understandable in the excitement of pulling off a semi-long con for the first time. And at least this way he'd recouped one of the cams. Dorian slid it back into his pocket, pensive.

For a little while he rewound the footage and sourly watched Nahm blowing kisses on loop, then finally he put the tablet away. He still had enough cash stowed to take a domestic down south and start over from there.

A fresh wave of tourists would soon be showing up on the islands, and Pattaya just wasn't doing it for him anymore.

Alex Irvine writes books (*Buyout, The Narrows, New York Collapse*), games (*Marvel Avengers Alliance, The Walking Dead: Road to Survival*), and comics (*Daredevil Noir, Deux Ex: Children's Crusade*). He lives in Maine.

NUMBER NINE MOON

Alex Irvine

They came in low over the abandoned colony near the eastern rim of Hellas Basin, deciding which landing spot gave them the best shot at hitting all the potential motherlodes in the least time. The Lift was just about done, and everything on this side of Mars was emptied out. The only people left were at the original colony site in the caldera of Pavonis Mons, and they would be gone inside twenty-four hours. Steuby, Bridget, and Marco figured they had twelve of those hours to work, leaving enough time to zip back to Pavonis Mons and pay for their passage back in-system on the freighter that was currently docked at the top of the Pavonis space elevator.

"Quick visit," Marco said to no one in particular. "We're just stopping by. Quick trip. Trips end. People go home. That's what we're doing, boys and girls. About to go home, live out our happy lives."

Steuby really wished Marco would shut up.

"That's it right there," Bridget said. She pointed at a landing pad on the edge of the settlement. "Close to the garage, greenhouse, that's a lab complex. . . ."

"Yup," Marco said. "I like it."

He swung the lander in an arc over the settlement, bringing it back toward the pad. Nineteen years of work, people devoting their lives to establishing a human foothold on Mars, and now it was up in smoke because Earth was pulling the plug. It was sad, the way people were withdrawing. Steuby always wanted to think of human civilization like it was an eagle, but maybe it was more like a turtle. Now it was pulling its head in. Someday maybe it would start peering out again, but all this stuff on Mars would be junk by then. Everything would have to start over.

Or humanity would stay on Earth, and in a hundred years no one living would have ever set foot on Mars or the Moon or an asteroid.

"Shame," Bridget said. "All that work for nothing."

"I hate quitters," Marco said.

Steuby didn't mind quitters. He kind of admired people who knew when to quit. Maybe that was a function of age. He was older than both Bridget and Marco by a good twenty years. The older you got, the less interested you were in fighting battles you knew you couldn't win.

But to be agreeable, he said, "Me, too."

"They're not quitting," Bridget pointed out. "Earth quit on them."

"Then I hate Earth," Marco said. "Just kidding. That's where I'll end up, when I'm old."

Nobody knew they were there, since what they were doing was technically illegal. The sun was going down, washing the landscape in that weird Martian blue dusk that made Steuby think he'd had a stroke or something every time he saw it.

"Time to see what the Lift left," Marco said, for maybe the hundredth time since they'd taken off from PM. Steuby was ready to kill him.

Their collective guess was that the Lift had left all kinds of useful things. People always did when they had to get out in a hurry. In the thirty days since the Mid-System Planning Authority announced it was ending logistical support for all human activity beyond the Earth-Moon Lagrange points, everyone on Mars had started lining up to get off-planet and back under the MSPA umbrella. Even the asteroid miners, as antisocial and hardy a group as had existed since Vinland, were pulling back. Things on Earth were bad— refugee crises, regional wars over water and oil and room to breathe. When things on Earth got bad, everyone not on Earth was on their own. That wasn't a big deal for the Moon settlements, which were more or less self-sufficient. Much different story for Mars.

"Are we sure nobody's here?" Steuby wondered out loud. It would be kind of a drag to get arrested in the middle of a planet-wide evacuation.

"I listened to the MSPA comm all night," Marco said. "Last people out of here were on their way to Pavonis before midnight."

Since the easiest way off-planet was the space elevator at Pavonis Mons, that was where the remaining colonists were, hiding out in the caldera until it was their turn to go up. The Hellas Basin settlement, over which they were now circling, was completely deserted. It was newer than PM, so the pickings would probably be better here anyway. Steuby looked out the window. Mars looked different around here. The PM caldera felt like it was already halfway to space because it was so high and you could see so far from the rim, when the storms let you go out on the rim. The Hellas Basin settlement, built just a couple of years ago to take advantage of a huge water supply locked in glaciers on the basin's eastern slope, was about as far from Pavonis Mons as you could get both geographically and environmentally. Practically antipodal. Where Pavonis was high, dry, and cold, Hellas was low, water-rich, and comparatively warm. Stormy during the summers, when the planet neared perihelion.

Which was now. There were dust devils everywhere, the atmosphere in the area was completely scrambled by magnetic auroras, PM was sucking itself up the space elevator as fast as it could get there, and here were Steuby, Marco, and Bridget thousands of klicks away at HB exploring. Well, prospecting. Okay, looting.

"We're just here to plunder the mysteries, Ma'am," Marco said to an imaginary cop, even though the auroras meant they couldn't talk to any authorities whether they wanted to or not. He put the lander into its final descent and ninety seconds later they were parked on the surface of Mars. There was a sharp crack from below as the ship touched down.

"Nice going," Steuby said. "You broke the pad."

Marco shrugged. "Who's gonna know? You find me a concrete slab on Mars that doesn't have a crack in it. Steuby, what was it, ten years since we were here before?"

Steuby nodded. "Give or take." He and Marco had worked a pipeline project on the lower slopes of Pavonis. Then he'd gone back in-system. He preferred the Moon. Real Martians wanted to get away from Earth. Steuby preferred to keep the Earth close by in case he needed it. "Bridget, you've been here before, right?"

"I built some of the solar arrays on the edge of the Pavonis caldera," she said. "Long time ago. But this is my first time coming out to Hellas. And last, looks like."

They suited up and popped the hatch. Bridget went first, Steuby right behind her, and Marco appeared in the hatchway a minute later, after doing a quick post-flight check on the lander's engines. "Good morning, Barsoom!" he sang out.

Marco was three steps down the ladder when they all heard a grinding rumble from under the ground. Steuby felt the pad shift and scrambled backward. The lander started to tip as the concrete pad cracked and collapsed into a sinkhole that opened up right at Steuby's feet. Marco lost his balance and grabbed at the ladder railing. The sinkhole kept opening up and the lander kept tipping. "Marco!" Bridget shouted. "Jump!"

He tried, but he couldn't get his feet under him and instead he slipped, pitching off the ladder and falling into the sinkhole as the lander tipped right over on top of him. The whole scene unfolded in the strange slow motion of falling objects in Martian gravity, dreamlike and all the more frightening because even slowed down, the lander tipped too quickly for Marco to get out of the way. He disappeared beneath it as its hull scraped along the broken concrete slabs.

Before it had completely come to rest, Steuby and Bridget were clambering around the edge of the sinkhole, where large pieces of the concrete pad angled under the toppled lander. Steuby spotted him first, face down and not moving. He slid into the dust-filled space underneath the bulk of the lander, Bridget right next to him. Together they grabbed Marco's legs and tried to drag him out, but he was caught on something. They could pivot him around but not pull him free. "Marco," Bridget said. "Talk to me."

The dust started to clear and Steuby saw why Marco wasn't answering.

The ladder railing had broken off and part of it impaled Marco just inside his right shoulder blade. Blood welled up around the hole in his suit and ran out from under his body down the tilted concrete slab. Now Marco turned his head toward them. Dust covered his faceplate. He was moving his left arm and trying to talk, but his comm was out. His voice was a thin hum and they couldn't understand what he was saying. A minute later it didn't matter anymore because he was dead.

"Marco," Steuby said. He paused, feeling like he ought to say something but not sure what. After a while he added, "Hope it didn't hurt too much when we pulled on you. We were trying to help."

Bridget had been sitting silently since Marco stopped moving. Now she stood up. "Don't talk to him, Jesus, he's dead! Don't talk to him!"

Steuby didn't say anything.

All he could figure was that there had been some kind of gas pocket under the landing pad, frozen hydrates or something. They'd sublimated away gradually from the sporadic heat of a hundred or a thousand landings, creating a soft spot, and when Marco set down their lander, that last little bit of heat had weakened the pad. Crack, tip, disaster.

"What are we going to do?" Bridget asked in a calmer tone. It was a reasonable question to which Steuby had no good answer. He looked around. They were at the edge of a deserted settlement on Mars. The only other people on Mars were thousands of kilometers away, and had neither the resources nor the inclination to help, was Steuby's guess.

He shrugged. "Probably we're going to die."

"Okay," she said. "But let's say we didn't want to die. What would we do then?"

Compared to the Moon, everything on Mars was easy. It had water, it had lots of usable minerals that were easy to get to, synthesizing fuels was no problem, solar power was efficient because the thin atmosphere compensated for the distance to the sun . . . as colonizing projects went, it was a piece of cake. In theory.

In reality, Mars was very good at killing people. Steuby looked at the horizon. The sun was coming up. If he and Bridget couldn't figure something out real soon, Mars would probably add two more people to its tally. Steuby wasn't ready to be a statistic. Marco, well, Marco already was.

Now the question wasn't what the Lift had left, but whether they were going to be able to lift themselves or be left behind for good.

"We'll see," Steuby said.

Bridget looked up. "See what?"

"Nothing."

"You're talking to Marco."

"No, I'm not," Steuby lied.

"Here's a question, since you're thinking about him anyway. What should we do with him?"

"What do you mean, what should we do? It's not like we can strap him to the roof."

She let it go. They started walking toward the main cluster of buildings and domes that made up the Hellas Basin settlement.

Phobos was rising, big and bright. Sometimes sunlight hit Phobos a certain way and the big impact crater on its planet-facing side caught the shadows just right, and for an hour or so there was a giant number 9 in the Martian sky. Steuby wasn't superstitious, but when he saw that, he understood how people got that way.

Number Nine Moon was his favorite thing about Mars. He hoped, if he was going to die in the next few days—and due to recent developments, that seemed more than likely—he would die looking at it.

From behind him Bridget said, "Steuby. Stop looking at the moon."

Marco was the one who had pointed out Number Nine Moon to him, when they'd been on Mars before. "I knew him for a long time, Bridget," Steuby said. "Just give me a minute."

"We don't really have any extra minutes."

This was true. Steuby climbed up out of the sinkhole. "Come on, then," he said.

"Where?"

"We can't walk back to PM," Steuby said. "Can't drive. So we're going to have to fly."

"Fly what?"

Steuby didn't want to tell her what he was thinking until he had a little more than moonshine to go on. "Let's head to the garage over there. I'll show you."

They sealed the garage doors after they went inside. It was warm. Condensation appeared on their faceplates. "Hey," Steuby said. "There's still air in here."

He popped his faceplate and smelled dirt and plants. A passive oxygen system in the garage circulated air from a nearby greenhouse. The plants hadn't had time to freeze and die yet.

With the dirty faceplate off, he could see better in the dim interior. He found a light switch and flicked it on, just in case. "Hey, lights too."

Now for the real test. Along one wall of the garage were a series of spigots and vents, spaced out over underground tanks. Steuby walked along them, saying silent prayers to the gods of chemistry that one of the spigots would be tagged with a particular series of letters.

He stopped at the fourth and pointed out the letters. "MMH," Bridget read. "Monomethylhydrazine, right?"

"Yup," Steuby said. "Also known as jackpot. They must have made it down here for impulse thrusters. Landers would need to tank up on it before they took off again. You know what this means?"

"That we have a whole lot of a fuel that doesn't work in our ship, which is crashed anyway."

"No, it means we have half of a hypergolic fuel combination designed to work in engines just exactly like the one built into that rocket out there." Steuby pointed toward the garage's bank of south-facing windows. Bridget followed the direction of his finger.

"You're kidding," she said. "That thing is a toy."

"Au contraire, Mademoiselle," Steuby said. "I've seen those fly."

When he'd gotten out of the construction business after Walter Navarro's death and spent his next years fleecing tourists, Steuby had briefly worked on an amusement park project. A woman named Veronica Liu wanted to create an homage to classic visions of the Moon from the days before the Space Age. Lots of pointy rockets and gleaming domes. She'd built it over the course of a year, with rides specifically designed for the Moon's gravity, and then at the opening ceremony she had put on a big show of landing a fleet of rockets specifically designed to recall the covers of pulp magazines from the 1940s. They were pointy, finned, gleaming—and when the amusement park went under five years after Liu built it, they were sold off to other concerns. One of them was still on the Moon as far as Steuby knew, because she hadn't been able to sell it for a price that made the deal worth doing.

Another was now standing on a small pad a kilometer from the garage. Steuby had spotted it on their first flyover. He didn't know how it had gotten there, and he didn't care. All he cared about was finding out whether it would fly.

"That's a ridiculous idea. This whole thing was a ridiculous idea. You had to come up with a stupid scheme to get rich and now Marco's dead because you couldn't just get off Mars like everyone else." Bridget was working herself up into a full-on rage. Steuby thought he should do something about it but he didn't know what. His way of dealing with trauma was to pretend he wasn't dealing with it. Hers was apparently to blow off some steam a short time after the traumatic event. "You wanted to come see HB and loot the mysteries! You said we'd be out and back in no time flat, no problem! Now we're going to die because of what you said!"

This was the wrong time to remind her that the whole thing had been Marco's plan, Steuby thought. He wasn't good at dealing with people, or emotions, but since Bridget was the one with the expertise in battery systems and flight control, he needed her help. Maybe a useful task would help her cope and also keep them alive.

"Let's find out if it's ridiculous," he said. "Come with me and we'll do a preflight check." He dropped his faceplate and went to the door.

After a pause, she said, "Why not. If we're going to die anyway."

Bridget didn't really believe him, but given no other option she went along while Steuby climbed up the ladder and poked around in the rocket. From the hiss when he opened the access door he could tell it had been sealed against the Martian dust—as much as anything could be sealed against Martian dust.

She looked at clusters of cables and wires, followed connections, popped open recessed coves in the floor, and eventually said, "We're still going to die, but electronically all of this looks intact."

"Perfect," Steuby said.

"For certain values of perfect," Bridget said. They climbed back down and Steuby checked the thruster assembly, feeling a surge of optimism as he opened panel after panel and found that the rocket had been staged and left. Nobody had stripped it for parts. Probably they'd looked at it and—like Bridget—thought it was just a toy.

But Steuby knew better. All this rocket needed was juice in its batteries to run the control systems, and fuel in its tanks to fire the engine.

"You watch," he said. "We're going to get out of here yet."

Bridget regarded the rocket with open scorn. "If by out of here you mean out of our bodies into the afterlife, I completely agree."

"I will be willing to accept your apology when we reach orbit," Steuby said. "Come on. We need charged batteries and a few tons of dinitrogen tetroxide." He headed for the garage, and she went with him.

They had ammonia, all they wanted, held in another of the underground tanks. It was useful enough that the base had kept a supply. Steuby was willing to bet that one of the machines in the garage either was designed to oxidate ammonia or could be configured to do so. NTO was a standard liquid fuel for all kinds of rocket models. All they had to do was find the right machine.

"We used to do this on the Moon," Steuby said. "You mix the ammonia with regular old air, and as nitrogen oxides form you add nitric acid to catalyze more nitrogen oxides. After that, you cool the mixture down and compress it, and the oxides combine to make NTO. It's just shuffling atoms around. Doesn't even need heat. All you need is compression at the right time and a way to siphon off the NTO. I would bet Marco's last dollar there's an NTO synthesizer somewhere around here."

They went looking for it and found it within ten minutes. There was even a generator, and the generator even still had power left in its fuel cells. For the first time since Marco's death, Steuby started to recover his natural state of irrational optimism.

They ran a hose from the ammonia tank over to the synthesizer, fed it a fair bit, and fired it up. Then they wheeled over a smaller tank of nitric acid and pumped some of it in, Steuby doing the figures in his head. They didn't have to be exact. The reaction, once it got going, just needed continual adjustment of ammonia, air, and nitric acid at the right pressures, and the holding tank on the other end of the synthesizer would fill up with nasty, corrosive, carcinogenic, and in this case life-saving NTO.

The synthesizer rattled to life. Steuby waited for it to explode or fall apart, but it didn't. It appeared to work. He watched the capacity readout on the tank. It stayed at 00 for a very long time . . . and then it ticked over to 01. Bridget looked on, and the readout ticked to 02 . . . 03. . . . "Keep this up and I'll start to believe you know what you're doing."

"Love it," Steuby said. "This is my favorite machine. Now all we need to do is make sure we can fuel up and take off before the storm gets bad and keep the rocket going straight up and escape the gravity well and make the rendezvous and convince the freighter to slow down and take us on board."

"When you put it like that," Bridget said.

Steuby nodded. "Now let's charge the batteries."

The sun was all the way up by the time they found the solar array's charging transfer board and ran cables all the way out to the rocket. Possibly it would have been quicker to pull the batteries and bring them to the charging station, but Steuby was nervous about disturbing anything on the rocket. There were charging ports built into the battery housing, and there was enough power cable lying around to reach Jupiter, so that was the most straightforward way. Still, it took a few hours, and both Bridget and Steuby stood around nervously watching the battery-charging readouts as the morning sky passed through its spooky blue dawn into its normal brownish-yellow.

"Good thing about solar arrays is they're pretty low maintenance," he said, to pass the time.

The charging indicators on the batteries lit up.

"Wonder how the NTO synthesizer is doing," Bridget said. She looked up at the sky. They knew what time it was, but that didn't matter. The only thing that mattered was the position of Phobos, zipping around three times a day. They were practically in Apollo 13 territory. The plan was this: watch until Phobos was in more or less the right place, then touch off the rocket's engines, and if they'd avoided fatal errors they would launch, achieve orbit, and then run out of fuel about when the freighter came along. The freighter's schedule was always the same: wait until the moons passed by, dock with the elevator, split before the moons passed by again. Once the freighter had decoupled from the elevator terminus, it would fire an escape burn. It took two hours or so to prep that burn. Bridget knew this because she had worked the Belt before deciding she liked to experience gravity once in a while. Even Martian gravity.

In this case the freighter wouldn't be doing a drop. Instead it would be taking on people and supplies, but the time frame was more or less the same. Counting two hours in Phobos' orbit from when it passed the elevator terminus put the little Number Nine Moon right on the western horizon. They had about an hour from then to fire their rocket, so they could be at escape velocity when they got close to the freighter, which would probably make an emergency burn to save them, but maybe not. Everything would be much more certain if they could match the freighter's velocity as closely as possible, which meant putting the rocket in a trans-Earth trajectory.

Problem was, if they did that and the freighter didn't pick them up, they would die long before they got to Earth. The rocket, if it had any fuel left, would do an automated Earth-orbit injection burn and the Orbital Enforcement Patrol would board it to find their desiccated bodies. Steuby hoped he wouldn't die doing something embarrassing.

Actually, he hoped he wouldn't die at all. You had to remind yourself of that once in a while when you were in the middle of doing something that would probably kill you. You got so used to the idea that you were going to die, you started trying to make the best of it. It was a useful corrective to articulate the possibility that you might survive.

The day on Mars was forty minutes longer than the day on Earth. Phobos went around about every eight hours, rising in the west because it orbited so much faster than Mars rotated. They needed to get the rocket up to a little more than five kilometers per second for escape velocity. Steuby liked the way those numbers went together. Forty, eight, five. Factors. Of course they had nothing to do with each other, but given the chaos of recent events, Steuby was willing to take his symmetry where he could find it.

Waiting for the tank to fill again, he looked around at the abandoned settlement. HB seemed nice, more like a real place to live than just a colony outpost. There was even public art, a waist-high Mount Rushmore of Martian visionaries carved from reddish stone. Wells, Bradbury, Robinson, Zhao. Marco probably would have wanted to take it if he was still alive, and if they could have justified the weight.

"No can do," he said out loud. "We're fighting the math. Man, Marco, when I was a kid, you could get anything. Strawberries in January. We were on our way. Now we're on our way back. Pulling back into our shell."

"Stop talking to him," Bridget said. "He's dead."

"Look." He was crying and hoped it didn't show in his voice. His helmet was so dusty she wouldn't be able to see.

Then she wiped the dust away with her gloved hand and said, "Steuby. I get it. He was an old friend and you're sad. Stop being an ass about it and stop trying to pretend you're not doing it, because if you divide your attention you're going to make a mistake and it will kill us. Okay?"

"Right," he said. "Okay."

He kept an eye on the NTO tank while Bridget did something to the monitors on the solar array, but he kept thinking: I'm millions of miles from Earth waiting for a robot left over from a failed Mars colony to finish refueling my rocket and hoping a dust storm doesn't stop us from making a semi-legal rendezvous with a freighter coming back from the asteroid belt. How had he gotten into this situation?

Steuby was sixty-two years old, born in 2010, and had only ever seen one other person die in front of him. That was back on the Moon, where he'd worked for almost fifteen years. A guy named Walter Navarro, looking the wrong way when someone swung a steel beam around at a construction site. The end of the beam smashed the faceplate of Walter's helmet. The thing Steuby remembered most about it was the way Walter's screams turned into ice fog pouring out and drifting down onto the regolith. By the time they got him inside he was dead, with frozen blood in his eyes from where the shards of the faceplate had cut him. Steuby had gotten out of the construction business as soon as he'd collected his next paycheck. After that he'd run tourist excursions, and seen some weird shit, but nothing weirder than Walter Navarro's dying breaths making him sparkle in the vacuum.

They found a tractor that would run and hooked the tank carriage to it. The tractor's engine whined at the load, but it pulled the tank as long as they kept it in low gear. The rocket's fueling port was high on its flank, on the opposite side from the gantry that reached up to the passenger capsule in the nose. Ordinarily a crew would refuel it with a cherry-picker truck, but neither Steuby nor Bridget could find that particular vehicle in or near the garage and they didn't have time to look anywhere else. So they had to tie two ladders together and lean them against the rocket. They flipped a coin to see who would climb, and Bridget lost. Steuby watched her go. "Hey, if you break your leg you're gonna have a hell of a time getting in the rocket," he said.

Bridget didn't miss a beat. "Better shoot me and leave me, then. Like Marco."

For some reason her tone of voice made Steuby think she was trying to make him feel bad.

"I didn't shoot Marco," he said defensively, even though he wasn't sure what he was defending.

Once the nitrogen tetroxide was topped off, they had to go back and clean the tank out, then fill it with hydrazine. Together the compounds would fuel a rocket via a hypergolic reaction. One of Steuby's favorite words, hypergolic. Like just being golic wasn't enough. Neither chemical would do a thing by itself—well, other than poison and corrode anything they touched. Together, boom.

Usually transfers like this were done in clean rooms, by techs in clean suits. Steuby and Bridget were doing it in a dust-filled garage wearing worn-out spacesuits that probably had a dozen microscopic leaks each. He hoped they wouldn't have to do any maneuvering in hard vacuum anytime soon.

When they cranked the fresh hose onto the nipple and locked it into place, Bridget and Steuby looked at each other. "Just so we're clear," Steuby said, "this will blow up and kill us both if there's any trace of the tetro still in there."

"Yup," Bridget said.

"Okay then." Steuby paused over the dial that would open the synthesizer and start dumping the MMH into the tank. "I'll try not to talk to Marco anymore," he said.

"That's the least of my worries right now."

"It's just . . . this is going to sound weird, but I talk to him even though he's dead because if I talk to him, it's like he's not dead, which makes me think I might not die."

"Turn the knob, Steuby," she said.

"I don't want to die."

She put her gloved hand over his, which was still resting on the dial. "I know. Me neither. But let's be honest. If we really wanted to be one hundred percent sure of living, we wouldn't be on Mars."

This was true. Bridget started to move Steuby's hand. The dial turned. Monomethylhydrazine started dumping into the tank. It did not explode.

Riding another spike of optimism, Steuby ran to the door. Phobos was visible. They had about eight hours to get the hydrazine topped off and transferred, and then get themselves aboard the rocket. He checked the batteries. They were still pretty low.

"How much of a charge do we need?" Bridget asked.

"I have no idea," Steuby said. "A few hours at least. It won't take long to reach orbit, but once we're out there we'd better be able to get the freighter's attention and keep pinging them our position until they can get to us."

"Assuming they want to get to us."

"They will. The whole point of the Lift is to evacuate people, right? We're people. We need evacuation."

Bridget spent some time in the rocket's crew capsule testing the electronics, which were in fine shape and included an emergency beacon on a frequency that was still standard. "Should we just set it off?" Steuby wondered. Bridget was against it on the grounds that nobody could get all the way across the planet to them and still make the last ship out, whereas if they sent an SOS from near-Mars space, a rendezvous would be easier. Steuby didn't want to go along with this, but he had to admit it made sense.

Other than that, most of the work they had to do—filling tanks, keeping the solar array focused, monitoring the mix in the synthesizer—was in the shop, away from the omnipresent Martian dust. Most of it, anyway. Humankind had not yet invented the thing capable of keeping Mars dust completely out of an enclosed space. Even so, they couldn't do everything inside. Bridget found some kind of problem with one of the battery terminals in the rocket, and they had to go out and pop the cover to see what was wrong. While she worked on it, Steuby watched the horizon.

A huge dust devil sprouted on the plain out past the edge of the settlement. They were common when Mars was near perihelion and its surface warmed up. Steuby and Bridget watched it grow and spiral up into the sky, kilometers high.

If that dust devil was a sign of a big storm developing, they were going to be in trouble. The rocket's engines themselves wouldn't be affected, but a bad dust storm would slow the recharging of the batteries by, oh, ninety-nine percent or so. That put the full charge of the rocket's batteries, and therefore their departure, on the other side of their teeny-tiny launch window.

They could get into the rocket either way and hope it was charged up enough for its guidance systems not to give out before they achieved orbit, but that was one risk Steuby really didn't want to pile on top of all the others they were already taking.

Steuby knew he was getting tired after a dozen runs back and forth to the rocket, and the hours spent working on machines without eating or sleeping. His ears rang and he was losing patience with Marco, who was saying maybe the rocket's placement was for the best because this way they wouldn't have to worry about the rocket's exhaust pulverizing anything important when they lifted off.

Steuby just looked at him.

Oh, right, Marco said.

"Steuby!" Bridget shouted, and Steuby snapped out of his daydream. "That's freaking me out. I'm alive. You want to talk to someone, talk to me. You want to go crazy and have conversations with dead people, do that after we're on the rocket. Okay?"

He didn't answer. She walked up to him and rapped her glove on his faceplate. "Okay?"

"Okay," he said.

She took a step back. Over their local mic he heard her sigh. "Let's get these batteries covered up."

It only took them a minute, but the dust devil was coming fast, and before they'd started the tractor again, it swallowed them up. Winds of this velocity would have flung them around like palm fronds on Earth, but in Mars' thinner atmosphere it felt like a mild breeze. The sensory disconnect was profound. You saw a powerful storm, but felt a gentle push. Your mind had trouble processing it, had to constantly think about it the way you had to plan for Newton's Second Law whenever you did anything in zero-G. In space, instincts didn't work, and on Mars, they could be pretty confusing, too.

Steuby froze and waited for it to go away. It was only two or three hundred meters across, and passed quickly. But as the day went on, there would be more. Steuby looked at the sky, to the west. Phobos had risen. It was all Steuby could do not to mention it to Marco. He's dead, he told himself. Let him be dead.

"Another hour going to be good enough for those batteries?" he asked. They got on the tractor and headed back toward the shop.

"Do we have more than another hour?"

"Not much."

"Then there's your answer." Bridget paused. She swiped dust away from her faceplate. "Look, Steuby. We're ready, right? There's nothing else we need to do?"

He parked the tractor. "Soon as the last tank of NTO is onboard, that's it. That's all we can do."

Bridget was quiet the whole time Steuby backed the tank into the airlock, closed the outer door, uncoupled the tank and pushed it into the shop, and closed the inner door. Then she said, "While you're filling the tank, I need to borrow the tractor for a minute."

"Borrow it? Why, do we need milk?"

"No, we need Marco."

He dropped the hose coupling with a clang. "Are you nuts?"

"We have to bring him, Steuby. It's the right thing to do."

"Math," Steuby said.

"Fix the math. Throw out what we don't need. You said it yourself. If we don't catch the freighter we're going to die. What's the point of having a month's worth of food for a three-month trip? Or a three-hour trip? That might be all we need."

"How the hell do we know what we're going to need?" Steuby shouted. "Have you done this before? I haven't!"

"I thought you hated quitters," she said.

"I—" Steuby stopped. She had him. He looked up at the sky. Phobos was low on the horizon, maybe ten degrees up. Less than an hour until they needed to fire the engines. He remembered Marco talking about going back to Earth, and he knew Bridget was thinking the same thing.

"All right," Steuby said. "Look. We'll do it this way. You go get him. I'll babysit the synthesizer. But if you're not back by the time Number Nine is overhead, I'm going without you."

"You will not."

"Try me."

She left without saying anything else. Steuby didn't know if he was serious or not. Yes he did. He was serious. If she was going to make a dead body more important than two living people, those were priorities that Henry Caleb Steuben was proud not to share.

On the other hand, he couldn't really climb up into the rocket and leave her to die. That wouldn't be right.

On the other other hand, who the hell did she think she was, endangering their rendezvous with the freighter?

On the . . . what was this, the fourth hand? . . . it would be pretty ironic if Steuby took off without her and then missed the rendezvous anyway, so both of them got to die cursing the other one out.

There was also the entirely plausible scenario of them taking off on time and still missing the freighter, so they could die together.

While the synthesizer poured NTO into the tank, Steuby suggested to himself that he adopt a more positive outlook. Maybe we'll make the freighter, he thought. It's only six klicks to where Marco is. An hour out there and back, tops. Unless—

He called Bridget up on the line-of-sight frequency. She was just visible. "What?"

"So, um, you have something to cut that piece of the railing, right?" he asked.

"No, Steuby. I survived twenty years working in space by forgetting tools." She broke the connection. Fine, he thought. Be pissed if you want.

Another dust storm rolled in maybe ninety seconds later. Figures, Steuby thought. Right when I have to go outside again.

One human-equivalent amount of mass had to come out of the rocket. Steuby stuck his head in the crew compartment. Dust blew in around him and he clambered in so he could shut the hatch. What could he get rid of? He started to panic. What if he threw something away and they needed it?

"Marco, help me out," he said. Bridget wasn't around. She couldn't give him a hard time. He wished he'd been able to crunch all the launch calculations and see whether they had an extra eighty kilos of payload slack. Maybe he was worrying over nothing.

He wriggled through a tight hatch into the storage space below the cockpit. There were lockers full of crap back here. Five extra helmets and suits. He pushed three of them up into the cockpit. He found spare electronics and computer components. They piled up in the pilot's seat. There were two water tanks. He took a deep breath and vented one of them even though he'd just filled it an hour ago. That saved almost a human's worth of mass right there. Now that he'd started, though, Steuby couldn't stop. What if one more thing thrown out the hatch was the difference between making that five point oh three kilometers per second and making a bright streak in the sky as they burned up on reentry?

He stuck his head into the cockpit and saw that the dust storm had blown through again. The suits, spare gear, and a bunch of other stuff went out the hatch, banging against the gantry before falling to litter the launch pad.

In the west, Phobos was high, nearly forty-five degrees. Steuby pulled empty metal boxes out of the storage compartment and threw them out the hatch. Then he had to head for the shop and make sure the last fuel tank was topped off with NTO, or nothing he'd done in here would matter.

When Bridget got back, Steuby was standing in the open airlock. She backed the tractor in and he hooked up the tank. Marco lay face-up in the small equipment bed behind the tractor's seats. The whole front of his suit was soaked in blood and caked in dust. Steuby climbed onto the tractor and Bridget drove them out to the rocket. "You connect the hose and I'll carry him up," Steuby said.

"This is Mars," Bridget said. "He only weighs about sixty pounds. I'll take him. You know more about the fuel system than I do."

"Whatever," Steuby said. He still had that teetering sensation that panic was right there waiting for him. He started the last fuel transfer and watched Bridget climb the gantry with Marco slung over her back. She pushed him in ahead of her and then climbed in. "Shut the hatch!" Steuby shouted. She couldn't hear him. A few seconds later she came back out, shut the hatch, and climbed down.

They stared at the hose where it was connected to the NTO tank. "Think it's enough?" Bridget asked.

The tank's feeder valve clicked shut. "That's all she'll take," Steuby said. "It'll have to be enough."

He disengaged the hose and backed the tractor away. "So how do we move the gantry?" Bridget asked.

"We don't," Steuby said. "The exhaust will do it for us."

"Not ideal," she commented.

"Neither was holding everything up to go collect a body." Steuby looked around. "Anything else we need? Time is short."

She was already at the base of the gantry ladder again. "Then let's move."

Steuby waited for her to get all the way in, then slid feet-first through the hatch. He turned and tried to push the gantry back, but it didn't move. "Forget about it, Steuby," Bridget said.

"I don't want it to tip against the rocket and tear a hole in us while we're lifting off," he said.

She jammed herself into the hatch next to him and together they shoved at the gantry. It still didn't move. "You think the exhaust will push it far enough away before it starts to tip?" she panted.

"If I thought that, I wouldn't be trying to push it myself," he said.

"I mean is it likely? Can we take the chance?"

"It's the only chance we've got," he said. He backed into the cockpit and Bridget closed the hatch.

They buckled themselves into the pilot's and copilot's seats, lying on their backs and looking at the sky. Old-fashioned, Steuby thought. Like we're off to fight Ming the Merciless or something. By accident he ended up in the pilot's chair. "You want to be the pilot?" he asked.

"There is nothing in the world I care about less," Bridget said. She powered up the onboard flight-control systems and saw that their battery life read about four hours of full operation. Steuby saw it, too.

"Sure hope that freighter answers fast," he said. "Where's Marco?"

Bridget adjusted herself in her seat. "Down in the back. Get us out of here, Captain Steuby."

"Blastoff," Steuby said. He flipped the failsafes on the fuel-mixing system, took a deep breath, and pressed the rectangular button labeled IGNITION.

Liftoff was like nothing Steuby had ever felt. He'd never actually been in an old-fashioned rocket before. Every time he'd gone from Earth to space he'd used the space elevators out of Quito or Kismaayo. This was multiple Gs, what the old astronauts had called eyeballs-in, sitting on top of a bomb and riding it into orbit. Steuby was terrified. He couldn't breathe, he couldn't see very well, he didn't know if they were going in a straight line or curving off into a fatal parabola . . . he wanted to start screaming but he was afraid if he did he wouldn't be able to get a breath again. As it was he could only gasp in little sips of air that felt like they weren't making it all the way down into his lungs. Bridget wasn't making any noise either, which on the one hand comforted Steuby because it meant she wasn't giving him a hard time but on the other hand upset him because she was solid and reliable and he wanted to hear her say something reassuring.

At first the sound was loud, overwhelming, but as the atmosphere thinned out it modulated down into a rumble they felt more than heard. The rocket didn't shake itself apart. It didn't shred from a hole caused by the gantry. It went straight up like it had been made to do, and if Steuby had been able to speak he thought he might have cheered. They'd done it. If they managed to live long enough to rendezvous with the freighter, people would be telling this story for decades. Also they might end up in jail, but at the moment that was fine with Steuby. Jails had air and food and water.

The thruster cut out. Their velocity was five point seven kilometers per second, plenty for escape velocity. They were nine hundred and sixty-one kilometers from Phobos, which arced away from them toward the horizon. They rose through its orbital plane. The rocket started to tip sideways, aligning its long axis with the direction of Mars' rotation. They were curving up and out of its gravity well, and now they could see the vast reddish emptiness of the southern highlands. Storms tore across the eastern limb, where it had been daylight the longest. Olympus Mons peeked over the horizon far to the northwest, its summit high above the weather.

"We did it," Bridget said.

"We sure did. There's a little fuel left," Steuby said. "Trans-Earth burn, or do we park here and wait for help?"

Bridget leaned over and activated the rocket's emergency beacon. "Park it here," she said. "We don't really have anywhere to go."

Steuby slowed them a little, right down to the edge of escape velocity. He didn't want to get into a parking orbit in case the freighter wanted them to do a rendezvous burn. He looked toward the Tharsis plateau, now visible as their silver museum piece of a rocket rose higher and arced west, following Number Nine Moon. They would be coming up on the freighter if they were lucky. They'd already had a lot of luck, and just needed a little more.

"Hope somebody comes back," Bridget said. "It would be a shame to let all this go to waste."

"Somebody will," Steuby said.

But it wasn't going to be him. No, sir. He was done with everything that didn't obey the gravity of Planet Earth. I might go back to the Moon, Steuby thought.

"You were right," he said to Bridget.

"About what?"

"Bringing Marco. I gave you a hard time about it."

She shrugged in her harness. "Doesn't matter."

The ship's comm crackled. "This is Captain Lucinda Nieto of the freighter *Mary Godwin*. We are responding to a distress call. Over."

Steuby toggled his mic. "This is . . . well, I don't know what the ship is called. But we sure are glad to hear from you."

"We have a fix on your location. If you are able, stabilize your altitude and stand by for rendezvous. How many on board?"

"Two," Steuby said.

"Three," Bridget said at the same time.

He looked at her. Then he leaned into the mic. "Sorry, three," he said.

"And what the hell are you doing out there, exactly?" Captain Nieto asked.

"Not quitting, Captain," Steuby said. "We sure appreciate you giving us a lift."

Sam J. Miller is a writer and a community organizer. His fiction has appeared in *Lightspeed, Asimov's, Clarkesworld, Apex, Strange Horizons,* and *The Minnesota Review,* among others. His debut novel *The Art of Starving* (YA/SF) will be published by HarperCollins in 2017, followed by *The Breaks* from Ecco Press in 2018. His stories have been nominated for the Nebula, World Fantasy, and Theodore Sturgeon Awards, and he's a winner of the Shirley Jackson Award. He lives in New York City.

THINGS WITH BEARDS

Sam J. Miller

MacReady has made it back to McDonald's. He holds his coffee with both hands, breathing in the heat of it, still not 100 percent sure he isn't actually asleep and dreaming in the snowdrifted rubble of McMurdo. The summer of 1983 is a mild one, but to MacReady it feels tropical, with 125th Street a bright beautiful sunlit oasis. He loosens the cord that ties his cowboy hat to his head. Here, he has no need of a disguise. People press past the glass, a surging crowd going into and out of the subway, rushing to catch the bus, doing deals, making out, cursing each other, and the suspicion he might be dreaming gets deeper. Spend enough time in the ice hell of Antarctica and your body starts to believe that frigid lifelessness is the true natural state of the universe. Which, when you think of the cold vastness of space, is probably correct.

"Heard you died, man," comes a sweet rough voice, and MacReady stands up to submit to the fierce hug that never fails to make him almost cry from how safe it makes him feel. But when he steps back to look Hugh in the eye, something is different. Something has changed. While he was away, Hugh became someone else.

"You don't look so hot yourself," he says, and they sit, and Hugh takes the coffee that has been waiting for him.

"Past few weeks I haven't felt well," Hugh says, which seems an understatement. Even after MacReady's many months in Antarctica, how could so many lines have sprung up in his friend's black skin? When had his hair and beard become so heavily peppered with salt? "It's nothing. It's going around."

Their hands clasp under the table.

"You're still fine as hell," MacReady whispers.

"You stop," Hugh said. "I know you had a piece down there."

MacReady remembers Childs, the mechanic's strong hands still greasy from the Ski-dozer, leaving prints on his back and hips. His teeth on the back of MacReady's neck.

"Course I did," MacReady says. "But that's over now."

"You still wearing that damn fool cowboy hat," Hugh says, scoldingly. "Had those stupid centerfolds hung up all over your room I bet."

MacReady releases his hands. "So? We all pretend to be what we need to be."

"Not true. Not everybody has the luxury of passing." One finger traces a circle on the black skin of his forearm.

They sip coffee. McDonald's coffee is not good but it is real. Honest.

Childs and him; him and Childs. He remembers almost nothing about the final days at McMurdo. He remembers taking the helicopter up, with a storm coming, something about a dog . . . and then nothing. Waking up on board a U.S. supply and survey ship, staring at two baffled crewmen. Shredded clothing all around them. A metal desk bent almost in half and pushed halfway across the room. Broken glass and burned paper and none of them had even the faintest memory of what had just happened. Later, reviewing case files, he learned how the supply run that came in springtime found the whole camp burned down, mostly everyone dead and blown to bizarre bits, except for two handsome corpses frozen untouched at the edge of camp; how the corpses were brought back, identified, the condolence letters sent home, the bodies, probably by accident, thawed . . . but that couldn't be real. That frozen corpse couldn't have been him.

"Your people still need me?" MacReady asks.

"More than ever. Cops been wilding out on folks left and right. Past six months, eight people got killed by police. Not a single officer indicted. You still up for it?"

"Course I am."

"Meeting in two weeks. Not afraid to mess with the Man? Because what we've got planned . . . they ain't gonna like it. And they're gonna hit back, hard."

MacReady nods. He smiles. He is home; he is needed. He is a rebel. "Let's go back to your place."

When MacReady is not MacReady, or when MacReady is simply not, he never remembers it after. The gaps in his memory are not mistakes, not accidents. The thing that wears his clothes, his body, his cowboy hat, it doesn't want him to know it is there. So the moment when the supply ship crewman walked in and found formerly frozen MacReady sitting up—and watched MacReady's face split down the middle, saw a writhing nest of spaghetti tentacles explode in his direction, screamed as they enveloped him and swiftly started digesting—all of that is gone from MacReady's mind.

But when it is being MacReady, it *is* MacReady. Every opinion and memory and passion is intact.

"The fuck just happened?" Hugh asks, after, holding up a shredded sheet.

"That good, I guess," MacReady says, laughing, naked.

"I honestly have no memory of us tearing this place up like that."

"Me either."

There is no blood, no tissue of any kind. Not-MacReady sucks all that up. Absorbs it, transforms it. As it transformed the meat that used to be Hugh, as soon as they were alone in his room and it perceived no threat, knew it was safe to come out. The struggle was short. In nineteen minutes the transformation was complete, and MacReady and Hugh were themselves again, as far as they knew, and they fell into each other's arms, onto the ravaged bed, out of their clothes.

"What's that," MacReady says, two worried fingers tracing down Hugh's side. Purple blotches mar his lovely torso.

"Comes with this weird new pneumonia thing that's going around," he says. "This year's junky flu."

"But you're not a junky."

"I've fucked a couple, lately."

MacReady laughs. "You have a thing for lost causes."

"The cause I'm fighting for isn't lost," Hugh says, frowning.

"Course not. I didn't mean that—"

But Hugh has gone silent, vanishing into the ancient trauma MacReady has always known was there, and tried to ignore, ever since Hugh took him under his wing at the age of nineteen. Impossible to deny it, now, with their bare legs twined together, his skin corpse-pale beside Hugh's rich dark brown. How different their lives had been, by virtue of the bodies they wore. How wide the gulf that lay between them, that love was powerless to bridge.

So many of the men at McMurdo wore beards. Winter, he thought, at first—for keeping our faces warm in Antarctica's forever winter. But warmth at McMurdo was rarely an issue. Their warren of rectangular huts was kept at a balmy seventy-eight degrees. Massive stockpiles of gasoline specifically for that purpose. Aside from the occasional trip outside for research—and MacReady never had more than a hazy understanding of what, exactly, those scientists were sciencing down there, but they seemed to do precious little of it—the men of McMurdo stayed the hell inside.

So. Not warmth.

Beards were camouflage. A costume. Only Blair and Garry lacked one, both being too old to need to appear as anything other than what they were, and Childs, who never wanted to.

He shivered. Remembering. The tough-guy act, the cowboy he became in uncertain situations. Same way in juvie; in lock-up. Same way in Vietnam. Hard, mean, masculine. Hard drinking; woman hating. Queer? Psssh. He hid so many things, buried them deep, because if men knew what he really was, he'd be in danger. When they learned he wasn't one of them, they would want to destroy him.

They all had their reasons, for choosing McMurdo. For choosing a life where there were no women. Supper time MacReady would look from face to bearded face and wonder how many were like him, under the all-man exterior they projected, but too afraid, like him, to let their true self show.

Childs hadn't been afraid. And Childs had seen what he was.

MacReady shut his eyes against the McMurdo memories, bit his lip. Anything to keep from thinking about what went down, down there. Because how was it possible that he had absolutely no memory of any of it? Soviet attack, was the best theory he could come up with. Psychoactive gas leaked into the ventilation system by a double agent (Nauls, definitely), which caused catastrophic freak outs and homicidal arson rage, leaving only him and Childs unscathed, whereupon they promptly sat down in the snow to die . . . and this, of course, only made him more afraid, because if this insanity was the only narrative he could construct that made any sense at all, he whose imagination had never been his strong suit, then the real narrative was probably equally, differently, insane.

Not-MacReady has an exceptional knack for assessing external threats. It stays hidden when MacReady is alone, and when he is in a crowd, and even when he is alone but still potentially vulnerable. Once, past four in the morning, when a drunken MacReady had the 145th Street bus all to himself, alone with the small woman behind the wheel, Not-MacReady could easily have emerged. Claimed her. But it knew, somehow, gauging who-knew-what quirk of pheromones or optic nerve signals, the risk of exposure, the chance someone might see through the tinted windows, or the driver's foot, in the spasms of dying, slam down hard on the brake and bring the bus crashing into something.

If confronted, if threatened, it might risk emerging. But no one is there to confront it. No one suspects it is there. Not even MacReady, who has nothing but the barest, most irrational anxieties. Protean fragments; nightmare glitch glimpses and snatches of horrific sound. Feedback, bleedthrough from the thing that hides inside him.

"Fifth building burned down this week," said the Black man with the Spanish accent. MacReady sees his hands, sees how hard he's working to keep them from shaking. His anger is intoxicating. "Twenty families, out on the street. Cops don't care. They know it was the landlord. It's always the landlord. Insurance company might kick up a stink, but worst thing that happens is dude catches a civil suit. Pays a fine. That shit is terrorism, and they oughta give those motherfuckers the chair."

Everyone agrees. Eleven people in the circle; all of them Black except for MacReady and an older white lady. All of them men except for her, and a stout Black woman with an Afro of astonishing proportions.

"It's not terrorism when they do it to us," she said. "It's just the way things are supposed to be."

The meeting is over. Coffee is sipped; cigarettes are lit. No one is in a hurry to go back outside. An affinity group, mostly Black Panthers who somehow survived a couple decades of attempts by the FBI to exterminate every last one of them, but older folks too, trade unionists, commies, a minister who came up from the South back when it looked like the Movement was going to spread everywhere, change everything.

MacReady wonders how many of them are cops. Three, he guesses, though not because any of them make him suspicious. Just because he knows what they're up against, what staggering resources the government has invested in destroying this work over the past forty years. Infiltrators tended to be isolated, immersed in the lie they were living, reporting only to one person, whom they might never meet.

Hugh comes over, hands him two cookies.

"You sure this is such a good idea?" MacReady says. "They'll hit back hard, for this. Things will get a whole lot worse."

"Help us or don't," Hugh said, frowning. "That's your decision. But you don't set the agenda here. We know what we're up against, way better than you do. We know the consequences."

MacReady ate one cookie, and held the other up for inspection. Oreo knock-offs, though he'd never have guessed from the taste. The pattern was different, the seal on the chocolate exterior distinctly stamped.

"I understand if you're scared," Hugh says, gentler now.

"Shit yes I'm scared," MacReady says, and laughs. "Anybody who's not scared of what we're about to do is probably . . . well, I don't know, crazy or stupid or a fucking pod person."

Hugh laughs. His laugh becomes a cough. His cough goes on for a long time.

Would he or she know it, if one of the undercovers made eye contact with another? Would they look across the circle and see something, recognize some deeply hidden kinship? And if they were all cops, all deep undercover, each one simply impersonating an activist so as to target actual activists, what would happen then? Would they be able to see that, and set the ruse aside, step into the light, reveal what they really were? Or would they persist in the imitation game, awaiting instructions from above? Undercovers didn't make decisions, MacReady knew; they didn't even do things. They fed information upstairs, and upstairs did with it what they would. So if a whole bunch of undercovers were operating on their own, how would they ever know when to stop?

MacReady knows that something is wrong. He keeps seeing it out of the corner of his mind's eye, hearing its echoes in the distance. Lost time, random wreckage.

MacReady suspects he is criminally, monstrously insane. That during his black-outs he carries out horrific crimes, and then hides all the evidence. This would explain what went down at McMurdo. In a terrifying way, the explanation is appealing. He could deal with knowing that he murdered all his friends and then blew up the building. It would frighten him less than the yawning gulf of empty time, the barely remembered slither and scuttle of something inhuman, the flashes of blood and screaming that leak into his daylight hours now.

MacReady rents a cabin. Upstate: uninsulated and inexpensive. Ten miles from the nearest neighbor. The hard-faced old woman who he rents from picks him up at the train station. Her truck is full of grocery bags, all the things he requested.

"No car out here," she says, driving through town. "Not even a bicycle. No phone, either. You get yourself into trouble and there'll be no way of getting out of here in a hurry."

He wonders what they use it for, the people she normally rents to, and decides he doesn't want to know.

"Let me out up here," he says, when they approach the edge of town.

"You crazy?" she asks. "It'd take you two hours to walk the rest of the way. Maybe more."

"I said pull over," he says, hardening his voice, because if she goes much further, out of sight of prying protective eyes, around the next bend, maybe, or even before that, the insane thing inside him may emerge. It knows these things, somehow.

"Have fun carrying those two big bags of groceries all that way," she says, when he gets out. "Asshole."

"Meet me here in a week," he says. "Same time."

"You must be a Jehovah's Witness or something," she says, and he is relieved when she is gone.

The first two days pass in a pleasant enough blur. He reads books, engages in desultory masturbation to a cheaply printed paperback of gay erotic stories Hugh had lent him. Only one symptom: hunger. Low and rumbling, and not sated no matter how much he eats.

And then: lost time. He comes to on his knees, in the cool midnight dirt behind a bar.

"Thanks, man," says the sturdy bearded trucker type standing over him, pulling back on a shirt. Puzzled by how it suddenly sports a spray of holes, each fringed with what look like chemical burns. "I needed that."

He strides off. MacReady settles back into a squat. Leans against the building.

What did I do to him? He seems unharmed. But I've done something. Something terrible.

He wonders how he got into town. Walked? Hitchhiked? And how the hell he'll get back.

The phone rings, his first night back. He'd been sitting on his fire escape, looking down at the city, debating jumping, though not particularly seriously. Hugh's words echoing in his head. *Help us or don't.* He is still not sure which one he'll choose.

He picks up the phone.

"Mac," says the voice, rich and deep and unmistakable.

"Childs."

"Been trying to call you." Cars honk, through the wire. Childs is from Detroit, he dimly remembers, or maybe Minneapolis.

"I was away. Had to get out of town, clear my head."

"You too, huh?"

MacReady lets out his breath, once he realizes he's been holding it. "You?"

"Yup."

"What the hell, man? What the fuck is going on?"

Childs chuckles. "Was hoping you'd have all the answers. Don't know why. I already knew what a dumbass you are."

A lump of longing forms in MacReady's throat. But his body fits him wrong, suddenly. Whatever crazy mental illness he was imagining he had, Childs sharing it was inconceivable. Something else is wrong, something his mind rejects but his body already knows. "Have you been to a doctor?"

"Tried," Childs says. "I remember driving halfway there, and the next thing I knew I was home again." A siren rises then slowly fades, in Detroit or Minneapolis.

MacReady inspects his own reflection in the window, where the lights of his bedroom bounce back against the darkness. "What are we?" he whispers.

"Hellbound," Childs says, "but we knew that already."

The duffel bag says *Astoria Little League*. Two crossed baseball bats emblazoned on the outside. Dirty bright-blue blazer sleeves reaching out. A flawless facsimile of something harmless, wholesome. No one would see it and suspect. The explosives are well-hidden, small, sewn into a pair of sweat pants, the timer already ticking down to some unknown hour, some unforeseeable fallout.

"Jimmy," his father says, hugging him, hard. His beard brushes MacReady's neck, abrasive and unyielding as his love.

The man is immense, dwarfing the cluttered kitchen table. Uncles lurk in the background. Cigars and scotch sour the air. Where are the aunts and wives? MacReady has always wondered, these manly Sundays.

"They told me this fucker died," his father says to someone.

"Can't kill one of ours that easy," someone says. Eleven men in the little house, which has never failed to feel massive.

Here his father pauses. Frowns. No one but MacReady sees. No one here but MacReady knows the man well enough to suspect that the frown means he knows something new on the subject of MacReady mortality. Something that frightens him. Something he feels he has to shelter his family from.

"Fucking madness, going down there," his father says, snapping back with the unstoppable positivity MacReady lacks, and envies. "I'd lose my mind inside of five minutes out in Alaska."

"Antarctica," he chuckles.

"That too!"

Here, home, safe, among friends, the immigrant in his father emerges. Born here to brand-new arrivals from Ireland, never saw the place but it's branded on his speech, the slight Gaelic curling of his consonants he keeps hidden when he's driving the subway car but lets rip on weekends. His father's father is who MacReady hears now, the big glorious drunk they brought over as soon as they got themselves settled, the immense shadow over MacReady's own early years, and who, when he died, took some crucial piece of his son away with him. MacReady wonders how his own father has marked him, how much of him he carries around, and what kind of new terrible creature he will be when his father dies.

An uncle is in another room, complaining about an impending Congressional hearing into police brutality against Blacks; the flood of reporters bothering his beat cops. The uncle uses ugly words to describe the people he polices out in Brooklyn; the whole room laughs. His father laughs. MacReady slips upstairs unnoticed. Laments, in silence, the horror of human hatred—how such marvelous people, whom he loves so dearly, contain such monstrosity inside of them.

In the bathroom, standing before the toilet where he first learned to pee, MacReady sees smooth purple lesions across his stomach.

Midnight, and MacReady stands at the center of the George Washington Bridge. The monstrous creature groans and whines with the wind, with the heavy traffic that never stops. New York City's most popular suicide spot. He can't remember where he heard that, but he's grateful that he did. Astride the safety railing, looking down at deep black water, he stops to breathe.

Once, MacReady was angry. He is not angry anymore. This disturbs him. The things that angered him are still true, are still out there; are, in most cases, even worse.

His childhood best friend, shot by cops at fourteen for "matching a description" of someone Black. His mother's hands, at the end of a fourteen-hour laundry shift. Hugh, and Childs, and every other man he's loved, and the burning glorious joy he had to smother and hide and keep secret. He presses against these memories, traces along his torso where they've marked him, much like the cutaneous lesions along Hugh's sides. And yet, like those purple blotches, they cause no pain. Not anymore.

A train's whistle blows, far beneath him. Wind stings his eyes when he tries to look. He can see the warm dim lights of the passenger cars; imagines the seats where late-night travelers doze or read or stare up in awe at the lights of the bridge. At him.

Something is missing, inside of MacReady. He can't figure out what. He wonders when it started. McMurdo? Maybe. But probably not. Something drew him to McMurdo, after all. The money, but not just the money. He wanted to flee from the human world. He was tired of fighting it and wanted to take himself out. Whatever was in him, changing, already, McMurdo fed it.

He tries to put his finger on it, the thing that is gone, and the best he can do is a feeling he once felt, often, and feels no longer. Trying to recall the last time he felt it he fails, though he can remember plenty of times before that. Leaving his first concert; gulping down cold November night air and knowing every star overhead belonged to him. Bus rides back from away baseball games, back when the Majors still felt possible. The first time he followed a boy onto the West Side Piers. A feeling at once frenzied and calm, energetic yet restive. Like he had saddled himself, however briefly, onto something impossibly powerful, and primal, sacred, almost, connected to the flow of things, moving along the path meant only for him. They had always been rare, those moments—life worked so hard to come between him and his path—but lately they did not happen at all.

He is a monster. He knows this now. So is Childs. So are countless others, people like Hugh who he did something terrible to, however unintentionally it was. He doesn't know the details, what he is or how it works, or why, but he knows it.

Maybe he'd have been strong enough, before. Maybe that other MacReady would have been brave enough to jump. But that MacReady had no reason to. This MacReady climbs back to the safe side of the guardrail, and walks back to solid ground.

MacReady strides up the precinct steps, trying not to cry. Smiling, wide-eyed, white, and harmless.

When Hugh handed off the duffel bag, something was clearly wrong. He'd lost fifty pounds, looked like. All his hair. Half of the light in his eyes. By then MacReady'd been hearing the rumors, seeing the stories. Gay cancer, said the *Times*. Dudes dropping like mayflies.

And that morning: the call. Hugh in Harlem Hospital. From Hugh's mother, whose remembered Christmas ham had no equal on this earth. When she said everything was going to be fine, MacReady knew she was lying. Not to spare his feelings, but to protect her own. To keep from having a conversation she couldn't have.

He pauses, one hand on the precinct door. Panic rises.

Blair built a spaceship.

The image comes back to him suddenly, complete with the smell of burning petrol. Something he saw, in real life? Or a photo he was shown, from the wreckage? A cavern dug into the snow and ice under McMurdo. Scavenged pieces of the helicopter and the snowmobiles and the Ski-dozer assembled into . . . a spaceship. How did he know that's what it was? Because it was round, yes, and nothing any human knew how to make, but there's more information here, something he's missing, something he knew once but doesn't know now. But where did it come from, this memory?

Panic. Being threatened, trapped. Having no way out. It triggers something inside of him. Like it did in Blair, which is how an assistant biologist could assemble a spacefaring vessel. Suddenly MacReady can tap into so much more. He sees things. Stars, streaking past him, somehow. Shapes he can take. Things he can be. Repulsive, fascinating. Beings without immune systems to attack; creatures whose core body temperatures are so low any virus or other invading organism would die.

A cuttlefish contains so many colors, even when it isn't wearing them.

His hands and neck feel tight. Like they're trying to break free from the rest of him. Had someone been able to see under his clothes, just then, they'd have seen mouths opening and closing all up and down his torso.

"Help you?" a policewoman asks, opening the door for him, and this is bad, super bad, because he—like all the other smiling white harmless allies who are at this exact moment sauntering into every one of the NYPD's 150 precincts and command centers—is supposed to not be noticed.

"Thank you," he says, smiling the Fearless Man Smile, powering through the panic. She smiles back, reassured by what she sees, but what she sees isn't what he is. He doffs the cowboy hat and steps inside.

He can't do anything about what he is. All he can do is try to minimize the harm, and do his best to counterbalance it.

What's the endgame here, he wonders, waiting at the desk. What next? A brilliant assault, assuming all goes well—simultaneous attacks on every NYPD precinct, chaos without bloodshed, but what victory scenario are his handlers aiming for? What is the plan? Is there a plan? Does someone, upstairs, at Black Liberation Secret Headquarters, have it all mapped out? There will be a backlash, and it will be bloody, for all the effort they put into a casualty-free military strike. They will continue to make progress, person by person, heart by heart, and mind by mind, but what then? How will they know they have reached the end of their work? Changing minds means nothing if those changed minds don't then change actual things. It's not enough for everyone to carry justice inside their hearts like a secret. Justice must be spoken. Must be embodied.

"Sound permit for a block party?" he asks the clerk, who slides him a form without even looking up. All over the city, sound permits for block parties that will never come to pass are being slid across ancient well-worn soon-to-be-incinerated desks.

Walking out, he hears the precinct phone ring. Knows it's The Call. The same one every other precinct is getting. Encouraging everyone to evacuate in the next five minutes if they'd rather not die screaming; flagging that the bomb is set to detonate immediately if tampered with, or moved (this is a bluff, but one the organizers felt fairly certain hardly anyone would feel like calling, and, in fact, no one does).

And that night, in a city at war, he stands on the subway platform. Drunk, exhilarated, frightened. A train pulls in. He stands too close to the door, steps forward as it swings open, walks right into a woman getting off. Her eyes go wide and she makes a terrified sound. "Sorry," he mumbles, cupping his beard and feeling bad for looking like the kind of man who frightens women, but she is already sprinting away. He frowns, and then sits, and then smiles. A smile of shame, at frightening someone, but also of something else, of a hard-earned, impossible-to-communicate knowledge. MacReady knows, in that moment, that maturity means making peace with how we are monsters.

Ken Liu is an author and translator of speculative fiction, as well as a lawyer and programmer. A winner of the Nebula, Hugo, and World Fantasy Awards, he has been published in *The Magazine of Fantasy & Science Fiction, Asimov's, Analog, Clarkesworld, Lightspeed,* and *Strange Horizons,* among other places.

Ken's debut novel, *The Grace of Kings* (2015), is the first volume in a silkpunk epic fantasy series, The Dandelion Dynasty. It won the Locus Best First Novel Award and was a Nebula finalist. He subsequently published the second volume in the series, *The Wall of Storms* (2016), as well as a collection of short stories, *The Paper Menagerie and Other Stories* (2016).

In addition to his original fiction, Ken is also the translator of numerous literary and genre works from Chinese to English. His translation of *The Three-Body Problem,* by Liu Cixin, won the Hugo Award for Best Novel in 2015, the first translated novel ever to receive that honor. He also translated the third volume in Liu Cixin's series, *Death's End* (2016), and edited the first English-language anthology of contemporary Chinese science fiction, *Invisible Planets* (2016).

DISPATCHES FROM THE CRADLE: THE HERMIT—FORTY-EIGHT HOURS IN THE SEA OF MASSACHUSETTS

Ken Liu

Before she became a hermit, Asa <whale>-<tongue>-π had been a managing director with JP Morgan Credit Suisse on Valentina Station, Venus. She would, of course, find this description small-minded and obtuse. *Call a woman a financial engineer or a man an agricultural systems analyst, and the world thinks they know something about them,* she wrote. *But what does the job a person has been channeled into have to do with who they are?*

Nonetheless, I will tell you that she was responsible for United Planet's public offering thirty years ago, at the time the biggest single pooling of resources by any individual or corporate entity in history. She was, in large measure, responsible for convincing a wearied humanity scattered across three planets, a moon, and a dozen asteroid habitats to continue to invest in the Grand Task—the terraforming of both Earth and Mars.

Does telling you what she has done explain who she is? I'm not sure. *From cradle to grave, everything we do is motivated by the need to answer one question: who am I?* she wrote. *But the answer to the question has always been obvious: stop striving; accept.*

A few days after she became the youngest chief managing director for JPMCS, on Solar Epoch 22385200, she handed in her resignation, divorced her husbands and wives, liquidated all her assets, placed the bulk of the proceeds into trusts for her children, and then departed for the Old Blue on a one-way ticket.

Once she arrived on Earth, she made her way to the port town of Acton in the Federation of Maritime Provinces and States, where she purchased a survival habitat kit, one identical to the millions used by refugee communities all over the planet, and put the pieces together herself using only two common laborer automata, eschewing offers of aid from other inhabitants of the city. Then she set herself afloat like a piece of driftwood, alone on the seven seas, much to the consternation of her family, friends, and colleagues.

"Given how she was dressed, we thought she was here to buy a vacation villa," said Edgar Baker, the man who sold Asa her habitat. "Plenty of bankers and executives like to come here in winter to dive for treasure and enjoy the sun, but she didn't want me to show her any of the vacant houses, several of which have excellent private beaches."

(Despite the rather transparent ploy, I've decided to leave in Baker's little plug. I can attest that Acton is an excellent vacation spot, with several good restaurants in town serving traditional New England fare—though the lobsters are farmed, not wild. Conservationists are uncertain if the extinct wild lobster will ever make a comeback in the waters off New England as they have never adapted to the warmer seas. The crustaceans that survived global warming were generally smaller in size.)

A consortium of her former spouses sued to have Asa declared mentally incompetent and reverse her financial dispositions. For a while the case provided juicy gossip that filled the XP-stations, but Asa managed to make the case go away quickly with some undisclosed settlements. "They understand now that I just want to be left alone," she was quoted as saying after the case was dismissed—that was probably true, but I'm sure it didn't hurt that she could afford the best lawyers.

Yesterday I came here to live. With this first entry in her journal, Asa began her seaborne life over the sunken metropolis of Boston on Solar Epoch

22385302, which, if you're familiar with the old Gregorian Calendar, was July 5, 2645.

The words were not original, of course. Henry David Thoreau wrote them first exactly eight hundred years earlier in a suburb of Boston.

But unlike Thoreau, who often sounded misanthropic in his declarations, Asa spent as much time alone as she did among crowds.

Excerpted from Adrift, by Asa <whale>-<tongue>-π:

The legendary island of Singapore is no more. But the idea of Singapore lives on.

The floating family habitats connect to each other in tight clan-strands that weave together into a massive raft-city. From above, the city looks like an algal mat composed of metal and plastic, studded with glistening pearls, dewdrops or air bubbles—the transparent domes and solar collectors for the habitats.

The Singapore Refugee Collective is so extensive that it is possible to walk the hundreds of kilometers from the site of sunken Kuala Lumpur to the surviving isles of Sumatra without ever touching water—though you would never want to do such thing, as the air outside is far too hot for human survival.

When typhoons—a near-constant presence at these latitudes—approach, entire clan-strands detach and sink beneath the waves to ride out the storm. The refugees sometimes speak not of days or nights, but of upside and downside.

The air inside the habitats is redolent with a thousand smells that would overwhelm an inhabitant of the sterile Venus stations and the climate-controlled domes of the upper latitudes. Char kway teow, diesel fumes, bak kut teh, human waste, raja, Katong laksa, mango-flavored perfume, kaya toast, ayam penyet, burnt electric insulation, mee goreng, roti prata, sea-salt-laced reclaimed air, nasi lemak, charsiew—the heady mixture is something the refugees grow up with and outsiders can never get used to.

Life in the Refugee Collective is noisy, cramped, and occasionally violent. Infectious diseases periodically sweep through the population, and life expectancy is short. The fact that the refugees remain stateless, so many generations after the wars that stripped their ancestors of homelands, seems to make it impossible for a solution to be envisioned by anyone from the Developed World—an ancient label whose meaning has evolved over the centuries, but has never been synonymous with moral rectitude. It was the Developed World that had polluted the world the earliest and the most, and yet it was also the Developed World that went to war with India and China for daring to follow in their footsteps.

I was saddened by what I saw. So many people clinging to life tenaciously on the thin interface between water and air. Even in a place like this, unsuitable for human habitation, people hang on, as stubborn as the barnacles on pilings revealed at every low tide. What of the refugees in the deserts of interior Asia, who live like moles in underground warrens? What of the other floating refugee collectives off the coasts of Africa and Central America? They have survived by pure strength of will, a miracle.

Humanity may have taken to the stars, but we have destroyed our home planet. Such has been the lament of the Naturalists for eons.

"But why do you think we're a problem that needs solving?" asked a child who bartered with me. (I gave him a box of antibiotics, and he served me chicken rice.) "Sunken Singapore was once a part of the Developed World; we're not. We don't call ourselves refugees; you do. This is our home. We live here."

I could not sleep that night.

This is our home. We live here.

The prolonged economic depression in much of North America has led to a decline of the region's once-famous pneumatic tube transportation networks that connected the climate-controlled domed cities, so the easiest way to get to the Sea of Massachusetts these days is by water.

I embarked in balmy Iceland on a cruise ship bound for the coast of the Federation of Maritime Provinces and States—November is an excellent time to visit the region, as the summer months are far too hot—and then, once in Acton, I hired a skiff to bring me out to visit Asa in her floating habitat.

"Have you been to Mars?" asked Jimmy, my guide. He was a man in his twenties, stocky, sunburnt, with gaps in his teeth that showed when he smiled.

"I have," I said.

"Is it warm?" he asked.

"Not quite warm enough to be outside the domes for long," I said, thinking about the last time I visited Watney City on Acidalia Planetia.

"I'd like to go when it's ready," he said.

"You won't miss home?" I asked.

He shrugged. "Home is where the jobs are."

It's well known that the constant bombardment of the Martian surface with comets pulled from the Oort Cloud and the increased radiation from the deployment of solar sails, both grand engineering efforts began centuries ago, had managed to raise the temperature of Mars enough to cause sublimation of much of the red planet's polar dry ice caps and restart the water cycle. The introduction of photosynthesizing plants is slowly turning the atmosphere into something resembling what we could breathe. It's early days yet, but it isn't impossible to imagine that a habitable Mars, long a dream of humanity, would be reality within two or three generations. Jimmy might go there only as a tourist, but his children may settle there.

As our skiff approached the hemisphere bobbling over the waves in the distance, I asked Jimmy what he thought of the world's most well-known hermit, who had recently returned to the Sea of Massachusetts, whence she had started her circumnavigation of the globe.

"She brings the tourists," he said, in a tone that strove to be neutral.

Asa's collected writings about her life drifting over the ruins of the world's ancient sunken cities has been a publishing phenomenon that defies explanation. She eschews the use of XP-capturing or even plain old videography, instead conveying her experiences through impressionistic essays composed in a florid manner that seems at once anachronistic and abiding. Some have called her book bold and original; others said it was affected.

Asa has done little to discourage her critics. *It was said by the Zen masters that the best place for hermits to find the peace they sought was in the crowd,* she wrote. And you could almost hear the disgusted groan of her detractors at this kind of ornate, elusive mysticism.

Many have accused her of encouraging 'refugee-tourism' instead of looking for real solutions, and some claim that she is merely engaging in the timeless practice of intellectuals from privileged societies visiting those less fortunate and purporting to speak for her subjects by 'discovering' romanticized pseudo-wisdom attributed to them.

"Asa Whale is simply trying to soothe the neuroses of the Developed World with a cup of panglossian chicken soup for the soul," declared Emma <CJK-UniHan-Glyph 432371>, the media critic for my own publication. "What would she have us do? Stop all terraforming efforts? Leave the hellish Earth as it stands? The world needs more engineers willing to solve problems and fewer wealthy philosophers who have run out of ways to spend money."

Be that as it may, the Federation of Maritime Provinces and States tourist czar, John <pylon>-<fog>-<cod>, claimed earlier this year that the number of tourists visiting the Sea of Massachusetts has grown fourfold since the publication of Asa's book (such rises in Singapore and Havana are even higher). No doubt the influx of tourist money is welcomed by the locals, however conflicted they may be about Asa's portrayal of them.

Before I could follow up on the complicated look in his eyes, Jimmy turned his face resolutely away to regard our destination, which was growing bigger by the minute.

Spherical in shape, the floating dwelling was about fifteen meters in diameter, consisting of a thin transparent outer hull to which most of the ship's navigation surfaces were affixed and a thicker metal-alloy inner pressure hull. Most of the sphere floated below the surface, making the transparent bridge-dome appear like the pupil of some sea monster's eye staring into the sky.

On top of the pupil stood a solitary figure, her back as straight as the gnomon of a sundial.

Jimmy nudged the skiff until it bumped gently against the side of the habitat, and I gingerly stepped from one craft to the other. Asa steadied me as her habitat dipped under my added weight; her hand felt dry, cool, and very strong.

I observed, somewhat inanely, that she looked exactly like her last public scan-gram, when she had proclaimed from the large central forum of Valentina Station that United Planets was not only going to terraform Mars, but had also successfully bought a controlling stake in Blue Cradle, the public-private partnership for restoring Earth to a fully habitable state.

"I don't get many visitors," she said, her voice tranquil. "There's not much point to putting on a new face every day."

I had been surprised when she replied to my request to stay with her for a few days with a simple "Yes." She had never so much as granted an interview to anyone since she started her life adrift.

"Why?" I had asked.

"Even a hermit can grow lonely," she had replied. And then, in another message that immediately followed the first, she added, "Sometimes."

Jimmy motored away on his skiff. Asa turned and gestured for me to descend through the transparent and open 'pupil' into the most influential refugee bubble in the Solar System.

The stars are invisible from the metal cocoons floating in the heavy atmosphere of Venus; nor do we pay much attention to them from the pressurized domes on Mars. On Earth, the denizens of the climate-controlled cities in habitable zones are preoccupied with scintillating screens and XP implants, the glow of meandering conversation, brightening reputation accounts, and the fading trails left by falling credit scores. They do not look up.

One night, as I lay in the habitat drifting over the balmy subtropical Pacific, the stars spun over my face in their habitual course, a million diamantine points of crisp, mathematical light. I realized, with a startled understanding reminiscent of the clarity of childhood, that the face of the heavens was a collage.

Some of the photons striking my retinas had emerged from the crease in the rock to which Andromeda is chained when nomadic warriors from the last ice age still roamed Doggerland, which connected Britain to the European mainland; others had left that winking point at the wingtip of Cygnus when bloody Caesar fell at the feet of Pompey's statue; still more had departed the mouth of Aquarius's jar when the decades-long genocidal wars swept through Asia, and aerial drones from Japan and Australia strafed and sank the rafts of refugees fleeing their desertified or flooded homelands; yet others had sparked from the distant hoof of Pegasus when the last glaciers of Greenland and Antarctica disappeared, and Moscow and Ottawa launched the first rockets bound for Venus. . .

The seas rise and fall, and the surface of the planet is as inconstant as our faces: lands burst forth from the waters and return beneath them; well-armored lobsters scuttle over seafloors that but a geologic eyewink ago had been fought over by armies of wooly mammoths; yesterday's Doggerland may be tomorrow's Sea of Massachusetts. The only witnesses to constant change are the eternal stars, each a separate stream in the ocean of time.

A picture of the welkin is an album of time, as convoluted and intricate as the shell of the nautilus or the arms of the Milky Way.

The interior of the habitat was sparsely furnished. Everything—the molded bunks, the stainless steel table attached to the wall, the boxy navigation console—was functional, plain, stripped of the elaborate 'signature' decorations that seem all the rage these days with personal nanites. Though the space inside was cramped with two people, it seemed larger than it was because Asa did not fill it with conversation.

We ate dinner—fish that Asa had caught herself roasted over an open fire, with the canopy open—and went to bed silently. I fell asleep quickly, my body rocked by the gentle motions of the sea and my face caressed by the bright, warm New England stars that she had devoted so many words to.

After a breakfast of instant coffee and dry biscuits, Asa asked me if I wanted to see Boston.

"Of course," I said. It was an ancient citadel of learning, a legendary metropolis where brave engineers had struggled against the rising sea for two centuries before its massive seawalls finally succumbed, leaving the city inundated overnight in one of the greatest disasters in the history of the Developed World.

While Asa sat in the back of the habitat to steer and to monitor the solar-powered water-jet drive, I knelt on the bottom of the sphere and greedily drank in the sights passing beneath the transparent floor.

As the sun rose, its light gradually revealed a sandy floor studded by massive ruins: monuments erected to long-forgotten victories of the American Empire pointed toward the distant surface like ancient rockets; towers of stone and vitrified concrete that had once housed hundreds of thousands loomed like underwater mountains, their innumerable windows and doors silent, empty caves from which shoals of colorful fish darted like tropical birds; between the buildings, forest of giant kelp swayed in canyons that had once been boulevards and avenues filled with steaming vehicles, the hepato-cytes that had once brought life to this metropolis.

And most amazing of all were the rainbow-hued corals that covered every surface of this urban reef: dark crimson, light orange, pearly white, bright neon vermillion. . .

Before the Second Flood Wars, the sages of Europe and America had thought the corals doomed. Rising sea temperature and acidity; booming algae populations; heavy deposits of mercury, arsenic, lead, and other heavy metals; runaway coastal development as the developed nations built up the machinery of death against waves of refugees from the uninhabitable zones—everything seemed to spell doom for the fragile marine animals and their photosynthesizing symbiotes.

Would the ocean become bleached of color, a black-and-white photograph bear-ing silent witness to our folly?

But the corals survived and adapted. They migrated to higher latitudes north and south, gained tolerance for stressed environments, and unexpectedly, devel-oped new symbiotic relationships with artificial nanoplate-secreting algae engi-neered by humans for ocean-mining. I do not think the beauty of the Sea of Massachusetts yields one inch to the fabled Great Barrier Reef or the legends of long-dead Caribbean.

"Such colors. . ." I murmured.

"The most beautiful patch is in Harvard Yard," Asa said.

We approached the ruins of the famed academy in Cambridge from the south, over a kelp forest that used to be the Charles River. But the loom-ing presence of a cruise ship on the surface blocked our way. Asa stopped the habitat, and I climbed up to gaze out the domed top. Tourists wearing GnuSkin flippers and artificial gills were leaping out of the ship like selkies returning home, their sleek skin temporarily bronzed to endure the scorching November sun.

"Widener Library is a popular tourist spot," said Asa, by way of explanation.

I climbed down, and Asa drove the habitat to dive under the cruise ship. The craft was able to submerge beneath the waves as a way for the refugees in coastal raft-cities to survive typhoons and hurricanes, as well as to avoid the deadly heat of the tropics.

Slowly, we descended toward the coral reef that had grown around the ruined hulk of what had once been the largest university library in the world. Around us, schools of brightly colored fish wove through shafts of sunlight, and tourists gracefully floated down like mermaids, streams of bubbles trailing behind their artificial gills.

Asa guided the habitat in a gentle circle around the kaleidoscopic sea floor in front of the underwater edifice, pointing out various features. The mound covered by the intricate crimson folds of a coral colony that pleated and swirled like the voluminous dress of classical flamenco dancers had once been a lecture hall named after Thoreau's mentor, Emerson; the tall, spear-like column whose surface was tiled by sharp, geometric patches of coral in carmine, cerulean, viridian, and saffron had once been the steeple of Harvard's Memorial Church; the tiny bump in the side of another long reef, a massive brain-shaped coral formation whose gyri and lobes evoked the wisdom of generations of robed scholars who had once strolled through this hallowed temple to knowledge, was in fact the site of the renowned 'Statue of Three Lies'—an ancient monument to John Harvard that failed to depict or identify the benefactor with any accuracy.

Next to me, Asa quietly recited:

> *The maple wears a gayer scarf,*
> *The field a scarlet gown.*
> *Lest I should be old-fashioned,*
> *I'll put a trinket on.*

The classical verses of the Early Republican Era poet Dickinson evoked the vanished beauty of the autumns that had once graced these shores, long before the sea had risen and the winters driven away, seemed oddly appropriate.

"I can't imagine the foliage of the Republican Era could be any more glorious than this," I said.

"None of us would know," Asa said. "Do you know how the corals get their bright colors?"

I shook my head. I knew next to nothing about corals except that they were popular as jewelry on Venus.

"The pigmentation comes from the heavy metals and pollutants that might have once killed their less hardy ancestors," said Asa. "They're particularly bright here because this area was touched by the hand of mankind the longest. Beautiful as they are, these corals are incredibly fragile. A global cooling by more than a degree or two would kill them. They survived climate change once by a miracle. Can they do it again?"

I looked back toward the great reef that was Widener Library, and saw that tourists had landed on the wide platform in front of the library's entrance or against its sides in small groups. Young tour guides in bright crimson—the color of Harvard achieved either by skin pigmentation or costume—led each group in their day-excursion activities.

Asa wanted to leave—she found the presence of the tourists bothersome—but I explained that I wanted to see what they were interested in. After a moment of hesitation, she nodded and guided the craft closer.

One group, standing on what used to be the steps ascending to the entrance of Widener, stood in a circle and followed their guide, a young woman dressed in a crimson wetsuit, through a series of dance-like movements. They moved slowly, but it was unclear whether they were doing so because the choreography required it or because the water provided too much drag. From time to time, the tourists looked up at the blazing sun far above, blurred and made hazy by a hundred feet of intervening water.

"They think they're doing taiji," said Asa.

"It looks nothing like taiji," I said, unable to connect the languorous, clumsy movements with the quick, staccato motion I was familiar with from sessions in low-gravity gyms.

"It's believed that taiji once was a slow, measured art, quite different from its modern incarnation. But since so few recordings of the pre-Diaspora years are left, the cruise ships just make up whatever they want for the tourists."

"Why do taiji here?" I was utterly baffled.

"Harvard was supposed to have a large population of Chinese scholars before the wars. It was said that the children of many of China's wealthiest and most powerful inhabitants studied here. It didn't save them from the wars."

Asa steered the craft a bit farther away from Widener, and I saw more tourists strolling over the coral-carpeted Yard or lounging about, holding what appeared to be paper books—props provided by the cruise company—and taking scans of each other. A few danced without music, dressed in costumes that were a mix of Early and Late Republican fashions, with an academic gown or two thrown in for good measure. In front of Emerson, two tour guides led two groups of tourists in a mimed version of some debate, with each side presenting their position through ghostly holograms that hovered over their heads like comic thought bubbles. Some tourists saw us but did not pay much attention—probably thinking that the drifting refugee bubble was a prop added by the cruise ship to provide atmosphere. If only they knew they were so close to the celebrity hermit. . .

I gathered that the tourists were re-enacting imagined scenes from the glory days of this university, when it had nurtured the great philosophers who delivered jeremiads against the development-crazed governments of the world as they heated the planet without cease, until the ice caps had collapsed.

"So many of the world's greatest conservationists and Naturalists had walked through this Yard," I said. In the popular imagination, the Yard is the equal of the Athenian Acropolis or the Roman Forum. I tried to re-envision the particolored reef below me as a grassy lawn covered by bright red and yellow leaves on a cool New England fall day as students and professors debated the fate of the planet.

"Despite my reputation for romanticism," said Asa, "I'm not so sure the Harvard of yesteryear is better than today. That university and others like it once also nurtured the generals and presidents who would eventually deny that mankind could change the climate and lead a people hungry for demagoguery into war against the poorer states in Asia and Africa."

Quietly, we continued to drift around the Yard, watching tourists climb in and out of the empty, barnacle-encrusted windows like hermit crabs darting through the sockets of a many-eyed skull. Some were mostly nude, trailing diaphanous fabrics from their bodies in a manner reminiscent of Classical American Early Republic dresses and suits; others wore wetsuits inspired by American Imperial styles, covered by faux body armor plates and gas mask helmets; still others went with refugee-chic, dragging fake survival breathing kits with artfully applied rust stains.

What were they looking for? Did they find it?

Nostalgia is a wound that we refuse time to heal, Asa once wrote.

After a few hours, satiated with their excursions, the tourists headed for the surface like shoals of fish fleeing some unseen predator, and in a way, they were.

The forecast was for a massive storm. The Sea of Massachusetts was rarely tranquil.

As the sea around us emptied of visitors and the massive cloud-island that was the cruise ship departed, Asa grew noticeably calmer. She assured me that we were safe, and brought the submersible craft to the lee of Memorial Church Reef. Here, below the turbulent surface, we would ride out the storm.

The sun set; the sea darkened; a million lights came to life around us. The coral reef at night was hardly a place of slumber. This was when the luminescent creatures of the night—the jellies, the shrimp, the glow-worms and lantern-fish—came out of hiding to enjoy their time in this underwater metropolis that never slept.

While the wind and the waves raged above us, we hardly felt a thing as we drifted in the abyss that was the sea, innumerable living stars around us.

We do not look.

We do not see.

We travel millions of miles to seek out fresh vistas without even once having glimpsed inside our skulls, a landscape surely as alien and as wondrous as anything the universe has to offer. There is more than enough to occupy our curiosity and restless need for novelty if we but turn our gaze to the ten square meters around us: the unique longitudinal patterns in each tile beneath our feet, the chemical symphony animating each bacterium on our skin, the mysteries of how we can contemplate ourselves contemplating ourselves.

The stars above are as distant—and as close—as the glowing coral-worms outside my portholes. We only have to look to see Beauty steeped in every atom.

Only in solitude it is possible to live as self-contained as a star.

I am content to have this. To have now.

In the distance, against Widener's cliff-like bulk, there was an explosion of light, a nova bursting in the void.

The stars around it streaked away, leaving inky darkness behind, but the nova itself, an indistinct cloud of light, continued to twist and churn.

I woke Asa and pointed. Without speaking, she guided the habitat toward it. As we approached, the light resolved itself into a struggling figure. An octopus? No, a person.

"That must be a tourist stranded behind," said Asa. "If they go up to the surface now, they'll die in the storm."

Asa switched on the bright lights in front of the habitat to get the tourist's attention. The light revealed a disoriented young woman in a wetsuit studded with luminescent patches, shielding her eyes against the sudden glow of the habitat's harsh lights. Her artificial gill slits opened and closed rapidly, showing her confusion and terror.

"She can't tell which way is up," Asa muttered.

Asa waved at her through the porthole, gesturing for her to follow the habitat. There was no airlock in the tiny refuge, and we had to go up to the surface to get her in. The young woman nodded.

Up on the surface, the rain was torrential and the waves so choppy that it was impossible to remain standing. Asa and I clung to the narrow ridge around the entrance dome on our bellies and dragged the young woman onto the craft, which dipped even lower under the added weight. With a great deal of effort and shouting, we managed to get her inside, seal the dome, and dive back underwater.

Twenty minutes later, dry, gills removed, securely wrapped in a warm blanket with a hot mug of tea, Saram <Golden-Gate-Bridge>-<Kyoto> looked back gratefully at us.

"I got lost inside," she said. "The empty stacks went on and on, and they looked the same in every direction. At first, I followed a candy-cane fish through the floors, thinking that it was going to lead me outside, but it must have been going around in circles."

"Did you find what you were looking for?" asked Asa.

She was a student at Harvard Station, Saram explained—the institution of higher learning suspended in the upper atmosphere of Venus that had licensed the old name of the university lying in ruins under us. She had come to see this school of legend for herself, harboring romantic notions of trying to search through the stacks of the dead library in the hopes of finding a forgotten tome.

Asa looked outside the porthole at the looming presence of the empty library. "I doubt there's anything left there now after all these years."

"Maybe," Saram said. "But history doesn't die. The water will recede from here one day. I may live to see when Nature is finally restored to her rightful course."

Sarah was probably a little too optimistic. United Planets' ion-drive ships had just succeeded in pushing six asteroids into near-Earth orbits earlier in the year, and the construction of the space mirrors had not even begun. Even the most optimistic engineering projections suggest that it will be decades, if not centuries, before the mirrors will reduce the amount of sunlight reaching Earth to begin the process of climate cooling and restoring the planet to its ancient state, a temperate Eden with polar ice caps and glaciers on top of mountain peaks. Mars might be fully terraformed before then.

"Is Doggerland any more natural than the Sea of Massachusetts?" Asa asked.

Saram's steady gaze did not waver. "An ice age is hardly comparable to what was made by the hands of mankind."

"Who are we to warm a planet for a dream and to cool it for nostalgia?"

"Mysticism is no balm for the suffering of the refugees enduring the consequences of our ancestors' errors."

"It is further error that I'm trying to prevent!" shouted Asa. She forced herself to calm down. "If the water recedes, everything around you will be gone." She looked outside the porthole, where the reef's night-time denizens had returned to their luminescent activities. "As will the vibrant communities in Singapore, in Havana, in Inner Mongolia. We call them refugee shantytowns and disturbed habitats, but these places are also homes."

"*I* am from Singapore," said Saram. "I spent my life trying to get away from it and only succeeded by winning one of the coveted migration visas to Birmingham. Do not presume to speak for us or to tell me what it is we should want."

"But you have left," said Asa. "You no longer live there."

I thought of the lovely corals outside, colored by poison. I thought of the refugees around the world underground and afloat—still called that after centuries and generations. I thought of a cooling Earth, of the Developed World racing to reclaim their ancestral lands, of the wars to come and the slaughter hinted at when the deck of power is shuffled and redealt. Who should decide? Who pay the price?

As the three of us sat inside the submerged habitat, refugees enveloped by darting trails of light like meteors streaking across the empyrean, none of us could think of anything more to say.

I once regretted that I do not *know the face I was born with.*

We remake our faces as easily as our ancestors once sculpted clay, changing the features and contours of our shells, this microcosm of the soul, to match the moods and fashions of the macrocosm of society. Still unsatisfied with the limits of the flesh, we supplement the results with jewelry that deflect light and project shadows, smoothing over substance with ethereal holograms.

The Naturalists, in their eternal struggle against modernity, proclaim hypocrisy and demand us to stop, telling us that our lives are inauthentic, and we listen, enraptured, as they flash grainy images of our ancestors before us, their imperfections and fixed appearances a series of mute accusations. And we nod and vow to do better, to foreswear artifice, until we go back to our jobs, shake off the spell, and decide upon the new face to wear for the next customer.

But what would the Naturalists have us do? The faces that we were born with were already constructed—when we were only fertilized eggs, a million cellular scalpels had snipped and edited our genes to eliminate diseases, to filter out risky mutations, to build up intelligence and longevity, and before that, millions of years of conquest, of migration, of global cooling and warming, of choices made by our ancestors motivated by beauty or violence or avarice had already shaped us. Our faces at birth were as crafted as the masks worn by the ancient players in Dionysian Athens or Ashikaga's Kyoto, but also as natural as the glacier-sculpted Alps or sea-inundated Massachusetts.

We do not know who we are. But we dare not stop striving to find out.

Carolyn Ives Gilman is a museum exhibit developer by day and a science fiction writer by night. Her latest novel is a space exploration adventure, *Dark Orbit*. Her short fiction has appeared in *Clarkesworld, Fantasy & Science Fiction, The Year's Best Science Fiction, Lightspeed, Interzone, Universe, Full Spectrum, Realms of Fantasy*, and others. She has been nominated for the Nebula Award three times and for the Hugo once.

Gilman lives in Washington, DC, and works at the National Museum of the American Indian (Smithsonian Institution). She is also author of several nonfiction books about North American frontier and Native history.

TOURING WITH THE ALIEN

Carolyn Ives Gilman

The alien spaceships were beautiful, no one could deny that: towering domes of overlapping, chitinous plates in pearly dawn colors, like reflections on a tranquil sea. They appeared overnight, a dozen incongruous soap-bubble structures scattered across the North American continent. One of them blocked a major Interstate in Ohio; another monopolized a stadium parking lot in Tulsa. But most stood in cornfields and forests and deserts where they caused little inconvenience.

Everyone called them spaceships, but from the beginning the experts questioned that name. NORAD had recorded no incoming landing craft, and no mother ship orbited above. That left two main possibilities: they were visitations from an alien race that traveled by some incomprehensibly advanced method; or they were a mutant eruption of Earth's own tortured ecosystem.

The domes were impervious. Probing radiation bounced off them, as did potshots from locals in the days before the military moved in to cordon off the areas. Attempts to communicate produced no reaction. All the domes did was sit there reflecting the sky in luminous, dreaming colors.

Six months later, the panic had subsided and even CNN had grown weary of reporting breaking news that was just the same old news. Then, entry panels began to open and out walked the translators, one per dome. They were perfectly ordinary-looking human beings who said that they had been abducted as children and had now come back to interpret between their biological race and the people who had adopted them.

Humanity learned surprisingly little from the translators. The aliens had come in peace. They had no demands and no questions. They merely wanted to sit here minding their own business for a while. They wanted to be left alone.

No one believed it.

Avery was visiting her brother when her boss called.

"Say, you've still got those security credentials, right?" Frank said.

"Yes . . ." She had gotten the security clearance in order to haul a hush-hush load of nuclear fuel to Nevada, a feat she wasn't keen on repeating.

"And you're in D.C.?"

She was actually in northern Virginia, but close enough. "Yeah."

"I've got a job for you."

"Don't tell me it's another gig for Those We Dare Not Name."

He didn't laugh, which told her it was bad. "Uh . . . no. More like those we *can't* name."

She didn't get it. "What?"

"Some . . . neighbors. Who live in funny-shaped houses. I can't say more over the phone."

She got it then. "Frank! You took a contract from the frigging *aliens*?"

"Sssh," he said, as if every phone in America weren't bugged. "It's strictly confidential."

"Jesus," she breathed out. She had done some crazy things for Frank, but this was over the top. "When, where, what?"

"Leaving tonight. D.C. to St. Louis. A converted tour bus."

"*Tour* bus? How many of them are going?"

"Two passengers. One human, one . . . whatever. Will you do it?"

She looked into the immaculate condo living room, where her brother, Blake, and his husband, Jeff, were playing a noisy, fast-paced video game, oblivious to her conversation. She had promised to be at Blake's concert tomorrow. It meant a lot to him. "Just a second," she said to Frank.

"I can't wait," he said.

"Two seconds." She muted the phone and walked into the living room. Blake saw her expression and paused the game.

She said, "Would you hate me if I couldn't be there tomorrow?"

Disappointment, resignation, and wry acceptance crossed his face, as if he hadn't ever really expected her to keep her promise. "What is it?" he asked.

"A job," she said. "A really important job. Never mind, I'll turn it down."

"No, Ave, don't worry. There will be other concerts."

Still, she hesitated. "You sure?" she said. She and Blake had always hung together, like castaways on a hostile sea. They had given each other courage to sail into the wind. To disappoint him felt disloyal.

"Go ahead," he said. "Now I'll be sorry if you stay."

She thumbed the phone on. "Okay, Frank, I'll do it. This better not get me in trouble."

"Cross my heart and hope to die," he said. "I'll email you instructions. Bye."

From the couch, Jeff said, "Now I know why you want to do it. Because it's likely to get you in trouble."

"No, he gave me his word," Avery said.

"Cowboy Frank? The one who had you drive guns to Nicaragua?"

"That was perfectly legal," Avery said.

Jeff had a point, as usual. Specialty Shipping did the jobs no reputable company would handle. Ergo, so did Avery.

"What is it this time?" Blake asked.

"I can't say." The email had come through; Frank had attached the instructions as if a PDF were more secure than email. She opened and scanned them.

The job had been cleared by the government, but the client was the alien passenger, and she was to take orders only from him, within the law. She scanned the rest of the instructions till she saw the pickup time. "Damn, I've got to get going," she said.

Her brother followed her into the guest room to watch her pack up. He had never understood her nomadic lifestyle, which made his silent support for it all the more generous. She was compelled to wander; he was rooted in this home, this relationship, this warm, supportive community. She was a discarder, using things up and throwing them away; he had created a home that was a visual expression of himself—from the spare, Japanese-style furniture to the Zen colors on the walls. Visiting him was like living inside a beautiful soul. She had no idea how they could have grown up so different. It was as if they were foundlings.

She pulled on her boots and shouldered her backpack. Blake hugged her. "Have a good trip," he said. "Call me."

"Will do," she said, and hit the road again.

The media had called the dome in Rock Creek Park the Mother Ship—but only because of its proximity to the White House, not because it was in any way distinctive. Like the others, it had appeared overnight, sited on a broad, grassy clearing that had been a secluded picnic ground in the urban park. It filled the entire creek valley, cutting off the trails and greatly inconveniencing the joggers and bikers.

Avery was unprepared for its scale. Like most people, she had seen the domes only on TV, and the small screen did not do justice to the neck-craning reality. She leaned forward over the wheel and peered out the windshield as she brought the bus to a halt at the last checkpoint. The National Park Police pickup that had escorted her through all the other checkpoints pulled aside.

The appearance of an alien habitat had set off a battle of jurisdictions in Washington. The dome stood on U.S. Park Service property, but D.C. Police controlled all the access streets, and the U.S. Army was tasked with maintaining a perimeter around it. No agency wanted to surrender a particle of authority to the others. And then there was the polite, well-groomed young man who had introduced himself as "Henry," now sitting in the passenger seat next to her. His neatly pressed suit sported no bulges of weaponry, but she assumed he was CIA.

She now saw method in Frank's madness at calling her so spur-of-the-moment. Her last-minute arrival had prevented anyone from pulling her aside into a cinderblock room for a "briefing." Instead, Henry had accompanied her in the bus, chatting informally.

"Say, while you're on the road . . ."

"No," she said.

"No?"

"The alien's my client. I don't spy on clients."

He paused a moment, but seemed unruffled. "Not even for your country?"

"If I think my country's in danger, I'll get in touch."

"Fair enough," he said pleasantly. She hadn't expected him to give up so easily.

He handed her a business card. "So you can get in touch," he said.

She glanced at it. It said "Henry," with a phone number. No logo, no agency, no last name. She put it in a pocket.

"I have to get out here," he said when the bus rolled to a halt a hundred yards from the dome. "It's been nice meeting you, Avery."

"Take your bug with you," she said.

"I beg your pardon?"

"The bug you left somewhere in this cab."

"There's no bug," he said seriously.

Since the bus was probably wired like a studio, she shrugged and resolved not to scratch anywhere embarrassing till she had a chance to search. As she closed the door behind Henry, the soldiers removed the roadblock and she eased the bus forward.

It was almost evening, but floodlights came on as she approached the dome. She pulled the bus parallel to the wall and lowered the wheelchair lift. One of the hexagonal panels slid aside, revealing a stocky, dark-haired young man in black glasses, surrounded by packing crates of the same pearly substance as the dome. Avery started forward to help with loading, but he said tensely, "Stay where you are." She obeyed. He pushed the first crate forward and it moved as if on wheels, though Avery could see none. It was slightly too wide for the lift, so the man put his hands on either side and pushed in. The crate reconfigured itself, growing taller and narrower till it fit onto the platform. Avery activated the power lift.

He wouldn't let Avery touch any of the crates, but insisted on stowing them himself at the back of the bus, where a private bedroom suite had once accommodated a touring celebrity singer. When the last crate was on, he came forward and said, "We can go now."

"What about the other passenger?" Avery said.

"He's here."

She realized that the alien must have been in one of the crates—or, for all she knew, *was* one of the crates. "Okay," she said. "Where to?"

"Anywhere," he said, and turned to go back into the bedroom.

Since she had no instructions to the contrary, Avery decided to head south. As she pulled out of the park, there was no police escort, no helicopter overhead, no obvious trailing car. The terms of this journey had been carefully negotiated at the highest levels, she knew. Their security was to be secrecy; no one was to know where they were. Avery's instructions from Frank had stressed that, aside from getting the alien safely where he wanted to go, insuring his privacy was her top priority. She was not to pry into his business or allow anyone else to do so.

Rush hour traffic delayed them a long time. At first, Avery concentrated on putting as much distance as she could between the bus and Washington. It was past ten by the time she turned off the main roads. She activated the GPS to try and find a route, but all the screen showed was snow. She tried her phone, and the result was the same. Not even the radio worked. One of those crates must have contained a jamming device; the bus was a rolling electronic dead zone. She smiled. So much for Henry's bugs.

It was quiet and peaceful driving through the night. A nearly full moon rode in the clear autumn sky, and woods closed in around them. Once, when she had first taken up driving in order to escape her memories, she had played a game of heading randomly down roads she had never seen, getting deliberately lost. Now she played it again, not caring where she ended up. She had never been good at keeping to the main roads.

By 3:00 she was tired, and when she saw the entrance to a state park, she turned and pulled into the empty parking lot. In the quiet after the engine shut off, she walked back through the kitchen and sitting area to see if there were any objections from her passengers. She listened at the closed door, but heard nothing and concluded they were asleep. As she was turning away, the door jerked open and the translator said, "What do you want?"

He was still fully dressed, exactly as she had seen him before, except without the glasses, his eyes were a little bloodshot, as if he hadn't closed them. "I've pulled over to get some sleep," she said. "It's not safe to keep driving without rest."

"Oh. All right," he said, and closed the door.

Shrugging, she went forward. There was a fold-down bunk that had once served the previous owner's entourage, and she now prepared to use it. She brushed her teeth in the tiny bathroom, pulled a sleeping bag from her backpack, and settled in.

Morning sun woke her. When she opened her eyes, it was flooding in the windows. At the kitchen table a yard away from her, the translator was sitting, staring out the window. By daylight, she saw that he had a square face the color of teak and closely trimmed black beard. She guessed that he might be Latino, and in his twenties.

"Morning," she said. He turned to stare at her, but said nothing. Not practiced in social graces, she thought. "I'm Avery," she said.

Still he didn't reply. "It's customary to tell me your name now," she said.

"Oh. Lionel," he answered.

"Pleased to meet you."

He said nothing, so she got up and went into the bathroom. When she came out, he was still staring fixedly out the window. She started making coffee. "Want some?" she asked.

"What is it?"

"Coffee."

"I ought to try it," he said reluctantly.

"Well, don't let me force you," she said.

"Why would you do that?" He was studying her, apprehensive.

"I wouldn't. I was being sarcastic. Like a joke. Never mind."

"Oh."

He got up restlessly and started opening the cupboards. Frank had stocked them with all the necessities, even a few luxuries. But Lionel didn't seem to find what he was looking for.

"Are you hungry?" Avery guessed.

"What do you mean?"

Avery searched for another way to word the question. "Would you like me to fix you some breakfast?"

He looked utterly stumped.

"Never mind. Just sit down and I'll make you something."

He sat down, gripping the edge of the table tensely. "That's a tree," he said, looking out the window.

"Right. It's a whole lot of trees."

"I ought to go out."

She didn't make the mistake of joking again. It was like talking to a person raised by wolves. Or aliens.

When she set a plate of eggs and bacon down in front of him, he sniffed it suspiciously. "That's food?"

"Yes, it's good. Try it."

He watched her eat for a few moments, then gingerly tried a bite of scrambled eggs. His expression showed distaste, but he resolutely forced himself to swallow. But when he tried the bacon, he couldn't bear it. "It bit my mouth," he said.

"You're probably not used to the salt. What do you normally eat?"

He reached in a pocket and took out some brown pellets that looked like dog kibble. Avery made a face of disgust. "What is that, people chow?"

"It's perfectly adapted to our nutritional needs," Lionel said. "Try it."

She was about to say "no thanks," but he was clearly making an effort to try new things, so she took a pellet and popped it in her mouth. It wasn't terrible—chewy rather than crunchy—but tasteless. "I think I'll stick to our food," she said.

He looked gloomy. "I need to learn to eat yours."

"Why? Research?"

He nodded. "I have to find out how the feral humans live."

So, Avery reflected, she was dealing with someone raised as a pet, who was now being released into the wild. For whatever reason.

"So where do you want to go today?" Avery said, sipping coffee.

He gave an indifferent gesture.

"You're heading for St. Louis?"

"Oh, I just picked that name off a map. It seemed to be in the center."

"That it is." She had lived there once; it was so incorrigibly in the center there was no edge to it. "Do you want to go by any particular route?"

He shrugged.

"How much time do you have?"

"As long as it takes."

"Okay. The scenic route, then."

She got up to clean the dishes, telling Lionel that this was a good time for him to go out, if he wanted to. It took him a while to summon his resolve. She watched out the kitchen window as he approached a tree as if to have a conversation with it. He felt its bark, smelled its leaves, and returned unhappy and distracted.

Avery followed the same random-choice method of navigation as the previous night, but always trending west. Soon they came to the first ridge of mountains. People from western states talked as if the Appalachians weren't real mountains, but they were—rugged and impenetrable ridges like walls erected to bar people from the land of milk and honey. In the mountains, all the roads ran northeast and southwest through the valleys between the crumpled land, with only the brave roads daring to climb up and pierce the ranges. The autumn leaves were at their height, russet and gold against the brilliant sky. All day long Lionel sat staring out the window.

That night she found a half-deserted campground outside a small town. She refilled the water tanks, hooked up the electricity, then came back in. "You're all set," she told Lionel. "If it's all right with you, I'm heading into town."

"Okay," he said.

It felt good to stretch her legs walking along the highway shoulder. The air was chill but bracing. The town was a tired, half abandoned place, but she found a bar and settled down with a beer and a burger. She couldn't help watching the patrons around her—worn-down, elderly people just managing to hang on. What would an alien think of America if she brought him here?

Remembering that she was away from the interference field, she thumbed on her phone—and immediately realized that the ping would give away her location to the spooks. But since she'd already done it, she dialed her brother's number and left a voicemail congratulating him on the concert she was missing. "Everything's fine with me," she said, then added mischievously, "I met a nice young man named Henry. I think he's sweet on me. Bye."

Heading back through the night, she became aware that someone was following her. The highway was too dark to see who it was, but when she stopped, the footsteps behind her stopped, too. At last a car passed, and she wheeled around to see what the headlights showed.

"Lionel!" she shouted. He didn't answer, just stood there, so she walked back toward him. "Did you follow me?"

He was standing with hands in pockets, hunched against the cold. Defensively, he said, "I wanted to see what you would do when I wasn't around."

"It's none of your business what I do off duty. Listen, respecting privacy goes both ways. If you want me to respect yours, you've got to respect mine, okay?"

He looked cold and miserable, so she said, "Come on, let's get back before you freeze solid."

They walked side by side in silence, gravel crunching underfoot. At last he said stiffly, "I'd like to re-negotiate our contract."

"Oh, yeah? What part of the contract?"

"The part about privacy. I . . ." He searched for words. "We should have asked for more than a driver. We need a translator."

At least he'd realized it. He might speak perfect English, but he was not fluent in Human.

"My contract is with your . . . employer. Is this what he wants?"

"Who?"

"The other passenger. I don't know what to call him. 'The alien' isn't polite. What's his name?"

"They don't have names. They don't have a language."

Astonished, Avery said, "Then how do you communicate?"

He glowered at her. She held up her hands. "Sorry. No offense intended. I'm just trying to find out what he wants."

"They don't want things," he muttered, gazing fixedly at the moonlit road. "At least, not like you do. They're not . . . awake. Aware. Not like people are."

This made so little sense to Avery, she wondered if he were having trouble with the language. "I don't understand," she said. "You mean they're not . . . sentient?"

"They're not conscious," he said. "There's a difference."

"But they have technology. They built those domes, or brought them here, or whatever the hell they did. They have an advanced civilization."

"I didn't say they aren't smart. They're smarter than people are. They're just not conscious."

Avery shook her head. "I'm sorry, I just can't imagine it."

"Yes, you can," Lionel said impatiently. "People function unconsciously all the time. You're not aware that you're keeping your balance right now—you just do it automatically. You don't have to be aware to walk, or breathe. In fact, the more skillful you are at something, the less aware you are. Being aware would just degrade their skill."

They had come to the campground entrance. Behind the dark pine trees, Avery could see the bus, holding its unknowable passenger. For a moment the bus seemed to stare back with blank eyes. She made herself focus on the practical. "So how can I know what he wants?"

"I'm telling you."

She refrained from asking, "And how do *you* know?" because he'd already refused to answer that. The new privacy rules were to be selective, then. But she already knew more about the aliens than anyone else on Earth, except the translators. Not that she understood.

"I'm sorry, I can't keep calling him 'him,' or 'the alien,'" Avery said the next morning over breakfast. "I have to give him a name. I'm going to call him 'Mr. Burbage.' If he doesn't know, he won't mind."

Lionel didn't look any more disturbed than usual. She took that as consent.

"So where are we going today?" she asked.

He pressed his lips together in concentration. "I need to go to a place where I can acquire knowledge."

Since this could encompass anything from a brothel to a university, Avery said, "You've got to be more specific. What kind of knowledge?"

"Knowledge about you."

"Me?"

"No, you humans. How you work."

Humans. For that, she would have to find a bigger town.

As she cruised down a county road, Avery thought about Blake. Once, he had told her that to play an instrument truly well, you had to lose all awareness of what you were doing, and rely entirely on the muscle memory in your fingers. "You are so in the present, there is no room for self," Blake said. "No ego, no doubt, no introspection."

She envied him the ability to achieve such a state. She had tried to play the saxophone, but had never gotten good enough to experience what Blake described. Only playing video games could she concentrate intensely enough to lose self-awareness. It was strange, how addictive it was to escape the prison of her skull and forget she had a self. Mystics and meditators strove to achieve such a state.

A motion in the corner of her eye made her slam on the brakes and swerve. A startled deer pirouetted, flipped its tail, and leaped away. She continued on more slowly, searching for a sign to see where she was. She could not remember having driven the last miles, or whether she had passed any turns. Smiling grimly, she realized that driving was *her* skill, something she knew so well that she could do it unconsciously. She had even reacted to a threat before knowing what it was. Her reflexes were faster than her conscious mind.

Were the aliens like that all the time? In a perpetual state of flow, like virtuoso musicians or Zen monks in *samadhi*? What would be the point of achieving such supreme skill, if the price was never knowing it was *you* doing it?

Around noon, they came to a town nestled in a steep valley on a rushing river. Driving down the main street, she spied a quaint, cupolaed building with a "Municipal Library" sign out front. Farther on, at the edge of town, an abandoned car lot offered a grass-pocked parking lot, so she turned in. "Come on, Lionel," she called out. "I've found a place for you to acquire knowledge."

They walked back into town together. The library was quiet and empty except for an old man reading a magazine. The selection of books was sparse, but there was a row of computers. "You know how to use these?" Avery said in a low voice.

"Not this kind," Lionel said. "They're very . . . primitive."

They sat down together, and Avery explained how to work the mouse and get on the Internet, how to search and scroll. "I've got it," he said. "You can go now."

Shrugging, she left him to his research. She strolled down the main street, stopped in a drugstore, then found a café that offered fried egg sandwiches on Wonder Bread, a luxury from her childhood. With lunch and a cup of coffee, she settled down to wait, sorting email on her phone.

Some time later, she became aware of the television behind the counter. It was tuned to one of those daytime exposé shows hosted by a shrill woman who spoke in a tone of breathless indignation. "Coming up," she said, "Slaves or traitors? Who *are* these alien translators?"

Avery realized that some part of her brain must have been listening and alerted her conscious mind to pay attention, just as it had reacted to the deer. She had a threat detection system she was not even aware of.

In the story that followed, a correspondent revealed that she had been unable to match any of the translators with missing children recorded in the past twenty years. The host treated this as suspicious information that someone ought to be looking into. Then came a panel of experts to discuss what they knew of the translators, which was nothing.

"Turncoats," commented one of the men at the counter watching the show. "Why would anyone betray his own race?"

"They're not even human," said another, "just made to look that way. They're clones or robots or something."

"The government won't do anything. They're just letting those aliens sit there."

Avery got up to pay her bill. The woman at the cash register said, "You connected with that big tour bus parked out at Fenniman's?"

She had forgotten that in a town like this, everyone knew instantly what was out of the ordinary.

"Yeah," Avery said. "Me and my . . . boyfriend are delivering it to a new owner."

She glanced up at the television just as a collage of faces appeared. Lionel's was in the top row. "Look closely," the show's host said. "If you recognize any of these faces, call us at 1-800- . . ." Avery didn't wait to hear the number. The door shut behind her.

It was hard not to walk quickly enough to attract attention. Why had she left him alone, as if it were safe? Briefly, she thought of bringing the bus in to pick him up at the library, but it would only attract more attention. The sensible thing was to slip inconspicuously out of town.

Lionel was engrossed in a website about the brain when she came in. She sat down next to him and said quietly, "We've got to leave."

"I'm not . . ."

"Lionel. We have to leave. Right now."

He frowned, but got the message. As he rose to put on his coat, she quickly erased his browser history and cache. Then she led the way out and around the building to a back street where there were fewer eyes. "Hold my hand," she said.

"Why?"

"I told them you were my boyfriend. We've got to act friendly."

He didn't object or ask what was going on. The aliens had trained him well, she thought.

The street they were on came to an end, and they were forced back onto the main thoroughfare, right past the café. In Avery's mind every window was a pair of eyes staring at the strangers. As they left the business section of town and the buildings thinned out, she became aware of someone walking a block behind them. Glancing back, she saw a man in hunter's camouflage and billed cap, carrying a gun case on a strap over one shoulder.

She sped up, but the man trailing them sped up as well. When they were in sight of the bus, Avery pressed the keys into Lionel's hand and said, "Go on ahead. I'll stall this guy. Get inside and don't open the door to anyone but me." Then she turned back to confront their pursuer.

Familiarity tickled as he drew closer. When she was sure, she called out, "Afternoon, Henry! What a coincidence to see you here."

"Hello, Avery," he said. He didn't look quite right in the hunter costume: he was too urban and fit. "That was pretty careless of you. I followed to make sure you got back safe."

"I didn't know his picture was all over the TV," she said. "I've been out of touch."

"I know, we lost track of you for a while there. Please don't do that again."

As threats went, Henry now seemed like the lesser evil. She hesitated, then said, "I didn't see any need to get in touch." That meant the country was not in peril.

"Thanks," he said. "Listen, if you turn left on Highway 19 ahead, you'll come to a national park with a campground. It'll be safe."

As she walked back to the bus, she was composing a lie about who she had been talking to. But Lionel never asked. As soon as she was on board he started eagerly telling her about what he had learned in the library. She had never seen him so animated, so she gestured him to sit in the passenger seat beside her while she got the bus moving again.

"The reason you're conscious is because of the cerebral cortex," he said. "It's an add-on, the last part of the brain to evolve. Its only purpose is to monitor what the rest of the brain is doing. All the sensory input goes to the inner brain first, and gets processed, so the cortex never gets the raw data. It only sees the effect on the rest of the brain, not what's really out there. That's why you're aware of yourself. In fact, it's *all* you're aware of."

"Why are you saying 'you'?" Avery asked. "You've got a cerebral cortex, too."

Defensively, he said, "I'm not like you."

Avery shrugged. "Okay." But she wanted to keep the conversation going. "So Mr. Burbage doesn't have a cortex? Is that what you're saying?"

"That's right," Lionel said. "For him, life is a skill of the autonomic nervous system, not something he had to consciously learn. That's why he can think and react faster than we can, and requires less energy. The messages don't have to travel on a useless detour through the cortex."

"Useless?" Avery objected. "I kind of like being conscious."

Lionel fell silent, suddenly grave and troubled.

She glanced over at him. "What's the matter?"

In a low tone he said, "He likes being conscious, too. It's what they want from us."

Avery gripped the wheel and tried not to react. Up to now, the translators had denied that the aliens wanted anything at all from humans. But then it occurred to her that Lionel might not mean humans when he said "us."

"You mean, you translators?" she ventured.

He nodded, looking grim.

"Is that a bad thing?" she asked, reacting to his expression.

"Not for us," he said. "It's bad for them. It's killing him."

He was struggling with some strong emotion. Guilt, she thought. Maybe grief.

"I'm sorry," she said.

Angrily, he stood up to head back into the bus. "Why do you make me think of this?" he said. "Why can't you just mind your own business?"

Avery drove on, listening as he slammed the bedroom door behind him. She didn't feel any resentment. She knew all about guilt and grief, and how useless they made you feel. Lionel's behavior made more sense to her now. He was having trouble distinguishing between what was happening to him externally and what was coming from inside. Even people skilled at being human had trouble with that.

The national park Henry had recommended turned out to be at Cumberland Gap, the mountain pass early pioneers had used to migrate west to Kentucky. They spent the night in the campground undisturbed. At dawn, Avery strolled out in the damp morning air to look around. She quickly returned to say, "Lionel, come out here. You need to see this."

She led him across the road to an overlook facing west. From the edge of the Appalachians they looked out on range after range of wooded foothills swaddled in fog. The morning sun at their backs lit everything in shades of mauve and azure. Avery felt like Daniel Boone looking out on the Promised Land, stretching before her into the misty distance, unpolluted by the past.

"I find this pleasant," Lionel said gravely.

Avery smiled. It was a breakthrough statement for someone so unaccustomed to introspection that he hadn't been able to tell her he was hungry two days ago. But all she said was, "Me, too."

After several moments of silence, she ventured, "Don't you think Mr. Burbage would enjoy seeing this? There's no one else around. Doesn't he want to get out of the bus some time?"

"He *is* seeing it," Lionel said.

"What do you mean?"

"He is here." Lionel tapped his head with a finger.

Avery couldn't help staring. "You mean you have some sort of telepathic connection with him?"

"There's no such thing as telepathy," Lionel said dismissively. "They communicate with neurotransmitters." She was still waiting, so he said, "He doesn't have to be all in one place. Part of him is with me, part of him is in the bus."

"In your *head*?" she asked, trying not to betray how creepy she found this news.

He nodded. "He needs me to observe the world for him, and understand it. They have had lots of other helper species to do things for them—species that build things, or transport them. But we're the first one with advanced consciousness."

"And that's why they're interested in us."

Lionel looked away to avoid her eyes, but nodded. "They like it," he said, his voice low and reluctant. "At first it was just novel and new for them, but now it's become an addiction, like a dangerous drug. We pay a high metabolic price for consciousness; it's why our lifespan is so short. They live for centuries. But when they get hooked on us, they burn out even faster than we do."

He picked up a rock and flung it over the cliff, watching as it arced up, then plummeted.

"And if he dies, what happens to you?" Avery asked.

"I don't want him to die," Lionel said. He put his hands in his pockets and studied his feet. "It feels . . . good to have him around. I like his company. He's very old, very wise."

For a moment, she could see it through his eyes. She could imagine feeling intimately connected to an ancient being who was dying from an inability to part with his adopted human son. What a terrible burden for Lionel to carry, to be slowly killing someone he loved.

And yet, she still felt uneasy.

"How do you know?" she asked.

He looked confused. "What do you mean?"

"You said he's old and wise. How do you know that?"

"The way you know anything unconscious. It's a feeling, an instinct."

"Are you sure he not controlling you? Pushing around your neurotransmitters?"

"That's absurd," he said, mildly irritated. "I told you, he's not conscious, at least not naturally. Control is a conscious thing."

"But what if you did something he didn't want?"

"I don't feel like doing things he doesn't want. Like talking to you now. He must have decided he can trust you, because I wouldn't feel like telling you anything if he hadn't."

Avery wasn't sure whether being trusted by an alien was something she aspired to. But she did want Lionel to trust her, and so she let the subject drop.

"Where do you want to go today?" she asked.

"You keep asking me that." He stared out on the landscape, as if waiting for a revelation. At last he said, "I want to see humans living as they normally do. We've barely seen any of them. I didn't think the planet was so sparsely populated."

"Okay," she said. "I'm going to have to make a phone call for that."

When he had returned to the bus, she strolled away, took out Henry's card, and thumbed the number. Despite the early hour, he answered on the first ring.

"He wants to see humans," she said. "Normal humans behaving normally. Can you help me out?"

"Let me make some calls," he said. "I'll text you instructions."

"No men in black," she said. "You know what I mean?"

"I get it."

When Avery stopped for diesel around noon, the gas station television was blaring with news that the Justice Department would investigate the aliens for abducting human children. She escaped into the restroom to check her phone. The internet was ablaze with speculation: who the translators were, whether they could be freed, whether they were human at all. The part of the government that had approved Lionel's road trip was clearly working at cross purposes with the part that had dreamed up this new strategy for extracting information from the aliens. The only good news was that no hint had leaked out that an alien was roaming the back roads of America in a converted bus.

Henry had texted her a cryptic suggestion to head toward Paris. She had to Google it to find that there actually was a Paris, Kentucky. When she came out to pay for the fuel, she was relieved to see that the television had moved on to World Series coverage. On impulse, she bought a Cardinals cap for Lionel.

Paris turned out to be a quaint old Kentucky town that had once had delusions of cityhood. Today, a county fair was the main event in town. The

RV park was almost full, but Avery's E.T. Express managed to maneuver in. When everything was settled, she sat on the bus steps sipping a Bud and waiting for night so they could venture out with a little more anonymity. The only thing watching her was a skittish, half-wild cat crouched behind a trashcan. Somehow, it reminded her of Lionel, so she tossed it a Cheeto to see if she could lure it out. It refused the bait.

That night, disguised by the dark and a Cardinals cap, Lionel looked tolerably inconspicuous. As they were leaving to take in the fair, she said, "Will Mr. Burbage be okay while we're gone? What if someone tries to break into the bus?"

"Don't worry, he'll be all right," Lionel said. His tone implied more than his words. She resolved to call Henry at the earliest opportunity and pass along a warning not to try anything.

The people in the midway all looked authentic. If there were snipers on the bigtop and agents on the merry-go-round, she couldn't tell. When people failed to recognize Lionel at the ticket stand and popcorn wagon, she began to relax. Everyone was here to enjoy themselves, not to look for aliens.

She introduced Lionel to the joys of corn dogs and cotton candy, to the Ferris wheel and tilt-a-whirl. He took in the jangling sounds, the smells of deep-fried food, and the blinking lights with a grave and studious air. When they had had their fill of all the machines meant to disorient and confuse, they took a break at a picnic table, sipping Cokes.

Avery said, "Is Mr. Burbage enjoying this?"

Lionel shrugged. "Are you?" He wasn't deflecting her question; he actually wanted to know.

She considered. "I think people enjoy these events mainly because they bring back childhood memories," she said.

"Yes. It does seem familiar," Lionel said.

"Really? What about it?"

He paused, searching his mind. "The smells," he said at last.

Avery nodded. It was smells for her, as well: deep fat fryers, popcorn. "Do you remember anything from the time before you were abducted?"

"Adopted," he corrected her.

"Right, adopted. What about your family?"

He shook his head.

"Do you ever wonder what kind of people they were?"

"The kind of people who wouldn't look for me," he said coldly.

"Wait a minute. You don't know that. For all you know, your mother might have cried her eyes out when you disappeared."

He stared at her. She realized she had spoken with more emotion than she had intended. The subject had touched a nerve. "Sorry," she muttered, and got up. "I'm tired. Can we head back?"

"Sure," he said, and followed her without question.

That night she couldn't sleep. She lay watching the pattern from the lights outside on the ceiling, but her mind was on the back of the bus. Up to now she had slept without thinking of the strangeness just beyond the door, but tonight it bothered her.

About 3:00 AM she roused from a doze at the sound of Lionel's quiet foot-step going past her. She lay silent as he eased the bus door open. When he had gone outside she rose and looked to see what he was doing. He walked away from the bus toward a maintenance shed and some dumpsters. She debated whether to follow him; it was just what she had scolded him for doing to her. But concern for his safety won out, and she took a flashlight from the driver's console, put it in the pocket of a windbreaker, and followed.

At first she thought she had lost him. The parking lot was motionless and quiet. A slight breeze stirred the pines on the edge of the road. Then she heard a scuffling sound ahead, a thump, and a soft crack. At first she stood listening, but when there was no more sound, she crept forward. Rounding the dump-ster, she saw in its shadow a figure crouched on the ground. Unable to make out what was going on, she switched on the flashlight.

Lionel turned, his eyes wild and hostile. Dangling from his hand was the limp body of a cat, its head ripped off. His face was smeared with its blood. Watching her, he deliberately ripped a bite of cat meat from the body with his teeth and swallowed.

"Lionel!" she cried out in horror. "Put that down!"

He turned away, trying to hide his prey like an animal. Without thinking, she grabbed his arm, and he spun fiercely around, as if to fight her. His eyes looked utterly alien. She stepped back. "It's me, Avery," she said.

He looked down at the mangled carcass in his hand, then dropped it, rose, and backed away. Once again taking his arm, Avery guided him away from the dumpsters, back to the bus. Inside, she led him to the kitchen sink. "Wash," she ordered, then went to firmly close the bus door.

Her heart was pounding, and she kept the heavy flashlight in her hand for security. But when she came back, she saw he was trembling so hard he had dropped the soap and was leaning against the sink for support. Seeing that his face was still smeared with blood, she took a paper towel and wiped him off, then dried his hands. He sank onto the bench by the kitchen table. She stood watching him, arms crossed, waiting for him to speak. He didn't.

"So what was that about?" she said sternly.

He shook his head.

"Cats aren't food," she said. "They're living beings."

Still he didn't speak.

"Have you been sneaking out at night all along?" she demanded.

He shook his head. "I don't know . . . I just thought . . . I wanted to see what it would feel like."

"You mean *Mr. Burbage* wanted to see what it would feel like," she said.

"Maybe," he admitted.

"Well, people don't do things like that."

He was looking ill. She grabbed his arm and hustled him into the bathroom, aiming him at the toilet. She left him there vomiting, and started shoving belongings into her backpack. As she swung it onto her shoulder, he staggered to the bathroom door.

"I'm leaving," she said. "I can't sleep here, knowing you do things like that."

He looked dumbstruck. She pushed past him and out the door. She was striding away across the gravel parking lot when he called after her, "Avery! You can't leave."

She wheeled around. "Can't I? Just watch me."

He left the bus and followed her. "What are we going to do?"

"I don't care," she said.

"I won't do it again."

"Who's talking, you or him?"

A light went on in the RV next to them. She realized they were making a late-night scene like trailer-park trash, attracting attention. This wasn't an argument they could have in public. And now that she was out here, she realized she had no place to go. So she shooed Lionel back toward the bus.

Once inside, she said, "This is the thing, Lionel. This whole situation is creeping me out. You can't make any promises as long as he's in charge. Maybe next time he'll want to see what it feels like to kill *me* in my sleep, and you won't be able to stop him."

Lionel looked disturbed. "He won't do that."

"How do you know?"

"I just . . . do."

"That's not good enough. I need to see him."

Avery wasn't sure why she had blurted it out, except that living with an invisible, ever-present passenger had become intolerable. As long as she didn't know what the door in the back of the bus concealed, she couldn't be at ease.

He shook his head. "That won't help."

She crossed her arms and said, "I can't stay unless I know what he is."

Lionel's face took on an introspective look, as if he were consulting his conscience. At last he said, "You'd have to promise not to tell anyone."

Avery hadn't really expected him to consent, and now felt a nervous tremor. She dropped her pack on the bed and gripped her hands into fists. "All right."

He led the way to the back of the bus and eased the door open as if fearing to disturb the occupant within. She followed him in. The small room was dimly lit and there was an earthy smell. All the crates he had brought in must have been folded up and put away, because none were visible. There was an unmade bed, and beside it a clear box like an aquarium tank, holding something she could not quite make out. When Lionel turned on a light, she saw what the tank contained.

It looked most like a coral or sponge—a yellowish, rounded growth the size of half a beach ball, resting on a bed of wood chips and dead leaves. Lionel picked up a spray bottle and misted it tenderly. It responded by expanding as if breathing.

"*That's* Mr. Burbage?" Avery whispered.

Lionel nodded. "Part of him. The most important part."

The alien seemed insignificant, something she could destroy with a bottle of bleach. "Can he move?" she asked.

"Oh, yes," Lionel said. "Not the way we do."

She waited for him to explain. At first he seemed reluctant, but he finally said, "They are colonies of cells with a complicated life cycle. This is the final stage of their development, when they become most complex and organized. After this, they dissolve into the earth. The cells don't die; they go on to form other coalitions. But the individual is lost. Just like us, I suppose."

What she was feeling, she realized, was disappointment. In spite of all Lionel had told her, she had hoped there would be some way of communicating. Before, she had not truly believed that the alien could be insentient. Now she did. In fact, she found it hard to believe that it could think at all.

"How do you know he's intelligent?" she asked. "He could be just a heap of chemicals, like a loaf of bread rising."

"How do you know *I'm* intelligent?" he said, staring at the tank. "Or anyone?"

"You react to me. You communicate. He can't."

"Yes, he can."

"How? If I touched him—"

"No!" Lionel said quickly. "Don't touch him. You'd see, he would react. It wouldn't be malice, just a reflex."

"Then how do you . . . ?"

Reluctantly, Lionel said, "He has to touch you. It's the only way to exchange neurotransmitters." He paused, as if debating something internally. She watched the conflict play across his face. At last, reluctantly, he said, "I think he would be willing to communicate with you."

It was what she had wanted, some reassurance of the alien's intentions. But now it was offered, her instincts were unwilling. "No thanks," she said.

Lionel looked relieved. She realized he hadn't wanted to give up his unique relationship with Mr. Burbage.

"Thanks anyway," she said, for the generosity of the offer he hadn't wanted to make.

And yet, it left her unsure. She had only Lionel's word that the alien was friendly. After tonight, that wasn't enough.

Neither of them could sleep, so as soon as day came they set out again. Heading west, Avery knew they were going deeper and deeper into isolationist territory, where even human strangers were unwelcome, never mind aliens. This was the land where she had grown up, and she knew it well. From here, the world outside looked like a violent, threatening place full of impoverished hordes who envied and hated the good life in America. Here, even the churches preached self-satisfaction, and discontent was the fault of those who hated freedom—like college professors, homosexuals, and immigrants.

Growing up, she had expected to spend her life in this country. She had done everything right—married just out of high school, worked as a waitress, gotten pregnant at 19. Her life had been mapped out in front of her.

She couldn't even imagine it now.

This morning, Lionel seemed to want to talk. He sat beside her in the co-pilot seat, watching the road and answering her questions.

"What does it feel like, when he communicates with you?"

He reflected. "It feels like a mood, or a hunch. Or I act on impulse."

"How do you know it's him, and not your own subconscious?"

"I don't. It doesn't matter."

Avery shook her head. "I wouldn't want to go through life acting on hunches."

"Why not?"

"Your unconscious . . . it's unreliable. You can't control it. It can lead you wrong."

"That's absurd," he said. "It's not some outside entity; it's *you*. It's your *conscious* mind that's the slave master, always worrying about control. Your unconscious only wants to preserve you."

"Not if there's an alien messing around with it."

"He's not like that. This drive to dominate—that's a conscious thing. He doesn't have that slave master part of the brain."

"Do you know that for a fact, or are you just guessing?"

"Guessing is what your unconscious tells you. Knowing is a conscious thing. They're only in conflict if your mind is fighting itself."

"Sounds like the human condition to me," Avery said. This had to be the weirdest conversation in her life.

"Is he here now?" she asked.

"Of course he is."

"Don't you ever want to get away from him?"

Puzzled, he said, "Why should I?"

"Privacy. To be by yourself."

"I don't want to be by myself."

Something in his voice told her he was thinking ahead, to the death of his lifelong companion. Abruptly, he rose and walked back into the bus.

Actually, she had lied to him. She *had* gone through life acting on hunches. *Go with your gut* had been her motto, because she had trusted her gut. But of course it had nothing to do with gut, or heart—it was her unconscious mind she had been following. Her unconscious was why she took this road rather than that, or preferred Raisin Bran to Corn Flakes. It was why she found certain tunes achingly beautiful, and why she was fond of this strange young man, against all rational evidence.

As the road led them nearer to southern Illinois, Avery found memories surfacing. They came with a tug of regret, like a choking rope pulling her back toward the person she hadn't become. She thought of the cascade of non-decisions that had led her to become the rootless, disconnected person she was, as much a stranger to the human race as Lionel was, in her way.

What good has consciousness ever done me? she thought. It only made her aware that she could never truly connect with another human being, deep down. And on that day when her cells would dissolve into the soil, there would be no trace her consciousness had ever existed.

That night they camped at a freeway rest stop a day's drive from St. Louis. Lionel was moody and anxious. Avery's attempt to interest him in a trashy novel was fruitless. At last she asked what was wrong. Fighting to find the words, he said, "He's very ill. This trip was a bad idea. All the stimulation has made him worse."

Tentatively, she said, "Should we head for one of the domes?"

Lionel shook his head. "They can't cure this . . . this addiction to conscious-ness. If they could, I don't think he'd take it."

"Do the others—his own people—know what's wrong with him?"

Lionel nodded wordlessly.

She didn't know what comfort to offer. "Well," she said at last, "it was his choice to come."

"A selfish choice," Lionel said angrily.

She couldn't help noticing that he was speaking for himself, Lionel, as dis-tinct from Mr. Burbage. Thoughtfully, she said, "Maybe they can't love us as much as we can love them."

He looked at her as if the word "love" had never entered his vocabulary. "Don't say *us*," he said. "I'm not one of you."

She didn't believe it for a second, but she just said, "Suit yourself," and turned back to her novel. After a few moments, he went into the back of the bus and closed the door.

She lay there trying to read for a while, but the story couldn't hold her attention. She kept listening for some sound from beyond the door, some indication of how they were doing. At last she got up quietly and went to listen. Hearing nothing, she tried the door and found it unlocked. Softly, she cracked it open to look inside.

Lionel was not asleep. He was lying on the bed, his head next to the alien's tank. But the alien was no longer in the tank; it was on the pillow. It had extruded a mass of long, cordlike tentacles that gripped Lionel's head in a medusa embrace, snaking into every opening. One had entered an ear, another a nostril. A third had nudged aside an eyeball in order to enter the eye socket. Fluid coursed along the translucent vessels connecting man and creature.

Avery wavered on the edge of horror. Her first instinct was to intervene, to defend Lionel from what looked like an attack. But the expression on his face was not of terror, but peace. All his vague references to exchanging neurotransmitters came back to her now: this was what he had meant. The alien communicated by drinking cerebrospinal fluid, its drug of choice, and injecting its own.

Shaken, she eased the door shut again. Unable to get the image out of her mind, she went outside to walk around the bus to calm her nerves. After three circuits she leaned back against the cold metal, wishing she had a cigarette for the first time in years. Above her, the stars were cold and bright. What was this relationship she had landed in the middle of—predator and prey? father and son? pusher and addict? master and slave? Or some strange combination of all? Had she just witnessed an alien learning about love?

She had been saving a bottle of bourbon for special occasions, so she went in to pour herself a shot.

To her surprise, Lionel emerged before she was quite drunk. She thought of offering him a glass, but wasn't sure how it would mix with whatever was already in his brain.

He sat down across from her, but just stared silently at the floor for a long time. At last he stirred and said, "I think we ought to take him to a private place."

"What sort of private place?" Avery asked.

"Somewhere dignified. Natural. Secluded."

To die, she realized. The alien wanted to die in private. Or Lionel wanted him to. There was no telling where one left off and the other began.

"I know a place," she said. "Will he make it another day?"

Lionel nodded silently.

Through the bourbon haze, Avery wondered what she ought to say to Henry. Was the country in danger? She didn't think so. This seemed like a personal matter. To be sure, she said, "You're certain his relatives won't blame us if he dies?"

"Blame?" he said.

That was conscious-talk, she realized. "React when he doesn't come back?"

"If they were going to react, they would have done it when he left. They aren't expecting anything, not even his return. They don't live in an imaginary future like you people do."

"Wise of them," she said.

"Yes."

They rolled into St. Louis in late afternoon, across the Poplar Street Bridge next to the Arch and off onto I-70 toward the north part of town. Avery knew exactly where she was going. From the first moment Frank had told her the destination was St. Louis, she had known she would end up driving this way, toward the place where she had left the first part of her life.

Bellefontaine Cemetery lay on what had been the outskirts of the city in Victorian times, several hundred acres of greenery behind a stone wall and a wrought-iron gate. It was a relic from a time when cemeteries were landscaped, parklike sanctuaries from the city. Huge old oak and sweetgum trees lined the winding roadways, their branches now black against the sky. Avery drove slowly past the marble mausoleums and toward the hill at the back of the cemetery, which looked out over the valley toward the Missouri River. It was everything Lionel had wanted—peaceful, natural, secluded.

Some light rain misted down out of the overcast sky. Avery parked the bus and went out to check whether they were alone. She had seen no one but a single dog-walker near the entrance, and no vehicle had followed them in. The gates would close in half an hour, and the bus would have to be out. Henry and his friends were probably waiting outside the gate for them to appear again. She returned to the bus and knocked on Lionel's door. He opened it right away. Inside, the large picnic cooler they had bought was standing open, ready.

"Help me lift him in," Lionel said.

Avery maneuvered past the cooler to the tank. "Is it okay for me to touch him?"

"Hold your hand close to him for a few seconds."

Avery did as instructed. A translucent tentacle extruded from the cauliflower folds of the alien's body. It touched her palm, recoiled, then extended again. Gently, hesitantly, it explored her hand, tickling slightly as it probed her palm and curled around her pinkie. She held perfectly still.

"What is he thinking?" she whispered.

"He's learning your chemical identity," Lionel said.

"How can he learn without being aware? Can he even remember?"

"Of course he can remember. Your immune system learns and remembers just about every pathogen it ever met, and it's not aware. Can *you* remember them all?"

She shook her head, stymied.

At last, apparently satisfied, the tendril retracted into the alien's body.

"All right," Lionel said, "now you can touch him."

The alien was surprisingly heavy. Together, they lifted him onto the bed of dirt and wood chips Lionel had spread in the bottom of the cooler. Lionel fitted the lid on loosely, and each of them took a handle to carry their load out into the open air. Avery led the way around a mausoleum shaped like a Greek temple to an unmowed spot hidden from the path. Sycamore leaves and bark littered the ground, damp from the rain.

"Is this okay?" she asked.

For answer, Lionel set down his end of the cooler and straightened, breathing in the forest smell. "This is okay."

"I have to move the bus. Stay behind this building in case anyone comes by. I'll be back."

The gatekeeper waved as she pulled the bus out onto the street. By the time she had parked it on a nearby residential street and returned, the gate was closed. She walked around the cemetery perimeter to an unfrequented side, then scrambled up the wall and over the spiked fence.

Inside, the traffic noise of the city fell away. The trees arched overhead in churchlike silence. Not a squirrel stirred. Avery sat down on a tombstone to wait. Beyond the hill, Lionel was holding vigil at the side of his dying companion, and she wanted to give him privacy. The stillness felt good, but unfamiliar. Her life was made of motion. She had been driving for twenty years—driving away, driving beyond, always a new destination. Never back.

The daylight would soon be gone. She needed to do the other thing she had come here for. Raising the hood of her raincoat, she headed downhill, the grass caressing her sneakers wetly. It was years since she had visited the grave of her daughter Gabrielle, whose short life and death were like a chasm dividing her life into before and after. They had called it crib death then—an unexplained, random, purposeless death. "Nothing you could have done," the doctor had said, thinking that was more comforting than knowing that the universe just didn't give a damn.

Gabrielle's grave lay in a grove of cedar trees—the plot a gift from a sympathetic patron at the café where Avery had worked. At first she had thought of turning it down because the little grave would be overshadowed by more ostentatious death; but the suburban cemeteries had looked so industrial, monuments stamped out by machine. She had come to love the age and seclusion of this spot. At first, she had visited over and over.

As she approached in the fading light, she saw that something was lying on the headstone. When she came close she saw that some stranger had placed on the grave a little terra cotta angel with one wing broken. Avery stood staring at the bedraggled figurine, now soaked with rain, a gift to her daughter from someone she didn't even know. Then, a sudden, unexpected wave of grief doubled her over. It had been twenty years since she had touched her daughter, but the memory was still vivid and tactile. She remembered the smell, the softness of her skin, the utter trust in her eyes. She felt again the aching hole of her absence.

Avery sank to her knees in the wet grass, sobbing for the child she hadn't been able to protect, for the sympathy of the nameless stranger, even for the helpless, mutilated angel who would never fly.

There was a sound behind her, and she looked up. Lionel stood there watching her, rain running down his face—no, it was tears. He wiped his eyes, then looked at his hands. "I don't know why I feel like this," he said.

Poor, muddled man. She got up and hugged him for knowing exactly how she felt. They stood there for a moment, two people trapped in their own brains, and the only crack in the wall was empathy.

"Is he gone?" she asked softly.

He shook his head. "Not yet. I left him alone in case it was me . . . interfering. Then I saw you and followed."

"This is my daughter's grave," Avery said. "I didn't know I still miss her so much."

She took his hand and started back up the hill. They said nothing, but didn't let go of each other till they got to the marble mausoleum where they had left Mr. Burbage.

The alien was still there, resting on the ground next to the cooler. Lionel knelt beside him and held out a hand. A bouquet of tentacles reached out and grasped it, then withdrew. Lionel came over to where Avery stood watching. "I'm going to stay with him. You don't have to."

"I'd like to," she said, "if it's okay with you."

He ducked his head furtively.

So they settled down to keep a strange death watch. Avery shared some chemical hand-warmers she had brought from the bus. When those ran out and night deepened, she managed to find some dry wood at the bottom of a groundskeeper's brush pile to start a campfire. She sat poking the fire with a stick, feeling drained of tears, worn down as an old tire.

"Does he know he's dying?" she asked.

Lionel nodded. "*I* know, and so he knows." A little bitterly, he added, "That's what consciousness does for you."

"So normally he wouldn't know?"

He shook his head. "Or care. It's just part of their life cycle. There's no death if there's no self to be aware of it."

"No life either," Avery said.

Lionel just sat breaking twigs and tossing them on the fire. "I keep wondering if it was worth it. If consciousness is good enough to die for."

She tried to imagine being free of her self—of the regrets of the past and fear of the future. If this were a Star Trek episode, she thought, this would be when Captain Kirk would deliver a speech in defense of being human, despite all the drawbacks. She didn't feel that way.

"You're right," she said. "Consciousness kind of sucks."

The sky was beginning to glow with dawn when at last they saw a change in the alien. The brainlike mass started to shrink and a liquid pool spread out from under it, as if it were dissolving. There was no sound. At the end, its body deflated like a falling soufflé, leaving nothing but a slight crust on the leaves and a damp patch on the ground.

They sat for a long time in silence. It was light when Lionel got up and brushed off his pants, his face set and grim. "Well, that's that," he said.

Avery felt reluctant to leave. "His cells are in the soil?" she said.

"Yes, they'll live underground for a while, spreading and multiplying. They'll go through some blooming and sporing cycles. If any dogs or children come along at that stage, the spores will establish a colony in their brains. It's how they invade."

His voice was perfectly indifferent. Avery stared at him. "You might have mentioned that."

He shrugged.

An inspiration struck her. She seized up a stick and started digging in the damp patch of ground, scooping up soil in her hands and putting it into the cooler.

"What are you doing?" Lionel said. "You can't stop him, it's too late."

"I'm not trying to," Avery said. "I want some cells to transplant. I'm going to grow an alien of my own."

"That's the stupidest—"

A moment later he was on his knees beside her, digging and scooping up dirt. They got enough to half-fill the cooler, then covered it with leaves to keep it damp.

"Wait here," she told him. "I'll bring the bus to pick you up. The gates open in an hour. Don't let anyone see you."

When she got back to the street where she had left the bus, Henry was waiting in a parked car. He got out and opened the passenger door for her, but she didn't get inside. "I've got to get back," she said, inclining her head toward the bus. "They're waiting for me."

"Do you mind telling me what's going on?"

"I just needed a break. I had to get away."

"In a cemetery? All night?"

"It's personal."

"Is there something I should know?"

"We're heading back home today."

He waited, but she said no more. There was no use telling him; he couldn't do anything about it. The invasion was already underway.

He let her return to the bus, and she drove it to a gas station to fuel up while waiting for the cemetery to open. At the stroke of 8:30 she pulled the bus through the gate, waving at the puzzled gatekeeper.

Between them, she and Lionel carried the cooler into the bus, leaving behind only the remains of a campfire and a slightly disturbed spot of soil. Then she headed straight for the freeway.

They stopped for a fast-food breakfast in southern Illinois. Avery kept driving as she ate her egg muffin and coffee. Soon Lionel came to sit shotgun beside her, carrying a plastic container full of soil.

"Is that mine?" she asked.

"No, this one's mine. You can have the rest."

"Thanks."

"It won't be him," Lionel said, looking at the soil cradled on his lap.

"No. But it'll be yours. Yours to raise and teach."

As hers would be.

"I thought you would have some kind of tribal loyalty to prevent them invading," Lionel said.

Avery thought about it a moment, then said, "We're not defenseless, you know. We've got something they want. The gift of self, of mortality. God, I feel like the snake in the garden. But my alien will love me for it." She could see the cooler in the rear view mirror, sitting on the floor in the kitchen. Already she felt fond of the person it would become. Gestating inside. "It gives a new meaning to *alien abduction*, doesn't it?" she said.

He didn't get the joke. "You aren't afraid to become . . . something like me?"

She looked over at him. "No one can be like you, Lionel."

Even after all this time together, he still didn't know how to react when she said things like that.

RECOMMENDED READING

"The Art of Space Travel" by Nina Allen, Tor.com, July 2016

"Mika Model" by Paolo Bacigalupi, *Slate*, April 2016

"Fifty Shades of Grays" by Steven Barnes, *Lightspeed*, June 2016

"A Fair War" by Taiyo Fuji, *Saiensu Fikushon 2016*, edited by Nick Mamatas and Masumi Washington

"The Mutants Men Don't See" by James Alan Gardner, *Asimov's*, September 2016

"My Generations Will Praise" by Samantha Henderson, *Interzone*, November/December 2016

"Origins" by Carlos Hernandez, *The Grim Future*, edited by Erin Underwood

"Stories of the Trees, Stories of the Birds, Stories of the Bones" by Kat Howard, *The Grim Future*, edited by Erin Underwood

"One Sister, Two Sisters, Three" by James Patrick Kelly, *Clarkesworld*, October 2016

"Kit: Some Assembly Required" by Kathe Koja, *Asimov's*, September 2016

"The One Who Isn't" by Ted Kosmatka, *Lightspeed*, July 2016

"Sleep Factory" by Rich Larson, *Analog*, October/November 2016

"Innumerable Glimmering Lights" by Rich Larson, *Clockwork Phoenix 5*, edited by Mike Allen

"Seven Birthdays" by Ken Liu, *Bridging Infinity*, edited by Jonathan Strahan

"Elves of Antarctica" by Paul McAuley, *Drowned Worlds*, edited by Jonathan Strahan

"Not Quite Taterona Kempi" by Ryan W. Norris, *Analog*, May 2016

"Travelling into Nothing" by An Owomoyela, *Bridging Infinity*, edited by Jonathan Strahan

"Unauthorized Access" by An Owomoyela, *Lightspeed*, September 2016

"A Song Transmuted" by Sarah Pinsker, *Cyber World*, edited by Jason Heller and Joshua Viola

"Red in Tooth and Cog" by Cat Rambo, *The Magazine of Fantasy & Science Fiction*, March/April 2016

"Passelande" by Robert Reed, *The Magazine of Fantasy & Science Fiction*, November/December 2016

"Those Shadows Laugh" by Geoff Ryman, *The Magazine of Fantasy & Science Fiction*, September/October 2016

"Firstborn, Lastborn" by Melissa Scott, *To Shape the Dark*, edited by Athena Andreadis

"The Whole Mess" by Jack Skillingstead, *Asimov's*, September 2016

"Licorice" by Jack Skillingstead, *Now We Are Ten*, edited by Ian Whates

"Everybody from Themis Sends Letters Home" by Genevieve Valentine, *Clarkesworld*, October 2016

"La beauté sans vertu" by Genevieve Valentine, Tor.com, April 2016

"The Mind Is Its Own Place" by Carrie Vaughn, *Asimov's*, September 2016

"That Game We Played During the War" by Carrie Vaughn, Tor.com, March 2016

"First Light at Mistaken Point" by Kali Wallace, *Clarkesworld*, August 2016

"Passion Summer" by Nick Wolven, *Asimov's*, February 2016

"Painter of Stars" by Wang Yuan, *Clarkesworld*, December 2016

PERMISSIONS

ABOUT THE EDITOR

Neil Clarke is the editor of *Clarkesworld* and *Forever Magazine*; owner of Wyrm Publishing; and a four-time Hugo Award Nominee for Best Editor (short form). He currently lives in NJ with his wife and two children. You can find him online at neil-clarke.com.